THE LYING LADIES

A rich woman's maid is brutall
believe that the young man wh
innocent? What do you do whe

the prosecutor want to close this case without looking at any of the contradictory evidence? If you're news reporter Dan Banion, you start digging. After all, a man's life is on the line. Does Mrs. Hibley, the maid's employer, know more than she admits to? Could Beth Ridgely, owner of the local cat house, be involved? Is Mrs. Hibley's daughter, Gail, to be trusted? And what of the murder victim herself? Is she who she appears to be? With the help of a local farmer and a courageous prostitute, Banion risks his life and career to cut through the lies and set things right.

THE BANDAGED NUDE

Dan Banion has returned from the war and moved to San Francisco, writing for the local paper. Today he is sitting in a bar called The Wreck. There used to be a popular nude painting behind the bar, but someone bought it. The artist himself walks in, trying to find out who purchased it. But no one remembers. Later that evening, a dead body is found inside a spaghetti crate and Banion gets a look at the corpse in the morgue. To his surprise, it is the young artist, poisoned to death. Banion starts his own investigation, and tracks down a number of suspicious characters, including the artist's ex-wife, a jealous lawyer, a shady detective, a vengeful photographer, a distraught girlfriend and a fellow artist. But who has been buying up all the artist's work—and why? And which one of them wanted him dead?

MANY A MONSTER

There is a killer at large, a fiend who hacks up young women. The police have arrested Rogan Lochmeister and are sure they have the right man. The murder weapon is found in his room along with his bloody clothes. But Rogan is a shell-shocked vet and doesn't remember a thing. And now he has escaped. The very next victim is Rogan's sister! She was convinced of his innocence, and had shared her thoughts with Dan Banion right before she met her own bloody end. And Banion is out to prove her right. All the evidence points to Rogan, but Banion finds a lot of suspicious characters in Rogan's circle of friends, including his old army buddy, his ex-wife, the woman who lived in the upstairs apartment, and his fellow workers at Wyler's department store. Could one of them have set him up?

ROBERT FINNEGAN BIBLIOGRAPHY

Novels:
Dan Banion series —
The Lying Ladies (Simon & Schuster, 1946)
The Bandaged Nude (Simon & Schuster, 1946)
Many a Monster (Simon & Schuster, 1948)

Short Stories:
The Sacred Thing (1933, as Paul Ryan)
Business Before Bullets (*Esquire*, Sept 1, 1947)

As Mike Quin

Non-Fiction / Essays:
Dangerous Thoughts (1940)
The Enemy Within (1941)
On the Drumhead: A Selection (1948)
More Dangerous Thoughts (1948)
The Big Strike (1949)

THE LYING LADIES
– – – – – –
THE BANDAGED NUDE
– – – – – –
MANY A MONSTER
– – – – – –
by Robert Finnegan
INTRODUCTION BY TOM CANTRELL

STARK
HOUSE

Stark House Press • Eureka California

THE LYING LADIES / THE BANDAGED NUDE /
MANY A MONSTER

Published by Stark House Press
1315 H Street
Eureka, CA 95501, USA
griffinskye3@sbcglobal.net
www.starkhousepress.com

THE LYING LADIES
Originally published by Simon & Schuster, New York, and
copyright © 1946 by Robert Finnegan. Reprinted in paperback
by Bantam Books, New York, 1948.

THE BANDAGED NUDE
Originally published by Simon & Schuster, New York, and
copyright © 1946 by Robert Finnegan. Reprinted in paperback
by Signet Books, New York, 1950.

MANY A MONSTER
Originally published by Simon & Schuster, New York, and
copyright © 1948 by Robert Finnegan. Reprinted in paperback
by Bantam Books, New York, 1949.

"Robert Finnegan's Dan Banion Trilogy" copyright © 2022
by Tom Cantrell

ISBN: 978-1-951473-81-5

Book design by Mark Shepard, shepgraphics.com
Cover design by Jeff Vorzimmer, ¡caliente!design, Austin, Texas
Cover art from the original edition of *The Bandaged Nude*
Proofreading by Bill Kelly

First Stark House Press Edition: January 2022

ROBERT FINNEGAN'S DAN BANION TRILOGY
By Tom Cantrell

Mystery fiction was a booming genre in the mid-1940s and one of the new names that appeared on three murder mysteries published in hardcover under Simon Schuster's Inner Sanctum imprint from 1946-1948, and by Boardman in London in 1949-1950, was Robert Finnegan. The fourteen years of experience William Paul Ryan had as a journalist publishing under the pseudonym of "Mike Quin" provided real depth to the fictional investigative crime reporter Dan Banion he created as mystery author "Robert Finnegan." The first novel published was *The Lying Ladies* (1946), then *The Bandaged Nude* (1946), followed in 1948 by *Many a Monster*. Each novel's main character was newspaper reporter Dan Banion, who in each case cleared a person wrongly suspected by the police of murder by exposing the actual murderer. There are recurring police and newspaper characters in the books that are well characterized and engage in cooperation, conflict and lively banter with Banion. The first edition of *Many a Monster* was published posthumously, as were all paperback editions.

The Lying Ladies, set shortly before World War II, takes Dan Banion to Sager Creek, a small city and its surrounding rural area to do an article on a local murder that an unemployed electrician drifting through town, a man named Ralph Flavin, has been charged with. The *Sager Creek Sentinel*, owned by a former colleague of Banion's, has assumed Flavin's guilt and framed their newspaper's coverage as being about the Great Depression's "Unemployed Character Menace." Banion argues that unemployment has no apparent connection to the murder, and chides his former friend from back when they'd both been reporters, for the sensationalist strategy he has adopted as owner of two small newspapers. Banion's employer, the urban newspaper *The Post-Tribune* has assigned him to travel outside their city in hopes of gaining rural subscriptions, when he happens across the murder story. By conducting a more open-minded murder investigation Banion uncovers a small-town brothel being run over a local bar and its surprising links to the prominent family that had employed the murdered woman as a housemaid. When he cracks the social and historical connections of the community, it is this combination that releases the innocent drifter Flavin and points to the previously well-concealed killer.

The Bandaged Nude opens in a San Francisco bar called The Wreck where WWII U.S. Army combat veteran Dan Banion drinks alone in the mid-afternoon lull. Another recently discharged combat vet named Kent enters, orders a drink, and asks the bartender about the identity of the buyer of a painting of a voluptuous nude woman that had previously hung on the wall behind the bar. The two customers introduce themselves by way of telling which combat outfits they had served in during the war. Kent is interrupted by the entry of Marian, an attractive woman he knows who asks him to leave with her. Kent's body will be accidentally discovered by police the next morning in the street when a crate supposedly containing damaged boxes of spaghetti on the way to the incinerator, but actually containing the corpse of a murdered man, breaks open in a delivery truck crash. Dan Banion becomes involved in the story the next day by coincidence during a visit to the courthouse he is making to introduce himself as a new reporter on the beat there. While being introduced to a homicide detective and the county coroner by a fellow reporter, Banion sees that the body being autopsied is that of Kent, whom he'd chatted with the previous afternoon. Banion seizes this coincidence as an opportunity to seek Kent's murderer by immediately infiltrating the social group of Kent's friends before he is reported deceased, thus increasing his access to information about the murder before people become guarded and are questioned officially.

He soon finds that Kent was a painter, last name Kipper, who had done the missing nude painting that had once decorated the bar where they had their first and only talk. This leads Banion to the San Francisco bohemian artist bars named The Iron Cat and the Black Pot where Kent's friends and associates gathered, then to their private house parties where he learns of their hedonistic lives intertwined into a confusing tangle of love and hostility that he must unravel to redeem some dignity for Kent, fallen in peace time, while searching post-war for "a world to live in." There were actually two famous bars in the bohemian history of San Francisco called The Black Cat and The Iron Pot whose names the author Finnegan reworded as names of the bars in this novel. Descriptions of Kent's apartment resemble one that might have been of the three-story tenement of bohemian apartments and studios called "The Monkey Block" that stood where today the Transamerica Pyramid skyscraper looms over North Beach. As a native observer of San Francisco who had been born there in 1906, Paul William Ryan (Robert Finnegan) wrote fine descriptions of the city's people and places, providing an atmosphere for mystery much the way L.A. itself was often Raymond Chandler's subject. In the first reviews of Finnegan's novels he was often compared to Chandler, whom he was also akin to in mapping elaborate and often unexpected social connections behind a city's façades.

Many a Monster builds from a car wreck that knocks out the police who are escorting a prisoner, freeing him to escape while being transported to a hospital for the criminally insane. Dan Banion covers the story of the search for the at-large convicted serial sex-murderer by going undercover as a roomer in the San Francisco boarding house where the sister of the escapee lives, hoping that her fugitive brother will try to contact her. The sister is murdered in the basement and Banion comes on the scene while the killer is still there but is unable to clearly identify the killer or capture him. The woman's murder is attributed to her brother, the escapee, but Banion defies his own paper and the local police authority's theory of the string of murders, to seek the real murderer. He proves the convicted Ira Rogerson's innocence by uncovering a deception involving gender in this 1940s case that would seem more likely to occur in a 1980s murder movie directed by Brian DePalma.

Robert Finnegan was a pseudonym Paul William Ryan used for his mystery novels. His other pseudonym of Mike Quin was well known for years before Ryan began mystery writing. Mike Quin was a columnist for West Coast communist newspapers such as *The People's World* in San Francisco. Several books contain excerpts from Ryan's career in journalism. *Dangerous Thoughts* (San Francisco, People's World, 1940) and *More Dangerous Thoughts* (San Francisco, People's World, 1941) were collections of his newspaper columns, many written in the form of parables with morals in support of labor activists and workers' economic interests, and others that were humorous dialogues between two fictional workingmen on political issues. After Ryan died in his early '40s of cancer, a tribute was published in the form of a collection of his columns, entitled *On The Drumhead: A Selection from the Writings of Mike Quin* (San Francisco, Pacific Publishing, 1948) and edited by Harry Carlisle, who'd once been his editor at the *People's World*. (Carlisle was deported to Britain in 1962 as an "alien" belonging to the Communist Party.)

A book by Mike Quin, *The Big Strike*, is an excellently detailed version of the Longshoremen's strikes in 1934 and 1936. Ryan also served the organized labor cause with his talents by being "The CIO Radio Reporter," for the final two years of the war doing news on a syndicated national radio network. Begun at the end of the war, his mystery writing career was undertaken to earn some financial support for his new wife and their baby. With income from the mysteries the family was able to move from a Telegraph Hill apartment in San Francisco to an old ranch he bought in Olema, near San Francisco, shortly before his death.

A mystery reader would likely not notice a pro-communist cast to his mystery trilogy but in places that influence emerges, often humorously, as in this exchange at the conclusion of *The Bandaged Nude* when the murderer is trying to buy Banion off, and he starts offering a bribe of $75,000. Banion refuses it and then the increases which are offered until the frustrated murderer says for him to name his price. When Banion replies that he wants one million dollars the murderer declares, "Banion, I can raise seven-hundred-thousand, but that's all." Banion replies, "If I couldn't be a millionaire I wouldn't want to be a lousy petty bourgeois. Connect me with Inspector Gallagher at Homicide Bureau." Other evidence of the author's political concerns is evident in Banion's battles with fascist American vigilante groups that become obstacles to his murder investigations and must be neutralized, sometimes violently. In *Many A Murder* Banion is shooting at "The White Knights," a group of anti-Semitic vigilantes, when fellow reporter Nix tells him "You're not in uniform now, you know," to which Banion replies, "My kind of uniform doesn't come off."

Ryan wrote verse, for example a poem appearing at the end of his pamphlet "And We Are Millions" entitled "Little Boy Blue" in which a young man who "took to the road in search of a job" to help his "starving" parents" fell under the wheels of a freight in Merced / And his frail little body is mangled and dead..." to which the poet replies to the parents who say "Go Wake Him! Go Wake Him! / Oh, no. Not I. / But I'll waken a storm. That will tremble the sky." His discourse encourages the reader to notice more extensive connections among citizens than are usually considered when considering one's personal problems, with a goal of worker and citizen solidarity against injustices. Many of his columns are humorous and poignant dialogues about serious subjects of politics and war. One describes a couple waking before dawn to get ready for work; she as a welder and he as a ship builder. He keeps bringing the conversation back to the need to open a second front in the War. He satirizes the government propaganda he is hearing on the radio for claiming morale is the issue. He says, give us a second front and we will bring morale. Quin was good at interweaving everyday life with larger events in the world.

Paul William Ryan was born in 1906 in San Francisco of Irish-

American parentage where he grew up with a brother and sister in the Mission District, raised by his mother and grandmother, as his father, a traveling salesman, had drifted away from the family. His mother was a dressmaker who referred to all the customers she made gowns for as "Mrs. Richbitch" and his grandmother ran a rooming house they sometimes lived in. In an article he later recalled seeing her witness a male boarder spying at a woman tenant through a bathroom keyhole and promptly kicking the man in the ass so hard he had a black eye from colliding with the door knob. Ryan said he learned that crime doesn't pay and even small pleasures were frowned upon in the world he lived in. Ryan quit school at age 15 to help his family and had jobs making deliveries, working at a stock brokers office, and an insurance office before shipping out at age 19 as a merchant seaman for three years. His family moved to L.A. and he joined them there from 1925-1929 where he got a job in a Hollywood bookshop. He joined The John Reed Club in Hollywood where he attended discussion groups and wrote for the club magazine *The Partisan*. One of his articles, "And We Are Millions: The League of Homeless Youth" (as Mike Quin) was published in 1933 by the Hollywood John Reed Club as a pamphlet. While employed at the Hollywood bookshop he continued to write at night, as he had for years, submitting but never selling his stories. This changed when he channeled into a story the anger he felt that so few of the books he inventoried on the shelves of the store addressed the desperation and grimness of the Depression. The result was his short story "The Sacred Thing" about a cop whose job was rousting the homeless from a public square by clubbing and kicking them, which was published in *Scribner's Magazine* and anthologized in *The Best Short Stories of 1934*. The policeman is badly shaken after he clubs and kicks a man off a park bench and then realizes he was already dead from starvation. What really bothers him, the cop tells his wife, was that he did that to a man "who was already in the presence of God." Ryan had a way of pointing to the ironies of the accepted social rules.

Ryan returned to San Francisco from L.A. where he became involved in 1933 as a journalist in the city's dynamic labor movement, one that resulted in the 1934 Longshoremen's strike, that led to the 1936 San Francisco General Strike. In 1936-37 he was employed in the WPA to write a history of cotton farming. His coverage in union papers the *Waterfront Worker* and *The Dispatcher*, and the communist paper the *Western Worker* (later *People's World*) of the heated, and sometimes violent struggle between police and the National Guard versus strikers and their supporters was later elaborated on by him in a book entitled *The Big* Strike by Mike Quin (Olema, Olema Publishing Company, 1949), published posthumously.

After the Nazis invaded Poland on September 1, 1939, Ryan, as Quin, wrote a pamphlet that was published by The Maritime Federation of the Pacific called *The Yanks Are Not Coming* which was in keeping with the change in the Communist Party line after Russia and Germany signed an agreement not to attack each other. In 1941, a series of articles he'd written for *The People's World* were collected and published by the paper as a pamphlet entitled *The Enemy Within*. The pamphlet with its arguments against intervention in Europe by America was widely read, and Walter Winchell referred to Mike Quin as the most dangerous man in America. When Hitler's Nazis broke their non-aggression pact by invading Russia on June 22, 1941, Mike Quin's column advocated the U.S. intervening in the war in Europe, in line with the overnight change in the Communist Party line.

Ryan died at age 41 on August 14, 1947 from a rapidly spreading cancer. At a memorial service ILWU leader Harry Bridges read a letter Ryan had written two months earlier to be delivered to the ILWU in which he told them, "Although I carry no card in the Longshore or Warehouse Union, I want you to know I have been your brother for a long time," and in which he exhorted them to "carry their appeal to the rank-and-file of any union" when the going gets tough as he predicted it would in the "Red Scare." Robert Finnegan was written about by Melvyn Barnes in an entry in *Twentieth Century Crime and Mystery Writers*, Second Edition (St Martin's Press, N.Y., 1985) who summarized that Finnegan "produced a handful of books demonstrating a very real talent...Finnegan painted his backgrounds and characters, whether of low or high-life, with a sure touch... It is a tragedy that Banion, with his streak of social conscience could not have appeared in a longer series. There have been too few writers as good as Finnegan." (pg. 312).

A longer critical evaluation is the 28-page article "Progressive Nostalgia: The Post-War Crime Fiction of Paul William Ryan" by Victor Cohen, published in the *Journal of Narrative Theory*, Volume 37, Number 3, Fall 2007, Eastern Michigan University. Cohen's article focuses on looking at how "Taken together as a project, these books show that Ryan was not so much formulating an analysis of post-WWII social relations, but keeping alive the memory and ambition of the progressive politics of the pre-war era in direct opposition to the emerging reactionary political 'common sense' of the Cold War" (pg. 2 of 28). Cohen contrasts Finnegan's Dan Banion with Mickey Spillane's anti-communist Mike Hammer. Cohen looks at how Robert Finnegan's mysteries were Paul William Ryan using "these stories to create a counter-hegemonic political sensibility that used the language of anti-fascism as a means to signal to his audience the range of, and validity to, the progressive and radical politics of the 1930s."

An example of the political controversy around interpretations of the Longshoremen's strike is a review of *The Big Strike* by Mike Quin (Olema Publ., 1949) in the *Pacific Historical Review*, Nov. 1950, by Hyman Weintraub. The reviewer's opening sentence: "If one is aware of the fact that Mike Quin was a 'party line' hack writer for the *Daily Worker*—a fact which is nowhere revealed in this book—it will help orient the reader in this account of the 1934 strike in the West Coast maritime industry," suggests the politically charged atmosphere his writing engaged. Weintraub states that Quin's "book itself is an example of how the Communists attempt to use the legitimate grievances of labor for their own purposes." Weintraub states that the only other book on the strike is less true to the facts than Quin's, and "in some cases gives an entirely erroneous impression. Quin has certainly succeeded much better in presenting the attitude of the men." (pg. 437) Weintraub faults Quin for not giving a "rational explanation of the employer's actions." I think the fact that by 1950 there were only two studies of the 1934 strike, a major event in the history of labor relations, suggests how controversial the politics of it were to write about. Paul William Ryan, aka Mike Quin the beloved labor journalist, aka Robert Finnegan the rising mystery novelist, was a committed communist who was able to succeed in the capitalist book business with his well-reviewed and internationally reprinted trilogy of noir mysteries; whodunits on the hard-boiled side that can make you strain your brain along with the protagonist Dan Banion to determine the murderer's identity from a group of intriguing suspects.

—October 2021

....

Tom Cantrell is the author of *The Mysteries of Roy Huggins and the Deportation of Harry Carlisle* (Hekate Publishing 2021) available as an Amazon paperback. He contributes articles to *Paperback Parade* magazine.

THE LYING LADIES

by Robert Finnegan

PROLOGUE

The very front yard gate looked as if it would resent not being carefully closed. It was cleanly painted and efficient on its hinges; the catch fitted perfectly. Ralph shut it behind him almost apologetically as he entered on an errand as ancient as hunger.

The lawn, he noticed, was lightly sprinkled with leaves from the giant shade trees, but its trimness matched the white picket fence and the gate. Every blade of grass looked of identical height. In an open space an automatic sprinkler cast spray in every direction, whirling giddily from the force of the water.

The spray was the only sign of life, yet the whole atmosphere of the place, he thought, was potent with awareness—sensitive—resentful of his intrusion. Not a sound but the crunching of gravel and the whirling of the lawn spray. Silent respectability on a hot afternoon.

Why he had chosen this house instead of any other was a mystery of mathematics. You might multiply the hunger in his stomach by the weariness of his feet, divide it by indecision, and subtract inhibitions— the result would be this gate.

Without thinking, he put one foot on the front step—then he remembered his status and took the gravel path around the side of the house—tiptoeing, he did not know why.

The path brought him in view of a garage that had once been a stable. The double doors were partly open, and through them he could see the maroon rear fender of a car, with a brightly polished bumper.

Why was he doing this anyhow? Why was he intruding on these strangers in a strange town? What was the name of the town? Hamilton. That's what it said on the road sign. Who had ever heard of it before?

Books and movies were full of this sort of thing—tramps asking for a handout at back doors. It seemed like the thing to do. Ralph didn't think of himself as a tramp, but the tradition held.

He didn't look like a tramp either, although his suit was pretty badly out of press, his face unshaven, and his shoes dusty.

As a matter of fact, a tramp would have had better sense than even to have walked through such a neighborhood.

He was just rounding the rear corner of the house when he heard the harsh sliding of wood on wood. "What do you want?" asked a woman's voice from overhead.

He looked up to a second-story window. The woman had the meanest face he had ever seen on a human being. He removed his cap politely. "Excuse me," he said. "If you have any work ... any windows to wash or anything ... I'm not exactly begging..."

"Get out of here," she said. "Get out of this yard or I'll call the police!"

"Excuse me," Ralph said. He started back toward the street, stepping quickly and gingerly.

"Get out of here!" the woman repeated in a tone that was slightly hysterical.

Ralph, still instinctively tiptoeing, retreated up the gravel path in a hurry. He didn't look back until he had closed the gate carefully behind him and was standing on the sidewalk. Then he saw that the woman had come out on the front porch and was beckoning to him.

She didn't shout; she just stood there beckoning with one arm. Her silence was queer. But now that he thought of it, she hadn't shouted from the back window either. Her voice had been audible enough but, in spite of its hysterical quality, not loud enough to carry. Maybe somebody was sleeping in the house.

Ralph pointed foolishly to his chest as if to inquire if it was him she was beckoning. The woman nodded fiercely and motioned again.

He didn't want to go back, but an obedient sense of politeness impelled him. He opened the gate carefully, shut it quietly, and crunched back through the flower beds to the porch.

"What are you looking for?" she asked. "Food?"

"I didn't mean to disturb you," Ralph said.

"Go on around in back," she said quietly. "Maybe I can find you something."

He followed the gravel path again, and she watched him until he rounded the corner of the house. When he got to the back door, however, she was already there, holding it open for him. As he entered, she smiled in a mirthless pretense of hospitality, but her eyes had a frightened, preoccupied look.

"I don't like to trouble you," Ralph said.

"It's all right. Come in," she mumbled.

The kitchen matched the garden in its immaculate order. It was old-fashioned. It made him remember his childhood. Flour bins under a fixing table. An ornate, iron, wood-burning stove. A sink with polished brass faucets.

"Sit down," she said, indicating a chair. "You're hungry. Is that it?"

"Yes ma'am. I'm willing to work, though." He removed his cap and, not knowing what to do with it, kept it in his lap. The shades were partly drawn, and the room was cool after the long, hot road.

"Where do you come from?" the woman asked bluntly. She was

moving around in what must be the pantry. He heard the familiar, solid slam of an icebox door, and the click of the handle.

"I started out from Philadelphia a couple of days ago," he said. "But I really come from Wilsie, Minnesota. That's where I was born. I'm on my way to join a friend of mine in California. He's got a job out there. I didn't have the fare, so I'm hitchhiking. I had a little money when I started out, but—"

"You have any friends around here?" she snapped.

"No ma'am. I just happened to land here—just passing through. I got a ride this morning that left me stuck out by—"

"Here's something, anyhow," she said, putting a plate of cold roast beef, a couple of cold boiled potatoes, and a glass of milk in front of him.

"Thank you very much," Ralph said. He noticed that the roast beef had been chunked off very inexpertly, also that she had to look in several drawers before discovering the one in which the knives and forks were kept.

"Where's your family? You got a wife or anything?" she asked.

"No, I don't have any family," Ralph mumbled through a mouthful of cold potatoes. "My parents died. I never had any brothers or sisters. This friend of mine in California—"

"How about your wife? Didn't you say you had a wife?" She snapped her words and bit off her sentences abruptly.

"No ma'am," Ralph answered. "I'm not married." Her questions were beginning to get on his nerves. He wondered if every tramp had to go through such a catechism. She sat in the chair opposite him, drumming her long, painted nails on the table, and not taking her eyes from his face.

Ralph stole a quick glance at her, and the thought occurred to him that she didn't belong in this house. To begin with, those fingernails. And take the dress she was wearing—a black silk dress with pink flowers scattered all over it—so many that you wouldn't know whether to call it a black dress or a pink one.

Ralph didn't know much about women's clothes, but he could recognize the difference between the sort of dress a woman might wear on the street, or to go visiting, and the kind she might wear in her own house on a hot afternoon.

Her face, too, seemed as out of place in this trim house and this quiet, old-fashioned kitchen as her dress and her painted nails. As he ate hungrily, with his eyes on his plate, and conscious of her fixed scrutiny, he tried to think of a word that would describe such a face.

She had evidently been quite beautiful at one time, and could still probably pass as quite good-looking at a distance. When you looked closely, however, you saw that the flesh was pudgy and there were deep lines on either side of her mouth.

Her eyes were so intensely cruel that he thought they could not possibly stay like that all the time. There must be some reason for it at this time—perhaps something in this house. She was laboring under a strong emotion. Her nervousness—her smoldering anger—the abruptness of her speech ...

A board creaked loudly somewhere in the quiet house. The sound seemed to come from upstairs—a stealthy sound as of someone walking on tiptoe.

The woman's eyes fled in the direction of the sound. She stood up. "You—eat," she said. "I'll be right back."

Relieved of the woman's eyes when she left the room, Ralph ate rapidly. "I've got to get out of here," he thought. He couldn't help feeling curious. But the feeling that something was very wrong in this house was even stronger than his curiosity.

He had an idea of finishing the food and getting out before she came back, but the woman returned almost immediately.

"You can do a little work when you're finished," she said, "and I might even pay you something."

His heart sank. He would have to earn his meal; there was no honorable escape from that. Every instinct told him to get out, but his moral training would not let him.

"Some furniture needs moving," she said. "Just a few things."

"That's okay." He finished the plate and the milk. "Thanks for the meal," he said. "I hadn't eaten anything since early this morning."

"It's upstairs," she said, opening a door that led into the house.

Ralph got a glimpse of a white marble statue—a draped nude—on a shining mahogany stand. He followed her into the hall where a cool, eerie light, tinted by the varicolored panes of glass in the front door, glanced off heavy oil paintings lining the wall, and gleamed on the polished banister of the thickly carpeted stairway which led above.

The top stair creaked loudly under her weight, and she looked back over her shoulder as if to make certain he was following. The stair creaked again as Ralph's foot pressed it—the same sound he had heard from the kitchen. He realized now that somebody else was in the house and he had been a fool to stay.

As the woman walked along the upper hall, she looked back again to make sure he was coming. He wanted to run, but with her eyes on him, he didn't have the courage.

Now she was opening a door—standing aside to let him enter.

Ralph hesitated; he stepped across the threshold in growing panic, and saw a portrait of a grimly respectable old man peering at him from the opposite wall. Too late, he sensed something behind him. Through the frilly curtains of a square-barred window, the sunlight seemed to explode.

CHAPTER ONE

When Tom Regan went out to mend the fence in his south pasture, he found a man lying in the grass nearby where the irrigation ditch came through.

The early morning sunlight was sparkling the dew on the grass. Birds were awake and chirping brightly. Insects were buzzing near the ground. The sky was clear. It looked like a fine day, and here was this fellow sprawled in the grass sleeping soundly.

Or was he dead?

No man would pick a place like that to lie down and go to sleep. The posture of his body looked more as if he'd fallen down or been thrown there.

He was a mess; a young fellow in his twenties, Regan judged. His shoes and his soiled, rumpled suit indicated a city man. Probably an unemployed hitchhiker. Some kind of a bum.

Any diversion was welcome. Regan didn't feel like fixing the fence anyhow. He leaned over the man and caught the unmistakable reek of whiskey.

"It's a good thing he crawled into my field and not Swanson's across the way," Regan thought. Swanson was a moral man and might have jabbed him with a pitchfork. Regan prodded him gently with a stick.

The man blinked his eyes and turned his head slightly. Regan poked again. It took several pokes before the man came hazily to his senses and sat up. Instantly he put his hand to his head and closed his eyes in pain.

"Come on, boy. Snap out of it," Regan said.

The young fellow seemed to have difficulty focusing his eyes.

"What kinda stuff you been drinkin'?" Regan asked.

"Excuse me. I—I—my head hurts."

"Excuse you? You ain't done nothing to me. This is my field, but I don't own the earth. You musta had a load last night."

"A load?"

"Yes, a load. You musta been stewed to the eyes."

"Stewed?"

"Come on, son. You better get up off that grass. Why'n't you go over to the ditch there and wash your face. Wake yourself up. You'll feel better."

Regan helped him to a shaky footing. The man kneeled beside the ditch and dipped his face again and again in the water, then groped for a dirty handkerchief and wiped his face.

"How'd you happen to get way out here so stewed?" Regan asked.

"I don't know," said the young fellow. "I don't know. There's something funny."

"I ain't seen you around here before. Where'd you get it? In Sawtooth? You look like you been in Beth's place."

"Get what?"

"The booze."

"I wasn't drunk."

"Now, son," Regan said. "Now, son."

The young fellow lifted his coat sleeve and sniffed. "It smells like whiskey," he said, "but I wasn't drunk. I didn't even have one drink."

"You must have been someplace," the man said.

"I'm going to California," said Ralph. "I'm hitchhiking. I got into a little town—Hamilton, I think the name was."

"That's just a whoop and holler down the road from here," said the man.

Briefly, Ralph described his experience at the immaculate white house—the woman who had called to him—how he went upstairs—the portrait in the room—and finally his waking up in the field.

The man listened thoughtfully and patiently, sucking comfortably on a pipe. "I'd call you a liar," he said when Ralph had finished, "except you described the Hibley home to a T. That's old lady Hibley's place. I know. I done some work around there for her. I used to live in Hamilton. That was 'fore I got this place out here. Most particular woman alive. Damn my soul! Put some fences up for her. Couldn't please her. Don't recollect the woman you speak of, though. Old lady Hibley has a daughter, lives in New York now. Doesn't sound like her, though."

"She didn't look like she belonged in the place at all," said Ralph. "I kept thinking that right along."

The man knocked the ashes out of his pipe and blew through it like a whistle. "You better come over to the house and let the old lady fix you some coffee," he said. "You don't make sense."

"Thanks. You see, I'd run out of money and I was figuring—"

"Sure. Sure. You'll feel better with a little coffee in you."

Regan led the way to a weather-worn house nearby. As they entered the kitchen Mrs. Regan, a stout woman washing dishes at the sink, cursed him for dragging in every bum that drifted by on the road. "Tom, I think there's a limit," she said. Nevertheless, she began preparing coffee.

"Don't mind her," said Regan. "She's the sweetest thing alive."

"I didn't mean to cause you any trouble," said the young man.

"It's not your fault," said Mrs. Regan. "It's his. God knows I'm not here to judge anyone, least of all the hungry. But you don't know what I put up with. You better have some eggs, too. You look sick, young man."

A small boy leaned his chin on Tom Regan's knee and stared at the stranger. A little girl watched from a nearby doorway. Regan stuffed his pipe comfortably.

"He's sick," said Amy. "Anybody can see he's sick."

"I feel better now," Ralph said. "I've still got a headache. But I think this coffee will help."

"Good," said Tom. "Drink it up. Coffee always helps."

"You drink too much of it," said Amy. "Your heart's like an outboard motor."

Tom ignored her. "What I suggest," he said, "is that you go straight in to Sager Creek—that's the county seat—and explain the whole thing. That is, if you're not lying."

"I'm not lying. What I told you is the truth," said Ralph.

"I don't know what it is," said Amy, "but don't lie. The world is strangling with lies. The newspapers lie to the people and the people lie to each other. It'll end in war. Watch and see."

"She can't stand liars," explained Tom, as if revealing some eccentric intolerance on his wife's part.

"Whatever it is, don't lie," counseled Amy. "We're poor, mister, and we're not geniuses. But we don't lie. It's the only decent thing I can say about Tom; he's not a liar."

"Thank you," said Tom solemnly.

"I'm not lying," Ralph protested. "I'm telling the truth. What should I do? Go to the police?"

"Keep away from the police," advised Amy.

"I'll tell you what I think you'd better do," Tom said to Ralph. "But first, that story of yours just don't make sense. Old lady Hibley's the tidiest thing in creation."

"And a liar," added Amy. "Mark my word, she's a liar. There's a lie behind that face. What people try to look like on the surface is what they're not underneath. You ought to stay here a few weeks, young man, and I'd put some weight on you."

"Amy," Tom protested, "please let us talk. This young man is in trouble."

"You talk about trouble like it was something unusual," said Amy.

"All right—all right. Please leave us alone just a few minutes."

"What's he done?" demanded Amy. "What have you done, young man? You can speak freely. We don't judge people. Heavens, the best of us are bad enough."

"Please, Amy, let him eat his eggs."

"The only thing you haven't dragged home is a murderer," she said, "and I suppose that'll come next."

"Pay her no heed," said Tom. "Now what I suggest you do is this: if your head feels all right, you go into Sager Creek and report everything to the sheriff there. Then you'll be in the clear."

"Why Sager Creek? Why not Hamilton?" Ralph asked.

"Sager Creek is the county seat and so close to Hamilton, they're almost like one town. That's the place to report. Fact is, there are three towns all sittin' in each other's laps, sort of. The other's Sawtooth, but it don't amount to much."

"Maybe I'd better just forget about it and keep right on going," Ralph said.

Tom sucked at his pipe and nodded his head. "On second thought, that would be the best advice. Why go looking for trouble?"

"Forget about what?" said Amy.

"Never mind, my sweet," said Tom. He puffed silently for a moment. "No," he added, "you better report. It's all so damn peculiar. If you report, then you're in the clear. You know, it's a funny thing, young man—I damn well know you're telling the truth. I believe you. I can mostly tell when a man is lying or if he's telling the truth. But what you say is plain crazy."

"What are you talking about, Tom?" demanded Amy.

"You wouldn't be interested," he said.

"I wouldn't be interested! Listen to him talk. Whatever it is, I'll be paying the freight on it. I feel it in my bones."

"To be fair all around," Ralph said, "I think I ought to report it."

"Hmmmmmm, I don't know," said Tom, frowning at his feet. "One minute I think yes, and another minute something tells me no."

"It's only fair to Mrs. Hibley that I report it," Ralph said.

"Well, I suppose so," Tom agreed. "Are you finished your eggs?"

"Yes, I have—and thank you very much. I feel much better now. I don't know how to thank you."

"Oh, pish," said Tom. "We'll hop in the Ford and I'll drive you in."

"Aren't you going to mend the fence?" asked Amy.

"Now, Amy, I'm just going to give this lad a lift into Sager Creek,"

Tom said.

"Here it goes all over again," sighed Amy. "This is the way it always starts."

Ten minutes on the road had brought them in sight of the church steeples and windmills of Sager Creek. Tom Regan's car was a Model A truck on which everything had apparently been neglected but the motor. One door was broken and secured with wire, so that both Ralph and Tom had to slide in under the steering wheel from the door on the driver's side. But the motor roared along with youthful vigor.

"I hope this doesn't take much time," Ralph said. "I want to be on my way to California. I have a long way to go."

"You won't find no work out there," said Tom. "Some of the folks around here have been out there and come back."

"Looks like there's been a wreck up ahead," said Ralph.

Just outside the town the road was blocked in the middle by a car parked zigzag. A motorcycle was leaning nearby, and an officer was questioning somebody in a coupe who had tried to steer around the obstruction. He waved the other car on just as they approached, and motioned for Tom to stop.

"Hell of a place to park a car," remarked Tom. "I don't see no wreck." He applied the brakes, then leaned his head out the window. "Hey, Sid! Get that thing off the road. What the hell's going on around here?"

The officer approached leisurely, tucking a notebook into his leather jacket. A bone-handled forty-five gleamed in its holster at his side. "What's your hurry, Tom? Who's your friend?"

"Young fellow I'm ridin' into town. What's the idea of parkin' a car in the middle of the road?"

"Keep your shirt on, Tom. Who are you, young fellow?"

"My name is Flavin," Ralph said. "Ralph Flavin. I come from Philadelphia."

"Philadelphia," said the officer in a mocking voice. "You're a long way from home, aren't you?"

"I'm going to California," said Ralph.

"You're goin' to California," said the officer, still in a mocking voice. "Now ain't that nice? It's pretty out there, I hear."

"Quit playing smart guy, Sid," Tom said. "I've known you since your mother used to dress you in velvet pants and a lace collar like a little girl."

Sid drew his forty-five and backed away a step. "Come on," he barked. "Get out! Both of you!"

"For the love of Pete," Tom said.

"Make it snappy," Sid roared. "Come on. Out in the road—both of you. And keep your hands up."

"Well, I'll be damned," muttered Tom. He fumbled the door open and slid out. "If this don't beat all!"

Ralph followed with slightly lifted hands.

"Higher," barked Sid.

Ralph lifted his hands higher above his head. Sid approached and slapped him around the hips and chest, then turned to Tom, who was standing sullenly with his hands in his pockets.

"You're next, Tom," said Sid.

"You goose me and I'll tell Florence on you," snapped Tom.

Sid hesitated, then abandoned the idea. "Where's your hat?" he said to Ralph.

Ralph rolled his eyes upward. "I must have lost it," he said. Turning to Tom, he added, "I must have left it in that house."

"What house?" demanded Sid.

"The widow Hibley's house over in Hamilton," Tom said. "The place where he got banged on the head."

The revolver began to shake in Sid's hand. His eyes widened. He groped wildly for his whistle, found it, rammed it in his mouth, and began blowing shrilly.

Ralph and Tom looked at each other questioningly.

In less than a minute a car with three men in it roared up the road and stopped beside them. Two of the men were officers; the other, a fat man in a gray suit, was Sheriff Horgan.

"All right, Sid," he said, jumping out of the car, "what have you got?"

"This guy was at Hibley's," said Sid, nodding at Ralph.

"Listen, Horgan," Tom cut in, "if you'll let us get a word in edgewise—"

"Put the cuffs on him, boys," said Horgan, indicating Ralph. "How do you know he was at Hibley's?"

"He said so," explained Sid.

"I said so," Tom interrupted. "I said he was at the Hibley's. He didn't say so. I did. Maybe he was and maybe he wasn't. What's this all about? Quit playing cowboy and Indian and tell us what's up."

"What's Tom Regan got to do with this?" Horgan asked Sid.

"He was riding with Tom in his car," Sid declared.

"I might have known it," said Horgan. "If there's anything screwy going on anywhere, you'd have your nose in it. Who is this guy, Tom? Where'd you pick him up?"

"Found him in my field this morning," said Tom. "He was knocked on the head, dead to the world—just lying there. We was comin' into town to see you."

"To see me?"

"Yeah, to see you."

"Well, I'll be—put him in the car, boys." Ralph was handcuffed and held by an officer on each arm. "You'll have to come along, too, Tom," said Horgan.

Tom gave Ralph a reassuring look. "Don't worry, son," he said. "It's all a lot of damned rigmarole." He started to climb in his Model A.

"Hold on there," said Horgan. "You're going in our car." Tom looked at him in disgust. "Oh, now, Horgan, don't be a damned fool."

"All right. Then you ride with him, Sid."

Sid tried to get in the door that was wired up and Tom had to steer him around to the other side. "You, pointin' a gun at me, Sid Evans," he said. "So help me! You who used to run around in lace pants."

CHAPTER TWO

The sheriff's office of Sager Creek was located in the jail just behind the courthouse. Earl Grimes, the County Attorney, was questioning a sad little man who sat very straight in his chair, alternately nodding and shaking his head.

"So then you got off the freight at Hamilton," said Grimes.

"No, sir," said the little man. "I got off at Sawtooth. Like I told you, I've never been to Hamilton."

"Where did you lose your hat?" asked Grimes.

"Like I told you, I never wear a hat."

"You never wear a hat."

"No, sir, I never wear one."

"Then what's this?" Grimes jerked a soiled cap from a desk drawer and threw it down in front of him.

"That isn't a hat," said the little man. "It's a cap."

"Your cap," said Grimes.

"I never wear a cap either. I never saw it before," said the little man.

"You never saw it before," repeated Grimes.

"No, sir. I never saw it before."

At this point Sheriff Horgan came into the office leading Ralph Flavin, in handcuffs, and followed by two officers.

"What's this—another one?" asked Grimes.

"This is the guy," said Sheriff Horgan. "We picked him up on the highway riding in a car with a fellow named Regan."

Grimes sat up straight and snuffed his cigar hastily in the ash tray. "Take this bum out of here," he said to the officers, indicating the sad little man. "Put him with the rest."

"This is the guy," said Sheriff Horgan proudly. "He admits it."

The little man looked solemnly at Flavin as the officers led him out.

"This isn't another gag of yours, is it, Jeff?" asked the County Attorney. "You've picked up half the stiffs in the state. They're piled three deep in every cell."

"This is the right one," said Horgan smugly.

"Bring him around here," said Grimes, motioning to the chair the little man had just left. When Flavin was seated, Grimes threw the cap in front of him. "That your cap, son?"

Flavin reached for the cap, but the handcuffs restrained him. He leaned over and looked at it. "Yes," he said. "I think so."

"Where'd you last see it?" Grimes asked quickly.

"I think I left it at a lady's house in Hamilton," Flavin said. "But there was something funny about that house. I was on my way here to tell you when they stopped us on the highway."

"Us? Who's us?"

"A fellow named Tom Regan," Horgan explained. "He owns a piece of land up the road a way. He had this guy in his car driving into town. Evans has him out in the anteroom. I thought you'd like to see this guy alone first."

Grimes tilted back in his swivel chair with a springy squeak. "So you were on your way here, you say. What were you coming here for?"

"I wanted to report something I thought I'd better tell you," said Flavin.

"Tell us what?"

"Well, you see, it was this way: I stopped yesterday afternoon at a house in Hamilton. That is, I went around to the back door to ask for something to eat. That is, I was willing to work for it."

"In plain words, you're a vagrant," said Grimes. "Where'd you come from?"

"I started out from Philadelphia a couple of days ago. I'm going to California. I'm hitchhiking."

"Well, go on. So you got to Hamilton, and you went around to the back door of this house. Then what?"

A bald man with horn-rimmed glasses stuck his head in the room. He was Vance Dalbert, editor of the Sager Creek *Sentinel*. "Am I interrupting something?" he asked.

"Come in, Vance. Come in," said Grimes. "I want you to hear this."

Dalbert adjusted his glasses and stared uneasily at Flavin as he entered. "Is this—?"

Grimes nodded shrewdly. "Go on," he said to Flavin. "You went around to this house. Then what?"

"A lady—a funny looking lady—leaned out a window and told me to go away."

"Told you to go away. All right, go on."

"So I started to go, and I got out to the sidewalk, and then she called me back."

"So you went back."

"I went back and I went around to the kitchen and she gave me something to eat. Then she said she had a job she wanted me to do. She wanted me to move some furniture and asked me to come upstairs."

"So you went upstairs," said Grimes. "Then what?"

"I'm telling you the truth," said Flavin. "I know it sounds screwy, but I'm telling you the truth."

"All right, so you went upstairs. Then what?"

"Then she told me to go in a room, and I went in, and somebody must have hit me over the head, because that's all I know. When I woke up, I was out in a field somewhere. Mr. Regan found me and offered to drive me in here to see you. We were on our way here when they stopped us just outside of town."

Grimes looked at Horgan. "Did you search him?"

"Well," said Horgan, "to tell you the truth, I thought you were in a hurry to question him, and—"

"Search him," said Grimes dryly.

Horgan dived his hands into Flavin's pockets and brought forth a dirty handkerchief, a notebook, a knife, a razor, a toothbrush wrapped in a piece of waxed paper, a fountain pen, several pencils, another notebook— "What's this?" he suddenly asked. He drew out a small roll of bills and threw them on the desk. "And this?" He laid an amethyst brooch, a gold bracelet, and three ladies' rings beside the bills.

Grimes leaned forward eagerly to examine them.

"Those things aren't mine," Flavin said hysterically. "I never saw them before. They're not mine. I never saw that money before."

Grimes selected a cigar from his pocket, bit off the end, and struck a match. Nobody said a word.

"What is this?" asked Flavin. "Why don't you tell me what's happened? I was coming here of my own accord, wasn't I? Do you think I'd come here to see you if I'd done anything?"

"You kind of left a few things out of your story, didn't you, son," said Grimes calmly.

"No. I told you what happened. I never saw those things before."

"For instance," said Grimes, "you had a few drinks. Did you forget about that?"

"I never had one drink. Flavin paused and sniffed himself. "I know what you're thinking. I meant to tell you about that. When I woke up I smelled of whiskey. But I never had one drink."

"You meant to say that," said Grimes with a cold smile, "but you didn't."

"I couldn't tell you everything all at once. I was—"

"Oh, then you didn't tell us everything."

"I don't mean that. I told you everything. I mean like this lady acted strangely. She didn't act like she belonged to the house."

"She wasn't a blonde lady, was she?" asked Grimes.

"No, sir, she wasn't blonde."

"You say she wasn't blonde?"

"No, she wasn't blonde. She was very dark-haired. Brunette."

Grimes dipped his cigar ashes into the tray and leaned forward in a getting-down-to-business attitude. "Your memory isn't what it ought to be, son. You had a bump on the head, you say."

"Yes, sir. It still aches. You can feel the bump."

"I believe you. You've got a few scratches on your face, too. Did you know that?"

Flavin moved his hands as if to feel his face, but the handcuffs restrained him again. "No, sir. I haven't seen a mirror. Where are the scratches?"

"Right down the side of your face. Three of them. Looks like fingernails might have done it. Have you noticed your right hand coat cuff?"

There was a thick, dark stain on the cuff.

"I was lying in that field," Flavin said. "I must have rolled in something."

Horgan leaned down and examined the cuff, then nodded at Grimes.

"That's a bloodstain, son," Grimes said. "Quite a lot of blood."

Flavin paled and looked frightened.

"Take a look at that knife, Horgan," said Grimes.

Horgan picked up the clasp knife he had taken from Flavin's pocket, and opened the blade. Again he nodded at Grimes.

"Do you know what's on your knife, son?" asked Grimes.

Flavin gritted his teeth and shook his head. His eyes were watering.

"Blood," said Grimes.

Sheriff Horgan jumped, but not quickly enough. Flavin's stomach emptied, partly on the desk and partly on Horgan's leg. For a moment he was convulsed as his stomach retched again and again.

"Goddamn it!" Horgan swore.

Dalbert hastened to open a window. Then he stuck his head out and emptied his own stomach onto the lawn, to the amazement of several people who were passing.

Horgan wiped his leg with a handkerchief.

Grimes shoved his swivel chair back from the desk. "Tsch—gad—get a mop—get a rag, one of you." He lost interest in his cigar and parked it in the ash tray.

One of the officers went out and came back with a mop and a handful of rags.

"That's a new one on me," said Horgan.

Dalbert drew his head in the window and wiped his face with a handkerchief. "Good heavens," he said. "I never did that before. I don't know what struck me."

"Open another window," said Grimes. "Get some air in here, damn it."

Flavin stopped retching and lifted his head. Water streamed from his eyes. "I'm sorry," he said. "I'm terribly sorry, but I had to do it."

"He's confessing," said Dalbert.

Grimes picked up his cigar again. "That's better," he said. "Now suppose you start all over again from the beginning. Why did you do it?"

"Do what?" asked Flavin.

Grimes looked sadly at Horgan. Horgan pointed a finger to his head and drew circles in the air.

"The house," said Grimes. "The big white house. The little blonde girl. Remember? You were telling us about the house and the little blonde girl."

"It was a lady," said Flavin. "A dark lady. She had on a black dress with pink flowers on it—lots of them. So it was almost a pink dress. Only it was black. She had puffy cheeks and deep lines around her mouth. Her eyes were black. She had long painted fingernails."

"Put him away," said Grimes impatiently. Then to Dalbert, "Well, I guess you got a story, eh, Vance?"

One of the officers asked, "What are we gonna do with that mob of bums we got caged in there?"

"Turn 'em all loose and give 'em twenty-four hours to get out of town," said Sheriff Horgan. "If you find any of them around after that, it's thirty days."

"You know how to handle this story, I hope," Grimes said to Dalbert.

"Aren't you going to tell me what happened?" sobbed Flavin. "Please tell me what happened." Tears were streaming down his face.

Grimes motioned to an officer. "Put him away. And you'd better have an extra guard sleep in the place tonight. We don't want any mob stuff. Better have plenty of men on hand, just in case."

"I haven't got any money," said Flavin, "but I didn't do anything. I was just passing through. I told you the truth."

An officer gripped him by the arm and shoved him through the door. Horgan followed, and Grimes was left alone in the room with Dalbert.

"Isn't it peculiar how they'll lie even when you've got them cold turkey," said Grimes.

"Well, I guess they figure they haven't got anything to lose," Dalbert said.

"That fellow didn't show much imagination in his story."

"He's a little cracked, that's obvious," said Dalbert.

"It's a dirty shame," said Grimes. "The country's overrun with them. You know how to handle the story, I hope."

"Well, let's see. Mad wolves of the city roaming the countryside. How's that?"

"No, no, no," said Grimes. He picked up his cigar, sucked on it, and discovered it had gone out. "Lay off baiting the city. That's out from now on."

"I don't get you. It's what they like."

Grimes revived his cigar with a match. "Get that out of your head, Vance. It's not what we want. Quote me like this: city and country must unite against unemployed menace."

"I don't get it, Earl. Our readers don't care about the city."

"The city voters do."

"What of it? They don't elect you."

"They elect the governor," said Grimes. He winked slyly.

"Well, I'll be damned," said Dalbert. "So that's it. I believe you could do it, Earl. I believe you could. So that's it."

"It's pretty well set," said Grimes, "but keep it under your hat. I've been talking to a few pretty influential people. You can see where this story will be important from that angle. The crime wave, linked to the unemployment problem, will be our main line. I want you to play up the idea of, 'Is your daughter safe?' and 'Is your home safe?' and lay the blame right at the door of the administration. Coddling the unemployed and all that."

"I get the idea, Earl. But that's what I've been doing."

"Yeah, but the country against city angle is out from now on. Understand?"

"Oh, sure. Hell, I'm not dumb."

"You ought to be able to figure a good editorial out of this."

"How's this?" asked Dalbert. "We head it: Who Are the Unemployed?

Then we use this case as an example."

"It's fair," said Grimes. "But call me up and let me hear it before you print it."

CHAPTER THREE

The offices of the Sager Creek *Sentinel* were located in a long, low, one-storied building a few blocks from the courthouse. As Vance Dalbert entered, the round-faced Norwegian girl who took care of circulation and advertising, in addition to serving as a receptionist, said, "There's a man to see you, Mr. Dalbert. He says he works for the *Post-Tribune* in the city. I told him to go in and wait."

In the narrow, glass-enclosed cage that served as Vance's editorial office, a man was seated with his feet on the roll-top desk reading a magazine and smoking a pipe.

Evidently the Lord had intended him to be handsome but had been called to the phone in the middle of his creation. All of his features were in the direction of being good-looking but just missed. In trying to pour into him enough ego to keep himself well-groomed, the supreme artist had overdone it and given him so much that he didn't even consider it necessary to keep his pants pressed. A great deal of indecision was apparent in the color of his hair, which was such a cloudy brown it was neither one thing nor the other.

Obviously the maker of men had tried his hand at something better, but the effort had been so self-conscious that the job was blotched.

"Well, for the love of heaven—Dan!" said Vance with genuine pleasure.

Dan looked up with the satisfied expression of a man who knows he is creating a surprise. Vance reached out and grabbed him by the shoulder.

"Good Lord! Dan Banion. How long have you been here?"

"Not long," said Dan. "You're looking fine, Vance. Maybe a little fat. So you're a publisher now."

"Don't laugh," said Vance. "I've got this paper and another over in Winfield—the *Bugle*. I tell you, Dan, it's the only thing. Be your own boss. Remember how we used to talk? Doggone!"

"It's been a long time, Vance."

"Say, hasn't it. We've got a lot to catch up on. You're with the *Post-Tribune*, the girl says."

"They sent me down here on a fishing expedition, Vance. Our rural circulation has been falling off—particularly on the Sunday edition. The editor thinks we ought to juice it up with a few country items. I've been touring the tank towns and just hit this one."

"Let's see—you must be working for Ainsley. Great guy, that Ainsley."

"Yeah, if you like heels, I guess he's about the biggest."

"Now, Dan, I don't think you mean that."

"Skip it, Vance. Can you give me any steers around here? I need a story."

"Well, you walked right into a nightmare. Get up out of that chair, Dan, and let me sit down. I've got the hottest story in the state right here. I've got to hammer out some copy on it, then we can talk."

"What is it? Rape among the rhubarb?"

"It's a pretty serious proposition, Dan. We had a murder over in Hamilton, and they just picked up the fiend."

"You don't mean to tell me you have fiends around here?" Dan got up and let Vance into his swivel chair.

"All right, Dan. Lay off the sarcasm. This story is due for a big play. It has political angles. Here. Read this. It'll give you the background." He tossed Dan the last edition of the Sager Creek *Sentinel*. "You don't mind if I ignore you for a while? I've got to get this written up."

"Bang away," said Dan. He opened the paper. "This is a cheesy make-up you've got here, Vance."

"Shut up, Dan. I'm trying to concentrate." Vance fitted a sheet of paper into the typewriter, then scowled at the blank page and screwed up his mouth. The phone rang.

"Yes, Fergus," said Vance. "Go on down to the jail. Tell Horgan I sent you. They've got the Hibley murderer there. A young fanatic. I want you to get a couple of pictures. Get him in the cell and cut a background of bars in if you can. And listen—bring out his character. Get him wild-eyed. Take your time. Talk to him. Get him worked up. I don't want anything that looks like anybody's nephew. You know what to do. Go to it."

"Why not get them to twist his leg while they're photographing him?" asked Dan. "Or better still, use an old picture of Boris Karloff."

"Shut up, Dan. I'm really up against a deadline," said Vance, staring into the typewriter.

Dan tilted his chair against the wall and read:

HIBLEY MAID MURDERED

Half Nude Body Found in Bedroom

Vagrant Suspected

Her clothes torn from her young body, her throat gashed by an unknown fiend, the body of Esther Berglan, comely housemaid in the home of Martha Hibley, widow of the late Vern B. Hibley, former state attorney-general, was found in the Hibley mansion at 813 Bruce Street in Hamilton yesterday.

The body was discovered by the widow's son, Ronald G. Hibley, when he returned home from his real estate business at six P.M. yesterday.

It is believed Miss Berglan was assaulted and murdered by a vagrant whom she admitted to the house in the absence of the family, and to whom she served food in the kitchen.

Mrs. Hibley had been away all day on a business trip to Frenton. The other servants had the day off. Miss Berglan was alone in the house during the afternoon.

Mrs. Garland, the cook, who returned earlier than Mr. Hibley, found a soiled cap on the kitchen table beside a plate on which food had been served. When Mr. Hibley arrived home, she showed him the cap. It was then that he examined the rest of the house and found Miss Berglan's almost nude body on the floor of Mrs. Hibley's bedroom upstairs.

It was evident that the girl had put up a desperate fight against her attacker. The room was in great disorder, furniture tipped over, and even some pictures knocked from the walls. Miss Berglan had a heavy lead statuette clutched in her hand like a club, with which she had evidently tried to defend herself.

Sheriff Harry Horgan of Sager Creek remarked that the girl's throat had been cut by a small knife—evidently a clasp knife—which was too short for stabbing. Several incisions in the girl's breast and shoulder indicated that the murderer had attempted to stab her before cutting her throat.

The bedroom had been ransacked thoroughly, and a strong cupboard concealed in the wall had been forced open. The contents were scattered on the floor, and a metal strong box, evidently taken from it, pried open with some heavy tool.

Mrs. Hibley, upon her return from Frenton, reported missing about $175 in currency, three rings of moderate value, and a few minor items of jewelry.

None of the other rooms evidently had been disturbed. But Mr. Hibley, when seeking a stimulant after the shocking discovery, found that the only bottle of whiskey in the house was missing from the dining room.

Coroner Armand Federson, after preliminary examination, declared that the girl had evidently been murdered at about four P.M.

yesterday afternoon.

County Attorney Earl Grimes issued orders for a round-up of all vagrants and a blockade of the highways and railroad yards.

"This is clearly another result of the tidal wave of degenerates that has swept our country in recent years," said Grimes. "They touched our pocketbooks, and we complained. But now they are reaching filthy hands at our womanhood, and we will show them all the wrath of awakened lions. Vagrants, from this day on, will find Patterson County a flaming torch of punishment and retribution. Honest and thrifty citizens will find their elected representatives warriors in their defense against the drunkards, murderers, rapists, and union organizers of Moscow-inspired rebellion."

Alongside the story was a ten-point type editorial headed: "Hamilton Murder Bares Unemployed Character Menace."

It started off: "Tolerate idleness and shiftlessness? Perhaps we have. But tolerate a murderous assault on our womanhood? No!"

Dan removed the pipe from his mouth. "What the hell has happened to you, Vance?" he asked. "Have you gone crazy?"

Vance stopped typing and blushed. "I don't get you."

"Well, this story—the way you've handled it. And this editorial. My God, Vance."

"I've just printed the facts, that's all, Dan." Vance's face, however, indicated a certain anguish.

"This stuff about the unemployed, Vance. That has nothing to do with the case."

"That's a matter of opinion," said Vance defensively.

"Don't give me that. This is as phony as a rubber doughnut."

"I've seen the same thing, almost word for word, in the *Post-Tribune*, time and again."

"That's not the point, Vance. That's Ainsley. This is you. My God! Have you forgotten the talks we used to have?"

Evidently Vance hadn't, because his face radiated a kind of guilty embarrassment. "I still believe in those things," he said. "But I'm not going to sit back and let foreigners come over here and run our country—let alone rape our women."

"Is this fellow a foreigner—this fellow they arrested?"

"That's not the point, Dan."

"Is he?"

"No."

"Then what the hell are you talking about?"

"Everything's related in the world today, Dan. You know what's going on."

"Yes, and it's enough to make me gag."

"Dan, you're the last man in the world I want to get in an argument of this kind with."

"All right, skip it, Vance. What about this murderer? They picked him up, you say."

"They've got him in the jail."

"Where is this jail?"

"You go up one block to your left, and another to your right. You can't miss it. Ask for Earl Grimes. He's the County Attorney, and he'll be a big man in this state someday, Dan. I'd go with you, but—"

"That's all right, Vance."

"And listen, Dan. Don't let's quarrel. That's no good. Come back when you're through. We've got a lot to catch up on."

"Sure, Vance," said Dan. "Shuck your corn and take it easy."

CHAPTER FOUR

When Dan explained he was from the *Post-Tribune*, he had no trouble getting in to see Grimes.

"Very glad you came," Grimes said. "Sit down. The publisher of the *Post-Tribune* is a very good friend of mine. Splendid man, Ainsley. So you're Dan Banion. I'm familiar with your by-line, Mr. Banion. It's a pleasure to meet you."

"I thought I might have a look at this fiend of yours," said Dan. "It didn't take you long to round him up."

"We know our business," said Sheriff Horgan, who was resting one hip on the corner of Grimes' desk.

"We've a very capable organization down here," said Grimes. "By the way, on this case I think it's time city and country saw eye to eye on this unemployed situation. In my opinion this is a statewide problem. The Hamilton murder brings it to a head."

"Have you been having a lot of murders?" asked Dan.

"Well, no. I wouldn't say that," said Grimes.

"There was that Blivens shooting in 1914," said Horgan. "That got a lot of notice."

Grimes shook out a match impatiently and puffed on his cigar. "That's not the point," he said. "We don't intend to let things get out of hand. Incompetents and degenerates are roaming our highways. We propose to make this case an example—a rallying point for action."

"What kind of action?" asked Dan.

"Well, that is to say, something ought to be done. It's a statewide problem. We must demand responsible measures by the state government."

"You aren't thinking of running for governor, are you?" Dan asked.

Grimes eyed him coldly. "What put that idea in your head?"

"Skip it," said Dan. "Our paper will run the story. They want something to revive our rural circulation. Besides, needling the present state and national administrations is Ainsley's meat."

"I think you'll find," said Grimes, "that Ainsley will understand my point of view on this. We're very close, you know. In fact, I had a talk with him just the other day."

"My job is to get the story," said Dan. "I don't care about the political angling. Ainsley takes care of that up in the city, no matter what I send in."

"In my opinion," said Grimes, "Ainsley is one of the most brilliant men in the country."

Dan bluntly changed the subject. "Are you sure you've got the right man in this murder case?"

Sheriff Horgan chuckled. "Show him the dirty pomes we found in his pocket."

Grimes was not satisfied. "I don't think you appreciate the far-reaching significance of this matter," he said.

"Listen," assured Dan, "when Ainsley gets through slanting it, you'll think the governor and the administration in Washington were both guilty. The other day a horse was hit by a trolley car on Tenth Street, and he managed to put a political angle on it. What I'm interested in is, have you got the right man? Did he confess?"

"Yes, he did," Grimes said, "but he was ranting so much you could hardly make anything out of it."

"He puked all over the joint," said Horgan.

"What did he say?" asked Dan. "Why did he do it?"

"He just said, 'I'm sorry. I had to do it,'" said Horgan.

"Had to throw up?"

Horgan pondered. "Say, Earl," he said, "maybe that's what he meant."

Grimes shook his head. "It's all beside the point. Here are the facts. He admits being at the Hibley house at the time of the murder. The girl was alone in the house—"

"Who is he?" asked Dan.

"A vagrant. We picked him up on the highway riding with a fellow who has a little farm just outside town. This fellow found him unconscious in a field, and says he was driving him into town to see Horgan."

"Who's Horgan?"

"Horgan's the sheriff. This is Horgan," said Grimes.

"I'm Horgan," added Horgan resentfully.

"Well, I don't get it," said Dan. "Why was he coming to see you?"

"Wait till I give you the whole story," said Grimes. "The guy was daffy. He didn't know if he was coming or going. We got him up here and he gave us a cock-and-bull story about calling around to the back door of the Hibley house and asking for food. He said a woman let him in and fed him, then he was knocked over the head and dumped out in a field."

"Who knocked him on the head?" asked Dan.

"That's all bunk," said Grimes. "The girl probably hit him with a statue when he was attacking her, but not enough to lay him out. The thing is, we found the murder knife in his pocket. It's still crusted with blood. We found the money on him that had been stolen, and the jewelry. He had scratches on his face where the girl clawed him. There was blood on the cuff of his coat, and he still smelled of whiskey. Now I ask you!"

"And the dirty pomes we found on him," added Horgan.

"Oh yes," said Grimes. "There was a lot of crackpot, sexy poetry in his pockets."

"He was probably high on marihuana when he did it, and hasn't come out of it yet," said Horgan.

"Can I see the knife?" asked Dan.

Grimes looked at him oddly. "Sure," he said. He opened a drawer in his desk. "I know what you're thinking," he added. "It's a simple case of a sex-starved bum. That's why I've been trying to explain to you the larger aspects of the thing. If this was an isolated case, Banion, I'd say forget it. Give it a little write-up and let it go at that. But it ties right in with the whole situation we're facing in the nation right now. Somebody's got to take a stand somewhere."

He handed Dan the knife and continued, "Certainly, if a man's up against it and needs a helping hand, I'm all for it. I'd be the first to suggest giving him a lift. But this thing of pampering idleness and catering to a lot of—"

"Do you mind if I open the blade?" asked Dan.

"Go ahead," said Grimes. "This catering to a lot of criminals and degenerates, and teaching people to depend on handouts and expect to be cared for—"

Dan closed the knife with a click. "What's this guy's name?" he asked.

"Flavin," said Horgan. "Ralph Flavin."

"Can I see the poetry?" asked Dan.

"Sure," said Grimes. He fumbled in the drawer while Horgan leaned over with a grin on his face.

The notebooks and the sheets of paper tucked into them were smudged and worn and shaped to the owner's body from long carrying. Dan sorted them on the edge of the desk and relit his pipe before reading them.

"You'll get a boot out of this," chuckled Horgan.

Dan read quietly for a few moments, then said, "It's a little corny, but I don't see anything dirty about it."

"It's mostly a lot of starry-eyed tripe," said Grimes.

Dan read a line at random: "A touch of starlight on your mind can wed you with the wind."

"Le'me show you some of the hot ones," said Horgan impatiently.

Dan pushed his hand aside. "I'll find them. Take your time. This one isn't bad:

> In narrow caves of conscience, called themselves,
> Too many live alone like frightened elves."

"What's good about it?" asked Horgan. "Let me show you the hot ones."

"Is this what you mean?" asked Dan. He read again:

> "Bright stars that guide the ships upon the ocean
> Cause men to trust the beauty of the skies;
> But I have something warmer to believe in,
> For my love has them shining in her eyes."

"Naw," said Horgan. "Le'me show you." He grabbed one of the notebooks and thumbed through it. "Take a gander at that."

Dan read again:

> "What hero ever sat so high
> He never reached for a woman's thigh?
> Our Presidents sought with all the rest
> The comfort of a woman's breast.
> Washington crossed the Delaware
> Dreaming of Martha's golden hair.
> Abraham Lincoln felt the need,

And mark how well the Roosevelts breed.
Great conquerors have knelt to beg
Warm favors of a silken leg.
How many heroes, long since dust,
Once paced the floor in lonely lust?
How many geniuses and braves
Lie still unsatisfied in their graves?"

"He had women on the brain," said Grimes.

"Le'me show you another," said Horgan eagerly. He reached over and thumbed avidly at the pages.

"You seem to have given it a very thorough going over," said Dan.

"Naw, I just skipped through till I saw something hot. Read that."

Dan obligingly read:

SONG OF THE WITCHES

"Wens on our noses, warts on our faces,
We are not fashioned for lovers' embraces.
Bent in the middle and hairy of breast,
Never the glance of lover has blessed,
Never the hand of love caressed,
Never the mind of man undressed,
In passionate dream, the hairy form
Of witch, nor warmed to heated storm
At thought of a witch's shriveled hips
Or the fuzzy kiss of her mustached lips.
Woe be the draughts of hell we brew;
An ounce can turn a man into
A beast, a bird, a bear, a bug,
But cannot win from him a hug."

"It's pretty disgusting stuff," said Grimes.

"A total screwball," said Horgan.

"Of course," said Dan, "you're just picking out certain things here and there. Most of this stuff might have been written by any lonely kid."

"My God, Banion," said Grimes. "That garbage? It's a lot of moonstruck crap."

"If any kid of mine started scribbling such stuff I'd break his neck," declared Horgan.

"I may want to copy some of it for the story," Dan said. "Is that okay?"

"Help yourself," said Grimes. "If I'm not here, Horgan will let you see it."

"Stick in the one about the Presidents feeling up dames," said Horgan. "That'll knock their eye out."

"And now, how about having a look at the guy?" said Dan.

"Certainly," said Grimes. "Horgan, you'll take him back there, won't you?"

"Come on," said Horgan. "You won't get much sense out of him, though. If you ask me, he's been on the weed."

CHAPTER FIVE

The long hallway between the cells smelled of antiseptics and stale tobacco smoke. The sun beating on the roof had heated the place like a waffle iron, but little sunlight penetrated. In the hot, gloomy cells as they passed, Dan could see forlorn men lying on cots, trying to sleep, or playing cards. A few looked resentfully after them.

Sheriff Horgan had been called to a telephone in the outer office and had delegated a stubby man called Mitch to "show Dan the screwball," as he put it.

Mitch loved the sound of the keys clanking in a ring on his belt. He opened iron doors with as much noise as possible, and closed them violently.

"You learn to know people in this work," he said, "and you pretty soon find out you can't trust any of them. The more innocent they look, the worse devils they are. You ain't nervous, are you?"

"I think I'll bear up," said Dan.

"There's nothing to be afraid of," said Mitch. "I've handled all kinds of characters in here. I know their psychology. And I know the only kind of reasoning that makes any impression on them." He patted the gun in his belt, and the hard little sap hanging beside it.

Flavin was locked off to himself in a kind of special felony cell apart from the rest. Through the bars, Dan could see him sitting with his head in his hands as they approached.

Mitch rapped harshly on the cell door with his sap. "Come on, son," he said; "Here's a man come to see you. He's gonna put your pitcher in the paper."

Flavin rose slowly and walked to the bars, eying Dan mistrustfully. He was plainly sick and frightened.

"Don't be nervous, fellow," Dan said. "I'm a newspaper reporter. I'm from the *Post-Tribune*. I just want to talk with you a little." Then, to Mitch. "Can't you open the door? Do we have to stand here like this?"

"You don't want to go in there, do you?" asked Mitch in amazement.

"Sure, you don't expect us to talk this way, do you?"

"Well, it ain't reg'lar, but it's your funeral." Mitch unlocked the door noisily. When Dan stepped into the cell, he banged the door and locked it again. "I'll be right out here when you're through," he said, and settled himself on a wooden chair nearby.

"Sit down, fellow," Dan said.

"You haven't a cigaret, have you?" Flavin asked.

"I smoke a pipe," said Dan. "But wait a minute." He walked to the bars. "Hey, pop! Got a cigaret on you?"

Mitch handed him a squashed pack.

"I'll keep 'em and get you another. Okay?"

Mitch grunted and resumed his seat.

Flavin sat on the cot, lit up, and puffed eagerly.

"That better?" asked Dan.

"Thanks," said Flavin.

Dan pulled up a stool. "Where did you come from?" he asked. "Have you got any family or friends anywhere?"

"I've got an aunt and uncle in—but I wouldn't want them to know about this. Listen, I don't know what you're thinking, but I didn't do this thing. It's all crazy. Will you let me tell you just what happened? It doesn't make sense, I know. But it's the truth. I didn't have anything to do with it."

"Let me ask you a few questions," Dan said. "This aunt and uncle—have they got any money?"

"They're broke. Uncle Fred's on WPA. There's no sense in worrying them."

"Haven't you any parents?"

"No. They're both dead. My aunt and uncle brought me up."

"How about friends? Do you have any friends who might help you?"

"I've got this friend out in California. I was going out to join him. But he hasn't any money. He just got a job out there, and he thought I might find a job, too, if I came."

"What do you do? What's your line?"

"Electrician, mostly. Or I guess you'd say electrician's helper. That's what I worked at last. But I've worked at a lot of odd jobs. I went to sea for a while."

"Isn't there anybody else might help you? A girl, maybe?"

"Well, nobody that I could ... no, I don't know anybody with money, or anybody I could ask for money."

"How about your poetry? Did you ever have anything published?"

"They've been reading my notebooks," Flavin said resentfully.

"Any of it ever published?"

"No, and I don't give a damn whether anybody likes it or not."

"That's a lot of moonshine," said Dan. "Sure you care. But we're wasting too much time. Do you know what they're accusing you of?"

Flavin pointed to a copy of the Sager Creek *Sentinel* on the cot. "Just what I read in there. But it doesn't make any sense. It's all crazy."

"All right, you tell me what happened—everything that happened—in your own words. I want everything in detail."

Flavin related his story more completely than he'd had time to do before the County Attorney, and Dan took careful notes.

"What kind of dress did she have on?" Dan asked. "Did you notice any jewelry or anything?"

"Well, it was a black dress, you might say, with pink flowers on it. But there were so many pink flowers it was almost a pink dress. Pink and black. Kind of low V-shaped in front, with a little lace. It was silk or rayon or something like that."

"Tight fitting?"

"Well, kind of. I think she wore a girdle. It looked like that."

"And no jewelry?"

"None that I noticed. I don't remember any."

"Are you any good at drawing?"

"Yeah. Pretty good. As a matter of fact, I took lessons. I was going to take it up once."

"Good. Think you could draw me a picture of this woman from memory?"

"I can try."

Dan handed him the notebook and pencil, and Flavin set to work. "I used to draw pictures of the guys on the ship," he said.

"I figured you'd gone to sea," Dan said. "That's where you got that knife, wasn't it?"

Flavin paused in his drawing. "Yeah. I've been thinking about that knife. If what it says in that newspaper is true, then—"

"I noticed it myself," said Dan. "I wouldn't say anything about it yet. Keep it as an ace up your sleeve. It doesn't prove anything, but you might be able to use it to advantage later on. Tell me what you saw when you first went in the gate. You say there wasn't anybody around."

"Nobody at all. And it was quiet. The only sound was the lawn spray—one of those whirligig kind that spins around and around."

"Notice anything else?"

"Well, around in back there was a garage that looked like it might have once been a stable. The door was partly open, and inside I could see a dark red automobile with a highly polished bumper."

"How about the house? What was it like?"

"It was clean, just like the fence and garden and everything else. Everything was immaculate. It was the most immaculate house I've ever seen. Everything was old-fashioned, and quiet, and immaculate."

"Now about the woman again. You say she acted strangely?"

"She seemed nervous about something, and I had a feeling she didn't live there. She had to hunt around for things, like she wasn't familiar with the kitchen. Another thing, she had long fingernails painted bright red and they didn't seem to go with the house. Nothing about her was like the place."

"You said you thought there was somebody else in the house."

"Well, yes. That was because once, while I was eating, a board creaked somewhere, like somebody walking on tiptoe. Right after that she left the kitchen for a few minutes. Then when we went upstairs, the top stair creaked when she stepped on it, just like I'd heard. And it creaked again when I stepped on it."

"And that's all you noticed?"

"Well, it's about all I can remember. Here's the picture. That's the best I can do. It's a pretty good likeness, I think. Her face isn't hard to draw."

"I haven't seen anything like this since I married and settled down," said Dan. "She looks like a woman used to manage a house in Albany."

"Now that you mention it, she did kind of look that way."

"You're pretty clever with your pencil."

"What are you going to do with it?"

"The first thing is to try to find out if there is any such woman."

"You don't think I did it, do you?"

"I don't think you did or you didn't. I don't know. But I'm going to try to find out."

"God, won't anybody believe me?"

"This is an age in which nobody will believe anything much. But don't worry. If you're telling the truth and there's any way of proving it, I'll find out. Meanwhile, sit tight and I'll have some magazines and cigarets sent in to you. I'll do the best I can."

Dan banged loudly on the cell door. "Come on, pop. Wake up!"

Mitch came to life grunting and blinking. He had fallen asleep on the chair tilted against the wall. "Goddamnit," he said, "I ate some cabbage last night and had heartburn all night long. Didn't sleep a wink. You get any sense out of him?"

CHAPTER SIX

Brannigan's barroom was full of stuffed birds. They stared in dusty, glass-eyed gloom from every niche and corner. They perched behind the bar, in the window, and even on the chandelier. Brannigan collected them, and they were his pride.

As Dan entered with Vance Dalbert, a storm of laughter was raging that all but swayed the dead birds on their perches.

Brannigan mopped a smooth area of the bar. "Evening, Mr. Dalbert. What'll it be?"

"What's all the laughing about?" asked Vance.

"Oh, some of the boys are needling old Regan," said Brannigan, nodding toward the other end of the bar. "He's trying to tell them that guy they arrested for the Hibley murder is innocent."

Vance laughed heartily. "He's a card. What'll you have, Dan?"

"Regan—isn't that the guy who was driving the kid into town when they picked him up?" Dan asked.

"That's right," said Vance. "Make mine a martini, Bran. What will you have, Dan?"

"Shot and a beer," said Dan. "Let's go talk to him. We might find out something."

"Still drinking the old boilermakers, I see. You don't want to talk to him, Dan. It's a waste of time. He's a town character. So you're married now, you say? Well, who'd have ever thought it?"

Dan glanced down the bar and saw the man they indicated to be Regan gripping a glass of beer as if he were hanging on to it to keep from being blown away in a cyclone. "You're a pack of unholy skunks," he was saying. "Every one of you goes sneaking in and out of Beth's every weekend, yet you want to hang a young lad because he mentions a woman's leg in a rhyme."

"Not to mention rape and murder, in addition to the poetry," added a fat man, and the whole bar roared.

Brannigan adopted the tone of voice one would use in addressing an authority. "Tell me, Mr. Dalbert, what do you think of this Czechoslovakian business? Do you think there's going to be another war?"

Vance shook his head scornfully. "This Sudeten business is nothing to worry about. It's just a lot of talk."

"That's what I figured," said Brannigan, "but, of course, I didn't know. How about the Russians?"

"They're no factor," said Vance. "Hitler's moving east. But the Russians haven't any army to speak of, and no industries. It doesn't amount to anything. Isn't that what you say, Dan?"

"I can't say as I agree with you," said Dan. "The whole thing is dynamite."

"Here's your martini," said Brannigan, sliding the thin-stemmed glass delicately toward Vance: Then he drew a beer for Dan and eased the whiskey into a shot glass.

"Come, Dan, aren't you being a little alarmist about the whole thing?" Vance asked.

Dan downed his shot and picked up the glass of beer. "I'd like to talk to that guy Regan," he said. He strolled down the bar and approached Regan.

"I might as well be trying to talk sense to those dead birds," Regan was saying.

"Whatsamatter, pop? They taking you for a ride?" Dan asked.

Regan jerked his head around, surveyed Dan contemptuously, then turned his back again. Then, as suddenly, he jerked his head around once more and said, "He didn't do it."

A roar of laughter went up from the bar. Regan stared angrily into his beer.

Vance came up behind Dan, winking at the others. "I think you're right, Regan," he said. "I don't think he did do it. I think you did."

Regan turned with slow dignity. "Vance Dalbert, you're a cow pie," he said. "If you want to know what I think of you, you're a cow pie."

Laughter exploded again, but no one could have said whether it was at Regan's expense or Vance's. Vance blushed deeply, as if he privately suspected he might be a cow pie after all. Dan gathered from the subtleties that Vance was not the most popular man in town.

"Come on," said Vance, pulling at Dan's coat. "We've got to get home. You're coming home to dinner with me. I've already phoned the wife."

Dan protested, "Not tonight, Vance—really."

"I won't take no for an answer," Vance said. He knuckled Dan in the ribs. "You old hyena, we've got a lot to catch up on."

"Some other night," said Dan. He leaned through a V-shaped aperture between Regan and the next man, and thumbed his empty glass on the bar. "Another of the same," he said to Brannigan, "and give him whatever he wants." He jerked a thumb at Regan.

"What the hell do you think I am?" asked Regan. "A B-girl? I don't even know you."

"Well, do you want the drink or not?" Dan asked.

Regan reflected for a moment, then emptied his glass and shoved forward. "Willful waste makes woeful want," he declared. "Who am I to be proud?"

"Make mine another martini," said Vance. "And listen, Dan, if you think I'm going to take no for an answer, you're badly mistaken."

"Go way and leave him alone," said Regan. "Can't you see he don't want to go home with you?"

The fat man next to Regan turned and poked a finger at Vance's coat lapel. "What we oughta do," he said, "is blockade the roads at the state border. Keep those bums out of here."

"And what are they going to do with our own bums?" Regan asked. "Round them up in other states and ship them back? There are more bums per capita from here, hitting up back doors all over the country, than from any other state in the union—including your brother. By the way, what do you hear from him, Frank?"

Another laugh went up. But the men were beginning to lose interest and split up into separate groups of argument.

"You don't think the kid's guilty, do you?" Dan said to Regan.

"I most certainly do not," said Regan. "You're new around here, aren't you, young fellow? I haven't seen you before."

"I'm a reporter from the *Post-Tribune* in the city," said Dan.

"Then you wouldn't be interested in the truth," Regan said.

"What have you got there?" asked Vance. He tried to twist his head around and look.

Dan had taken Flavin's attempt at a portrait from his pocket and was studying it. "Nothing," he said. "I picked it up on the sidewalk. Some kid must have drawn it." He handed it to Regan. "Did you draw that, pop?"

Regan examined it curiously. "Hell, no. I can't draw nothing. It's a good likeness, though."

Brannigan leaned across the bar, and Regan showed him the drawing. "Goddamn," Brannigan said. "That's pretty good. Her eyes look a little goofy, but otherwise it's Beth, all right."

"Let's see it," said the fat man. He held the drawing conveniently to his vision, and laughed until his chins danced. "Somebody's drew Beth's pitcher," he chortled. "Put it over the bar, Brannigan."

"Yeah, with the other dead birds," said Regan.

"Who's Beth?" asked Dan.

"You wouldn't be interested," said Vance. "You're a married man."

"She runs a joint down to Sawtooth," said Regan.

"It's a honky-tonk," said Brannigan. "A kind of bar and dance hall, with a cat house upstairs."

"Where's Sawtooth?" Dan asked.

"No you don't, Dan. Not tonight," said Vance. "You're coming home to dinner with me."

"Leave him alone," said Regan. "He don't want to go home with you."

"Sawtooth's a crossroads about a mile below Hamilton," said Brannigan. "A sort of shanty town. These three towns are so close together they're almost like one—Sager Creek, Hamilton, and Sawtooth. Only, respectable folks don't recognize Sawtooth."

"Just the same," said the fat man, "you'd like to have the dough Beth takes into her joint every Saturday night."

"Any night, for that matter," said Brannigan. "It's the biggest gold mine in the country." The phone rang, and Brannigan answered it behind the bar.

"Who is this Beth?" asked Dan, putting the picture back in his pocket. "Is she from around here?"

"It's for you, Mr. Dalbert," Brannigan said, holding his hand over the mouthpiece. "Are you here?"

"Yeah. I'll take it in the booth," said Vance. "That's the wife, Dan. We've got to get going."

"Honest, Vance, not tonight," Dan pleaded. "Some other night. I'm not hungry."

Vance shrugged his shoulders and went off to the phone booth.

Dan pulled Regan by the arm. "Do you mind if I have a word with you, pop?"

Regan objected, "I wish you'd quit calling me pop. Maybe I look used up, but I could swing you around my head and throw you through the transom." But he slid off the stool and accompanied Dan to one of the tables along the opposite wall.

"Can you keep your mouth shut?" Dan asked.

"I have no reputation for it," said Regan. "I'm the village idiot, as they must have informed you. A dull wit in a community of intellectuals."

Dan eyed him carefully and decided to take a chance. "You think the kid they have in the jail is innocent, don't you?"

"I know it," Regan said.

"Maybe you're right and maybe you're wrong. But what are you going to do about it?"

Regan lost his assurance. A tired look came into his eyes. "What can I do? They won't listen to me."

"Then you ought to stop blowing your mouth off."

"What do you mean? Stop talking? Never. Stand up like a man and tell them what you think. That's my way."

"And if they don't believe you, what good is it? The thing to do is get some proof. And you can get that better by keeping your mouth shut."

Regan nodded thoughtfully. "You're right, of course, that's been my trouble all my life. I blow my mouth and kid myself that I'm not taking anything from anybody. Then they kick my behind all over the lot. It's results that count, not talk." He meditated for a moment, then barked defensively, "Goddamn it, though, young fellow, somebody's got to be honest and speak the truth somewhere along the line. All this playing games—I hate it."

"Just the same," Dan said, "I'm asking you to keep your mouth shut about what I tell you now."

"All right, son. When you're trapped in a low cave, I guess you've got to crawl to get into the light. I'll play your game."

"Remember the picture I showed you?"

"The one of Beth? Yeah."

"The kid drew that. He drew it in jail today. She was the woman who gave him food at the Hibley house."

"Well, I'll be—but it's impossible."

"Just the same, he drew that picture. Do you want to go down to that joint with me tonight and see what we can find out?"

"Well, sure—but it's impossible."

Vance came back rubbing his hands together. "I got out of it, Dan, old boy. Did I have to do some explaining! I told her you were interested in investing some money in the business, and I had to pamper you. We're going to make a night of it, you and me. By the way, you wouldn't be interested in buying in, would you?"

Regan eyed Vance with a kind of nausea. Dan, however, greeted him for once with warmth. "Now you're talking, Vance. Pull up a chair." He yelled to Brannigan at the bar for another one all around. "Regan here's going to take us down to Beth's place in Sawtooth."

"You ought to be ashamed of yourself," Vance said to Regan. "You, with a wife and kids."

"I'm just a vulgar old man at heart," Regan said coldly.

"You're not going to back out on us, are you, Vance?" Dan asked.

"How does it go?" said Vance recklessly. "What you do when you're drunk and in foreign countries doesn't count."

"Beth's going to drop dead when she sees you walking in the front door instead of sneaking in the side entrance," Regan said.

Vance shot him a look of raw hatred.

Dan pushed back his chair. "I'll just let you two old cronies chat while I put in a phone call."

In the booth, he deposited a coin and called a Frenton number.

"Hello—Al? I called you at home because I couldn't talk very well over the office phone this afternoon. That switchboard girl listens to everything and carries it to Ainsley. Look—that kid they picked up in the Hamilton case. The one they arrested. There's no certainty he's guilty. He may not have done it. They're willing to hang it on him without giving him a chance.

"There isn't much you can do, Al, I know. They'll try to make the kid look like Dracula. When the story goes through your desk, try to tone it down as much as you can, will you? Give the kid a break. And print those poems I included. They might help.

"I know you can't do much, Al, but I wanted you to know the facts. Do the best you can. No, you won't get your neck in a jam. I know it's none of my affair. Nothing is any of my business. You're the city editor. You ought to be able to do something.

"Sure I'll take care of myself. What do you think I am, a chump? All right, then, I am. I'll call you back tomorrow night and give you some bulletins."

When he had hung up, Dan dropped another coin, lifted the receiver, and called another Frenton number.

"Ethel? Gee, darling, it's good to hear your voice. Sager Creek. I'm in Sager Creek. Sure I'm coming home, just as soon as I can. How do I know where Sager Creek is? I never heard of it before. When? Well, I might be held up here a few days. Nothing important. No. I don't know why you say that. I sound funny? That's nonsense.

"I'm going to a movie. I am not lying. My God, Ethel! Instinct, my neck! That's imagination. Woman's intuition—for the love of Pete. There isn't any such thing. I tell you, I'm going to a movie.

"Listen, darling, I can't come home tomorrow. No reason. I just can't. The office phoned me and said I had to stay here a couple of days. I'm not lying. You ask Al.

"He isn't a liar. Listen, darling, don't talk like that. I tell you I'm going to a movie. It's the deadest town I ever saw. Not a thing going on. They pulled in the sidewalks an hour ago.

"Cut out that feeling things in your bones. Yes, darling. Yes, darling. Of course, darling. Of course, darling. Good night, sweetheart. Good night, you little bum. That's a good girl. Good night."

Coming out of the booth, Dan mopped his brow with a handkerchief. "Come on, fellows," he said. "Let's get going."

"This is my night to howl," Vance said recklessly.

"The old lady's going to give me hell for this," said Regan.

CHAPTER SEVEN

The immunity of Beth's place from interference by the police was an accepted miracle in the county. Others who sought to open similar establishments evoked the quick wrath of the law. Shutting them down and prosecuting the proprietors was a rapid and simple process.

In coping with Beth's place, however, the authorities developed a unique blindness and ineptitude. The task seemed fraught with unsurmountable difficulties and complications. Evidence which in the other instances was a crude matter of herding patrons and personnel into jail, became elusive and impossible to obtain regarding Beth's place.

Officials, when called on by protesting delegations of housewives, would furrow their brows and admit that there seemed to be a situation in Sawtooth that needed some investigation, and as a matter of fact, proper steps had already been taken to look into it. If the allegations proved true, then certainly this was not a thing to be tolerated.

But it went right on, year after year, until Sager Creek, Hamilton, and the other surrounding towns came to accept it as an unavoidable evil, more practically combated by right teaching in the schools and promotion of all-out church attendance than by enforcing the law.

Beth's place was an ornate, two-storied, wooden building that had once been a hotel, and still was, theoretically—the Queen Anne Hotel, transient, with the Crystal Bar underneath. It was situated on a corner, with entrances on both streets, and a third entrance into a dark vacant lot in the rear that served as a parking area. The barroom itself made a fourth entrance, for it was connected with the hotel above by a stairway.

The "Jersey Bounce" was blaring from a red, purple, and green juke box as the three men entered. Almost all of the tables were occupied by loudly chattering groups of men, interspersed with heavily rouged women in cheap evening gowns. The smell of tobacco smoke and strong perfume mingled in the air.

The bar was pretty thickly clustered, but they managed to find two stools and elbow room for one down near the end.

Vance had been telling a dirty story all the way from the parking lot and was still at it. It was one of those stories which build up through endless repetition and unnecessary detail to a surprise punch line, and depend upon the skill of the narrator at imitating dialogue—something for which Vance had no talent at all. Both Dan and Tom Regan had heard it a dozen times before, but let him go ahead.

"So," said Vance, "she went to a third drugstore. The clerk came out and said, 'What can I do for you, madam?'"

Regan nudged Dan and nodded toward the end of the bar. Dan recognized the woman instantly from Ralph's drawing. She was seated on a high stool behind the bar, from which vantage point she could command a view of the whole establishment. The look of fear and nervousness was not in her eyes. Otherwise, she fitted the picture. The heavily lined mouth was set in a kind of permanent, insincere grin, and the eyes were dark and cruel. She was chatting easily with a couple at the bar.

"What'll it be, gentlemen?" said the bartender, mopping an area in front of them.

"Shootin' any pool lately, Ray?" asked Regan.

"I don't know you from a hole in the ground," said the bartender. "Last time you were in here you went out without paying for some drinks."

"That's a damn lie," Regan protested.

"What'll you have, gentlemen?" the bartender repeated. "Is Tom with you?"

"We're all together," said Dan.

"Listen to what I'm saying," Vance insisted. "So then she went into a fourth drugstore."

While the bartender called Ray fixed their drinks, Dan studied him with interest. He was a towering man, well over six feet, with thick arms and a sagging, bag-like stomach that swayed when he moved. There was a sweaty unpleasantness about his whole person. His face was white and pasty, in odd contrast with his bright red hair. Mean little eyes of milky blue peered from under unusually long eyelashes. On the pale skin of his forearm was a large, faded tattoo of a dagger with a snake coiled around its length. The snake had the head of a woman, with a fanglike tongue darting from her mouth.

When their drinks were served, Regan looked around him and suggested they move to a table near the wall.

"That guy's served a lot of time," Dan said as they settled in chairs, "and if I'm not mistaken, he's had some ring experience."

"You mean Ray?" said Regan. "He used to be some kind of champ in the Navy."

"Listen," said Vance, "so when she came to the next drugstore—" He delivered the punch line and roared with amusement.

"Ha, ha, ha," said Regan flatly. "Thank God that's over. What makes you think he served time?"

"That gray look, and those eyes," said Dan. "I couldn't be wrong."

A chubby brunette, in satin slacks pulled so tightly over her seat they looked at the point of bursting, came up with a tray. "If you boys are gonna sit at a table, why do you get your drinks at the bar?" she asked. "All I make's a commission on what's sold at the table."

Dan slipped her a dollar bill. "I'm sorry," he said, "we didn't know."

Vance tried to wrap an arm around her, and she slapped him off. "If you want to play, go upstairs," she said. "I'm here to wait on table. How about another one, or are you gonna nurse those?"

"Give us the same all around," Dan said.

Two willowy girls in rayon evening gowns floated casually up and hovered near the table. Dan rose gallantly. "Can we ask you to have a drink with us?" he said.

They smiled indulgently. One was a brunette with a nose like a bird's beak. The other was a platinum blonde with a flat, Norwegian face. Her hair fell loosely in a long bob, and she had a tiny bouquet of artificial flowers fixed on the exact top of her head. Dan guided her to a seat next to him because she looked as if she had a sense of humor.

The brunette ordered expensive Scotch, and the blonde asked for a King Alphonse.

"She's Madge, and I'm Shirley," said the blonde.

"Don't give your right names, boys," said Vance with a chuckle.

The girls gave him a contemptuous look. Regan stared into his glass in embarrassment.

"That's a nice thing you've got in your hair," Dan said, indicating the bouquet on Shirley. "I don't think I ever saw one before. It looks swell with your kind of hair."

Shirley's eyes flashed happy gratitude.

"She made it herself," said Madge. "Gee, she's clever. She makes all her own hats and things. Gosh, I wish I could do something like that. I think it's swell to be good at something, don't you?"

"You made that yourself?" asked Dan in an incredulous tone. "Well, by gosh!" He leaned over and examined it closely. "All those little flowers—do you mean you made all those?"

Shirley glowed quietly.

"Sure," said Madge proudly. "She can make anything."

"Or anybody, I'll bet," said Vance, laughing at his own wit.

Dan gave the girls an apologetic look. "It's funny," he said. "Some people are clever at doing things, and some people aren't."

"If I try to do anything like that, it just turns out a mess," said

Madge.

Shirley unpinned the bouquet from her hair and held it out for inspection. "That blue was an old piece of blouse," she said. "The yellow centers are from an old felt hat I had. The wire, you buy."

"It's pretty, kid," said Madge.

"Move your elbow," said the girl with the tray. "Here's your drinks."

"Did you make the dress, too?" asked Dan.

"No, that's bought," said Shirley. "I make most of the things I wear when I'm not working, though."

"Didn't I see you downtown the other day in a kind of black and pink dress?"

"Black and pink? I don't think so. Not me."

"Well, it had a kind of black background and pink flowers. But so many pink flowers it was almost a pink dress. Black and pink. Wasn't that you?"

"Beth has a dress like that," said Madge. "She had it on yesterday. But you couldn't have mistaken Beth for Shirley. Gosh!" A harsh but hearty feminine voice descended from over their heads. "You getting along all right here, boys?"

It was Beth, making her periodic back-slapping tour of the floor.

"No complaints," said Dan. "Won't you sit down?"

Beth eyed Vance and grimaced. "Well, how do you do? This is an unexpected honor, Mr.—"

Vance put one finger to his lips. "Incognito," he said.

"I get it," said Beth. "Well, you don't have to worry in here. Are you all being taken care of all right?"

"Everything's fine," said Dan. "Won't you sit down?"

"Well, just a short one," said Beth, easing into a chair. "But this one will be on the house." She waved to the girl with the tray.

"Wasn't that a terrible thing about that murder in Hamilton," said Madge. "I was reading about it in the paper."

"Well," said Dan, "they've evidently caught the guy, so that's the end of it." He watched Beth's face, but there was not the slightest movement or change of expression.

"They caught him running around with a bloody knife in his hand," said Madge.

"What a screwball," said Shirley.

"What kind of woman is Mrs. Hibley?" Dan asked.

"Search me," said Madge. "She wouldn't be apt to come in here."

Beth took an interest in Shirley's artificial flowers. "You'd better put those in your hair, honey, or you'll lose them."

"We were talking about dresses," Madge said. "This gentleman thought he saw Shirley in one like you have. That black and pink one you had on yesterday."

That did it. Dan saw the smile on Beth's mouth harden into a straight line, and a flash of fear light her eyes.

"I don't know what you're talking about, Madge. I don't have any such dress," she said.

"Yes, you have. I saw you in it yesterday afternoon," Madge insisted.

"You're crazy," said Beth angrily. "You must be drunk." Her voice was so hard that Madge backed down. "Well, of course, I might have been mistaken."

Dan attempted a rescue. "As I remember," he said, "it wasn't a dress, but a skirt. And it may not have been pink. Maybe yellow. It was just a girl I saw yesterday afternoon. I thought it was Shirley here."

Beth's eyes did not relax. "You're new around here, aren't you?" she asked.

"I'm a reporter from the *Post-Tribune* in the city," Dan answered. He decided to throw the issue in her face. "What's your opinion of this Hibley murder, Mrs.—or Miss—I don't think I got your name."

"The name's Ridgely," said Beth. "And it's Mrs.—but everyone around here just calls me Beth."

Vance jerked a thumb at Regan. "Tom here thinks the guy they arrested is innocent, don't you, Tom?" He chuckled and winked at the others.

Regan looked at Dan for a signal, but getting none, stuck to his own frankness. "All right, I do," he said. "I don't give a damn what you say, I think he's innocent."

"How could he be?" asked Madge. "The paper said they found him with the knife and all."

"He couldn't be," said Vance. "He's the man, all right. I was there when he confessed."

"What were you doing there?" asked Shirley.

Vance suddenly remembered his incognito and was embarrassed.

Beth eyed Regan sharply. "It says in the papers that you were the one who picked him up and brought him into Sager Creek—weren't you?"

"I did," said Regan. "I found him in my field."

"Golly," said Madge. "I would have been scared to death."

"Did you get any reward?" asked Shirley.

"Scared, shucks," said Regan, "he's just a nice young kid. He didn't do it at all. "

Beth looked sharply at Dan. "What's your opinion?" she asked.

"It's a simple case," said Dan, knocking his pipe out into an ash tray.

"The kid was probably sex-starved and broke. He discovered the girl was alone in the house—probably tried to take advantage of her, she started to yell, he got scared and killed her. Then he thought he might as well rob the place. He found a bottle of whiskey. Maybe he had a few drinks before, for that matter. Anyhow, he was scared and nervous, so he kept on drinking, 'til he didn't know what he was doing. He got well outside of Hamilton, then was so drunk he either fell down, or else decided to lie down and take a nap. He slept all night, and Regan found him the next morning. That's all there is to it."

"Say, Dan," said Vance suddenly. "Show Beth the picture you found of her. The one you were showing in the bar."

"Oh, that? I lost it," said Dan. "I left it there on the bar."

"No you didn't. You put it in your pocket. I saw you," said Vance.

Reluctantly, Dan fished in his pocket and drew out the picture. "They say it's a picture of you," he said. "I don't know. I picked it up on the street. Maybe there's a slight resemblance."

Beth looked at the drawing and whitened noticeably. Madge leaned over to get a view. "That's you, Beth," she said. "And see, you've got the dress on that I was saying."

"That's not me," snapped Beth. "My God! If I looked like that I'd hang myself."

"Well, I didn't say it looked *exactly* like you," said Madge.

"It doesn't look anything like me," said Beth.

"I don't think it looks like you either," said Dan. "It's just a piece of paper I picked up, and that was on the back."

"Who drew it?" asked Beth.

"I don't know," said Dan. "I just picked it up."

Beth drained her glass and stood up. "You boys enjoy yourself. I've got this place to watch after."

"Can I have the picture back?" asked Dan

"What do you want with it?" asked Beth.

"Oh, nothing," Dan said.

"Then keep it," said Beth. "Shirley—Madge—you see that these gentlemen have a good time." She wandered off toward the bar.

"Do you want to dance?" Madge asked.

Vance wrestled out of his chair and wrapped himself around her.

"How about you?" Shirley asked, putting one hand on Dan's arm. "What's that you're doing?"

"I need one of these for drinking in my room," said Dan. "You just say nothing about it." Taking a handkerchief from his pocket, he had carefully wrapped it around Beth's shot glass and stowed it in his pocket.

"That's a funny thing to steal," Shirley said. "It only costs about a nickel."

Dan gave her a dollar. "Look," he said, "you get that changed and put some nickels in the juke box. What do you say?"

"Anything particular you want to hear?"

"Whatever you like," said Dan.

As soon as she was gone, Regan leaned close. "You're a hell of a detective," he said. "All you've done is put her wise. She's on to you. Beth's no fool."

"I know," Dan said, "but it got out of control. What could she have been doing in the Hibley house?"

"It doesn't make the slightest bit of sense to me," said Regan. "But look over there. She's talking to Vance."

Beth had called Vance and Madge off the dance floor to the bar, and she was apparently questioning Vance intently.

"She's worried plenty," Dan said. Under the table, he slipped a bill to Regan. "When the girl comes back, you excuse yourself and go to the can. But don't come right back here. Stop at the bar and buy yourself a shot. When that bartender, Ray, serves it to you, pick it up carefully by the rim, drink it, and then when nobody's looking, wrap it in your handkerchief and stick it in your pocket."

"You want his fingerprints?" asked Regan.

"That's right," Dan said. "Can you do it?"

"Sure, but I don't need this." Regan tried to give him back the bill.

"Keep it," said Dan. "I have an expense account."

When Shirley returned, Regan excused himself and disappeared onto the crowded floor.

"Do you want to go upstairs?" Shirley asked Dan.

"Let's have another drink first. Were you in here yesterday afternoon?"

"Yesterday was my day off," said Shirley. "That's always my day off, if you're interested."

"Is Beth usually here in the afternoons?"

"Sometimes. She wasn't here yesterday afternoon. I know because I came back to my room early in the evening and saw her drive into the parking lot. She lives on the place—has an apartment in back, upstairs. You're not interested in me, are you?"

"Why do you say that?" Dan took one of her hands in his own. The drinks were beginning to muddle his brain.

"Gosh, kid, you're pretty," she said. "You're nice. I guess a girl would be a chump to fall for you. Especially a girl like me."

"You're nice, Shirley." Dan looked around the dance floor for Madge and Vance, but they had disappeared. Beth was behind the bar on her observation stool. Regan sauntered out of the men's room and leaned against the bar.

"Yeah, but I'm not your kind," said Shirley. "You'd never fall for a girl like me."

"What makes you think I'm any better than you are?"

"Someday I figure to have a little dress shop of my own," Shirley said. "Someday I'm going to meet a man I can trust, and have him for myself. You know, they say girls like me make the best wives. These little chippies you see around, just out of high school—they don't know anything."

"Doesn't that stuff ever have any effect on you?" asked Dan, nodding toward her drink.

"That? Oh, that's just syrup and water. They don't serve us anything real."

"Never anything real. Always just pretending. Is that the way it is?" Dan asked.

"You don't think a girl like me could ever feel things, do you?"

"Listen," said Dan, "people are just people to me. I'm no snob."

"A girl like me can give you a better time than any of these little dopes who think you owe them your life if you so much as put your hand on them."

"How long have you been working around here?"

"I've been here about a month. But I was other places before. I won't kid you. I'm not going to stay here, though. I don't like her." Shirley nodded toward Beth, who was still behind the bar. "I'm a chump to talk to you this way. Listen, if you don't want to go upstairs, I can't sit here long. She likes us to circulate around."

Dan drained his glass. "All right, let's go upstairs."

CHAPTER EIGHT

Tom Regan was leaning on the bar as they passed. Vance was nowhere in sight. They entered a hall at the side of the bar and climbed a carpeted stairway to the floor above. Here was a maze of passageways with numbered doors, and the strong smell of antiseptics.

Shirley led the way to her own room, unlocked it, and snapped a light switch inside. It was a tiny bedroom, with a cheap oriental bedspread, a dressing table covered with bottles and powder boxes, and a lot of floppy, stuffed dolls thrown about.

"Did you make the dolls?" Dan asked.

"Yeah," said Shirley. "I made the lampshades, too. Do you want to give me the money now? I have to check in with the maid, down the hall, so they know where I am."

Dan slipped a bill out of his wallet and handed it to her.

"Do you want any change?" she asked. "If not, we can take our time."

"Keep it," said Dan. He relaxed on the bed, picked up a doll, and studied its face.

"I'll be right back, honey," she said, and eased out the door. Alone, Dan rubbed his face vigorously, and shook his head. He was tired and would have liked to have gone to sleep right there on the bed. But he knew he had work to do.

He got up and stuck his head out the only window in the room. It opened, he saw, into a narrow light well. Directly across from him was another dark window which he could reach out and touch. Behind him, he heard the door open and shut.

"You're not sick, are you, honey?" Shirley asked.

"I was just getting a breath of air," Dan said, drawing his head back into the room.

"'Cause if you are, the bathroom's right down the hall." She was already fumbling with the ribbons of her dress, untying them.

"Don't do that, kid," said Dan. "I don't want to do anything but just sit and talk. I like you, but I'm a married man."

"Married men are nothing new in here," she said. "What's the matter, doesn't your wife give you a good time?" She stopped fumbling with her ribbons, but didn't tie them again. From the dressing table she took a pack of cigarets, slipped one out, and lit it.

"That's not it," Dan said. "I came here for a different reason."

"Maybe you're not so different as you think?" she said, taking a deep drag of the cigaret, and reclining on the end of the bed. "All these guys think they're different. Their wives don't know what it's all about, so they come to us. I don't know why they don't marry us in the first place. What's the good of a wife you can't—"

"My wife and I get along fine," said Dan defensively.

"You don't have to apologize to me, honey."

"Listen," said Dan, changing the subject forcibly, "what's that window just across the light well from this room?"

"That's Beth's apartment. Sit down. Don't be afraid. Do you think the world would explode if you touched me?"

"Does Beth ever come upstairs this time of the night?"

"No, but stop worrying about her. What are you afraid of, honey? You're not doing anything wrong. What do you care what Beth thinks?"

"I don't," said Dan. "That's not the point."

Shirley put one hand gently on his arm. "Tell me, honey—tell me what's troubling you. You've been worried all evening. Sometimes it does a man good to get things off his chest. You love your wife, but what? What is it? You just can't let yourself go with her. Is that it?"

"It hasn't anything to do with my wife," Dan said. "It's that kid they've got in jail over in Sager Creek for that murder."

"Oh," said Shirley in a disappointed voice. She removed her hand from his arm. "What about him?"

"It's possible he didn't do it at all."

"That's tough. But what's that got to do with me?"

"I think Beth did have something to do with it."

"Something to do with what?"

"Something to do with that murder."

Shirley stood up and snuffed her cigaret in a little porcelain ash tray on the dresser. "I don't want any part of this," she said coldly. "I get it now. You're a cop."

"I'm not a cop. I'm a newspaper reporter. But I wouldn't sit back and see a young kid take the rap for something an old bitch like Beth had a hand in."

"What is he, your brother or something?"

"I never saw him before this afternoon."

"What makes you think he didn't do it?"

"Well, I'm not sure. But he's entitled to a break."

"I'll be damned," said Shirley.

"Why do you say that?"

"I've been in jail a lot of times, honey, but nobody ever came along like you to give a damn what happened to me. You better get out of here. I can't afford to have any trouble with Beth or anybody else."

"Look. All I want you to do—"

"Will you get out of here?" asked Shirley angrily. "What do you want to do, drive me crazy? Can't you see I've had enough trouble?"

Dan stood up. "All right," he said, "I should have had better sense."

"I'm sorry," Shirley said, handing him his hat, "but I have my own troubles."

"I know, I should have had better sense." Dan put his hand on the doorknob.

"What were you figuring on doing?" asked Shirley.

"I just thought I could climb across the light well and take a look in Beth's apartment for a minute. I might find something that would help clear the kid."

"Yes, and maybe it's a gag and you just want to swipe something."

"That's not so, and you know it," Dan said.

"I've had all the trouble I want. Nobody ever went crawling across light wells to help me."

"Well, I'm sorry."

"And suppose Beth should come up here while you're in there? That would be my neck."

"Where's the door to her apartment?"

"Down the hall and around the corner."

"Is there any way of reaching it except past this door?"

"No."

"Then you could listen at this door, and if you heard anybody coming you could whistle across the light well and I'd be out of there in plenty of time."

"And run the chance of getting my neck in a jam? Don't make me laugh."

"Well, you asked me what I was thinking of."

"Why should I stick my neck out for you?"

"It isn't for me, it's for that kid in jail."

"I don't even know him."

"Neither do I."

"If you want to be a damn fool, that's your business. I've got myself to think about."

"All right, skip it. I was a damn fool to ask you."

"Wait a minute," said Shirley. "Then hurry up and get it done with. Don't waste so much time."

"You mean—"

"Hurry up and get it done with," said Shirley angrily.

"You're a swell kid," Dan said.

"I'm a damn fool," she replied, pressing her ear against the door.

Dan wasted no time leaning out the window into the light well. He found the opposite window half open and pushed it all the way up. He gripped the sill and swung himself across, elbowing his way into a dark room. His head bumped a chair, which he pushed aside, and he clambered to the floor.

Looking back across the light well, he could see Shirley with her ear pressed against the door of the room he had just left. He struck a match, saw the outlines of a door, and a switch beside it. Another instant and he had the lights on.

It was a gaudy sitting room. Through the open door of another room, he could see the foot of a bed. He entered the bedroom and snapped on another light, opened a closet door, thumbed through the dresses lined up on hangers, and found the black and pink flowered one.

Under the dresses he saw a small, flat trunk. He tried the lid and found it locked. Closing the closet door, he tackled a small writing desk. Over it hung a photograph which appeared to be Beth in her younger days, in the frilly tights and spangles of a chorus girl. Dan eyed it appreciatively. She had been something to whistle at in her time.

In the long drawer under the desk top was a jumbled assortment of papers, address books, check stubs, blotters, and other junk. A brownish newspaper clipping caught Dan's eye. It was an obituary notice of Vern B. Hibley, clipped from a Frenton paper. The date on it was February 28, 1928. It mentioned Hibley's long service as Attorney General.

A stiff, blue sheet of letter paper that looked fairly new lay near the clipping. There was no date on it, nor any indication of where it came from. It read:

> Dear Beth: June should arrive on about the fifteenth. I'm expecting you to take care of her. If not, I'm sure you realize what I am capable of. I may be in the same boat with you, but I don't care as much whether it sinks or not as you do. If the rest of my life is going to be like it's been so far, I'd just as soon drag us both down as not. This is the first thing I've asked of you, and I guess you know I mean business.

It was signed "Franz." The handwriting was in a square, angular pattern that suggested a European background—probably German.

Just then, Dan heard a soft whistle. He shoved the letter in his pocket, closed the drawer, and made a dive for the light switch. In the sitting room, he snapped out the light and lunged through the window, grabbing the opposite sill and flinging himself through.

Shirley helped him as he rolled onto the floor, and she quickly pulled down the shade. "We'd better make a noise like business," she said.

Dan peeked under the blind and saw the lights go on in the sitting room he had just left. Shirley pulled him away from the window and turned on the water in the basin, noisily.

"You sure know your onions," she said loudly. "Are you going to come back and see me often, honey?" Her serious face was really frightened. She waved her hand in a manner that implied "Give, brother, give."

Dan took his cue. "Baby, you've got what it takes," he said in a voice perhaps a little too loud. "Come on, let's play some more."

With rapid hands, she mussed his hair, pulled his necktie loose, and unbuckled his belt. Then, motioning for him to finish the process, she jumped on the bed and made a noise with the springs, meanwhile indicating the door with her thumb.

Dan slipped out of his trousers, jerked his necktie off, fairly ripped the buttons off his vest, and began fingering frantically at his shirt buttons.

There was a loud knock at the door.

Shirley slipped out of her dress and threw it on the floor. "What do you want?" she yelled at the door. "Go away or I'll call Ray."

"This *is* Ray," said a voice in the hall. "Open this goddamn door."

Dan was down to a convincing state of undress, and Shirley threw her last unmentionable at the chair as she unlocked the door.

"What the hell's the idea?" said Dan loudly. "Is the place pinched?"

Ray stuck his head into the room. "Shut up, Buster," he said. He looked around and was evidently impressed by the show of licentiousness. Dan by this time was sprawling on the bed in an attitude of drunken stupor.

"What's the idea of embarrassing my gentleman friend?" Shirley demanded in a show of anger.

"Is it a pinch?" Dan asked with a look of stupid terror.

"All right, put your pants on," said Ray.

"Well, of all the nerve," said Shirley. "Busting in here like this."

"Shut up," said Ray. "You ain't hurt. Neither of you are hurt. Sorry, mister. Just keeping an eye on things. Better put your pants on." He backed out the door and closed it.

Dan began to climb into his clothes again.

Shirley came close to him. "For God's sake," she whispered, "don't leave me here tonight. Don't leave me. Please take me with you."

"They don't know anything," said Dan. "You've got nothing to worry about."

"I don't know what they know or what they don't know," she whispered desperately. "I don't know what the hell's going on. But don't leave me here. You don't know them."

"But, my God," said Dan, appalled by looming complications.

"I stuck my neck out for you. Please don't leave me holding the bag. They'll question me and question me, and I'm no good at lying. They'll know I'm lying. You don't know them. Don't walk out on me."

"All right. Hell," said Dan, "pack your stuff and come along." Shirley dragged an old cardboard suitcase from the closet and began ramming clothes into it.

"You ought to wear some of them," Dan suggested.

"Oh yeah. Gosh!" She began stepping and elbowing into fluffy underthings.

"I don't know how we're going to engineer this," Dan said as he jammed down the lid of the suitcase and snapped the clasps. "Are you going to leave all those dolls and stuff?"

"All I care about is getting out of here. We can go down through the side entrance of the hotel. Have you got a car?"

"Yeah, it's in the parking lot out back. But I came with a couple of guys downstairs. I oughtn't to leave them."

"You don't seem to realize the jam you've got me into. Can't they take care of themselves?"

"Looks like they'll have to. Are you ready? Lead the way."

Dan followed the girl around two different turns in the hallway then down a narrow stairway to a glass paneled door on which he could see the words "Queen Anne Hotel" backwards through the pane. Once in the street, she grabbed his hand and steered him around the corner of the building, and down a narrow cement walk to the parking lot. He found his coupe and opened the door.

"Is that you, Banion?" said a voice.

Shirley's fingernails dug into Dan's arm.

"It's only me—Regan," said the voice. "I got the glass."

"Okay," Dan said. "Move over. We've got company."

"What's this?" asked Regan. "What have you been up to?"

"Shut up," said Dan, "and move over." He pushed Shirley and her suitcase into the seat beside Regan, then ran around the car and climbed in under the wheel.

"Where's Dalbert?" asked Regan. "You're not going to leave him in there, are you?"

"I'm going to get the hell out of here," said Dan. He stepped on the starter, shifted gears, and eased the car out of the lot onto the road.

"Hey, what's going on here?" said Regan. "I'm damned if I know what you're doing from one minute to the next."

"Neither do I," said Dan. "Look back. Do you see anybody following us?"

Regan twisted around. "No. The road's clear." He looked at Shirley, who sat gripping her suitcase between her legs. "This young lady— do you mind if I ask—"

"I got her in a jam," said Dan, "and had to bring her along."

They were well out of Sawtooth now, and the headlights were racing over a strip of asphalt between two dark fences. The smell of fresh alfalfa came to them from cool fields.

"What are you going to do with her?" Regan asked.

"I'm damned if I know."

Shirley began to sniff. "I wish I was dead," she sobbed. "I wish I was dead."

"Now, now," said Dan. "You shouldn't say that, Shirley. There's nothing to worry about."

"Are you positively convinced of that statement?" said Regan. "We've got to find a place for her to stay. You haven't got an extra bed in your house, have you?"

"Well, by all the gods," Regan blurted. "You've got your nerve. How long have you been living this way, young fellow? Do you just help yourself to people and things wherever you go? I've already committed petty larceny for no other reason but that you suggested it."

"I wish I was dead," sobbed Shirley. "I'm going to kill myself."

"Don't say such a thing," said Dan.

"Everybody thinks of everybody else, but I just get kicked around," sobbed Shirley. "I don't count. Somebody else gets in trouble and everybody breaks their necks trying to help him out. I get in trouble and nobody cares. You only brought me along because you had to. Now you don't know what to do with me and I'm a nuisance."

"I told you," Dan said, patiently, "there's a kid in the Sager Creek jail in an awful jam. I'm just trying to help him."

"I wish I was in jail. I wish I was accused of murder. Then maybe somebody would care about me. But no. I don't count. So far as you're concerned, I'm just a—"

"That's not the way it is at all," said Dan.

"No, Banion," said Regan. "You're wrong. By heaven, what this girl says is true. The world is nothing but a madhouse."

"I'm going to kill myself," Shirley said.

"No you're not," said Dan. "You're going home with Regan."

"What are you talking about, Banion? My wife would kill me."

"Nobody wants me." Shirley began to cry again.

"The world is a screaming nuthouse," said Regan.

"What do you say we stop for a hamburger somewhere," Dan suggested.

In the cozy warmth of an all-night lunch counter, with the smell of hot coffee and scorched grease, Shirley's morale improved. A fat hamburger with plenty of onions and mustard renewed her desire to live. Besides, she sensed now that she was "in," and that whatever happened, these peculiar men were bound to her by conscience.

Dan let Regan get halfway through his sandwich before prodding him again with, "Did I hear you say you had an extra bed?"

"What's wrong with a hotel?" Regan asked, licking his fingers.

"At a hotel, they'd have a line on her in a minute. Beth and that gorilla of hers would be on her neck in an hour."

"What the hell do you think I live in—a fort?"

"I hardly think you'll need a fort. Besides, they won't know she's at your house. They'll expect to find her with me."

"I want to go with you," said Shirley, patting Dan's arm.

"Well, you can't. That's out of the question."

"Then I guess I'll have to go with Mr. Regan," she said, eying Regan speculatively.

"Okay," said Regan gloomily, "but don't blame me if my wife murders us both."

"That's fine," said Dan. "That is, I mean she'll be all right at your place until tomorrow, anyhow. In the meantime, I'll have time to think things out."

"My God," said Regan, pausing in the act of sipping his coffee, "haven't you been thinking up to now?"

"What about you?" Shirley said to Dan. "Beth will be awful mad. She might send Ray or somebody after you."

"I don't think so," said Dan. "Besides, I can take care of myself. They're experts at bullying women. But they'll think twice before tackling a man."

"Why don't you come to Mr. Regan's house, too? I'm sure he won't mind."

Regan choked on his coffee and had to wipe off his shirt front. "Bring your whole family," he said. "Let's move the whole county in."

"That won't be necessary," said Dan. "By the way, have you got that shot glass you took from Ray? You didn't smear it with your fingers, did you?"

Regan fished the glass out of his pocket with elaborate delicacy. It was swathed in his dirty handkerchief. "He had his sweaty paw all over it," Regan said proudly.

On the road into Sager Creek, a tired quiet settled on them. Regan yawned and apologized several times. "Among other things, I've got to think up what to tell my wife for staying out so late," he remarked.

"I imagine she's used to it," said Dan.

Shirley leaned her head on Regan's shoulder and dozed off.

Dan drove them to the place near Brannigan's bar where Regan had parked his dilapidated Ford truck. "I'll drive over to your place tomorrow," he said, "probably in the afternoon. I'm going to go over to Hamilton in the morning and have a look at this Hibley house."

"How in the hell am I going to explain this girl to my wife?" Regan asked.

CHAPTER NINE

The chambermaid, banging her broom and dustpan in the hall, roused Dan to a sunlit room shortly after ten o'clock the next morning.

While shaving, he had time to realize that so far as any tangible evidence of Flavin's innocence was concerned, he had arrived at nothing. Beth was the woman who had served him food in the Hibley house. Of that he was sure. But how could he prove it? And what was she doing there, anyhow? She would be certain to have an airtight alibi to account for her whereabouts that afternoon.

Some connection obviously existed between Beth and the Hibleys. The newspaper clipping he had seen in the drawer of her desk indicated that. Whatever it was, it was beyond the imagination of most people in the community. The letter he had taken from the drawer might not have the slightest connection. Then again, it might. It indicated at least that she was under some pressure. This man Franz, whoever he was, had something on her.

The letter said: "June should arrive on about the fifteenth." But who was June? And in what manner was Beth expected to "take care of her"?

It all must have been fairly recently, because the sheet of stationery had a reasonable freshness about it.

As to whether Beth was the actual murderer, he wasn't sure. She didn't appear to be a woman who would do her own killing. Besides, Flavin's story indicated the presence of a third party in the house on that afternoon.

Possibly that bartender, Ray. He had forgotten to ask Shirley if Ray had been at the Queen Anne that afternoon. Somehow he felt that Ray figured in the picture somewhere, but that was purely a hunch. He must ask Shirley more about him.

The chambermaid stuck her head in the door when Dan was buttoning his shirt. She couldn't understand how anyone could sleep this late if he weren't sick. When he asked her if she could find him a cardboard box and some excelsior, she couldn't understand that either.

Dan told her that he collected birds' eggs and wanted to mail some specimens home, but that was reckless, as he soon found out. It happened that her nephew collected birds' eggs, and she concluded they should get together for a talk.

"He's a lonely man," she explained, "and doesn't make friends easily.

It would do him good to get together with someone who was interested in the same things. It might bring him out of himself."

She found Dan an old shoe box and a handful of excelsior, but he had to promise tentatively that, if he could find time, he would drop around and look at Ferguson's collection. He even had to write down the man's address before he could get rid of her.

When she was gone, Dan swore to himself never to lie again. He packed the two shot glasses carefully and addressed them to a street number in Frenton. Then he removed the lid from his portable typewriter and wrote several letters.

Before breakfast, he dropped by the post office and mailed them all, sending the box special delivery.

It occurred to him to drop by the office of the *Sentinel* and inquire how Vance had got home the night before—if he had got home. But he decided that he had wasted too much time already, and that he'd better visit the Hibley house before anything happened to close their door against him. Besides, Beth wouldn't be apt to harm anybody in Vance Dalbert's position in the community.

After a meal of sausage and eggs at a lunch counter, he headed his car toward Hamilton. With little difficulty, he found 813 Bruce Street, drove a few doors past it, and parked. The wide trees, shading the walk from the midday sun, and the carpet of brown leaves beneath them carried his mind back to childhood. He had a sudden inclination to take off his shoes and feel the ground with his feet. Instead, he strolled up to the Hibleys' trim picket fence, entered the gate, and crunched up the gravel path.

The place was just as Ralph Flavin had described it. On the lawn near the porch, a round-shouldered, middle-aged man in a floppy panama hat was coiling a garden hose as Dan approached. He stopped in his work and stared at Dan questioningly.

Casting his eyes over the garden quickly, Dan decided that the flower bed below the porch rail was the most probable point of vanity, and nodded in its direction. "Those are the finest looking asters I have ever seen. Pardon me for saying so, but they're remarkable."

The man was taken off guard. His eyes softened and he grinned wryly, showing yellow teeth. "They're Lady Wentworths. My own cultivation. I developed 'em myself. They won the prize last year in the Sager Creek show."

"Mind if I look at them?" Dan kneeled beside the flower bed.

"This one's about the best specimen right now," said the man. He stooped and took one of the flowers delicately in his wrinkled brown hand, and bent it forward for Dan's attention.

"They're amazing," Dan said. "I don't suppose it would be possible to get some seeds?"

"Well, now, I don't know. Maybe I could spare you a few."

"I'd be glad to pay for them."

"Oh, no—no. Nothing like that. Be glad to let you have them. Was you looking for somebody in particular?"

"Yes, Mrs. Hibley, if she's in."

"Well, I don't know. It's a bad time. A terrible thing happened here day 'fore yesterday. Maybe you read about it in the paper?"

"I'm a newspaper reporter," said Dan. "I want to get a statement from Mrs. Hibley."

"Tsch, tsch," the man clucked, "I haven't got over it myself. Can't understand why the government lets those fiends roam the country. They'll have to do something about it now. People won't stand for such goings on."

"You're the gardener, I take it?"

"Yes, sir. And I tell you, there wasn't a sweeter girl anywhere in this county than Esther. Quiet, kind little soul. I'd like to get my hands on that devil."

"Did you get a look at him at all?"

"Look at him? I wish I'd been here. He wouldn't have got in that gate. Too kindhearted, she was. They don't fool me. If a man can't earn his living in this country, there's something wrong with him. I never begged a penny in my life."

"Wasn't anybody around—anybody who might have heard her call for help?"

"Not a soul. Widow Hibley went to Frenton that day. I took in the matinee downtown. This *Mutiny on the Bounty*. That guy Laughton is in it. Have you seen it?"

"Yeah, I saw it twice in the city."

"Wasn't it a pip? Say, that guy's good. The place where he tried to blame the guy for swiping the cheese, and he'd swiped it himself. That was a swell picture. But I wish I hadn't gone now. I wish to God I hadn't gone."

"Do you suppose Mrs. Hibley will see me?"

"I don't know. Mostly she's been in bed. Her son's here. Maybe you can talk to him. He was the one discovered it. And her daughter came in from New York this morning."

"Can I find you later? I'd like to get those seeds, if you really mean it."

"Sure, I'll be around the place, or out back by the garage. My name's Farnsworth—Otis Farnsworth. Just ask for Otis."

Dan climbed the porch steps and rang an old-fashioned pull-bell beside the screen door. A stout, pink-cheeked woman answered the bell.

Dan removed his hat. "I'm Banion of the *Post-Tribune*. I wonder if I might see Mrs. Hibley—or her son, Mr. Hibley?"

"What is it?" asked a girl's voice in the hall.

"A newspaper man from the city," the housekeeper replied.

"I'll take care of him," said the girl.

The screen door opened on a trim figure in a stylishly tailored suit. Confident, twinkling brown eyes looked at Dan from under a riot of soft brown hair cut in a long, careless bob. A cigaret burned between long, red-tipped fingers.

"You know your mother asked you not to smoke in the house," the stout woman said as she retreated down the hall.

"Come in," the girl said. "Park your hat on a buffalo horn." She pointed to an elaborate hall tree with horns for hat hooks.

Dan followed her into a parlor that looked like a Mid-Victorian museum. Its neatness was almost frightening. Every object was dusted and polished and placed in such precise order that the idea of sitting down seemed sacrilegious.

"Find some jagged corner and impale yourself," said the girl.

"You're Mrs. Hibley's daughter, I take it?"

"If you can take it, I guess I can," she answered. "Smoke?" She extended a pack.

"I smoke a pipe," said Dan, "but I'd as soon smoke a pipe in here as set off firecrackers in a chapel."

"Go ahead. Don't let it scare you."

"No, thanks. I'd feel guilty. You came in this morning, the gardener tells me."

"Yes, and am I glad to see you! I'm Gail Hibley, incidentally. What's your name?"

"Dan Banion of the *Post-Tribune*."

"Dan Banion! My God, I know a man who thinks you're the second coming of Shakespeare. Let me look at you. Red Creighton of the *Planet*. Remember him?"

"Red? Well, for the love of—listen, Red and I—what's he doing now?"

"He's on the New York *Planet* doing rewrite. I work on the *Planet* myself."

"You—Well, I'll be damned. Listen, Red and I—but say, you live here, don't you?"

"I was born in this museum. I got a hurry-up telegram from mama about this business. She seemed to think the sky was falling. Mama gets excited easy. So, down I came. Grisly, isn't it?"

"What do you think about it?"

"Think about what? You mean the murder? My God! It's been happening all over the country. I don't blame anybody. These guys go broke, their socks get dirty, they have nothing to keep them occupied, every signboard and magazine cover blares sex—sex—sex. Legs and buttocks and bosoms dangled in pictures wherever they look. So they go crazy. I wouldn't guarantee what you might do under similar circumstances. When you get hungry, your brain gets looney."

A tall, serious-looking man strode into the room. "Gail," he said, "mother wants to see you now. Please don't smoke cigarets in the house. You know how it upsets her. Oh—" He noticed Dan.

"This is Mr. Banion of the *Post-Tribune*. And please, Ronny, don't act silly with him and scare him away." She pointed a long, red-tipped finger at Dan. "Don't you go 'way, see. If you forsake me in this Godforsaken dump, I'll poison the mind of your best friend against you. You be here when I get back."

"I'll hold the fort," Dan said.

With a shake of her silky bob, Gail whirled into the hall and tripped up the stairs. The top step creaked loudly. It startled Dan and recalled him to his business. Ralph Flavin's story checked to the last detail.

"Impetuous girl," said Ronald Hibley. "You'll pardon it, I'm sure, Mr.—"

"Banion."

"Yes, to be sure. I'm Ronald Hibley, Mrs. Hibley's son. This has been really very frightful. We really didn't want to see any newspaper reporters, but then, if you're a friend of Gail's—"

Ronald Hibley's head was egg-shaped and partly bald. His shoulders curved downward too sharply, and his stomach was slightly paunched. Dan noticed that his co-ordination was not all that it should be. In sitting down, he bumped the chair arm, then sat on the edge of the chair, fidgeted, and presently got up to pace the floor.

"They tell me you discovered the body," Dan said.

"Yes." Ronald Hibley's voice cracked. He cleared his throat. "Yes," he said uncertainly, putting his hand to his throat.

"You had been downtown all day at your business, I assume."

Ronald Hibley blushed crimson, tried to smile, then gave it up. Instead of speaking, he nodded his head.

"It was when you returned home from your real estate business that you—"

Ronald Hibley walked unsteadily to a door that led into the dining room, turned, and said in a voice that was badly choked, "Do you mind if I get a drink?" He took one step, then looked over his shoulder. "Do you want one?"

"Thanks," said Dan. What was the matter? This fellow was near the end of his rope. Something was damned near killing him inside.

Ronald returned with some whiskey already poured in a glass, and a bottle in his other hand. The glass shook so much the liquor danced.

Dan relieved him of both the glass and bottle. "Listen, fellow," he said. "Make it easy for yourself. You can trust me. This is just between us. Hell, anybody's nerves can get shaken. It doesn't mean anything."

"Thank you," said Ronald. He relaxed into a chair and began to cry softly.

"Did you do it?" asked Dan quietly.

"Oh, my God, no. Whatever made you say that?"

"Because that kid they've got in the Sager Creek jail—the one they picked up—didn't do it either."

Ronald looked at him blankly. "I don't understand."

"Just this: I've checked that kid's story piece by piece. He didn't do it. You can take my word for it."

"I don't understand what you're saying."

"You can understand this: that kid didn't do it, and I'm going to find out who did. I don't know what's eating you, but you might as well tell me. I'll find out anyway. If you're on the level in this thing, you can trust me. If not, God help you. Now get it off your chest."

Upstairs, a door closed.

"I can't talk to you now," Ronald said. "My sister mustn't see me like this. I'll talk to you later."

"Wait a minute. Where are you going?" Ronald Hibley had risen from his chair and was hurrying toward the hall. He jerked his hat from the hall tree. "Hey, wait a minute, Hibley. Will you be at your office?"

"All right, anything, anywhere, but not now. I'll be at my office."

"Well, see that you are," called Dan as the front door slammed behind Ronald Hibley.

"What's the fuss about?" asked Gail, coming down the stairs.

"Tramps aren't the only ones who look at signboards and magazine covers," said Dan.

"You mean him?"

"No offense intended."

"If you could imagine him astride anything but a hobby horse, you're another Jules Verne," she said. "Why did he take a powder?"

"I don't know. I guess he got excited."

"Excited about what?"

"Just excited. Maybe he has an appointment."

Gail looked curiously at the front door, and at Dan. "I heard what you said to him. What did you mean by, 'Well, see that you are'?"

"Nothing. I'm going to see him later, that's all. We were talking and he had to go."

She spotted the whiskey bottle on the table. "You don't mean to say he gave you a drink? I've been trying to find where they had that bottle hidden ever since I got here. Say, what's going on around here, anyhow?"

"I think your brother is nervous, that's all. This business has upset him."

"I noticed he was acting kind of moody. We might as well have another drink." She got another glass from the dining room.

"Is that what your mother talked to you about, upstairs?" Dan asked as she poured the drinks. "Is she worried about your brother?"

"That, Banion," Gail said, "is none of your business."

"I don't suppose I could see your mother and talk to her myself?"

Ignoring the question, Gail handed him his glass. "Listen, Banion— or suppose I call you Dan? I love my family like you might love a tribe of cannibals you escaped from. Just the same, they're my family, and blood is thicker than water. Or what am I talking about?"

"I don't think you know."

"Maybe I don't," she admitted.

"When a house catches fire, the skeletons in the closets get hot. Is that what you mean?"

"Ronald's all right," she said, ignoring his question again. "He's a prude and a moron. But he's all right. He wouldn't hurt anybody. What did you mean by, 'Well, see that you are'?"

"Curious, aren't you?"

"Oh, cut it out. You make me feel like an idiot. I just don't want anybody to hurt him. What's up, anyhow? You came here for a story. What did Ronald tell you? I'm all in the dark."

"What did your mother tell you, upstairs?"

"Nothing," said Gail, slumping into a chair and crossing her legs. "Nothing at all." Noting a glint of appreciation in Dan's eyes, she pulled the hem of her skirt down sharply. "You're acting very silly. She only said that Ronald hasn't been well and that he needed a rest. She's upset by this gruesome business. She was afraid a lot of men like you might come around bothering her, and—"

"And that Ronald had been having an affair with the girl who was killed, and she was afraid it might leak out," Dan added, making a reckless guess.

"Oh, hell, all right. What if he had, Dan? It has nothing to do with this business. Ronald's a baby. Don't be so cheap as to crucify him just to bulge out a dirty story that oughtn't to be played up in the first place. Red said you had some integrity."

"So I should leave your brother out of it."

"All right, if you want to put it that way. You're making me feel very awkward. Why do you act this way? It's a simple enough business. I don't know why you're bothering so much about it."

"I guess if it came to a showdown, you'd be for your family, right or wrong."

"My family isn't to blame for this. But they have to live in this respectable, stuffy community, and there's no sense in adding scandal to murder. Especially since they've got the man who did it."

"You can't judge the respectability of a community by how much noise the church bells make on Sunday morning," said Dan. "I've been having a look around, and if you ask me, this isn't a community, it's a rabbit hutch."

"The natives manage to propagate themselves, if that's what you mean."

"What you don't seem to realize," said Dan, "or I wonder if you do— is that your family is in a first-class jam. Just to calm you down—to begin with, I don't think your brother did it."

"Didn't do what?"

"Didn't murder that girl."

Gail froze. "What do you mean by saying such a thing? Of course he didn't."

"All right, now calm down. I don't think he did. But that kid they've got in Sager Creek didn't do it either. At least I've got good reason to believe he didn't."

"That tramp, you mean. The one they arrested."

"Yes."

"Don't be ridiculous. He confessed. And they found the knife on him. It's all in the paper."

"If you've got any sense, you'll listen to what I have to say."

"What did you tell Ronald while I was upstairs?"

"I told him the kid didn't do it."

"Dan, that's insane. You ought to know better than to tell him a thing like that, in the condition he's in. Who else thinks this fellow is innocent besides you? Nobody, I take it."

"No, and they're not apt to. They're so anxious to stick it on him and use the story for political capital that I'm not likely to get much co-operation."

"Did it ever occur to you that you might be a screwball, and the others might be right? What makes you think this fellow didn't do it?"

"Right now," Dan said, "I'm beginning to be careful of you. This is your family, remember, and from all indications, they're mixed up in it somewhere."

"Well, my people aren't murderers, if that's what you mean. They're a little stupid, I admit."

"Will you do me a favor?" Dan asked.

"Don't make it too complicated."

"Well, stop being so damned sophisticated. I think you're all right. In fact—well, you're swell. Relax. You don't have to put on a front for me."

She bit her lip in annoyance. At the same time, her eyes shaded, and for an instant he could see through the surface of smart confidence to a gnawing loneliness inside her.

Almost involuntarily, he repeated a couple of lines he had read in Ralph Flavin's notebook, and that now came into his mind: "These narrow caves of conscience called ourselves, wherein we dwell alone like frightened elves."

"What's that apropos of?" she asked.

"Nothing," he said. "Just poetry. Do you like poetry?"

"Aren't you being a trifle on the adolescent side?"

"You've written your share of sloppy verse and mooned over it in privacy. I'll bet you used to lock yourself in your bedroom in this very house and scribble all sorts of languid nonsense."

"Oh, for Pete's sake, Dan. Come out of it. Don't tell me you're one of these amateur psychologists who thinks he can see right through people. If there's anything more boring!"

"All right, skip it."

Her annoyance, however, needed more expression. "These guys who read a Haldeman-Julius Blue Book of Psychiatry Simplified, and then go around glooming into people's libidos, imagining secret frustrations in everybody's pants. They even analyze the fire hydrants. If there's anything gives me a pain—"

"You've evidently been bit bad by one."

"I almost married one," she said, snuffing her cigaret angrily in a flower dish, since no ash trays were about. "Now leave me alone. Yes, I was a goofy, frustrated child, if that's what you want to know. What were you? A quiz kid?"

"My puberty was awkward enough to frighten God," said Dan. "But we're getting off the track."

"It's a good thing I came down here, if for no other reason than to revive your sense of humor. Here, let me give you another drink. Go on with your pipe dream about this maladjusted creature they've got in the jail."

"He's just a lonely kid," said Dan. "Now listen—" He patiently repeated Flavin's story, leaving out his own experiences at checking it. "His poetry's not bad at all. You'd like the fellow," he said as he finished.

Gail rose thoughtfully, poured them both another drink, and held the bottle up to the light. "We might as well kill this. You're a very sweet guy, Dan."

"You don't believe his story, do you?" he asked.

"I'm sorry, Dan. I don't like you any the less for it, but do you have any idea of what your reputation is?"

"The kid's telling the truth."

"Red told me about you. He said you're the swellest guy who ever walked, bar none, and that if you ever got sense enough to sit down and work you'd be a genius. But that you're a screwball, and for heaven's sake, if I ever met you, not to be taken in by any of your pipe dreams. You still believe in Santa Claus."

"Red's got it all wrong. Red doesn't stop to think—"

"He told me all about the Kelly affair."

"That man Kelly would have fooled anyone," said Dan. "How was I to know he'd forged the President's signature?"

"Yes, I know, Dan. How were you to know? But sooner or later you have to grow up. This fellow Flavin's story—things don't happen like that. Sure he's a nice kid. I don't doubt it. That's what's causing you to make a fool of yourself, Dan. That's what you can't get through your head. It's possible for a nice kid in this world to commit murder. Did you know that?"

"Certainly I know that."

"No you don't. You don't know that even the nicest people can burn with terrible feelings at times. That things sometimes get beyond their control, and—"

"Now you're getting subjective."

"Who would pull a silly frame-up like that? Dan, use your head."

"Listen. Do me one favor," Dan said. "Let me look in the girl's room. Will you let me do that?"

"Why, certainly." Gail began to laugh. "I get it. You're playing detective."

"Never mind. Just let me have a look in her room."

"Well, I wouldn't want you to think the Hibleys were hiding anything. Come on."

She led the way through the hall toward the kitchen. "You went to see the guy, and he turns out to be a nice kid. He writes poetry. He seems like a good fellow. So you assume from that he could do no wrong. Lots of good guys have done wrong. Lots of good guys have got themselves in awful jams, Dan, and been guilty as hell. You've got a lot to learn yet."

"Shut up and lead the way," said Dan.

As they passed through the kitchen Mrs. Garland, the housekeeper and cook, stopped scouring a pan and said, "Miss Hibley, they're wrong about Esther having served food to that tramp. He must have helped himself to it."

"What makes you say that?" asked Gail.

"Well, Esther didn't carve that roast. I know that much. Esther knew how to carve. I taught her just how to do it. That roast was chunked off like somebody had whittled it, and they didn't even use the carving knife."

"Are you sure she couldn't have been nervous?" Gail suggested.

"No matter how nervous she was, she wouldn't have done it that way. Besides, I gave her strict instructions she was not to touch that roast. And Esther never disobeyed."

"Did he put the roast back in the icebox?" Dan asked. "Or did he leave it out on the table?"

"That's another silly thing," said Mrs. Garland. "He put it back in the icebox."

"You were away all day, I take it," Dan said.

"I spent the day with my daughter in Sager Creek. It must have been five-thirty when I returned. I didn't notice exactly, but Mr. Hibley came in a short while after. I had found that dirty cap on the kitchen table here, and the plate where somebody had eaten."

"Didn't you wonder where Esther was?" asked Dan.

"Well, I called through the house for her several times, but she didn't answer, so I thought she'd gone out somewhere. When Mr. Hibley came in, I showed him the cap. He looked upstairs and—" Mrs. Garland began to sob, and lifted the corner of her apron to her eyes.

"Why don't you go and lie down, dear," Gail said. "Let these things go."

"No, I feel better doing things," said Mrs. Garland. "Besides, there's dinner to think about."

"We're just going to take a look in Esther's room," Gail said.

"It's terribly untidy, I suppose," apologized Mrs. Garland. "I haven't had the heart to go in there. I suppose we'll have to pack her things and send them off to her relatives."

Esther's room was off a little hall that entered from the kitchen. Another door at the end of the hall led into the back yard. The room was small, but comfortable, and had the same frilly curtains that seemed to prevail throughout the house. The bed was made, but rumpled, as if someone had been lying on top of it.

"It's even simpler now," said Dan. "Apparently he attacked and murdered her, then, without any trouble, went and got the bottle of whiskey from its hiding place—the bottle which even you couldn't find. He then got drunk, went to the icebox and chunked himself off some roast beef, carefully putting the roast back where it belonged. After eating heartily, he walked out and left his cap on the kitchen table. I wonder why he didn't wash the dishes?"

"Don't be a ham, Dan. Let me show you where your reasoning is cockeyed. When he saw she was alone in the house, he went barging around to see what he could find. He discovered the roast. She told him not to touch it, but he helped himself anyhow, using the first knife that came to his hand. While he was stuffing himself, she put the roast back in the icebox. Afterward, he demanded something to drink. She was frightened and got him the bottle from its hiding place. He got drunk and started to attack her. She broke away from him and ran upstairs. He followed her."

Dan was peering in one of the drawers of the dresser. "Okay, you win. But what's this?" He pulled out an artificial leather make-up kit. It contained everything from deep red lipstick to false eyelashes.

"That was her own affair," said Gail. "You're a regular Peeping Tom. The girl probably dreamed of being glamorous some day."

"This stuff is all well worn," said Dan. "It's been used plenty."

Gail opened the closet door and examined the clothes on the hangers. Everything was as simple and modest as possible. "She might have got that glamour kit secondhand from somebody. This stuff looks homely enough."

Dan went over and took a look. "You're kind of naïve," he said. "Do you notice all this stuff is practically new? Why isn't there an old or worn dress somewhere? Look at those dresses closely. You're the woman. Not me."

Gail reluctantly felt the material, and thumbed through the cotton dresses.

"If I'm not mistaken," said Dan, "all that stuff was bought on the same day. What's this?" Under some hats on the shelf, he found a book, took one look at it, and handed it to Gail. The title was *Prospective Motherhood*.

Gail looked worried.

"The first thing we'd better find out," Dan said, "is how far things had gone between your brother and this girl."

"Listen, Dan. Slow down a minute. You've got my head swimming. All this doesn't necessarily mean anything. If anybody examined your room and started jumping to conclusions, they'd swear you were a lunatic. She might have been keeping that make-up kit for somebody. Maybe she was robbed, or in a fire, and had to buy a whole new wardrobe all at once. The book might belong to her aunt. As a matter of fact, I have a copy in my own room."

"How did you happen to get a copy?"

"That's none of your business. Those drinks are beginning to unravel me." She sat on the bed and ran her fingers through her thick, silky hair. "You jump to too many conclusions, Dan."

"Oh, don't worry. I intend to check on everything. Move your feet." He pulled a suitcase from under the bed. It was locked. Dan searched through the dresser until he found a purse, and in it a bunch of keys. Before trying them, he lifted a card from the purse and read a phone number: "Sawtooth 141-J."

"I suppose that's very significant, too," said Gail.

"I'll lay you an even bet I know whose telephone number this is."

"Which means you probably do. Whose is, it?"

"Never mind. We'll check it later."

"It wouldn't be Santa Claus, would it?"

"Get your feet off that," said Dan. He jerked the suitcase, almost upsetting her onto the floor.

"I don't know why I tolerate you," Gail said.

"The idea is, you don't want me to think you Hibleys are hiding anything," said Dan. He tried the most probable key and it fitted. The suitcase opened in an explosion of bright rayon and satin. There were sheer slacks and cheap, filmy under-things. Dan selected a red evening dress of the dance hall variety and held it up for inspection. "I don't know what all this suggests to you," he said, "but how long had Esther been working here?"

"About two months, according to what mother says." Gail felt the material of the dress. "I admit it's kind of funny. Still, any girl is apt to want nice things."

"Even you, I suppose," said Dan, holding up an item of black lace underwear. "Is this the type you would—"

"Oh, shut up. What would all this have to do with it anyway? It doesn't change anything."

"There's one thing you seem to overlook, and that is that I might know a lot more about this case than I've let you in on. Do you mind if I use your phone?"

"Well, I think I do, Dan. Whatever all this may mean, it has nothing to do with the murder. I don't see what you hope to accomplish by dragging Ronald into it."

"Listen," said Dan, "get this straight. I'm not dragging anybody into anything. If you want to keep your brother's name out of it, then you'd better find out everything you can about what went on here."

"What I object to is you poking your nose into it."

"My nose is already in up to the elbow. I know more about this than you think."

"You're holding something out on me. Is that the idea?"

"Yeah. Now where's your phone? I want to check on something."

"What, for instance?"

"I happen to know the woman who was here in this house Wednesday afternoon. Unless I'm mistaken, this phone number I found in Esther's purse is hers. If you won't let me check it on your phone, I'll just go outside and do it. So what's the difference?"

For the first time, Gail appeared worried. She led him through the house to the telephone in the hall and waited while he called the number. As soon as Dan heard a voice say, "Queen Anne Hotel," he hung up.

"Check," he said. "Just what I expected."

The ominous creak of the top stair sounded from above. A voice called, "Gail, what is this man doing here?"

Dan looked up to see a white-haired woman in a Paisley shawl limping down the stairs with the aid of a cane. Her face wore the annoyed expression of a neat person in a disorderly world.

"Mother, this is Dan Banion, of the *Post-Tribune*," Gail said.

"I hope I didn't disturb you by using your phone," said Dan.

"Gail, you've been smoking again. I can smell it."

"Well, mother, if you want me to come and see you, you've got to put up with a few things."

"A few things! After what I've gone through the past two days, I'd think you'd show a little consideration." She reached the bottom of the stairs and limped into the living room. She pointed at the whiskey bottle with her cane. "Gail, how dare you touch that whiskey?"

"Now, mother. All right. Nobody has hurt a thing." Gail removed the bottle and glasses.

Mrs. Hibley eased herself slowly into a chair. "That girl has changed in the past few years. Mr. Banion, I hope you don't smoke."

"Not in the house," lied Dan.

"I cannot abide smoking. Mr. Hibley never smoked when he was alive."

"I realize, Mrs. Hibley, that you've been quite upset. I wouldn't like to disturb you anymore, but I wonder if I might ask you a few questions?"

"I'm afraid you'll have to talk to my daughter," said Mrs. Hibley. "I'm in no condition to be annoyed anymore."

Gail returned into the living room. "Come on, Dan," she said. "Mother really should be let alone."

"Just one question," said Dan. "I was wondering, Mrs. Hibley, how you happened to hire this girl, Esther Berglan. Where did she come from? Who recommended her to you?"

"I don't consider that any of your business," snapped Mrs. Hibley. "Gail, I must ask you to take this young man out of here."

"All right, one more question. Did you ever hear of a woman named Beth Ridgely—or Elizabeth Ridgely?"

Dan noticed that her fingers tightened on the handle of the cane, and her mouth hardened. "Certainly not. Why are you asking me these impertinent questions?"

"Dan, will you please leave mother alone? She isn't well," Gail repeated.

Dan ignored her. "I'm asking these questions in a completely friendly spirit, Mrs. Hibley," he continued. "If they don't mean anything to you, then forget about them. If they do—well, then you'll realize their importance, and I'd advise you to be frank. If you are worried about your son's relationship with Miss Berglan, I know all about it. I intend to keep it confidential, if possible. Your co-operation can help make it possible."

"Dan, how can you be so crude?" Gail said.

"Young man, is this blackmail? Gail, did you talk to this young man?"

"He already knew about Ronald," Gail said.

"Mr. Banion, what do you mean by forcing yourself into this house and spying on my son?"

"Don't misunderstand me," said Dan. "I'm not saying your son had anything to do with the murder. But I do know that the boy they've arrested and are folding in the Sager Creek jail didn't kill Miss Berglan."

"That's perfectly ridiculous," said the old lady.

"Well, at least I want you to hear his story and tell me if you know anything that might throw any light on it." Dan very briefly repeated Flavin's story of what had happened to him. Mrs. Hibley listened impatiently. Gail, obviously annoyed, looked out the window.

When he had finished, Mrs. Hibley said, "Young man, I have never heard anything more preposterous in my life. I'll thank you to leave this house immediately, and don't come back. Gail, I have no idea how you could permit this man to come here and—"

"I'm afraid I must insist that you leave, Dan," said Gail coldly.

"All right," said Dan, "but in case you change your mind." He scribbled hastily on a sheet of notebook paper. "Here's the name of my hotel in Sager Creek. If I'm out when you call, just leave a message. Just say you're Mrs. Flannagan, and I'll know who you are, and get in touch with you." He gave the note to Mrs. Hibley. Surprised, she accepted it.

"Well," she said. "Well!"

"I'll be getting along now," Dan said. He turned to Gail. "Are you coming with me?"

"Not while I'm in my right mind. If I were a man, I'd knock you down. The idea of talking to my mother that way! Haven't you any consideration?"

"Sure," said Dan. "Lots of it. My own grandmother can't move a step without a cane. I've watched her getting around on it for years."

"Young man," said Mrs. Hibley, "I'll thank you to get out of my house."

"Incidentally, Mrs. Hibley, let me give you a tip. Don't point with your cane while you're standing. Another thing, you considerably overdid that business of coming downstairs. Make up your mind which foot you intend to limp on. Don't experiment with one and then the other in front of an audience. If you want to follow me, Gail, I'll be down at the coroner's."

Dan took his hat from the rack and banged out the screen door.

CHAPTER TEN

As Dan descended the Hibley front steps, already ashamed of having lost his temper, he heard the calm voice of Mr. Otis Farnsworth, the gardener.

"Do you still want those seeds?"

Dan blinked in the sunlight. Otis was standing on the lawn, furling more lengths of rubber garden hose.

"Oh, yes. If it wouldn't be too much trouble."

"Not a bit," said Otis. He dropped the hose, wiped his hands on a dirty handkerchief, and led the way around the house to the garage. "Take lots of water, these lawns," he remarked. "Especially this time of year. Got to watch them every minute. Ya talk to the widow?"

"A little," said Dan. "I didn't like to bother her. She's pretty well shaken up."

"Awful thing to have happen," said Otis. "I'd like to get my hands on that devil, just once." He opened the garage door. "Government ought to do something about these tramps."

Dan looked about him. The converted stable was large. There was space for two cars, a workroom, and considerable storage. A green Ford truck of even older vintage than Regan's—a model T—was the only car in sight; but grease drippings on the floor showed where another one was kept. A stairway led above, evidently to Otis' living quarters. There were large sliding doors on both ends of the garage. The rear doors were slightly open.

"You don't live around here, do you?" asked Otis. "Did you want the seeds for your own garden?"

"I live in Frenton," said Dan. "My wife and I have a little place there. I want them for her." He looked through the rear door into the alley beyond.

"This used to be a stable," said Otis, busying himself with a brown paper parcel he reached down from a shelf. "You can drive in or out either way. Generally, they drive in the front and go out the back. It saves turning around."

"I'm not putting you to too much trouble, am I?" Dan turned from the door to watch the gardener.

"No trouble at all." He couldn't untie the knot on the parcel, so he cut the string with his knife. "But you came just in time. I had these wrapped up to mail to a friend of mine in Florida. Last ones I have, but you're welcome to some. Work on a newspaper, you say?"

"*Post-Tribune*," said Dan.

"Can't believe a word you read in these papers," Otis said. "No offense to you. Take all this talk about Hitler. Think there is going to be a war?"

"It's nasty business," said Dan. He stooped to examine a heap of old magazines under the work bench.

"Foreigners are a sneaky bunch," continued Otis. "You can't trust one of them. You take this murderer, I bet he's a foreigner. That's my guess."

"I couldn't say. Who reads all the magazines? Mrs. Hibley?"

"Gosh, no. Are you lookin' at those?" Otis colored slightly. "Those are just down there to be thrown out. I read 'em sometimes, just for the fun of it. They ain't no good."

Dan tossed a copy of the *Screen Beauty Parade* back on the pile and brushed his hands together. "How long had this girl been around here?

Had she worked here long?"

"Esther? About two months. Sweetest little thing you ever saw. If I ever could lay hands on that devil—"

"Was she a Hamilton girl? Was she born around here?"

Otis spilled a few seeds into his hand from the brown paper bag. "There you are. I better put them in something for you." He opened a drawer in the work bench and fished around.

"Did she live around here before she came to work?" asked Dan.

"I'll be darned if I can keep a paper bag in this place. The mice must carry 'em off."

"Did her family live around here—this girl Esther?"

"Oh, you mean Esther?" said Otis. "Her last name was Berglan. Esther Berglan. This ain't a very clean bag, but it'll hold 'em. You figure to be around here long?"

"Not very long," said Dan. "You were telling me about this girl Esther. Did she live around here?"

"Why, she lived right here in the house. And a sweeter, nicer girl you'd never want to meet."

"But I mean—"

Dan was cut off by Mrs. Garland's voice calling Otis from the kitchen door.

"Doggone it! Now there's that fool woman wanting something. Well, there's your seeds, and I hope your little wife likes 'em." Otis stepped into the back yard where Mrs. Garland was still shouting. "I hear you. I hear you," he called.

"Well, why don't you answer?" snapped Mrs. Garland angrily. "Mrs. Hibley wants to see you. Do you think I have nothing else to do but stand here and yell my lungs out?"

"I'm comin'," said Otis. "I'm comin'." Then to Dan, "Well, young fellow, good luck with your dahlias."

As the kitchen door slammed behind Otis Farnsworth, Dan followed the gravel path to the street.

He found his car, stepped on the starter, and headed in the direction of the small business section of Hamilton. When he had gone about a block and a half, he saw a familiar figure footing along the sidewalk going in the same direction. He pulled in to the curb and honked his horn. "I'm sorry," he said. "I really am,"

Gail opened the door and slid in beside him. "Dan," she said, "speaking to my mother that way was unnecessary."

"What I can't seem to get through your head," he said, "is that I haven't any time to waste. And that goes for your sake as well as anyone else's."

"My sake?"

"Yes. I'm trying to tell you this is serious."

"Well, where do I come in?"

"It's your family. I can't help it if they're mixed up in this, but I've got to find out to what extent, and in what way. And you ought to be interested in finding out, too. If you don't know already." He looked at her strangely. For some reason he had been taking her at face value, and now he wondered why.

"What business is it of yours, aside from a story? And I can't believe you're such a heel as to— "

"Are we going to go all over that again? I told you that kid they picked up is innocent. That makes some difference to me." Dan felt his temper slipping again. He pulled in to the curb and stopped the car. "If it doesn't make any difference to you, Gail, then get out. And I mean it."

"Dan, you're serious."

"I'm dead serious."

"Well, you don't have to lose your sense of humor."

"There isn't any sense of humor about this. You special people make me so goddamn mad, I could ... listen, you sophisticated smart aleck. That kid in the Sager Creek jail is all alone. He hasn't got anything or anybody to look to. I don't want to hurt your family, but if it lands the whole bigoted crowd of you in jail—including you—I'm going to get at the truth of this. I won't stop at anything. Now get out. I'm fed up with smart people."

She didn't move.

"I mean it," said Dan. "Get out."

"Please don't say that, Dan. I'm sorry."

Dan suddenly noticed that his hand was shaking. He shifted gears and stepped on the gas. They were silent for a couple of blocks. Then Dan said, "Your mother isn't sick. I didn't want to hurt her, and I didn't hurt her. But I wanted to plant those things in her mind. That cane was a fake, wasn't it?"

"Yes, it was. But that doesn't mean anything. She just didn't want to be bothered, and that was a good excuse."

"Someday, maybe, you'll get into trouble and run into a lot of people who can't be bothered. Then you'll realize why I get so mad. Even a nice little girl like you could get into trouble, you know."

"Don't I know it."

"Where would the coroner be located? Have you any idea?"

"Yes, keep on going down this street. But what do you want at the coroner's?"

"For somebody who works on a newspaper, you can ask more foolish questions. Stick around, and maybe you'll learn how to cover a story."

"Like the Kelly affair."

"Never mind about the Kelly affair. A man's entitled to a certain quota of mistakes."

A sign, ARMAND FEDERSON, MORTUARY, over a remodeled residence, marked the coroner's establishment. He evidently held the job as a sideline to his regular business.

The tinkle of a two-tone doorbell chime brought a serious-faced little man in horn-rimmed glasses to the door. He seemed to recognize Gail.

"Miss Hibley," he said, "I'm so sorry about what happened. But do come in. Is there any way I can help? And this is—" He eyed Dan questioningly.

"This is Mr. Banion from—" Gail began.

"I'm a very close friend of the family," Dan cut in.

Gail gave him an annoyed look, but let it pass.

"I hope you'll convey my sympathy—my deepest sympathy—to your mother," Federson said, as he ushered them into his office. "It was an extremely unfortunate thing. Extremely unfortunate."

"Sheriff Horgan has cautioned us about keeping the intimate details confidential," said Dan. "I hope we can depend on you to co-operate."

"Oh, absolutely," said Federson. Then he caught himself. "I don't believe I quite understand."

"We're aware of the situation," said Dan. "It isn't that we want to conceal anything, but there is simply no point in saying anything, particularly to the press."

"Then you know," said Federson hesitantly.

"Of course. And while we know Sheriff Horgan cautioned you, both Miss Hibley and myself wanted to appeal to you directly. I'm sure you understand."

"Oh, my goodness, yes."

Gail sat in a chair and looked at Dan in bewilderment.

"How soon do you think she would have become a mother?" Dan asked.

"Well, I'd say—but Horgan insisted I was not to discuss this with anyone. I really don't—"

"I'm sure that you'll be discreet," said Dan. "And I hope you don't misunderstand our anxiety."

"I quite understand," said Federson. "The whole thing is most unfortunate."

"There couldn't have been any mistake in your examination, could there?"

"Oh, no. That would be impossible."

"You're quite positive she was pregnant."

"Definitely," said Federson.

"Do you mind if I have a look at the body?"

"I'm afraid that's out of the question. I have definite orders in that respect."

"I hardly think that applies to us," said Dan.

Federson reached for a telephone. "Do you mind if I call Horgan and get an okay on it? Just a formality. It will put me in the clear."

"I wouldn't advise you to call anyone," said Dan. "It won't put you in the clear. It will put your neck in a jam."

"I don't understand this at all," said Federson.

"Well, to be plain with you, I'm a reporter from the *Post-Tribune*. I didn't know whether the girl was pregnant or not. But I tricked you into admitting it. Now, do you want to call Horgan and tell him that?"

Federson put down the phone. "That was a contemptibly dirty trick," he said.

"Well, it's one way of getting the truth."

"Now, I'll thank you to get out of here."

"If I get out of here, I'll spread that story over every newspaper in the state. But if you'll listen to reason, nobody will know a thing about it."

"I wouldn't take your word for anything, after what you just did."

"Well, take your choice."

"You put me in a very unfair light. I had no desire to withhold information. But I'm not the government."

"If Horgan is the government, then George Washington crossed the Delaware in vain."

"Listen," said Federson, "if you want the plain truth, I'm not the least bit afraid of you or Horgan either. As far as I'm concerned—and please pardon me for this, Miss Hibley—you can both go to hell. Every time I try to do someone a decent favor, something like this seems to happen."

"Did it ever occur to you," said Dan, "that the young fellow they arrested for this murder may not be guilty?"

Federson's face became very serious. "No, come to think of it. Is there any doubt about it?"

"Well, I've been looking into the thing, and I'm satisfied that he's innocent. That's why I want a look at the body. It may help me prove something."

Federson was thoughtful for a moment. "This is very humiliating," he said. "As a matter of fact, I'll let you see the body regardless. But if you could keep the matter confidential, I'd appreciate it."

"I'll do the best I can," Dan said.

"It's silly, and I suppose selfish. But, frankly, I need the money. This coroner's job only pays a few hundred a year, but it helps. I can't afford to have trouble with Horgan. Of course, if it's necessary, go right ahead. Don't let a little thing like this stand in the way. I'm only saying, if you can get along just as well without mentioning it, I'd appreciate it."

"Well, as I say," said Dan. "I'll do the best I can. My only interest is seeing that the kid they've arrested gets a square break."

Federson got up to lead the way. "If there's any doubt, then let's be sure. By the way, is Miss Hibley coming with us?"

"She'll wait here."

"I will not," said Gail, rising from her chair.

"She will not," said Dan. "Let's go."

Federson led the way to what had formerly been the kitchen of the house, but was now his workroom. The shades were pulled down, and the light was dim. A figure lay on a long porcelain table in the middle of the room.

"That's not her," said Federson solemnly. "That's Mr. Bloor, God rest him. Be careful passing that stool. That pail has liquid in it." He passed through the workroom, unclamped a heavy door, opened it, and snapped an electric switch inside. Chill air swept out in their faces.

One look, and Gail sagged. Dan caught her as she fell.

"Oh, dear me," said Federson. "I was afraid of that."

Dan picked her up in his arms and carried her back into the office. Federson, shuffling ahead, cleared a litter of articles from a leather-covered couch.

"Put her there," he said. "I'm dreadfully sorry. I was afraid it would be like that."

Dan put Gail on the couch and patted her hand. Federson found a bottle of whiskey and a glass. "Poor girl," he said. "They just never seem to understand. No matter how much you warn them, they still insist."

Gail was beginning to stir. Dan pressed a glass of whiskey against her lips. Her hand came up and grasped it.

"You all right, kid?" he asked.

"Sip a little," said Federson. "Just sip." He sipped from an imaginary glass in pantomime.

Gail sipped, then gurgled. The whiskey spilled down her chin. She blinked her eyes.

"Do you want to throw up?" Dan asked.

Federson looked frantically around him for a pail.

"I'm sorry," Gail said. "I'll be all right. I'm a damned baby."

"You lie here and take it easy," said Dan. "We'll be right back."

"Use this, if you have to," said Federson, shoving an enameled pail beside the couch.

"She'll be all right," said Dan. "Let's go back and have a look."

"I'm terribly sorry," said Federson, as they passed through the kitchen-mortuary again. "I shouldn't have allowed her. Mind that stool, won't you?"

When they returned to the office, Gail was sitting in a chair replenishing her make-up. "Don't you dare ever tell a soul about this," she said.

"My heavens, that's nothing to be ashamed of," said Federson.

"You don't look so good yourself," said Gail, looking at Dan.

"I don't feel so good," he said. His face was the color of the sheet that covered Mr. Bloor.

"Sit down," said Federson. He poured out a stout whiskey. "Here. You'd better have a little of this."

"Thanks," said Dan. "You must have nerves like piano wire."

Federson laughed lightly. "People are not bodies," he said. "It's the confusion of the person with the body, and the absence of the person from the body that upsets you. People are—" He shrugged his shoulders. "We know so little. We come, we go. The body is part of the earth. It belongs in the earth when the spirit is gone. When you understand that, it doesn't bother you."

"I want to apologize for the way we came in here," Dan said.

"Oh, that's all right. As a matter of fact, if I'd had the slightest idea there might be any question as to guilt, I never would have hesitated. Do you think there is any question?"

"I'm sure of it," said Dan. "By the way, if I called on you to make a statement about those wounds, and the kind of weapon that caused them, would you do it?"

"Unquestionably. I certainly would. I wouldn't want to endanger my job as coroner if I could help it. But you must feel free to do what you believe is right." He poured himself a drink. "It's unfortunate the way things happen, but I really don't know what to do about things, Mr. Banion. I really don't. I sometimes wonder where things are heading." He tossed off the drink.

"So do we all," said Dan. "But we can do our best. I must say you're an encouraging relief, as people go."

CHAPTER ELEVEN

"What's this about wounds?" Gail asked when they had returned to the car.

"I could stand something to eat," Dan said. "I haven't had any lunch yet."

"Do you mean to tell me you could eat after that?"

"You're not so tough as you pretend, are you?"

"Never mind about that. Tell me about the wounds."

Dan ignored her question. He drove to a place called the Brock Hotel that had a coffee shop connected with it. In the lobby, he bought a copy of the *Post-Tribune*. "That heel Ainsley has his neck out a thousand miles," he said.

Gail glanced over his shoulder and pointed to the headline: EUROPE PEACE SEALED BY PACT AT MUNICH. "That's dynamite," she said. "It's like pacifying a maniac by giving him a rusty butcher knife."

"I don't mean that," Dan said. He pointed to a secondary story beneath the headline: POET FIEND, KILLER OF BEAUTY. Beside the story was a picture of Ralph Flavin, evidently supplied by Vance. It had been taken right after his session in Grimes' office. He was badly shaken and looked wild enough for anything.

"Your boy scout looks a trifle maladjusted," said Gail.

"They'd just scared hell out of him," Dan said. "I'd like to have photographed you after you had a look in that icebox a while ago."

The story was peppered with "brutal assault," "fiendish outrage," "mad killer," "sex maniac," and similar phrases. Beside it was a companion item: "Rural Crime Wave a State Problem, Says County Attorney." It was a long statement by Earl Grimes that squeezed the last ounce of political capital out of the affair.

Dan noticed that Al had managed to slip into the story a fairly complete account of Flavin's own version. Al Wilson was the unhappy city editor who had the job of making the paper reflect the ideas of Ainsley—ideas with which he disagreed almost entirely. He endured this by convincing himself that if he didn't do the job, somebody else would, and jobs were hard to get. Besides, he had to earn a living for his wife and two children.

None of Flavin's poems were on the front page, but when Dan turned to the jump inside, he saw the ones he had selected printed in ten-point type. Al was doing his best.

"Will you excuse me a minute?" Gail asked. "I ought to call mother. She'll be worried about where I am." She reached for her purse.

Dan flipped a nickel across the table.

"Thanks," she said. "I'll only be a moment."

As soon as she was out of sight, Dan picked up her purse and opened it. Among keys, cosmetics, and customary articles was a yellow telegram which he opened quickly. It was addressed to Gail Hibley at a New York address:

VERY MUCH WORRIED ABOUT WHAT I TOLD YOU IN LAST LETTER. GOING TO FRENTON WEDNESDAY TO SEE HOWARD. WIRE ANSWER. MOTHER.

It was dated five days before the murder.

Dan also found a railroad ticket stub from New York dated the day before the murder. He put the stub and the telegram in his pocket and returned the purse to where Gail had left it.

When Gail returned, she said, "I'll have to go, Dan. Mother is worried half sick. You won't do anything rash until you've talked to me, will you?"

"You're making a mistake not telling me everything you know," Dan said. "Whatever you're trying to hide, I'll find out anyway. It may be pretty awkward for you later on."

"What is it you want to know, Dan? What are you driving at?"

"Where did your mother hire that girl? Who recommended her?"

"I don't know."

"Is there any connection between your mother and a woman named Beth Ridgely, who runs a cat house and honky-tonk called the Crystal Bar in Sawtooth?"

"For God's sake, no. And what has that got to do with it?"

"Does your mother have much money? Does she own any property?"

"Well, she isn't a millionaire. Dad left us pretty well off. She owns a couple of apartment houses in Frenton, and she has a few stocks and bonds. I think she lost a little money in the crash, but we've never had to worry. Dan, I simply have to go now. Please promise me you won't do anything rash without talking to me first."

"I can't promise you anything."

"Well, at least get in touch with me tonight. Please do. After dinner. Pick me up and we can take a drive. I'll need it."

CHAPTER TWELVE

After dropping Gail at the Hibley house, Dan headed directly for Ronald Hibley's real estate office, the sign of which he had noticed on the main street of Hamilton as they were driving to the Coffee Shop.

A thin, sour-faced woman in the outer office told him that Mr. Hibley was in, but was busy with some gentlemen. Just then the door of the inner office opened and County Attorney Earl Grimes stepped out, followed by Sheriff Horgan and Vance Dalbert.

"I'd just forget about it, if I were you, Mr. Hibley," Grimes was saying. "And if this fellow Banion bothers you again—well, I'll see that he's properly dealt with."

At that, they all stopped in their tracks and stared at Dan. "Are you referring to me?" Dan asked.

Grimes bit hard on his cigar. "I guess now is as good a time as any to have this out," he said. "I'm glad you're here, Banion. Do you mind coming in here with us for a minute?"

Dan kicked open the swinging gate that led to the inner office. "I thought I heard you mention my name."

"Come in," said Grimes. All of them filed back into the office. Vance Dalbert looked at Dan, half resentful and half scolding.

Ronald Hibley sat down behind his desk as if the seat were filled with eggs. The others grabbed the chairs, and left Dan standing. He eased one buttock onto the corner of the desk.

"All right, Banion," said Grimes, "just what is this you've been telling Mrs. Hibley and her son about Flavin being innocent? Suppose you tell me about it."

"So you've talked to Mrs. Hibley, too," said Dan.

"Never mind. I'm asking the questions."

"All right, go ahead and ask them." Dan lit his pipe and puffed smoothly.

"I asked you, what's the idea of telling Mrs. Hibley and her son that Flavin is innocent? What's your game, Banion? What are you trying to do?"

Dan looked at Vance. "Get home all right last night?" he asked.

Vance blushed to the roots of his hair.

"I know all about that little affair, too," said Grimes. "Don't try to evade the question. What's your object?"

"So you know all about last night, do you? Then you must know all about Beth's place. That's quite an admission for a man who wants to be governor."

Grimes calmly removed his cigar from his mouth and studied it. "Listen, son, I think you're out over your head. You're not the first newspaper reporter with a head that got too big to fit his hat—or should I say job?"

"If anybody's out on a limb, Grimes, it's you. You're moving too fast. You're overanxious. You'd better slow down until you know what you're doing. This case could make you. Then, on the other hand, it could break you."

Ronald Hibley's eyes jerked from one speaker to another, as if he were watching a tennis match.

"I asked you a question," said Grimes. "I'm waiting for an answer."

"You'll wait politely, too," Dan said. "You can't push me around, Grimes. If you want answers to your questions, then ask them decently, and respectfully. I can answer you or not, just as I see fit."

"I simply asked you, Banion, what's the idea of going around telling people Flavin is innocent?"

"Well, what are you so damned mad about? You act as if it were a crime to suggest that someone was innocent. Every man is considered innocent until he's proven guilty."

"But he confessed," said Vance.

"He did not. He said he was sorry because he puked on Horgan's rompers when you scared him with a lot of gore. You were all so anxious to have him guilty that you took an apology for a confession."

"I thought that might be it," said Horgan.

"You fellows keep out of this," said Grimes. "That's neither here nor there, Banion. The evidence is clear. You still haven't answered my question. Why are you going around telling people he's innocent?"

"Because he *is* innocent. He didn't do it. And if you have any sense you'll listen to me before you stick your neck out any farther on this case."

"I'm listening, but I'm not hearing a damned thing."

"In the first place," Dan said, "the crime couldn't possibly have been committed with the knife you found on the kid."

"Don't be ridiculous," said Grimes.

"That knife was made for cutting ropes. It has no point on it. It has a rounded end like a Barlow knife. It had nothing but an edge, and a mighty dull edge at that. You couldn't have stabbed anyone with it. If you want to take it into court, I'll let you stab me with it as much as you want. You won't even puncture my vest."

"But the girl wasn't stabbed," said Vance. "Her throat was cut."

"Before her throat was cut, she was stabbed in the breast several times. The blade wasn't large enough for the purpose, and that's why the murderer had to cut her throat. It's written up in your own paper, Vance, and I believe Sheriff Horgan is the one you quoted on it."

"By God, that's right," said Horgan.

"It's not conclusive in any way," said Grimes. "I'd have to examine the knife again before I'd even concede what you say. Furthermore, Flavin might have tried first with some other weapon, and then resorted to the knife."

"What other weapon?" asked Dan. "And where is it?"

"Well, that's what we'll have to look into. He probably disposed of it."

"You mean he disposed of the weapon he stabbed her in the breast with, and kept the knife he cut her throat with in his pocket—not even bothering to wipe it off? You'd better trim your sails, Grimes."

"Compared with the other circumstantial evidence," said Grimes, "the knife is almost incidental."

"If it's circumstantial evidence you want," Dan said, "there were plenty of motives for killing that girl. And plenty of motives for framing Flavin."

An instant of silence followed. Grimes cleared his throat. "I don't understand you, Banion. What do you mean?"

"For one thing," said Dan, "the girl was pregnant. For another, she was misrepresenting herself in the Hibley household. She wasn't a maid. What do you know about this girl? You haven't even tried to find out. Who was she? Where did she come from?"

Ronald Hibley's face turned white.

"Who was she, Mr. Hibley?" Dan asked.

"Don't answer any of his questions," said Grimes. Then, facing Dan, "What do you mean by saying the girl was pregnant? You're taking a lot on your shoulders, it seems."

"You know what I'm talking about. Don't try to act dumb."

"I don't. I don't know what you're talking about, Banion."

"Wait a minute," said Ronald Hibley. "Yes, she was going to have a baby—my baby. Don't stop me, Mr. Grimes. I would give my soul if I could have her back. Listen to me, Mr. Banion, and believe me. I want to know who did this thing. And I want him killed. Do you hear me? I want to kill him with my own hands. I want to get my hands on him!"

Sheriff Horgan put a hand on Hibley's shoulder. "Come on, now, Ronny," he said. "Take it easy."

"I'm sorry," Dan said. "But I can assure you, Mr. Hibley, it will be better for everyone concerned if you'll tell the truth."

"I'm not trying to hide anything," said Hibley. "As far as I'm concerned, I have nothing to live for anymore. I have nothing to be afraid of."

"We'd better get out of here," said Grimes. "We've upset Mr. Hibley enough."

"We'd better stay right here and let him get this off his mind," said Dan.

"We can take care of criminal investigations in this county," said Grimes. "We don't need your interference."

"You're not trying to investigate anything," said Dan. "You're only interested in finding a man guilty."

"You'd better get out of here, Banion," Grimes said.

"Try to put me out of here now and I'll make a bigger monkey of you than King Kong."

Vance, in his quiet way, had brought Ronald Hibley a paper cup of water from the cooler in the corner. Ronald drank it. "I'm all right now," he said. "I loved Esther. I know that now. I wish I'd known how much she meant to me before. I'm not ashamed. She was the best thing that ever happened to me."

"Have you any idea who might have killed her?" Dan asked.

"No, I haven't. That is, if this man they've arrested didn't do it. And you say he didn't—then I can't imagine who would have done it."

"You don't have to answer any of this fellow's questions," said Grimes.

"I think I can trust Mr. Banion," Hibley said. "I've absolutely nothing to hide. I don't mind answering his questions."

The phone rang, and Hibley answered it. "Yes, mother. Yes, I'll be along. I have some gentlemen here. No, mother. Yes, mother. Mr. Grimes and some other gentlemen. No, don't wait dinner. Yes, mother. No, mother. I'll speak to her."

Hibley put his hand over the receiver. "My sister wants to speak to me. She's down from New York. I'm sure you'll excuse me." Then he spoke into the phone. "Yes, Gail. Mr. Banion, you say? He's here now. Did you want to speak to him? No. No. No. But I have nothing to hide, Gail. Mr. Grimes is here, too. But I don't understand. Yes, I did. Well, Gail, I don't understand. I really don't care. Why should I? Yes, he's right here. Why, certainly." He turned to Dan. "She wants to speak to you. Do you mind?"

Dan took the phone and Gail's voice came through. "Dan, for the love of heaven, take care of him. He's a baby. He can't take care of himself. God knows what he'll tell them. Believe me, Dan, he had nothing to do with this."

"Keep your shirt on," said Dan. "He hasn't done anything."

"Please, Dan. I'm serious."

"So am I."

"I'm trusting you, Dan."

"Your brother can take care of himself. He's all right."

"Then call me later. Please don't forget."

"Sure. And stop worrying. The truth isn't going to hurt any innocent person."

When he hung up, Dan said, "Just a social call. Now, where were we?"

Grimes glared at him. "I don't know what your game is, Banion, but I'm getting fed up with your methods."

Dan ignored him and turned to Ronald Hibley. "Who was Esther Berglan? Where did she come from? Who recommended her to your mother?"

"Don't answer him," said Grimes.

"I don't see that there's anything to hide," said Hibley. "She came from Omaha. At least, that's where she grew up. She went to high school there, I believe. Mother got her from an agency in Frenton."

"Why didn't she hire some girl from right here in Hamilton?" Dan asked.

"You'd have to know mother to understand that. She isn't easy to get along with. We had several girls from around here. They wouldn't stay. Mother's very particular. She felt that a girl who wasn't acquainted here would do less running around."

"Did Esther have any family anywhere?" asked Dan.

"Her parents were dead, and she never mentioned any brothers or sisters. She was alone in the world."

"She told you this herself."

"Yes, of course."

"And did your mother know about your relationship with her?"

"Yes, she did. She found out about a week ago."

"And she didn't like it, I gather."

"No."

"Did she know the girl's condition?"

"Yes. I think she would have tried to put her out of the house, if it hadn't been for that."

Grimes tried to interrupt. "You're a damned fool to tell this man all your private business," he said angrily.

"As long as he already knows as much as he does, I want him to know the truth."

"Were you going to marry the girl?" Dan asked.

Ronald Hibley looked at his hands. "I hadn't made up my mind yet," he said hesitantly. "But I wish I had. I wish I'd married her right away. She was the best thing that ever happened to me."

"Did anybody else know she was pregnant?" Dan persisted.

"Nobody. Just mother. I'm quite sure nobody suspected."

"Did your mother's trip to Frenton that day have anything to do with Esther Berglan?"

"I don't see how it could have. Mother always goes to Frenton, at least once a month. She has an attorney there who looks after her business interests. She likes to keep a close check on everything."

"She owns some real estate, doesn't she? I should think you would be the logical one to look after it."

"Her attorney was my father's old business partner. He always looked after things."

"Yes, I think I remember his name. Howard, isn't it?"

"Howard Marnell," said Hibley. "How did you know?"

"It stuck in my mind," said Dan. "Tell me, did you see Esther at any time on the day of the murder?"

"In the morning. I saw her in the morning. Then she phoned me early in the afternoon. She said she wanted to see me. I wish now that I'd gone. She sounded very strange."

"You mean she phoned you here in the office?"

"Yes. She said she wanted to tell me everything. She said she had to see me right away—that it was important."

"What did she mean by 'tell you everything'?"

"I really don't know."

"Well, what did you think at the time?"

"I didn't know what to think."

"Well, didn't you go to see her?"

"No. I knew she'd been upset, and I thought she just wanted to— well, go over the whole thing all over again. I had some people here who wanted to see a farm I've been trying to sell. I couldn't very well pass up the opportunity. I'd been trying to get these people to look at that farm for weeks. I'd promised to drive them out."

"What did you tell Esther?"

"I told her I couldn't come. She insisted. We quarreled, and—" Ronald's thick lower lip quivered.

"And what?" asked Dan.

"I hung up on her," said Ronald. Burying his head in his arms, he sobbed bitterly.

"For God's sake, leave him alone," said Grimes. "Come on. Let's get out of here. I've had enough of this. Can't you see the man's upset?"

"Go ahead," said Dan. "Beat it, if you want to."

"Be reasonable, Banion. This has absolutely nothing to do with the case," Grimes said.

Vance toddled from the water cooler with another paper cup.

Sheriff Horgan clamped a fat hand on Ronald Hibley's shoulder. "Buck up, Ronny, old boy," he said. "Hell, anybody's apt to get in a jam. We're all your friends here."

"I'd like to ask just one more question," Dan said.

Ronald raised his head and mopped his face with a handkerchief. "I'm all right," he said. "Go ahead."

"Are you familiar with the story this boy Flavin told when he was arrested?"

"Just what I read in the *Sentinel.*"

"The *Sentinel's* not the most accurate source of information in the world," said Dan, with a look at Vance. "Listen, and I'll repeat it briefly."

"I thought this was to be just one more question," said Grimes.

"It's all right," said Ronald. "We want to get at the truth."

Dan repeated Flavin's account of what had happened. "Does that make any sense to you?" he asked, concluding.

"No, it doesn't," said Ronald. "No sense at all. There isn't any such woman who might have been in our house."

"Banion, this is all a lot of damned nonsense," said Grimes.

"Think carefully," said Dan. "Are you absolutely sure you don't know such a woman?"

"Well, I'm as positive as a man can be," said Ronald. "It just doesn't make sense."

"You're making a fool of yourself and wasting our time," said Grimes. "Mrs. Hibley told us what you were up to."

"Yeah? What did she say?" asked Dan.

"She said you threatened her about her son's relationship with the girl. She said she caught a hint of blackmail in your voice, and I think she was right. And I think it's a damned good thing we happened to be here when you came sneaking around to talk to Mr. Hibley."

"You know that's a lot of malarkey, Grimes. Why do you try to pull such stuff? What else did she tell you?"

"That's all. And I told her I'd see to it that you didn't bother her again. Just to make damned sure you wouldn't, I phoned Ainsley. If you'd take time out to call your office, you'd save all of us a lot of time. The days of the smart aleck newspaper reporter are over, Mr. Banion. In fact, they never really did exist. There are ethics in journalism today which you don't seem to comprehend."

"You shouldn't have done that, Grimes," Dan said.

"Don't expect any sympathy from me," said Grimes. "You had it coming to you."

"But didn't she tell you anything else?" Dan persisted.

"Didn't who tell me anything else?"

"Mrs. Hibley. Didn't she say that I questioned her about another woman—someone well-known around here?"

"She didn't say so."

"She didn't mention it, huh?"

"What other woman?" asked Sheriff Horgan.

"Don't pay any attention to him," said Grimes. "He's just trying to talk himself out of a hole."

"Oh, a smart guy. Is that it?" asked Horgan.

"Yes," said Grimes. "But in this case, just a little too smart for his britches. Don't you think you'd better phone your office, Banion?"

"The way you put it," said Dan, "there would be a lot more sense in calling the *Banner*. Isn't that the Frenton paper that's supporting Governor Emerick for re-election?"

"You're not a newspaperman," said Grimes. "You're a contemptible blackmailer."

"You're a cheap, bigoted politician," said Dan, "and by the time I'm finished with you, you won't be able to be elected dogcatcher in Sawtooth, even with Beth Ridgely's support. So you called up Ainsley and got me fired. You're going to pay through the nose for this."

"Please, please, gentlemen," said Ronald Hibley. "This isn't going to help anything."

"You can't bluff me, Banion," said Grimes. He rose, and Vance Dalbert and Sheriff Horgan rose with him. At the door, he paused and looked back at Dan. "Go ahead," he said. "Call the *Banner*. I hope they run your cock-and-bull story—your cheap attempt at blackmail. All crimes intrude upon the unfortunate personal affairs of the victims. And if you want to take advantage of that, go ahead, and see where it lands you."

With that, he banged out the door, Vance and Horgan following at his heels.

"I'm sorry it all turned out this way," said Ronald Hibley. "I feel as you do, that every possible aspect of this thing should be investigated. Believe me, Mr. Banion, I want to know the truth."

"You're not satisfied, are you?" Dan asked.

"No, I'm not. I seem to feel there's more to it. I want to know."

"I may be calling on you for some help before I'm through," Dan said.

"Then feel free to do so," said Ronald Hibley. "I have only one concern in the matter. I want to know who is guilty, and I want that person punished—no matter who it may be."

"Are you sure you mean that?" asked Dan. "No matter who it may be?"

"Yes," he said coldly. "No matter who it may be!"

CHAPTER THIRTEEN

Tom Regan had given Dan directions how to reach his place. They were all vague in his mind now, but he remembered a few landmarks Tom had mentioned, and trusted to them. It was almost sundown as he drove along the cooling fields.

The day had been hot and he cranked down a window to take advantage of a breeze that was brushing the grass and swaying the trees gently. He breathed in the clear air and marveled at the calm order of fields and orchards and growing things, compared with the tangled lives of those who owned or tilled them.

Before leaving Hamilton, he had stopped in at a drugstore and phoned his friend Al Wilson, city editor of the *Post-Tribune*. Grimes had done his dirty work, all right. Ainsley had given orders that Dan should drop the Hibley story and return to Frenton at once, and Al had instructions to fire him the minute he put his nose in the place. Worst of all, this meant that his expense account would be ended.

He had told Al that he intended to stay on the story, and to stall things along, if he could. He didn't know what Al would be able to do. Al was already in a jam about the poems. Letters and phone calls were pouring in to the city desk from readers who believed Ralph innocent and wanted something done about him, and from others who merely asked for more poetry, seemingly indifferent to the fact that the author was in prison accused of murder.

Printing such a detailed account of Flavin's story had also stirred the readers' imagination. Hundreds found it more convincing than the fiendish attack angle. And Ainsley was too shrewd an editor to accept all this as naïveté on Al's part.

Dan had also told Al about the shot glasses, purloined from Beth's place the night before. He had mailed them to a fingerprint expert, and asked Al to pick up the photographs of any prints on them and have them checked through police connections. Al had told him to go to hell, but Dan was sure he'd take care of it.

Finally, he had asked Al to dig everything he could out of the *Post-Tribune's* morgue on former State Attorney General Vern B. Hibley, and his business associate, Howard Marnell, and to forward what he found by special delivery. Al had told him to go jump in the lake, but again Dan felt he'd come through.

After that, Dan had phoned his wife, Ethel, but got no answer. He was worried. He had an understanding with Ethel that he'd call her at the same hour every night, and she had never failed to be there before. There could be a hundred different explanations, but he felt uneasy.

As far as proving Flavin's innocence was concerned, Dan realized he was still shooting in the dark. He doubted if he could really talk the *Banner* into challenging Grimes' case. It was the opposition paper, so far as Ainsley and his crowd were concerned, but it had no guts, and couldn't be expected to move excepting on a sure thing. Arthur Dempsey, its editor, had made a modest financial success of liberalism, and championed the truth fearlessly whenever it seemed reasonably certain the truth would win. But he had never been known to stick his neck out.

The knife angle was sound, but Dan doubted if it would stand up in court against the mass of circumstantial evidence against Flavin. There was enough to pin the murder on him without the knife.

Accusing Ronald Hibley would be a convenient way of creating a controversy. But if he really had shown those people the farm that afternoon, he had an airtight alibi.

Behind its respectable front, the Hibley family seemed to have closets filled with old bones that they didn't want dragged out. In spite of the fact that he had emphasized Beth Ridgely in his conversation with Mrs. Hibley, she had failed to mention it to Grimes. That couldn't have been an oversight. Some connection obviously existed there.

What the business about Gail and Howard was, he couldn't imagine. Evidently it was Howard Marnell, her father's old business partner. But even that was just an assumption.

The letter Dan had taken from Beth Ridgely's desk was still an enigma. It referred to a girl named June, and was signed "Franz." It might have nothing to do with the case.

This looked like the three trees where Regan had told him to turn off the highway. Dan nosed the car onto a dirt road, bounced along a few hundred yards, and swung into the Regans' yard. Mrs. Regan was jerking washing off a line.

"Are you Mr. Banion?" she said as he opened the car door.

"Yes. Is Tom around?"

"He's in the kitchen. Your wife is out with Lawrence, bringing in the cows."

Cold panic seized Dan. "My wife!"

"Yes, who did you think I meant?"

"Oh yes, of course," said Dan, "my wife."

"Go right in," said Mrs. Regan hospitably. "You'll find Tom listening to the radio. Did you figure to stay to dinner?"

"Oh, no. I'm afraid not. Thanks."

"You might as well. We put your name in the pot. Go on in. Tom's expecting you."

Dan entered the kitchen and found Tom Regan on his hands and knees in front of an old radio. "Shush!" he said. "It's that fool Chamberlain, from London."

"Listen," said Dan, "what the hell did you—"

"Shush!" said Regan. "Come over here if you want to listen."

Dan settled into a Sears Roebuck rocker to wait. Presently, Tom clicked off the radio and stood up. "He's done it now, the damn ass. Peace for the next generation! Peace, my behind! I was in the last war. When will they get some sense?"

"Listen, what did you tell your wife?"

"It was easy," said Tom. "She's the sweetest thing alive. I said Shirley was your wife, and you was going to be out on business, and didn't want to leave her in the hotel by herself overnight. It was simple. Don't think another thing about it."

"You didn't have to say she was my wife!"

"Listen, young fella, do you think I'm in the habit of bringing blondes home in the middle of the night? Maybe I should have said she was a heifer, and put her out in the barn with the cows?"

"Yes, but good grief!"

"It ain't going to hurt nothing. Besides, you could do a lot worse, even if she was your wife. Look at the way she cleaned this place up, and helped the wife with the washing. What did you find out? Anything?"

Amy came reeling in from the back yard, her arms loaded with washing. "Tom," she said, "are you going to get that wood? Or do you expect me to do that, too?"

"Right away, my darling. I was just listening to that Neville Chamberlain."

"A liar," said Amy, dumping the washing on a couch. "A liar if there ever was one. Mr. Banion, I hate liars. Tom is no good, but he's not a liar."

A little girl about seven years old came sauntering in from another room. "Mama," she said, "if you were a big bear, and I was little Goldilocks, and you found me sleeping in your bed, what would you say?"

Amy turned and attempted a ferocious expression. "I'd say grrrrrr grrrrrrr growl—now I am going to eat you for supper."

The child made a wild dash across the room and hid behind the couch. "Oh please, Mr. Bear, don't eat me up," she shouted joyfully.

"Now keep out from under mama's feet, won't you, darling," said Amy gently. "All day long that child keeps this up, till I'm nearly wild. Tom, go get the wood or, so help me, I'll burn your *National Geographic* magazines in the stove."

With a loud galloping of feet, Shirley and Murphy (Lawrence to his mother) burst in the door. "Bang! Bang! Bang!" yelled Murphy, flourishing a toy pistol. "You're kilt. Fall down dead."

"Not now," said Shirley. "I'm all out of breath." She was wearing an old shirt and overalls, evidently Regan's.

"You're kilt," screamed Murphy. "Fall down dead."

"That child can hardly wait until he grows up and can shoot somebody," said Amy. "I don't know where he gets it."

Shirley looked at Dan. "Well," she said, her eyes twinkling, "if it isn't my old man."

"Hello," said Dan weakly.

Shirley put both arms around him and planted a slow kiss on his lips.

"Ain't that cute," said Amy. "Tom, look. Don't it remind you?"

Tom kissed Amy and slapped her on the seat. "I'm going to get the wood," he said, and banged out the door.

The little girl jumped up on the couch and waved her arms. "I'm the wicked troll that lives under the bridge, and I'm going to turn you all into frogs."

"Connie, if you get your feet on that washing, I'm going to spank you," said Amy. Then, sweetly, to Dan, "Why don't you two young people take a walk before supper. You want to be alone, I know."

"Can't I help you with things?" asked Shirley.

"Get along, darling. There isn't a thing you can do. You'll only get under my feet. Tom will set the table."

"I'm goin', too," said Murphy.

"You're going to stay right here and behave yourself," said Amy. "Get along, now, you two. And don't be too long. Things are almost ready."

The yard was pleasantly cool, and the sky was aflame in the east. Great golden clouds hung almost motionless against the sky. Shirley took Dan's hand and led him along the dirt road.

"I thought I told you I was married," Dan said.

"It's just pretend," she said. "Just let me kid myself a little. It won't hurt anything. Gosh, it's pretty. Don't say anything. Let's just walk."

Dan was tired and confused enough for that to be agreeable. He made no effort to separate his hand from hers. After a while, he lifted her hand and examined it.

"Where'd you get the wedding ring?" he asked.

"It's just five and ten. I carry it in my purse. It comes in handy when you're trying to get rid of a guy."

"I'm going to have to ask you more about Beth's place. How long had you been there?"

"You're still worried about that guy in jail, aren't you?"

"I'm not going to let them stick a murder on an innocent kid."

"You got ideals. How come I always fall for guys like you?"

"They don't seem to have done very well by you. How long were you at Beth's?"

"About a month. But I'm not kidding you; I'd been in other joints before. I'm not a nice girl."

"People aren't always to blame for what they are, or what happens to them. We're a long way from understanding things in this world, Shirley."

"You're sympathetic with everybody, aren't you?"

"Don't let that fool you. When a man is tolerant and understanding of others, it's usually because he is burdened with so many weaknesses and crazy things in himself. You can't understand in others what you've never felt in yourself. I sometimes wonder about Christ. I wonder if we grasp the true symbolism of the cross he carried."

"I don't always know what you're talking about."

"It doesn't matter. About Beth's place; have you noticed anything funny going on around there in the past month? Anything at all. Whether it makes sense to you or not, tell me about it."

Shirley thought for a minute. "Well, I don't know if it means anything, but that night at about eight o'clock, when Beth got back—"

"The night of the murder, you mean."

"Yes. It was my day off, but I happened to be going back to my room at about eight o'clock. I was passing the parking lot and saw Beth drive in. But she wasn't in her car. It was one of those red convertible club roadsters that belonged to a guy who'd been drunk there for a couple of days."

"One of the customers?"

"Yes. A guy named Stanley Ross. He's an awful case. He comes from someplace out of town, I think from Frenton. He goes on eight and ten day drunks. They say he has a wife and two kids. I feel sorry for them."

"Is Ross his right name?"

"Yes."

"How do you know?"

"Well, if you must know, I peeked in his wallet one night. I wasn't going to take anything. I was just curious."

"And you say he was at Beth's place that day?"

"Well, he'd been there the night before. He usually slept it off the next day and started in again in the evening. Madge says that sometimes his car is parked there for a week or more. I figured he was on another bender, and Beth had borrowed his keys and used his car. That's all."

"Was he there last night, while we were there?"

"No. The next day they wouldn't give him anything more to drink. They sobered him up and made him go home, or at least get out of there. And was he sore!"

"Did you notice anything else in the past month? Anything at all?"

Shirley was thoughtful again. "Well, only one thing, and it's hardly worth mentioning. There was a funny looking guy with a kind of big nose who used to come around once in a while. And when he did, Beth would leave the bar and go upstairs to her apartment with him."

"Do you think she had a crush on him?"

"No, I don't think so. He didn't look like a guy anybody would ever have a crush on. Besides, she was always kind of sharp with him. I figured they had some business they talked over."

"How did he dress? Did he look like a businessman?"

"No, he looked like he worked with his hands somewhere, and just dressed up when he went out. His face was kind of tan, like as if he was in the sun a lot."

"Can you think of anything else to describe him? What color were his eyes?"

"They were grayish, and kind of nervous. It's hard to describe. He acted like he'd been ashamed to have been caught in such a place. Don't you think we'd better go back? Mrs. Regan will probably have dinner ready."

As they neared the house, Murphy approached them, yelling, "Aunt Shirley! Aunt Shirley. Ma says dinner is ready to go on the table."

Back in the Regan kitchen, Tom was wrestling with the cork of a bottle. "This is some of my own raisin wine," he said. "It's my own invention, mostly. Wait 'til you taste it."

"Tom, put that away," Amy said. "You'll have gas on your stomach again. Remember what happened last time."

"This is just for special occasions," said Tom. "Sit down here. And you right beside her. Murphy, take your fingers out of that. Wait until everybody's ready."

During dinner, Tom expounded one of his favorite themes. "Radio will never amount to much," he said, "as long as the advertisers control it. Take books, for instance. Suppose every man who wrote a book had to bring it to a toothpaste manufacturer to have it published. All our literature would be to the taste of toothpaste manufacturers. And when the books were published, they'd have advertising all over the jackets, and scattered through all the pages."

Amy presided over a lamb stew that sent all plates back for extra helpings. She dished with pride and deprecated the present sample of her culinary art, explaining that it should have a little more of this, and a little less of that.

The raisin wine proved to have remarkable powers of transforming the earth. Wrinkles and blemishes seemed to disappear from everybody's faces when you drank it. Discouraging factors of life retreated into insignificance. Impossibilities seemed easy of accomplishment. Comedy attached itself to everything, and the simplest puns drew the wages of wit. Amy herself sipped a glass, and her great bosom danced with laughter at the merest indication of a joke.

The children, taking advantage of the situation, threw balls of bread at each other and rollicked on the fringe of rare adult abandon.

Dan began viewing the Hibley mess with great optimism, and described loudly what he was going to do to Grimes and Ainsley, and the whole political setup of the county and state. Suddenly, he noticed that he had his arm around Shirley. She kissed him, and he did nothing but laugh.

Tom fussed with the knobs of the radio, and soon a boisterous polka dominated the room. Tom grabbed Amy by her hands and pulled her out of her chair. They danced merrily.

Murphy and little Connie joined them on the floor in clumsy, faltering imitation of their parents' antics. Tom, obviously proud of his grace, lept buoyantly through difficult steps and routines which Amy, for all her bulk, was able to follow with neat and agile response. Tom waved one arm in frantic invitation. Dan and Shirley joined them.

Shirley was a perfect little dancer and melted into his arms with the music. The sides of the room raced past Dan's eyes, and a warm joy throbbed inside him. Somewhere in the dim recesses of his brain, a sober voice was saying, "You're a married man. Who killed Esther Berglan? You're a married man. Who killed Esther Berglan?" But it all seemed unimportant compared with the warm rhythm of the moment.

"Why shouldn't people love each other?" Dan shouted above the music. "Why must they always fight with each other?"

"It would interfere with business," was Tom's reply.

At that instant, Dan felt a cold draft. A hard voice said, "All right. Cut it." Dan turned in the direction of the voice and saw a large man in the door: He wore a white cloth over his face, with slits cut for his eyes. Other men wearing similar masks crowded behind him

Tom dived for the shotgun in the corner, but two of the men grabbed him. He slammed one of them in the face with his fist, but the other slugged him neatly on the head with a sap, and he collapsed on the floor.

Murphy charged the man's leg like an angry terrier, his little fists swinging, his teeth biting. The man kicked and sent him sprawling. The strains of the polka still came grotesquely from the radio.

Two of the men headed for Dan. He waited until they were ready to lay hands on him, then shot one fist up like lightning. There was a loud, fleshy impact, and the man went down with a clatter. The other man wrapped an arm around Dan's neck in a choking embrace.

Shirley grabbed a large serving fork from the table and jabbed it into the man's hip with unmerciful force. With a howl of pain, he released Dan and lunged for her. Dan whirled around and kicked his legs from under him. He fell to the floor where Shirley, with quick teamwork, picked up the stew bowl and broke it over his head. Dan turned again, just in time to duck a blow from the man who had entered first.

A deafening report shook the room. Amy had got her hands on the shotgun. One of the men screamed and fell to the floor, blood oozing from a mangled leg.

"The next man gets it in the face," screamed Amy.

Two of the men fled out the door. The wounded man rolled on the floor and moaned. The man Dan had hit was out cold. The big man hesitated, uncertain.

"Move a whisker and I'll blow your head off," said Amy.

It was so grimly plain she meant it that the man's hands trembled as he raised them above his head. Dan slid his hands over his chest and pulled out a snub-nosed revolver. Shirley caught the idea, stooped, and removed an automatic pistol from the man who had been knocked out.

As she moved to do the same to the wounded man, he reached toward his shoulder.

"Uh, uh, uh!" said Amy, in a tone that made him withdraw his hand. Shirley reached under his coat and removed another gun. Then, without losing a single motion, she examined his leg.

"Murphy," said Shirley, "get me a scissors, quick."

"It's all right," Dan said to Amy. "I've got him covered." He had the revolver pointed at the big man, but had drawn back a sufficient distance so that he could cover the door, too.

Amy set the shotgun on the couch and leaned beside Tom. "Tommy darling," she said. "Tommy dear."

Tom was just beginning to come to. He was blinking his eyes.

Dan reached over and jerked the white cloth mask from the big man's face. It was Ray, the bartender from Beth's place.

Murphy had brought the scissors to Shirley, and was now fetching a pitcher of water to Amy. Shirley was cutting away the man's trouser leg.

The radio still babbled insanely. "Evol, friends, is the gentle laxative," a voice was saying. "Spell it backwards, and it spells Love."

"Connie, darling, turn off the radio," sobbed Amy. "Tom! Tom! Are you all right?" She sopped water onto his head, and he came spluttering to life.

Ray eyed Dan contemptuously. "You ain't goin' to get by with this, Buster," he said.

"Aren't you a little mixed up on who's trying to get by with what?" asked Dan.

"We've got to get this man to a hospital," said Shirley, still working over the wounded man. "Murphy, bring me a towel or something, and a stick." She had removed the mask from the man's face. He was a hard-faced young man with greasy black hair. He was scared white, and moaning.

Dan stooped and pulled the mask from the third man, lying unconscious on the floor. He was a puffy-faced, half-bald man, just beginning to regain consciousness.

Tom had rolled to a sitting posture, and was rubbing his head. "What did they hit me with?" he asked. "What happened?"

"It's all right, darling," said Amy. "I scared them away. That was the one who hit you, over there. I blew his foot off."

"We've got to get this guy to a doctor," repeated Shirley.

"Do you know any of these fellows, Tom?" Dan asked. "Aside from our old friend Ray here?"

Tom blinked at them and shook his head. "Never saw them in my life before. What's the matter with you, Ray? Have you gone crazy?"

Shirley fashioned a tourniquet and twisted it around the man's leg. "We've got to get him to a doctor," she repeated insistently.

"Have you got a phone?" Dan asked.

"No," said Tom. "But it will only take a few minutes to run him into Sager Creek."

"Do you feel all right enough to tie these monkeys up while I hold a gun on them?" Dan asked.

"I'll do that," said Amy eagerly. She left the room for a moment, came back with a length of rope, and began tying the hands of the unconscious man in a businesslike way. By this time he was blinking and stirring.

Dan turned to Ray. "Sit down. Maybe you and I had better have a talk."

"You can't get away with this," Ray said. "You're just a damned fool."

"Just the same, we're going to take you in to Sager Creek and turn you over to Sheriff Horgan," said Dan.

"Go ahead," Ray said. "See where it gets you."

"What was your idea, busting in here?" Dan asked.

"You're the smart guy," said Ray. "You know all the answers."

"If you want to tell us what the idea is, Ray, we might listen to reason. We don't want to turn you in unless we have to."

"As far as I'm concerned, you can go to hell," said Ray.

Amy approached Ray with a rope. "Now for you, young man. Put your hands behind you."

Ray eyed Dan, who had the revolver leveled at him. "You wouldn't dare shoot," he said.

"Well, I wouldn't mind blasting one foot off you," said Dan.

Ray hesitated a moment, then submitted.

"Now what the devil?" said Tom. "You can't go out there with those other two gorillas roaming around. And there might be more of them."

"We've got to get this guy to a doctor somehow," said Shirley.

"How does it happen you fellows didn't use any of this artillery you had on you?" Dan asked, hefting the revolver he had taken from Ray.

"We didn't need it," said Ray. "If it hadn't been for that damn fool woman, we could have taken care of you. As for you, I'm going to take care of you personally before I'm finished."

"You can't go out with those other guys roaming around," repeated Tom "You'll have to wait till morning."

"By that time, this guy might lose his leg," said Shirley. "I'm no Florence Nightingale. I don't even know what I'm doing here, much."

"I don't think we have to worry about them as long as they know we're armed," said Dan. "And the sooner we turn these three over to Horgan the better. Besides, they'll sleep better in the jail. Won't you, Ray?"

"You ain't so goddamn smart as you think," Ray said.

Out in the yard it was dark and cool, but bright stars were shining overhead. Dan backed his car up near the kitchen door. Tom suggested leaving Ray and the other man in the house, and sending Horgan out to pick them up later, since there wasn't much room in the coupe. But Dan didn't like the idea of endangering the Regan family by their presence.

He opened the spacious storage compartment in the rear of the car, and made Ray and the other man squeeze in. Ray complained nastily and threatened vile revenge, but complied when Amy suggested clubbing him over the head.

Dan then slammed down the lid and locked it.

"That's a right good idea," said Tom. "I never would have thought of it. But won't they choke to death?"

"They may get a little bruised up when we go over the dirt road," said Dan. "But they're tough."

As they lifted the wounded man into the front seat, Tom instructed Dan how to get to the Sager Creek hospital. Amy stood in the doorway holding the shotgun in eager readiness.

"They won't come back here," she said. "If they do, I'll blow their heads off."

At the last minute Shirley, clutching the revolver she had taken from the wounded man, climbed in beside them. Dan objected, but she insisted on going along. Tom thought he'd better stay there with Amy, in case the men came back.

As they bounced over the dirt road leading from the farm, Dan held the revolver in one hand. But when they reached the main road where there was an assuring amount of traffic, he slipped it in his pocket.

"You're a fancy looking sight in those overalls, to be driving into town," he said to Shirley. "Put that gun away. They won't start anything with all this traffic. Do you know this guy here?"

"I saw him in Beth's place once. But I don't know who he is."

"Not very talkative," Dan said.

The wounded man, slumped between them, didn't even look up.

"We're risking our necks and going to an awful lot of trouble to save your foot," said Dan. "I don't know exactly why."

"The cat's got his tongue," said Shirley.

The man looked up sullenly. "You ain't so smart, kid."

"What was your idea?" Dan asked. "What did you guys figure to do, smashing in on us like that?"

"What do you think? You're supposed to know all the answers."

Dan located the hospital and parked in front of it. "Run in and get somebody to help me with him," he told Shirley.

She returned in a moment with a white-coated man who smelled of antiseptics. "Oh, oh. What have we got here? Tsch, tsch, tsch! How did he do that?"

"I think we can carry him, if you'll help me," Dan said. "It's just his foot. He's a very smart man. A genius. Goes around kicking little boys. So he got in the way of a shotgun."

"You ain't so smart," growled the wounded man.

Dan and the attendant made a seat with their hands and carried him into the hospital. Shirley ran ahead to open the door.

Inside, Dan phoned the sheriff's office. Horgan wasn't there, but a deputy on duty said he'd send some men right over. Since it was only three blocks away, they arrived before Dan had finished answering the questions of the hospital authorities.

Sid Evans and two other officers strode importantly in, their heavy pistols swaying in holsters at their sides. "You're the newspaper guy, aren't you," Sid said. "Well, what's your trouble now?"

Dan explained briefly, meanwhile leading them to the door. "They're out here in my car. Come on, I'll show you. I've got 'em locked in the storage compartment." He stopped short as they reached the sidewalk.

"What car?" asked Sid.

"They've stolen my car," said Dan.

"What car?" asked Sid.

"My car. It was parked right there."

"It was there just a minute ago," said Shirley, who had followed along.

"If it was parked here a minute ago, then where is it?" Sid demanded.

"That's what I'm telling you. Somebody stole it."

"They told me all about you," said Sid. "You're crazy. People don't steal cars around here."

"He's right, Sid," said the hospital attendant. "It was parked right there. I saw it. We took the man out of it."

"What man? What are you talking about?"

"The man who was shot in the foot. He's inside now."

"Shot in the foot!"

"Yes," said Dan. "Shot in the foot. That's what I've been telling you."

"Who's she?" asked Sid, indicating Shirley.

"She's with me," Dan said.

"You been drinkin'," said Sid. "Your breath smells of booze. So does hers."

"Listen," said Dan, "get busy and find that car. It's important."

"Do you think we've got nothing to do but chase around after drunks?" asked Sid.

"I tell you there were two men locked in the luggage compartment—two men of a gang that attacked us out on Regan's farm. Look. Here are their guns. Give me that gun, Shirley." He took the revolver from her and handed both guns to Sid. The automatic, taken from the third man, he had left with Tom Regan.

"There's something fishy about you two," said Sid. "Where'd you get these guns?"

"I just told you. We took them off those men."

"The one who was shot in the foot is inside now," said the hospital attendant. "Why don't you talk to him?"

Inside the hospital, the wounded man stubbornly refused to talk. He insisted on his right to see an attorney. His pockets yielded no identification whatsoever. Sid assigned a man to guard him. "You two will have to come with me," he said, turning to Dan and Shirley. "There's something fishy about the whole thing."

At the station they were greeted by Sheriff Horgan, who had been called away from a bowling tournament, and was none too happy about it. "What the devil is it now, Banion?" he demanded. "Don't you ever let up? Excuse me. Here's your wife. She's been looking for you all evening."

The added complication was more than Dan's brain could manage, and it lapsed into total confusion. Ethel was accompanied by Vance Dalbert, who hovered in the background as she swooped forward and seized Dan by the shoulders.

"I thought you were mixed up in something," she said. "I just knew it. What is it, Dan? What have you been doing?"

"She came around to the *Sentinel* office looking for you," explained Vance. "I sort of took her under my wing. We were having dinner at my house when they phoned me about this business, and we came right along."

Dan put one arm around his wife and patted her shoulder. "Ethel, you shouldn't have come down here. There's nothing wrong."

"That's what you always say. Vance has been telling me about this thing you're mixed up in. Dan, how can you be such a fool?"

"But there's absolutely nothing to worry about," said Dan. "Everything's all right."

"Here's a couple of guns he claims he took off a gang of thugs," said Sid, handing the revolvers to Horgan.

CHAPTER FOURTEEN

Shirley appraised Ethel quickly. Class and education stood out all over her—the kind of woman who could pick her man and hold him. She looked versatile enough to keep a perfect home or be a good drinking companion, as the occasion required. Beauty, brains, a sense of humor—good in the kitchen and probably fun in bed. It was too much. Shirley's heart sank.

"And who is this?" asked Ethel, nodding toward Shirley. "I don't believe we've met."

"Oh," said Dan lightly, "this is Shirley. Shirley—"

"Peterson," said Shirley honestly, discarding, she knew not why, her business name of La Rue.

"She's a friend of mine," added Dan.

"Excuse my overalls," said Shirley. "We just came from a riot."

"Yes," said Dan jauntily. "Just a little riot."

"Just a little riot," repeated Ethel sarcastically.

Sheriff Horgan walked around in back of his desk and settled squeakily in the swivel chair. "Now suppose we skip the social chatter," he said, "and get down to business. Banion, what was this you were telling Sid here about a fight at Regan's place?"

Dan started to tell about the attack, but Horgan interrupted. "But what were you doing when this happened?"

"When they came busting in?"

"Yeah. When they came busting in."

"Well," said Dan, "we'd just finished dinner, and we were dancing."

"You were dancing."

"Yes, we were dancing."

"Have anything to drink?"

"Well, yes. A little raisin wine."

"You'd had a little raisin wine and you were dancing. Who were you dancing with?"

"Well, let's see. We were all dancing. I was dancing with Shirley."

"That's this girl here, I take it."

"That's right."

"Okay, so you were dancing. Then what happened?"

Horgan listened patiently and nodded his head from time to time as Dan described the battle, the drive into Sager Creek, and the disappearance of the car.

When Dan had finished, Horgan reached for the phone. "We can find out pretty quick about that bartender," he said. He called a Sawtooth number, and presently had Beth Ridgely on the phone. They talked for quite a while. Horgan nodded his head and said "Yes"; nodded, said "yes"; nodded, said "yes"; nodded, said "yes."

"It was all just fun," Dan said to Ethel, while Horgan was phoning. "We drank a little raisin wine, and then we danced. That's all."

"I heard you the first time," said Ethel. "I thought you told me they took the sidewalks in at sundown in this town."

Sheriff Horgan hung up the receiver. "We'd better discuss this in private, Banion. If your wife doesn't mind."

"Dan, what have you done now?" Ethel demanded.

"See here," said Dan, "I haven't done a damned thing. There isn't anything concerning me that my wife isn't welcome to listen to."

"Well, it's your funeral," said Horgan. "If you don't care, it's all right with me. I always like to give a guy a break, though." He stared at Shirley. "What's your name again, young lady?"

"Shirley Peterson."

"It wouldn't be La Rue sometimes, would it?"

"Maybe," Shirley gulped and began to cry.

Dan reached over and ruffled her hair. "Come on, kid. Don't let 'em get you down."

"Don't mind me," said Ethel coldly. "After all, I'm not supposed to be here."

"Oh, don't be crazy, Ethel," said Dan.

Shirley sniffed and searched futilely in her overall pockets. Ethel opened her purse, took out a handkerchief, and offered it condescendingly to Dan. He handed it to Shirley.

"Thanks, kid," she said, looking gratefully at Ethel. Ethel arched her eyebrows and looked away.

"Remember, Banion," said Horgan. "You took this on yourself. I tried to give you a break."

"Okay," Dan said. "Let's have it."

"Well, Beth says this girl, Shirley, was Ray Goldman's girl—Ray being the bartender in her joint. You went to Beth's place last night and took her away from him—gave her some kind of a line and got her to ditch Ray. Beth says Ray found out you took her to Regan's house and were having the time of your life with her there. He rounded up some of his pals and went out there to bust up the party. He didn't show up for work tonight, so she figured he'd gone on a rampage. Did you take Shirley out of Beth's place last night?"

"Well, to tell you the truth, I did," said Dan. "But it wasn't the way Beth told you at all."

"Were you Ray's girl?" Horgan asked Shirley.

Shirley blushed deeply. "Well, he was kind of stuck on me, all right. But I wasn't his girl! I couldn't see him for sour beans."

Horgan threw down his pencil, as if that settled the matter. "I can't understand you, Banion. You've got a nice wife. What I ought to do is lock you and this girl up overnight for protection, and make you clear out of here tomorrow."

"You try anything like that, Horgan, and I'll see to it that it costs you that badge you're wearing."

"I don't think anything like that will be necessary, Horgan," said Vance Dalbert.

Ethel had risen to her feet. Her face had colored deeply. "Dan, I'm afraid all this is a little thick."

"Ethel, for God's sake don't pay any attention to this nonsense."

"I happen to have a little pride, you know."

"I told you to stay in the city. You don't understand things like this."

"No, I'm afraid I don't. Let's go, Mr. Dalbert. Please."

"Certainly," said Vance, popping out of his chair. "You're welcome to stay at our house tonight."

"Listen, Ethel, I can explain this whole damned thing."

"I'm afraid, Dan, I'm getting a little tired of explanations. Can we go, Mr. Dalbert?"

Dan followed them out in the hall, protesting, but she quickened her pace and fairly ran down the steps, with Vance hopping along at her side.

When Dan walked back into Horgan's office, Shirley said, "What a sap! Walking out on a guy like you."

"We just got a report on your car," said Horgan. "It was found five miles out of town. They ran it off an embankment into a creek."

"I suppose that's just considered child's play around here," said Dan. "Or do you intend to try to find out who did it?"

"I sent out word to pick up Ray Goldman. As for the others, we don't know who they are. We'll do the best we can, Banion, but you ought to have better sense than to get yourself into such jams. Why don't you try to patch it up with your wife and go back to Frenton. You're not doing yourself any good down here. By the way, did you have any insurance on that car?"

"No, damn it, I didn't. Ethel has been pestering me for a month to have it renewed and I never got around to it."

"Then forget you had a car. It's in the bottom of a ravine. It would cost you more to pull it out than you could sell it for junk."

"I'm just bad luck," said Shirley. "All I do is bring people bad luck."

CHAPTER FIFTEEN

Outside in the street, Dan and Shirley wandered like a pair of unwanted orphans.

"I could have told you you wouldn't get nowheres with those hick bulls," Shirley said. "They're retarded."

"Well," said Dan, "I've lost my job, lost my wife, and lost my car. What else can happen?"

"I could walk out on you," said Shirley. "But I don't suppose you'd notice it."

"There's one nice thing about being on the bottom; you've nowhere to go but up. Let's get a cup of coffee. That's always a good idea when you're stumped."

They entered a coffee shop a block away from the station and were settled in a booth before they noticed that Ethel and Vance were sitting in the booth across the aisle. Dan got up and leaned over their table.

"Don't talk to me," said Ethel. "I don't want to talk to you."

Dan looked at her for a minute. "All right," he said, "don't." He went back and sat down with Shirley.

"Gee, kid, I'm sorry I messed things up for you," Shirley said.

"It isn't your fault."

"Maybe you oughta patch things up with her and go back home. Maybe you can even get your job back."

"I'm not walking out on this job. I've started something, and I'm going to finish it."

"Move over," said Ethel. She had a determined look.

Dan moved and made room for her. "I thought you didn't want to talk to me."

"I changed my mind," said Ethel, edging into the booth. She fixed Shirley with a glare. "If she thinks she's going to walk off with my husband, she's crazy."

"If you think I wouldn't do it if I could, you're crazy, too," said Shirley. "But I can't. He can't see me for beans."

"Dan," said Ethel, ignoring Shirley, "doesn't our marriage mean anything to you at all? You've got a good job now. Please don't do anything crazy and lose it."

"I've already lost it," Dan said. "Ainsley fired me this afternoon. At least my walking papers are waiting for me the minute I show up."

Ethel sighed and rolled a paper napkin into a ball. "I suppose we'll live like savages again."

"Why don't you calm down and catch up on what's happening?" Dan said. "You don't even know what I've been doing. Aren't you interested?"

"Mr. Dalbert told me all about it. Dan, why don't we get in the car and go home? I'm sure Mr. Ainsley will give you another chance if you'll be sensible."

"Well, for one thing, the car is in the bottom of a ravine. Somebody stole it tonight. They wrecked it."

"Dan, did you have that insurance renewed?"

"No, I didn't. Go ahead and howl."

"How do you expect me to be patient? You haven't any more responsibility than a jack rabbit."

"Are you taking that lace panty Dalbert's word against mine?" Dan looked across the aisle at Vance as he spoke. Vance was sucking the straws of a malted milk, making a gurgling sound in the bottom of the glass.

"Dan, it isn't just Vance. Everybody says the same thing. Don't you think the police can handle their own murders? It's their business, not yours."

"Listen, Ethel, that kid they've got in jail is innocent. He didn't do it. He didn't have anything to do with it."

"Don't be childish."

"Call it whatever you like, but I'm sticking. You might as well make up your mind."

"Now you're really being childish. What'll you use for money? You've lost your job."

"I've got enough for a few days."

"Then what? Dan, please be sensible. Let's go back to town."

"Ethel, you should never have come down here. This isn't your kind of dish. Why don't you go back to town yourself? I'll clean up this business in a few days and then come home."

"And leave you here with her?" said Ethel, looking at Shirley.

"For heaven's sake, we're just friends. What's got into you?"

"I'm just one of the neighbors' children," said Shirley. "But if you want to know what I think, I think you don't deserve a man like him."

"Nobody asked you for your opinion," said Ethel.

"Nobody ever asked me for my opinion," said Shirley, "and nobody ever will. Just the same, you can't control a guy like Dan. You're wasting your time."

"I wouldn't want to control any man," said Ethel. "I wouldn't want a man I could control."

"No, but just the same you'll break your neck trying to control him, and then if you ever succeed, you'll lose respect for him and get interested in the butcher boy. I've seen it too many times."

"I don't see where this is any of your business," said Ethel.

"My business ain't so very different in the long run, honey. Only it's more democratic, or something, I guess."

"Dan, are you going to sit there and let her talk to me that way?"

"Yes. She isn't hurting you."

"I'm entitled to a little respect," said Ethel.

"And a man's entitled to expect his woman to back him up," said Shirley. "He's got his neck in a jam, and instead of helping him, you side with everybody against him. All you care about is your own goddamn comfort. What if he has lost his job? He's doing what he thinks is right. Maybe he's a chump. I don't know. But you're not going to change him. You ought to make up your mind whether you want him or you don't want him. Either play or get off the piano."

"You don't know what I've had to put up with," said Ethel. "This is the first decent job he's had in over a year."

"So maybe you'll have to go to work for a change," said Shirley.

"I'll have you know I've earned my living before. How do you think we kept alive this past year?"

"Listen," Dan said, "this isn't getting us anywhere."

"Well," said Shirley, "she ought to make up her mind whether she's for you or against you."

"Shirley, if you were in Ethel's place, you'd be acting just the same way."

"The hell I would!"

"I think I'm entitled to some explanation," Ethel said.

"Now we're getting somewhere," said Shirley. "Tell her, Dan."

Vance leaned into the booth apologetically. "I don't like to butt in," he said, "but I was getting very lonely." He edged into the seat beside Shirley. "By the way, there's no hard feelings, I hope, Dan."

"None in the least," said Dan. "I think you're a sterling example of citizenship and manhood."

"Oh, skip it," said Vance. "As a matter of fact—I was going to say— I see no reason, Dan, why I couldn't speak to Grimes and have him put in a good word for you with Ainsley. Nobody's really sore about this thing. You just—well, man, you always were an old rebel, and this time you kind of went astray. Don't we all, once in a while?" He tailed off into indulgent laughter.

"By the way, how'd you get home from Beth's the other night?" Dan asked.

Vance colored like a firecracker.

"Did you go to that awful place with Dan?" Ethel's voice was filled with loathing.

"Didn't he tell you about it?" Dan winked at Shirley, and she chuckled joyously.

"See here, Dan, that's not quite fair," said Vance.

"You're dead set on hanging that young kid they've got in jail, aren't you?" Dan said.

"Now, Dan, that's not a fair way to put it. I'm not interested in hanging anybody. He's an unfortunate case, and has to be dealt with."

"And you're jumping on it with both feet to make political capital for Grimes. You won't even listen to any possibility of the kid's being innocent."

"Dan, you're talking like a fanatic. I'm perfectly willing, for the sake of old times, to talk to Grimes and—"

"You can take Grimes, and Ainsley, and the *Post-Tribune*, and add your own *Sentinel*, and shove them all up your ego," said Dan.

"Well, if that's the way you feel about it, Dan, I might as well go."

"No," said Dan, changing his tone to deep earnestness. "Don't go. Listen, Vance, you used to have some kind of principles. Why don't you listen to reason on this? Grimes and Ainsley have their necks out a mile. So have you, for that matter. Give me two more days, and I'll not only prove to you that Flavin is innocent, but I'll tell you who the murderer is."

"If I thought there was any chance he was innocent, I'd be the first person to offer help. But you're imagining things."

Ethel dug her fingers into Dan's arm. "Dan, you stick with it. I don't know what it's all about, but you go right ahead and show them. And if you ever crawl out, I'll leave you so damned fast that—"

"Well, cut my legs off and call me shorty," Shirley said.

"To hell with the butcher boy," said Ethel with a smile.

"She's human!" said Shirley.

"But who else could possibly have done it?" demanded Vance.

"Up to a few hours ago," Dan said, "I was working in the dark. Now I have a pretty good idea."

"You know who the murderer is?" Vance asked incredulously.

"I have a pretty good idea."

"Whom do you suspect?"

Dan ignored the question. "How about driving us back to Regan's place? They're still sitting there, waiting for something to happen."

"I'll drop you off, but I still think you're acting damned unreasonable.

Whom do you suspect?"

As they slid out of the booth, Shirley took Ethel's arm. "Gee, kid, you're not mad at me, are you?"

"I'm not mad at you yet," said Ethel. "But if you ever try to cut in on Dan, I'll chew you limb from joint. I'll dismember you and throw the pieces out different windows."

CHAPTER SIXTEEN

In the back seat of Vance's sedan, Ethel and Dan had an opportunity to get warmly reacquainted.

"I'll get a job," she said. "Maybe that malted milk shop could use me. I've still got a pretty good shape, you know. And that's what counts in making malts."

"Well, not exactly," said Dan. "It's when you lean over to pour it in the glass. You've got to have a loose—"

She slapped him loudly. Vance and Shirley turned around.

"When a man's married to you," Ethel said, "he seems to feel he can take liberties."

"Ain't they cute," said Shirley. They returned their eyes to the road.

"Anyhow, I'll get a job," Ethel said. "And then, no matter how long it takes, you can pitch in and give them hell."

"It won't take that long. It's just a matter of fitting the pieces together, and I think I've got the important ones now."

"Well, if you finish in a few days, then maybe we could get jobs harvesting fruit. I've always wanted to be a fruit tramp. Wouldn't it be wonderful? We could travel from crop to crop."

"It's not such a picnic as you may think. Everybody's always looking for the easy life. There is no easy life, Ethel. Not in the world today. Everything's fixed so you have to keep pounding your brains out, or working your hands off, day in and day out. No rest. No peace of mind."

"What's the sense of it, Dan? There's plenty of everything."

"Yes, but people haven't waked up to the fact. All I've ever wanted is an easy life, and I've tried everything. There's no escape from this frantic grubbing, grubbing, grubbing."

"Here we are," said Vance, rolling into the Regans' yard.

The lights were still on in the house, but they had to bang on the door several times before there was an answer. Amy made them identify themselves before she would open up. Shotgun in hand, she greeted them warmly. Regan was lying on a couch, looking at pictures in *National Geographic* magazines.

"They didn't come back," Amy said. "At least I don't think so. There was a noise out by the road. I hollered, 'Who is it?' Nobody answered, so I shot the gun off once, just to show them. But I don't think they'll come back again. Would you like some coffee?"

"I wish they would," Regan said. "I'd mash them with my bare fists. I knocked two of them cold as clams."

"One of them, if any," corrected Amy.

"Well, it's hard to tell, when you're milling around that way," said Tom.

"They're safe in jail, I hope," Amy said. She put one arm around Shirley. "Sit down, Mrs. Banion, you look tired."

Ethel stiffened sharply. Dan remembered the situation and felt a cold sweat on his brow.

"I don't think we know all these people," said Amy. "That's Vance Dalbert who runs the *Sentinel*," said Tom. "I don't know the lady."

"Oh, her," said Dan, grabbing Ethel by the arm and digging his fingers in. "Well, this is—well—she's my sister."

"Isn't this nice," said Amy. "We're meeting your whole family. Mr. Dalbert. So you run the *Sentinel*. Tell me, who invents those awful recipes you've been printing? I tried one for a cake and it came out like a piece of cheese."

"Your sister!" said Vance in amazement.

"Yes," said Dan, "my sister." He kicked Vance in the leg. "You knew she was my sister, didn't you?"

Shirley began to laugh and buried her head in her arm on the table.

"Brother dear," said Ethel bitterly, "I wonder if I could have a glass of that wonderful raisin wine you told me about?"

"I was going to suggest coffee," said Amy.

Tom rolled up off the couch. "So you liked that wine, Dan? There's plenty of it. It's my own invention, in a manner of speaking. That is, I do things to it that other people don't know about."

"What are you laughing at, darling?" Amy asked, putting a hand on Shirley's shoulder. "Are you hysterical?"

"Maybe we should all have a glass," said Tom. "It's been something of a night, you know."

Ethel leaned over and mumbled to Shirley, "Wait until I get you alone. I'll rip every hair out of your head."

"It's nothing," whispered Shirley. "Dan will explain."

"Your brother has a lovely wife," Amy said to Ethel. "She's been staying with us, as you know."

Shirley continued to laugh. Tom handed her a glass of the thick yellow wine. "Drink that. It will calm you. Women haven't the stamina we men have."

"I feel a little faint myself," said Ethel.

Tom poured her a generous glass.

"None for me, thanks," said Vance.

"Don't be a wet blanket," said Dan. "It'll give you new ideas."

"What did the police say when you dragged those criminals in to the jail?" asked Amy.

Dan related their experiences at the hospital and the station, leaving out the part where Horgan phoned Beth Ridgely.

"This county's a jungle," declared Tom. "The only one who gets any protection from the police is Beth's joint in Sawtooth."

"Oh, I wouldn't say that," said Vance.

"You wouldn't say anything Grimes didn't tell you to say," Tom snapped.

Ethel took advantage of their preoccupation to reach down under the table, take a large pinch of Shirley's thigh, and twist it. Shirley jumped.

"Goodness, your nerves are all on edge," said Amy. "Mr. Banion, why don't you stay here with your wife tonight? We could put your sister up, too."

"I'm afraid that's impossible," Dan said. "I have some things to attend to in town."

"You haven't stayed here one night with your wife. I don't understand it," Amy said.

Ethel looked somewhat relieved. As they walked through the dark yard to the car, Shirley followed along and whispered to Ethel, "It was just a gag to get me a place to stay. Dan didn't have anything to do with it. It was Tom's idea. You aren't mad at me, are you?"

"You've got to admit, I'm taking plenty," said Ethel.

"Please don't be mad at me," said Shirley. "It hurts to have people mad at you."

CHAPTER SEVENTEEN

In the morning, Ethel had to roll Dan like a lump of dough, and then pull the covers off him to wake him up.

"Don't do that, damn it," he said. "That's not funny. Cut it out." He pulled the covers over himself, nosed into the pillow, and closed his eyes.

"If some of these romantic girls knew how you snored at night, they wouldn't be so anxious to take you over," she said. "Now get up. It's ten o'clock."

"Just a few minutes," he moaned.

"Are you sure you told me everything last night?"

"Please leave me alone, Ethel. What time is it?"

"It's ten o'clock. Now get up."

"Just another hour. Go away and let me sleep. Please."

"You get up and get busy. You've started something, and you're going to finish it. And I don't want it to take all year. Who is this Mrs. Flannagan? I don't remember you mentioning her last night."

"I don't know any Mrs. Flannagan."

"Think hard. Maybe you're Mr. Flannagan, and it's all a mistake."

"I never heard—wait a minute!" Dan sat up, and rubbed his head. "Mrs. Flannagan? What about her?"

"You should have looked in your box when we came in last night. The clerk gave me a message for you. A Mrs. Flannagan called last night, and wants you to get in touch with her."

Dan whipped back the covers and sat unattractively on the edge of the bed, blinking in the sunlight. "Where's my pants?"

"They've been walking around the room looking for you. I think they got tired and sat down over there."

Dan grabbed his pants off the chair and lunged his legs into them, sliding into both underwear and trousers at once in a splendidly perfected maneuver. "Mrs. Flannagan is Mrs. Hibley. Remember? I told you I gave her a key name to use if she wanted to get in touch with me."

"Maybe she'll confess and let us go home."

"I thought you wanted to pick fruit," said Dan, gawking at himself in a mirror. "God, what a head! If I ever reach for any of that raisin wine again, I hope you'll tie me up."

"It certainly has an amorous effect. I think it's a good thing I came when I did. That Shirley is cute. The dope."

"You could get the same effect by beating yourself over the head with an empty bottle," said Dan.

There was a knock at the door.

"It's me, Mr. Banion," called the chambermaid. "Do you want any more boxes?"

"No more boxes," called Dan. "I haven't been able to find any more birds' eggs."

The chambermaid popped her head in the door. "Oh, a lady," she said.

"My wife."

"How do you do?" said the chambermaid. "I talked to Mr. Ferguson, and he's anxious for you to come over and see his collection. He says, could you come to dinner tonight?"

"I'm afraid not. Maybe some other time."

"Oh, that's too bad. He'll be so disappointed."

"Who is Mr. Ferguson?" Ethel asked.

"My nephew," said the chambermaid. "He collects birds' eggs, like your husband. I was so hoping they could get together."

"Maybe some other time," said Dan.

"It would be so good for him to see you. It might sort of bring him out of himself. Ferguson doesn't make friends easy. So few people collect birds' eggs."

"The field is not at all crowded," said Dan.

"He mentioned a very rare one he had. Some kind of a bird. I forget the name. But he said you'd be surprised. Was it a sturgeon? Let's see. Funny, ain't it—how things get away from you?"

"The sturgeon is a fish," said Dan.

"Then it wasn't a sturgeon. What was it? It's on the tip of my tongue."

"Maybe it was a pelican," said Ethel.

"No, that wasn't it. Do you collect birds' eggs too, Mrs. Banion?"

"If you'll excuse us," said Dan, "my wife and I have some things to talk about."

"Oh, goodness, don't let me intrude."

"It's quite all right," said Dan.

"It's so nice that you're married. I wish Ferguson could find a good wife. It might bring him out of himself. But these girls nowadays, my heavens! If you worked in a hotel, what you'd see. I wouldn't trust one of them as far as I could fling a cat."

"My husband gets around considerably," said Ethel.

"Collecting birds' eggs, I should imagine. Do you have to climb a lot of trees, Mr. Banion?"

"In many respects he is much like a monkey," said Ethel.

"I declare, Ferguson's the same way. If you want to find Ferguson, look up in a tree. He was up a tree the other day when that girl was murdered in Hamilton. Wasn't it terrible? I suppose you heard about it."

Dan stopped combing his hair. "What tree?" he asked.

"I shouldn't have mentioned it. He's always climbing trees, that's all. He happened to mention that he climbed a tree on Bruce Street the day it happened, and looked right down into the Hibleys' yard. When I think that the fiend might have been murdering her right while Ferguson was up that tree! Well, I have my rooms to do. You will try to see him tomorrow night, won't you, Mr. Banion?"

"Wait a minute," said Dan. "What else did he say he saw?"

"I shouldn't have said anything. People are so curious about murders. He just looked down into their yard, that's all."

"What did he see?" Dan persisted.

"Well, he saw the yard, of course."

"Is that all?"

"Well, certainly that's all."

"Come to think of it," said Dan, "that rare egg he has is a blue-crested floogle, isn't it?"

"No, that doesn't sound like what he said."

"I'm sure that must be it," said Dan. "Darling, this is what I've been looking for for years. The blue-crested floogle is the rarest bird in the world."

"You sound just like Ferguson," said the maid.

"Give me his address again," said Dan. "Maybe I can drop by and see him sometime today. Does he work?"

"No. At least he's not working now. He spends most of his time in the library or climbing trees. If he isn't home, you'll most likely find him in the library. Dewey Ferguson is his full name, but mostly we just call him Fergy."

When the maid had gone, Ethel looked at Dan. "For a warrior in the service of truth, you're the most all-around liar I've ever seen. Will you tell me what this is all about, if it isn't asking too much?"

"It was just an accident," said Dan. "But it may be the biggest break we've had yet." He explained the business of the whiskey glasses and his slip of the tongue regarding birds' eggs.

"So now you're going to fly off at a tangent in search of the blue-crested floogle," Ethel said.

"No," said Dan. "You are. While I'm running down these other things, you're going to go and see Mr. Ferguson and find out what he saw in that yard."

"Which was probably nothing."

"And which might be anything. Just the same, you're going to find out. Another thing I want you to do is drop by the jail and see that kid Flavin. Find out how he's doing, and tell him not to worry. Bring him some cigarets and magazines."

"Dan, aren't you overlooking the main thing? You ought to find out who that girl Esther Berglan was. That's important."

"And that's what I intend to find out from Mrs. Hibley."

"Shall I disguise myself as a bird's egg when I go around to see this goof?"

"Don't be silly. Ask him in detail everything he saw."

"Suppose he didn't see anything?"

"He couldn't help but see something. I don't mean he saw anybody chasing another person with an axe, or anything like that. Probably he didn't see anybody at all. But he saw the yard. Have him describe the yard and everything that was in it, however slight. Also, find out exactly what time it was, and write down everything he tells you."

"You mean you want to know about benches, flower beds, clotheslines—things like that?"

"Everything."

"Okay, you're the boss, but it sounds kind of pointless."

"People never give themselves away on big things. It's always some silly little detail that traps them. Go over Flavin's story again with him, too. Ask him to describe the grounds of the Hibley house as he remembers them. Ask him to describe the kitchen. I may have missed something when I talked to him."

"Suppose they won't let me in to see him?"

"Use your charm. Flatter them. If that doesn't work, call Vance. He can get you in. And he seems to have a crush on you."

"Speaking of crushes, what will you be doing all this time? What's this Gail Hibley like? I suppose she's stuck on you, too."

"Don't be ridiculous. She thinks I'm a screwball."

"So do I. Women love screwballs, don't you know that, darling?"

Before going to breakfast, Dan phoned the Hibley house. Mrs. Hibley wouldn't say what was on her mind, but she wanted to see him as soon as possible. It wasn't quite what Dan had expected. Her voice was as arrogant and commanding as ever. There was no note of apology or conciliation. Nevertheless, he agreed to come.

At breakfast he studied the latest issues of the Sager Creek *Sentinel* and the *Post-Tribune*. Grimes and Ainsley seemed as determined as ever to stick out their necks a thousand miles on the Hibley murder case. It received almost equal prominence with the Munich pact which, incidentally, both papers hailed as the most glorious diplomatic achievement of the age.

The editorial on the Hibley case began: "The economic ills of our nation cannot be cured by subsidizing crime, which after all is what the nightmare of wasteful extravagance in Washington amounts to. The decent unemployed of America do not want relief, but a preservation of the sink-or-swim, do-or-die individualism that the early pioneers ingrained in our national personality. As Earl Grimes, the County Attorney of Patterson pointed out yesterday—"

Ethel's voice cut in on his reading. "Do your girl friends know that you hide behind a newspaper at meals and merely grunt when you're talked to?"

Dan slapped the paper with the back of his hand. "I don't give a damn if I never get a job on a paper again. Read that." He handed it to her.

"You're not responsible for the editorial policy," she said.

"That's what Al Wilson mumbles in his whiskey glass every night."

"They're sticking their necks out pretty far," said Ethel, glancing over the paper. "Can't you make them slow down?"

"I tried to," said Dan. "But now I think the farther they stick their necks out the better. It will end Grimes' chance of becoming governor, and the state will be that much better off."

CHAPTER EIGHTEEN

Mrs. Garland, the housekeeper, admitted Dan to the Hibley house, and he tossed his hat once more on the horned rack. Mrs. Hibley received him in the museum-like parlor.

She appeared much stronger than on the previous day, and the cane had been discarded. There were, however, unmistakable lines of worry in her face. She pointed to a litter of dead rose petals under a vase on the table and snapped irritably at Mrs. Garland. "Must I tell you how to do everything? That trash must have been there for two days."

"I can't do everything," said Mrs. Garland. "Cooking meals and taking care of this house is more than one body could do. You'll have to get another girl." She moved to scoop up the rose petals with her apron.

"Not now. Never mind it now. Good heavens!" barked Mrs. Hibley.

The housekeeper sighed, shrugged her shoulders, and stomped off toward the kitchen.

"Such stupidity," said Mrs. Hibley bitterly. "It's impossible to get intelligent servants, Mr. Banion. If I didn't continually call attention to everything in this house, nothing would ever get done."

"That's too bad," said Dan, not knowing what else to say.

"You may sit down, Mr. Banion. I called you because, frankly, I was quite upset about the things you said yesterday."

"I'm very sorry," Dan said.

"Your attitude was extremely disrespectful, and I felt that some reprimand was necessary. I am not accustomed to being addressed in quite that manner."

"I'm extremely sorry."

"I understand that Mr. Grimes instructed your employer to discharge you."

"I'm afraid that's so," said Dan, attempting to look humble and unhappy. "I was only trying to get a good story for my paper. I didn't know I was going to get myself in bad."

"You have a great deal to learn, Mr. Banion, about how to get on in this world. You're a very young man."

"Yes, ma'am."

"You should have learned by this time that a great deal depends upon a proper attitude toward the right people."

"I'm trying to get a break. I don't intend to spend my whole life as a newspaper reporter."

"Your intelligence seems to be above the average. I have no use for men who are not ambitious."

Dan tried to make his attitude seem as ingratiating as possible, "Perhaps if you would speak to Mr. Grimes," he said, "or to my employer, they might—"

"It may be," said Mrs. Hibley, "that I could speak to some people in Frenton and find some other opening for you—something even more to your liking."

"I'd appreciate that very much."

"That will all depend, of course. In the meantime, I think there may be something you could do for me."

"I'd be only too glad."

"What was your interest in the matter concerning Esther Berglan and the incompetent they have under arrest?"

"I thought it would make a good story for my paper."

"And now?"

"Well, now I don't have any job, so what difference does it make?"

"Yesterday, you mentioned a woman named Beth Ridgely. Exactly what connection did she have in your mind?"

"It was just a shot in the dark. She seemed to fit the description. That's all."

"But what made you think she could have been near this house?"

"I didn't know. I was just guessing."

"Do you still feel that tramp is innocent?"

Dan shrugged. "What do you think?"

"What happens to such people doesn't matter. I'm not interested in tramps, one way or another. I am interested, however, in knowing more about this occurrence. I suppose that's why you left me that telephone number."

"I thought you might be interested."

"I think you understand that I cannot be intimidated, Mr. Banion."

"I didn't exactly mean it that way."

"No, but you're an ambitious man."

"I admit, I want to get ahead."

"That's nothing to be ashamed of. Perhaps, as I said, if you could be of some service to me, I might be able to put in a good word for you."

"What is it you want me to do?" asked Dan.

"I want to know who that girl Esther Berglan was, and where she came from."

This wasn't what Dan had expected. Evidently she didn't know. "Where did you hire her?" he asked.

"She was sent to me by an employment agency in Frenton. They thoroughly examine the references of all the people they handle. It's an entirely reliable firm. They sent me a full report on the girl before I hired her. She had worked for several very good families, and was excellently recommended. I am very particular about these things, so I checked several of the references myself, and the reports were excellent."

"But now you have reason to believe there was something wrong about her?"

"I examined the things in her room, as you did, Mr. Banion."

Dan asked Mrs. Hibley the name of the agency in Frenton. Then he asked if he could use the phone, and soon had them on the line. It took some time for them to check the records, and he had to explain and ask questions through several clerks before he got the information he wanted. Then he asked them to check again, to be absolutely certain.

Returning to the parlor, he caught a glimpse of Mrs. Hibley in a dejected attitude. When she heard his step, however, she stiffened into her defiant manner again.

"It seems," Dan said, "that Esther Berglan was sent to you by the agency, but she never arrived at this house. According to their records, and what they can remember, Esther Berglan came here to go to work, but was told that you had already hired someone else. You are supposed to have given her a week's pay for her trouble, and sent her back. Later, they placed her with a family that moved to Seattle, and they assume she went with them."

"But she had an introduction from the agency," Mrs. Hibley protested. "It was one of their forms, with her name on it, introducing her to her employer."

"They also say they sent you a formal letter thanking you for paying the girl for her trouble, and hoping they could be of service some other time."

"I never received any such letter."

"They say they placed Esther Berglan with a Mr. and Mrs. Almon Stevenson of Seattle. Do you mind if I make a long distance call on your phone?"

Mrs. Hibley did not object, so Dan asked the operator to get him Esther Berglan in the Almon Stevenson home in Seattle, and to ring him back when the call had been put through.

When he returned to the parlor, he asked Mrs. Hibley, "Do you remember how the girl arrived? Did you have someone meet her at the train?"

"Why, yes, I believe it was Ronald. Or it may have been Otis. I don't remember."

Mrs. Garland was summoned. Her memory told her it was Otis, and he, in turn, was called from the garden. He remembered picking up Esther at the train. "I liked her the minute I saw her," he said. "A nice, quiet girl."

He couldn't recall anything wrong when he met her. He had been late in getting there, and she had had to wait for some time. "You remember," he said to Mrs. Hibley, "you didn't tell me until it was past train time, and I had to drop everything and drive down there right away."

"I don't remember anything of the kind," said Mrs. Hibley.

Otis was inclined to argue about it, but she sent him back to his lawns and flower beds. "He's the stupidest man we've ever had about the place," she said.

"I think maybe we'd better have another look at Esther's things," said Dan. "There must be something there that will give us a line on who she was."

Mrs. Garland had packed Esther's things, but Dan unstrapped the suitcases and poured through them. There was not a thing to identify her past; not a letter, a photograph, an address book, nor any of the usual things you would look to for identification.

In the simple garments she had worn while employed in the Hibley household, he noticed the labels of Frenton stores. From the fancier dresses and articles, evidently identified with her past, Dan could learn little.

The vanity case, however, bore the imprint of a San Diego department store. A pair of slacks also bore the label of a San Diego shop, and one pair of high-heeled shoes had faintly distinguishable labels from a San Diego store.

Dan had just finished shoving the things back in the suitcases when Mrs. Garland announced there was someone on the phone, long distance. It was the call he'd put through to Seattle.

While Dan talked, Mrs. Hibley stood behind him anxiously. When he hung up, she asked, "What did she say?"

Dan walked thoughtfully into the parlor before replying. He took out his pipe and began fingering tobacco into it from his pouch.

"If you don't mind," said Mrs. Hibley. "I cannot endure smoking in my house. What did the girl say?"

"Oh, excuse me," said Dan. Regretfully, he returned pipe and pouch to his pocket. "It was exactly as the agency said. Only she claims she was met at the train by you, and that you told her to go back."

"That's ridiculous."

"I know," said Dan. "She described you, and it wasn't you."

"Who was it?"

"According to the girl's description, it was Beth Ridgely."

Mrs. Hibley grew suddenly pale. Her hand trembled as she put it to her forehead.

"Are you all right?" Dan asked.

Mrs. Hibley lowered herself into a chair. "I'm all right," she said. But her eyes glowed with anger. "How can we find out who that girl was? I've got to find out."

"If you don't mind my putting through another long distance call," said Dan.

"Make all the calls that are necessary. Only find out."

Dan put through a person to person call to Ike Miller on a San Diego newspaper, again asking the operator to ring him back when the call was through. As he hung up the receiver, Gail came in the front door.

"What are you doing here?" she asked. "Mother will scalp you."

"It's all right, my dear," said Mrs. Hibley, from the parlor. "Mr. Banion is doing something for me."

"Dan, what are you up to?"

"It's all right," said Dan. "Now don't get excited. I got fired from my job on the paper, so now I'm helping your mother run down a little information."

"Dan, are you still—"

"Mr. Banion apologized for his actions yesterday," said Mrs. Hibley. "Now, if you don't mind, my dear, I'd like you to leave us alone. This matter doesn't concern you."

Gail plunked herself down in an uncomfortable chair. "I want to know just exactly what's going on between you two."

"We are just inquiring to find out where Esther Berglan lived so that we can send her things on to her family," said Mrs. Hibley.

"Such a reverent regard for private property," said Gail. "Have you found out anything?"

The phone rang and Dan hopped to answer it. "Hello, Ike?" he said. "This is Dan. Dan Banion. Never mind. Listen to what I say. Shut up, will you? This is costing dough. I'm calling halfway across the continent. I want you to check on any female fugitives from justice around there. I said justice. From justice. The little men with the badges, who blow whistles. That's right, from the cops. You don't have any crimes there, huh? Only rape. Listen, take down this description. No, I'm not a stool pigeon. Pay attention. There may be a good story in it for you."

Dan gave him as complete a description as possible of the girl who had posed as Esther Berglan. "How long ago? Well, let's see. Anywhere from four to six months—maybe a year. Do you remember anything? I don't know. She might have done anything. That sounds kind of gory. Have you got a description of her there? How do I know? Look it up anyhow, will you? I'll wait, but make it snappy."

"What's he say, Dan?" asked Gail, who was right at Dan's elbow.

"I don't know. He's looking it up. It sounds kind of gruesome, though."

Presently, Ike returned. For a while, Dan just kept saying, "Yes. Yes. Yes," into the phone. Then he took out a notebook and began scribbling. "Oval-shaped, birthmark behind left ear. Yes. Scar on underside right arm, midway between elbow and hand. Yes. Caesarean operation scar. Yes. Anything else? Crooked finger, broken and reset wrong. Which finger? Is that all? It's plenty. No, I don't think so. This doesn't seem probable. Listen, Ike, check with the cops. Find out about anything that fits the description. What was the name of this one again? No, I don't think so. What was the fellow's name, just in case. Sure I'll let you know. You check and I'll call you back. How long will you be there? I'll call you before then. But listen, if I get anything hot, I'm going to reverse the charges. Okay?" Dan hung up.

"What is it?" asked Gail.

"What did he say?" asked Mrs. Hibley, who was standing in the entrance to the parlor.

"It's probably crazy," said Dan. "I'm only fumbling in the dark." He thumbed through the telephone directory on the stand beside the phone.

"But what is it?" asked Gail.

"I'll tell you in a minute," said Dan. He called Armand Federson's number, and soon had the undertaker on the phone. "I just want to ask you a few questions about that girl," he said. Federson answered his questions readily, without having to check.

When he hung up the receiver, Dan again walked silently into the parlor, sat down, and began to finger tobacco into his pipe, ignoring the questions of Gail and Mrs. Hibley.

"Mr. Banion, if you don't mind, I cannot tolerate smoking," said Mrs. Hibley.

"Oh, excuse me," said Dan, once more returning the pipe and pouch to his pocket.

"Mother, don't be so damned crotchety," said Gail. "Dan, what did you find out?"

"Wait a minute," said Dan. "Let me think."

"I think we're entitled to some courtesy," said Mrs. Hibley.

"Yes. Excuse me," said Dan. "It's more than I figured on. I'm afraid I owe you both a sincere apology. This makes a lot of things clear. But not everything."

"Dan, will you stop being cryptic, and tell us what you found out?" asked Gail.

"All right, here goes. It seems your Esther Berglan was June Heidelmann of San Diego. And it seems that about four months ago she shot a movie actor named Renton Brownell full of holes in the bathroom of an auto court bungalow, and then disappeared. Before that, she'd been working in a San Diego taxi dance place."

Dan rose just in time to grab Mrs. Hibley and save her from a fall. He eased her into a chair, while Gail rushed for the traditional Hibley whiskey bottle.

"I'll be all right," said Mrs. Hibley after a moment. "It's just that all these things, one right after another—Gail, take that nasty whiskey away."

"You'd better take just a little, mother. It will make you feel better." Gail pressed the glass against Mrs. Hibley's lips and made her sip a little. "You might as well take one too, Dan," she said, nodding at the bottle.

Dan accepted the invitation.

"I'm all right now," said Mrs. Hibley. "Was there anything else you were going to say, Mr. Banion?"

"Just that it appears your household has been used as the hide-out for this girl without your knowledge. That's what I want to apologize about."

"Did you think we were implicated in this?" asked Gail with a trace of anger in her voice.

"Well, I didn't know," said Dan.

"I don't think it's necessary for you to trouble yourself any further about this matter," said Mrs. Hibley. "I've found out what I wanted to know."

"No, of course not," said Dan. "But, if you'll excuse me now, I have some things to take care of."

"What do you intend to do?" asked Mrs. Hibley.

"I'll have to inform the police, of course," said Dan.

"Do you think that is necessary?" asked Mrs. Hibley. "After all, Mr. Banion, we've been inconvenienced enough."

"Just you put your mind at ease, Mrs. Hibley. You haven't a thing to be concerned about," Dan said. "I'll take care of everything."

Gail took her beret from the hall rack and jammed it on her head.

"Where are you going?" asked Dan.

"I'm going with you."

"I didn't invite you."

"I know, but try and get rid of me."

As they paced down the gravel path toward the gate, Dan said, "Maybe this will teach you to recognize a story when you see one."

"You're not such a dope as I thought you were," said Gail. "Let me in on the rest of it. Come on, give."

"Everything in good time," said Dan. "First, I've got to get to a phone."

"What's the matter with the phone in the house?"

"I want a private phone," said Dan, flinging open the door of the car.

"What's this? Where's your car?"

"It's a rented car. A gang of goons stole mine and wrecked it last night."

"Is that why you didn't phone me? Dan, what happened?"

"There's more been happening around this poky little town than you have any idea. Now be quiet a minute and let me think. We know who Esther Berglan was, and we know she was masquerading in your house, using it as a hide-out. But we don't know who killed her, or why."

Dan was thinking about the letter he'd taken from the drawer in Beth's room. It referred to a girl named June about to arrive in Hamilton. That must certainly have meant June Heidelmann.

"Maybe the tramp did it after all," said Gail.

"My, but you're dumb. Stubborn and dumb. Shut up and let me think. I've got so many pieces to put together, I can't keep track of them all."

"Dan, if this story is going to break, I want to phone it to my paper. Renton Brownell is national news. This town is going to be swarming with reporters."

Dan pulled up at the first drugstore he saw. "You don't deserve it," he said, "but I'll give you a break. First, though, you've got to let me put in a call. Wait here. I'll be right back."

From a booth in the drugstore, Dan called the Frenton *Banner*. It took a while to get Arthur Dempsey, the managing editor, on the phone, but Dan refused to talk to anyone else. Dempsey was inclined to be doubtful, at first, but as Dan unfolded the particulars, his interest warmed to a frenzy.

"It's your chance to pull the chain on Ainsley, Grimes, and their whole crowd," Dan explained. "But I want one thing understood. There's a job in this for me, and I could use some expense money, too."

Dempsey was more than willing.

"If you're going to beat them to the punch on this," Dan said, "it's worth an extra as soon as you can get it out. Am I on your payroll?"

Dempsey fairly screamed his assurances.

"Well, here's what you can say definitely. Esther Berglan is alive and working in Seattle. You can check on that yourself if you want to. The body they have here hasn't been identified as June Heidelmann yet, but you can say it answers the description exactly.

"No, I haven't notified the police. Do you think I'm crazy? You get your extra out first, and don't do anything to tip your hand until it's on the street. I'll give you all the particulars in a minute. You'll have to move fast. And don't forget to take credit for a *Banner* reporter digging all this up. Will this make a horse's rump of Grimes, or won't it? Sure I want a by-line. What do you thing I am, reticent?

"And listen," Dan added, "put in as many inferences as you can that Flavin is innocent. No, I can't prove it yet. You can imply it safely, though. Play up his alibi. Start raising the question: 'Who was the mysterious woman in the house?' Sure I know who it was, but I can't prove that yet either.

"The real Esther Berglan will be able to identify her, and so will Flavin. But let's save that for the follow-up. Yes, I think I know who did it, but I can't prove it. Get busy on what I've given you. That's enough for a start. Esther Berglan is still alive, and the body here fits the description of June Heidelmann. And make a chump of Grimes. Official negligence—*Banner* reporter easily uncovers what County Attorney is too dumb even to look at. Apprehension over the obvious crudeness with which the case was being handled caused *Banner* to investigate.

"No, I'm not trying to tell you how to run your paper. But listen, you've got to move fast, because I've got to give a fellow named Ike Miller on the San Diego *Enterprise* a break on the story. Also, there's a girl down here from the New York *Planet* who will be phoning in a story in an hour or so. No, she doesn't know everything, but she knows enough to break the story."

When Dan came out of the booth, a fat lady remarked, "I should think some people would realize that other people want to use the phone too. Hanging onto the phone for hours when other people have important calls."

"I'm sorry," said Dan.

"You're not the only one who has to use the phone."

"Well, there it is," said Dan. "I'm sorry."

"Some nerve!" she said, banging the folding door shut on herself.

Gail's greeting was no more cordial. "I suppose you've got yourself credit for the story in every paper in the country by now. There's nothing like greasing your own ambitions with other people's troubles. For an idealist, you're as big a ghoul as the next fellow."

"After all, I did dig up the story. It's not my fault if you can't see a story when it's sitting right in your lap. Let's get something to eat."

"What about my story?"

"Well, phone your paper that—well, what do you know about it? Tell them as much as you know."

"All I know is that the girl in the morgue fits the description of one June Heidelmann, who shot a man full of holes in a San Diego auto court. What were those identification marks? I didn't take any notes."

"There you are," said Dan. "A good reporter takes notes."

"I know I'm a ham. Help me, will you?"

"Let's get something to eat. Then I'll tell you what to phone your paper."

CHAPTER NINETEEN

Dan drove to the Brock Hotel Coffee Shop where they had eaten the day before.

"Can you get a check cashed in this town?" he asked Gail. "I'm running out of cash."

"Don't change the subject," she said. "Let me in on what's going on. Give with some information, and then maybe I'll get a check cashed for you."

"I said I'd give you a break, and I will. But there's another guy who's entitled to a break first. You sit here and order me a ham and Swiss cheese double-decker, and a glass of milk. I'll be right back."

"Are you going to disappear into one of those phone booths again?"

"You just sit easy. I'll just be a minute."

"Dan, have a heart."

"I told you what to do, but you didn't take the hint."

Dan went to the phone booth in the lobby of the hotel and called Ike Miller in San Diego, reversing the charges. He told Ike that the girl in the Hamilton morgue fitted the description of June Heidelmann, and gave him some particulars on the Hibley murder, reserving the information on the real Esther Berglan being in Seattle, so that the *Banner* could have that exclusive.

"By the way," Ike said, "this guy Brownell's wife has offered a five-thousand-dollar reward for June, dead or alive. This puts you in line for it. It also puts me in line for a case of whiskey, because I'm the only guy who can guarantee you were the one who delivered."

"Find out what's the cheapest brand, and order yourself a case," said Dan. "If I could reach you, I'd kiss you. I need that dough. How I need that dough!"

"If you're going to kiss me, I'll have to ask for two cases," Ike said. "Why don't you move out here to California? Sunshine all the time. We go barefoot and bare-bottom eleven months of the year."

"This is long distance," said Dan. "Cut the social chatter."

"The paper is paying for it," said Ike. "What do we care? The old fag who owns this sheet has so much money he buys horses and runs them around in circles just to get rid of it. They tell me you're married now. I don't believe it."

"Man, I've got a wonderful wife, Ike. I'm not kidding you."

"They've all got the same general equipment," said Ike. "I like to play with them, but I never wanted to own one. What the hell do you do with one when she's on your hands day in and day out? You can't neck all the time. It must be hell."

"Oh, you take 'em to the movies, walk 'em around the park, and talk about life and philosophy," said Dan.

"Jesus!" said Ike. "You poor guy."

"What happened to the book you were writing?" Dan asked.

"I'm still writing it," said Ike. "It's an artistic job, all about how people feel inside, and what a pain in the neck everything is outside, and the writhing of their souls as they long for something real after all this sham of modern existence. I call it 'Witha.'"

"With a what?" asked Dan.

"Just 'Witha.' It's from the classical quotation: 'Let us now be up and doing *with a* heart for any fate.'"

"You're insane," said Dan.

"I'm nothing of the kind. I'm a child of nature trapped in a mechanical civilization. A thousand years ago I'd have been a simple shepherd, tending my flocks, with never a cruel thought in my brain."

"Don't you think we've run up enough of a bill on this boss of yours?"

"Oh, don't worry about him. He doesn't feel he's getting anything unless it costs him plenty. He's got life solved. No wives for him, only horses. He's crazy about horses. But if you ask me, it's the jockeys he's interested in."

"Listen, Ike, nail that reward for me, and I'll drown you in whiskey. I'll be calling you back later to give you further developments."

When Dan hung up on Ike, he dropped another coin in the phone and called Al Wilson in Frenton. It was too early to call him at home, so he got him on the line in the *Post-Tribune* office.

"I suppose you know you're fired," Al said. "Furthermore, Ainsley said if you ever get another job on a paper in this country, it will be over his dead body."

"Well, I can always learn Chinese," said Dan. "They're a more mature civilization anyhow. They invented gunpowder, didn't they?"

"Yes, and they've been shot at ever since. What's the number of that phone you're calling from? Gladys has big ears on that switchboard. Did you hear me, Gladys? I'm about to go out for a cup of coffee, and I'll call you right back."

Dan gave him the number and hung up. As he stepped out of the booth, he saw Gail busy at another phone behind the hotel desk. Her face was serious, and she was talking fast. The sight warmed Dan's heart. He liked her. He couldn't help it.

She hung up the receiver almost as soon as he came out of the booth. "So you decided to use your own head after all," Dan said.

"Don't make fun of me, Dan," Gail said. "I'm not half as smart as I pretend to be. But I've got to make good at my job. You don't know how important it is to me. You don't know what a tough time I had breaking away from that atmosphere in mother's house."

"What did you tell your paper?" Dan asked.

"I took the hint from you and told them everything I knew. Help me, Dan. I don't know what I'm doing."

"That's what you should have done in the first place. Phone your paper what you know before the other fellow can. Then get more later. That's all they have to know—that the girl here answers the description of June Heidelmann. They'll get people on the phone and run down the rest. You don't have to have the whole story from beginning to end. They'll print what they can prove, or twist it to suit their phony editorial policies. Meanwhile, you get busy and dig up more."

"You don't think I'm dumb, do you, Dan?"

"Kid, I'm in favor of you one hundred per cent. But always be sure to let your paper know what you can confirm. Don't try to give them guesswork as facts. Just because we have lousy papers to work for doesn't mean we have to be lousy reporters. Turn the story in accurately. What they do to it after that is a crime. But you turn it in straight."

The telephone rang in the booth.

"That's for me," said Dan. "You go back and finish your sandwich and I'll be along in a minute."

"What is all this phoning you're doing?"

"Never mind," said Dan. "Go eat your sandwich."

Al's excited voice came over the phone. "For once you've hit on something, Dan. Those fingerprints were dynamite. Beth Ridgely isn't Beth Ridgely at all. She's Adelaide Gwinn, the musical comedy star of about twenty years ago. Do you remember the famous Malnick case in 1913? Yeah, I know it was before your time. Anyhow, Adelaide Gwinn was her stage name. She was married to Alliston Malnick, the insurance man.

"Yeah. That's the original Malnick of the Malnick Insurance Company. Anyhow, this guy Malnick died under very peculiar circumstances. He was poisoned. A waiter named Heidelmann was accused—Franz Heidelmann. He was acquitted, and later on opened a big restaurant in St. Louis. But get this: It was Vern B. Hibley who defended him. That was Hibley's first big case—the one that got him into the limelight. As a matter of fact, it's what started him on his career."

"Did they ever find out who did it?" Dan asked.

"No. But that's not all. That made me curious, so I did some inquiring among old-timers with long memories. There was quite a bit of gossip about Hibley and Adelaide Gwinn. If you ask me, she was his mistress."

"What about the other fingerprints—those of the bartender."

"He's just an ordinary crook. He served some time for a clumsy assault and robbery around 1919, but there doesn't seem to be any connection. You were asking about this guy Howard Marnell, too. I don't know why I didn't remember when you mentioned him. There's a hell of a mess, if you like family troubles. His son, Howard Junior, was recently accused of contributing to the delinquency of minors, and he tried to kill himself. The old man's an alcoholic, and was committed to a sanitarium last Tuesday.

"But that's not all. I find that old man Marnell and Vern B. Hibley were not only business partners, but rivals for the hand and the rest of the anatomy of Ruth Kenyon, who finally married Hibley, and is now the Mrs. Hibley you're dealing with down there. In later years, Marnell hovered around in the role of the understanding friend of the family. How do you like that for a nightmare?"

"Good work, Al. Tell me more about this Howard Junior."

"Well, he was a psychology student at the University. He was studying up to be a bug jockey—a psychiatrist. You know. One of these guys who manipulates the maladjusted. Does all this make any sense to you?"

"Gradually," said Dan. "It's an appalling picture of life on the planet Earth. You say old man Marnell is in a sanitarium. Who took over his business—his law practice?"

"Oh, hell, he didn't have any. He was practically retired. Ralph Grovenor was his partner. He'd be taking care of anything there was to take care of. I know him well, if you want me to check on anything. We drink in the same bar, and I've done a lot of favors for him."

"Call him up, will you, Al, and ask him if he's taking care of Mrs. Hibley's property. Use any excuse. Find out what her property amounts to, if you can, and what connection Marnell had with it. But first, tell me more about Adelaide Gwinn. What happened to her as time went on?"

"She went to hell, in a manner of speaking. Was hauled in for running disorderly houses several times. While he was alive, Vern B. Hibley evidently pulled her out of the messes she got in. I wouldn't be surprised if he set her up in that joint down there. In fact, that's my guess."

"Well, give this guy Grovenor a ring and call me back, will you, Al? Can you do it right now? I'll stick around and wait."

Dan left word at the hotel desk to call him when the phone rang in the booth. Then he joined Gail in the Coffee Shop.

"Dan, what is it? All these phone calls. I don't get it," she said.

"You will," Dan said.

"And what you said to mother and me. Something about owing us an apology."

Dan chewed his sandwich thoughtfully. "I don't know, I'm all up in the air. For a while, I thought it was getting clear. Now it's all mixed up again."

"I have absolutely no idea of what you are talking about."

"You won't like the way things are shaping up, Gail. But I can't help it. Your family closet is so full of skeletons, nobody could hide them all."

"Well, there's no use dragging us in the mud just to make copy, if that's what you mean."

"I can't keep your brother out of it any longer. The girl was pregnant, and he was responsible. It's bound to come out sooner or later, so we might as well break it."

"I don't think he cares, particularly. All that worries me is that everybody will jump to the conclusion that he killed her."

"He has an airtight alibi, if he's telling the truth. By the way, who is this Howard Marnell? What's his relation to you?"

"How did you know about him?"

"Never mind. Who is he?"

"He was daddy's law partner. Somehow, Uncle Marnell was closer to us children than our own father."

"Was he your uncle?"

"No, but we called him uncle."

"When you told me the other day that you almost married an amateur psychologist, that was his son, wasn't it?"

"Yes, how did you know?"

"What happened that broke it up?"

"Nothing, really. We grew up together, as children. Uncle Marnell always hoped we'd marry. I guess that's the only reason we were engaged. Later we went to different colleges and grew apart from each other. He got morbid and became interested in psychology in a wrong way—like a nasty little boy pulling the wings off flies. Everybody he met he'd psychoanalyze. He never saw anything but morbid and perverted tendencies in people. I couldn't stand him anymore, and he wasn't interested in me either. We just broke it off."

"Well, what about Marnell. What happened to him?"

"Uncle Marnell was a very unhappy man. He began to go to pieces as he got older. He began to drink terribly. I was about the only one who could reason with him. He was always very fond of me. His son got in a nasty mess recently. I guess you know about that, too."

"Yes."

"Well, it broke Uncle Marnell up completely."

"Is that why your mother wired you to come down from New York?"

"That's right."

"And instead of coming straight to Hamilton, you stopped in Frenton to see Marnell."

"Yes, how did you know that?"

"You met your mother in Frenton, but she came back to Hamilton the same evening that the girl was murdered. You stayed over another night in Frenton and came in to Hamilton the next morning."

"That's right."

"And to simplify things, you told me you'd come directly from New York, and let me think your mother had wired you because she was worried about Ronald."

"Yes, but I didn't see any point to going into all these particulars, Dan. Besides, mother was worried about Ronald, so it wasn't entirely untrue."

"Are there any other lies you've told me along the line that might be futzing up my calculations?"

"I don't think so. And I still don't see how all this has any connection."

"It has this much connection; when you tell me one thing and I find out something entirely different, how am I to know whether it's significant or not?"

The clerk from the hotel lobby interrupted. "That phone call you were expecting," he said.

Dan returned to the phone booth. It was Al Wilson again from Frenton. "Marnell didn't have any law practice left," he said. "Grovenor says they let him keep an office with his name on the door for the sake of old times. But he was hardly ever in it. As for Mrs. Hibley's property, she hasn't got any. Marnell was taking care of it before the crash, but she was wiped out. Yes, Grovenor was sure of it. I didn't even have to ask him. He said that was what washed Marnell up completely. Marnell told him all about it. So far as he knows, Mrs. Hibley hasn't got a nickel. That's what Marnell told him. Marnell felt responsible, and worried a lot about it, and was always talking about it to Grovenor."

"One more thing, Al. What became of this Franz Heidelmann, the waiter who was accused of poisoning Adelaide Gwinn's husband?"

"I told you, after he was acquitted he opened a high-class restaurant in St. Louis. Some years later it went broke. Since then, nobody seems to know. By the way, how is all this going to affect the murder case down there? Are you getting to first base?"

"Buy a copy of the *Banner*, and read all about it. They ought to have an extra out by this time that will fry Ainsley in his pants."

"My God, Dan, you can't do this to me. Ainsley will be half crazy. He already half suspects I've been playing along with you. I've got a wife and kids. You had no business ringing me in on this."

A cold sickness swept though Dan as he realized what he had done. "Listen, Al, I'm not letting you down."

"Not letting me down! For the love of Pete, man. You ask me to do you a favor and then—"

"Listen, Al, I'm not letting you down. Do you hear?"

"If you've given the *Banner* a scoop—you got the job here because I recommended you. Remember?"

"But Al, we can't hang an innocent kid and elect the biggest heel in the state governor just to keep your job for you."

"I'm no crusader. I take the world as I find it. Let God look after his own business. He started all this. I'm not trying to save the world. All I want to do is pay my rent."

"Al, please—"

"Of all the goddamn, double-crossing screwballs. Am I dumb! Just ask me a favor again and see where you light."

"Will you listen to me, Al? I told you I'm not letting you down."

"The meek shall inherit the earth. Tell me where my acres are. Of all the trusting chumps, I win the cup. Am I a boy scout!"

"But Al—"

Dan heard the click of the receiver as Al hung up in his ear. For a minute, he wished he were dead. He stood there staring at the phone and feeling very much alone. There was no turning back now, and no telling how many more complications would pile up around his ears before he was finished. He put another coin in the phone and called Ike Miller in San Diego. Ike's voice came booming in.

"I told them I located June Heidelmann on a Ouija board, and they're going to give me the reward. They love Ouija boards out here. They don't give a damn what the living say, but man, how they want to talk to the dead."

"Shut up, Ike, and answer one more question," Dan said. "What about June Heidelmann's father? Is he around there anywhere?"

"He runs a hamburger joint down near the docks, that caters to the fleet. That's where June got her early training. Tell me what makes these dames go for the Navy? Is it the tight pants? I've often wondered."

"Just to make sure, Ike, what's his name?"

"Franz Heidelmann. F for—"

"That's enough. I heard you."

"By the way, Dan, if you're holding out any angles of this story on me, you can kiss that reward good-by. I'm not making a horse's rump of myself for a lousy case of whiskey."

"The case of whiskey will do that. Anyhow, here's a new lead for your next edition." Dan gave Ike the dope about the real Esther Berglan being in Seattle. "When I get anything more I'll let you know. Now nail that reward for me, Ike. I need the money. I need it badly."

Ike was willing as ever to skyrocket his employer's telephone bill with horseplay, but Dan cut him short. He deposited another coin and called Arthur Dempsey at the *Banner*.

"It was a bombshell," said Dempsey. "We can't print papers fast enough. Ainsley is howling mad. I even got a call from Grimes. They've got a dragnet out for you. Don't tell them a thing. How much did they pay you on the *Post-Tribune?* Hell, I'll make it eighty a week. Listen, they'll be making you offers. Don't listen to them. You've got security here. Have you got anything new?"

"I've got an avalanche," said Dan. "But you'll have to move fast on it."

"Let's have it."

"First, there's something serious. I couldn't have handled this story without the help of a certain guy on the *Post-Tribune* who ran down the facts for me. Now he's going to be fired. That guy's got to have a job."

"See here, I've already got a full staff, and the Guild has me hog-tied with a contract whereby I have to grant dismissal pay for anybody I fire. What the hell do you think I'm running?"

"I tell you, he's got to have a job."

"He's not the only one. I'm not responsible for all these guys. I'll tell you what I'll do, I'll recommend him for a WPA job."

"That won't do. This guy has kids. He's got to have a job."

"I've promised you a damned good job, and you're going to get it. But that's all."

"All right, forget about me. Give this guy a job and you don't have to worry about me."

"I'm not worried about you. I want you."

"I'm just a stooge. This guy Al did all the brain work."

"I think you're a liar."

"Then you can go to hell. I'll phone the new developments to the *Post-Tribune*. You said they were willing to bargain."

"This is blackmail."

"I got that guy fired, and I'm going to get him another job. Either that, or I'll throw this story down a sewer."

"All right, son, he gets it. Now what else have you got on this story?"

"Just a minute. This stuff I've got is hot. It's worth more solid cash to you and your crowd than this guy would cost you in a hundred years."

"I said I'd hire him."

"Well, he always wanted to be a drama editor."

"That's out—strictly out. So forget it."

"Yeah, but you don't know. He knows his stuff. He's really good. He—"

"All right, goddamn it, he's my drama editor. Will you please give me what you've got on this story?"

"You're giving me your word on this, remember."

"I give you my word. And I'll tell you right now, my word is a damned sight more reliable than my checks."

"I'm really doing you a favor. He's one of the best newspapermen in the country. He's Al Wilson."

"Yes, I know Wilson."

"Will you call him right away and tell him about it, and tell him I fixed it?"

"I'll call him. I'll send a taxi for him. I'll have a carpet unrolled when he arrives. I'll hire an orchestra. Give me that story."

"Well, for one thing, the murdered girl was pregnant, and Mrs. Hibley's son Ronald admits he was responsible."

"It's worth another extra."

"But wait a minute. That's not half of it. June Heidelmann's father was Franz Heidelmann, who was accused of poisoning Alliston Malnick, the founder of the Malnick Insurance Company, back in 1913. He was acquitted, but Vern B. Hibley was the attorney who got him off. He now runs a hamburger joint on the San Diego waterfront."

"Son, I'd be happy to hire your whole family if you wanted."

"Wait a minute. That's not all. Alliston Malnick was the husband of Adelaide Gwinn at the time he was killed. She was the well-known musical comedy star. Later there was gossip about Vern Hibley and this Adelaide Gwinn. In any case, she now runs a hotel and bar—cat house and honky-tonk, if you want the truth—in a town called Sawtooth, only a couple of miles from Hamilton."

"What is this? Does Lincoln's assassination figure in it, too?"

"You can check it all. Adelaide Gwinn is now known as Elizabeth Ridgely—better known around here as Beth."

"It's all amazing, but what's the connection?"

"For one thing, I found Beth Ridgely's telephone number in the murdered girl's purse. We can't prove anything yet, but I'm positive Esther Berglan can identify Beth as the woman who met her at the railroad station here and decoyed her from the Hibley house. I'm also positive that Flavin can identify her as the woman he saw at the Hibley house the afternoon of the murder."

"If anything goes wrong about this, I'll murder you with my own two hands."

"You can't go wrong. Print what you can check and what you can prove, and save the rest for follow-ups. Drag out the old Malnick murder case again. Play it up. Raise questions. Emphasize that it's never been solved. And give that kid Flavin a break. Run his poems again. Get some literary critics to comment on them."

"I know how to run my paper. Remember, that kid could still have done it, all this notwithstanding."

"I tell you, he didn't. But anyhow, you don't have to say anything one way or another. You're just printing the facts."

"Yes, and facts have a way of looking different from every angle you look at them. I'm sending a man down there to help you. He ought to be there sometime this evening. Pete Corbett. I think you know him."

"Pete Corbett? Fine. I can use him."

CHAPTER TWENTY

When Dan returned to the table where Gail was waiting, he said, "I meant to ask you, is your mother pretty well off financially? Does she have much money?"

"Well, you see how we live. Say, you asked me that once before."

"Did I? I must have forgotten."

"Dad left us pretty well off. Mother owns a couple of apartment houses in Frenton, and some stocks and bonds. I don't know how much, but we've never had to worry."

"Then you've never had to help out from what you earn?"

"No. In fact, mother has helped me out once in a while."

"And Ronald, you say, doesn't make much from his real estate business?"

"No. Mother has to keep stringing him along. What are you getting at?"

"Come on. We've sat here long enough. I think I need one or two more pieces before this puzzle fits together. I'd better take you home."

"You're not taking me home."

"Now be reasonable."

"Once you dump me off there, that's the last I see of you. I'm going wherever you go."

"Well, don't blame me for whatever happens. If you'd been with me last night, you might have got your block knocked off."

"I'll take my chances," said Gail.

When they returned to the car, Dan took the road toward Regan's farm. It was the edge of the evening, almost the same time he had driven over it the night before.

Gail snuggled in the seat beside him and leaned her head on his shoulder. Her hair was soft. Dan thought to tell her to sit up straight and behave herself, but let it slide. The fragrant fields and soft sky seemed to impel affection. He told himself it was all brotherly.

"I'm glad you didn't marry that bug," he said. "If I weren't married myself, I'd get my hair cut and see what I could do."

She straightened up. "Dan, you didn't tell me you were married."

"Sure I did."

"You did not." She hesitated a moment, then asked, "What's she like?"

"Crazy. Who else would marry me? She's swell."

"Is it serious?"

"Do you think I go around marrying people as a joke?"

"You don't act like a married man."

"I still enjoy life, if that's what you mean."

"I mean the way you look at other women. There's a certain way."

"You mean the way I look at you?"

"Not necessarily. You looked at the waitress in the restaurant that way too."

"She was pretty."

"I guess all men are the same, aren't they?"

"My God!"

"Well, aren't they?"

"What a nose dive for a conversation to take."

"Well, aren't they?"

"Listen, before I was married, every time a good-looking girl in a thin summer dress walked by me, my eyes went after her."

"And now?"

"And now it's just the same. Why wouldn't it be? I'm the same guy."

"Yes, but when you're married!"

"What do you think I got married for?"

"Now you're talking silly."

"I'm not talking silly. I'm exactly the same man I was before I married. And if I ever stop glancing after pretty girls I won't have any more reason to be married."

"Dan, there's someone following us."

"What makes you think so?"

"I can see them in the mirror. Ever since we left Hamilton they've been right behind us."

"Maybe they're just going the same way."

"I tell you, they're following us. I've been watching them."

"Well, I'll give them a little of the old Barney Oldfield and see what they do." Dan stepped down on the gas. The roadster got as busy as her old bolts would allow.

The other car, a new eight-cylinder job, increased its speed and kept pace with them easily. The old roadster rattled as if it were going to fling its parts in every direction.

"This is silly," Gail said. "We can't get away from them in this mousetrap."

As far as Dan could see, the road ahead was empty of traffic. Nor were there any houses in this particular area. He heard a roar to his left, and the car behind pulled up even. It was a touring car. Four men were in it.

"Hang onto your head," Dan said, and stomped the brakes.

The other car shot ahead a few hundred yards. There was a screeching of rubber tires as the driver applied his own brakes. Dan stepped on the gas and turned the car around, bumping over the edge of a field in the process. He headed back in the direction of Hamilton, his foot clear down on the accelerator, and the old roadster trembling with epileptic effort.

The beauty of the old car trying to do its best made an impression on Dan in spite of the urgency of the moment. It occurred to him that there is poetry in nuts and bolts. In the mirror, he could see the other car back, turn, and come roaring after them.

"Damn it, Gail, I told you to stay home," he said in a kind of desperation,

As the touring car drew even again, Dan jammed the brakes once more. The road here was too narrow to turn around, so he put the car in reverse and backed down the road as rapidly as he could.

The other car screeched to a stop. Three of the men piled out and ran toward them. When they were close enough, Dan geared the car ahead and aimed as if to run them down. They scattered to the sides of the road. Dan rattled past the stopped touring car full speed ahead toward Hamilton. In the mirror, he could see the three men run to the touring car and pile in. It lunged after them again.

Gail's fingers were digging into Dan's arm. The big car drew even again, shouldering Dan toward a ditch beside the road. He braked again. The big car stopped, and this time the men were out of it and after them before Dan could back away. One of them jumped onto the running board and shoved a revolver against his chest.

"All right, Buster, cut the goddamn peek-a-boo."

The driver of the big car walked up to Dan. "You ain't so goddamn smart," he said.

"Oh, it's you guys again," said Dan.

"Get outa that damn buggy," said the man. "You, Ed, take this heap and follow us."

They forced Dan and Gail into the back seat of the big car, with a gun-packing guard beside them. The other two got in the front seat. The fourth man followed along behind with the roadster.

"Do you mind telling me what this is all about?" Dan asked.

"He wants to know what it's all about," said the man beside him, laughing.

"I thought you was the smart guy," said the driver. "I thought you knew all about everything."

"Don't you know all the answers?" asked the third man.

"I know that this is kidnapping," Dan said. "And it carries a heavy rap. If you fellows are doing this as a favor for someone, you're making a mistake."

"Well, ain't that cute," said the driver. "So now you're a couple of little kiddies."

"Were you one of the guys who made tracks last night when an old lady shot off a shotgun?" Dan asked.

The man at the wheel turned. "You ain't so goddamn smart." The car almost ran off the road, and he had to wrestle the wheel to steady it.

They drove for nearly an hour. It was just getting dark when they turned off a road into a dilapidated farm that evidently had not been worked for several years. Dan didn't see the house until they pulled into the yard. It stood behind a row of poplar trees—a colorless, weather-beaten, two-story structure with an air of vacancy and desertion.

Boards creaked resentfully under their feet as they mounted the sagging porch. In the mouldy parlor, Ray Goldman was reading a copy of *Weird Crimes* magazine by the light of an oil lamp he'd evidently just lit. The remains of a bachelor dinner of sardines, crackers, and cheese littered the table in front of him. The smell of the oil lamp and the food mingled with a general odor of decay.

The original furniture of the house had long since been removed, but there was a dirty couch, an old Morris chair, and a few plain wooden chairs.

Ray Goldman slapped down the magazine and rose to his feet as they entered. "Who's this dame?" he demanded.

"I dunno," said the driver of the car. "She was with him."

"Who said anything about bringing a dame?"

"Well, she was with him."

"I didn't tell you to bring no dame."

"She was with him."

"What the hell difference does that make? You've loused up the whole business."

"What did you expect us to do? She was with him."

"Who are you, girlie?" Ray asked Gail.

"Don't answer him," said Dan.

"Oh, still a smart guy," said Ray. "We'll take that out of you. Give me her purse, Ben."

The man who had driven the car jerked the purse out of Gail's hand and threw it to Ray. He turned it upside down and emptied the contents on top of the table. Picking up her driver's license, he read: "Gail Hibley. That sounds familiar. Gail Hibley. Where the hell have I heard that name?"

"That's the old lady in Hamilton, where that murder came off the other day," said one of the men.

"Sure, that's right," said Ray. "That's right. Some bird raped a dame, wasn't it?"

"And carved her up."

"They've got him in the can," said Ben. "We don't want any part of that."

"You any relative of that old dame?" asked Ray.

"She's her daughter," said Dan.

"Shut up, wise guy. Is she your mother, girlie?"

"Yes," said Gail. "She's my mother." Her voice cracked. Dan could see that she was badly scared.

Ray glared at Ben. "You sure have loused things up."

"All I know is you said to bring him. She was with him and—"

"Yeah, you said all that. I suppose if the Mayor was with him, you'd have brought him." Ray turned to Gail. "What're you doin' runnin' around with this bum?" He indicated Dan with his thumb.

A loud pounding and kicking interrupted them. It came from a door to an adjoining room. "Go shut her up," said Ray. "No. Wait a minute. Maybe smart pants, here, would like to see his girl friend."

Ray unlocked the door and pushed it open. Shirley staggered into the room. Dan hardly recognized her. Both eyes were blacked and there was a smear of blood under her nose. She still had on Regan's overalls. She was sobbing hysterically.

Dan took one step forward, then drew back. He didn't say a word. His fists clenched so hard that his fingernails dug into the palms of his hands. But he didn't move. He felt a hot flush of blood to his forehead, and could almost hear his heart pounding. He felt insanity rising in him, but held on.

"Dan, go away," screamed Shirley. "Do anything he says, but go away."

Ray held her by the wrists. "Is that any way to talk to your boy friend?" he asked. Then turning to Dan, "Ain't you got anything to say, smart pants?"

Dan dug his fingernails deeper into his palms, but didn't say a word.

"Ray, let him go," pleaded Shirley. "I'll do anything you want, but let him go. Please let him go."

"That's enough, sweetheart," said Ray, dragging her back toward the room.

She wrenched one hand free and began hitting at him, but he seized it again and dragged her through the door out of sight. There was a sound of unmerciful slapping, and Shirley cried like a child.

Ray came back into the room, locking the door behind him. "The dirty little bitch," he said. "Now, smart pants, you're going to get yours."

Dan made a sound as if he were going to speak.

"You got something to say, smart pants?"

Dan stood quietly.

"All right, boys," Ray said. "You just keep the lady company here while smart pants and me go down in the basement."

Gail began to cry. "Don't. Don't. Please don't," she begged.

"Your boy friend likes to lock people in the backs of cars and bump them over rough roads. This ain't any of your worry, lady. Just pick your friends better after this." He took another oil lamp from the mantel and lit it carefully. "So you was going to get a cut on the business or you'd louse things up. Was that it? Well, well, well."

"Listen to me," Dan said, eyeing the four men who had brought them there. "If any of you so much as lay a finger on this girl while I'm out of the room, I'll kill you. Is that plain?"

Ray paused in putting the chimney back on the lamp. The other men looked at Dan oddly, too. It wasn't so much what he said, but the way he said it. It sounded convincing. There was something in his voice that hit clear to the marrow.

Ray studied Dan for a minute, then put the chimney back on the lighted lamp. Then, as if not satisfied, studied him again.

In the back of Ray's brain, a bit of reasoning was trying to shape itself, but his intellect was not equal to the thought. What his brain was trying to tell him was that if this man would kill somebody for touching a girl, he would kill him for what he had done already. He tried to grasp this reasoning, failed, and shrugged it off as just a "funny feeling."

"Come on, smart pants," he said. "You're going to find out what happens to small-time pimps who try to muscle in on big-time rackets."

"Ray, I don't like the idea of this dame being here, with her tie-in with that business in the paper," said the man called Ben.

"You brought her here, didn't you?" said Ray.

"Yeah, but—"

"Then you worry about it." Ray took a revolver from the pocket of a coat thrown over a chair, held the lamp in one hand, and motioned Dan toward the kitchen door. "Come on, smart pants."

"No," sobbed Gail. "Don't."

Dan gave her arm a squeeze, and walked ahead of Ray into the kitchen. The flicker of the lamp danced over the bare walls of a room, greasy and worn from much living and eating. Ray kicked open a slanting door and motioned with the revolver. Dan groped his way down the stairs. As Ray came after him, the light of the lamp showed a wide cellar, partially paved with flat stones.

Ray set the lamp on a high ledge and laid the revolver beside it. The ledge was well out of Dan's reach. Beside the towering bulk of Ray Goldman, Dan was a pigmy.

"You didn't know I was heavyweight champ of the Pacific fleet at one time, did you, pimp?" said Ray.

Dan said nothing.

Ray stripped off his shirt and bared a hairy chest. He flexed his muscles. "When I finish with you, the girls ain't going to think you're so pretty."

Dan unbuttoned his coat and vest and threw them against the wall, stripped off his shirt and threw it after them. The cellar, by the light of the oil lamp, was a gloomy hell. Ray's hairy chest and pale flesh gave him the aspect of an unhealthy beast.

"So you're gonna fight, are you, you dirty little pimp. Well, ain't this somethin'?" Ray said.

Dan's fists were like knobs of hate, and his eyes gleamed with a kind of insanity. The muscles fitted around his bones like wrappings on wire. He crouched as Ray came at him, and ducked the first three blows. The fourth got him in the face and rocked him against the stone wall of the cellar. A trickle of blood came from a cut in the side of his mouth.

Ray laughed and moved on him slowly. Dan ducked under his arm and retreated to the opposite wall. Ray followed in leisurely amusement. "That wasn't nothin'," he chortled. "Now I'm gonna loosen some of those teeth." He lunged at Dan suddenly, clipping him hard just over the left eye. Dan lost his footing and went down. He was on his feet again immediately, ducked another blow, and retreated.

For a while, Ray pursued him from one corner of the cellar to another. Dan had not attempted a single blow. He presented a spectacle of clumsy helplessness. When Ray swung at him, his arms went up in a frantic and ineffectual effort to ward off the blows. Several times he cowered, as if trying to hide his head in his arms.

Ray dropped all pretense of boxing and began mauling Dan at will. No longer anticipating any fight from Dan, he made no attempt to guard himself. Once he even turned and spat, ignoring Dan completely.

Dan let the carelessness develop. Ray was taking his time. When he got bored, Ray intended to move in and pound Dan to a pulp without any nonsense, and Dan knew it. For the moment, Ray was amused. Soon, however, the game got monotonous.

"Oh hell," Ray said, "that's enough playing, smart pants. Now we're gonna get down to business." He turned to spit again, leaving himself wide open.

Dan's whole body moved to the punch. There was not a flicker of drawback or preparation. His fist shot from his side in one flashing, forward movement, with all the weight of his shoulder behind it. He aimed deep under Ray's jaw, at the soft glands and nerve centers. Or, rather, he aimed at an imaginary goal a foot beyond.

This was something he'd learned from one of the top men in the ring. If you aim exactly for the goal of your fist, there's a psychological slowing down when you get there. Aim beyond it, and let your fist strike in full strength and flight. Let your fist seem to keep right on going through a man's head, as if the head were in the way.

The muscles in Ray's neck, grown flabby from the licentious gossip of bartending, were no protection from Dan's bony knuckles. The glands and nerves filled his brain with screaming pain, and he fell with a thud of bones and flesh on the stone floor of the cellar.

Dan didn't give him an instant to recover. Marquis of Queensbury rules were designed for the sensibilities of gentlemen, and there were none present. Before Ray could blink an eye, Dan was on top of him, pounding a sharp knuckle with merciless force into the soft place of Ray's temple. Ray went out with a gasp of agony.

Dan stood up, breathing hard. There was no sound in the cellar but the panting of his chest. He was badly out of condition, and he knew it. As he looked down at Ray's pasty face, he wanted to beat it with his fists, stamp it with the heel of his shoe. That's what he had intended to do after seeing Shirley upstairs. But too much civilization had been drilled into him. He felt the futility of revenge.

He stood there, panting and looking at Ray for a minute, then slipped back into his shirt, tucked it in his pants, and elbowed into his coat and vest.

Ray moaned and stirred a little on the cellar floor. Dan walked over and kicked hard at the soft place in his temple. With a kind of slurp and gurgle, Ray went quiet.

Dan found a box, climbed on it, and took the revolver and the lamp from the ledge. Setting the lamp on the floor, he examined the gun. All six chambers were loaded.

He became conscious that his teeth were clenched tightly and his lips were bared. He didn't know himself. It was as if he moved in a different body—thought with a different mind.

He walked over to Ray, took another look at him, and spat on him for good measure. The gun trembled in his hand. He reached with the other hand and steadied it.

Then he picked up the lamp and climbed the cellar steps.

CHAPTER TWENTY-ONE

When Dan left the room with Ray, Gail closed her eyes and almost froze with fright. She felt entirely alone. The four men around her seemed like beings from another planet. She couldn't imagine their psychology. They were capable of terrible things.

Behind Gail's closed eyes, in the dark privacy of her mind, a voice seemed to be saying, "What does Dan want you to do? What would Dan do?"

She opened her eyes and saw the four men looking at her. Somehow, she sensed that Dan's warning had made a strong impression on them. They wouldn't touch her. They knew as well as she knew that Dan had meant what he said—that he would kill them, and that he was capable of doing just that.

So they were human beings after all. That's what Dan would have told her. She remembered his words: "Go ahead on what you know and dig up the rest as you go along."

She was surprised to hear herself saying, "You don't know what you're doing. Dan Banion's a reporter from the *Post-Tribune*. You're going to get yourselves in trouble." The sound of her own voice lessened her fear.

The man called Ben, who had driven the car, said, "He's a cheap pimp, lady. We've taken plenty of his kind down the line."

"You don't know what you're talking about," Gail repeated. "He's a reporter from the *Post-Tribune*. He's covering the murder case in my mother's house."

A thin, slick-haired young man spoke up. "What gives you the idea he's a reporter on any paper?"

"I'm a reporter myself. I'm with the New York *Planet.*"

"What the hell kind of a line are you giving us?" said Ben.

"Look in my purse," Gail said. "Look on the table. You'll find my police pass there."

"Police pass!" The man called Ben leaned over the litter of her purse on the table, and thumbed through the articles. "Well I'll be a—"

"What's up, Ben?"

"It's the McCoy. Look." He held up the card in alarm.

"We're being played for a bunch of suckers," said the slick-haired man. "I knew that guy didn't look like no pimp."

"This is serious."

"What are we gonna do?"

"Goldman's a goddamn fool. He told me this guy was a city pimp trying to muscle in on Beth's business. I don't want no part of this for a lousy fifty bucks."

"Lady, are you sure this guy ain't a pimp?" asked a bald-headed man.

"I tell you, he's a reporter from the *Post-Tribune.*"

"I'm gettin' out of this right now."

The fourth man, who had been sitting quietly until now, got up and examined the police card. "Don't forget," he said, "that we're already in this thing up to our ears. There's no pulling out now. If Ray's played us for chumps, we'll take care of him all right. Meanwhile, nobody's going to do nothing until we've had a talk with him. Is that understood?"

"Sure, Eddy, nobody's going to go flying off half-cocked."

"Then let's hear no more about anybody getting out," said Eddy. "If we've been played for chumps, that ain't going to cut any ice when the law steps in." Eddy was a dark, broad-shouldered man who looked as if he needed a shave. His words seemed to carry some weight with the rest of them.

"Ray told me the law was fixed," Ben said.

"If he said it's fixed, then it's probably fixed," said Eddy. "Ray's no fool. We'll find out soon enough. Meanwhile, don't let anything this dame says panic you."

"But look at the police card she's got," said Ben. "I don't want no part of this for a lousy fifty bucks."

"You're already in up to your ears."

"I'm a married man," said the bald man. "Ray told me this was all on the up-and-up or I wouldn't have touched it. He said the law was fixed, and we had a green light."

The pounding on the door from the adjoining room was repeated.

"Don't let that trouble you, lady," Ben said. "She's just one of Beth's girls who got out of line."

Gail swallowed hard before she spoke. "Nothing is fixed so far as my paper is concerned, and unless you open that door and let that girl out I'll see that every one of you is brought to trial."

"That's a lot of bunk," said Eddy. "She can't do a damned thing."

"You'll find out what I can do," said Gail.

"There's no reason for getting mad at us, lady," said the bald man.

"If that's all she wants, just the door opened, what the hell?" said Ben. "That ain't going to hurt nothing."

The bald man walked to the door and turned the key. "I'll have you notice, lady, I'm opening the door."

Shirley reeled into the room. "He'll break his nose," she sobbed. "Ray will break his nose. That's what he does. Just for meanness."

Gail took her by the shoulders. "Help me talk to these men. I'm trying to make them understand."

"She ain't nobody," said Ben. "She's just one of Beth's girls."

"If one of you bastards moves a hair, I'll kill you," Dan said from the kitchen door.

The dark man called Eddy lunged for the door and managed to get it open. Dan shot and he crumpled to the floor. The man called Ben tripped Dan as he entered. They all ran for the door before Dan could pick himself up again. One of them, in his hurry, knocked against the table. The lamp crashed to the floor and spread an area of flame.

Gail helped Dan to his feet. "Where's Shirley?" he asked.

"Right here," answered Shirley.

Dan pushed them through the door. Flames were spreading rapidly over the oil-soaked floor behind them. As they crossed the yard, Gail gripped Dan's arm. "That man," she said, "—the one you shot. He's still in there."

Dan shoved her along toward the car.

"But that man," she repeated. "He'll be burned."

Without a word, Dan pushed her into the car. He backed the roadster out of the yard and stepped on the gas. They bumped along toward the highway with flames mounting behind them.

"Dan," Gail said, "you've got to listen to me. That man is in there."

"I know it," said Dan.

"And that other man. The one you went down in the basement with."

Dan said nothing.

"Dan, he's in there, too!"

"I know it," said Dan coldly. "He's in the basement."

Shirley was trying to wipe the blood from Dan's battered face while he drove.

"Are you all right, kid?" he asked.

"Sure," she said. "I'm all right."

"But Dan—" Gail began.

"I never said I was a nice guy," said Dan. "Maybe that was just a mistaken idea you got."

CHAPTER TWENTY-TWO

Dan asked the old roadster for all it could give on the road back. He learned from Shirley that the same men who had stopped him and Gail on the highway had taken her from the Regan farm shortly after lunch. She and Murphy had been taking a walk. Murphy, it seemed, had fought them as valiantly as his little fists and feet could manage, but had received a kick that sent him sprawling in a ditch.

Dan wanted to drive straight into Sager Creek, but Shirley was so worried about Murphy, he agreed to stop there on the way.

Gail sat quietly, her brain gripped by the thought of the flaming house and the two men in it. Her feeling toward Dan was now mingled with fear and awe. She realized that when he said, "I won't stop at anything," he meant it.

As they swung into the dark yard of the Regan farm, Sid Evans, from Sheriff Horgan's office, stepped onto the running board and flashed a light in Dan's face. "We been looking for you," he said.

"As a matter of fact, we could have used you," Dan replied. The yard was well populated with officers, who now came out of their hiding places.

"Don't tell them anything until we've had a chance to phone our papers," Dan said to Gail. "Shirley, you keep quiet, too."

"Grimes will have plenty to say to you," said Sid.

"Well, it won't be half as interesting as what I have to say to him," said Dan.

As they entered the kitchen, Mrs. Regan rushed to Shirley and put her arms around her. "What have they done to you, darling? Mr. Banion, thank heaven you found her."

"Where's Murphy. Did they hurt Murphy?" Shirley asked.

"The child's all right," said Mrs. Regan. To confirm it, Murphy ran from the bedroom and grabbed Shirley by the hand.

Sid fixed Dan with an accusing look. "Where the hell have you been? What's the matter with your face?"

One of Dan's eyes was black, and the cut at the side of his mouth gleamed redly. "We've been where you ought to have been," he said.

"Mr. Banion, they have Tom in the jail," said Mrs. Regan. "They put Tom in jail."

"That makes about as much sense as everything else they've done," said Dan. "What's the idea of arresting Tom?" he asked Sid.

"He tried to shoot up the Crystal Bar in Sawtooth," said Sid.

"He did right," said Mrs. Regan. "Tom knew Horgan wouldn't do anything about Shirley because he wouldn't do anything about what happened last night. So when Lawrence came back all kicked and bleeding, and crying, and your wife kidnapped, he rounded up his friends and went after them."

"He had all the screwballs in town out with shotguns," said Sid. "They blew hell out of Beth's place—smashed the mirror in back of the bar. I'll bet that thing cost fifty bucks, if it cost a nickel."

"If you can take your mind off cat houses for a minute, I'll tell you where you can find some real destruction," Dan said. "About twenty miles or so north of here, you'll find an old abandoned farmhouse burning down—if it hasn't burned down by this time. And if I'm not mistaken, you'll find a couple of bums, including Ray Goldman, thoroughly barbecued in the mess."

"What the hell are you talking about?" Sid scratched his head.

"You heard me. If you want to investigate it, go ahead. If not, forget it."

"That sounds like the old Krueger place," said Sid.

"I don't know whose place it is or was, but you'd better look into it."

Sid instructed a couple of his men to go and investigate. "I never know whether to trust anything you say or not," he said. "But I have orders to bring you to Grimes."

In the room outside Horgan's office, Ethel was waiting anxiously. "Dan," she said, seizing him by the lapels, "your face! Where have you been? What happened?"

"I'm all right," said Dan. "Just a little fight, that's all. You ought to see the other guy."

Pete Corbett of the *Banner* came forward and squeezed Dan's arm. "Dempsey sent me down to—"

"I know," said Dan, "and man, do I need you!"

Vance Dalbert and two reporters from the *Post-Tribune* crowded in and began firing questions.

"Who hit you, Dan?"

"Where have you been?"

"Who slugged this girl?"

"Who is this girl?"

"What's your name, Miss?"

Dan warned Shirley, "Don't tell them anything." To Gail he whispered, "Phone in the story to your paper, but don't tell these guys a thing. Let the implication be that we were kidnapped for investigating the case."

Gail slipped out the door in search of a phone.

"What did you, tell her?" asked Vance. "Be reasonable, Dan."

Dan pulled Pete Corbett aside and began whispering in his ear, while Pete took rapid notes. When he had finished, Pete ducked out the door.

"Dan, this isn't like you," complained Vance.

"You know me, Banion," said one of the Post-Tribune reporters. "Someday you may be asking favors yourself."

"This story cost me a black eye," said Dan. "That makes it exclusive."

"We'll get it all from Grimes later anyhow."

"All right, here are the facts," said Dan. "Grimes is the murderer. He's an anarchist and resents the idea of servants, so he just killed the girl. He also blacked this girl's eyes because he hates aristocracy and she's the Princess of Luxembourg traveling incognito. He knows his game is up, and he committed suicide an hour ago."

"Banion, I want a word with you," roared Grimes. He was standing in the doorway to Horgan's office.

"I'll bet you do," said Dan.

"Banion, for the love of God, be reasonable. Come in here."

Dan followed him into the office where Horgan was sitting with a heaped up ash tray that was evidence of a long session.

"See here, Banion," said Grimes when the door was closed, "if you had information on this case, why didn't you—what in the name of heaven has happened to your face?"

"One of your pals did that to me. Never mind it now. What were you going to say?"

"One of my pals—see here, Banion, you've got me all wrong."

"That eye looks pretty bad," said Horgan.

"Skip it," said Dan. "I want to hear what you were going to say."

"It's just that if you had information on this case, Banion," said Grimes, "why didn't you bring it to me? After all, that's what I'm for. To get at the truth."

"It seems to me I did mention that the kid was innocent, so you got me fired from my job." Dan pushed the nauseous ash tray away from him. "Do you mind?"

"After all," said Grimes, "there still isn't anything to indicate he didn't do it. As for your job, you shouldn't have taken that seriously.

I called Ainsley this afternoon. He's willing to overlook everything. Empty this damn ash tray, will you, Horgan?"

"It's a little late," said Dan. "I've gone to work for the *Banner*."

"That's a hell of a thing to do after all the trouble I've gone to. There's a good future with Ainsley. The *Banner* doesn't amount to anything."

Horgan took the ash tray and glanced around, wondering what to do with it.

"Thanks just the same," said Dan. "I'll stick to the *Banner*."

"You're not as smart as you think you are," said Grimes.

"I spent the early part of the evening with a group of gentlemen who said the same thing. One of them gave me this shiner."

"Yeah? Who was that?"

Horgan finally decided to dump the ash tray in the wastebasket.

"One of them was Ray Goldman, the bartender from Beth's place. The others were four muscle men."

"Is that so. Where are they now?"

"Well, Ray Goldman, I believe, burned to death in an old farm about an hour's ride up the road. Another one I shot. The other three got away, or I'd have shot them, too. There's the gun I used." Dan tossed the revolver on the desk.

Grimes and Horgan leaped out of their chairs.

"Why didn't you tell us? What's this all about?"

"If your department can't give people any protection, they've got to protect themselves. The story has been phoned to the *Banner* by this time, and I asked them to play up the angle of your inefficiency. That's two nights in a row I was attacked by thugs, and your office hasn't even lifted a finger to investigate. All you've done is to throw a decent man in jail who was somehow trying to protect himself and his family. I'm going to see that angle is played up, too."

"You mean Regan?" said Horgan. "He tried to shoot up Sawtooth. We had to arrest him, and the gang of dopes he had with him."

"It's too bad Regan doesn't make enough on his farm to pay you for protection, or he'd be as immune from arrest around here as Beth and her crowd."

The phone rang. It was one of the men Sid had sent to investigate the fire. Farmers nearby had been attracted by the blaze, but were unable to put it out. The officer couldn't say if there were any bodies in the wreckage or not.

"That's a hell of a thing," said Horgan, as he hung up the receiver.

"I want to know what you were doing out at that farm," said Grimes.

Dan told the story briefly, and Horgan noted the descriptions of the men.

"I ought to book you for murder," said Grimes.

"That's all that would be needed to make you out a complete ass."

"You think I couldn't do it?"

"In the first place, we were kidnapped, and anything I wanted to do to get us out of there was legitimate. In the second place, you don't even know if they're dead or not. Maybe they got out. Maybe the others came back and dragged them out. In the third place, there is no law saying I have to risk my neck in a burning building to rescue a couple of thugs."

"Did you say you phoned that story to the *Banner?*" asked Grimes.

"I had a *Banner* reporter in the outer office phone it in while we were sitting here. Also, Mrs. Hibley's daughter has phoned it to the New York *Planet* by this time."

Grimes leaned back in his chair and closed his eyes for a minute. "You've been extremely unfair in this whole matter, Banion," he said finally. "You've put this office in an extremely unfair light."

Dan shrugged his shoulders. "Are you going to arrest Beth Ridgely?"

"Why?" asked Grimes.

"Because enough evidence has already appeared in the papers to show plausible connection with the murder of Esther Berglan. Because Ray Goldman was the bartender in her joint. And finally, because if she manages to slip out on you, you're going to look twice the damn fools you do already. If I'm not mistaken, you'll find her packing her bags right now."

Grimes took out a fresh cigar, bit off the end, and chewed it for a moment without lighting it. Then he said to Horgan very calmly. "Tell Sid to go pick up Beth Ridgely. Book her on anything that will hold her."

Horgan whistled through his teeth. "You better be sure of what you're doing, Earl."

"I'll take the responsibility," said Grimes.

"And you'd better tell Sid to get over there in a hurry," added Dan, "or you'll find she's skipped."

Horgan left reluctantly. When he had gone, Grimes turned to Dan with a reasoning air. "After all, you've got to recognize my position. There isn't anything to indicate that tramp we have in jail didn't kill that girl."

"You've read the papers," said Dan. "Suppose Flavin can identify Beth Ridgely as the woman who served him food at the Hibley house? And suppose the real Esther Berglan, in Seattle, can identify her as the woman who sidetracked her at the railroad station from going to the Hibley house?"

"Do you believe Beth murdered the girl?"

"No, I don't think she did."

"Then who do you think did do it? That is, assuming the tramp didn't, and I'm not ready to concede that by any means."

"Look here, Grimes, suppose we bury the hatchet and start co-operating."

"You're a hell of a one to talk about co-operation."

"So far, we've been working at cross purposes and it hasn't worked out very well for you."

"I'll admit that," said Grimes. "But the final word hasn't been said yet."

"Why don't you play ball, and give me a chance to prove who did it?"

"And make a damned fool of myself in the bargain, I suppose."

"That's what you've been doing all along—making a damned fool of yourself. I mean start acting sensible."

"Listen, Banion, you haven't dug up a single thing that indicates in any way that this fellow Flavin didn't commit the murder. As far as I'm concerned the evidence against him is airtight. All the rest of this stuff is just coincidence."

"Grimes, you've got the thickest head I've ever seen on a human neck."

"Yeah? Well, we'll see who has the final laugh. I've asked Ainsley to take you back and he's decent enough to talk business. If you insist on playing it your way, I don't see that there's any more I can do."

"There's one more thing," said Dan. "How about letting Regan and his gang out of jail and dropping the charges?"

"You can go to hell," said Grimes angrily. "I'm trying to be reasonable with you, Banion, but I've taken just about all I intend to. They smashed up a bar, and they're going to take the consequences. We're responsible for law and order around here, and we don't intend to play any favorites."

"Then why have you let Beth's place stay open so long?"

"It's a hotel and bar," said Grimes.

"My paper may call it something different," said Dan.

"Are you trying to blackmail me?"

"Pouncing on Regan and his friends for smashing up the county cat house is the only instance of efficient law enforcement that has occurred down here. Go ahead and prosecute those guys if you want to. But if you've got any sense you'll drop the case right now. Regan had good cause for what he did. His house was entered and his family attacked last night, and you didn't even lift a finger to find the guilty parties. Horgan laughed in my face when I told him about it.

Both you and Horgan are getting a payoff from Beth's joint and you know it."

"That's a goddamn vicious slander," said Grimes. "But rather than let you spread your dirty lies, I'm going to let those men go. I hope you appreciate, Banion, that I'm being more than fair in this matter. I try to treat other people decently, and expect them to do the same to me. I'll let them go. But frankly, my patience is about at the breaking point."

"Then you'll let them go and drop the charges."

"As a matter of fact," said Grimes, "we never intended to do more than keep them locked up overnight to cool them off.'"

CHAPTER TWENTY-THREE

If Regan and his associates gained anything from the experience of being locked in the Sager Greek jail, it wasn't humility. Mitch, the turnkey, was cursed every inch of the way as he led them, keys clanking, down the corridor of cells to the outer office.

"This is going to cost you your job, you fat Hitler, you blab-mouthed Mussolini," Tom shouted.

"You tell 'em, pop," called the vagrants from the cells.

"And give us back our shotguns," yelled a lanky man who followed at Tom's heels.

Mitch took it all with puffing discomfort. The jail had been a madhouse ever since Tom and his friends had been brought in. First they had sung "Glory, Glory, Hallelujah," and all the vagrants had joined in. Tiring of that, they switched to "We'll hang lousy Grimes from a sour apple tree," varying it occasionally to include, "We'll hang Sheriff Horgan," and "We'll hang dirty Mitch."

Later, forgetting their crusade, and carried away entirely by their singing, they indulged in such numbers as, "Mammy's Li'l Baby Loves Shortn'n Bread," and "Who Threw the Overalls in Mrs. Murphy's Chowder?"

"I ain't got a goddamn thing to do with it," said Mitch. "As far as I'm concerned, I'm just doing my duty."

"Just as soon as you give me back my gun, I'm going to blow your head off," said a round little man, shaking his finger in Mitch's face.

They exploded into the outer office in a riot of noise. Tom was reciting at the top of his voice, "When in the course of human events it becomes necessary for one people—"

"You, Horgan," yelled the tall, lanky man, "don't you ever send your boy around to buy chickens from me again. I'm going to put a sign: 'Horgan is a dog' on the back of my truck, and it stays there until after the next elections."

"Give me my shotgun," yelled a husky, bronzed man wearing a sailor hat, a striped T-shirt, and greasy khaki pants.

"We hold these truths to be self-evident," continued Tom. He broke off at the sight of Shirley. "Who blacked her eyes? Who hit that girl? Horgan, if you blacked that girl's eyes—"

"You stinking pig," said the fat man to Horgan, accepting the question for the fact. "Take that badge off for five minutes and come outside with me."

"He didn't do it," said Dan. "Everything's okay now. All charges are going to be dropped, and Sheriff Horgan apologizes. Don't you, Horgan?"

"Well, goddamnit," said Horgan. "Well, hell, you know I ain't got nothing against you boys."

"Give us back our guns," shouted the lanky man.

Regan's army consisted of five men. The lanky man was Slim Stevens, who ran a little poultry farm outside Sager Creek. The man in the sailor hat and greasy britches owned an independent gas station. The fat man was Leonard Elkins, a janitor in the railroad station. An elderly man with a bulbous nose was the town's most persistent drunk, and was indebted to Tom for abundant favors. His single claim to virtue was the oft-repeated statement that he'd cut off his arm "up to there" for Tom Regan. The fifth man was a printer from Vance Dalbert's *Sentinel*.

Their shotguns restored to them, they all jammed into the combination malted milk and coffee shop nearby to relive their glory. Dan, Ethel, Gail, Shirley, and the assembled newspaper reporters went along as an audience.

"I pointed my gun bang square at that big mirror," said Tom. "'Hand over that girl,' I said, 'or I'll blow it to hell.'"

"Ed, here, got his foot caught in a spittoon," said the fat man. "I thought I'd die laughing."

"You wouldn't have laughed if you'd had that woman swinging at you with a bottle," said the bulbous-nosed man.

"I flang one of them pipe chairs," said Slim, "and it bounced clear up to the ceiling, jes' like a spring."

"You shoulda heard them girls scream," said the printer. "Why didn't you shoot your gun off when that guy came at you with the club?" asked the fat man.

"Oh hell, it won't shoot. It ain't even got a trigger."

"I shot, and down came the mirror with a splash," said Tom.

"Ed and me ran upstairs," said the gas station man. "And you should have seen them monkeys come piling out of those rooms. One guy didn't have nothing on but—"

"Shut up. There's ladies present," said bulbous-nose.

"Who do I see running at me in his undershirt but the cashier of the bank," roared the fat man.

"That's nothing," said Slim. "Do you know who that guy was that fell down the light well? Sure, he thought he was jumping out a window, and landed in the bottom of the light well. It was Brinsley. Sure, it was Brinsley."

The conversation boiled for an hour or more, then, one by one, the warriors departed.

Dan managed to corner Tom Regan quietly, and catch him up on events.

The printer was hardest to get rid of. He had written a book on a new monetary system of his own invention and wanted to explain it to Dan then and there.

"You got literary experience," he said. "You could go over it and straighten out the sentences."

Dan excused himself to grab Leonard Elkins, the fat man who was janitor at the railroad station, and who was about to depart.

"Can I have a word privately with you?" Dan asked.

"Sure," said Elkins. They retired to an empty booth, and Dan motioned to Pete Corbett to join them.

"Did you say you saw the cashier of the bank running out of Beth's place in his undershirt?" Dan asked.

"I did."

"Does he know you saw him?"

"He does. He ran slap bang into me, and begged me not to tell anybody. I guess I was kind of a heel to mention it tonight."

"Is he married?"

"Married, and has two kids. I shouldn't have said anything, should I? Hell, I was just excited."

"Do you want to help in this business—help clear that kid they've got in jail?"

"Tom says he didn't do it, and I'd believe Tom any day. Tom took my wife and kids into his house and kept them for three months while I was in the hospital last year. Me on relief, I didn't have a nickel. Now he won't take a penny for it. Sure, I believe anything Tom says. Do you know what he did for Slim over there? They was gonna take Slim's farm away from him. Regan says, sign the farm over to me, just like as if I bought it. So Slim signs the farm over to Regan before they can get an attachment on it. Slim takes his time paying his debts, then Tom signs it back to him. Tom thought that up himself. Tell me he ain't smart."

"Listen," said Dan, "we've got to find out about a couple of bank accounts around here, and that cashier can give us the dope. I think he'd do you that favor."

"I'll ask him, if that's what you want."

Dan outlined what he wanted to know. "Pete," he said, "you go with Elkins tomorrow and see what the two of you can find out."

CHAPTER TWENTY-FOUR

Before he sat down to breakfast in the morning, Dan bought copies of all available papers. The *Banner* exploited every opportunity of making Grimes an ass. The affair at the abandoned farm, Regan's revolution, and the attack on Regan's place the night before were featured under a head: "Gangsterism Rampant in Patterson County." Regan and his five-man army were described as justified citizens forced to defend themselves in the face of official indifference.

The *Post-Tribune*, on the other hand, called them radical trouble-makers who were quickly squelched by the efficient arm of the law. The abandoned farm affair was attributed to "a roving army of malcontents invading every decent community in the nation."

Ainsley saw fit to turn the abduction of Dan and Gail to his own advantage in an editorial that read: "This ruthless and wanton attack on peaceful American citizens, following close on the heels of the brutal murder by a vagrant sex-maniac in Hamilton, emphasizes once more the necessity for action, as pointed out by County Attorney Grimes yesterday." The blame was laid at the door of the Administration in Washington.

The identity of the murdered girl was handled in a separate story headed: "Act of Fiend Bares Masquerade of San Diego Slayer." The story began: "By a strange trick of fate, one killer struck down another in the Hamilton murder case, as the mounting wave of crime that is sweeping the nation struck at the peaceful County of Patterson."

Relation of the affair to the old Malnick case was isolated in still another story, headed: "Famous Malnick Case Recalled in Hamilton Murder."

By thus chopping the story into various parts and scattering them, Ainsley succeeded in dodging the worst implications. A front page cartoon showed a leering criminal loading his revolver from an ammunition box labeled WPA, which was being held out to him by a gibbering idiot in the gown of a college professor. Under it was an editorial: "Subsidizing Crime."

The story in the *Banner*, however, linked up all the events in their full complexity. It raised strong doubts as to the guilt of Ralph Flavin, and reprinted excerpts from his poems prominently. The main editorial fried Grimes in proper style, giving a point by point analysis of the whole case.

Dan noted two significant things; first, that the body of the murdered girl had definitely been identified as that of June Heidelmann; and second, that no human remains had been found in the ruins of the burned farmhouse. Evidently, Ray and Ben had either crawled out, or their companions had returned and dragged them out.

Vance Dalbert's *Sentinel* handled the matter with sedate rewrites of the *Banner* stories, leaving out all implications. An editorial appealed for sober common sense on the basis that competent authorities would certainly investigate all facts.

"What kind of boondoggling do you have in mind for me today?" Ethel asked, as Dan put aside the papers.

"First let's hear how you came out yesterday," he said. "What did you learn from the bird's egg?"

"Ferguson? Nothing. He doesn't know anything. What a sad little dope. He even looks like a bird's egg. That was a waste of time."

"Well, tell me what he said."

"In the first place, he didn't climb the tree until six-thirty. By that time the body had been discovered."

"Well, what did he see?"

"Nothing. He saw the gardener come home and start digging in the garden. That's all."

"Nothing else?"

"Nothing that he can remember."

"How about Flavin? Did you get in to see him?"

"Yes, and Dan, I think you're right. That kid didn't kill that girl. I'm sure he didn't."

"Did he tell you anything new?"

"We checked over everything he could remember about the Hibley place when he went there. I wrote it all down, if you want to look at it."

Dan checked over the notes, but they added nothing to what Flavin had already told him.

"Today," he said, "we're going to check some alibis. You'd better write this down. First, I want you to go to the Acme Theatre in Hamilton and check on what movie was showing there the day of the murder, what time the matinee started—if they had a matinee—and what time the feature was over. Maybe you can do that on the phone."

"What's that got to do with it?"

"Maybe nothing. But that gardener, Farnsworth, at the Hibleys' claims he went to the movies that afternoon and saw *Mutiny on the Bounty*. Find out if it was playing, and what else was on the program."

"You don't think he might have done it?"

"I'm not thinking anything, but we've been neglecting him."

"You don't miss much, do you?"

"I miss plenty. Otherwise I'd be able to make some sense out of this. Also, I want you to locate Mrs. Garland's daughter—she lives somewhere in Sager Creek—and find out if Mrs. Garland visited her on that day."

"Let's see, she was the housekeeper. Is that right?"

"Correct. And just in case she might have primed her daughter for an alibi, check with the neighbors if you can."

"You're going to make an awful snoop out of me."

"Don't worry, darling. Maybe when this is over I'll get some kind of an honest job."

"Dan, you will be careful today, won't you. What are you going to do?"

"First, I want to see if they managed to pick up Beth. Then I'm going to try to talk some sense out of Mrs. Hibley."

"And where will I see you?"

"I'll see you back at the hotel around dinnertime."

"And you won't do anything foolish, will you?"

"I don't know what you'd call foolish."

"Just don't take any chances."

"Well, I'll look both ways crossing the street. You don't have to worry, honey. Today's just going to be routine. I think we've got some of these characters around to the place where they'll have to do some talking."

It was almost noon when Dan called in at the Sager Creek jail. As he expected, Beth had skipped before Horgan's men could nab her.

"Bag and baggage, off she went. Nobody knows where," said Horgan. "I can't understand it. We really didn't have a thing on her. Here's a wire from San Diego says that guy Heidelmann—the girl's father—skipped out too. Dropped out of sight a week ago. Not a trace of him. We got Ray Goldman and his boys, though. They were picked up at the state line—some of them. Ray and another one, Ed Rankin, turned up in the hospital. The others dumped them on the steps and then scrammed."

"Then they didn't burn."

"No. They were fried good, though. What do you make of it all?"

"You've closed the insane asylum door after all the leading nuts have escaped. I don't think Ray and his gang are going to do you much good. I don't think they know anything."

"To top it all off," said Horgan, "Ronald Hibley's disappeared. It looks like he took a powder, too."

"When did this happen?"

"He shoved off some time last night. Didn't say good-by to anybody. His bed wasn't slept in last night."

"Are you sure he wasn't hit over the head and thrown in some ditch somewhere?"

"Well, he packed a suitcase. Grimes is fit to be tied."

"You don't seem to be worrying much."

"What the hell, I've just about given up all idea of being re-elected anyhow. I'm getting along in life, and I've got a little piece of land. Earl, he's different. He's ambitious."

"Do you still think that kid Flavin did it?"

"How the hell do I know? It's anybody's guess now, isn't it?"

"Well, while you're waiting to retire, do you intend to do anything to earn your pay?"

"Oh, I'm thinkin' about it. I was just sittin' here thinkin' about it. I'm tryin' to get an idea. You got any ideas?"

Dan called the Hibley house and got Gail on the phone. She had nothing to add to Horgan's account of Ronald's disappearance. He had packed a suitcase, his bed hadn't been slept in, he was gone. "I've been trying to reach you all morning," she said.

Dan agreed to come over as soon as possible.

In the outer office Pete Corbett, the reporter Dempsey had sent down to help him, was waiting. "Well, we got the dope," he said. "The bank cashier was a little nasty about the whole thing, but that fellow Elkins handled him all right." He handed Dan a piece of paper on which he had scribbled the information. "You'll notice Beth Ridgely's account shows regular monthly withdrawals of five hundred dollars for more than a year. A little over a year ago, there was a withdrawal of five thousand dollars. There are other items, of course, but those stand out.

"Now look at Mrs. Hibley's account. It shows deposits of five hundred dollars a month for the same period of time, and approximately on the same dates. A little over a year ago, on the same day that Beth

Ridgely withdrew five thousand dollars, Mrs. Hibley deposited the same amount. It might be a coincidence, but I doubt it."

"Well, at least we know who was shaking down whom—if it was a shakedown," Dan said.

"I thought about that. You don't suppose, on the q.t., the old lady owns that clip joint Beth operates, do you? That would be a hot one."

"No, I don't think so," said Dan. "But you'd better check on it just the same. See if you can find out who owns the real estate, if there are any mortgages on it, and all that."

Dan rented the same rattletrap car he'd driven the day before and set out for Hamilton.

Farnsworth was dragging the sprinkler across the lawn as Dan entered the gate. "Afternoon, Mr. Banion," he said. Then, after a cautious look at the house, "Can I have a word with you, Mr. Banion?"

Dan paused. "Yeah, sure. What's on your mind?"

"Maybe we better go 'round in back."

Dan followed him to the garage-workshop. Farnsworth fished an envelope out of his back pocket. It was addressed to Dan. While Farnsworth eyed him expectantly, he ripped it open and read:

> I have to leave in a hurry, and for reasons you will understand later, do not want my whereabouts known. I think I see this whole thing clearly now. In any case, I'll know very soon. If I do not return home in twenty-four hours, I will be at my cabin near Lake Farrow. I hope that you will come. Farnsworth knows where it is and will drive you if you like. You can trust him. But don't bring anyone else, and please—please—do not mention any of this to my family or to anyone else. You will understand when you come. I believe that your efforts in this matter have been sincere. The information you have uncovered so far has been invaluable to me in figuring this out.

It was signed: Ronald Hibley.

"Anything serious?" asked Farnsworth.

"What do you think?"

"I don't know as I'm doin' right or not. He gave it to me last night, just before he pulled out. Said not to say a word to anybody, but to give it to you first opportunity I had. I'm worried, Mr. Banion."

"What do you think he was up to?"

"I don't know, but he was mighty fond of that girl. If he thinks he knows who did it—well, he's one of these quiet ones, Mr. Banion. I don't know what he might do."

"Did he mention where he was going?"

"Not a word."

"Here, read it," said Dan. He handed Farnsworth the letter.

Farnsworth read it through twice, very slowly, then shook his head. "I'll leave it to you, Mr. Banion, to decide what you think is best."

"Suppose we let it ride for the present," said Dan. "Then, if he isn't back by tonight, could you drive us up there?"

"Sure. Glad to. Just say the word."

"All right. You'll be here, will you, if I have to get in touch with you?"

"I'll stick right around close."

At the front door of the Hibley house, Dan gave his hat to Mrs. Garland and asked for Mrs. Hibley instead of Gail. Mrs. Hibley was seated in the parlor, looking somewhat shattered, but still defiant. As Dan had hoped, Gail was out of the room.

"Have they found that woman?" asked Mrs. Hibley.

"What woman? Do you mean Beth Ridgely?" Dan asked.

"Certainly I mean her. She's responsible for everything. She killed that girl. Ronald didn't have anything to do with it. He was a fool to run away. If Mrs. Garland had had the sense to keep her mouth shut on the telephone, we wouldn't have this embarrassment."

"What did Mrs. Garland do?"

"When the police called, she told them his bed hadn't been slept in."

"Well, isn't it time, Mrs. Hibley, that you started being frank with someone? You can't go on hiding things and expect everyone to believe your family is entirely in the clear."

The old lady glared hatefully. "You've caused enough trouble already with your snooping and spying. I don't see that any of this concerns you in the least."

"Mrs. Hibley, if your family is innocent in this matter, then it's all to your interest to find out who killed that girl and why."

"That woman did it."

"Do you really have any reason for saying that?"

"She's an evil woman."

"What reason did she have for planting June Heidelmann in your house."

"I haven't the slightest idea."

"Mrs. Hibley, do you think Beth Ridgely had anything to do with poisoning her husband back in 1913?"

"I don't know what you are talking about."

"Franz Heidelmann was accused and your husband defended him. You can't be as ignorant of all this as you pretend."

"It has nothing to do with me."

"Mrs. Hibley, I'm going to be frank with you. I happen to know that you lost all of your income properties over a year ago. Since then you've been receiving money from somewhere. I don't want to drag this all out in the open if I can help it. But you're going to have to be reasonable."

"Are you trying to blackmail me? Is that what I am to understand?"

"I don't want anything from you but the truth. And if you don't speak truthfully to someone pretty soon, things are going to come crashing down around your ears."

"Dan, what are you talking about?" It was Gail who, attracted by their voices, had come down from upstairs.

"I'm simply trying to get your mother to face facts," Dan said.

Gail addressed the old lady impatiently. "Mother, is there anything you're not telling us? If so, for heaven's sake let's have it out. It's going to come out anyhow."

Mrs. Hibley avoided her daughter's eyes. "If this young man would mind his own business—"

"Mother, don't be silly."

The old lady began to sob. She rose to leave the room, but paused at the entrance to the hall. "I have done my best all my life to give you and Ronald every advantage. Neither of you have ever had a word of appreciation. Neither of you have had the slightest consideration." She turned and hurried upstairs, sobbing as she went.

"I don't know what to do with her," said Dan.

"It may be, you know, Dan, that she really doesn't know anything more than she's told us."

"I think she does. All this linking up with the old Malnick case can't be coincidence. Do you know, Gail, that a year ago your mother lost all her income property in Frenton? Yet since that time, her bank account shows monthly deposits of five hundred dollars. That money must be coming from somewhere."

"Lost all her property!"

"Yes. Of course, she might have some other income property around here that nobody knows about. I think you ought to do some checking up."

"Are you sure about this, Dan? How did you find out?"

"I checked. I'm sure enough. But, Gail, I think you ought to check for yourself. And I think you ought to have a good talk with your mother. Have you any idea where Ronald went?"

"Not in the slightest. Dan, I'm worried. He hasn't been right for days. I'm positive, Dan, that he didn't have anything to do with this thing."

"All right, I'll tell you what I think you'd better do. Check on this question of your mother's property. Find out what's what if you can. And see if you can't get some sense out of her. Meanwhile, I'll see what I can find out about Ronald."

"But, Dan, I want to see you later."

"I think we ought to have a look at Ronald's office. Suppose I meet you there?"

"All right, Dan. Make it four-thirty. Or let's say between four-thirty and five."

"Between four-thirty and five in Ronald's office."

"Yes, but, Dan, be there. I'm counting on you."

"I'll be there," Dan said. "Meanwhile, see what sense you can get out of your mother. If she doesn't talk soon, people are going to start talking for her."

CHAPTER TWENTY-FIVE

Gail hadn't arrived yet when Dan called at Ronald Hibley's real estate office, so he sat down to wait. The thin, sour-faced woman in the outer office discreetly told him that Mr. Hibley was away on business, and gave him a magazine to read, the *Real Estate Journal*. Dan glanced at the leading editorial: "Is Public Housing Bolshevism?"

"Can Americans choose the kind of houses they want to live in, or are they to be regimented into public dormitories of the type the government is now squandering taxpayers' money on in many parts of the nation?"

The sound of the telephone interrupted his reading. He could tell from the way the thin woman talked that it was Gail. Suddenly she clamped her hand over the mouthpiece and spoke to him. "It's Miss Hibley. She says she'll be a little late. She says for you to wait."

"Tell her I'll wait," said Dan.

The thin woman relayed his message and added, "But, Miss Hibley, I was about to close. Yes, it's one minute to five. Well, do you think that would be all right? Well, I suppose if you say so. Yes, I'll tell him."

She hung up the receiver. "I'm sorry, but I'm going to have to close up. Miss Hibley said it would be all right for you to wait inside, though. It's a spring lock. You can let her in when she comes."

After perching an infinitesimal hat on her hair and jabbing it in place with a hatpin, she put the rubber cover on her typewriter and banged out. Before walking away, however, she tugged and jolted at the knob to make certain the door was locked.

Dan returned his eyes to the editorial. "What people should be reminded of," it said, "is that Abraham Lincoln was born in a log cabin, not a Federal housing project."

Dan threw the magazine across the room, got up, and prowled around. The door to Hibley's private office was open, so he went in and established himself in the swivel chair.

A framed motto on the desk read: "It's easy enough for a man to smile when life goes along like a song, but the man worth-while is the man who can smile when everything goes dead wrong."

In the top drawer, Dan found an assortment of crossword puzzles clipped from newspapers, a lot of odds and ends of junk, rubber bands, paper clips, leads for automatic pencils. A side drawer contained current correspondence, mostly about houses and lots and farms Hibley was trying to sell.

Dan skipped through them, reading one here and there. One in particular held his attention. It was painfully scribbled on cheap notebook paper:

Dere Mr. Hibley: The bank ses I have got to pay them sum intrest or they will forklose and they will take the farm. Mr. Hibley my crop was dam good. It was fine. You could see for yorseif wen you was out last and if you wood like sum more peeches you can have them just help yourself. But the company will not by my crop they say there is too much everywhere and they do not want it. But I reed all the time in the Sentnel where peeple in the city are hungry and sum-buddy must be lires. Also they will not let me take my crop to the city and sell it because I don't have no license they say. How can I pay the bank sum intrest wen they wil not by my crop and they wil not let me sel my crop? Mr. Hibley, everybuddy nose that Mr. Collingwood who owns the paking company is the president of the bank to. If they wil not by my crop then how can I—

Suddenly Dan sensed another presence in the room. He looked up straight into the muzzle of a revolver in the hand of a short man who was standing just inside the door. The man was smirking. He had a nervous tick in the corner of his left eye, and it was twitching. His face, though deeply lined, had an air of arrogance and distinction.

"I thought I'd find you in here," he said. "I knew your secretary was lying this afternoon when she said you were out."

Although he spoke in excellent English, there was a slight, guttural,

German quality to his voice.

Dan was too surprised to say anything.

"You killed my daughter," the man said.

"Now wait a minute," said Dan.

"Now I'm going to kill you, Hibley."

"You're making a mistake," Dan said urgently.

"You didn't think my daughter was good enough for you."

"Listen, I'm not—"

The man's voice became abrupt and commanding. "Where's Adelaide?"

"I'm not Hibley," said Dan. "You're making a mistake."

"Where's Adelaide? I've been to her place and she's gone."

"I tell you I'm not—"

"Talk fast, Hibley. Where is she? You're both going to pay for this. You goddamn rotten nobody."

"I tell you, I'm not Ronald Hibley."

"You're a liar." The man moved closer to the desk.

"I'm not even any relation to him. I was just sitting here in his office."

"You're a liar and a coward."

"I'll show you my press credentials." Dan reached for his pocket.

"Keep your hands on the table," the man barked.

"If you'll only let me show you my credentials, you'll save yourself from making a mistake."

"What are doing here if you're not Hibley?"

"I'm a newspaper reporter. My name's Dan Banion. I work for the *Banner* in Frenton. Ronald Hibley has disappeared. I'm just trying to get a line on him."

"You're a liar."

"If you'll let me show you—"

"Stand up and put your hands over your head. Move around here." The man felt Dan's coat and rear pockets, looking for a gun. Then he began reaching in pockets, pulling out whatever was there and throwing it on the desk. Dan noticed uneasily that the letter Farnsworth had given him earlier was among the pile.

The man sat in Hibley's chair and began examining the contents of Dan's wallet: driver's license, press card, Guild card, Social Security card.

"Maybe you are Banion," he said. "If so, where's Hibley?"

"He's gone. He left last night without telling anyone where."

"You're lying. Where is he?"

"I don't know."

"Where's Adelaide?"

"Do you mean Beth Ridgely?"

"Yes. Where is she?" The man's left eye was twitching erratically.

"She pulled out last night, too. I don't know."

As he talked, the man had been thumbing through the rest of the things he had taken from Dan's pockets. He came to the letter, opened it, and read it several times.

"You're a liar," he said. "You knew where he was."

"I don't know that he's there. I don't even know where Lake Farrow is."

"You and I are going to find out. Who's this Farnsworth he refers to?"

"He's the gardener at the Hibley house."

"Well, I guess you and I can find this place without him. Keep your mouth shut and do what you're told, Banion, and I'll give you quite a story. Cause me any trouble and I won't have the slightest compunction about shooting you. You don't mean a damn thing to me. Is that clear?"

"It's too clear."

"Do you have a car?"

"No."

"You're a liar, Banion, and a fool. There's a receipt for a deposit on a rented car from a garage right here among your papers. I haven't much time to waste, Banion. If you don't change your attitude, I'd just as soon kill you right now."

Dan led the way to where he had parked the roaster. As they left the office, he looked up and down the street for Gail, but she was not in sight.

The man sat in the seat beside him with the revolver out of sight, but poked against his ribs. "The first thing you're going to do," he said, "is get some gas and find out where this Lake Farrow is."

At a service station on the edge of town, Dan picked up a road map and learned that Lake Farrow was in hunting and fishing country about seventy-five miles north of Hamilton. For some distance they rode quietly. Then Dan said, "I take it you're Franz Heidelmann."

"That's right."

After a few moments more of quiet, Dan said, "Adelaide Gwinn poisoned her husband, didn't she?"

"That's right."

"Why?"

"For his money. He was no good anyway. A fool."

"What was your part in it?"

"None of your business. I stood trial and was acquitted."

"Did Vern Hibley know that she was guilty or implicated?"

"Certainly. He charged plenty for keeping his mouth shut. He blackmailed her for years afterward. He made her sign a confession that he kept for his protection."

"What do you mean by that?"

"So that she wouldn't poison him or do away with him. If anything happened to him, the confession would be found and she'd take the consequences."

"He must have been a pretty shrewd character."

"He wasn't any good. He was a fool."

"What happened to the confession after he died?"

"I guess his wife must have found it. She's been blackmailing Beth with it for over a year."

"Doesn't the confession implicate you?"

"I stood trial and was acquitted. You can't try a man twice on the same charge. You can't hold a man in double jeopardy."

"That puts you in the clear."

"Certainly I'm in the clear."

"Well, how did it happen that—well, why didn't you—"

"I got my share after the trial. Is that what you mean?"

"Yes."

"I got fifty thousand out of it. I should have got more."

"Tell me, Heidelmann, why do you think Beth planted your daughter in the Hibley house?"

"To locate the confession, of course. She wanted to get her hands on the confession and thought June could locate it or steal it for her. She had no business using June like that. I'm going to pay her off for that."

"What makes you so sure Ronald Hibley killed your daughter?"

"It stands to reason, doesn't it? He made her pregnant."

"He didn't necessarily kill her."

"If he didn't, Adelaide did. I'm going to fix them both."

"Well, why kill him if he isn't guilty?"

"He messed around with my daughter. He's no damn good. Why not kill him?"

CHAPTER TWENTY-SIX

It was well into the night when they reached Larkinville, the nearest town to Lake Farrow. The garage attendant knew Ronald Hibley well and told them how to get to his cabin.

"It's pretty far up the mountain," he said, "and I don't think you'll find anyone there. At least, Mr. Hibley usually drops in here on the way up, and we haven't seen him for a good many months. It isn't likely he'd have gone up there without letting somebody in town here know."

As a parting shot he called, "Once you turn off on the dirt road, you can't go wrong. Just keep right on going. But be careful. That road's plenty bad in some places."

It was worse than bad. Once they left the main road, Dan had to feel his way forward slowly and jerkily. The dirt road twisted and turned and climbed upward, following every contour of the mountainside. The headlights turned the curtain of dark ahead into flashes of forest, and occasionally steep drops that made haste unwise. Once, turning a corner, the headlights picked up a startled deer.

Heidelmann rode quietly, hardly uttering a word after they left Larkinville.

Ultimately, the dirt road led into a flat clearing, and the lights fell on Hibley's big black sedan parked to one side.

"This must be it," Dan said.

"You keep quiet. Understand?" Heidelmann warned. "Turn off those headlights."

Dan flipped the switch, and they were in darkness. Not a light showed anywhere, nor was there any sign of a house.

"Turn on the dash light," said Heidelmann.

Dan turned on the small light over the dashboard. "Have you got a flashlight in this car?"

"I doubt it," Dan said.

Heidelmann explored the compartment in the dashboard. There was no flashlight, but he found a long, stout cord. "Hold your hands out," he ordered.

Dan extended his wrists, and Heidelmann bound them tightly, leaving a long end dangling, which he held like a leash.

"Now you go ahead of me," he said. "And if you make any stupid move you'll regret it."

Dan sidled out of the car, and Heidelmann followed.

"Which way?" asked Dan.

"There's an opening through the trees over there to the right. We'll try that."

Dan groped forward vaguely. Behind him, Heidelmann lit a match. He could see the opening, and entered it, feeling his way cautiously with his feet. It felt like a path. Heidelmann lit matches every few yards until they reached another clearing where they could make out the dark shape of a cabin.

"No light," said Dan.

"Call him," said Heidelmann. "He was expecting you."

Dan called weakly, "Anybody home?"

"Louder."

"Anybody home?"

"Call his name."

"Hi, Hibley. Anybody home?"

There was no answer from the cabin.

"We'll go in," said Heidelmann. "You lead."

Stumbling ahead, Dan found a porch and mounted it. Heidelmann lit a match. A door appeared a few feet away. Heidelmann tried the knob.

"It's open. Go in."

Dan walked forward and felt himself in a room. Another match lit behind him showed it to be a kitchen. It was empty, but a door was ajar into another room.

"Go ahead," said Heidelmann.

Dan groped to the other door and went through. His foot kicked against something on the floor. Somehow, he knew what it was.

"Go ahead," repeated Heidelmann.

Dan groped around the thing on the floor and continued a few steps. Heidelmann evidently kicked against the same object. He grunted and lit a match. The flickering light revealed a woman face down on the floor. An oil lamp could also be seen on a nearby table. Heidelmann went over and lit it.

The interior of the cabin was finished in knotty pine boards. A number of deer heads on the wall seemed to leap out of the darkness as the wick of the lamp flared higher.

Heidelmann kneeled beside the figure on the floor, then took hold of it and rolled it over. It was stiff as a frozen side of beef. The front of the dress pulled loose from a clotted stain on the floor with a slight ripping sound. There was a darker clot in the middle of the chest. The body thumped as it rolled over on its back.

The eyes caused Dan to widen his mouth and gasp in revulsion. They were fixed in a kind of giddy terror. The face had an expression he had only seen on insane persons whose nerves had snapped and who had lost all control of the muscles of their faces. The jaw was jerked to one side, so that the lips did not meet properly. It was as if all the fear and weakness this face had concealed in life revealed itself in death.

"Who is she?" asked Heidelmann.

"It's Beth," said Dan.

"No."

"Yes, it is."

"Jesus Christ!" Heidelmann leaned closer and stared.

"She must have been dead quite a while," said Dan.

"My God, it is her," said Heidelmann.

"Sure it is."

"My God, I'd never have recognized her."

"It's her all right."

"My God, what happened to her?"

"She's been shot."

"I mean her face—her—my God, you should have seen her twenty-five years ago."

"I saw a picture of her."

"She was beautiful."

"Yeah. I know."

"Jesus Christ!" Heidelmann stood up. He looked around the room. Suddenly his eyes fixed on something and his brow wrinkled. The twitching corner of his eye seemed to be working like an excited pulse.

Dan followed his stare and saw a man's feet protruding from behind a table. Heidelmann went over and looked down at it. "Jesus Christ!" he said.

Dan looked over his shoulder. "That's Hibley—Ronald Hibley."

"Hibley?"

"Yes. Hibley."

"Good God!"

Hibley was lying as if he had fallen from the chair at the table. A Savage automatic was gripped in his fingers. A dried pool of blood was under his head and a dark clot in his temple.

"You're sure that's Hibley?"

"Yes. Positive," said Dan.

Heidelmann went back and stared down at Beth. "What happened to her? What must have happened?"

"Time changes people," said Dan.

Heidelmann looked over to Dan as if appealing for understanding. "There wasn't anything else I could do. I had to send June somewhere. I didn't know what else to do. I shouldn't have trusted her, but what else could I do?"

Dan leaned over and studied the way Hibley had fallen. Heidelmann stared some more at Beth, then went over and sat on a cot. "If I'd known anywhere else to send her. But Adelaide was the only one I knew that I thought I could trust. You can understand that, can't you?"

"It must have happened some time last night," said Dan. He backed away from the table and began circling around with his eyes on the floor.

"I'd never have sent her—never—if I'd had any idea. I never would have believed. What are you doing that for?"

"I'm looking for shells," Dan said. "That's an automatic pistol and would have ejected the shells."

"If I'd had any idea what Adelaide was like. If I'd realized what she'd become. Here's one of them."

Heidelmann stooped and picked up a shell near his foot.

"Yes, that would be about right," Dan said. "He could have been standing over there when he shot Beth." He stooped and picked up another shell not far from the table.

"June was the only thing I had in the world," said Heidelmann. "What's the matter? Is something wrong?"

"I don't know," said Dan. "The gun ejects shells to the right, and this is way over to the left."

"It might have rolled."

"It might have, but I hardly see how."

"He was pointing the gun at his head. There's no telling what direction the shell would have gone in."

"Maybe not. But according to the wound, and assuming he was sitting at the table, it would have gone almost straight ahead and landed on the table top or in front of it."

"Not necessarily."

"Almost necessarily. In any case, I don't know how it could have got over here. And it's funny that there isn't any note."

"Why would there be a note?"

"Well, he'd hardly commit suicide without leaving a note to explain it. Especially since he expected me to come up."

"Do you think something's wrong?"

"I think it's just possible somebody shot both of them and rigged it up to look as if Hibley shot Beth and then killed himself."

"Who would do that?"

"Well, that's what I don't know."

"You're just guessing. I don't see that he'd have to leave a note."

Dan held out his wrists. "Suppose you untie these. I want to have a look at the rest of this place."

"I've no reason to think I can trust you," Heidelmann said.

"Well, you've got no reason not to trust me anymore. They're both dead. You can't shoot them. Nobody has anything else on you."

"You could make some trouble against me for holding a gun on you."

"Just untie me and we'll call it square. I'm not causing any more trouble for anybody."

Heidelmann untied the cord. "I don't care much what happens anyhow," he said. "June was all I had left in life."

Dan rubbed his wrists and began examining the room in detail. Then he lit another lamp, explored the kitchen, and went outside to look around the house. When he returned, Heidelmann was sitting in a chair staring at Beth.

"She had the softest skin you ever touched," he said. "Her hair was like fine silk. She used to wear flowers in it."

"We'd better get out of here," Dan said. "I can't find anything that looks out of line."

"Jesus!" said Heidelmann. "How Adelaide changed."

Coming down the dirt road off the mountain, Dan turned one of the many sharp curves and was momentarily blinded by the lights of a car coming up. He applied the brakes and the two cars halted almost bumper to bumper. A big man in a canvas hat came up and stuck his head in. "Where you two men headed?"

"We've been up at the Hibley cabin," Dan said.

"See anything of Hibley up there?"

"He's dead."

"Dead?"

"Yes, shot. There's a woman up there shot, too."

Three other men from the car ahead came up. The big man turned a flashlight in Dan's face. At the same time, he exhibited a badge.

"I'm the sheriff from Larkinville. You fellows better get out."

Standing in the road, they were searched, and one of the men took Heidelmann's gun from him.

CHAPTER TWENTY-SEVEN

Dan's head wasn't thinking too clearly after a night spent in the Larkinville jail, with very little sleep. Still, he couldn't accept the sudden end matters had come to.

County Attorney Earl Grimes was jubilant, glad to see it over with, anxious to forgive all concerned, especially himself.

"Certainly I made some mistakes in the beginning," he said. "I'm perfectly willing to admit it. None of us are infallible. But in the end, Banion, I think we've given a splendid example of all-around teamwork. And that's the angle I think we ought to stress. Co-operation between the press, the public, and the police as the only democratic answer to crime."

"I think it's all been a goddamn mess," said Sheriff Horgan. "The less we say about it, Earl, the better."

"I don't think that's a constructive attitude at all. Do you, Banion?"

"Right now I'd favor a crusade to reform the jails," said Dan. "Why do you have to make them so uncomfortable? A man's supposed to be considered innocent until he's proven guilty. Why not give him a decent bed to sleep in while you're finding out? That can in Larkinville is a worse dungeon than Devil's Island."

"I'm sorry, Banion," said Grimes. "Sheriff Moynes there didn't know. He had to hold you until we could investigate. Those things happen. Chalk it all up to experience, eh?"

"I'm still not satisfied," Dan said. "I don't think this thing makes sense at all."

"Now don't start messing things up again, Banion. Please," said Horgan nervously.

"You're just unstrung," said Grimes. "You just need a good sleep, that's all."

"If Hibley had shot himself he would have left a note," said Dan. "And you still haven't taken those shells from the automatic into consideration."

"Banion, listen," Grimes said, "you've no way of telling which direction Hibley was sitting in the chair when he shot himself. The shells might have lit anywhere. Furthermore, you and Heidelmann had time to kick them all over the place before you ever thought to look for them. We can't go on anything like that."

"But you still have no proof of who killed that girl June or why?" Dan insisted.

"Beth killed her," said Grimes. "Hibley found that out. When she tried to run away, he followed her. He caught up with her somewhere and took her up to his cabin. He made her confess, and then shot her. Then he shot himself."

"That's all guesswork," said Dan. "Why did Beth kill June in the first place?"

"You as good as explained that yourself, Banion. The girl discovered Beth was implicated in her husband's murder back in 1913. She was going to tell."

"June had a murder rap hanging over her own head. Why would she tell?"

"Listen, Banion, we've been all over that—over and over and over it. She was pregnant. She'd been harassed all she could take. She had reached the point where she didn't give a damn, and was going to turn herself in, too."

"All this is assumption, Grimes. You can't prove any of it. Besides,

Flavin says there was somebody else in the house. Somebody else hit him over the head—not Beth."

"You can't go on that, Banion. Flavin walked into a room. He was hit from behind. Beth was behind him. He can't guarantee whether it was somebody else or not. That's just an impression he has. Ask him."

"Besides," Horgan cut in, "lots of guys commit suicide without leaving notes. Maybe he forgot. Maybe he didn't have a pencil." His voice was pleading.

"I still contend," Dan said, "that Beth was working with somebody else in the Hibley household. Otherwise, how did she know Mrs. Hibley had ordered a new maid from a Frenton employment agency?"

"That, I admit, I don't know," said Grimes. "But there are so many possible ways, your assumption isn't justified. She could have found out from the agency. Then there's gossip. Mrs. Garland no doubt mentioned it to others. It got mouthed around. Beth heard about it, and—"

"Yes, but the exact timing at the railroad station. Grimes, use some sense."

"Banion, you've just gone fanatic on this case. I've admitted my mistakes. Now why don't you be reasonable? Flavin's free. We dropped the charges against him. He's waiting with Tom Regan and your wife in the outer office now. What in the hell more do you want out of this?"

"I'm just not satisfied. I'm not convinced."

"All right, who did it then? Who else do you suspect?"

"I don't know. I don't know what to say. Good God, I'm tired."

"Well, there you are, Banion. Get yourself a sleep and the whole thing will look simpler."

"Get yourself a couple of stiff shots and a little shut-eye," said Horgan. "Pull yourself together."

"What are you going to do about Heidelmann?" Dan asked.

"Nothing," said Grimes. "Turn him loose, I guess. We haven't got anything on him, unless you want to bring any charges."

"No, to hell with it," said Dan. "Do as you please. I'm going to get some sleep."

In the outer office, Ralph Flavin greeted Dan with a speech he'd evidently been rehearsing over and over in his mind. "I sure want to thank you, Mr. Banion. If it hadn't been for you—"

Tom Regan cut him short. "You're gonna come out to the house," he said. "Amy's baked a ham. You can stretch out on the bed till things are ready."

"Dan," Ethel said, "I'm proud of you. Everyone's proud of you. You look tired, darling. You look all played out."

"Jesus, I'm sleepy," Dan said.

"He's tired," said Regan. "Let's bring him out to the house, and—"

"No, Tom. I've got to get some sleep," Dan said.

"Well, that's what I'm telling you," Regan insisted. "You can stretch out on the bed. Nobody will bother you. We've planned a little celebration."

"Whatever you feel like, darling. You're to do just as you want," said Ethel.

"Well, all right. Let's go. But I'm going to sleep. My God! Night after night. I'm fed up with the whole business. I'm through. Let 'em do as they please."

At the Regan house, Shirley was festooning the walls with strips of colored crepe paper. "Oh, you came too soon," she said. "It's not ready yet."

Amy was laboring fiercely at the stove, pushing hot pans around and tapping a big spoon on the edges. "Now everybody sit down," she said. "There isn't a thing to be done. Everything's cooking."

Regan was fighting with the cork on a bottle of raisin wine. "All's well that ends well," he chanted. "I knew it would wind up with Grimes being a jackass. Get some glasses, young fellow."

"I'm really tired," Dan said. "Where's this bed you were talking about?"

"Tom," Amy called from the stove, "the poor man is half dead. Leave those bottles alone and show him to the bedroom."

"He wants a little drink first," said Tom.

"No, thanks," Dan said. "Just show me where I can lie down."

"Come on, darling. We'll let you sleep," said Ethel. "Where shall I take him?"

"This way," Shirley said. She led them to the Regans' bedroom. Dan fell onto the springs and closed his eyes. Ethel began taking his shoes off.

"You got a peach of a man," said Shirley.

"If I can keep him in one piece," said Ethel.

"God, this feels good," said Dan.

Shirley heaved a quilt over him. "You did a good job," she said. "You sure know the angles on springing people from the can. I wish you'd work a miracle for me sometime."

"Now go to sleep," said Ethel. "Do you want us to wake you when dinner's ready?"

"Say, Ethel," Dan said, "what about Mrs. Garland's daughter and that movie. How'd you come out on those things?"

"Oh, Dan, that doesn't matter now. You get some sleep."

"How'd you come out? Tell me."

"Well, Mrs. Garland had visited her daughter, just as she said. They've got the funniest baby, Dan. I wish you could have seen it."

"How about the movie. What show was there?"

"*Mutiny on the Bounty*, just what Farnsworth said. Darling, it doesn't matter now. Your brain's on a merry-go-round."

"I guess you're right."

"Do you want us to wake you when dinner's ready?"

"No. No. Don't wake me. I want to sleep. I want to forget the whole damn thing. Don't wake me."

"All right, darling, now you sleep."

In the kitchen, Murphy and Connie were sitting bored and annoyed on the couch. Amy was shaking her spoon at them. "And you're to be perfectly quiet so that Mr. Banion can sleep," she warned.

"Try this," said Regan, handing Flavin a glass of raisin wine.

"Mr. Banion doesn't seem to be satisfied," said Flavin.

"Well, everybody's out of jail," said Regan, "and that's good enough. If we investigate any further the whole county may land in the penitentiary."

In the bedroom Dan found to his annoyance that he couldn't sleep. The elements of the case kept circling around in his mind. Several times he dozed off, only to wake with the happenings of the past few days all mixed with dreams in his brain.

Finally he sat up and lit a cigaret from a pack he found on a side table. He didn't know how long he'd been lying there, but the clatter of dishes and murmur of voices from the kitchen indicated dinner was in progress. Somehow he wasn't hungry.

The cigaret tasted good. Maybe he should trace the whole thing over in his mind. Maybe that would satisfy him. If he could only convince himself that Beth was the murderer, he could rest. Until then, his brain wouldn't relax.

Step by step he relived every moment of the past few days in his memory, puffing slowly at the cigaret. Then he studied each participant, his conversation, actions, and behavior. Finally, he began trying out each person as a possible accomplice of Beth. Suddenly he sat straight up in bed and threw back the quilt.

That might be it. A trivial, silly thing, but it might be it.

He snuffed out the cigaret, got up, and paced the floor in his socks. Then he searched through the pockets of his coat. Yes, there was the address on the back of an old envelope. It was a wild guess, but possible. If it didn't work, people might think he were crazy.

He paced the floor a while longer deliberating, then began putting his shoes on. There was only one way to find out. After all, he reasoned, civilization would never have progressed at all if men had been afraid of making damned fools of themselves on occasion.

When his hand was on the doorknob, he hesitated. There was no sense in going out there and trying to explain to them. They'd think he was delirious. They'd argue him out of it.

Through the open window he could see the rattletrap roadster he had rented parked in the Regans' yard. That would be a better way. He scribbled a note, pinned it to the pillow, and climbed out the window.

The car made a lot of noise starting, but he hoped the hilarity of the dinner table would drown it out. Another minute and he was on the highway speeding toward Hamilton.

CHAPTER TWENTY-EIGHT

A tall, sick-looking woman answered the door at the cottage Dan called at.

"Dewey? Yes, Dewey's here," she said. "Dewey," she yelled into the back of the house. "Dewey. A gentleman's here."

A short, thin-faced man in horn-rimmed spectacles came slowly through the hall, his head cocked inquisitively to one side.

"Are you Dewey Ferguson?" Dan asked.

"Yes," he said with a kind of defensive caution. He relaxed when Dan introduced himself. "Yes, my Aunt Minnie told me about you. I'm so glad you called. I talked with your wife the other day. I have quite a few specimens you're going to be quite interested in."

"Well, that will have to wait," Dan said. "Right now I want you to take a ride with me. It shouldn't take us more than an hour."

Dewey's caution returned at the suggestion. When Dan explained what he wanted, he was all the more reluctant. "I don't feel it's our business to intrude," he complained.

Dan turned on all the high-pressure persuasiveness he could muster.

"Well, if you say Mrs. Hibley wishes it."

"She insists on it," Dan lied.

"Well, then, I suppose there'd really be no harm." Dewey put on a rounded Panama hat that looked like a child's Sunday headgear, and went along.

Dan parked some distance from the Hibley house, and they approached on foot. When they reached the edge of the picket fence, he held Dewey back and peered into the garden. It was deserted.

"What are you looking for?" Dewey asked.

"Nothing," Dan said. "I just thought I saw something."

They entered the gate, and Dan led the way around to the rear of the house.

"Hadn't we better go in and speak to Mrs. Hibley?" asked Dewey.

"She's taking a nap," said Dan. "She doesn't want to be disturbed."

"Oh," said Dewey.

"Now show me exactly where you saw the gardener digging that afternoon when you were up in the tree."

"It was that tree," said Dewey, pointing to the neighboring yard.

"Yes, that was the tree. Now where did you see him digging?"

Dewey put one finger on his chin and circled around over quite an area. Several times he looked back at the tree, then at the ground. "There," he said, pointing to a particular spot. "As nearly as I can remember, it was about there."

Dan glanced around, saw a shovel leaning against the garage, and secured it. He began to dig. Not trusting Dewey's memory too much, he dug widely. Soon he had made quite a trench and was beginning to feel panicky. This would be hard to explain.

He began digging the whole area a little deeper.

"I don't understand what you're doing," said Dewey.

"It's a sort of WPA project," said Dan.

"Oh, for the government," said Dewey seriously.

Dan cursed under his breath and dug frantically. Suddenly a corner of cloth appeared under the shovel. He threw the shovel aside and began scraping with his hands. In a moment he stood up and unfurled a dirt encrusted khaki shirt. As he did so, a large clasp knife fell from its folds and landed at his feet.

"It's a shirt," said Dewey.

Dan examined the front of it. There were dark stains all down it and on the sleeves. He stooped to pick up the knife, and his nerves froze at the sound of a voice in back of them.

"Give me that."

He picked up the knife and turned. A genuine fear gripped him inside as he did. This was no joke.

"Give it to me," ordered Otis Farnsworth. He held a revolver in one hand and reached out with the other. Dan handed him the shirt and the knife.

"Now head for that garage, quick."

Dewey was trembling so badly he could hardly walk. Inside the garage, Farnsworth motioned toward the stairway leading above.

They mounted to his living quarters under the eaves. He tossed the shirt and knife on a table and nodded to a couch covered with an old army blanket. "Sit down."

A kettle was boiling on a small electric stove. "I always like a cup of tea this time of the afternoon," he said. "You drink tea?"

"Not with a gun pointed at me," Dan said.

"Hmm! Sensitive nerves. Some people are like that. It's a good thing I looked out the window. You're pretty sharp, Banion."

"I wondered why a man would come home from the movies and start digging in the garden immediately," Dan said.

With his free hand, Farnsworth poured hot water into a teapot on the table, and settled into a spindle rocking chair to wait for it to seep. "How'd you know that?"

"Ferguson here saw you. He was up a tree in the next yard."

Farnsworth eyed Ferguson sadly. "Always somebody to see. Always eyes somewhere."

"And I wondered whether a gardener would go off to the movies and have a lawn spray going. Ralph Flavin saw it when he came in the gate. You never went to the movies at all. Well, you almost got by with it," Dan said.

"Almost?"

"You might as well put that gun away. It's not going to help you."

"Well, that's something we don't know yet, Banion."

Dewey Ferguson sat staring wide-eyed through his horn-rimmed spectacles. He said nothing, but looked from one to the other as they spoke.

"You killed Hibley and Beth, didn't you," Dan said.

"They won't be missed."

"How about the girl?"

"She was wanted for murder. Her life wasn't worth anything." Farnsworth tested the tea in a cup, then poured. "You said you were a gardener."

"An amateur," Dan said.

"Well, that's enough. You've weeded out a garden. You've killed a plant here and there so another could live. You've killed snails and pests. You're dealing with life there—with living things—beautiful living things. People aren't beautiful, Banion."

"Aren't they?"

"Beth, for instance. Was she beautiful?"

"Once."

"Not ever, Banion. She may have had a beautiful face. That's all. Change your mind about tea?"

"No. Go ahead and talk. You've been hungry to talk. Now's your chance."

"You're pretty sharp, Banion."

"Maybe if you talk enough you can convince yourself."

"Don't get me wrong, Banion. I never wanted to kill anybody. All I ever wanted was to be let alone. I didn't want to kill that girl any more than I wanted to kill Beth or Hibley or any of the others."

"Others?"

"You didn't think it began with them, did you? Where do you think I learned gardening?"

Dan shrugged.

"San Quentin. You know what that is."

"It's a penitentiary in California."

"That's it. I had plenty of time to learn. Got real fond of it. I've got what they call a green thumb. I can make anything grow."

"Was that for murder?"

"No, that was forgery. Later, when I got out—well, it was an accident, you might say. I didn't intend to kill the guy. It was over a woman."

"But you killed him."

"Well, yes. And that would have been the end of it, but another fellow found out and blackmailed me. I paid him for a while." Farnsworth was thoughtful.

"And then?"

"And then, Banion, I reasoned it out. This fellow was no good. He was a weed. In a garden you pull weeds. In life you let things get overrun with them. I killed him."

"That made two."

"Yes, that made two. But it wasn't as easy as I figured. I made some fumbles and had to pull out. I came here."

"Why here?"

"Well, I went to Frenton first. Got a job in a big nursery there. Changed my name to Farnsworth. I faked a lot of references and the guy never bothered to check up. I stayed there quite a while."

"What's your real name?"

"Gerwig. Leonard Gerwig. I'd have been all right if I'd stayed there. But Hibley was fixing things up down here. He ordered a lot of plants and trees from this nursery, and I was sent down here to put them in. I sort of took a liking to the place. Hibley—that was Vern Hibley—offered me the job. I took it. I was a fool. He was State Attorney General. In his business, he soon found out who I was. Well, as it happened, I'd been keeping my own eyes open. I had something on him, too. Enough to keep his mouth shut. He was a shrewd man."

"So I've noticed."

"He was shrewder than I thought. When he died, I figured that was the end of it, and I'd be let alone. I like it here. That's all I ever wanted was to be let alone. I was a fool not to let matters be."

"Well, what happened?"

"A man's a man. I got in the habit of going to Beth's place in Sawtooth every once in a while. I got to know her, and one night she made me a deal. Some way she'd found out Mrs. Hibley wanted a new maid. She had this girl she wanted to get a job for. 'You get that job for her,' she said. 'Say she's your cousin or some relative. And I'll give you fifty bucks.'"

"Did you know who the girl was?" Dan asked.

"Of course not. I thought it was just a girl needed a job. Anyhow, Mrs. Hibley wouldn't go for it. She was set on this girl from the agency. Then Beth thought up this thing about meeting the agency girl at the station—offered me a hundred dollars if I'd co-operate."

"Didn't that make you suspect there was something more involved?"

"I wasn't using my head, I guess. I wanted that hundred dollars. I've been saving up to get a piece of ground of my own. I'm going to buy a lot down in Sawtooth. I expect to move down there next spring."

The positive calm with which Farnsworth said this sent a chill through Dan. "You mean you actually expect—"

"Well, next summer at the latest."

"But how—"

"I didn't know about what was really going on," Farnsworth continued, "until the day Mrs. Hibley went to Frenton, and Mrs. Garland went to visit her daughter. I went in the house and I heard Esther on the phone saying to somebody she wanted to tell everything. I thought she meant she was going to say how she got her job. So when she hung up I asked her not to do that because she would get me fired."

"What did she say then?"

"She said, 'You and Beth have threatened me all you are going to. I know all about you and Beth. I know all about you, Mr. Gerwig.'"

"How did she know your real name was Gerwig?"

"That hit me hard. I didn't know. I began asking questions. It seemed she'd found some papers in the house—found 'em hid in a hollow bedpost in Mrs. Hibley's room. One of them was about Beth, and some other ones were all about me; where I was wanted and everything. Stuff Vern Hibley had left."

"Then Mrs. Hibley must have known about you, too."

"No, the papers only referred to Leonard Gerwig. Mrs. Hibley never thought of them in connection with me. But this girl did because she thought I was in with Beth on the whole business. That was on account of the way we met her at the railroad station. The other paper was about Beth, so she took it for granted the rest were about me. And she was right."

"Did she show you the papers?"

"Not at first, but I made her show me where they were."

"How did you do that?"

"I damn near had to kill her."

"And then—"

"Well, then I did kill her. There wasn't anything else I could do. She was hysterical."

"What did you do with the papers?"

"The ones about me, I burned. The one about Beth, I kept. That was for my own protection."

"Well, how did Beth happen to come on the scene that day?"

"She came a short while after. She knew Mrs. Hibley had gone to Frenton, and she came out to try to make Esther give her the paper. She was plenty scared when she saw what had happened. I said, 'Beth, you'd better help me, or I'll turn that paper over to the police.'"

"Then what?"

"Well, Beth moved her car into the garage to get it off the street out of sight. She was scared. We didn't have much time to think. Then that young fellow came looking for food. That gave us an idea."

"It was a pretty silly idea."

"It might have worked if you'd kept your nose out."

"Why did you kill Hibley?"

"There wasn't anything else I could do. When he gave me that note, I steamed it open and read it."

"The note to me?"

"Yeah. I figured he was after Beth. I got up to the cabin before him and kept out of sight. He brought Beth in. I guess he followed her when she tried to run away. He was going to kill her. He was crazy about that girl. Beth got scared and told him about me. I had to kill them both." Farnsworth put his teacup aside.

"It almost worked," said Dan.

"Why almost?"

"You've kind of reached the end."

"I hope so," said Farnsworth. "All I want is to be let alone. I guess you've got a car around here somewhere."

Dan said nothing.

"I asked you if you had a car around here," Farnsworth repeated.

"I'll drive you to the police station," Dan said. "That's the only thing left, Farnsworth."

"Is that your opinion? Where's your car?"

"Put that gun away and I'll tell you."

Farnsworth stood up and leveled the revolver at them. "Start moving," he said.

"Where to?" Dan asked.

"Start moving. I know the car you've been using, Banion. I guess we'll find it all right."

As they passed through the garage downstairs, Farnsworth selected a shovel and took it along. Outside, he put the gun in his pocket, but kept his hand there. In the street, he quickly spotted the roadster.

"You two get in first," he said, "and if either one of you opens his mouth, you'll both get it right then." He climbed in after them.

"Where to?" Dan asked.

"Just you drive the way I tell you. Keep on this street till we get out of town."

Dan put the car in gear and followed instructions. Ferguson was still silent. He had stopped trembling, but his face was pale and his eyes frightened.

Dan reasoned every possible diversion along the way, but couldn't bring himself to take a chance. Farnsworth was too coldly serious. There was a place where he could have swung the car into a pole, not twenty feet from a highway patrolman, but he knew that it would have been suicide.

Outside the town, Farnsworth directed him to follow the main highway for about twenty miles, then ordered him to turn onto a dirt road. It led farther and farther from all signs of habitation. Any hope of attracting attention now was gone.

The road entered a thick forest, and when they were some distance into it, Farnsworth ordered Dan to pull over to the side and stop.

"Get out. This is the place," he said.

"What's the idea?" Dan asked when they were standing in the road.

"Go on. Into those trees. Do as I tell you," Farnsworth said.

A short distance through the thicket, they came to a slight clearing. Farnsworth handed the shovel to Dan. "Start digging," he ordered.

"What for?" Dan asked.

"What do you think? You seemed to like digging."

It occurred to Dan to swing at him with the shovel and take his chances, but Farnsworth kept too much distance between them. Dan removed his coat and began digging.

"Don't go too slow, Banion. I'm not in an awful hurry, but I can't waste too much time."

"I ought to tell you to go to hell and let you do this yourself," Dan said.

"You won't."

Dan hesitated a moment, then resumed digging. Fear and panic were mounting in him. To Farnsworth he was no more than a snail or a weed. The man had rationalized all sensibility about killing out of his head. Human beings were as casual as plants or bugs to him.

After a while, Farnsworth said, "That's enough for now. Let him spell you." He motioned the revolver at Ferguson.

Without a word, Ferguson rose from the ground where he'd been sitting and accepted the shovel from Dan. Then he dug as if trying to make good on a job. The dirt flew furiously. Dan became uneasy at the speed with which the grave was deepening.

"For God's sake, Farnsworth, have some humanity," Dan implored. "You can't get by with this." His voice cracked badly. He felt the sickness of fear gripping his stomach.

"You won't be missed, Banion."

"It won't help you any at all," Dan argued. "For God's sake don't kill us for nothing. They're going to catch you."

"You're a fool, Banion. And this fellow—I don't know who he is—but he's nobody."

"He's a human being. What would you call somebody?"

"Well, not him. What's his name?"

"Ferguson. Dewey Ferguson."

Ferguson went on digging as if they were not referring to him.

"Look at him," Farnsworth said scornfully. "What use do you think he is to himself or anyone else? He's like a worm. Just crawling muck. That's what most people are, Banion. Crawling muck. And you think it's wrong to kill him."

"He wants to live. I want to live."

"So does a snail."

"So do you."

"If you want to live, you've got to kill. Everything lives by killing. You ought to know that, Banion. I don't have any choice. All I ever wanted was to be let alone. I've got what they call the green thumb. I make things grow. I'm a good gardener."

"You're a murderer."

"There are a lot worse things than murder, Banion."

"You've got a twisted brain like a diseased plant. You ought to be in an institution," Dan said.

"You shut your goddamn mouth, Banion."

"You're crazy, Farnsworth."

Farnsworth gripped the revolver tightly and clenched his teeth. Then he changed his mind. "All right, you," he said to Ferguson. "Lay off. Let Banion do the digging."

"Is this punishment?" Dan asked.

"Take the shovel and dig," snapped Farnsworth.

Ferguson stopped and wiped his brow with the back of his sleeve. He dragged the shovel over toward them.

"Give it to him," said Farnsworth.

Ferguson suddenly snapped like a spring. It was too fast for Dan's eye to catch. There was a metallic, crunching sound as the shovel struck Farnsworth's head, then a thump as he hit the ground. The shovel was flailing like mad in Ferguson's hands, hitting again and again.

Dan had to hold his arms to stop him.

"Crawling muck," panted Ferguson. "Crawling muck, he said."

"Hold it," said Dan. "Hold it. That's enough. Stop."

Ferguson dropped the shovel and stood off panting.

"Jesus Christ!" said Dan. Farnsworth's head was a mass of blood. Dan picked up the revolver and put it in his pocket.

"Crawling muck, he said," repeated Ferguson.

"Come on. Give me a hand. We've got to get him out of here."

Ferguson kneeled to help. "Crawling muck," he repeated. "Did you hear him?"

"My God, you're all right. I couldn't think of anything," Dan said.

Ferguson began to weep hysterically. "I'll kill him, Mr. Banion. I'll kill him."

"Easy, Ferguson. You did swell. Get him up to the car."

CHAPTER TWENTY-NINE

"Well, don't it beat hell," Ike Miller said over the phone from San Diego when Dan had given him the final details. "What a picture! You digging your own grave. I think you're giving me a lot of malarkey. You made that part of it up. But it's good."

"I'm telling you the truth," Dan said. "He had a gun on me. What else could I do?"

"Yes, yes, yes. And who would dig his own grave when he knows he's gonna be shot anyway?"

"That's the thing, Ike. You never lose hope. So you dig your grave and hope for a miracle."

"And the bird's egg got you out of it. Why didn't you slug him, you dope. If it hadn't been for the bird's egg you'd be underground."

"Well, I guess Farnsworth wasn't expecting anything from him, and wasn't watching him so much. It surprised me as much as it did him."

"You never can tell about these little people. Is he going to live?"

"The best doctors in the state are trying to pull him through in order that they can electrocute him in the correct manner."

"The world is nuts, Dan. What are you going to do now?"

"Take a vacation."

"With that five grand reward money you can go around the world."

"I've got plans for that dough, Ike."

"Yeah? What are you cooking?"

"Well, for one thing, I'm going to set a little dame here up in a hat shop. Her name is Shirley."

"Oh, oh. I knew that marriage racket wouldn't last long."

"No, you've got it wrong. It isn't that way at all."

"That's what they all say. But nobody ever sets a guy up in a hat shop. It's always a blonde. She is blonde, isn't she?"

"Yes, but—"

"You're a sucker, Dan. There's blondes all over the beach out here and all you have to buy 'em is an ice-cream cone."

"Ike, you're filthy-minded."

"I'm the little folks, Dan. I'm the hope of the world. What else are you planning?"

"Well, for another thing, I'm going to buy a washing machine for a woman named Amy."

"As I said, the world is nuts."

Dan was phoning from Vance Dalbert's office. When he hung up, Vance said, "If you had any sense, Dan, you'd listen to what I say and come in with me. I've got this paper and another one over in Winfield—the *Bugle*."

"Well, you can blow it. I'm taking a vacation, then heading west."

"Sooner or later, Dan, you're going to have to settle down and take things seriously."

"Take things seriously!"

"Yes, take things seriously."

"Like you."

"If you want to put it that way, like me. You can't be irresponsible all your life."

"Irresponsible!"

"Yes. Irresponsible. Erratic."

"Let me get this straight, Vance. You're responsible, and I'm erratic."

"That's right. That's what it amounts to, doesn't it?"

"Listen, Vance, if it had been up to you and Grimes, you'd have sent Flavin to the chair."

"I wouldn't say that. The evidence was very misleading."

"Yet you're responsible and I'm a screwball."

"I didn't say screwball, Dan."

"Erratic."

"Yes, erratic. It's time you settled down."

"Like you."

"Very well, like me."

"Listen, Vance, the only interest you have left in the world is making money for yourself."

"Well, aren't we all?"

Ethel, coming in, interrupted them. "Dan, Tom's waiting to drive us to the station. We haven't much time."

"Well, let me know if you change your mind," said Vance. "There's a good opportunity here."

As the train pulled out, Tom Regan and Shirley stood on the platform waving until they were out of sight.

"I'm going to do nothing but lie in the sun and loaf for two weeks," Dan said.

"You deserve it, darling," Ethel agreed. "And after that—"

"After that I've got a surprise for you."

"I don't want any surprises. After that, I was thinking, now that you've got a good job—"

"I was thinking we might go to San Francisco," Dan said. "I've got a friend out there, and according to what he writes—"

"No."

"Well, you haven't heard what I was going to say."

"The answer is, no."

"That's a remarkable city, and I thought—"

"Dan, you've got a job. You've got a good opportunity. Mr. Dempsey thinks the world of you."

"Yeah? He'll think I'm the world for about one week. After that he'll decide I'm a spoonful of dirt."

"Dan, aren't we ever going to amount to anything? Or are we going to be kicking around from one cheesy apartment to another all our lives?"

"But you'd like San Francisco. You've never been there."

"Dan, I was looking at houses in Frenton before I came down.

Houses with roofs and yards. Nobody upstairs and nobody downstairs.
Your own house. We have enough with this reward money to—"

"But, Ethel. That's how you learn things; from the people upstairs
and the people downstairs."

"Dan, we've simply got to settle down sometime."

"You don't want to live in Frenton all your life, do you?" Dan's voice
was shocked.

"Dan, I sometimes wish that some of these little squirts who think
you're such a dream could have you for a while. It would punish them
enough. What would you do in San Francisco? I suppose the streets
are paved with gold out there."

"To tell you the truth, Ethel, you probably won't believe it, but that's
exactly what this friend of mine says."

THE END

THE BANDAGED NUDE

– – – – – – –

by Robert Finnegan

CHAPTER ONE

When the young fellow came into the bar and straddled a nearby stool, Dan Banion hardly noticed him at first. Dan had thoughts of his own, and a barroom in midafternoon is sometimes a good place to think. It's like a lull in a battle. The noon rush is over, and the five o'clock going-home business won't start for some time. The evening riot is a long way off. You can sip your beer in peace without drunks lurching against you or the juke box pounding sentimentality in your ears.

This particular bar was called The Wreck. It was new to Dan, as was the whole city. New, and yet the same old thing. How many cities had he given a try since his discharge from the army? New York, Chicago, New Orleans, and now San Francisco.

The others had all got on his nerves within a week or so. He had to get out of them. San Francisco seemed no different, but maybe he'd stay here. He had been here about a week and had managed to get a reporter job on the *Journal*. The *Journal* didn't seem to be a bad setup as newspapers went. Anyhow, he'd have to settle down sooner or later.

Maybe it was just a world without Ethel that got on his nerves. His wife had died while he was in the army, and it made a particularly empty homecoming. But probably it was more than that. Other people felt it too. He could see it in their eyes and sense it in their conversation. Restlessness. Dissatisfaction. An uncertainty about the world and about themselves. The war had left everybody on edge.

The conversation between the young fellow who had come in and the bartender began to intrude on Dan's thoughts.

"Did you manage to remember that name, Chuck?" the young fellow asked.

The bartender, a stout, bald Irishman with fat hands and stubby fingers, stopped polishing a glass, removed a cigar from his mouth, and looked wistfully at the ceiling. "Jefferson? Jeffries? Jepperson?" He put the cigar back in his mouth and resumed shining the glass. "I can't remember, Kent. He was a lawyer, I think. A cheap, shyster lawyer. That's what he looked like. What'll you have, Kent?"

The young man was wearing a brand-new tweed suit of the hasty reconversion variety being sold to veterans. Dan spotted the familiar "ruptured duck" in his lapel. Closely cropped brown hair showed under the rim of his hat, shoved back on his head. Dan liked the face.

"What about the boss?" the young fellow said, looking rather worried. "Didn't he have any record? Give me an ale, Chuck."

Chuck wrinkled his nose in disgust. "Naw, hell, that fool don't keep a record of anything if he can help it. He can't remember." He shuffled his giant bulk lazily toward the refrigerator case.

Dan held up an empty glass significantly as he passed.

Chuck grunted. "Be with you in a minute, Bud." The glass door was below the bar level, and he had to stoop for it.

"Mine's an ale too, while you're at it," Dan said.

"You guys'll go batty drinkin' that stuff." Chuck stood up with two bottles clutched between the fingers of one hand. With the other he dusted ashes from his protruding stomach. "All the winos down on skid row are off the muscatel and are drinkin' ale." He eased the caps off the bottles and thumped them with glasses in front of the two men.

Dan turned the bottle in his hand. "What's the idea?"

"Three bottles are enough to get you drunk," the young fellow said, with a smile.

"Enough to send you to the dippy bag, you mean," Chuck corrected. "I think they needle it with somethin' to give it a stronger kick."

The young man poured his ale thoughtfully. "You've got to get a kick out of something, Chuck. It's a wonder we're not all bugs."

"You'll get over it," Chuck said. "There've been wars before."

"Not like that one," the young fellow said.

"What outfit were you in?" Dan asked.

"104th—Timberwolves."

"You had it tough. I was with the 90th."

"The 90th!" The young man reflected. "You had your share."

"All I want," Dan said.

The young fellow raised his glass. "Here's to making some sense of things from now on."

Chuck grunted. "If you can make any sense of this mess, you're a genius. I was in the last one."

"A guy needs a world to live in," the young man said. Chuck arched his eyebrows. "What's this we're standin' on? Ain't this a world?"

"Skip it." The young man shrugged and assumed a back-to-earth tone. "Tell me, Chuck, if you ever saw that guy again, do you think you'd recognize him?"

"The guy who bought the pitcher?"

"Yeah."

Chuck nodded positively. "Oh yeah. I'd know him. I don't forget faces."

"If you ever see him in here again, try to get his name, will you?"

"Sure, Kent. Be glad to. Anything wrong?"

"I'm not sure. I'm just curious."

Chuck looked sorrowful. "The boss was a damn fool to sell that pitcher. It brought a lot of guys in here. I used to look at it myself." He swiveled his head and gazed up at a huge sepia print of a redwood tree that hung above the bar. The tree had a tunnel chopped in its base, and an old-fashioned automobile was driving through. "That goddamn thing!" he sneered in disgust.

"I'd give a lot to know who bought it," the young man said.

Chuck turned to Dan. "Jesus, it was a lovely thing! Pitcher of a dame. Nothin' on. What hips! Whew! And a pair of tomatoes that would make your mouth water." He poised his fat hands over his chest to indicate size. "Used to hang right up there over the bar."

"I just want to know who got it," the young man repeated doggedly.

Chuck's shoulders heaved with laughter. "Guys used to sneak in here to eye it." He leaned on the bar and imitated a man sneaking a look. "They pretended they wasn't even interested. Just drinkin' their liquor. Soon as they thought nobody was watchin' them, up goes their eyes." He rolled his eyes upward lasciviously.

She had come in so quietly they hadn't noticed her. "Kent," she said in a soft voice. They all turned, startled.

"Oh, hello, Marian," the young man said. "Can I buy you a drink?" His voice was easy and casual.

Chuck polished a glass fiercely and looked shy at having been caught in the middle of such a story.

Dan had difficulty taking his eyes off her. He looked away, but found his eyes creeping back again. She noticed it. He turned his back and watched her reflection in the mirror behind the bar.

Her voice was urgent. "No, Kent. Can't we go somewhere and talk? I've got to talk to you."

"Certainly." Kent was polite and matter-of-fact—a little artificially so, Dan thought. He drained his glass and slid from the stool. "See you later, Chuck."

As the girl turned to go, she caught Dan's eyes in the mirror. Her dark eyes were troubled and appealing. For an instant they looked deeply in his, then snapped away.

As the door closed behind them, Dan said, "Wow!"

Chuck leaned against the back bar and sighed. "Sweet dish, ain't she? I go for brunettes." Nevertheless, he shook his head with an air of disapproval.

"Anything wrong?" Dan asked.

Chuck woke gradually from his reverie. "Wrong? Oh, no. At least nothin' you got to worry about."

"Do you have any more like her in this town?"

"Good-lookin' dames? Sure. All shapes and sizes." Chuck spoke proudly, as if he'd fathered them all. Suddenly his eyes sparkled with amusement, and he leaned closer. "Pipe this comin' in. He's one of my regulars."

A bony, gray little man in a seedy suit wandered in talking to himself at a rapid rate in an angry, challenging voice. He chose a distant stool, but his jabbering was plainly audible. "Clean it up," he said indignantly. "Clean it up. As if they knew. The damn fools! Five bucks, she says. Five bucks for what? Hell! Forty years for nothin'. I saw them. Christ! It was all over the place. Clean it up yourself. Ninety dollars a pound. The muckin' liars. Don't tell me. I was there. Shove it yourself. Who wouldn't run? Give her the steam, goddamn it, give her the steam. Ninety dollars a pound. As if you wouldn't know the difference. Starch in their pants! Humph! Starch in their pants. Ask me. I'll tell you."

"What's he talking about?" Dan asked.

Chuck shrugged his shoulders. "Search me. I've listened to him for hours. Can't make head or tail of it."

Without even asking the little man what he wanted, Chuck uncapped a bottle of ale, put it down in front of him, and scooped up fifteen cents. When he returned, he said, "That guy never stops talkin' day or night. I've got another one comes here is stone dumb. Can't speak a word. Ain't it a kick?"

CHAPTER TWO

At about eleven the next morning, a truck driver named Steve Hannegan was hauling a load of packing cases along Valencia Street. He was thinking about his wife, who had been moody and irritable ever since he got out of the Marines. His mind was not on his driving.

Suddenly, a little brown coupe coming head on shocked him out of his thoughts. It was too late. He swung the wheel frantically to the right and stomped the brakes, but his big truck smashed the plate glass window of a barber shop before it stopped. The coupe sideswiped the rear end of the truck, ripping loose several cases which fell to the street with a loud crash.

The coupe careened crazily and came to a stop still upright, but with the left side badly smashed. The crash, followed by the sound of tinkling glass, brought people out of their houses for a block around.

The barber, with a razor in his hand, and a man half-shaved, with the cloth still around his neck, came out of the shop bug-eyed.

Slowly, cursing to himself, Hannegan stepped down from the cab of the truck. A glance at the coupe showed a badly scared woman being helped out by spectators. Useless for him to vent his wrath there. Silently he began to inspect his truck.

"What's the matter with you?" the barber shouted. "You crazy? You pay for that window, every cent."

Hannegan ignored him. With the dignity of a gladiator, a storm mounting inside him, he walked slowly around and examined the rear end of the truck.

"What happened?" a man asked foolishly from the gathering crowd. "Was it an accident?"

Hannegan turned, looked the man up and down without saying a word, and spat.

The crowd moved in to get a look. The woman from the brown coupe, pale and quivering, was being helped to the sidewalk by a man. Hannegan shook his head gravely. "Tsch, tsch, tsch, tsch."

"She doesn't seem to be hurt," said the man helping her. "Just shock."

"Somebody better call an ambulance," Hannegan said.

A cop swam through the crowd, his arms pushing and flailing about him. "Clear out. Make room. Stand back. Make way."

"It was the lady's fault," a voice volunteered. "I saw it. She was on the wrong side of the street."

"She tried to pass at a bad time," said another.

Hannegan was quietly writing down the names and addresses of witnesses with a tiny stub of a pencil, which he licked again and again for each new name.

"What happened?" the cop demanded.

Hannegan waved the stub of a pencil at the truck. "Dame comin' up the wrong side of the street. Swung in here to miss her." He resumed his writing.

The cop put the backs of his hands on his hips and looked the wreck over. He shook his head disapprovingly, then turned and began abusing the crowd. "Come on, now. Get back. Go on home. Get out of the street. Make a passage here."

In due time the crowd lost interest and scattered away. The ambulance had come with its awful wail, and the creepy white stretcher had carried away its trembling burden. When the siren dwindled in the distance, they knew there was nothing more to see.

A group of eager men and boys had rolled the damaged coupe out of the street. The barber was sweeping broken glass out of his shop.

"All right," the cop said to Hannegan. "I don't think your truck's hurt much. You can pull out any time."

Hannegan drew the back of a dirty hand across his mouth. "I could do with a shot first." He surveyed the street.

"There's a little place around the corner," the cop suggested. "Mickey's."

"You want one?"

"Well, now, I don't know. Against the rules."

"What the hell? Let's go."

The cop pointed to the rear of the truck. "Don't you want to load those cases back on?"

"I damn near forgot." Hannegan walked around in back. Three of the long cases had fallen. Only one of them was badly smashed. He stooped and examined it.

"What's in it?" the cop asked.

"Spaghetti," Hannegan said.

"Spaghetti?"

"Yeah. Either that or macaroni."

"In those dirty old cases?"

Hannegan didn't seem to hear the question. He squatted beside the broken case, silent and motionless.

The cop repeated, "In those dirty old cases, spaghetti?"

Hannegan still didn't seem to hear. He had lifted an edge of the crate and was now staring at it with an expressionless face. He was looking at a naked human foot protruding from the box.

CHAPTER THREE

Inspector Gallagher was going rapidly insane, but he was determined not to show it. He mopped an enormous hand over his flabby face and felt the button at the end of his pug nose as if to see if it were still there. Then he poked at his thinning, gray hair with his fingers.

He didn't look correct behind a desk. He was too big. He looked more like a moving man who had just hauled the desk into the room on his back, then sat down behind it to rest. The desk itself looked neglected; a piece of furniture constructed to have complicated business transacted over it, and used only for people to put their feet on. Its top bore nothing but an overloaded tin ash tray and a newspaper that had been unfolded, read, and then folded back again on the wrong creases, so that its corners stuck out fanlike at odd angles.

Inspector Gallagher, sensing that he was being put on the defensive, decided to employ sarcasm. He fixed Steve Hannegan with his small blue eyes. "So Mrs. Hannegan's pride and joy was drivin' out of town with a corpse on his truck, and he didn't even know a thing about it."

Hannegan was a nerveless mountain of bored flesh. "That's the fact," he said, calmly.

"And tell me, where were you headed with this dead body?"

"I didn't know it was there," said Hannegan.

"I asked you, where were you headed?"

"To the incinerator plant."

"What incinerator plant?"

"Our incinerator plant."

"And who," asked Gallagher, "is 'our'?"

"Ours," Hannegan snapped. "The Hogby and Engles Salvage Company"

"And what were you going there for?"

"To burn the spaghetti," said Hannegan, bluntly.

Gallagher leaned forward on his elbows and put the tips of his fingers together. "And what's the idea of burning spaghetti?"

"It's no good."

"Well, what's wrong with it?"

Hannegan eyed him as he would an idiot. "Salt water. It's off the *Albert C. Decker* that was sunk in shallow water, and was raised. We bought her cargo."

Gallagher relaxed back, and the joint of his swivel chair squeaked. He smiled dryly. "Why the 'we'? Are you one of the owners?"

"No. I drive the truck."

"Then why the 'we'?"

Hannegan looked offended, and crossed his legs. "That's my way of lookin' at things."

Gallagher squeaked up in his swivel chair. "All right, the firm bought the bum spaghetti. What did they do that for?"

"We bought the whole cargo. It wasn't all spaghetti. But there were three thousand cases of it. We didn't want the spaghetti, but we wanted the other stuff. It was all or nothing. Now we got to get rid of the spaghetti. We got a lot of stuff like that. That's why we've got this incinerator."

"Do you have to burn it?"

"What else would you do with it? It's no good. It takes up space. There's no place to dump it. If you dump it in the ocean, it floats and piles up on the beach. Then you'd be jumpin' down our necks.

Warehouse space is valuable. So we burn it."

Gallagher fished in his pocket and drew out a smashed pack of cigarettes. He slid one out and poked it in his mouth. "Where is this incinerator of yours?"

"About a mile below Daly City."

"And you were on your way there?"

"I been haulin' cases of spaghetti down there all week. Three thousand cases is a lot."

Gallagher reached in his pocket and drew out a thick, wooden kitchen match, which he poised between his fingers. "And what do you do with it, when you get it down there?"

"I told you, we burn it."

"In the incinerator?"

"Certainly in the incinerator."

Gallagher scratched the match under the edge of the desk and lit the cigarette in his mouth. "What's this incinerator like?"

"Like hell, I'd imagine."

"I mean, how does it operate?" Gallagher shook out the match and deposited it on top of the mounting pile in the ash tray.

"It's just a big furnace."

"Closed in?"

"Certainly, closed in."

Gallagher gestured with one hand vaguely. "This stuff you burn. Is it out in the open? Can you see it? Or do you open a door, shove it in, then close the door?"

"You close the door, of course. Stick your nose in there and it'd burn the face off you."

"You can't see it burning."

"Not after you close the door, no. How could you?"

"I see. And this spaghetti you were burning. Did you take it out of the cases to burn it?"

"What the hell would be the sense of that?"

Gallagher inhaled deeply of his cigarette and blew the smoke in a kind of gasp. "I'm not asking you what's sensible or not sensible. Do you take it out of the cases?"

"No."

"Just pitch the cases in the way they come off the truck?"

"Yes."

"Where have you been taking these cases from?"

"They're in a lot about a block away from Pier 33. The *Albert C. Decker* is tied up there—what's left of her. We unloaded it onto the dock, and we couldn't leave it there. So we moved it to the lot, and we can't leave it there. So we're taking it down to the incinerator and burning it."

Gallagher swiveled around sideways so that he could stare out the window and across the dirty roof of a building nearby. "Has there been any guard over this stuff? A watchman or anything?"

"What's the sense of guarding a pile of bum spaghetti? If anybody wants some, they can help themselves. It'll damn near kill 'em if they try to eat it. The *Albert C. Decker's* been on the bottom over a year. It's plenty salty. Not to mention a lot of crude oil that seeped in."

"Then anybody, any hour of the day or night, could drive by there, pick up a case, and drive off. And nobody'd think anything of it."

"That's right."

"They could take it someplace, dump the spaghetti, put a corpse in its place, nail the lid back on the case, drive down and put it back with the rest, and nobody would know the difference."

"That's right."

Gallagher swiveled around from the window, and his blue little eyes ate into Hannegan's features. "Except the man who loaded it onto the truck."

Hannegan didn't even blink. "Aw, nuts."

"You loaded the truck, didn't you?"

"I loaded the truck."

"And you mean to tell me when you lifted a box with a corpse in it, you couldn't tell any difference between that and a box of spaghetti?"

"No."

"It was heavier, wasn't it?"

"No."

"How much do those boxes weigh?"

"I'd say about a hundred and fifty pounds."

Gallagher looked all the scorn in the world. "And you just pick up hundred-and-fifty-pound cases and toss them around like candy, I guess."

Hannegan shifted his weight in the chair and looked bored. "I had a guy helping me."

"You didn't say that."

"You never asked me."

"What's this guy's name?"

"Carlson never had anything to do with it."

Gallagher's voice barked angrily, "That's for us to determine. How do you know he didn't?"

Hannegan raised his voice to match the Inspector's. "I'm tellin' you, that's all."

"Why wasn't he on the truck with you?"

"Because he's busy over at Pier 33 with the rest of the cargo, that's why. He just came over to give me a hand."

"You don't have to shout. I'm not deaf."

"Well, you're shouting."

Gallagher lowered his voice. "Let's see, now, how about down at the incinerator? Do you unload the truck there?"

"There's another guy down there helps me."

"And you help him burn it."

"So what?"

Gallagher assumed a grave tone. "Understand this, Hannegan. Whoever put that stiff in the box knew exactly where those cases were going, knew what was going to be done with them, and knew what the incinerator was like. They knew exactly what circumstances they'd be disposed of in."

"So maybe they did. Any number of people would know. Hell, we've been using that incinerator for years. We do jobs for all kinds of people. Anybody could know. Anybody could find out. Anybody could have done it."

Gallagher's eyes narrowed, and his voice became grim. "Or, for that matter, you could have done it."

Hannegan uncrossed his legs and crossed them again in the other direction, sighed, and looked at Gallagher as if he pitied his ignorance. "Inspector, use your nut. If I was gonna murder a guy, I'd pick somebody I knew, wouldn't I? Somebody I didn't like. What would I murder that guy for? I don't even know him."

CHAPTER FOUR

Nix Peters opened one half of a large double door and stood aside so that Dan Banion could stick his head in and look around. "In here is where they try the dopes, pickpockets, prostitutes, wife-beaters and suchlike small enterprises," he said. "Of course, it's not in session now."

"Crummy-looking joint," Dan observed.

"Oh, well, now, you take a big-time embezzler, or some society dame who bumps off her husband; we've got regular temples to try them in." Nix closed the door and led the way down the marble-floored corridor.

"Nice of you to show me around," Dan said.

"It's nothing at all, son. Besides, I'm expecting you to loan me money when I run short. In there's the traffic court. Nothing to look at. It's just the same."

Nix Peters was a reporter from a rival paper, the *Herald-Dispatch*. He was six feet tall and towered above Dan. The knobs of his shoulders, elbows, and knees showed under a suit that needed pressing. His hat looked as if it had been put on his head by someone else, and a slight alcoholic flush reddened his cheeks on either side of a prominent, pointed nose. His eyes were friendly, but shy.

Dan was younger and his clothes fitted him better, but they were almost as badly in need of pressing. He was of average height, with features that just missed being handsome. His eyes, thoughtful and inquiring, were what people noticed first about him, and remembered. They were the eyes of a man who never told all that he was thinking.

As they turned a corner of the corridor, Inspector Gallagher came out of his office and started down the hall.

Nix called, "Hey, Neil."

Gallagher paused and looked around. "Don't bother me now, Nix."

They overtook him. "I want you to meet Dan Banion, Neil. He's with the *Journal*. Dan, this is Inspector Gallagher—Homicide Bureau."

"Glad to know you. I'm busy. See you some other time." Gallagher stopped in front of the elevator and poked the button.

"Anything new on the spaghetti-case stiff?" Nix asked.

Gallagher looked at him resentfully. "They just brought it in a half an hour ago. What the hell do you guys think I am?"

"What about the truck driver?" Nix asked.

"He doesn't know his hind end from his elbow."

"What's the stiff look like?"

The elevator arrived. "I'm goin' down to look at it now. Come along, if you want."

The morgue seemed to have strange acoustics, but that wasn't altogether true. Actually, it was because most people's voices change in the presence of the dead.

Inspector Gallagher, Nix Peters, Dan Banion, and a deputy coroner stood around a porcelain-topped table on which the corpse lay covered by a sheet.

Nix prepared himself with an expression of frank and unashamed honor. Dan's face was tense, but controlled. Inspector Gallagher affected hard-boiled cold-bloodedness. The deputy coroner was matter-of-fact. "Of course, there's been no time for an autopsy," he explained.

"Take the sheet off and let's have a look at it," Gallagher said.

The deputy coroner flipped back the cloth.

Nix clapped one hand over his mouth, and slowly dragged it across his chin. The muscles pinched around Inspector Gallagher's eyes.

Dan's mouth fell open in a startled expression.

"You know him?" the deputy coroner asked quickly.

"No such luck," Gallagher said.

"I mean him." The deputy coroner nodded at Dan.

Gallagher looked up at Banion. "You recognize this guy?"

"Well, no."

"What do you mean, 'well, no'? Do you?"

"No."

Gallagher looked at the coroner. "What made you ask?"

"He looked that way. The way he looked when I uncovered it."

Gallagher looked back at Dan. "What did you think you saw?"

"Nothing," Dan said. "I just—" He shrugged his shoulders. "Nothing."

"It's nothing," the deputy coroner said. "I just thought for a moment he looked as if he knew the man. That's all."

"You don't, do you?" Gallagher asked again, eyeing Dan closely.

"No."

Gallagher looked back at the deputy coroner. "You're imagining things."

The deputy coroner shrugged. Gallagher returned his eyes to the naked corpse. Young face. Maybe twenty-seven or twenty-eight. Closely cropped brown hair. Nice-looking kid. Mouth curled slightly at the corners in a sort of smile. What was most remarkable was that the lips were stained bright green in places.

"Got any l-l-line on him?" Nix asked in a quavery voice. His face was white, except for the red-veined spots on his cheeks.

Gallagher looked at him scornfully. "What the hell's the matter with you? Didn't you ever see a stiff before?"

"They always give me the goddamn creeps," Nix said.

Gallagher sneered. "You're a hell of a sissy."

"I don't give a damn," Nix said. "Have you got any line on him?"

"No, but we will have. We're checking his fingerprints. Then somebody always turns out to be missing in a case like this."

"That green on his lips," Dan said. "What is it?"

The deputy coroner frowned professionally. "We can't say yet. There hasn't been an autopsy."

Gallagher eyed him. "What's your guess?"

The deputy coroner shrugged. "I'd say leunatine. But I wouldn't want to be quoted."

"Leunatine? What's that?" Nix asked.

"Understand, you're not to quote me," the deputy coroner said. "It's just my guess. It's an extremely rare poison. I've only seen one instance of its being used like this, and that was a great many years ago. It leaves that green stain on the lips."

"Where would anybody get a hold of such stuff?" Gallagher asked.

"It would be rather difficult, I should imagine. There are small quantities of it in a few chemical laboratories in this country. But it's rarely used, even for experiments."

"Evidently it's pretty deadly," Dan said.

"I should say it is. Practically instantaneous in the very smallest amount. It's made from a plant that grows in Africa. You've got to refine about a ton of it to get a thimbleful of poison. It comes in the form of tiny green crystals which dissolve into clear, colorless liquid. Then, when it dries, it turns green again. That's why it leaves a green smear on the lips."

"Then you figure this guy was poisoned?" Nix said.

"I'm not saying anything for publication until there's been an autopsy. I'm just saying what it looks like to me, off the record."

Gallagher clenched his jaw and shook his head. "Some shrewd bug dreamed this one up. This is gonna be a pain in the neck. I can feel it. How long's he been dead?"

"Oh, roughly, I'd estimate about twelve hours."

Gallagher put his tongue in his cheek and reckoned. "That would place it at about 2:00 A.M. this morning."

Dan cleared his throat before speaking. His voice had an ominous quality. "What kind of clothes was he wearing?"

"What's wrong with you?" Gallagher demanded. "You chicken-livered, too?"

"It kind of has an effect on you," Dan said, quietly.

The deputy coroner answered his question. "He didn't exactly have clothes. Pajamas and a bathrobe. And there was a pair of slippers in the crate."

Gallagher pulled the sheet farther back. "He was a well built lad. Any marks?"

The position of the body was grotesque from rigor mortis. The fingertips were still smudged with ink where they'd taken prints.

"A mole on the left leg. Small scar on the right arm. We may find something more in the autopsy."

"Just think," Nix said morbidly, "this time yesterday he was walkin' around."

"Clever skunk did this," Gallagher remarked. "Everything planned to the last detail. If it hadn't been for that traffic accident, nobody would ever have found out."

"A chance in a million," Nix reflected.

"Makes you feel there's a higher power," Gallagher said thoughtfully.

"How come?" Nix asked. "You mean God made that dame bump into the truck?"

"Don't joke about such things," Gallagher said.

"Dirty trick on the dame. How's she coming?"

"Scared the wits out of her. She isn't hurt."

"What did God go ahead and let the poor guy get poisoned for if he was going to get mad about it later?" Nix asked.

"You don't know anything about God, so don't try to talk."

"Neither do you, Neil."

"Maybe I don't," Gallagher said. "But at least I don't go around blowin' my mouth off. If there isn't a God, then what the hell is life all about?"

"You got me, Neil."

Gallagher's voice was a blend of irritation and anxiety. "There must be somethin'. Otherwise, hell, man, what's the sense of it? A guy's alive, and he works himself into a lather about this, that, and the other thing. Then he dies. And what's the sense of it? Cover it up, Jeff. Let me know when you cut it open and find out what's inside. Come on, fellows. Let's get out of here."

CHAPTER FIVE

When Dan Banion left the Hall of Justice, he headed for Montgomery Street walking fast. A strange anger burned in him. He had lied to Inspector Gallagher and the others in the morgue. Certainly he had seen that face before. He had seen it casually in a barroom the day before. He had seen it warm and full of life and good nature. A man like himself, returned from the war and trying to pick up the threads of his life where he had left off. A man who, in his own words, wanted to "make some sense of things," and wanted "a world to live in."

Now he lay dead in the morgue, and Dan felt a personal sense of enmity toward his killer. He felt a strong compulsion to seek that man out and destroy him.

How much time would he have? It might take Inspector Gallagher twenty-four hours or more to identify the corpse. In the meantime, no one would know the man was dead. That is, no one but the murderer and his accomplices, if any. The murdered man's friends and associates would still be thinking of him and talking of him as a living person.

Ordinarily the atmosphere of a man's life dies with him. The very news of his death alters or negates the delicate balance of emotions and relationships which, while he is living, are as much a part of his life as his breathing or thinking.

The man Dan had just seen in the morgue was not entirely dead yet. His heart had stopped. The blood in his veins no longer flowed. His hand was cold. But this other part of him lived on. He still lived in the hearts and minds of his associates. He was still a living factor and would remain so until news of his death got around.

Dan felt strongly that if he could find this man's friends and go among them before the news got out, it might give him a long head start toward finding the killer.

Often before he had followed cold trails through the altered pattern of a dead man's life. This was a chance to enter the living environment of a man and study the attitudes of people before his death was known.

What did he know of this man? Kent, the bartender had called him. There was some conversation about a picture. A nude painting that had once hung over the bar. The man was trying to find out who had bought it. Then there was the girl with the troubled eyes who came in and interrupted.

It had rained earlier and the sidewalk was still damp. The five-after-five crowd of clerks and stenographers from the high office buildings along Montgomery Street were hurrying toward streetcars with a noticeable air of liberation. Dan wove his way among them until he came to The Wreck bar.

Inside was a noisy confusion of thumping dice boxes, laughing voices, and juke-box rhythm. The businessmen were having their end-of-the-day drinks.

Dan straddled a stool between two groups of dice-box thumpers. The stout bartender, Chuck, assisted by another, was pouring drinks and stirring highballs as rapidly as he could move, meanwhile chattering incessantly with the customers.

Dan ordered a beer, and as Chuck eased it into a glass, said, "By the way, do you remember that fellow who was in here yesterday afternoon?"

Chuck raised his eyebrows and seemed about to reply, when a tall, serious-faced man in a neat business suit reached an arm over Dan's shoulder and said, "Have you got my stick, Chuck?"

"Your stick? Oh, sure, Larry." Chuck reached under the bar and handed him a wooden stick about two feet long. Other customers began shouting for attention farther down the bar, and Chuck took off in their direction, forgetting Dan's question.

The man with the stick walked over to the pink and blue illuminated juke box, studied the selections seriously, and inserted a nickel. Then he backed away a few steps and stood waiting, a bored, matter-of-fact expression on his face. Dan swiveled around on his bar stool to watch. No one else paid any attention.

Suddenly the man's body tensed. He made a swift flourish with the stick in exact time with the first note of music. If you hadn't known about the juke box, you'd have sworn the orchestra had been alerted by his stick—that the eyes of obedient musicians were intent on his baton.

It was a popularized arrangement of Tchaikovsky's *Symphony Pathétique*. The man's left hand rose delicately to supplement the guidance of his baton. His head swung vigorously, and his whole body entered into the strenuous work of directing the orchestra. There was anxiety in every muscle as he strove to draw the best out of each instrument and caution those who made too much of their parts. Drops of perspiration formed on his brow. Several times he frowned angrily and gestured to soften an overenthusiastic horn or to stimulate a violin to greater passion. At other times he would smile in patronizing satisfaction—a rewarding sign that they were beginning to understand.

When the record ended, the man sighed deeply and his whole body relaxed. He took a handkerchief from his pocket and mopped his brow. Swinging his stick carelessly, he returned to the bar and straddled the stool next to Dan.

"I get a kick out of it," he said to Dan. "Nothing gives me such a whale of a boot."

"Are you a musician?" Dan asked.

"No. I wish I was."

Chuck, taking advantage of a momentary lull, sauntered down to where they were sitting. He peeled the paper band from a cigar, bit the end off, and spat. "Goddamn rush hour gets me down." He touched a match to the cigar.

The man with the stick ordered a bourbon and soda. While Chuck eased the whisky into a glass, Dan said, "I was in here yesterday afternoon. Do you remember the fellow who was here at the same time? You called him Kent."

Chuck nodded. "Yeah. I remember you. You're the newspaperman."

Dan persisted. "Do you remember that fellow who was in here? He sat right about there. You called him Kent."

Chuck looked at the ceiling. "Oh, hell, you mean Kent." He turned to the man with the stick. "He means Kent. Yeah. Sure. Kent Kipper. He'll be in pretty soon." Chuck looked at the clock. "It's early for him.

He'll be in after a while."

The man with the stick pursed his lips and nodded gravely. "Very nice guy, Kipper. Very nice guy indeed. I like that lad."

Chuck pointed his cigar at the print of the giant redwood tree over the bar. "Kent's lookin' for that pitcher he painted. The pitcher of a dame that used to hang up there. You remember it, Larry?"

"Oh yes. I remember it."

"What is he? An artist?" Dan asked.

"A very good artist." Larry said.

Chuck leered. "You oughta seen that dame."

"Well, that isn't a fair example," Larry said deprecatingly. "He just painted that for the hell of it."

Chuck removed the cigar from his mouth indignantly. "It was goddamn good."

"It was all right," Larry said. "But it was just a nude. He did it more or less as a favor for Falletti, and for the free drinks."

"It was real enough to spank," Chuck said. He grinned. "I got a kick out of the bandage."

"That's what I mean," Larry said. "It was just a gag."

Chuck leaned his elbows on the bar and explained to Dan. "That was a panic. He paints this pitcher, see. Just a nude for over the bar. But what a nude! It would melt in your mouth. And here's this dame stretched out on a couch, and everything's perfect except her toe. Her goddamn toe is bandaged, just like she'd stubbed it. Just a clumsy rag bandage like you see on kid's fingers. I tell you, it was a kick."

"What happened to the picture?" Dan asked.

"Well, Falletti," Chuck said, "—that's the guy who used to own the place—he sold out."

"That was while Kent was overseas," Larry added.

"He sold out," Chuck continued, "and this new guy—his name's Dolan—had to put all the cash he could scrape up into the deal. He needed ready dough. So along came some guy and made him an offer for the pitcher. At first he wouldn't sell. The thing kind of gave the place class. But the guy raised his ante, so Dolan got money-hungry and let it go. I still think he was a damn fool."

"Who was the guy who bought it?" Dan asked.

"Well, that's what beats me. I'm damned if I know. I can't remember the guy's name. It began with a *J*, like Jefferson, or Jessel, or something like that."

"How about Dolan," Dan asked. "Doesn't he know?"

"Dolan can't remember nothin'. The guy paid cash, and Dolan never even wrote down his name. I'd recognize the guy, though. I'd remember him if I saw him. He'll come in here someday, and I'll remember him."

"Is that how Kipper made his living—makes his living?" Dan said. "As an artist?"

"If you can make your living that way," Chuck said. "I don't know. He tries to."

"Kent's worked at a lot of things," Larry said. "He was on the ships at one time. Then he worked in a warehouse. I believe he once drove a taxi, didn't he, Chuck?"

"I think he did. Mainly, what Kent likes to do is paint, though. He's only been out of the army about four months."

"Who was that girl who met him in here yesterday? The hot-looking brunette," Dan asked.

"Oh, her?" Chuck flipped his cigar ashes with his little finger. "That's Marian."

Larry seemed surprised. "Not Marian Cleave?"

"Sure."

"Don't tell me he's going around with her again!"

"I don't know what's the situation. I see 'em together once in a while."

"Well, I'll be damned!"

"Why? What's the matter?" Dan asked.

"They used to be married," Chuck said. "But they split up. That was before the war."

"She's a beautiful girl," Larry remarked.

"She's a dish, all right," Chuck agreed, "but she's no good for Kent. If you ask me, she's hot pants. All those dames with big cow eyes are hot pants."

"She hasn't got cow eyes," Larry said. "She's got beautiful eyes."

"I suppose a cow's eyes ain't beautiful!" Chuck declared.

"Of course not."

"You're crazy. Did you ever look in a cow's eyes?"

"What would I be doing looking in a cow's eyes?"

"Well, there you are. You don't know what you're talking about." Chuck walked off to attend some customers who were clamoring for service.

When he was gone, Larry turned to Dan seriously. "Do you think a cow's eyes are beautiful?"

Dan took a neutral position on the question and tried to get the conversation back to Kent Kipper, but Larry wanted to talk about cows. Chuck had become involved in another conversation farther down the bar and had forgotten them.

Dan finished his drink, extricated himself from the conversation about cows, and went out.

CHAPTER SIX

Kent Kipper an artist! That simplified things. Artists usually ran in cliques, frequented the same neighborhoods, hung out at the same bars.

Who would be apt to know artists in San Francisco? Nix Peters might. Still, that would be a dirty trick to make use of Nix without cutting him in on the story. Somehow, Dan didn't feel it was a story he was after. It cut him deeper than that. He felt a personal anger about the man in the morgue. Maybe it was pent-up anger about a lot of things that had occurred in recent years. Things he couldn't do much about.

True, he didn't even know the man who had been murdered. But even a casual contact had left the strong impression that he was a good guy. And Dan was tired of seeing good guys kicked around.

No, he didn't want to team up with Nix in a greedy scramble for headline copy. But if not Nix, who else?

He remembered Ike Miller. Ike would know the artists in this town if anybody did. Ike always hobnobbed with artistic people. Being a frustrated novelist himself, Ike usually gravitated to those circles. And he owed Ike a visit anyhow.

The studio of Station KZY was not far from The Wreck bar. Dan found Ike in the newsroom amidst the clatter of a half-dozen teletypes.

"Sure," Ike said. "I know Kenton Kipper. Know him well. What about him?" Ike was a sandy-haired man with a boyish face and bright, enthusiastic eyes.

"Nothing particular," Dan said. "A friend of his asked me to look him up."

"As a matter of fact, I'll probably be seeing him tonight," Ike said. He removed a green eyeshade and dropped it in a desk drawer. "I was just about to knock off. Why don't you come along with me? We'll have a good feed and I'll show you a little of the town."

According to Ike, some people named Hobart were giving a little party, and Kipper was almost certain to be there. Dan welcomed the idea of going along. It would give him a chance, he thought, to size up the crowd Kipper ran around with.

Ike had a battered coupe parked outside, and drove them to a Basque restaurant in the North Beach district. Dan tried to steer the conversation to Kipper, but Ike was in a mood for reminiscing about the "old days" of newspapering prior to the war.

They hadn't been seated long before a tall, sleepy-looking man with a brown mustache, and two girls approached their table. Ike was all hospitality and they joined parties.

The sleepy-looking man was introduced as Arnold Winkleman. Dan gathered from the conversation that he was an artist. One of the girls, Lorna Cargill, was a slim, dark-eyed brunette with a long, tousled bob that slanted across her face almost obscuring one eye. The intimate bickering that went on between her and Ike suggested a relationship more than casual.

The other girl, Janey Navarro, had reddish-brown hair and a nose that turned up slightly at the end. The curves of an excellent figure asserted themselves even through the rough tweed suit she was wearing. There was a warm gleam in her eyes that Dan guessed was attributable to some man. He studied Winkleman for the role, and decided it couldn't be. The dull stare of the artist's red-lined eyes and the indifferent manner in which he addressed both girls made him an improbable lover.

Ike suddenly turned to Janey and said, "Where's Kent?"

The warm look in her eyes leaped higher. "He had to go to Berkeley today," she said. "He's going to meet me at the Hobarts' later."

"Dan, here, wants to meet him," Ike said. "He knows an old friend of his, or something. What was it, Dan?"

When Dan tried to use his voice, he found it husky and had to clear his throat. "I met a guy in the army who knew him. He told me to look him up."

"Who was it?" Winkleman asked.

Dan groped to invent a name. "Jeff—ah—Jeff Warren." They all reflected, repeating the name to themselves, but none could recollect it.

Ike took the occasion to turn the conversation to art, and a fairly heated dispute resulted. Apparently Winkleman didn't think very highly of Kipper's work. Janey Navarro defended his merit with fury, and finally said, "Just because Kent doesn't paint people with triangular heads and their insides falling out, some people think it isn't art."

The gibe evidently hit home, because Winkleman flushed angrily and said, "All right. Let's drop the subject. You asked my opinion and I told you."

Later on, Ike remarked that Winkleman was looking tired.

"I guess I can't take it like I used to," Winkleman said. "I was down the Peninsula last night with Lance and Foisie. Maybe we drank too much. Anyhow, I had an awful head this morning. We stayed all night at Lance's place down there. They were hung over this morning, too. So I guess I'm not the only one."

Dinner finished, Ike drove them to the North side of Telegraph Hill. The girls squeezed into the front seat with Ike. Dan and Winkleman took the rumble seat.

From where they got out of the car, they could see a whole panorama of the harbor, with lights twinkling far across the bay. Ike led them through an old iron gate into a dark garden that smelled of fresh fertilizer. They walked over stepping-stones toward a cottage in the rear. There were lights in the windows, and they could hear a turmoil of voices and laughter inside.

A plump blonde woman let them into a room full of chattering people. A dozen arguments seemed in loud progress on as many different subjects. Winkleman and the two girls disappeared into the mob. Ike steered Dan to a table where an enormous man with a sagging, bag-like stomach was pouring Scotch from a bottle.

"My God," Ike said, "is that Blue Thistle?"

"This, Ikey boy," the fat man said, "is Blue Thistle, and, what's more, pre-war. I was down the Peninsula last night with Lance and Arnie. Lance ran across four bottles he'd forgotten all about. I persuaded him to bring two of them along tonight."

Ike introduced Dan, and the fat man said, "Danny boy! So glad to know you." He took Dan's hand between his own great flabby ones and held it as if trying to warm it. Dan extracted it with the same sensation he would have had pulling it from the mouth of a cow.

The fat man's name was Guy Foisie and he wanted to talk about water colors, but the plump blonde woman interrupted and hauled him off to another part of the room.

"What the hell kind of party is this?" Dan asked, when Foisie was gone.

"Don't let it bother you," Ike said. "You'll meet all kinds of people here." He wandered off in the direction of Lorna, leaving Dan to shift for himself.

Dan strolled around the room, listening on the fringes of one argument and then another, and wondering if he hadn't been a little crazy to imagine he could learn anything from an abstract confusion of jobber-jabber such as this.

The sight of Janey Navarro sitting quietly in a corner, watching the hallway expectantly every time the doorbell rang, disturbed Dan and made him feel like a fraud. If Kipper was responsible for the warm light in her eyes, he could be credited with having had very good taste.

As Dan was watching Janey, another figure moved in between

them, obscuring her for a minute. Someone he hadn't noticed in the room until now. It was the girl he had seen in The Wreck bar with Kipper the previous afternoon—the one the bartender said was Marian Cleave, Kipper's ex-wife. Her eyes met Dan's, and they had the same troubled, appealing look Dan had noticed before. She looked questioningly at him for a few seconds, and Dan thought there was a flash of recognition. Then her eyes snapped away and she continued across the room.

An ex-wife and a present girl friend in the same room! Or was Dan imagining things? No, that look in Janey's eye was unmistakable. As for Marian Cleave, an ex-wife who meets a man in a bar and says she has to speak to him alone may not be entirely in the "ex" category.

Dan remembered the casual "keep your distance" attitude with which Kipper had greeted her in the bar. That might mean an ex-wife trying to maintain a grip, and an ex-husband trying to get away. Whatever it was, Marian too seemed to confirm the murdered man's good taste. Tonight she had fixed a white gardenia in her coal-black hair. The strange, anxious look in her eyes added something to her beauty.

Dan's thoughts were interrupted by a slap on the back from Ike. "Dan, I want you to meet a couple of guys." He introduced a stubby little man with thick black hair and a black mustache; and a tanned, athletic-looking man, well into middle age, with slightly graying side chops and alert eyes.

The stubby man was Mark Wiener, a psychiatrist. The athletic-looking, gray-tinged man was Lance Mallory, who acknowledged the vague occupation of "investments." They launched into a discussion of the atomic bomb. Dan let it proceed for a few minutes, then interrupted to ask if anyone had seen Kenton Kipper.

They all stood on their toes and looked around the room. "I thought I heard someone mention his name," Lance Mallory said.

"I think he was here and left," said Mark Wiener. Ike didn't think he'd arrived yet.

The walls of the room were hung with a number of original paintings. Dan nodded toward them and asked if any of them happened to be by Kipper.

Mark Wiener stopped the plump blonde woman who was passing with a tray of glasses. "Kay, didn't you have a few water colors by Kipper?"

"I did have, Mark, but I lost them," she said. "Either that or they were stolen. It just makes me sick to think of it."

Guy Foisie, the big man with the sagging stomach, interposed himself. "Water colors, did you say? What water colors?"

"The ones Kent did of clotheslines," the blonde woman said. "You remember them. I lost them."

"You lost them? How in the world? I don't understand."

"It must have been when we moved from the other house. That's the only thing I can think."

"No. God, what a pity," Foisie said.

"I've looked everywhere," said the blonde woman. "I don't know how it could have happened, because I packed everything so carefully."

Glancing toward the hallway, Dan noticed a new arrival entering. He was a dark-haired man with dazed, drunken eyes, making a task of each individual step. His features were well formed, but grooved by dissipation. His hair was disheveled, his fly unbuttoned, and there were powdery marks on his blue suit where he had leaned against something.

As he tottered drunkenly into the room, he kicked a low table, upsetting a vase of flowers. The blonde woman leaped to rescue them, and the man apologized incoherently. Lance Mallory grabbed him and guided him to a chair, where he sat swaying and blinking around the room.

The distraction ended the conversation about Kipper's paintings. The others were attracted in various directions, and Dan was left once more to himself. He observed that the drunken man was leaning out of his chair and feeling around the floor with his hands. Dan wandered over and asked him if he'd lost something.

The man blinked up at him. "Pipe. Lost my pipe." He leaned over too far and fell out of his chair. Dan hoisted him back to it. "Pipe," he mumbled. "Had my pipe and I lost it."

"Sure you had it with you?" Dan asked.

The man didn't seem to hear. His eyes had narrowed, and he was staring across the room. Dan followed his gaze and saw that he was looking at Marian Cleave. Suddenly the man rose to his feet and staggered across the room in her direction.

As he approached Marian, Ike stepped in between and tried to get him to sit down. He shook himself free and took a wild, drunken swing at Ike, missing him widely. Lance Mallory stepped forward, held the man by the arms, and began talking to him. He seemed to have a calming influence.

In the meantime, Marian Cleave, appearing very much upset, had started toward the door. As she passed Mark Wiener, she said, "Please, Mark, take me home."

A few minutes later, Lance Mallory guided the drunken man out, saying, "Come on, now, Greg. Let's you and me get some air."

When they were gone, the fat man, Guy Foisie, said, "Good heavens! What's come over Greggy? He used to be the sweetest chap."

Arnold Winkleman, the artist, shook his head. "It's too damn bad. It's a damn shame."

"You've known him a long time, Arnie. You ought to have a talk with him," Foisie said.

"Talking's not much good with Greg," Winkleman said. "I knew him at college. We were in the same class at Stanford. Even then he was pretty hard to reason with. But I think there's two sides to this question."

"You mean Marian? Heavens, you can't blame her."

The blonde woman, evidently sensing a delicate subject, interrupted with, "I think we all ought to have another drink."

Ike came over to Dan and said, "Do you want to wait around for that guy Kipper, or shall we get the hell out of here and I'll show you some of the town?"

"Maybe we could drop by Kipper's place and see if he's in," Dan suggested. "Do you know where he lives?"

Ike punched Dan's shoulder. "Good idea." He tried to persuade Lorna Cargill to come with them, but she wouldn't leave.

CHAPTER SEVEN

When they got in the car, Dan said, "What was all that business back there about the drunk? I didn't get it."

"You mean Greg? Oh, that's nothing. He used to be married to that dame, Marian Cleave. They split up and he's been hitting the bottle ever since."

This was a new complication. Dan thought about it for a moment, then said, "I thought she used to be married to Kenton Kipper."

"How'd you know that?"

"Somebody mentioned it."

"You interested in Marian Cleave?"

"Not particularly," Dan said. "Why do you ask?"

"It just struck me funny, that's all. She cornered me up there at the party and asked all about you. Now you start asking about her."

"She doesn't even know me."

"Well, she does now."

"What did you tell her?"

"What do you think I told her? I gave you a build-up, of course."

"She was married to Kipper, wasn't she?"

"Yeah. But that was a long time ago. Before the war. She busted up with Kent and married this guy Gregory Fallon."

"How come?"

"Oh, hell, Dan, it's a long story. You know how those things go. She was away visiting her mother. The old lady was sick or something. She died, in fact. Anyhow, while Marian was away Greg got mixed up with some blonde. The blonde's husband caught them in bed and raised hell. He sued Greg for alienation of affections, and it all came out in the papers. It was a hell of a mess. Anyhow, she's getting a divorce from him. This is where Kipper lives, but I doubt if he's in."

Ike turned the car into a narrow alley and pulled up to the curb. He leaned his head out and looked up at the windows. "No light. I guess he's not home."

Dan opened the car door and stepped out in the street. The alley was only one block long, and it was lined with dirty-looking wooden flats built right out to the sidewalks. The air was cold and moist. An arc light high on a pole gave illumination.

"Which house?"

"Right across the street. The one with the brown front."

The building Ike indicated was three stories of ramshackle tenement. "He's number 183 on the top floor," Ike said. "We could go in. He keeps the key over the door. But what's the use? There's no light."

Dan looked up at the dark, silent windows—as lifeless as the eyes of the man in the morgue. "Let's have a look, anyway," he suggested. "He might be in back."

"No, he's not. Get in. Let's go down to the Black Pot. We'll like as not run into him there."

"What's the name of this alley?"

"Prawn Street."

Dan got back in the car. "It looks like pretty much of a dump."

"It isn't bad. It's a damn sight better than where I live." Ike started the car again.

"Kipper hasn't much money, I take it."

"Kent? Hell, no. He had some luck while he was in the army, though. A lot of his paintings sold. Stuff he'd left here with one dealer or another. I guess people had more dough to spend on such stuff during the war."

"What happened between him and Marian?"

"Oh, Christ, that's a long story, Dan."

"Just couldn't hit it off, eh?"

"It was more than that. Money had a lot to do with it. She just isn't right for him."

"Why do you say that?"

"Well, she had money and he didn't. That doesn't seem to work out. Not that I wouldn't mind trying it myself."

"What does this Gregory Fallon do?"

"He's an attorney downtown. A pretty good one, I hear."

Ike drove them to a bar called the Black Pot. The walls of the place were hung with paintings for sale, and Ike explained that it was a hangout for local artists. He introduced Dan to a man named Andre de Carlo, who handled the art concession in the place.

Dan asked if they had anything by Kipper. De Carlo shook his head. They had had a couple, but he had sold them while Kipper was in the army. Kipper, he said, had been inquiring about them. He had given Kipper the name and address of the purchaser, but when Kipper tried to get in touch with her, he found that there was no such address. Her name was Miss Adele Wolgast, and all that De Carlo could remember about her was that she was a "big luscious blonde."

The next bar they went to was called the Iron Cat. A rusty, wrought-iron resemblance to a cat hung over the door. In the window were dusty printed signs marking the place "out of bounds" and "off limits" for army and navy personnel.

Inside was a yellowish, smoky atmosphere inhabited by discontented faces. As in the Black Pot, the walls were hung with paintings and sketches.

Everyone seemed to know Ike, and he nodded greetings to right and to left as they entered. At a table in the rear, a gloomy waiter mopped the oilcloth covering and asked them what they'd have.

While they were waiting for their drinks, Ike, who had reached the heart-to-heart stage, began talking of his personal bewilderments. "I've been thinking, Dan," he said. "You take livin' in goddamn hotels and flea traps, gettin' drunk night after night, dopin' your brain with this rotgut, and sleepin' around with a lot of floozies. A guy gets tired of it. A guy wants somethin' more than that. I've been thinking—"

That was as far as Ike got. A big man with thick shoulders and wavy brown hair leaned his knuckles on their table and fixed Ike with a scowl. "Where's Kipper?" he demanded.

Ike was startled. "Why, I don't know. Hasn't he been around?"

"You know damn well he hasn't been around."

The man was powerfully built, like a wrestler, but, in contrast, his eyes were large and brown, and he had long lashes like a girl's. Under his left eye was a wide, purple bruise.

"Well, what about it?" Ike asked.

"The bastard's laying low," the man snarled. "You tell him for me that when I meet up with him I'm gonna beat the goddamn muck out of him."

Ike laughed. "Aw, go sit down. Kent gave you one shiner. What do you want him to do? Black your other eye?"

The man reached out and grabbed Ike by the coat lapels. "Oh, a smart guy. I got a damn good mind to—"

Dan reached up and rapped his knuckles against the man's shoulder. "Let go of my friend."

The man released Ike and turned furious eyes on Dan. "Do you wanta make somethin' of it?"

"Just keep your hands off my friend," Dan said.

"I can take care of myself, Dan," Ike protested. But his voice was unconvincing.

The man glowered drunkenly at Dan. "Do you wanta come out in the alley and make somethin' of it?"

"I wouldn't walk across the street to spit on you," Dan said. "But if you don't get the hell away from this table and stop bothering us, I'll break a couple of your bones and maybe put one of your eyes out. Now beat it."

The tone of Dan's voice and his savage choice of words gave the big man pause. He hesitated, then said, "Just keep your nose out of my business, see?"

"I'm not interested in you. Beat it."

The big man poked a finger in the direction of Dan's face. "We're not through. Understand? This isn't finished." He strode back to his own table.

"Who's that moose?" Dan asked.

"Aw, he's a big bag of wind," Ike said. "Kent socked him the other night and blacked his eye. It's torturing his ego."

"What was the fight about?"

"I don't know. It was night before last up in Chinatown. Janey Navarro was with him. Maybe she knows. Kent pasted him and threw him out of a bar. Glotcher'll never get over it."

"Is that his name?"

"Yeah, Armand Glotcher. He does art photography. But if you ask me, he spends most of his time luring little dames to pose in the nude. God's gift to women, or so he thinks. Look who's here."

Arnold Winkleman and Lorna Cargill came up and joined them at their table. They had left the party shortly after Dan and Ike. Kent Kipper had not shown up, they said, and the party had kind of piffled out.

Dan noticed that Ike was considerably enlivened by the presence of Lorna Cargill, and wondered if she was the reason why Ike was suddenly fed up with boozing and sleeping around.

A stoop-shouldered, bleary-eyed little man, wearing soggy bedroom slippers, came over and sat at their table. Ike introduced him as Oliver Hinkleburger, the proprietor of the place, but everyone greeted him as "Hinky."

Just to see what would result, Dan asked him if Kenton Kipper had been in that night.

"Naw, he ain't," Hinky said. "I don't know about his painting. Who bought his painting? How do I know? Berlenbach. Does what de man said his name was. Dot's all I know."

"What are you talking about?" Ike asked.

"Dot Kipper," Hinky said. "He went off to de war. He left a painting. A man bought it, I give Kipper de money. Who is de man? he says. Where does he live? Berlenbach, I said. Paul Berlenbach. I gave him de piece of paper with de address. Now he can't find him. Fooey!"

"What picture was that?" Ike asked.

"De one of de dirty old lady. I gave him de money. What de hell should he care who bought it? Paint some more pictures, I told him. Earn your living. Don't sit around boozing wit dese bums."

Presently the waiter began picking up empty beer bottles and chanting, "Drink up. We're closing. Twelve o'clock. Everybody out."

Hinky took up the cry. "Get oud. Go home. All of you. Go earn your livings. Drunken bums. Go home and sleep."

CHAPTER EIGHT

Out on the sidewalk, Arnold Winkleman proposed Chinatown and noodle soup. The others were agreeable, but Dan felt it was time to stop drifting and get down to business on his own. He mumbled something about having to get up the next morning. They tried to persuade him, but he was firm.

They dropped him off at his hotel on Pine Street near Kearny. It seemed to take Ike some time getting the car started again, so, for the sake of appearance, Dan opened the door of the hotel and went in the small lobby. A gray little man behind the desk fished Dan's key out of its numbered pigeonhole. Halfway to the desk, Dan turned and saw the car pull away from the curb. He retraced his steps and went out into the night again.

The gray little man cursed and threw the keys back in the pigeonhole. It confirmed his belief that human beings were crazy.

Dan walked a few blocks through the darkening streets. Lights were going out behind the closed doors of bars. Only the hotels and all-night restaurants remained open. Drunks staggered homeward in the darkness. A few sailors and their girls whistled at taxicabs. It began to rain gently, and Dan buttoned the collar of his topcoat.

There was something unusual about the way Kipper's paintings never seemed to be available. First, the nude from over the bar in The Wreck. Same man had bought it and they couldn't remember his name. Something like Jeffries or Jeffers, Chuck had said.

Then the water colors that had been stolen from the Hobarts. Then the paintings from the Black Pot. At least that fellow De Carlo remembered the name of the purchaser. Adele Wolgast! Odd name. Something familiar about it.

Hinkleburger, in the Iron Cat, remembered the name of the man who had bought the picture there, too. Berlenbach! Paul Berlenbach! Where had he heard that name before? It had a strangely familiar sound.

Apparently Kipper had been making inquiries, trying to find out what had become of his pictures. That might be natural. An artist paints pictures, and then would like to know where they are. Kind of keep track of them. Maybe borrow them for an exhibit.

Up ahead on the street, Dan saw a taxi stop in front of a hotel. He quickened his pace. The taxi unloaded a fat man with his necktie askew, and a girl so drunk she couldn't stand without support. When the fare had been paid, and the fat man pushed and guided the tottering girl in the hotel door, Dan asked the driver to take him to the one hundred block on Prawn Street.

It was beginning to rain in earnest, and the wheels of the cab made a sizzling sound on the wet, slimy pavement. The best place to look for reasons why anybody would murder Kenton Kipper might be in his own apartment. Ike had said he kept the key over the door. Entering another man's house unasked and in his absence—even a dead man's house—was questionable business. Still, Dan had gambled a lot of his conscience on being able to discover something that night before news of the murder got around. So far, he'd encountered a lot of tangled personal relations, and that was all. Kipper's apartment was a last chance he couldn't overlook.

The matter was further complicated by a strange comradeship he felt for the murdered man. A feeling that this was something personal.

The rain was beating down heavily when the cab drew in to a curb in the narrow alley. "This is Prawn Street," the driver said. "Which house?"

"This is okay." Dan paid the fare and waited in a dark doorway until the cab drove off. Then, hugging the buildings to avoid the rain, he made his way to the ramshackle wooden building Ike had pointed out.

The entrance was a square of darkness. Dan lit a match and saw a wooden stairway leading above. It was inside, protected from the rain, but not closed off by any door.

Holding the lighted match, he started upward. When the match burned out, he guided himself by feeling along the banister. Presently he came to a small landing that indicated the second floor. He lit another match and saw two doors. Evidently there were two flats on each floor. Ike had said Kipper's place was number 183 on the top floor.

He continued up the rickety flight of stairs that creaked with every step. The flight turned sharply and doubled back on itself at regular intervals, and as Dan turned one of these corners, he stepped on something that almost threw him off balance.

Reaching down in the dark, he felt around with his fingers until he had it. His touch told him that it was a pipe. He remembered Gregory Fallon complaining drunkenly that be had lost his pipe. He put it in his pocket and continued upward.

The next landing seemed to be the top; there were no more stairs. A match showed two doors, the one on the right numbered 183. Dan studied the silent door until the match burned his fingers and he dropped it. Darkness was absolute. The little landing was sheltered from the rain, but not from its sound. The steady tempo of its beating on the roof, its eager splashing down drainpipes and dripping from every eave and projection of the building, was like something alive.

Dan took a pair of gloves from his topcoat pocket and put them on. In the darkness, he felt the door with his hands. Ike had said the key would be over the door. His fingers scraped dust on the ledge above, but there was no key. He felt for nails on which it might be hanging. There were none. Disappointed, he tried the knob. The door was open.

Inside was black silence. Dan stepped cautiously in and closed the door behind him. A board creaked under his foot, and a streak of fear shot through him. With his gloved hand, he felt along plaster walls for a switch and realized that his hands were trembling. No switch. In an old house like this, the lighting fixture was probably somewhere in the center of the room, worked by a cord. He lit another match, and dim shapes of furniture leaped at him from every side. He saw a lamp on a table, groped to it, found the switch and pressed it.

His fears vanished in the warm light. A comfortable, welcoming room clicked into being around him. The feeling was so friendly the furniture almost seemed to be laughing at him.

A little round-bellied iron coal and wood stove with a draft regulator like an exaggerated navel stood bowlegged almost in the middle of the room, its long stovepipe extending to a distant flue.

Dan pulled the cord of an overhead light and the cheerfulness doubled. The floor was plain, clean boards, except for a couple of worn Navajo rugs. The walls and ceiling were white-painted plaster, chipped in a number of places and showing a little yellow underneath.

Old-fashioned windows with squared panes overlooked the bay. A double studio bed was covered by a patchwork quilt. Backed off a comfortable distance from the stove was an old easy chair that looked as if it had come out of an ancient hotel lobby. A low table beside it was littered with ash trays, magazines, pencils, papers, a bottle of wine, several glasses, and other casual objects.

An old walnut chest of drawers with a marble top and a large mirror bore a scattering of brushes, combs, an electric razor, neckties, and toilet articles. Thrown carelessly on a chair was the brown tweed suit Dan had seen Kipper wearing on the previous afternoon. The coat was slung on the back of the chair, and the pants were thrown across the seat in the manner of garments a man had just taken off prior to going to bed. On the marble dresser top was a little heap of coins, a wadded-up dollar bill, a soiled handkerchief, and a paper matchbook. Things Kipper had probably taken out of his pockets before removing his clothes.

Dan remembered the deputy coroner explaining that the body had been clothed in pajamas and a bathrobe, and that a pair of slippers had been found in the crate.

Apparently, Kipper and come home and prepared to go to bed, taken his clothes off, put on pajamas, robe, and slippers—then what? Had the murderer called on him? That seemed the obvious answer. In all probability, then, Kipper had been poisoned right in this room.

Dan glanced around for any sign of a visitor. He went over and examined the wine bottle and glasses. The glasses were clean. The cork was firmly in the bottle. Only two cigarette stubs were in the ash tray, and they were of the same brand as a half-empty pack lying on the table.

Of course! The murderer would have had sense enough not to leave any evidence. But why hadn't he hung up Kipper's suit, or disposed of it? Why leave such obvious signs of a man having prepared for bed? And why was the door unlocked?

Dan noticed that the door to a closet was ajar. He went over and looked in it. The first thing that struck his eye was a khaki uniform with the familiar green and gray Timberwolf insignia on the shoulder. Kipper's wardrobe was sparse. One other suit, a gray one. A leather jacket. Two pairs of slacks. An overcoat and a raincoat. But no bathrobe.

Dan looked among the shoes on the floor. There were no slippers. He closed the closet. Over against one wall was a wide ledge with cupboards underneath and shelves above it. It was littered with painting and drawing materials. The shelves held books, ornaments, knick-knacks and what looked like souvenirs from many lands.

A screen hid one corner of the room. Dan looked behind it and found a small kitchen with a two-burner gas plate, a sink, shelves and dishes and cooking materials.

Another door led to a narrow room containing a shower and a toilet.

Beside one of the windows was a table that evidently served as a desk. Dan started in that direction, but stopped to examine one of the pictures on the wall. It was a colored etching of a rabbit. Every hair and whisker seemed alive. Dan's knowledge of art was small, but he recognized it as a Dürer.

There ought to be something of Kipper's around. He moved from one picture to another. Most of them were prints. Manet's "Boy with a Flute," a couple of Van Goghs, and several Dan could not identify. The signatures on them indicated that they were not Kipper's work.

Over near the front windows was an easel with its back to the room. This was where Kipper had evidently been working. Dan walked around it and stared at a piece of charcoal paper. There was an extension light clamped to a drawing board that had been fitted on the easel. He lit it for a sharper view of the drawing.

For several minutes he stood there looking at it. It was unfinished. The faces of children, a boy and a girl, sketched in charcoal. The heads and shoulders were complete. The rest was just sketched in. What held Dan's attention were the eyes.

The drawing matched a picture that was etched painfully in Dan's memory. Something he had seen in Europe that he could not, forget. Kipper had seen it too.

The eyes of children trapped in the frightening violence of an adult world they could not comprehend, but were determined to survive. A blend of anger, terror, and the will to live. Fighting eyes in little faces; a power of resentment that would change the face of the earth being burned into their brains.

He turned from the easel with a sense of dizziness. The complacent cheerfulness of the room disturbed him. The bow-legged stove, the fat armchair, the elderly-looking chest of drawers, all as if nothing had happened.

He went over to the armchair and sat down, felt in his pocket for his pipe, then changed his mind and took a cigarette from the pack on the low table. It was clumsy business getting one out with his gloved hands. As he held a match to the cigarette, he realized that he was angry. He shook the match out, started to drop it in the ash tray, then thought better of it. He pinched the end to be sure it was out, and put it in his pocket.

Beside the ash tray was a cheap dime-store notebook, pocket size. He picked it up and thumbed through it. Most of the scribbling was cryptic. Notes that read: "Chrome dress. Sienna cliff. Chinese boy with kite. Fat hands and worn currency, pinching each bill for fear they'll stick together. Naked store dummy with missing abdomen."

Evidently notes of things Kipper had picked up with his eye, wandering around town. Things he might want to recall.

Dan closed the book and reached for the wine bottle. Then he remembered the green stain on Kipper's dead lips, and withdrew his hand.

He got up and went to the table that seemed to serve as a desk. An unsealed envelope was lying face down beside an uncapped fountain pen. Dan turned it over. It was addressed to Marian Cleave. He slipped the letter out and unfolded it.

DEAR MARIAN:

A year ago, if anyone had told me I would be writing this tonight, I would have thought they were crazy. To have wanted something as much as I wanted you, and then to change so completely, isn't an easy experience. But it has happened. I have realized it for some time, but never so clearly as tonight. I think I understand you for the first time. Don't think I am critical or scornful. The Glotcher business does not shock or horrify me. If anything, it's silly. Disgusting, maybe, but more than that, silly. I think Lance is about the only one who has had your number right along.

Maybe you don't mean to hurt other people, but you do. And you'll go right on doing it. And I think in your heart you know it.

Here I am sounding critical. I don't mean to. I know you'd like to be different than you are. But what can anyone do?

We might as well be good sports about what neither of us can help. Your offer was a beautiful and generous one. I know it was sincere. But it just wouldn't work out.

I'm writing you this because, knowing you as I do, I don't think you took what I said tonight to heart. Believe me, I meant every word of it. I never felt more certain of just exactly what I intended to do. You've got to get it through your head that everything between us is past and closed.

If it will make it any more definite in your mind, I have decided to get married. That may hurt your ego for a little while, but soon you'll be off on another tangent. And God help the poor devil involved.

There I go sounding bitter. I'm not bitter. I just want you to be sensible and face facts. We're not to see each other again, and you're not to come here anymore. If we bump into each other at parties or anything like that, let's be friends.

I'm sorry you told so many people that we were going back together again, or gave them that impression. That was a mistake. There's nothing we can do about it now. You'll just have to pocket your pride and forget about it. I'm sorry, but that's the way it is.

Sincerely,
KENT

Dan read the letter twice, then folded it and put it back in the envelope. It annoyed him. What was the Glotcher business? In what way was Lance supposed to have "had her number"? Kipper said he wasn't bitter. Like hell he wasn't! "Your offer was a beautiful and generous one." What did he mean by that? And who was he intending to marry? Janey Navarro perhaps.

He put the envelope face down on the table the way he had found it. Farther back, near a row of books, was a neat little pile of letters, all in the same size envelopes. He picked them up. They were all sealed. He thumbed through them. They were addressed to various persons, with Kenton Kipper's return address in the upper left-hand corners. All of them had been returned by the Post Office marked "no such address" or "no such person at this address."

The top one was addressed to Mr. Paul Berlenbach, 426 Euclid Avenue, Oakland. Berlenbach! That was the man who was supposed to have bought one of Kipper's paintings from the Iron Cat.

An open clasp knife lay conveniently on the table. Dan hesitated a moment, pondering the advisability, then decided that caution too often continues ignorance. He slit the envelope and unfolded its contents.

DEAR MR. BERLENBACH:

I am informed by Mr. Hinkleburger, the proprietor of the Iron Cat, that about a year ago you purchased one of my paintings from him. It was of a destitute old woman against the background of a perfume advertisement.

I want to thank you for liking it well enough to buy it, and would like to ask you one more favor. I was recently discharged from the army, and have returned after a long absence. Naturally, as a prelude to getting my hand back to work, I'd like to see some of my old paintings and study them with what may or may not be more mature eyes.

I wonder if you could arrange to let me see the one you bought, or, if you no longer have it, if you would tell me where it now is.

Thanking you again for your interest, I am

Sincerely yours,
KENTON KIPPER

Dan folded it, put it back in the envelope, and thumbed through the others, all marked "return to sender" for one reason or another. They were addressed to Mrs. Frederick Steele, Miss Adele Wolgast, Mr. Samuel Mandell, Mr. James Goodrich, Mr. Robert Olin, Mrs. Louis Brouillard, Mr. John Henry Louis, Mrs. Peter Latzo, Mr. Frank Klaus, Mrs. Joseph Walcott, and Mrs. Benjamin Jeby.

Dan slit open a few more. The contents were about the same, except they named various establishments as places where the pictures were bought. A couple of letters mentioned the Bishop Gallery on Sutter Street.

So many wrong addresses didn't make sense. That was probably what had puzzled Kipper. There was something phoney about the whole business. Dan took out his notebook and copied down the names and addresses on the letters. They all had a vague flavor of familiarity. He tried to reason what it was, but failed.

He returned the pile of letters to its place near the books, and examined the table further. There was a wide, flat drawer under the top. He had pulled it open a fraction of an inch when he heard slow footsteps on the old stairs outside.

He quickly pushed the drawer back, and his eyes darted around the room. Again the complacency of the furniture and the pot-bellied, bowlegged stove seemed to mock his alarm. So far as he knew, there was no back door. At least, he hadn't thought to look for one.

But how did he know the footsteps were coming here? There was at least one other flat on this floor. It might be a person next door coming home late.

The footsteps became louder. The rain was still drumming steadily on the roof. He heard the boards creak directly outside the door. Feet stamped as if to shake off mud. It still might be for the other flat.

A light, sharp knock was repeated several times on the door. That settled that. For an instant Dan was panicky; then he reasoned that when you're caught, you're caught, and there's nothing else to do but brazen it out and take the consequences. The knock was repeated more sharply.

Whoever was knocking had seen the light in the window and knew someone was there. If no one answered, he would instinctively try the knob, and the door would open. There was only one sensible thing to do, and Dan did it, very much against his inclination. "Come in," he called.

Slowly the door opened, and a white-hooded, smiling face leaned in. "Oh," she said. "I didn't expect—"

"It's all right. Come in," Dan repeated.

Marian Cleave was wearing a hooded raincoat of white material, with white galoshes to match. She shook herself as she came dripping into the room. "Well, I didn't expect you." She smiled, as if she'd been caught at something, and intended to have a sense of humor about it.

Dan motioned awkwardly with his hands. "I was waiting for Ike— Ike Miller."

She unfastened her raincoat, slipped the hood from her head, and shook her hair. "Ike? Is Ike coming?"

"He said he'd meet me here. He had to go somewhere and he said he'd meet me up here." Dan tried to sound as casual as possible.

Marian slipped off her raincoat and held it dripping in one hand. She seemed relaxed and perfectly at ease. The look of troubled anxiety was gone from her eyes, and instead there was something almost mischievous in their gleam. "Well, you know how Ike is. He's probably got himself involved somewhere. Is Kent here?"

"No. There was no one here. The door was open, so I came in to get out of the rain. My name is Banion, incidentally. Dan Banion."

"Yes, I know." She hung the coat on a hook. "I know quite a bit about you." She didn't seem to think it unusual that the door should be open or that Dan should be making himself at home.

"From what Ike told you?"

"Yes. Why don't you take your hat off?"

Dan realized that he was still wearing hat, coat, and gloves. "I didn't know how long I'd be here. I had a taxi, but I let it go. I—"

"We might as well make ourselves comfortable." She sat in the big chair and unzipped her galoshes. Her black hair, wild from a mussing under the hood, spilled forward and hung down loosely as she stooped to the task. "Where is Kent? Do you know?"

Dan removed his hat and struggled out of his topcoat. "I don't know. Ike said he'd probably be here." He left the gloves till last, reluctant to remove them. Then he reasoned that fingerprints didn't matter much now that he'd been discovered in the place. He took them off and threw them on top of his coat, which he had placed across the writing table, concealing the letter that was lying there.

She sighed and threw the galoshes one after the other on the floor. "I'll bet he doesn't show up."

"Who? Ike?"

"No. Kent." She stood up and walked a few paces into the room, mussing her hair and rubbing her scalp with her fingers. "I love this room."

She wasn't drunk, but Dan estimated her to be near the border line. "It's a nice place," he said.

"Are you shocked?"

"Should I be?"

She kicked off her shoes and walked softly to the fat little stove. "If you want. We used to be married. Why didn't you make a fire?"

"I didn't think of it. Here, let me do that."

Marian had opened the lid of the stove, picked an old newspaper out of a box beside it, and was crumpling it in her hands. Dan took it from her and rammed it in the stove. She relaxed in the big armchair, took a cigarette from the pack on the low table, and lit it.

"Have you ever been married?" she asked.

There was wood in a box nearby and a scuttle of coal. Dan put some sticks of kindling in the stove, then a shovelful of coal. "Once," he said.

"What do you think of it?"

Dan lit a match and started the paper burning, then closed the lid and adjusted the draft. "It was good." He whisked his hands together to shake off coal dust.

"What happened?" She reached for the wine bottle. Dan remembered the green lips in the morgue.

"Don't drink that."

"Why not?"

He stooped quickly and took the bottle from her. "It's sour."

"How do you know?"

"I tasted it. It's sour." He walked to the sink behind the corner screen, removed the cork to pour it down the drain, then remembered it might be important evidence. He corked it again and put it on a high shelf.

When he returned, Marian was searching in one of the cupboards under the long ledge. She stood up with a fresh bottle. Dan went over and took it from her.

"There's a corkscrew hanging over the sink," she said, familiarly.

Dan examined the bottle. Cannelli Brothers California Burgundy. It had a factory seal that looked all right. He began peeling off the plastic material that replaced tin foil during the war.

Marian returned to the big chair. "What happened to it?"

"What happened to what?"

"You said you were married."

"I was, but she—well, she's dead."

"Oh."

"You want to know a lot of things for a person who's hardly met me." Dan picked up a couple of glasses, took them to the sink, rinsed them thoroughly, found the corkscrew and returned. Marian was leaning back in the big chair dreamily, her chin tilted in the air.

"Do you feel that way—as if you'd just met me?"

Dan put the glasses down and began twisting the corkscrew into the cork. "No."

"How *do* you feel?"

"I feel like having a drink."

"You're a strange person. You were in the bar yesterday when I met Kent. You stared at me. Why?"

Dan shrugged.

"Why don't you tell me? Is there any reason why you shouldn't tell me?"

Dan had been about to pull the cork. He hesitated and looked at her in exasperation. "All right. I guess there isn't. You happen to be very beautiful. Does that satisfy you?" He pulled the cork with a *plop* and began easing the wine into glasses.

She laughed pleasantly. "That would satisfy any woman. I'm not, though."

"Take my word for it, you are."

"You stared at me again this evening at the Hobarts' house."

"Same reason." He handed her a glass.

"You've heard awful things about me, haven't you?"

"No." Dan pulled up an old-fashioned wooden rocker.

"How long have you known Kent?"

Dan raised his glass. "Here's luck."

They sipped and she asked him again, "How long have you known Kent?"

"Not very long."

She studied him with her deep brown eyes. They had the imploring look Dan had noticed earlier. "We used to be married. You'll probably hear awful things about me. They're not true."

"What happened?"

"You mean with Kent and me?"

"Yes."

"It was my fault. I was selfish. Then, later, I was a fool." She got up and strolled around with the glass in her hand. "Seriously, what do you think of marriage?"

"My own?"

"Anybody's."

Dan rolled a little wine around in his mouth before swallowing. It was good—very good. He held his glass to the light to enjoy the ruby color. "Do you know what are the two most miserable things in the world?"

"What are they?"

"Married men and unmarried men."

She laughed. "I was asking you seriously."

Dan leaned back in the rocker. "I don't know the answer. You look at married people, and they seem bored to death. You look at unmarried people, and their lives are impossible. I think marriage is the thing. But there are a lot of difficulties and contradictions people seem unwilling to face squarely."

"Hell, isn't it?"

"It's a problem."

"I've been married twice."

"Maybe you just didn't hit it right."

"Being unmarried is no answer."

"You get lonely."

She looked at him with feeling. "You get terribly lonely."

"Among other things," Dan added.

"Yes," she said, with emphasis. "Among other things." She began walking around the room thoughtfully. She noticed the easel, went over and looked at the unfinished drawing. She stood there quietly staring at it for some time.

"What do you think of it?" Dan asked.

When she looked at him, her eyes had that imploring look. "Kent's too good for me. He always was."

"I don't know why you say that."

"I have faults."

"Who hasn't?"

She looked back at the picture. "It's wonderful, like everything he does."

The telephone rang. She went over to it, walking silently in her stocking feet, and lifted the receiver. "Hello. Yes. Yes, of course. No. I just happened to be here. No. All right. Yes, I am. No, not at all. I'm all right. Don't be silly. I just dropped in. I was lonely, I guess. I haven't any idea. I'm going home. Certainly not. I have my car. Certainly not. You know I am. All right. Good night. Good night."

When she hung up the receiver, her eyes had a mischievous look. Dan looked at her inquiringly: She just stood thoughtfully probing one cheek with her tongue. Finally she said, "It was Kent. He's not coming home. We might as well go. I have my car. I can drive you."

Dan started. "It was *who?*"

"It was Kent. Why do you look like that? He just said he's not coming home. We might as well go. I can drive you."

Dan said, "Oh, Kent. Sure. He's not coming home, you say."

"No. I wouldn't wait for Ike if I were you. He's probably got sidetracked somewhere." She began putting on her shoes. "Hand me my galoshes, will you, Dan. I can call you Dan, can't I?"

"Oh, certainly." Dan couldn't help feeling he was getting the rush act out of the apartment.

When he picked up his topcoat from the writing table, he saw the unsealed letter to Marian still lying there face down.

CHAPTER NINE

Driving through the rain, Marian Cleave suddenly said, "It's all over between Kent and me."

The windshield wiper snapped back and forth. Dan waited for her to continue.

"I'm a fool. I've made so many mistakes."

"Why? Has something happened?"

"In a way. But it didn't mean anything. It didn't mean anything at all. Kent should have realized that."

"Tell me about it."

"Oh, it was nothing. I suppose if it hadn't been that, it would have been something else. It's all over, though. I know it."

"Suppose we stop some place and get a cup of coffee."

"Yes, let's. Dan, you may hear all kinds of things about me. They're not true."

"I won't believe them."

She slipped one hand from the steering wheel and gave his arm a squeeze. "Thanks."

Soon they were climbing another hill, and the neighborhood didn't seem to be in the direction of all-night coffeehouses. On a quiet street, she turned into a driveway. The headlights flashed across a lawn and revealed a one-story shingle house. There was a crunch of gravel under the tires, and she stopped beneath a shelter.

"It's my place. It will be much nicer. Do you mind?"

"No. Not at all."

As Dan stepped out of the car, he got a moist fragrance of growing things and rain-wet earth. She fumbled for keys and let them in through a heavy door. Inside was the smell of floor wax and furniture polish characteristic of houses well cared for by servants. The snap of a switch lit an expensive table lamp made from a fat Chinese vase. She reached a hanger out of a hall closet. "Let me take your coat."

The main room had the inevitable windows overlooking the bay. Lamps in various parts of the room gave a subdued light. The walls were of natural-finish redwood with built-in bookshelves well stocked with books. A large pebble-stone fireplace was at one end.

"Sit down and I'll fix some coffee. I love to stay up late." She walked to a small bar and selected a bottle. "Scotch, while you're waiting?"

"Yes. Thanks." Dan settled in a large davenport before the fireplace. "You've got a nice place here."

"Try living in it alone and you wouldn't think so. Light the fire, will you?"

Paper, kindling, and logs were already stacked. Dan leaned forward and touched a match. She handed him a large glass of whisky and soda with an ice cube floating in it, then pressed a button on an automatic phonograph that started soft music. "Be comfortable, Dan, while I fix the coffee."

When she left the room, Dan relaxed and watched the flames lick their way up the logs. What a joint! He sighed deeply. A gust of wind threw a patter of rain against the windows. It was warm. It was nice. He felt a glow inside him, and ideas inconsistent with duty began to form in his head. He lifted the Scotch and soda to his lips, then hesitated. The green lips in the morgue came back to him.

He sniffed at the glass, then held it up and looked at it. Ridiculous! What a silly idea! He put it to his lips and sipped. Good. He took a large swallow and relaxed.

What the hell was all this leading up to? On second thought, that seemed a foolish question. Lonely girl reacting to emotional rebound. If only this murder wasn't hanging over everything! What was that telephone call in Kipper's flat? Maybe just somebody phoning Kipper who recognized her voice. But why had she said it was Kipper? What were all these cryptic comments? Would she ever get down to talking straight? He mustn't hurry her. Let her take her time. Let her get it off her chest. Let her cry on his shoulder, then—

Marian was gone for some time. When she returned, he noticed she had changed into black silk slacks and a frilly white blouse. She had a single large white daisy fixed in her black hair.

"The coffee's dripping," she said. "It's nice with the rain and the fire. I like rain, if I'm not alone." She sat beside him on the davenport and pulled her feet up under her. She wore sandals held on by strings across her bare feet. Her feet were delicately shaped. The toenails were painted deep red.

Dan motioned with his glass toward some pictures on the wall. "You don't happen to have anything by Kipper around, do you?"

She bit her lip and her eyes shaded darkly. "Greg burned them. I had three Kent did of me. I loved them. Greg was jealous and burned them."

"That was your second husband, the man who came into the Hobarts' drunk tonight, wasn't it?"

"Yes. He denied it, but he burned them."

"Tell me about it."

"Well, it was the summer of last year, when I was up at Lake Tahoe. Greg stayed in town. When I returned, the paintings were gone. One had been hanging in my room, another in the living room. The other I had in a closet. They were gone. Greg said they'd been stolen. He said he'd come home one night and noticed they were gone, and that someone must have stolen them."

"Maybe he was telling the truth."

"No, he wasn't. I went through the ashes in the fireplace and found the tacks that held the canvas to the frames. I also found pieces of the frames that weren't quite all burned, and even the wire that was used to hang them, with the little round screws still attached. The fireplace was screened over in the summer, so I didn't find them until it began to get cold, and I moved the screen to make a fire."

"Did he still deny it?"

"Yes, but I knew he was lying."

"Did you love him? Greg, I mean."

Marian got up and walked to the little bar. "Don't let's talk about it. It was awful." She poured herself a straight shot and downed it. "Please don't let's talk about it. It's all over. I can't stand to think about it."

"I'm sorry," Dan said. But to himself he cursed this blind alley of "don't let's talk about it" that every subject seemed to wind up in.

"The coffee ought to be ready." She went out and returned with a tray, walking awkwardly, arching her eyebrows and watching the cups. As she stooped to set it on a low table, Dan noticed that she wasn't wearing a brassiere.

"Let's have a little brandy in it." She went to the bar and returned with a bottle, from which she poured generously into the cups. "There." She nestled into the davenport. "Now tell me something about yourself."

"Oh, I don't know," Dan said. "There isn't anything much to tell." He sipped the coffee. "That's pretty good."

"You're not happy, are you?"

Dan looked a little annoyed. "I wish people would stop harping on that subject. Who would expect to be happy in a world gnawed to ribbons by depression and shot up by war? They're continually wondering why they're not happy and why other people aren't happy, when, my God, the reason's obvious enough for anyone to see."

She put her hand on his arm and looked at him seriously. "You've suffered a lot, haven't you?"

"No. Not like some people."

"Yes, you have. I can see it."

"A lot of things give me a pain in the neck, if that's what you mean." She moved closer to him. "Dan, you like me, don't you?"

He stared into the coffee cup. "Of course."

"I saw it in your eyes. I saw it when you looked at me in the bar."

She was so near that he could feel her breath on his face. He could smell her perfume. It wasn't just her. It was any beautiful woman. Years in the army. Months of haphazard wandering since. It was ordinary woman hunger. But how could he tell her that?

"I saw it again at the Hobarts'. It's in your eyes, Dan."

It's in the eyes of half the nation, he reflected. But he said, "I'm not denying it."

"Dan, you've got some sense. You can take things as they are. You can forget things that don't mean anything. You know how life is."

What was she referring to now? What difference did it make? He moved his arm and discovered that it was around her.

"Dan, don't leave me alone tonight. I can't stand to be alone. I'll go mad if I'm alone."

He took her lips and pulled her across him with both arms.

"Take me, Dan. Take me and don't let me go."

He stopped thinking. They were quiet together for a few minutes. Then she began to cry softly. "I've got to have someone. I can't be alone. I can't."

"Nobody ought to be alone." Dan had put his coffee on the low table and forgotten it. He reached up an arm and pulled the cord on the lamp over the davenport.

"That's nicer," she said.

There was only the light from the fireplace and a little reflection from lamps at the other end of the room. The tiny buttons in her blouse had come undone. Dan felt the zipper of her silk slacks under his fingers. He felt along it until he found the catch. Suddenly a harsh buzzer sounded through the room.

Her body stiffened, and she leaned up on one elbow. They were both tense and listening. The buzzer sounded again, long, as if someone was holding a finger on the button.

"What is it?" Dan asked.

"Shhhhh! The doorbell."

The buzzer kept sounding persistently. Marian sat up and began buttoning her blouse. Dan pulled on the light above the davenport.

Marian stood, shook her hair, and ran her fingers through it. Her face was annoyed. The buzzer kept sounding. Dan stroked his suit to remove wrinkles.

"Damn it," she said, under her breath, and moved slowly toward the hall, rubbing one arm.

Dan got up, buttoned his coat and smoothed his hair.

The buzzing stopped, and presently he heard a man's voice in the hall. He tiptoed closer to hear, but he couldn't make it out. The tone suggested an argument. Marian's voice was insistent. The man's was placating. They talked for quite a while, then Marian came in followed by Lance Mallory.

"You met Lance, I think," she said.

Lance came forward smiling, his hand out. "Banion, of course. Glad to see you, old boy."

Dan accepted the hand. It was a firm grip.

Marian said in a bored voice, "Will you have a coffee and brandy, Lance?"

"Coffee, yes. Brandy, no." He looked at Dan. "Just saw a light. Thought I'd pop in for a minute." He settled himself on the davenport.

"I could have killed Greg tonight," Marian said. "I don't know what

I'm going to do if he keeps on. It's terribly embarrassing." She handed Lance a cup. "I hope it's not cold."

He sipped it. "Warmish. It's all right. I took him outside and walked him around a bit—let him talk a little—get it off his chest. He's a child."

Marian sat beside Lance on the davenport. "He'll kill himself if he doesn't stop drinking."

"Oh, Greg's all right. Don't be so hard on him. He'll straighten out."

Marian looked wistfully at Dan. "I don't know what I'd have done the past year without Lance. He's been a real Dutch Uncle."

"My God! Anything but that. I'm neither Dutch nor anybody's uncle."

"Well, guardian angel, then."

"That's worse. You make me sound like a St. Bernard dog."

She gripped his shoulder and shook it. "That's what you are, darling, and you don't know it. And you can cook, too."

Lance looked at Dan patronizingly. "Get Dan another drink. Don't mind us, Dan. When I first met this kid she was reading Laurence Hope."

Dan dropped into an easy chair. He was annoyed at having been suddenly thrust back into the position of an outsider. Marian got up and slouched toward the bar. "Will you have one too, Lance?"

"No thanks. The stuff doesn't seem to agree with me lately. I had a session with Guy and Arnie last night down the Peninsula at the old house. I had an awful head this morning."

"I don't know how you can stand Foisie," Marian said.

"Oh, Foisie's all right. You shouldn't take him seriously."

"You're in a regular Pollyanna mood tonight. Everybody's wonderful. Foisie's wonderful. Greg's wonderful. The world's wonderful." She came back walking gingerly with another tall Scotch and soda for Dan.

Lance smiled indulgently. "Oh, come now, Marian. Everyone's taking things too seriously nowadays. Especially themselves. Loosen up."

"Maybe you're right."

Lance tilted his chin and recited to the ceiling:

> *"Have we lost the mood romantic*
> *That was once our right by birth?*
> *Lo! the greenest girl is frantic*
> *With the woe of all the earth!"*

"What's that from?" Marian said.

"That was John Davidson."

Dan jiggled the ice in his glass. "I believe he also said: 'So perhaps we are in hell, for all that I can tell, and lost, and damned, and served up hot to God.'"

Lance appeared surprised. "Oh, so you know him. Odd chap, wasn't he?"

"He grasped something."

"A little on the morbid side."

Dan stared into his drink. "He lost hope. Maybe he couldn't help it. He gave up."

Marian looked from one of them to the other. "What do you mean?"

Lance again cocked his head and recited:

> *"Sometimes I think that God himself is cursed,*
> *For all His things go wrong. We cannot guess;*
> *He is very God of God, not God of men:*
> *We feel His power, His inhumanity;*
> *Yet, being men, we fain would think Him good.*
> *Since in imagination we conceive*
> *A merciful, gracious God of men.*
> *It may be that our prayer and innocent life*
> *Will shame Him into goodness in the end.*
> *Meantime, His vengeance is upon us; so,*
> *My blessing and God's curse be with you all."*

"Good grief!" Marian said.

Dan took a gulp of his drink and set it down. "After writing that, he went out and shot himself."

Marian curled her lips disdainfully. "What a morbid mind!"

Lance shrugged. "His troubles were practical. He had too many children and couldn't feed them."

"He shouldn't have given up," Dan said.

Lance held his palms out. "What else could he have done?" "Nowadays when people can't feed their children they don't shoot themselves. They shoot someone else."

"How the devil did we get onto this subject?" Lance asked.

Marian sighed. "What a world!"

Lance reached over and rumpled her hair. "You worry too much about everything. Just forget it. A million years from now it won't make any difference. And now we're going to go home and let you get some sleep. Coming, Banion?"

Dan responded reluctantly. "Well, I guess so. Yes." He looked at

Marian. She sighed and pouted her lips.

Lance opened a door that led into the house. "Pardon me a moment. This is the way, isn't it?"

"Second door to your left," Marian yawned.

When they heard his footsteps going down the hall, Marian tiptoed over and pressed herself against Dan. "Call me tomorrow. The number's in the book." Her lips were reaching, so Dan took them.

"Call me in the afternoon. You won't forget?"

"I'll call."

"Be sure."

"I'll be sure."

Lance's footsteps were returning. They separated. Lance entered rubbing his hands together jauntily. "It's cold in that hall. Are you ready, old boy? Let's go."

As Lance Mallory was driving Dan back to his hotel, he said, "Marian's a fine girl. I'm very fond of her."

"Yes," Dan said.

"People don't understand her very well."

"No?"

"She's had a frightful amount of trouble. I'm hoping she can get herself straightened out now."

"You mean her divorce?"

"Yes, that and everything else."

Dan waited but Lance did not explain what he meant by "everything else." Finally Dan said, "You've known her quite a long while?"

"Oh yes. She's really a very fine girl. I've always been terribly fond of her." Lance's voice had the quiet warning quality of a vigilant protector.

"Yes," Dan agreed. "She's—ah—very charming."

"She's rather impressionable. Of course, she'll get over it. Right now is a rather difficult time for her."

"Yes, of course."

"I wouldn't want to see anyone take advantage of her."

"Of course not."

"She's too fine a girl." Lance peered out of the car. "Is this your hotel?"

As Dan opened the car door, Lance seemed on the point of saying something. Then he apparently changed his mind. "Good night, Banion."

CHAPTER TEN

As Dan entered his hotel, the gray little man behind the desk put down the newspaper he was reading, eyed him critically, fished his key out of the pigeonhole, and threw it on the blotter.

Dan stopped before he got to the desk and entered a telephone booth.

There was no sense in delaying any longer. This wandering like a ghost in the dead man's living environment could be carried too far. Further delay in identifying the body might work to the advantage of the murderer.

In a moment he had the city desk of the *Journal* on the line. "Rufe, this is Dan, I—"

"Where the hell have you been, son? Don't you have sense enough to call in once in a while?"

"Rufe, I've got something—"

"It's 4:00 A.M. Do you know that?"

"Do you want this, or don't you?"

"The boss wants you to get active on that corpse they found in a spaghetti box. It intrigues him."

"Oh, that."

"Yeah, just that. You better get off your dead bird. Where you been?"

"You want to know who killed the guy, is that the idea?"

"Well, find out who the guy was first, stupid."

"I know who he was."

"You what?"

"I know who he was."

The voice over the wire yelled so loudly Dan had to hold the receiver away from his ear. "Well, what are you gonna do? Write us a postcard. Unload, damn it, unload."

"If you'll shut up long enough to let me get a word in—"

"I'm asking you, who was it?"

"Kenton Kipper, an artist."

"Never heard of him."

"Too bad. Then I guess you're not interested."

"Cut the goddamn nonsense. Is this straight?"

"I've been up all night running it down. Get your pencil ready." Dan gave him the particulars.

"How do I know you're not just drunk?"

"Don't worry, I'm going to double check it. Get the story all ready to roll. I'm going to drag a witness out of bed and bring him down there to identify the body officially."

"Phone me the minute he makes the identification. And don't tell a soul before that. I'll have an edition ready to hit the streets. And God help you if there's any slip-up."

"There won't be."

"Have you any ideas on who might have done it?"

"I'm working on that. This story has what we educated people call ramifications."

"Keep right on it. Don't let it get away from you."

"You don't mind if I take time out for a little sleep, do you?"

"Yeah. I mind plenty. Get that identification and call me back before you start lying down. God knows when you'd wake up. And keep out of trouble. We don't want any law suits."

When Dan left the phone booth, he walked straight to the door and out into the street again.

The gray little man behind the desk looked after him with sour eyes. He picked up the key and threw it violently back into the pigeonhole.

Ike Miller had not been exaggerating when he said he lived in a dump. Dan could barely distinguish the number in the cracked and peeled gold lettering of the door. The knob pivoted loosely in his hand when he gripped it, because the screws that held it in place had fallen out, and no one had been interested enough to replace them. The lock appeared as if the key had been lost years ago and nobody cared. It was one of those buildings that had died long ago, but which had been revived for tenancy by the wartime housing crisis. Ike had said he was lucky to find even this.

The hall inside was lighted by feeble little bulbs burning nakedly in ancient fixtures. It smelled like the inside of an old shoe. There was carpet on the stairs, but it had evidently been tacked there twenty years ago and never swept.

Along the gloomy halls were cheap pine doors with aluminum numbers tacked on. The carpet was worn through in many places, and the halls were littered with old bedsprings, parts of stoves, mattresses, and other junk piled there for lack of storage space.

On the third floor Dan found 320. Some joker had painted the name "Ike" on it in flowery letters, with clumsy cupids flying around. Someone farther down the hall was snoring or strangling, it was hard to judge which. There would be three or four long, ripping, regular snores, then it would be tripped up in snarling, gasping confusion. Then the long, easy snores would continue for three or four more, and trip up in snorting chaos again.

Dan rapped his knuckles moderately and waited. Then he knocked louder. He heard bedsprings creak. He knocked again and heard whispered voices. He knocked a fourth time, and the bedsprings creaked louder. Presently he heard Ike's voice on the other side. "Who is it?"

"It's me. Dan. Open up."

"Who?"

"Dan. Dan Banion. Open up."

A bolt rattled and the door opened a few inches. Ike's sleepy face appeared in the crack.

"Let me in, Ike. I've got to see you."

"Jesus Christ! What time is it?"

Dan pushed a little against the door. "Let me in."

Ike held it firmly, grimaced, and jerked his head backward to indicate he had someone with him. To confirm him, the springs creaked again, and a sleepy feminine voice whined complainingly, "Who is it?"

Ike spoke back into the dark room in a half whisper. "It's Dan. Dan Banion."

The voice yawned, "What's he want?"

"Let me in," Dan repeated. "I've got to talk to you."

"Wait a minute," Ike said. "I'll put something on and come out."

"Oh, let him in," yawned the feminine voice. "What of it?"

Ike let go of the door. "Okay. Come on in." He turned on a small lamp that half lit the room.

Dan stepped inside and closed the door behind him. It was a large room with two windows and a naked-looking washbasin in the corner. It looked as if it had been ransacked by burglars who never found what they were after, but were thorough in their search. The dresser drawers were partly open, and tails and ends of clothing were hanging out of them. The toilet articles on top were all mixed up with cooking utensils, unclean coffee cups, salt and pepper shakers, books, and writing materials.

Clothes were heaped or strewn on all the chairs. A two-burner gas plate held dirty pans. A girl was lying in the bed face down. A few strands of long, dark hair and a pointed elbow were all that showed. Dan guessed her to be Lorna Cargill.

Ike was wrapped in a yellow bathrobe. He lifted a bottle with a few inches of sherry in the bottom. "I can't offer you much of a drink."

Dan pushed it aside. "Never mind a drink. Sit down. I've got to talk to you."

Ike cleared a couple of chairs by throwing the clothes on the floor. "Sit down. What's all the panic?"

"I hate to have to tell you this, Ike, but your friend Kipper is dead."

Ike blinked. "What are you talking about?"

"He's dead."

"Kent Kipper?"

"Yes. He's dead."

Ike's sleepy brain was gradually thawing out. "You don't mean— Jesus! I'm sorry to hear it. When did this happen?"

Lorna Cargill sat up in bed. "What—what did he say?"

Ike turned to her. "Kent Kipper. He says he's dead."

Lorna's eyes became agonized. She bit her knuckle and began to cry.

"When did it happen?" Ike asked.

"Night before last, or early yesterday morning."

Lorna threw herself on the pillow and wept in a torrent.

Ike rubbed his face. "How did it happen?"

"That's why I woke you up. He was murdered."

Ike's face jerked to attention. "No."

"You remember that corpse they found in a packing case yesterday?"

"The one off the truck?"

"Yes."

"You don't mean that was Kent?"

"It was."

"How do you know?"

"I saw it."

"You—" Ike's eyes became suspicious. "How long have you known about this?"

"Now don't get excited. I knew about it yesterday afternoon."

"So that's why you were asking me all those questions."

Lorna was sitting up in bed listening and poking at her nose with a knot of a handkerchief.

"I would have told you, but I sort of wanted to—"

"That's a hell of a goddamn thing to do."

"I'm telling you now. What the hell do you think I got you out of bed for?"

"Jesus Christ, Dan! Anybody else, I might expect it, but you and me—"

"Listen, Ike, I'm telling you now. You're the only one I have told. I phoned in my story a few minutes ago, but the body hasn't even been identified."

"How do you know it's him?"

"It's him all right. But I want you to come down to the morgue and make it official."

Dan turned his eyes to the window. Behind his back he could hear Lorna rustling into her clothes.

Ike said, "It doesn't make sense, Dan. Who the hell would want to kill Kent?"

"That's what I want to find out. Did he have any enemies?"

"Nobody who'd want to kill him. It's hard to say."

"That dirty little bitch," Lorna said in a hard voice.

Ike was disparaging. "Marian? Don't be crazy."

"What made you think of her?" Dan asked.

"Don't listen to her," Ike said. "She's got it in for Marian."

"I knew that dirty little bitch would kill him."

"Don't be ridiculous," Ike said.

Dan heard Lorna fussing with pans on the two-burner plate, and looked around again. She had her dress on and was rinsing out the coffee pot. Ike was floundering into his clothes.

Dan repeated, "What makes you say she might have done it?"

"She has driven every man crazy she ever had anything to do with."

Ike gestured with a sock he was about to put on. "That doesn't mean she'd kill anybody. Besides, how could she nail anybody up in a packing case?"

"She's not so weak."

Ike paused with his foot half into the sock. "Say, I just thought of something. There's that guy Glotcher."

"I was thinking of him," Dan said. "But he's too stupid."

"Maybe."

"How about Gregory Fallon?"

Ike pondered it. "He was jealous of Kent, all right. But, Dan, you know how it is. People you know—you can't imagine any of them as murderers."

A thin, blue light of dawn was beginning to show on the windows. The smell of hot coffee filled the room.

"You mark my words," Lorna said. "That little bitch had something to do with it."

CHAPTER ELEVEN

It was Kenton Kipper all right. Ike identified him instantly. So did Lorna.

Dan didn't wait around to see Inspector Gallagher. The longer he could postpone that encounter, the better. Besides, the strain of his all-night ramble was beginning to drag at his shoulder blades. He headed for his hotel, tumbled into bed, and let darkness take him.

He was awakened at noon by the ringing of the phone. He had left word at the hotel desk to call him at that hour. They had to ring quite a while before he staggered up to answer.

Now what? He scratched his head and looked back at the bed. It was tempting, but he didn't dare lie down again. He turned some cold water into the basin and doused his face until he was awake.

Things began coming back to him. A jumble of faces and places and tangled personalities. Marian Cleave! Lance Mallory! Gregory Fallon! Lorna! Janey Navarro!

He examined his face in the mirror with the usual critical lack of enthusiasm. He didn't feel so bad, considering all those drinks. He had phoned Rufe Robinson at the *Journal* immediately after the body had been identified. The edition must have hit the streets long ago. Everybody in town knew about it by this time. Inspector Gallagher was no doubt on the job with an army of photographers and fingerprint experts.

While he shaved, Dan tried to piece together his experiences of the previous night. There was something definitely screwy about the elusiveness of Kipper's paintings. Whenever you asked to see one, it was either lost or strayed or sold to someone who couldn't be located.

Then there was that telephone call in Kipper's apartment. Marian had answered it and said it was Kipper. That was a nice one! But who had it been?

How did Glotcher fit into the picture? God's gift to women! Not much of a gift, either. Kipper was supposed to have slugged him. Why was that? According to Ike, it had been in Chinatown, and Janey Navarro had been present. Maybe she could explain it.

Dan finished shaving and stepped into the freshly pressed trousers of his other suit. When it came to transferring the contents of the pockets from one suit to the other, he discovered a little saddle-bit bulldog pipe with a gold band. Real French briar. A beauty! Where had that come from?

He remembered picking it up on the stairs going up to Kipper's apartment. Someone must have dropped it there. Whoever it was would be eating his heart out. It was a jewel. Must have cost twenty bucks. Cut right out of the center of the burl. He put it to his nose. Smelled good, too.

The initials "G.V.F." were engraved on the gold band. That could be Gregory something-or-other Fallon. Middle name Victor, maybe. Or

Vincent.

What would he have been doing on Kipper's stairway? That's what you'd call a clue. He put it in his pocket and finished dressing.

Outside the sky had cleared, and the sun was putting a golden hand on the gray buildings. A busy little wind was ruffling skirts and awnings, though, and might bring more clouds or fog in off the ocean.

Dan had a hell of a time getting breakfast. All the restaurants were crowded with the noon-hour rush. When he asked for ham and eggs the waiter scowled at him and showed his teeth. No fry cook likes to stop in the middle of the noon hour rush to fry eggs. Dan compromised and ate a lunch with meat and potatoes, but it didn't seem right.

He had a copy of the *Journal* with him and read the account of Kipper's murder, considering it a very sloppy job of rewrite. They'd stuck his by-line over it. A few extra facts they'd dug up had been added. Kipper had been born in San Francisco, his parents were dead. There was no mention of other relatives. His father had been the captain of a tugboat. They had even found a photograph of Kipper somewhere. The poisoning had been confirmed by the morgue's toxicologist, who didn't name the poison, merely stating that it was deadly and quick acting.

Dan took out his notebook and studied the things he had scribbled during the previous night. The Bishop Gallery on Sutter Street! That would be as good a place as any to begin. He'd have to move fast. He read the list of persons who were supposed to have bought Kipper's paintings. Odd that they should seem so familiar.

Someone jabbed him fiercely in the ribs. "Why don't you go to the public liberry if you want to read?" A fat woman with artificial cherries on her hat was standing behind his lunch-counter stool waiting to take his place.

"I'm sorry."

"This isn't a liberry. People have to eat." She raised her voice in order to shame him before his fellow citizens. A look of mounting savagery gleamed in her eye. Dan knew when to accept defeat. He scrambled down rapidly.

She mounted the stool with the satisfied expression of one who had properly chastised an idiot. "Some people got all day. Others got to earn their livings."

The Bishop Gallery had a large store front on Sutter Street, with a few paintings displayed in the windows. Dan paused to study one of them, but couldn't make head or tail of what he saw. The picture appeared to be the insides of a clock with a lot of human anatomy mixed in. An enormous eye, divorced from its socket, was lying off to one side. A card on a little rack under the painting read: "Existophrenic Landscape by Arnold Winkleman." Dan gave it up and entered.

A nearsighted blonde woman wearing thick glasses and a tan smock came forward arching her eyebrows.

"Could I see the manager?" Dan asked.

"You mean Mr. Foisie?"

"Is he the manager?"

"Yes. I'll see if he's busy."

Foisie! Must be that fat—

Before Dan could finish the thought, Guy Foisie, the enormous man he had met at the Hobarts' place, came beaming from behind a partition. "Danny boy. You've come to see me."

"Well, not exactly," Dan said. He extracted his hand from Foisie's flabby grip.

"Have you heard about poor Kipper?" Foisie said. "I think it's simply frightful. I think it's the most awful thing I ever heard of."

"That's what I came to see you about."

"We've all been terribly upset," Foisie said.

"Yes, well, I understand you had some of Kipper's paintings here that you sold for him."

"Oh yes. But that was some time ago."

"Do you have any by him in the place now?"

"No. I'm sorry. No, we don't. We have a display of Arnie's things, though. I think you'll love them. Let me show you."

"No, thanks," Dan said. "Not right now. Tell me, had Kenton Kipper been inquiring about his pictures recently? Since he got out of the army?"

"Inquiring? Oh yes. We paid him, you know, what we had received for them. Less our commission, of course."

"I mean, had he been inquiring who had bought them."

The blonde woman, who had been hovering nearby, said, "We gave him the names and addresses of the purchasers, but he came in later and complained that he couldn't locate the people."

"Of course, we don't know anything about that," Foisie added.

"How many pictures did you have?"

"There were three, weren't there?" Foisie said.

"Yes. I sold one, and Miss Hollingsworth sold the other two," said the blonde woman.

"Do you remember anything about the people who bought them?"

"Why, yes. The man who bought one from me was rather heavy-set with thick eyebrows. The reason I happen to remember is because he impressed me as being not the sort of person you would expect to be interested in paintings."

"What do you mean by that?" Dan asked.

"Well, he dressed rather vulgarly and his manner of speaking was coarse."

"Do you recall his name?"

"Olin. Robert Olin. Mr. Kipper asked me these same questions when he was in."

"Oh well," Foisie said, "it's very likely the man moved out of town, or something like that. I don't think it's important."

"Where did you deliver the painting?" Dan asked.

"We didn't deliver it," said the blonde woman. "He paid cash and took it along in the car."

"How about the other lady you mention. Does she remember anything about the people who bought the other two paintings?"

"Now that you mention it, Mr. Kipper didn't get to talk to her. She was on vacation the day he was in here."

"Is she here now? Can I see her?"

"Why, yes. I'll call her." The blonde woman went behind the partition.

Foisie put a hand on Dan's shoulder. "I wish you'd let me show you Arnie's exhibit. The boy is really remarkable."

"Some other time," Dan said.

The blonde woman returned with a short, curly-haired brunette in a blue smock. "This is Miss Hollingsworth."

When Dan had explained what he wanted to know, she pursed her lips and opened her eyes widely. "I knew it. I knew there was something funny about that woman."

"Then it was a woman who bought them?" Dan said.

"Yes. A tall blonde."

"Good looking?"

"Some people might think so. I wouldn't. She lied about her name."

"How do you mean she lied about her name?"

"She lied. I saw her picture in the paper a few days later, and it was an entirely different name. The name she gave me was Mrs. Benjamin Jeby."

"What name did she have in the paper?"

"I don't remember. It was Dorothy something. She was the woman who was mixed up with that attorney, and whose husband got mad."

Foisie appeared startled. "Good heavens! You don't mean Gregory Fallon, do you?"

"Yes. That was the name of the attorney. I don't remember the woman's name."

"It's fantastic," said Foisie. "Utterly fantastic. I'm sure you must be mistaken."

"No, I'm not," Miss Hollingsworth said firmly.

"Are you positive," Dan said, "that the woman whose picture you saw in the paper was the same one who came in here and bought a painting?"

"Two paintings," Miss Hollingsworth corrected. "She bought two of them."

"Could you identify her, if you ever saw her again?"

"Yes. I'm sure I could."

"Thank you very much," Dan said.

"Is anything wrong?" Foisie asked.

"Just that a man's been murdered."

"Wait a minute. Aren't you going to look at Arnie's exhibit?"

"Some other time. Much obliged." Dan shot out of the place leaving Foisie with his mouth open. He headed straight for the offices of the *Journal*.

In the back files of the paper, he had no trouble finding the picture he was after. A luscious-looking blonde was posing on the edge of a table, showing plenty of leg. The caption above it read: "$50,000 Worth of Affection." The story was headed:

VET SUES 'OTHER MAN' FOR FIFTY GRAND

Howard Vane, 37, recently discharged from the army, has filed a fifty-thousand-dollar alienation of affections suit against Gregory Fallon, San Francisco attorney.

Vane asserts that he entered his wife's apartment about 1:00 A.M. last Monday morning and found his wife and Fallon in a "state of undress." A fight ensued. Neighbors called the police and both men were taken in custody. The wife, Mrs. Dorothy Vane, lives at 1262 Bush Street.

Fallon declined to comment on the suit. He is married, and a graduate of the University of California Law School.

From the *Journal's* morgue, Dan obtained a copy of the photograph, and tucked it in his pocket.

1262 Bush Street was a plaster-front apartment house. The brass mailboxes were brightly shined, indicating janitor service, at least. Dan rang the apartment marked Dorothy Vane. Presently, the lock of the iron-grilled door began to buzz.

The entrance hall was furnished with objects that it would be difficult to pick up and walk out with. A large plaster urn with ferns growing in it. A bench of cast cement, with a plush cushion.

The stairs had good carpet and were well padded. The clean white doors in the hall above had brass numerals. Number 20 opened the instant he put his finger on the buzzer. Dan saw a tall, buxom blonde with moist eyes and thin eyebrows, whom he recognized as the girl in the picture. She wore a blue dressing gown and was holding a piece of toast in her hand. Her taffy-colored hair was propped haphazardly on her head with pins. When she saw Dan, one hand went self-consciously to her hair, and the other was embarrassed by the piece of toast.

"Mrs. Vane?"

"Yeah," she said in a tentative voice.

"I'm a reporter from the *Journal*. I wonder if I could talk to you for a few minutes?"

She took a moment to think about that. "What for?"

"It's nothing that concerns you personally. Only, you may be able to give me some advice."

She thought about that for a moment, too. "Come in."

He followed her through a narrow hall to a small room that contained a chesterfield set, a rug, a standing lamp, a table with a few fashion and movie magazines on it, a standing ash tray, a Maxfield Parrish print of a naked girl in a swing, and absolutely nothing else. An extra-wide door that concealed a wall bed was partly closed, but the corner of a sheet was sticking out of it. The ash tray was littered with butts smeared with red lipstick. A tantalizing, womanish smell pervaded the room.

"I was havin' my breakfast." She giggled and rammed the piece of toast in her mouth. "Kinda late breakfast, huh?"

"Don't let me interrupt you."

She licked her fingers. "I was finished. Wait a minute." She disappeared through a door off the narrow hall. When she returned, she had lipstick on her wide, thick lips, her eyebrows had been penciled darker, and her hair was poked into some kind of pattern.

She slumped into an overstuffed chair and crossed her legs, slitting the dressing gown to above the knee. Her legs were well shaped, but pudgy. There was a black and blue mark on one of them.

"Have you seen the morning paper?" Dan asked.

"Uh-uh."

Dan unfolded his copy, leaned across, and spread it in her lap. She looked it over in an uninterested way, glancing from item to item. "They're lettin' all the boys out of the navy." She sounded disappointed. Suddenly she giggled. "A man was arrested for walkin' across Golden Gate Bridge with no clothes on."

Dan waited patiently.

"Know what he said when they took him to the station? 'Make the most of it.'" She laughed raucously. "Some people are dopey." Her eyes moved to another item. "Some guy got killed. Tsch, tsch, tsch, tsch! Murder." She started to move on to another item, then her eyes darted back seriously. The smile disappeared from her lips. She read it all, then folded the paper and handed it back.

"Did you read about Kenton Kipper?" Dan asked.

"Sure. It says a guy by that name was killed."

"Murdered."

"I read it."

"Some months ago, Mrs. Vane, you bought a couple of paintings by Kenton Kipper from the Bishop Gallery."

"I never did." She sat straighter and closed the gap in her dressing gown to less inviting width.

"The girl there can identify you."

"That's a lie. I never bought any paintin's in my life. What would I do with a paintin'?"

Dan wondered himself. "I'm not saying you had anything to do with Kipper's murder, but I would like to know about those paintings."

"You're crazy. I don't know anything about any paintin's. I don't know what you're talkin' about." She was almost convincing.

"Who did you buy them for?"

"I just told you I didn't buy 'em."

"If you're trying to protect someone else, it just won't work."

"What the hell's the matter with you? I told you I don't know anything about it."

"You bought those paintings for Gregory Fallon, didn't you."

"Gregory Fallon!" Her voice quieted. "What's he got to do with it?"

"You did buy them for Fallon, didn't you?"

"I tell you I didn't buy any paintin's for nobody."

"You're making a serious mistake in not being frank. You ought to put yourself in the clear on this thing as soon as possible. I can help you. But not if you keep denying everything."

"But I don't understand. What does Fallon have to do with it?"

"Fallon was married to Kenton Kipper's ex-wife. He had good reason to be jealous of Kipper."

"You mean Fallon's wife used to be married to this guy who was killed?"

"That's the situation."

She pondered a moment. "Do you think Fallon killed him?"

"I didn't say that. I do say he's mixed up in it. And you're going to be dragged in too, unless you clear yourself now. Why did you buy those paintings?"

"How could I be dragged in?"

"You know your connection with Fallon."

Her eyes were really worried. "It doesn't make sense."

"Why don't you tell me why you bought the paintings and what you did with them?"

"I didn't buy them."

"How would you like me to write a news story saying that you did, then leave it for you to prove otherwise?"

"That would be stinking."

Dan stood up, as if to go. "I guess there's no use trying to reason with you."

She rose quickly and held his arm, a look of stupid fear on her face. "Wait a minute. I don't know anything about this. But give me a couple of hours. I'll try to find out."

"I want the truth right now."

She widened her limpid eyes. "I'm telling you the truth."

"Then what is it you want to find out?"

"Please give me two hours. I think I can tell you what you want to know, if you'll give me two hours."

Dan looked at his watch. "If I come back in two hours and you're not here, the story goes in. Do you understand that?"

"I'll be here. You can phone me, if you want."

Dan took out his notebook. "What's the number?"

"Ordway 9578."

As he wrote it down, he got an idea. "Mind if I use your phone?"

"You're not going to call the cops?"

"No."

"It's in the hall."

He kept his notebook and pencil in hand. She stayed in the room pacing up and down.

It was just as he had hoped. Although there was no telephone pad outside, she was a wall-scribbler. The telephone was in a recess, and on the white woodwork beside it, an assortment of phone numbers had been penciled. For the sake of appearances, he dialed the number of the *Journal*, then began copying down the numbers.

When the switchboard girl at the *Journal* answered, he said: "Is Mr.

Loganberry there?"

"We don't have any Mr. Loganberry."

He skipped a few that were plainly marked grocery, hairdresser, and liquor, but copied down the rest. One in particular interested him. It was penciled blacker than the rest, had a circle around it, but no name attached.

"What time will he be in?"

"We don't have any Mr. Loganberry."

"Well, will you just tell him Mr. Banion called." He had finished the list, so he hung up.

As he slipped the notebook in his pocket, Dorothy Vane came into the hall with his hat. "Just two hours," she said.

"All right. And you'd better be here."

"Don't worry," she said. "I'll be here."

CHAPTER TWELVE

A block away from Dorothy Vane's apartment, Dan went into a bar called the Pearl Harbor, ordered a beer, and studied the list of names and numbers he'd copied. Joe, Tillie, Howard, Valerie, and Mike. The only number without a name was the one that had been circled.

Howard might be Dorothy's husband, Howard Vane. No harm in finding out. Dan stepped into the phone booth at the end of the bar and dialed the number.

A gruff voice said, "Flint Hotel."

"Is Mr. Howard Vane there?"

"No. He hasn't been here for months."

"Did he leave any forwarding address?"

The man at the other end yelled a question over his shoulder, then said, "No forwarding address."

"Any idea where he is?"

"No idea." The man hung up.

Dan dropped another nickel and called the nameless number that had been circled. The line was busy. He returned to the bar, drank a little more of his beer, and tried again.

"A man's voice answered. "Price Agency."

"Who's this speaking?"

"Barney Price."

"Wrong number," Dan said, and hung up.

The phone book was dangling nearby on a chain. He opened it and ran his finger along the *P*'s until he found "Price Detective Agency."

The number tallied with the one he had just called.

What in the blazes! Who would be apt to know about an outfit like that? Nix Peters, probably. He rang up Nix Peters in the pressroom of the Hall of Justice.

"Say Nix, do you know a guy named Barney Price?"

"I know a guy named Dan Banion who pulled a fast one on me yesterday, and I'm gonna put arsenic in his beer."

"Now take it easy, Nix. That wasn't any fast one."

"I belong to the old-fashioned school that still thinks a mile a minute is fast. You knew that cadaver Gallagher showed us."

"Well, not exactly. No, I didn't."

"Don't tell me you didn't have a line on that guy."

"I admit I saw him drinking in a bar. That's all."

"You know, son, we co-operate around here. Scoop hounds are a nuisance."

"You mean you snooze on that couch in the pressroom and wait for the stories to come in to you."

"That's modern journalism, son. Besides, I have corns. No hard feelings. I'm just ribbing you. What were you asking?"

"Do you know a guy named Barney Price?"

"You don't mean the Barney Price that runs that phoney detective agency?"

"That's him. What kind of an outfit does he have?"

"Keyhole peeping for divorce grounds, mostly. Though I don't think he'd turn down any dollar, however dirty. Years ago he was on the force. Later he went in the ring. He promoted prize fights for a time. Still does, once in a while. Divorces are his specialty, but I've heard he does a little fancy pimping on the side. That what you want to know?"

"Has he got much of an organization?"

"Barney? No. He's a one-man show. I guess he's got a few stooges around here and there he farms out work to, but that's about all. Strictly shoestring. That's Barney. Why are you so interested?"

"Just curious, Nix. Much obliged."

"You better keep out of Inspector Gallagher's way, son. He's wise to the way you slipped one over on him yesterday. He'd like to chew your ears off."

"I'll watch it, Nix. Thanks again."

"Don't mention it, son. Any time you run out of brains, just help yourself to mine. God knows I don't use them."

Price Detective Agency! That might mean anything or nothing. Barney Price might be one of Dorothy Vane's boy friends. Or maybe they had a business arrangement. Anyhow, it was worth looking into.

Dan took a taxi to the address indicated in the phone book. It was a dilapidated building on O'Farrell Street with a dingy entrance and a flimsy-looking automatic elevator. The directory of tenants on the wall listed the Price Detective Agency in room 408.

Dan wrestled the doors of the automatic elevator, pressed the button for the fourth floor, and the cage groaned slowly upward. On the fourth floor, the waiting shadow of a man appeared on the cloudy glass of the elevator door. Dan pushed back the door and found himself face to face with Armand Glotcher.

For a moment they stood there looking at each other, neither able to figure out what sort of greeting the occasion required. Glotcher was hatless and wore a loose brown overcoat with a green muffler.

Above the green muffler, Glotcher's dark eyes were startled and puzzled. Then his face relaxed into a sneer, as if he'd figured something out. He burst out laughing, pushed past Dan into the elevator, and slammed the door. When the cage started downward, Dan could still hear him laughing.

What was eating that guy? Instinctively, Dan looked down at his clothes to see if anything was wrong. What was so funny? Dan shrugged and went looking for room 408. Maybe this visit wasn't going to be a waste of time after all. What the devil was Glotcher doing here?

The hall was scarred and dimly lighted. The doors had panes of cheap frosted glass. He found the Price Detective Agency, and opened the door. A thick-shouldered, bull-necked man in shirt sleeves and unbuttoned vest sat behind a desk grunting into a phone. His hair was streaked with gray, but his eyebrows were thick and black. A fat cigar was gripped in his teeth. Without taking his attention from the phone, he raised one hand and fanned it toward himself, motioning for Dan to enter.

In addition to the desk, there was a filing cabinet, an old iron safe, and several yellow oak chairs that were thoroughly scratched and nicked. The walls, almost from ceiling to floor, were covered with framed photographs of prize fighters and ring scenes.

Presently the man said into the phone, "Hold it a minute." Clamping his hand over the mouthpiece, he gave Dan a quick scrutiny. "Grab a chair. I'll be with you in a jiff." He turned his attention again to the telephone. "Okay, shoot. What time was all this?" He continued grunting and nodding his head.

Instead of sitting down, Dan strolled about the room and looked at the pictures on the walls. Quite a collection. Huskies in black tights or loose shorts, crouching, scowling, threatening with their gloves. Hairy chests and hairy legs. Old-time outdoor ring scenes with men in derbies and handlebar mustaches crowding the ropes. John L. Sullivan, James J. Corbett, Al McCoy, Philadelphia Jack O'Brien, Stanley Ketchel, Paul Berlenbach, Ad Wolgast-

Dan halted with a sensation of excitement. Ad Wolgast, lightweight champ from 1912 to 1914. Adele Wolgast, the woman who was supposed to have bought two of Kenton Kipper's paintings from the Black Pot.

Paul Berlenbach, light-heavyweight champion from 1925 to 1926. That was the name given by the man who bought one of Kipper's paintings from the Iron Cat.

Behind Dan's back, Barney Price continued grunting into the phone. "Yeah," he said. "Well, I've got it now. You don't have to worry. I've got it here."

Dan skipped his eye over a few more pictures and came to Ben Jeby, middleweight title holder for 1932. Mrs. Benjamin Jeby was the name Dorothy Vane had given at the Bishop Gallery.

A little farther on was Joe Walcott, welterweight champ from 1901 to 1904. Mrs. Joseph Walcott was one of the names on the list of purchasers he'd copied from the returned letters in Kipper's flat. Next to Walcott was Sammy Mandell, lightweight champ from 1926 to 1930. Mr. Samuel Mandell was another of the alleged purchasers.

Other names under fiercely posed fighters along the wall continued to check with the list. Fred Steele, middleweight champ from 1936 to 1938. Jimmy Goodrich, lightweight champ of 1925. Bob Olin, light-heavyweight title holder from 1934 to 1935. Robert Olin was the name given by the man who bought one of Kipper's paintings from the Bishop Gallery. And the blonde woman there had said the man who bought it had thick eyebrows.

Dan turned and studied the bushy brows of Barney Price, who still crouched over his telephone with the round-shouldered concentration of a gorilla eating a banana. "I can't tell you now," he was grunting. "No, I can't tell you over the phone. It's impossible."

Dan resumed his inspection of the pictures. Lou Brouillard, welterweight champ in 1931. That checked with Mrs. Louis Brouillard. Pete Latzo, welterweight champ in 1926. That would be Mrs. Peter Latzo. John Henry Lewis, light-heavyweight champ of 1935 to 1936. Frank Klaus, who claimed the middleweight title in 1911 to 1913. And there was James J. Jeffries. That could be the name beginning with a J that Chuck Leary, the bartender in The Wreck, had such difficulty remembering. No wonder the names seemed familiar!

Behind him, Dan heard Barney Price bang down the receiver. He turned to see him thrusting the phone aside with both hands, as if it were something he wanted to be rid of forever. "Goddamn! This is my day for ass aches. What do you want, son?" Without even looking at Dan, he opened a yellow envelope on his desk, took out what appeared to be a photograph, studied it, and chuckled.

Dan took a chair. Barney Price continued to stare at the photograph. "That's really somethin'. Hot damn!" He slipped a negative out of the yellow envelope and held it to the light. A big ruby-like ring on his finger gleamed.

"What is it?"

"Wish I could show it to you. Private business. Some business, I'll say! Wouldn't mind a crack at that myself." He put the photograph and negative back in the envelope and dropped in into the top drawer of his desk. "What's on your mind, son?"

Dan inclined his head toward the pictures on the wall. "Nice collection."

"That's only part of it. I've got a lot more. You got me at a busy time, son. What can I do for you?"

"Then we might as well come right to the point."

"Shoot. What's your trouble?" Price leaned back in his swivel chair with a squeak.

"I'm interested in an artist named Kenton Kipper, and I'm interested in what happened to his pictures."

Price bounced forward in his swivel chair, caught himself, and relaxed. "Never heard of him."

"Somebody's been going around and buying up his pictures."

"That so?"

"Yes. I understand you bought one from the Bishop Gallery."

"I bought one!"

"Yes."

"You must be dippy, son. I wouldn't buy no pitchers, unless they might be fight pitchers."

"You bought one, all right."

"Say, what the hell is this? Who are you?"

"I'm a reporter from the *Journal*."

"Well, suppose you get your ass out of here, and get it out in a hurry." Dan stood up, as if to go.

Price cleared his throat. "No, wait a minute. Sit down. What the hell are you driving at?"

"Let's stop kidding each other. You know what I'm talking about."

"I'm damned if I do."

"I'm doing you a favor by coming to you directly and putting it to you squarely. If you want me to do it another way, say so."

"Sit down, son. Don't be so touchy. What's this all about?"

Dan took the chair again. "Kipper was murdered night before last. You know that."

"Kipper? You mean this artist you're talking about?"

"You know who I mean."

"No, I don't."

"It's all in the paper."

"I guess I must have missed it."

"Kipper was murdered. But before that, someone was going around buying up his pictures and giving fake names." Dan thumbed toward the fight pictures on the walls. "Wolgast, Berlenbach, Olin, Jeby, and others."

"What's that got to do with me?"

"You didn't use much originality in picking names. You just grabbed them off the wall over there."

Price pondered a moment, then laughed and slapped the desk. "Oh, hell, I get it. Somebody was buyin' up pitchers and givin' fight monickers for names, so you figured it might be me. That's a good one."

"Yes, and I think the lady in the Bishop Gallery can identify you. She can also identify Dorothy Vane."

Barney Price stopped laughing and looked puzzled. "Dorothy Vane? Who's that?"

"You know who she is. She's another one who was buying Kipper's paintings."

Barney scratched his head and grinned. "Son, you've got me completely in the fog. Who told you all this guff?"

"You and Dorothy Vane were buying those pictures for Gregory Fallon. Isn't that right?" Dan was beginning to feel he was pushing guesswork beyond reasonable limits, and his doubt showed in his voice.

Barney sighed, got up and walked to a window. He looked back and asked in an amused voice, "Who the hell is Gregory Fallon?"

Dan stood up. "All right, skip it. If you don't want to be reasonable."

Barney returned to the desk fanning one hand downward. "Sit down. Don't be so jumpy. Sit down." His manner was patronizing.

Dan resumed his chair. Barney uncapped a large pen, opened a legal tablet, and began writing. "You say this guy's name was Kipper. What was his first name?"

"You know his name."

"I guess I can get the particulars out of the paper. Who was this other guy you mentioned? Gregory Fallon. That was it, wasn't it?"

Dan said nothing.

"And Dorothy Vane." Barney studied what he had written. "Oh, yeah. The name of that joint. Bishop Gallery. Where's that?"

Dan was sullen. "On Sutter Street."

Barney wrote with a flourish. "I don't know why I'm doing this, son. Christ knows I have enough to worry about. You come back and see me about six o'clock. I'll see if I can't find out what this is all about for you."

"That ought to give you time to get in touch with the client you were buying those pictures for."

Barney capped his pen. "Don't be a chump. Somebody's evidently been pullin' your leg."

Dan got up. Barney came around the desk and walked to the door with him. "I know quite a few of the boys over at the *Journal*. Always glad to do a favor when I can. You never can tell when co-operation helps."

"Six o'clock, you say."

"Six, or around then. I'll see what I can find out. Looks to me like somebody's gone off their nut."

"If you're not here at six, when I come back, I'm going to run the story anyhow and let you worry about disproving it."

Barney grinned broadly. "Now, son, don't do anything screwy. I wouldn't do anything, if I were you, till we check up on this thing and see what the hell's going on."

CHAPTER THIRTEEN

Going down in the elevator, Dan felt like a man who had found the address he was looking for, but got tangled up in the revolving door and came right out onto the sidewalk again.

Getting any information out of Barney Price was like trying to shake a dime out of a piggy bank. And why not? Barney was shrewd as he was crude. Of course, there was always the chance that he really didn't know anything, and that his apparent implication was sheer coincidence. That would be stretching coincidence pretty far, but it was possible.

After all, what was there to go on? A telephone number scribbled on the wall of Dorothy Vane's apartment. The names of a dozen or so prize fighters which coincided with the phoney names given by the purchasers of Kipper's paintings. You couldn't swim very far in such a shallow puddle of guesswork. Barney Price would have to be slapped in the face with pretty solid evidence before he'd talk turkey.

In a drugstore phone booth, Dan called Marian Cleave's number. No answer. That was something he should have taken care of earlier.

It was a little soon for calling Dorothy Vane, but he tried it anyhow. No answer there either. That looked bad. Still, whatever she wanted to satisfy herself about may have required her to leave the house.

There was another bet; Janey Navarro. It seemed very probable that she was the person Kenton Kipper had in mind when he wrote to Marian that he had decided to get married. Her number wasn't listed in the phone book. Dan called Ike Miller at Station KZY.

"She hasn't got any phone," Ike said. "But she lives in the Casbah at 1125 Kearny Street."

"What's the Casbah?"

"It's a pile of old tenements up a flight of stone steps off Broadway. A lot of the poorer Bohemians have turned them into studios. They got the idea of calling it the Casbah from that movie."

"Anything new coming over the teletypes on the case, Ike?"

"Not a thing. The cops are probably taking Kent's flat apart and looking for fingerprints. You making any progress?"

"Round and round, Ike. Round and round."

"If I know you, you're a liar. But let me know if I can help you any. I've got a kind of personal interest in this."

Leaving the drugstore, Dan returned to the offices of the *Journal*. The girl in the morgue had some difficulty in finding a photograph of Barney Price, but finally managed to dig one up. He'd been photographed standing beside one of the fighters he'd promoted years before.

Dan's next stop was the Bishop Gallery. The blonde woman in the tan smock studied the picture carefully and declared without any doubt that Barney Price was the man who had bought a Kipper painting from her.

That was some help. Barney could still probably claim she was mistaken, but it gave Dan more assurance that he was on the right track.

From the Bishop Gallery, Dan took a cab to Kearny and Broadway. The car wouldn't negotiate the steep hill in the block where Janey Navarro's address was located, so the driver let him out at the corner. Stone steps replaced sidewalks. Halfway up the block, Dan found 1125 among a lot of other numbers painted beside a square opening in the basement of a dirty, three-story wooden building.

He entered a kind of tunnel that led through to still other buildings in the rear. A flight of wooden stairs took him to a long porch overlooking a view of the financial district's skyscrapers across the grimy roofs of near-by buildings.

Numerous doors off the porch apparently gave into small apartments. Some of them were gaily painted and decorated. Other were bare and shabby. Dan had to knock several times on 1125 before it opened a crack and Janey Navarro's eye appeared under a patch of her reddish-brown hair.

"I'm Dan Banion. Remember? We met last night."

Her voice was thick. "What is it?"

"I know you're upset, but I'd like to talk to you."

"Please, unless it's important, I—"

"It is important. It's about Kenton Kipper."

She hesitated. "Wait a minute."

The door closed and Dan waited. In a minute it opened again. Janey's eyes were red. She wore a gray tweed suit with a flouncy lace blouse. A three-quarter studio couch was unmade, but the covers had been pulled up. The room was small and furnished mostly with makeshift articles. Painted orange crates served as bookshelves. A decorated packing case was a coffee table. A portable phonograph rested on the floor with records strewn about it.

"The place is a mess," she said in a husky voice.

"You knew about—"

Her mouth tightened and she nodded her head.

"I'm a reporter for the *Journal*. But I don't want you to think that's the only reason I came here."

"Glotcher did it."

"How do you know?"

"Glotcher did it," she repeated doggedly.

"Are you sure?"

"Glotcher hated him. Glotcher did it."

"Why are you so sure?"

"He hated Kent. Kent hit him. I was there."

"You mean—was that in Chinatown a few nights ago?"

"Yes. They fought. He threatened Kent. He did it."

"Have you any other reason for thinking so, besides that fight?"

"No, but I'm sure he did it."

"Sit down. Tell me about it." Dan took a chair, but Janey paced up and down, distracted.

"There's nothing to tell," she said. "They fought and he told Kent he was going to get even if it was the last thing he did."

"Why did they fight? Where was this?"

"It was a bar. Glotcher was drunk. He showed Kent a piece of paper and laughed at him."

"What kind of a piece of paper?"

"It was a photograph, I think."

"You didn't see it?"

"Kent wouldn't show it to me."

"Well, what happened then, after he showed Kent the piece of paper?"

"Kent knocked him down."

"And they fought. Is that it?"

"Glotcher tried to fight. But Kent was strong. He twisted his arm in back of him and pushed him out onto the sidewalk. That was when Glotcher threatened him."

"Well, what became of the picture, or piece of paper, or whatever it was?"

"Kent tore it up in little pieces and threw it in a spittoon."

"Did you ask Kent what it was?"

"He wouldn't tell me."

"Have you told the police about this?"

"No. I got a newspaper on the way to work. When I read it, I didn't go to work. I came back here. I've just been sitting. I can't seem to think. I don't know what to do." She put her hands over her eyes and began to cry.

Dan sat quietly for a while and let her sob. Finally he said, "Why don't you come out with me and have a drink?"

She dabbed at her eyes with a handkerchief. "There's wine in the kitchen, if you want it." She hesitated, seemed to remember something. "Kent bought it." Her sobbing started anew.

Dan took the photographs of Dorothy Vane and Barney Price from his pocket. When her weeping subsided a little, he said, "Will you look at these, Janey, and tell me if you know these people?"

She took the pictures and studied them. "No."

"Have you ever seen them around anyplace?'

"No."

"You're sure."

"Yes."

Dan took the photographs and put them back in his pocket. He wanted to ask her if she and Kent had intended getting married, but couldn't bring himself to do it. Instead, he said, "Have you had anything to eat?"

"I'm not hungry."

"You ought to eat something. Let me take you out and get something."

"I couldn't eat."

"I don't like to leave you alone."

"I'm all right."

"Isn't there anything I can do for you? Anything at all?"

"No. But thanks."

Dan took out his notebook, scribbled on a page and tore it out. "This is my address and phone number. If there's any way at all that I can help—anything, no matter what—you call me."

"Thanks."

"Be sure."

"Thanks."

Dan put his notebook in his pocket and got up from the chair. "The police will probably be around to ask you questions. They might come any minute."

"Yes." She was indifferent.

"If they don't come, you ought to get in touch with them. You ought to tell them what you told me."

"Glotcher did it."

"There's no certainty of that."

"I remember how he looked when he threatened Kent. I know he did it." Her voice was bitter, her eyes dazed. Dan was reluctant to go. She hardly seemed conscious of his presence.

"If Glotcher did it," he said, "I'll find out, and he'll get what's coming to him."

It wasn't far from Janey Navarro's place to the Iron Cat, so Dan walked it. Clouds had blown in from the ocean since noon, and the sky was overcast. The streets were a dismal gray.

Light in the Iron Cat at this hour was an exhausted remnant, strained first through the clouds above, then through Hinkleburger's dirty front windows. It was like an aged pilgrim arriving at its destination too weary to remember its mission. Enough of it penetrated the front part to enable those at the bar to see each other and count their change. Farther back, around the tables, was a vague gloom. Not many patrons were on hand.

Hinkleburger sniffed closely at the photograph of Barney Price when Dan handed it to him. "Ya," he said. "Dot's de guy. Dot's de son of a bitch."

"You're sure," Dan said, "that he's the one who bought Kipper's painting?"

"Ya, sure. Berlenbach. Dot's him. Paul Berlenbach."

A florid-faced man on a near-by stool shook his head sadly. "Poor Kent. Too bad. Nice guy, he was."

"Ya," said Hinkleburger. "He paid his bills. He was all right. Why couldn't somebody have poisoned some of you no-good bums instead? Dot's what I can't figure."

As Dan's eyes became more accustomed to the gloom in the Iron Cat, things farther back became more discernible. He recognized Lorna Cargill drinking alone at a table. He picked up his beer and went back.

"Mind if I sit down?"

"No. Go ahead."

"Are you busy?"

"Do I look busy?"

"I wish you'd go up and sit with Janey Navarro. She's in kind of bad shape."

Lorna reached for her purse. "Poor kid. Of course."

"She's all alone up at her apartment. I was just there."

"I'll go right up." Lorna started to rise, but Dan stopped her.

"Just a minute. Before you go. I wish you'd look at these." He handed her the photographs of Dorothy Vane and Barney Price.

Lorna squinted at them, then got up and walked nearer the light. When she returned, she threw them on the table in front of him. "What about them?"

"Did you ever see either of those people before?"

"No."

"Are you sure?"

"I may have seen them around and just don't remember."

"Sit down a minute. You knew Kipper pretty well, didn't you?"

"What's it to you?"

"Did he and Fallon ever have any quarrels?"

"Not that I know of. They might have, though. Wherever Marian's involved, you can expect anything."

"You're pretty bitter about her, aren't you?"

"Every man she meets she tries to get, just to see if she can do it. And they fall for her, the dopes."

"What makes you think she had anything to do with Kipper's murder?"

"Kent was wise to her. Her line wasn't working on him anymore. She tried to get him back, and he wasn't interested. He was interested in Janey Navarro. That was something Marian couldn't take. Janey is real stuff, and Marian couldn't compete with her. You don't know what that means to a woman like her. Her cheap little ego couldn't take it."

"As I understand it, she left Kent long ago. What made her want to get him back?"

"She was on the loose. Kent was around. She wanted to see if she still had a hold on him. When she discovered she didn't, and that she couldn't get him back, she was frantic."

"That isn't convincing."

"Listen. You don't understand women like her. She wants every man until she gets him, and once she gets him, she, doesn't give a damn about him anymore. It's a complex with her. You don't think she was true to Greg Fallon, do you?"

"Wasn't she?"

Lorna smirked. "My God! Fallon is about the only one who doesn't know. Why do you think Arnie Winkleman goes around all the time looking as if he was half doped? What she did to him was pure sadism. And Greg Fallon is one of his best friends. They went to college together."

"Why? What did she do to him?"

"Nothing much that she didn't do to plenty more. Just gave him the old 'you and I understand each other,' and the rest that goes with it. Only he was too easy to get. She doesn't like the easy ones. I always felt that if she ever met a man she couldn't get, she'd kill him. And she did."

"But you haven't any actual evidence. That's just opinion."

"Evidence! Look at her. What's she got, except a lot of sex? That's all she's got to cling to. When that doesn't work, she's terrified. She might do anything."

"Were you in love with Kent?"

"Leave me out of it."

"You don't mind running down Marian Cleave, but when it comes to yourself, you want to be left out of it."

"I guess you can find plenty of people to run me down. They're a dime a dozen."

"I'd rather hear it from you."

"Of course, I was fond of Kent."

"Is that all?"

"Kent wasn't in love with me. We were honest with each other."

"How long ago was this?"

"Oh, it was a long time ago."

"Before he met Marian?"

"Yes. I used to pose for Kent sometimes. That was before I lost weight."

"And did Marian break things up between you and Kipper?"

"I wouldn't say that. Kent was never serious about me."

"Why not?"

"I'm not the type. Men like women who are just beginning to make their mistakes. I started making mine too early."

"From what you say, Marian has made plenty of mistakes herself."

"Yes, but she's making a career of it, and they don't seem to faze her." Lorna reached for her purse again. "I'd better go up and see Janey."

Dan knocked the ashes out of his pipe and dug at the bowl with a match. "You underrate yourself. You've got to pocket your losses along with experience, and keep on trying."

Lorna was thoughtful. "It takes two to make a try." She straightened her long bob with a shake of her head and stood up. "I'd better go to Janey. She's the one who needs a hand."

CHAPTER FOURTEEN

It was five-thirty when Dan left the Iron Cat. Light in the sky was fading, and the streets were again swarming with homeward-bound people.

Across the street in the Black Pot, Andre de Carlo was not in. No way to check whether he could identify the photograph of Dorothy Vane as the "luscious blonde" who had bought Kipper's paintings from him.

Dan paused long enough to ring Dorothy Vane's apartment again. No answer. That was bad. Maybe she'd taken a run-out on him. That would mean she was pretty thickly implicated. Barney Price might do the same. That seemed unlikely, though. To run away was like a confession of guilt. Barney was too smart for that. Dorothy Vane had probably lost her head.

The Wreck bar was only a few blocks away. Dan walked as rapidly as he could. The evening rush hour was well under way, but Chuck Leary abandoned some customers he was serving, and came forward shaking his head sadly. "Jesus! Did you hear that about Kent?"

Dan took out the picture of Barney Price. "I'm in a hell of a hurry, Chuck. Look at that and tell me if that's the guy who bought the picture from over the bar."

Chuck studied it for a moment, then his head began to nod. "That's him. That's the guy."

"You're sure."

"Oh yeah. That's him. Who is he?"

Dan put the picture back in his pocket. "Sorry to give you the rush act. I'm in a hurry."

Chuck's eyes popped. "What's up?"

"Tell you later, Chuck. Thanks. I've got to run."

Chuck remained staring after him with his mouth open. Outside, Dan had to yell and wave his arms at five different cabs before he stopped an empty one.

It was already a few minutes after six when the cab let him off in front of the dilapidated building on O'Farrell Street where Barney Price had his office. It was dark now. Street lamps and show windows were lighted.

Inside, Dan soon had the automatic elevator groaning upward. It stopped with a jerk on the fourth floor. Low-watt bulbs gave a dismal, yellow illumination to the corridor. The pane of milky glass in the door marked Price Detective Agency was dark. Dan gave it a couple of knocks. Silence.

Not so good. Dan checked his watch. Seven minutes after six. Allowing people periods of grace wasn't working out so well.

All the other doors in the hall were dark too. Dan strolled up and down and read a few. The Limpac Novelty Company. Wyantax, Inc., whatever that might be. Julian Goncourse, Trusses. Struggling, clawing little two-bit businesses. Isaac Goldman, Vest Maker.

He returned to Barney Price's door and stared at it in frustration. For no sensible reason, he rapped his knuckles on it again. Silence.

He rattled the knob. It was open. A widening slit showed darkness inside.

Dan glanced up and down the corridor to reassure himself. Silence everywhere.

He reached an arm inside and felt around the wall. His fingers found a switch and pressed it. Bright light filled the room. It had an effect on his nerves like noise, and his impulse was to turn it off before it attracted anyone's attention.

He pushed the door farther open. The pictures of fighters glared from every wall. The chair behind Barney's desk was empty. Everything appeared as he had seen it that afternoon, except that there was no one there. Then he noticed a shoe protruding from behind Barney's desk.

He stepped inside, closed the door, walked quickly to the desk and looked behind it.

Barney Price was lying face up, one hand clawing at his collar. The big ruby-like ring on his finger caught the light in an angry glint. The pupils of his eyes were dilated, and his face had a pinkish color. His lips were stained the same sickly green as those of Kipper.

Dan didn't have to touch him to know that he was dead.

On the desk was a half-empty bottle of cheap whisky—Old Thundercreek. There were two shot glasses beside it, and a green stain on the desk blotter where some of the liquor had spilled.

Dan returned to the door. There was no catch lock, but an ordinary bolt was screwed to the inside, which he slid into place. Then he put on his gloves.

Remembering the yellow envelope he had seen Price drop in the top drawer of his desk, he went over and looked. It was gone. There was a snub-nosed revolver, a notebook, and a litter of papers. But no yellow envelope.

He opened the other drawers, pulling them by the very edges of the handles to avoid disturbing any fingerprints that might be on them. There was a variety of junk, envelopes, letterheads, twine, ink bottles, a dirty shirt and some socks, a few old magazines, but no yellow envelope. The lower right-hand drawer—a deep drawer intended for files—was already open. It contained two pairs of boxing gloves and a few glasses. Dan guessed that the whisky had been kept in here.

He examined the other articles of furniture. The filing cabinet seemed to contain nothing but fight pictures. The safe was locked.

He went over and took another look at Barney Price. Then he lifted the phone and dialed "Operator."

"Give me the police department."

When he got them, he asked for Inspector Neil Gallagher. There was a short wait, and Gallagher's voice rasped on the other end.

Dan started, "This is Banion of the *Journal*. I—"

"Oh yeah. I want to see you, Banion."

"We've got another corpse, Gallagher."

"What?"

"I just located another corpse."

"Another what?"

"Another corpse. A stiff. Another murder. It's got green lips just like the last one."

"Are you sober?"

"I'm telling you, I found another one. It's right here. I'm looking at it."

"Where are you phoning from?"

"Office of Barney Price, a private detective, 316 O'Farrell."

"What's he got to do with it?"

"He's the corpse."

"Barney?"

"Yeah. Barney Price."

"What are you—never mind. You stick there. Stay right there. Do you hear me?"

"I'll be here."

"You stay there, see? I'm comin' right over. Who else is there?"

"Nobody. Just me."

"Well, you stay there and don't touch anything."

"Okay."

"You heard me, didn't you? Don't touch a damned thing."

When Gallagher hung up, Dan dialed the *Journal*. Charlie Dixon was on the desk. Before Dan could say anything, Charlie asked, "Wait a minute, Banion. Is this hot?"

"Red hot."

"Hold it till I cut in a rewrite. Get on that other line, Phil. Okay. Shoot."

Dan reeled it off in a monotonous voice, speaking precisely and going slowly for the sake of the pencil at the other end. "Barney Price of Price Detective Agency—p-r-i-c-e—murdered in his office, 316 O'Farrell Street, room 408. Time, between 4:00 and 6:00 P.M. Weapon, poison. Evidently same poison as killed Kenton Kipper. Same green-stained lips. Same appearance generally."

Charlie interrupted. "Is that what the cops say?"

"They haven't seen it yet. They're on their way. I just called them. I stumbled onto it myself. Don't interrupt me. You've got to get this down fast. It's exclusive."

"Okay. Shoot."

"Poison was evidently administered in whisky. Whisky bottle half full on desk. Old Thundercreek. Two shot glasses on desk blotter. Places where liquor spilled turned to green stain like on lips. Body discovered by *Journal* reporter at 6:07 P.M., while tracing clues on Kipper case."

Dan ground patiently through all the details of his finding the body, and outlined the riddle of Kenton Kipper's missing paintings. When he had finished, Charlie Dixon began shooting one question after another. Dan answered about twenty of them before he heard the motor of the automatic elevator start droning. That would be the cage moving downward for someone on the first floor.

"I've got to hang up, Charlie. The law's arriving. I'll call you back later. Better send a man over to help me on this."

The complaining drone of the elevator motor continued for a spell, then stopped. Gallagher would be battling the sliding doors down in the entrance hall. Presently, the droning started again. Gallagher was on his way up. When the droning stopped, Dan heard the metal doors sliding open down the hall. A moment later, the doorknob was rattling fiercely. Somebody banged knuckles on the glass panel.

Dan removed his gloves, put them in his pocket, and unbolted the door. Gallagher, followed by another plain-clothes man and two uniformed officers, pushed past him into the room. All were big men, and they gave Dan the sensation, as police often do, of being creatures from another, larger planet.

Gallagher shot Dan a hard look before his small blue eyes made a quick, circling examination of the room. He strode to the desk, looked down at the form behind it, and remained staring for about ten seconds, his body rigid. Then he relaxed, walked around to the other side of the desk and studied the top, with its bottle and two shot glasses.

The other men stood silently, just inside the door. No one had yet spoken a word.

Gallagher turned to the other plain-clothes man, a man in a belted, checkered overcoat, a brand-new gray hat with the store block still fresh on it, and a big black mustache. "You call the coroner, Mack?"

"He's coming."

Gallagher jerked a thumb toward the corpse. "Barney's finally collected in full." He kicked one of the yellow oak chairs to a new position facing the door, and sat down heavily.

The other plain-clothes man went over and studied the corpse. "It's Barney all right."

Gallagher sat leaning his elbows on his knees, his shoulders hunched, the tips of his fingers together. He looked steadily into Dan's eyes for a moment, without saying anything. Then he turned to the uniformed cops. "You fellows can wait outside."

The two cops filed out, closing the door behind them. Mack remained in the room.

Gallagher fished a crushed pack of cigarettes out of an inside pocket, stuck one in his mouth, and offered the pack to Dan. "Smoke?"

"No, thanks." Dan took out his pipe and pouch, and began scooping tobacco. Was Gallagher going to be friendly? This gesture might mean anything. Dan decided to hold his tongue and await developments.

Gallagher lit his cigarette with a thick kitchen match that he took from his overcoat pocket and scratched with his thumb. "This is a hell of a lot of work. I've got a touch of neuritis, and it's damn near killing me."

Dan said nothing. He was damned if he'd volunteer any information until Gallagher abandoned his game of smug silence and asked some questions.

Gallagher suddenly became interested in the fight pictures on the wall. His eyes narrowed. He got up and examined a few closely. When he returned to his chair, he said, "Ready, Mack?"

Mack whipped out a notebook and poised a pencil over it.

Gallagher crossed his legs and looped one arm over the back of the chair. "All right, Banion. Start talking."

Dan finished lighting his pipe. "Well, I came here to see Price this afternoon. He was busy and told me to come back at six o'clock. I came back at a little after six, so I opened the door and turned on the light. There he was, just as you see him now. So I phoned you."

"Why did you have the door bolted?"

"I didn't want anybody barging in until you got here."

"You didn't touch anything?"

"No."

"That's probably a damned lie. What did you come here to see him about?"

Dan pulled a chair into position and sat down. "I was trying to find out who's been buying up Kipper's paintings."

"Did you know Barney before?"

"No."

Gallagher's blue eyes narrowed, and he looked again at the pictures on the wall. "Did you think those had anything to do with it?"

"How do you mean?"

"Listen, Banion, I could cause you a lot of trouble. Don't make me. You were up in Kipper's joint last night. You recognized him in the morgue yesterday. You're playing the game altogether wrong with me."

"I didn't exactly recognize him. I'd seen him in a bar, that's all. I went back to the bar on a hunch to see if I could find out who he was. We didn't run any story until I brought in a guy to identify him officially."

"All right, Banion. Skip that stuff. You and I know what you've been doing. I got reports on you today from nearly every paper you ever worked on. You've done this kind of thing before. Well, you're not going to make any chump out of me."

"That's not the idea."

"That's exactly the idea. You're one of these performers. You've got a cop phobia. Well, get this straight. I don't think I'm any genius, and I don't want to be. Besides, I've got a touch of neuritis. If any guy wants to go running ahead of the routine digging up facts, that's all right with me. I can't stop him. I can make it tough for him here and there, but I can't stop him. All I ask is that he play the game on the level and co-operate. I've got a fixed routine for investigating these homicides.

It ain't perfect. It's kind of slow. But it gets there most of the time, and it's thorough. Naturally, some wise guy playing hunches, not having to stop and take a thousand fingerprints, or question all the neighbors, can get a mile ahead of me. I can't help that. He might get his ass in a jam, too. I can't help that either. The question is, are you and I going to co-operate like sensible guys, or are we gonna be a couple of goddamn prima donnas trying to outdo each other?"

Dan grinned and relaxed. "I like the way you talk."

"Good. Then let's stop kidding each other. Did you think those fight pictures on the wall had anything to do with the case? Is that why you came to see Barney?"

"No. I didn't connect the names of the people who bought Kipper's paintings with fighters until I came into his office this afternoon."

Gallagher's eyes gleamed. "There you are. There's an example. You weren't so smart. I tumbled to it the minute I saw the names on those letters in Kipper's place. Berlenbach, Wolgast, Mandell—I got it right away."

"You mean you thought of Barney Price?"

"Hell, no. I just knew they were fight names. What made you come to see Barney, if it wasn't that?"

"Well, that's kind of a complicated story." Dan explained how he'd traced some of the purchases from the Bishop Gallery to Dorothy Vane, and how the phone number on her wall had led him to Barney Price.

Gallagher listened intently, then massaged his chin with one hand. "That's goddamn cute work. I could use you on the force." He turned to Mack. "Phone the station to pick up that dame Dorothy Vane. Tell 'em to bring in her husband too—Howard Vane." He eyed Dan again. "If that Vane dame has skipped out, we can thank you for it."

"She'd have skipped anyhow, as soon as she read the papers."

"Maybe. Anyhow, what's your theory on all this business?"

"I think somebody hired Barney Price to buy up Kipper's paintings on the sly. Barney wasn't too bright, and he probably didn't take the job seriously anyhow. So, when it came to giving out fake names, he just grabbed them off the wall over there. Maybe he thought he was being funny."

"Where would Dorothy Vane fit in?"

"She was probably working for Barney."

"Could be. And the murderer would probably be whoever hired Barney to buy the paintings. Come in, Kennedy."

A stout little man in a black overcoat and a plaid muffler had stuck his head in the door. "Is this the room?"

Gallagher pointed to the desk. "It's on the floor back there. See what you can make of it."

The man set a black doctor's bag on the desk, looked down behind it, and began pulling off his gloves. He said, "Tsch, tsch, tsch, tsch!"

Photographers and fingerprint men came in and began unpacking their equipment.

"Let's get the hell out of here and let the boys do their work," Gallagher said. He led the way to the hall where a pleasant-faced, white-haired man in dirty corduroy pants was standing patiently beside the two uniformed officers. "Who are you?" Gallagher asked.

"I'm the janitor."

"Oh yeah? What time'd you come to work?"

"Six o'clock."

"Did you relieve somebody?"

"There's a day man. He left at six."

"Anybody else around who might have been here, say from four o'clock on?"

"No. There's another man helps me clean the offices. He's downstairs now. But he didn't come until six-thirty."

Gallagher looked up and down the hall. "We need another room. It's getting crowded in there."

The janitor took a large ring of keys from a hook on his belt. "There's a room right here across the hall. The people moved out, but there's still some furniture in it." He opened a door and snapped on the light. It was a bare room with a cheap flat-top desk and a few hard chairs.

Gallagher looked it over. "This'll do fine. You stick around outside. I'll want to ask you more questions. Come in, Banion."

Mack followed them in with his notebook. Gallagher took the chair behind the desk. "Let's see. Where were we? You say you think Barney Price was buying the paintings for somebody else. Who would that be?"

"I don't know. Whoever it was, they didn't want their name known."

"Why not?"

"I don't know. But they wouldn't hire a private detective to buy paintings under fake names if there wasn't something phoney about it."

"You're smarter than that, Banion. You have some ideas about it. Let's hear them."

"Well, there are several reasons why somebody might do such a thing. One would be that they thought the paintings were going to be valuable some day, and wanted to buy them up at a cheap price on the quiet."

"Do you think that fits this case?"

"No."

"Go ahead. What's the rest of it?"

"Another reason would be that they liked Kipper and wanted to help him out financially without his knowing who was doing it."

"Is that what you think?"

"No. It's not likely."

"Well, what is your opinion?"

"Another reason would be that somebody hated his guts and was buying the paintings to destroy them."

"That's screwy. What the hell would Kipper care what they did with his paintings, just so he got his dough?"

"That's not the way an artist reasons. The money doesn't mean so much to him as his paintings. His paintings are his life's work. It's just like killing an artist to destroy his paintings."

"Well, I guess it takes all kinds of people to make a world."

"If anyone had an impulse to kill an artist, that impulse might easily express itself first in a desire to destroy his works. They might start by destroying one painting out of spite. Then another, and another, until it became a mania. Finally it might lead to their killing the artist himself."

"That's some of this psychology stuff you're talking about, isn't it?"

"In a way, yes."

"I'm due to be pensioned in a couple of years. I'm glad of it. This business is getting beyond me. It's got so you have to know why a nut's a nut in order to operate."

Dan poked thoughtfully at his pipe bowl with a match. "There's another reason. Maybe it was professional jealousy."

Gallagher's eyes were alert. "You mean another artist?"

"Could be."

Gallagher nodded. "You never can tell what an artist might do. When a businessman's murdered, you know it's either money or women or both. An artist you can't figure."

"I'm not saying everything happened just that way in this case. I'm just giving you my ideas for what they're worth."

Gallagher worked his mouth, as if trying to masticate the idea. "If such a deal as that could be true, then you probably figure that Barney, knowing who'd been buying the pictures, put two and two together, and was wise to who murdered Kipper."

"Something like that. For another thing, if the missing paintings were traced to Barney, he'd be apt to tell who the real buyer was. If the real buyer had destroyed the paintings, it would be a dead giveaway."

"So the murderer had to get rid of Barney."

"It's just a rough theory, but it makes sense."

"Maybe. Of course, it's not established yet that Barney didn't commit suicide."

"Aw, don't be crazy."

"Just the same, he could have murdered Kipper, then lost his nerve and poisoned himself."

"I don't believe it."

"Neither do I."

"Barney was murdered, and whoever did it called on him here, sometime between four and six."

"Not necessarily," Gallagher said. "The poison could have been put in that bottle earlier in the day, or on the day before, for that matter. All we know is that Barney took a drink sometime between four and six."

"That's true. My hunch, though, is that the murderer was here this afternoon."

Gallagher clenched his hands on the top of the desk and studied the ceiling. "I might find something in Barney's papers, when those monkeys get finished in there and I have a chance to get at them. But I don't expect to find much. Barney wasn't the kind of a guy who kept records. Did you run across an attorney named Gregory Fallon in your wanderings last night?"

"He's Marian Cleave's last husband."

"Right."

"I got a look at him. That's about all. He was stewed."

"Done any thinking about him?"

"Yeah. I can't figure his connection with Dorothy Vane. She was the dame he was found in bed with, or something like that. Her husband raised hell, and that's why she got her picture in the paper, it broke up his marriage with Marian."

Gallagher cleared his throat. "And Dorothy Vane had been going around buying Kipper's pictures under take names."

"That's right."

"Ten to one she'll be the next stiff to turn up with green lips."

"I thought of that."

Gallagher leaned forward. "Try this on your psychology, just for size. Gregory Fallon was married to this Marian Cleave. Kenton Kipper was the Cleave dame's first husband. She was still kind of stuck on Kipper and that made Fallon jealous. He started buying Kipper's paintings and burning them. He didn't want to be seen buying them himself, so he got Dorothy Vane to do it for him. He'd been playing around with Dorothy Vane on the side, so it was natural for him to use her. Finally, Dorothy Vane's husband catches them together. There's a scandal. The Cleave dame leaves Fallon and starts running around with her former husband, Kenton Kipper. So Fallon dopes out a murder. Kipper is to be nailed in a spaghetti case and burned in an incinerator. He's just to drop out of sight. No evidence, no nothing. But it don't work out that way. A traffic accident busts open the case. Fallon's on the run. Sooner or later, somebody'll trace those paintings to Dorothy Vane. Sooner or later, Dorothy Vane may put two and two together."

Dan interrupted him. "Aren't you forgetting about Barney Price?"

"Barney! Oh yeah. Well, Barney could fit in there anywhere. Maybe, after a while, Dorothy Vane got tired of buying paintings, so Fallon had to hire Barney."

"That wouldn't explain why Dorothy Vane was using prizefight names when she made the purchases. Obviously, Barney was in on it from the first. He was giving Dorothy Vane her instructions. He was telling her what fake names to use. She was working for him."

"Well, maybe he was in on it from the start. That could be explained a number of different ways."

"One more thing. Dorothy Vane bought some of the paintings *after* the scandal between her and Fallon. Do you think he'd still have been using her after that?"

"It's possible."

"But not likely. I thought of Fallon first, too. He's still a possibility. But you need more evidence. All this is guesswork. You must have questioned Fallon today. What kind of alibi does he have for the night of Kipper's murder?"

"None at all. He was drunk, he claims. Came home about one o'clock. Went to sleep on top of the bed with his clothes on. Woke up shivering at about 5:00 A.M. Got up, took his clothes off, went to bed, and slept till the following noon. No witnesses at all to prove it. Lives by himself in an apartment on Sacramento Street."

"How about the others? You must have found that letter in Kipper's apartment."

"The one he wrote to Marian Cleave, and hadn't mailed yet?"

"That's the one."

"I found it. Nice of you to leave it there for me, damn you. I checked everybody mentioned in it. Marian Cleave had dinner with Kipper that night. Then they went to some gin mill and sat talking until the place closed at midnight. After that she drove him home. He didn't have a car. She says they sat in the car in front of his place for a while and talked. After that she drove home."

"She didn't go up to his apartment?"

"No. And probably she's telling the truth. There's a lady in the apartment underneath Kipper's who has insomnia. She says she remembers hearing a car drive up a little after twelve. She thought it might be her husband and looked out the window. The car stayed parked there for a while with its lights on. Later, she heard the car door slam, and Kipper came upstairs by himself. She's pretty sure he was by himself, because she heard the car drive away, and she knows the sound of people's feet on the stairs. She's a nosy old bag who keeps track of everybody's goings and comings in the building."

"There was a fellow named Glotcher mentioned in the letter. Did you look him up?"

"Oh yeah. Nasty character. Photographer. Quite a man with the ladies. No love lost between him and Kipper. However, his alibi's sound. He had a lot of people with him all the way up till about 4:00 A.M. They were drinking in a place called the Black Pot. After that they went to Chinatown for chop suey. Later they went up to Glotcher's studio and staged a party that lasted most of the night."

"In his letter Kipper referred to the 'Glotcher business.' Did you find out what he meant by that?"

"Well, it's pretty clear there'd been an affair between Glotcher and the Cleave dame. Kipper probably got wind of it and was disgusted."

"Did you ask Glotcher about it?"

"He won't admit it in so many words. He just says they were friendly, and sneers so you'd like to belt him across the mouth. Why? Do you think it's more than that?"

"You never can tell."

"Maybe you're right. I'd better scratch that Glotcher a little deeper."

"How about Mallory? Did you see him?"

"You've been getting around, Banion. The letter only mentions Lance. How did you know the last name was Mallory?"

"I met him last night."

"You evidently met quite a few people. It was Marian Cleave who told me she found you in Kipper's apartment last night."

"What was Lance Mallory's story?"

"He was out of town the night of the murder. He was down the peninsula at a place he has in Burlingame. A couple of other guys were with him. They spent the night."

"Kipper said in the letter he intended to get married. Who did he have in mind? Do you know?"

"You ought to know, Banion. You went to see her this afternoon half an hour before I did. She told me you'd been there."

"Janey Navarro?"

"Right. Didn't you have that figured out?"

"I wasn't sure. By the way did you talk to any of the neighbors around Kipper's place?"

"Spent most of my time on them this morning, when I wasn't being pestered by people wanting to rent the apartment."

"Wanting to rent Kipper's apartment?"

"Yeah. The housing shortage is terrific. They read about Kipper's murder in the paper, and looked up his address in the phone book. More than twenty people came around there before noon. Every time a death notice of any kind appears in the paper, there's a stampede of people trying to rent the house."

"What did the neighbors have to say?"

"The woman downstairs was the only one who had anything to say worth listening to. She sort of manages the building for the owner. Has insomnia. She heard Kipper come home, like I told you. After that she heard him walking around a little. At about one-thirty, she heard the phone ring in Kipper's place, and he answered it. She's sure of the time because she looked at her clock. Five or ten minutes later, she heard a car drive up in front and honk twice. She remembers that because it made her sore. Then she heard Kipper open his door and come down the stairs in his slippers. She's sure he was in his slippers because he wore them around the house a lot, and she knew how they sounded. She heard him go down to the street and talk to whoever was in the car. A few minutes after that, the car started up and drove away. She listened for Kipper to come back upstairs, but she didn't hear him. Finally, she fell asleep."

"Evidently the murderer didn't go up to the apartment; just phoned him and had him come down to the car."

"That's the way it looks. The next morning the landlady noticed that Kipper's door was ajar and the lights were, on. She knocked, but no one was there. She went in and turned the lights off, because it made her mad to have him wasting electricity. Then she closed the door, and meant to speak to him about it later."

"Didn't it occur to her that something was wrong?"

"Not in that neighborhood. They're used to people coming in and out at all hours, and acting screwy."

"Apparently, then, Kipper came home and got ready for bed. He put on his bathrobe and slippers, and sat down to write Marian a letter. Along about one-thirty, somebody telephoned. It must have been somebody he knew very well, because they evidently told him they were going to park down in front and blow their horn."

"I figure it was probably a woman," Gallagher said. "A woman would have an excuse for not wanting to go up to his apartment."

"Yes, but a man sometimes does that too. I remember once a friend of mine had been duck hunting. He called me up late on his way home, said he'd park down in front and blow his horn. If I wanted a couple of ducks, I could come down and get them."

"Did you do it?"

"Yes. Why?" Dan said.

"What did he do? Just hand you the ducks and drive off?"

"No. As I remember, he had a bottle, and offered me a drink."

"And what did you do?"

"I took it."

"Right there on the sidewalk?"

"No. I got in the car with him."

Gallagher nodded in satisfaction. "Sure, it happens all the time. Most natural thing in the world. It's happened to me. And I'll bet that's what happened to Kipper. Only in his case the drink was poisoned. That stuff acts quick. The murderer probably had the empty spaghetti case in the car. All he had to do was drive someplace, squeeze Kipper into it, nail down the lid, drive back to the lot where he got the case, dump it with the rest, and drive off."

"Have they found out what kind of poison it was yet?"

"Yeah. It's what Jeff thought it was. Leunatine."

"He said it was hard to get."

"It is. We're having all known supplies of it checked. But we can't count on much from that. It's been the experience where some rare or screwy poison like this turns up that the killer got a hold of it years before, and it's impossible to trace. Some people are that way, you know. Poison fascinates them. Romeo and Juliet, and all that junk. Most people play around with the idea of killing themselves at one time or another. Especially women. You'd be surprised how many people get a hold of bottles of poison and keep them for years. Mostly, they never use it. Sometimes the temptation gets the better of them. I hate poison cases."

"Why?"

"Because they're dirty. You take a gun. There's something honest about it. Your worst enemy can stand up and blow your head off with it. But poison—that's sneaky. It's nearly always dished out by somebody you trust. Somebody who pretends to be your friend. They say, 'Have a drink, pal,' and you take it in good faith, and strangle. It's sneaky. It's hypocritical. It's dirty." Gallagher fished a big gold watch out of his vest and squinted at it. "Those boys ought to be about finished in Barney's office. I better go have a look at his papers."

"Do you want me to hang around here anymore?"

"Sure. Stick around. No telling what we'll turn up."

"I haven't eaten a damn thing since noon."

"Neither have I. I'm gonna have 'em send in some sandwiches."

"No, thanks. I want a real dinner."

"Well, run down to the corner and get a bite. I'll give Barney's desk the once-over, and we'll have another talk."

"I've got a sort of a date, I hope."

Gallagher's eyes narrowed and he pointed a finger at Dan. "No more pulling any fast ones. We're co-operating. Remember?"

"Yeah, but that doesn't mean I'm going to cease all activities."

"I could hold you here, you know. You're the guy who discovered the body."

"That wouldn't be co-operation."

Gallagher scratched his chin. "No, you're right. Okay, Banion. You can beat it. But watch yourself, son. You're making yourself a likely candidate for one of those green mickeys this murderer is passing out."

CHAPTER FIFTEEN

While Dan and Gallagher were in the room, the hall had become congested with eager-eyed newspaper reporters and cameramen. As Dan pushed his way through them, Nix Peters waved a pencil excitedly and shouted, "Special privilege! Special privilege! What's the idea of letting him inside?"

"Now keep your pants on," Gallagher said. "He discovered the body. He's a witness." They clustered around Gallagher like a flock of hungry birds.

Dan spotted another man from the *Journal* among them, and pulled him aside. "I'm going to beat it," he said. "You better stick around. Gallagher may have something to say when he finishes going through Barney's pockets."

While the crowd was intent upon Gallagher, Dan slipped away and took the automatic elevator down to the street. In a nearby barroom, he found a phone booth and called Marian Cleave. Her voice almost climbed into the phone in negligee.

"Oh Dan. I've been wanting you to call. It's been terrible. The police were here. I don't know what to think."

"Have you had your dinner?"

"Yes, what little I could eat."

"I haven't. I'm starved."

"Dan, tell me where you're going to eat, and I'll meet you there. Make it some place we can talk."

"You know the town. Suggest a place."

"Go to Raoul's. It's quiet and they have booths. It's on Sacramento, just above Montgomery. Don't wait for me. Go ahead and eat. I may be a little late, but I'll be there."

Outside, the street was wet and the air moist and cold. Apparently it had rained a little and then stopped. The damp sidewalk glistened under the street light. An O'Farrell Street cable car, bulging with passengers, swayed past with a furious clanging of its bell.

Not quite sure which way to go, Dan walked a block in the wrong direction before he noticed he was headed away from the downtown area. He turned and retraced his steps. As he did so, he passed a big man in a gray hat and a black overcoat walking in the opposite direction.

At the corner of O'Farrell and Powell, Dan stopped to buy a copy of the *Journal*. Happening to glance back in the direction he had come, he saw the same gray-hatted, black-overcoated man pausing to concentrate on a shop window filled with women's corsets.

Dan crossed to the other side of the street, walked down a block, and turned a corner to his left. It was a shopping district with brightly lighted display windows. Before reaching the next corner, he glanced back over his shoulder. The big man in the gray hat was still coming along behind him.

Dan turned right on Geary Street, walked a block and a half, and looked back. The man was still coming. Dan turned left on Kearny Street and ducked into a barroom before the man could reach the corner. It was a tiny place, jammed with navy men. He took a stool far down at the end where he couldn't be seen from the door, and ordered a beer.

A few minutes later, the man in the gray hat slipped quietly in and straddled a stool at the other end of the bar.

Well, well! So Gallagher was having him tailed! Some cooperation! Maybe it was good sense from Gallagher's standpoint, but not allowable from Dan's. How to shake this gorilla?

Dan took one long gulp of his beer and, leaving the rest unfinished, walked quickly out of the place. Two doors to the left of the bar was an alley. He ducked into it and ran like hell.

The alley was lined with expensive-looking restaurants and bars.

Estimating that his pursuer could not possibly have rounded the corner yet, Dan shot into one of the bars. His entrance startled a bartender in the act of pouring a Martini.

Dan slowed down to a walk and continued toward the rear. The bartender followed him down the bar, eyeing him suspiciously. "Whatya lookin' for?"

"The can."

"Upstairs." The bartender thumbed toward a carpeted flight.

Dan took the stairs two at a time. There was a mezzanine lounge with low tables and clustered easy chairs. In back were two red doors marked "Boys" and "Girls."

Dan entered "Boys" and found himself in a narrow white-tiled room. He opened a frosted glass window to see if it might lead to a fire escape, but there were bars on the other side. He leaned against a washbasin and waited. After a while, the door opened. A thin man with a mustache smaller than an eyebrow came in, looked at him curiously, used the urinal, eyed him again, and went out.

Dan waited a while longer. Then he went out to the mezzanine and looked over the railing to the bar below. There sat Gallagher's bloodhound, twirling a glass of beer.

Dan descended the stairs and, ignoring a contemptuous look from the bartender, walked straight out of the place. A taxi had just unloaded two women at the curb, and the driver was about to take off. Dan jumped in. "Chinatown," he said.

The gray-hatted bloodhound came out of the bar just as the cab pulled away. Dan thought, "If he can find another cab soon enough to follow me, I'll buy him a dinner."

In Chinatown, he dismissed the cab and walked several blocks slowly, stopping to gaze in shop windows and look back over his shoulder. The gray hat did not appear. Satisfied he had shaken Gallagher's stooge, he turned down Sacramento Street toward the restaurant where he was to meet Marian Cleave.

Raoul's was a place with thick lace curtains in the windows that look as if it would charge five dollars for a lamb chop. A man who could have passed for the Duke of Luxembourg greeted Dan as he entered, raised his eyebrows, clicked his heels, and held out one hand, as if for a nickel.

"Do you have a booth? I'm expecting a lady."

The Duke snapped his fingers. A waiter came groveling in haste and led the way with bowed head and beckoning arm. The Duke followed close behind. At the booth, he plucked Dan's hat from him as if he were picking something off a bush, and helped him out of his overcoat.

Unaccustomed to the service, Dan was a little flustered. "Thank you," he said in a suppressed voice, and sidled into the booth while the waiter held aside the curtains.

The Duke thrust an enormous card into his hand and vanished. The waiter poised a pencil over a blank check.

The menu listed several hundred items in small type, variously priced from $3.75 to $20.

"If I may suggest," the waiter said, "the Rouennaise Duckling in Port Wine is excellent. Or, perhaps you would like Loins of Veal a la Chartreuse."

"Listen," Dan said. "I make about the same pay you do, and probably went to the same grammar school. What would you order if you wanted to be nourished and get out of here with carfare home?"

"I beg your pardon?"

"Oh, never mind."

The waiter thought a minute. "We have a very good ground round steak with mushrooms. Of course, it isn't called that."

"Well, bring it anyhow."

"Would you like a vegetable or some potatoes?"

"Don't you get anything with it?"

"Well, no. That's extra."

"Well, what the hell!"

"How about an order of hashed browns?"

"Okay. And bring me a bottle of beer."

"And a bottle of beer. Very good, sir."

The waiter turned to go, then paused. "What grammar school *did* you go to?"

"The General Grant in Minneapolis."

"No," said the waiter, disappointedly. "It isn't the same. Mine was P.S. 28 in New York."

"Did they ever make you clean blackboard erasers by slapping them together?"

The waiter's eyes brightened. He pointed his pencil at Dan. "Sure enough. You remember."

"It was all the same," Dan said.

Sighing visibly, the waiter departed carrying Dan's order and the weight of years.

Dan had almost finished his ground round steak when the booth curtains parted and Marian Cleave stepped in. He shoved back his chair.

"Don't get up," she said. She slipped off a fur wrap, revealing a pea-green dress with silver trimming, cut low in the front. A faint scent of perfume came with her. "I told Lance to meet us here. Do you mind?"

"Not a bit."

"Dan, there's something I want to know." She took the chair opposite him, and set a large white kid purse with a jade fastener on the tablecloth beside her. "Did you know about Kent when I found you in his apartment last night?" Her eyes were appealing.

Dan sipped his beer before replying. "Yes, I did."

"Dan, how could you?" Her lip trembled, as if she were going to cry.

"I was going to tell you."

"But, Dan, you didn't."

Dan groped in his mind for an excuse. "It all happened so fast."

"To have let me go on that way, and—"

"I'm sorry. I guess I hated to tell you."

A wary look came into her eyes. "What were you doing there?"

"I was hoping to run across something that would help me find out who killed him."

As if she could hold it back no more, she began sobbing.

"I'm terribly sorry," Dan said.

She reached for her bag, unfastened the jade clasp, and took out a handkerchief. "I'm all right. I'll be all right in a minute."

Her hand had disturbed the contents of her bag. From its opening, a yellow envelope was protruding. It recalled to Dan the yellow envelope he had seen Barney Price examining that afternoon. The color seemed identical.

"You'd better let me order you a drink." He pressed a button on the wall of the booth.

She tucked the handkerchief back in the bag, took a cigarette from a silver case, and tapped it nervously. "Dan, who could have done this? I can't understand. It frightens me."

"Somebody had a reason."

The waiter stuck his head through the curtains of the booth. Dan ordered an old-fashioned for Marian and coffee for himself.

"Have you any ideas?" he asked, when the waiter had gone.

"How could I? He didn't have an enemy in the world."

"How about Glotcher?"

She appeared alarmed. "But ... why?"

Dan struck a match and held it across to her. She puffed jerkily, and the cigarette trembled in her hand.

"That's what I'm asking you. Why?"

"You don't think it was Glotcher?"

"Glotcher hated his guts."

"Yes, but ... I still don't understand."

"Kipper beat him up and threw him out of a bar in Chinatown the night before he was murdered."

"But why?"

Dan took out his pipe and pouch. "I thought you might know why."

Her face colored. "Dan, I've been a fool."

Dan shrugged. "I've been a fool myself, lots of times. What was it?"

"Oh, Dan, it was nothing. It didn't mean a thing."

"Yes, but what was it?"

"Dan, please!"

"Listen. Kipper was a good guy. Somebody's a dirty, sneaking rat. We've got to find out who. Our own sensibilities don't matter. You can't shock me. Now, what was it?"

She began to cry. The waiter brought the drinks, appraised her, and shot Dan an accusing look as he departed.

She talked through gulps. "I met Glotcher. I went out with him a couple of times. That was all. It was just after I'd left Greg. I guess I was lonely. But Kent thought I'd been having an affair with him."

"Had you?"

"Oh, Dan, how can you ask?"

"Why did Kent think so?"

"You don't understand Kent. He was terribly jealous."

"Then there was nothing to it."

"Of course not. I was a fool ever to have spoken to the man."

"Hello. Am I interrupting?" Lance Mallory smiled through the part in the curtains. When he saw Marian's eyes red from weeping, his face became serious. "Is something wrong?"

She clutched his sleeve and pulled him into the chair beside her.

"Glotcher. He was asking about Glotcher."

"Well, for God's sake!" Mallory was angry. "Banion, you have no right to be torturing this stuff out of her. It's none of your damned business."

"It's all right," she said. "Dan thinks Glotcher did it."

Mallory was bewildered. "That pig? He's too stupid. Don't be ridiculous, Banion."

"Well, he figures in it somewhere." Dan threw a match into the ash tray in an annoyed gesture.

"What makes you think so?"

"He had a fight with Kipper the night before Kipper was murdered. He hated Kipper. Then, this afternoon I saw him coming out of the building where Barney Price had his office. He got in the elevator on the same floor as Barney's office."

"Who's Barney Price?" Mallory asked.

"Haven't you read the paper?"

"Not since about three o'clock."

"Well, hell. No wonder. It's in the late editions. Did you read it, Marian?"

"No. What?"

"Barney Price was a cheap private detective downtown. He was murdered in his office this afternoon. Poisoned. The same poison that killed Kipper."

Marian's eyes narrowed. "A private detective?"

"What's the connection?" Mallory asked.

"Well, it seems he'd been going around on the quiet, buying up Kipper's paintings. What he did with them, I don't know, because they seem to have disappeared. I think he was buying them for somebody else."

Marian looked vague. "It doesn't make sense."

"There's something very peculiar going on here," Mallory said in a quiet voice.

Dan related the particulars to the extent they would appear in the papers, omitting any mention of the yellow envelope he'd seen on Barney's desk.

When he had finished, Mallory gritted his teeth and shook his head. He began breaking a match into small pieces. First he broke it in half. Then he broke each of the halves. Then he started on the quarters.

"Lance, what are you thinking?" Marian said.

He glanced sideways at her, but said nothing.

"Do you think Greg—" Marian's voice broke slightly.

Mallory blew his breath through his teeth, and shook his head. "God, I hope not." He swept the broken pieces of the match into his hand and dumped them in the ash tray. "I'm afraid we've got some work to do."

"You're thinking of Gregory Fallon. Is that it?" Dan said.

"I don't know what to say." Mallory looked Dan in the eye. "But whoever it is will kill again and again. He's got to be found. He's got to be stopped." He turned to Marian. "You're not to stay alone in that place of yours another night."

"Lance, you don't think—"

"I don't know. But there's no sense in taking chances. We'll go by your place and you can pack a few things. You can stay at the Hobarts' tonight. Or maybe the Foisies can put you up."

"Not the Foisies. I couldn't stand it."

"Well, the Hobarts, then. But you're not to be alone. Banion, I'd appreciate it if you'd come along."

Dan waved his pipe. "Certainly."

"What are you going to do?" Marian asked.

"Nothing you have to worry about. But we can't sit back and let matters go on the way they are." Mallory removed her fur coat from the hook and held it for her arms.

Dan turned over the check which the waiter had left face down at his elbow, and gasped at the total. His wallet felt like an empty sausage skin when he had counted out the bills.

CHAPTER SIXTEEN

At Marian's house, Dan paced the floor and glanced at titles in the bookshelves. Marian had gone into her bedroom to pack a bag. Lance Mallory was in the hall telephoning.

Dan stared around the comfortable room and wondered if he would ever live in a house like this. Ethel had wanted this kind of thing. He'd never given her a chance. Always hotel rooms and crummy flats. Always with his nose in somebody else's business instead of his own.

Or was that right? Maybe this was his business. The tangled mess of other people's lives! How could anyone hope to lead a serene life in a disorderly world? Kipper had put it in an interesting way. You need a world to live in. You need an environment.

Dan was distracted from his thoughts by the sight of Marian Cleave's white kid bag lying on the table. She was still in her bedroom packing her things. Lance Mallory's voice in the hall indicated he was intent on the phone.

Dan flipped back the jade clasp, and the mouth of the bag gaped. The yellow envelope protruded like a tongue. He plucked it out and stuck a finger under the loose flap.

"Dan! Oh Dan!" Marian's voice came from the rear hall. The sound of her heels was coming closer. Instinctively, Dan snapped the bag shut. The envelope remained in his hand. He tucked it in his inside pocket.

"Dan!" Marian put her head through the door. "Help yourself to a drink. You know where it is."

"Thanks. I will."

Lance Mallory came in from the front hall. "I'm afraid you can't stay at the Hobarts'. They don't answer. You'll have to put up with the Foisies for one night. He says they've plenty of room."

"Oh, Lance, I won't do it."

"Listen. You have to be sensible."

"Oh, all right. He's such an old prune, though."

"Foisie's all right. Now hurry up."

Marian returned to her packing. Lance helped himself to a brandy. "She'll be all right at Foisie's. He's a little peculiar, but a good sort."

Foisie's house was an old-fashioned, bay-windowed, two-story wooden mansion on Pacific Avenue. An iron crane on the lawn pointed its beak scissors-like at the sky. The front door was paneled with leaded glass in a design of red and green. Guy Foisie opened the door.

"Come in, Lancey. Come in. And Marian, sweet. So good to see you, Danny boy." He put one of his big hands on Mallory's neck and fairly pushed him into the parlor. "Lancey, I want you to see the cutest thing. I bought it for my little niece Agnes. Come in, everyone. You'll love it."

The parlor had a pink rug, a marble fireplace, and bow-legged gilt furniture. In a large chair off to one side sat an enormous gray-haired woman with ankles swollen thick as stovepipes. Her dress was more of a bag to hold her sagging flesh than a garment. Her face was bloated, too thickly powdered, and highly rouged. Her eyes were indifferent as a cat's. She was knitting.

A fat young man with dark hair and pink cheeks stood near the fireplace where a log was blazing.

Foisie pranced with amazing sprightliness to a table on which was set a round box with a doll on top. The doll wore an apron and had a little tin knife in her hand. Around her feet were three small figures of mice. Foisie tripped a lever and a music box began playing "Three Blind Mice." As the music played, the mice ran round and round the feet of the doll and the knife moved up and down in her hand.

Foisie watched entranced. "Isn't it a love? I've almost worn it out playing it for my own delight."

When the music box had played itself out, Foisie inclined his head toward the bloated elderly woman. "That's my mother. She's deaf as a stone. I'd introduce you, but it's senseless. She can't hear you. Say anything you please." He extended an arm toward the fat young man at the fireplace. "This is Leonard, my buddy." He began rewinding the music box. "Do you want to hear it again?"

"No, Guy," Mallory said. "We can only stay a minute. That is, Dan and I have to go. Marian is staying."

Foisie drew himself up to his full height, put the back of one hand on his hip, and waggled a finger at Mallory. "By the way, I have a bone to pick with you."

"Now what?" Mallory said.

Still pointing at Mallory, Foisie looked at Leonard and announced, "This is the brute who got me drunk."

"*I* got you drunk!" Mallory laughed. "You got yourself drunk. You and Winkleman."

"I only had four little bitsy drinks. What in the world was that stuff?"

"It was good Scotch."

Foisie turned to Dan. "You know, we went down to Lancey's place in Burlingame night before last. Arnie Winkleman was with us. I had four little drinks and it knocked me, just like that. I went to bed at eleven o'clock and didn't wake up till almost noon. And, oh, did I have a head!"

"You're just an old woman, Guy," Mallory said.

"*I* am?" Foisie was indignant. "What about yourself? You passed out on the couch. Arnie and I had an awful time putting you to bed."

Mallory grinned. "Maybe we just can't take it like we used to. Guy, we have to go now. Take care of Marian, will you?"

"She'll be snug as a little chick. We'll put her in the blue room."

"Maybe she'd like to go to her room now," Mallory suggested. "She's had a rather trying day."

"Yes, I would," Marian said. "Do you mind?"

Foisie waved his arms as if scattering imaginary objections.

"Do I mind? What a question! Not a bit, my sweet."

"Call me in the morning," Marian begged. "I'll be so worried until I hear from you." She seemed to be addressing both of them, but she looked meaningly at Dan.

As Mallory headed his car back downtown, he said, "Odd chap, Foisie. Queer as a fish. But he has a wonderful heart."

"Doesn't he get on your nerves?" Dan asked.

"I guess I'm used to peculiar people, Banion."

"How well do you know Gregory Fallon?"

"Oh, I've known Greg a good many years."

"Suppose we drop in on him. Do you know where he lives?"

"Good suggestion. I doubt if he'll be in, though. We can try."

"Does he strike you as a man who might be capable of a thing like this?"

"Frankly, no. But that doesn't mean anything. You can't tell what a person might do if the compulsion was great enough. We're all savages under the skin, Banion. If he's in, suppose you let me do the talking. I think I know how to handle him."

Mallory seemed accustomed to being in charge of matters. Dan wasn't fond of the secondary status this placed him in, but he could think of no reason to object. Mallory drove to a level street atop Nob Hill and parked. Directly ahead, the street sloped off abruptly in a steep grade. Below them, the lights of the city glowed dimly through the fog.

"Greg's apartment is in the next block," Mallory said, "but it's easier to park here."

Dan was just about to open the door when Mallory held his arm. "Wait a minute. I think that's Greg coming up the hill now." He watched intently for a moment. "That's Greg, all right. Let's be quiet a minute and see what he does."

On the other side of the street, Dan saw a man walk briskly under a street lamp, pause at a parked coupe, and unlock the door.

"Shall we follow him and see where he goes?" Mallory whispered.

"It's okay with me," Dan replied.

As Fallon's car pulled away from the curb, Mallory stepped on his own starter. The red taillight of Fallon's coupe danced ahead of them down one grade after another, leveling off at intersections, and disappearing momentarily when it plunged over crests. It led straight down off Nob Hill until it reached Kearny Street, then swung to the left.

Although Fallon set a mad pace, once almost colliding with a cable car that clanged its bell hysterically, Mallory followed skillfully. At Kearny and Jackson, Fallon turned right entering the wholesale fruit and vegetable district, almost deserted at this hour.

As they approached this quiet area, Mallory slowed down and followed at almost a block's distance. When Fallon's car pulled in to a curb ahead, Mallory turned a corner and parked. Dan had the door open before the car came to a halt, and they managed to get up to the corner in time to see Fallon walk to the doorway of a two-story building and disappear inside.

Mallory gripped Dan's arm and gave him a slight push. "Walk down past the place and see what it is. Greg's not apt to recognize you if he comes out."

Dan was a little irked by Mallory's commanding attitude, but since it was what he intended to do anyhow, he strolled down the narrow, deserted street, lined on both sides with dilapidated two-story buildings. Downstairs were wholesale food establishments; upstairs were offices and rooming houses. Farther along the street, a few lights seemed to indicate cheap hotels.

Dan wasn't sure which doorway Fallon had entered. All were dark and narrow. The one that seemed most likely led to rooms or offices on the second floor. Dan stepped into the entryway and lit a match to read the names on the mailboxes. "Fergus Manley, Nature Illustrations." "Margot Lisner, Personality Building." "Armand

Glotcher, Art Photography."

Footsteps sounded on the stairway inside. Dan blew the match out. He walked quickly a few doors down the street and stood in another dark entryway. Two men came out of the building, walked to Fallon's car, and got in. Dan recognized one of them as Fallon. The other he couldn't make out. As the car drove away, he ran back to the corner where he had left Mallory.

Mallory was already in the car and had the engine started. As Dan lurched in, he swung around and headed down the street in the direction Fallon had gone. Several blocks distant, they saw a red taillight turn a corner to the right. It might have been Fallon. It might have been anyone. The engine roared as Mallory hurtled them through the quiet street. When they reached the corner where the taillight had turned, the street was empty.

Mallory cursed under his breath.

"Well, I guess that's that," Dan said.

"Who was with him? Could you see?" Mallory asked.

"I don't know. It was too dark."

"What was that place he went in?"

"Glotcher's studio is in there. His name is on the mailbox."

"I'll be damned!"

"Does Fallon know Glotcher?"

"I suppose so."

"Let's go back and see if Glotcher's there."

"Oh, I don't think he would be. That was probably Glotcher with Fallon. I've a hunch they may have gone back to Fallon's apartment. Let's have a look."

Mallory drove back to the top of Nob Hill. His guess had been a good one. Fallon's coupe was parked in the same place it had been before.

CHAPTER SEVENTEEN

Gregory Fallon lived in a gray stucco apartment house built for higher-income tenants. The brass mailboxes shone with mirror-like brilliance. The entrance hall gleamed with hardwood paneling.

When Dan and Lance Mallory came out of the automatic elevator on the third floor, Fallon already had his door open and was standing in the hall, having answered their ring below by clicking the electric door latch.

"Oh, it's you," he said, indifferently. He weaved slightly on his feet.

"Hello, Greg." Mallory motioned toward Dan. "I believe you met each other last night at the Hobarts'."

"I was too drunk to remember. Come on in." Fallon's breath smelled strongly of whisky. The apartment was expensively furnished in the taste of a professional interior decorator. The only mark expressing Fallon's own personality was a whisky bottle and some glasses on a low table.

Arnold Winkleman, the artist, was sitting in one of the chairs. He greeted them with a yawn.

Fallon lifted the whisky bottle. "What's on your mind, Lance?"

"Nothing special, Greg. Just thought we'd drop in."

Greg appeared annoyed. "That's a good one. Just thought you'd drop in! Will you have a drink?"

"No, thanks," Mallory said. "We were here earlier, but you were out."

"Just a friendly visit," Fallon said resentfully. "Why don't you tell the truth? You think maybe I killed Kipper, so you came here to feel me out. Well, I didn't. Does that satisfy you?" He motioned to Dan with the bottle. "How about you? Have a drink?"

"No, thanks," Dan said.

Fallon looked at him carefully. "What's the matter? Are you afraid you'll be poisoned?"

Winkleman intervened. "Take it easy, Greg. Don't be so damned sensitive."

Fallon wrinkled his mouth ironically. "That's right. Take it easy! You lose your wife, think nothing of it. Take it easy! People accuse you of murder. Take it easy! Let 'em walk all over you. Wonderful advice." He poured himself a drink.

"Nobody's accused you of anything," Winkleman said. "You've had enough to drink, Greg. Why don't you listen to reason and lay off for tonight?"

"I can take care of myself."

As if he felt obliged to explain, Winkleman said, "I met him in a bar downtown. We had a few drinks, then I brought him home."

"I don't need any nursemaid," Fallon said.

Winkleman got up. "I'm going to have to run along. Don't take anything he says too seriously."

Fallon's eyes became worried. He pointed the whisky bottle at Winkleman. "You're not going to forget what we talked about!"

"Oh, no. Don't worry." Winkleman laughed lightly.

"It's a promise," Fallon said. "Remember, you promised."

"I won't forget. Only have a heart, Greg, and lay off the booze for one night."

When Winkleman had gone, Fallon poured himself another drink.

"Well, I'm not afraid of being poisoned."

"Greg, I want you to tell me the truth," Mallory said. "Did you ever buy any of Kipper's paintings?"

Fallon corked the bottle, but forgot the drink he had poured. "Did *I* ever buy any of his paintings?"

"Yes."

"Listen, Lance, I've bought a lot of idiotic things in my life, but no one can say I ever bought one of that guy's pictures. I was sick enough of hearing Marian talk about him. Kent this, Kent that, and Kent the other thing. Kent with breakfast. Kent with lunch. Kent with dinner."

"Did you ever have anybody else buy some for you?"

Fallon was thoughtful. "I get it. You're thinking of that private detective who was poisoned this afternoon. I read all about it. For God's sake, Lance, lay off. I didn't have anything to do with killing Kipper or anybody else. Maybe I didn't like him. I admit that. But I didn't kill him."

Mallory's voice was cool. "Then how does Dorothy Vane fit into all this?"

"Dorothy Vane? What's she have to do with it?"

"Dorothy Vane had some connection with the private detective who was killed. And we happen to know that she had been going around buying up Kipper's paintings."

"You mean Dorothy Vane was buying Kipper's pictures?" Fallon seemed genuinely bewildered.

"Exactly."

"What for? I don't get the connection." Fallon's dark eyes narrowed.

Mallory appealed to Dan. "Tell him what you told me."

Dan had been sitting quietly taking it all in. He patiently related the way he had traced purchases of Kipper's paintings to Dorothy Vane and from there to Barney Price.

As Fallon listened, he picked up the drink he had poured, walked to a chair, and sat there staring thoughtfully at the glass in his hand. When Dan had finished, he got up and put the glass on the coffee table without drinking it.

"We had a couple of Kipper paintings in the house," he said, slowly. "Somebody burned them in the fireplace." He took a pipe from his pocket, leaned over, and began to fill it from a humidor. "Marian blamed me."

Dan reached in his own pocket, took out the bulldog pipe he'd found on Kipper's stairway, and handed it to Fallon. "There's a little pipe a man could fall in love with."

Fallon snatched it quickly and rubbed it with the palm of his hand, "Where'd you get it?"

"It's yours?"

"Certainly. Where'd you find it?"

"I found it on the stairs in front of Kenton Kipper's place last night."

Fallon put it in his teeth and breathed through it a couple of times. "I was afraid I'd lost it."

"The question is," Dan said, "how did it get where I found it?"

Fallon dipped the pipe in the humidor and stuffed it affectionately. "Thanks for returning it. I must have dropped it there last night."

"What were you doing at Kent's place last night?" Mallory asked.

"Well, that's kind of embarrassing."

"You don't have to worry about being embarrassed with us."

"Well, I was drunk, as usual. I wanted to see if Marian was there. I just went up to the door and listened. There was nobody there. It was a crazy notion."

"What time was this?" Dan asked.

"It was just before I went up to the Hobarts'. Maybe you don't understand that kind of thing. But a man does a lot of peculiar things when he's in love." Fallon walked to the window and looked out on the sparkling city.

"You still haven't explained why Dorothy Vane was buying those paintings," Mallory said.

Fallon continued looking out the window. "How can I explain it? I didn't even know about it until you just told me. I wish somebody would explain it to me."

"Tell me, Greg, how did you happen to meet that girl?"

"Dorothy Vane?"

"Yes."

"It was in a bar. She happened to be sitting next to me. We got acquainted, and—"

Mallory looked disapproving. "What in the devil ever made you do such a thing, Greg?"

"Do we have to go into that? I was crazy, I guess. Marian was up at Tahoe. We had quarreled before she left."

Mallory sighed. "I suppose it's the same old story."

Fallon turned from the window. "Well, you know Marian. You've known her longer than I have. She's not the easiest person to get along with. You ought to know that."

"It's always easy to blame the other party, Greg."

"I know. You think I'm a heel. Everybody thinks I'm a heel. Well, you don't know everything."

"I've always been very fond of Marian. You know that, Greg. I don't say she's without faults. But this is one thing you can't blame her for."

"All right. Skip it."

Mallory's voice became firm. "I'm going to have to be blunt with you, Greg. You haven't been telling us the truth."

"What do you mean?"

"Well, for one thing, you didn't meet Winkleman in a bar tonight. You met him in the building where Armand Glotcher has his studio."

"I say I met him in a bar."

"And I'm just as positive you didn't."

"It isn't any of your business where I met him."

"Perhaps not. But why do you want to deny having met him at Glotcher's?"

"What makes you think I met him at Glotcher's?"

"Because we followed you there. We saw you go in, and saw you come out."

"You followed me there!"

"Yes. Dan and I."

Fallon sat perfectly still for a moment. Suddenly he stood up. "Get out."

"I'm asking you to be reasonable," Mallory said.

"Get the hell out of here," Fallon shouted.

"Now, listen Greg—"

"Nobody's going to spy on me and get by with it. And you pretended to be my friend!"

"Greg, you've got to realize that—"

"I'm warning you to get the hell out of here."

Fallon's face was such a spectacle of rage, Mallory reached quickly for his hat. Dan had already walked calmly to the door and was waiting.

CHAPTER EIGHTEEN

Outside on the pavement, Dan said, "You shouldn't have told Fallon we'd followed him."

Mallory was nettled. "How could I have been expected to know he'd act that way?"

"No man likes to be spied on. You wouldn't like it either."

"I should have punched him in the face."

"Oh no. He had cause to be sore. When you lose a trick that way, the best thing to do is get out."

"Did you hear the way he talked to me?"

"He was talking to me, too."

"He'll have cause to regret that."

When they got in the car, Mallory said, "I've a hunch we ought to go back to Glotcher's studio and try to find out what he was doing there."

"At this hour? It's almost one o'clock."

"He wouldn't be in bed."

"Does he live there?"

"Well, I suppose so. Most of those people in that district live and work in the same studio. Of course, if you object—"

"Not a bit," Dan said. "By the way, do you know anything about Fallon's business connections?"

"A little. Why?"

"Those spaghetti cases were stored in a lot near the waterfront. They came off a salvaged ship. Whoever committed the murder must have had pretty intimate knowledge of where they were being taken and how they were to be destroyed."

"You're right. Come to think of it, I believe he does have some clients in the shipping business."

"Is there any way of checking?"

"Why, yes, I think so."

"Mind letting me know what you find out?"

"Not at all. That's a good suggestion. You call me at my office tomorrow. It's in the phone book. Mallory, Waller, and Wyatt. I wish you'd call me anyhow, Banion. There are several things I want to check up on in the morning and, well, you may be able to give me some advice."

Mallory drove to within a few doors of the building where Glotcher's studio was located, and parked. They got out and walked to the entrance. The door was open, and at the top of a dark stairway they could see a dim light burning in a hall. They started up, and each stair creaked an aged complaint under their feet. They were almost to the top when two explosions sounded in quick succession in the hall above.

Dan gripped the banister. Mallory recoiled and took several steps downward. A quick patter of heels sounded on the floor above. The silhouette of a girl with a gun in her hand appeared at the top of the stairs. She saw them and ran back the way she had come.

Dan took the remaining stairs three at a time. Mallory remained frozen to the banister. At the top, Dan looked down an empty hall. Somewhere around a corner he heard a window slide in its frame.

Behind him came a wild clatter of heavy feet on the stairs. Inspector Gallagher came puffing upward followed by Mack and the man in the gray hat who had followed Dan earlier in the evening. Gallagher held a big blunt revolver.

"Around the end of the hall. She got out a window," Dan said.

Mack and the other plain-clothes man took off down the hall, the tails of their overcoats whipping behind them. Gallagher scrutinized Dan and Mallory. "What were those shots?"

"We were coming up the stairs," Dan said. "A girl came running with a gun in her hand. When she saw us, she ran back. I heard a window open somewhere down the hall."

"Did you see who it was?"

"No."

Gallagher scowled and started down the hall looking at doors. Dan and Mallory followed. When he came to one with Glotcher's name on it, Gallagher tried the knob. It was locked. He banged his fist on it. "Come on. Open up."

There was no answer. He hammered again. "Open up. It's the police." Still no answer. "I know you're in there. Open up or I'll bust the door."

"Who are you?" came a muffled voice on the other side.

"Inspector Gallagher. The police. Open up."

The door cracked open disclosing Armand Glotcher. His face was milky pale, his hands trembling.

Gallagher pushed the door wide and led the way in. Glotcher backed up. He was shaking so badly he could hardly stand. The room looked more like a seduction chamber than a Photographer's studio. A low bed was covered by an Oriental spread. Subdued lighting came from rickety-looking lamps on low tables. A large camera stood spraddle-legged on a tripod. Pictures on the walls were mostly nude studies. A flat-top desk opposite the door was the only thing that gave the place any semblance of a business establishment.

Gallagher took a quick look around. "What the hell were those shots?" he demanded.

Glotcher leaned against the desk. He tried to talk, but no words came. He was scared speechless.

"You better sit down and cool yourself," Gallagher said.

Glotcher staggered to the chair behind the desk and flopped in it.

Mack and the other detective came in shoving Janey Navarro ahead of them. She stood rubbing her wrist where Mack had gripped her, and looking from one person to another with frightened eyes.

Mack took a small automatic pistol from his overcoat and displayed it. "Found her hidin' behind a chimney on the roof next door. She was packin' this."

Gallagher looked from Janey to Glotcher. "All right, now, what happened here?"

Janey began to cry.

Glotcher found his voice. "I just came home. I just came upstairs."

"I know," Gallagher snapped. "I saw you come in. I was sitting across the street in a car." He looked at Dan and Mallory. "I saw you two guys come in right after. Now what the hell happened?"

Dan moved close to Janey, slipped a hand under her arm, and squeezed reassuringly.

"They shot at me," Glotcher gasped. "I was just opening my door. I'd just put the key in the door when they shot at me."

"What do you mean, *they* shot at you?" Gallagher demanded.

"I did. I shot at him," Janey sobbed.

"They tried to kill me," Glotcher whined.

"Don't be foolish," Dan said. "If I'd shot at you, I wouldn't have missed."

Glotcher wiped a hand across his brow. "I ran inside and locked the door."

Gallagher looked closely at Janey. "Where were you? I didn't see you come in."

"I wish I'd killed him," she sobbed. "I wanted to kill him."

"Don't say that," Dan warned. "Wait till you calm down before you make any statements."

"For chrissake," Gallagher said. "Will you let me handle this, Banion?"

"I don't care what happens anymore," Janey sobbed.

"What was the idea of shooting at him?" Gallagher asked.

"He killed Kent. I know he did. He hated Kent."

"She's crazy," Glotcher said. "She's dangerous. She ought to be locked up."

"You shut your mouth," Gallagher ordered. "When I want to hear from you, I'll say so." He returned his attention to Janey. "What makes you say he killed Kipper?"

"He hated Kent. He swore he'd get even. Kent hit him, and he said he'd get even."

"Is that the only reason you have for thinking he killed him?"

"Yes, but he did. I know he did."

"She's a maniac," Glotcher said. "She ought to be put away."

Gallagher ignored him. "Tell me just what happened tonight."

"I'd just come in," Glotcher began, "and was opening my door, when—"

"I mean her," Gallagher snapped.

Janey mopped at her eyes with a handkerchief. "I came a long while ago. I had to wait a long time. I waited around the corner in the hall. When he came, I shot. I shot twice. I missed. I'm sorry I missed."

Glotcher, now somewhat restored, stood up and took a bottle of whisky and a glass from a cabinet. "She oughtn't to be let run around loose. It's not safe." He put the whisky on the desk and went to a corner basin to rinse out the glass.

"While you were waiting," Dan said, "did anybody else come in?"

"Yes," said Janey. "Arnold Winkleman came. He knocked on Glotcher's door, but there was nobody there."

"About what time was that?"

"At about eleven-twenty. He waited a while in front of the door, smoking a cigarette. Then Greg Fallon came, and they both went away."

"Did you hear them say anything?"

"Yes. Arnie said, 'The bastard isn't in.'"

Glotcher returned to the desk, snapping the glass to shake off the drops of water. "Did Arnie Winkleman say that?" His face was indignant.

"What else did they say?" Dan asked.

"Greg said something about should they wait. Arnie said he didn't think it would be any use, and they went away."

"Were they the only ones who came?"

Janey indicated Gallagher and his assistants. "These men came about half an hour ago. They knocked on the door for quite a while, then went away."

Gallagher had been listening intently, switching his small blue eyes from face to face as they talked. "We didn't go away. We were across the street in a car watching the joint." He turned his attention to Glotcher. "Where have you been all night? My men have been looking for you."

Glotcher's arrogance had returned to him. "I don't have to report to you. She tried to kill me. She admits it. Put her away. That's your business." He poured himself a drink.

Gallagher kicked a chair to a position facing Glotcher, and sat in it. "If you don't want to talk here, I can take you down to headquarters. Make up your mind."

"You're not going to question me unless I have my attorney with me. That's the law. I know my rights."

Gallagher had fished out his battered pack of cigarettes and was probing for one with his finger. "What I'm particularly interested in is your dealings with Barney Price."

Glotcher paused with the drink halfway to his lips, "Barney Price?"

"Yeah. The private detective who was murdered this afternoon."

"I don't know any Barney Price."

"Think hard. Your number was scribbled on his desk blotter."

"Must be a mistake." The glass trembled in Glotcher's hand as he raised it to his lips.

"There's no mistake. You—"

Gallagher never finished. Glotcher had risen from his chair and was clawing at his throat. His eyes bulged in terror and his face was turning pink. His head was jerking erratically.

Janey Navarro gave a little scream and hid her face in her hands. Mallory's mouth opened, and he looked away. Before Gallagher could get to him, Glotcher crumpled to the floor, his head striking the edge of the desk with a loud thump, and his body falling with a clatter.

There was a kind of snoring gasp from behind the desk, then a thin whistling sound that grew thinner and thinner. Gallagher, who had been leaning over him, straightened up, his face a conflict of embarrassment and rage.

"The guy have a stroke?" Mack asked.

Gallagher walked around in front of the desk and sat on it. The unlighted cigarette was still dangling from his lips. He lit a kitchen match with his thumbnail, and puffed. Mack walked around and had a look for himself.

"He's dead," Gallagher said.

"Leunatine?" Dan suggested.

Gallagher removed his hat and massaged his brow with a hand. "No doubt." He sighed with deep weariness. "Now we can begin all over again."

CHAPTER NINETEEN

It was 4:00 A.M. when Dan turned the key and entered his small hotel room.

Having a third murder committed before his eyes hadn't improved Gallagher's disposition. Repeated grilling of everyone present added nothing to the information already at hand. Someone, somehow, had put leunatine in Glotcher's whisky bottle. The possibility of suicide was not even worth considering.

By suggesting that the newspaper story could be so written as to obscure the fact that a murder had been committed under the very nose of an inspector of the Homicide Bureau, Dan had succeeded in convincing Gallagher that Janey Navarro should be booked for nothing more serious than possession of a concealed weapon. Gallagher was inclined to be liberal on the score, inasmuch as shooting at Glotcher seemed to him a perfectly understandable impulse.

Mallory had put up bail for Janey, and they had taken her home. Then Mallory had dropped Dan off at his hotel. In parting, he had advised Dan, through a yawn, that he would check on the business connections of Fallon tomorrow, and not to forget to call him.

Dan was almost too tired to think. He threw his overcoat and hat on the bed, unbuttoned his vest, and relaxed in a chair.

He was always conscious that coming home to this room comprised coming home to nothing. The single bed looked as if it had been made by a machine. The washbasin gleamed nakedly in a corner. A narrow window led to a fire escape, and looked out on the brick wall of another building. There was something elaborately foolish about the way a couple of curlicued arms held up the mirror on a cheap veneer-board dresser. His little beaten-up portable typewriter on the bedside table was the only warm and familiar thing. It reminded him of how many times he had pawned it to feed Ethel and himself before the war, during the depression that had followed the boom, which came after the depression which followed the last war, which had been preceded by the depression that followed the boom that—

Oh hell! Dan's thoughts were getting out of control. He yawned and removed his shoes. The relief of his feet from confinement almost cleared his brain. He stood up and took his coat off. As he did so, the yellow envelope he had taken from Marian Cleave's purse gleamed in his inside pocket. He had forgotten all about it.

Settled again in his chair, be turned the envelope in his hand and reflected for a moment before opening it. Then he pressed back the flap and removed a photograph.

He felt a slight rush of blood to the head. It took some time for his mind to bridge the gap between the make-believe world of daily living and the crude reality of this picture. The politeness and pretense of surface things were ripped away, and he was staring at the savagery beneath.

"What a naïve bunch of idiots we are," he thought.

He rose and poured himself a shot of whisky from a pint on the bureau. His hand was unsteady, and the whisky spilled over the edge of the glass.

No wonder Kipper had socked Glotcher! No wonder a lot of things.

So this was Marian! He remembered her plaintive voice, "You'll hear awful things about me, but they're not true." It was obvious from the picture that she had been drunk, but even so—

He raised his glass to his lips before he remembered how Glotcher had been poisoned, and set it down again without drinking. He returned to the chair and looked at the photograph again. Inside the envelope, he also found the negative. He had expected something compromising, but not rank pornography.

"Oh, Dan, it was nothing," she had said. "It didn't mean a thing." And earlier, "Dan, you've got some sense. You can take things as they are. You can forget things that don't mean anything. You know how life is."

He sat for some time in a kind of a daze. Was this the same yellow envelope he had seen Barney Price handle shortly before he was murdered? Not necessarily. Still, its appearance was identical.

If it was the same envelope, then it was reasonable to suppose Glotcher had just delivered it to Barney when Dan encountered him going into the elevator. But why would he bring it to Barney? And how did it get from there into Marian's purse?

Glotcher was not above a little blackmail. He had already shown the photograph to Kipper. That, no doubt, was the incident in Chinatown when Kipper hit him. It was worth something to Marian to get her hands on that negative. Maybe Barney was acting as the middleman in negotiations.

The conclusions Dan drew from this caused him to whistle through his teeth. He stood up to pace the floor, but the narrow room would only allow about three steps in any direction. It all seemed to hinge on one question; was this the same yellow envelope he had seen in Barney Price's hands? Nobody could prove this. Dan himself couldn't swear to it.

He checked his door to be certain it was locked, and got ready for bed. Before turning out the light, he picked up the photograph and had another long look at it. He shrugged his shoulders. "Hell," he said. "Who am I to criticize?" and snapped off the light.

CHAPTER TWENTY

Dan's waking the next day was a gradual experience. He lay for a long time dozing and blinking. At last he threw the covers back, rubbed his eyes, and massaged his scalp. The alarm clock on the dresser told him it was noon.

In a yawning daze he made a few sour faces in the mirror over the washbasin, brushed his teeth, shaved, and combed his hair. As he groped around getting into his clothes, he noticed the yellow envelope still lying on the cover of his portable typewriter. It recalled the events of the night before.

"Live and learn," he told himself briskly. "Live and learn."

While putting on his necktie, he thought over plans for the day. A showdown with Marian Cleave seemed in order. Perhaps he ought to turn the photograph over to Gallagher and let him handle it. But that seemed a dirty trick unless he was sure it had bearing on the murders. Better see Marian first, then decide what to do.

Suddenly his attention was attracted to the dresser top. He stood staring with his necktie half tied, his fingers halted in their task. The whisky he had poured the night before, and had not drunk, was still in the shot glass. Where his shaking hand had spilled some of the liquor on the dresser cloth, was a green stain.

For a while he stood motionless, looking at it. Then he emptied the shot glass down the washbasin, rinsed it thoroughly, and washed his hands. He rolled the whisky bottle in the stained dresser scarf, and wrapped them both in a newspaper. When he had finished dressing, he put the yellow envelope in his pocket, took the bundle under his arm, and left the room.

Through an open door down the hall he saw a maid cleaning one of the rooms. He questioned her. She had seen no one go in his room yesterday. But, of course, she couldn't be sure. She seldom noticed who came or went, and she spent only an hour or so a day on that floor.

The clerk at the desk in the lobby couldn't help Dan either. "We've seldom any thefts," he said. "Of course, people go in and out all day. Some of them live here and some of them don't. Why do you ask? Did you lose something?"

Dan didn't bother to explain. He stopped in the lobby phone booth and called the *Journal*.

"The boss says you're doing fine," Charlie Dixon said. "Keep right on the story and dig us up something new to keep it rolling."

"How would another corpse do?"

"That would be great."

"And suppose I was the corpse?"

"Don't overdo it."

"I'm not kidding you. Somebody slipped a dose of that screwy poison in a bottle of whisky I had in my room."

"You're making this up."

"The hell I am. I've got it under my arm. I'm on my way to show it to Gallagher now." Dan gave him the details of the story.

"Keep right on the job," Charlie said. "Don't let them scare you off. They're trying to bluff you."

"Would that have been bluffing if I'd taken a drink of that stuff?"

"You're not getting chicken, are you?"

"I'm scared spitless, if you want the truth."

"Don't run out on us, Dan. Don't be a quitter."

"Quit? How the hell can I? The murderer has me on his list now."

"That's the spirit, Dan. Stay with it. But be careful what you drink."

"Thanks for the advice."

The restaurants were again crowded with the noon-hour rush, but Dan managed to squeeze in at a lunch counter. Eating with a bottle of poison in his lap was a new sensation. He wondered what his neighbors to right and left would think if they knew what was in the package. While he ate, he read the *Journal's* account of Glotcher's murder, which he had phoned in early that morning.

In spite of the clamoring of troops overseas for transportation home, strikes and impending strikes, furious debates over ceiling prices, and conjecture as to whether mankind would blow itself up with the atomic bomb, the "Green-Lip Murders," as it had been characterized, still occupied the headlines. The weird killer who had corpses in spaghetti boxes and planted death in whisky bottles had captured the public's imagination.

The man on the stool beside Dan reached over and tapped a finger on the page. "That dame done it," he said positively through a mouthful of wieners and sauerkraut.

Dan was startled. "What dame?"

"That Cleave dame."

"What makes you think so?"

The man looked morbidly wise, chewed solemnly, and swallowed. "Love," he said. "'Each man kills the thing he loves.'"

"Yes, but you said the girl did it."

"Same thing, man or woman. Love a thing and you want to kill it. Sometimes I could wring my wife's neck." He speared a wiener viciously.

At the Hall of Justice, Inspector Gallagher was sitting behind his desk, red-eyed, plainly exhausted, but very calm. "What's on your mind, son?" he said in a patronizing voice.

Dan opened one end of his newspaper-wrapped bundle, slipped out the pint bottle, and set it on the desk in front of Gallagher. "You look tired. You look as if you could use a drink."

"Thanks, Banion, but if I took one drink of that I'd go to sleep in my shoes. I'm played out, and my neuritis is damn near killing me. Nice of you, though."

"It's just as well," Dan said, "because if you took one drink of that you'd turn red as a lobster and your soul would go hissing out through your false teeth."

Gallagher eyed the bottle warily. "What is it?"

"Whisky with just a touch of leunatine."

"Where'd you get hold of it?"

"It was on the dresser in my hotel room. Somebody, sometime yesterday, sneaked into my room and poisoned it. I came home last night—or rather, this morning—and started to take a drink. After I poured it, I changed my mind. I spilled some on the dresser scarf, though, and today when I woke up, it had dried a lovely shade of green. Here. Take a look at it." Dan unwound the dresser scarf and threw it on the desk.

"I'll be a son of a bitch. Sit down, son."

"Lucky thing I didn't drink the stuff or I'd be lying on the carpet right now while you went through my pockets."

Gallagher examined the scarf closely. "We'll have the stuff analyzed. But I haven't any doubt what it is. Did you question the hotel people?"

"Yes, but they don't know. People go in and out of a hotel all day."

"Have you any ideas?"

"No, have you?"

Gallagher tossed the scarf aside, leaned back in his swivel chair, and spoke with irony. "You need have no fear, my man. The police are on the case, and we expect to make an arrest any minute. You may quote me to that effect."

"Just what does that mean?"

Gallagher straightened up with an angry squeak of the swivel. "Just what it generally means. I don't know the seat of my pants from a Goodyear blimp. I'm no farther ahead than when I began. If this nut, whoever he is, goes on poisoning people, sooner or later he'll make a mistake and leave his calling card. Then I'll go after him with a siren blowing and make an arrest. In the meantime, there's nothing to do but wait for the next corpse to turn up. Seems that will probably be you."

"Unless he poisons you first."

"He couldn't do that. It's against the law. By the way, all this is off the record, you understand."

"What did you learn from Fallon and Winkleman?"

"They said they'd been invited to a party in Glotcher's studio, but when they got there the door was locked and nobody was in."

"That's a good one."

"It's a lot of baloney, I know. But they stuck to their story."

"What reason did they give for lying to Mallory and me?"

"They said they didn't think it was any of your business. Glotcher was in the habit of giving pretty wild parties, and they didn't want to advertise that they'd been there."

"Pretty thin."

"Yeah. There's another angle to this Fallon that looks bad. He's an attorney, you know."

"So I'm told."

"Well, it turns out he's the attorney for the Hogby and Engles Salvage Company. He handled some of the legal matters concerning the steamship *Albert C. Decker.*"

"That's the salvaged ship they took the spoiled spaghetti off."

"Right. And, as the attorney for the company, he'd be apt to know all about the deal."

"What does he say to that?"

"He denies knowing anything about it."

"Did you ask him about his connection with Dorothy Vane, and her buying Kipper's paintings?"

"He says it doesn't make sense to him. According to him, he hasn't laid eyes on her since that time when her husband caught them in bed."

"Whatever happened to the suit for fifty thousand dollars that guy Howard Vane brought against him?"

"That was ridiculous. The guy settled out of court for five hundred."

"How about Dorothy Vane? Any trace of her?"

"Not a sign. She packed a bag and left her apartment, and that's as far as we know. We have descriptions of her out everywhere. She'll be picked up."

"And her husband, Howard Vane?"

"We're after him, too. Last trace of him, he was running a dice game in Reno. We'll find him."

"Meanwhile, are you going to let this fellow Fallon run loose?"

"I haven't anything on him but circumstantial evidence, and damn little of that. I've got a tail on him, though. I'm having that artist Winkleman tailed, too. We're going to watch every move they make."

"Come to think of it, you put a tail on me yesterday."

"Why not? You've got a nose for corpses. You've smelled out two of them already. You know, Banion, if my instinct didn't tell me different, I'd be suspecting you."

"Do you think I'd try to poison myself?"

"No, but dragging this bottle and dresser cover in here, and claiming somebody tried to poison you, would be a pretty slick cover-up if you were guilty."

"If I was going to poison anybody, I could name a lot of people who'd be first on the list."

"Well, don't name them. They might turn up with green lips yet."

Dan crumpled the newspaper he'd wrapped the bottle in, and threw it in Gallagher's wastebasket. "How about it? When I leave here, will I have one of your bloodhounds tailing me?"

"It wouldn't be a bad idea, Banion. Let one of my boys follow you around for your own protection."

"I just don't like it."

"Suit yourself. It's impossible to tail a man if he knows you're doing it. There are too many ways of shaking him."

"Why put me to the trouble?"

"It's your stomach, Banion. If you want it poisoned, I guess I can't stop you. All I ask is that you remember my neuritis and give me a square deal."

"Then there's to be no tail?"

"No tail, Banion. You're on your own."

In the Hall of Justice pressroom. Dan looked up Guy Foisie in the phone book and called his home. A maid informed him that Marian Cleave had gone out early that morning and had not returned. She took her bag with her, so the maid didn't think she was coming back.

He called Marian Cleave's house and nobody answered. He looked up Lance Mallory and called his office, but he had gone out and they didn't expect him back.

A total score of zero so far as the telephone was concerned. Dan decided to drop by the *Journal* office and talk to Hal Swayne, the sports editor.

As he entered the *Journal* editorial room, the girl at the switchboard said, "A letter for you, Mr. Banion," and held out an envelope.

It was a plain five-and-ten-cent-store envelope postmarked "Redwood City." There was no return address. Inside Dan found a note scribbled on cheap, lined tablet paper: The Crow, Laurel and L Streets, Redwood City. Ask for Agnes. Come alone." It was signed, "Dorothy V."

"Where's Redwood City?" he asked the switchboard girl.

"It's down the Peninsula."

"How far?"

"Oh, less than an hour's ride. Some people commute on the train."

Dan pocketed the note and walked over to where Hal Swayne sat hunched over his typewriter like an angry bird. Hal had pure white hair, affectionate blue eyes, and a face that was as tanned and wrinkled as an old baseball mitt. "Whadda you know," he said, as Dan approached. "Billy Conn will get five hundred thousand for fighting Joe Louis, and the government will take four hundred thousand in taxes. How's a man ever to get out of the proletariat at that rate?"

"I can't tell you," said Dan pulling up a chair. "Do you know anything about this guy Barney Price who was murdered yesterday?"

"Barney Price? Sure. He was a welterweight for about a year. But he wasn't any good. That was a long time ago. Later, he taught boxing at Stanford University, but was thrown out for bootlegging gin to fraternity houses. That was during prohibition, of course. Then he ran a speakeasy somewhere down the Peninsula. After that, he managed fighters for a while, and finally turned up running that private detective agency of his. Oh yeah, somewhere along the line he was a cop. I think that was before he went in the ring. I'm not certain."

"When did he teach at Stanford? Do you remember?"

"Let's see. My boy was there at the time. That must have been—yes, it was 1920. I'm positive. I know Barney was working there then, and I believe that was the year he was thrown out."

"Your son might remember him."

Hal nodded his head thoughtfully. "Yes, he probably would."

"Is he in town? Can I call him up?"

"No." Hal stared into his typewriter. "My boy was killed at Iwo Jima."

"I'm sorry, Hal."

"Anything else I can do for you?"

"Where was that speakeasy Barney operated?"

"I'm not sure, but I think it was San Mateo. It was one of those towns down the Peninsula."

"That would be in 1921."

"That's right. Just after he left Stanford."

"Well, I guess that's all, Hal. Thanks a lot."

"Any time, Dan. Glad to help. I guess I know most of the old-timers around here. Boxers, ballplayers, jockeys, cops, pimps. I've got a head full of ghosts. That's why my hair is white."

CHAPTER TWENTY-ONE

Before leaving the *Journal* office, Dan phoned Marian Cleave's house again, on the chance that she might have come in. Her voice answered. "Oh, Dan, I was hoping it would be you."

"I'd like to see you, Marian."

"Please come right away. I'm alone. I simply couldn't stay with those Foisies. I couldn't do it."

To Dan there seemed an extra measure of anxiety in Marian's voice. The cab that he took rattled and thumped and tossed him about on the seat with springless violence. Finally he yelled to the driver, "This wreck is about ready for the junk heap, isn't it?"

"You ain't kiddin', buddy," the driver yelled in reply. "If we don't get new ones soon, the damn old thing is gonna let go of her bolts. She's ran day and night through the whole war. I'm tellin' you, she's hauled more sailors in the past year than a fleet of cruisers. Not to mention their dames. This here hack has gone farther than from here to Tokyo and back. They quashed all the stuffin' out of her seats, and all the bounce out of her springs, and the only thing that don't squeak is the windshield wiper, because that don't work at all."

The day was stinging cold, but clear and bright. As the cab groaned up Russian Hill, Dan got a look at the bay flecked with whitecaps. The grass on distant hills was green. The big white letters that had been painted on the side of Angel Island, "WELCOME HOME, WELL DONE," had been partially washed away by the rains, so that they now read, "WEL ME HOM W DONE." The word "done" alone remained intact.

Dan viewed Marian Cleave's house by daylight for the first time and found it quiet, unpretentious, and practical in a highly expensive way. A big lawn set off from the street by a well-trimmed hedge. Several shade trees almost obscuring the one-story shingle house in the rear. A sense of privacy, comfort, and well-being. Everything first class and well kept.

Marian herself, in white silk slacks and a peasant blouse, opened the door. She held out her hand and pulled him inside. "I'm not afraid anymore, now," she whispered.

Dan had only the vaguest impression of getting rid of his hat and overcoat. In the big room that overlooked the bay, she pressed herself against him and put her lips to his. His hands began to wander over the softness of silk, then he checked himself.

"Dan," she said, "take me away. Let's get away from all this."

Dan eased himself reluctantly from her embrace. "You're upset," he said. "Give me time to get my breath."

"No," she said. "No. Don't think. Thinking is no good. Thinking spoils it all. Let's go away together, right now, while we both feel this way." Her eyes pleaded with him.

Dan was having trouble assembling his thoughts. "Sit down a minute," he said. "Let's get our bearings. A few things have to be talked about."

"No. Dan. Let's not talk about anything. Let's just go. We can go to Mexico. I know just the place." Again she moved toward him.

Dan backed away and sat in a large armchair. "Yes," he said, "but Marian—"

"You're thinking of money? I have plenty of money." She sat on the arm of the chair and put her hand behind his neck.

From the moment he had entered the door, she had taken the initiative, and he didn't know how to get it away from her. "Listen, Marian, three murders have been committed. We can't—"

She looked provoked. "Dan, I'm afraid. Can't you understand? I'm afraid!"

"Yes, but—"

"I can't go away by myself, Dan. I need you. I'm being as honest as a person can be. I don't know where to turn. I'm throwing myself at your feet."

Dan made an effort to break the spell. "Listen. Go over there in that other chair and sit down, will you?"

She rumpled his hair with her finger. "Please don't scold me. You can talk to me here."

"Go over there and sit down!"

Very slowly, with pouting lips and hurt, plaintive eyes, she obeyed him. "Maybe it doesn't pay to be honest," she said. "I thought you'd understand."

At this distance, Dan felt in better control of things. "Marian," he said, "three people have been killed. This isn't a thing to take lightly."

"That's why I want to go away. I'm afraid."

"But you can't run away. You're implicated."

"Implicated!"

"Yes."

She looked puzzled. "But how?"

"Because of your relationship with Kipper." He paused. "And because of Glotcher."

"But I told you about Glotcher." Her eyes were earnest. "It didn't mean anything. I met him. I went out with him a couple of times. That was all. I was a fool to do even that. But I was so lonely and upset at the time. It wouldn't even be worth mentioning except that Kent was so terribly jealous. Don't you believe me?"

Dan thought he had never seen such sincere and plaintive eyes. In spite of himself, he almost believed her. Then he released the sandbag. "There's an important question," he said, "about a yellow envelope, and a photograph, and a negative."

Her face burned red. She got up hastily and took a cigarette from an ivory box on a table. Her hands shook. She had to thumb the lighter several times before the wick caught. With her back turned, she walked to the little bar and poured some brandy in a glass. When she turned to walk back, her face was no longer flushed. Her eyes were insolent and hard.

She stood in front of him. "Did you take that envelope out of my bag?"

"Yes," Dan said.

Her eyes narrowed. Dan's hand came up quickly enough to knock the glass aside as she tried to throw its contents in his face. The glass crashed to the floor. Dan jumped to his feet. She rushed him, slapping with both hands.

Dan seized her wrists and held them. She tried to bite his wrist, but he thumped her hard with the back of his hand, and held her off at arm's length.

Marian shook her black hair from her eyes. "Let go of me or I'll scream," she hissed.

"Now, Marian, stop this," Dan begged.

She screamed so loudly that he let go of her hands. Instantly, she was at him again, slapping and clawing. Dan tried to capture her wrists with one hand and clamp the other over her mouth. It was unsuccessful, so he pushed her in the face and sent her sprawling on the rug.

As she opened her mouth to scream again, he said, "Don't be a damn fool. If anyone comes, I'll have to give that picture to the police."

She sat on the floor breathing hard for a moment, but didn't scream. Suddenly, she scrambled to her feet and ran for the poker.

Dan grabbed a small chair and held it out as a guard. She tried to run around it, but he kept the legs pointed at her. She swung wildly with the poker, and the sharp end barely missed his nose. He grabbed it and wrenched it from her hands. "For God's sake, be reasonable," he said.

She came at him again, so Dan slapped her face hard enough to take her breath away, shook her violently, and threw her in an armchair. "If you don't stop this, I'll throw you in a cold shower," he said.

Her eyes were defiant. "Give me that envelope."

"First, you're going to tell me where you got it, when you got it, and how you got it."

"Give me that envelope!" she shouted.

"It won't do you any good to yell."

She stared angrily for a moment, then limped to the bar and poured herself another glass of brandy. "How much do you want for it?" she sneered.

"Nothing. All I want is to know how you got it." Dan smoothed his hair and tucked his necktie back in his coat.

"I'll give you a thousand dollars."

"I don't want your money." He sat in the armchair again.

A whimsical look came into her eyes, and the corners of her mouth turned up in a slight smile. She filled another glass with brandy. When she faced him again, with a glass in each hand, she was laughing. "We're acting like children," she said.

"You mean *you're* acting like a child. Like a child or a wildcat, I don't know which."

"And so are you." She limped toward his chair, making a wry face. "Ouch. You hurt me."

"Well, I couldn't let you knock my head off with the poker."

She laughed and handed him the drink. "Here, you bum."

He accepted the glass, and before he had a chance to indicate any choice, she snuggled in his lap, ran her fingers through his hair, and put her lips to his. "We understand each other," she said softly.

"Do we?" Dan said. "I wonder."

"I'm bad. I guess I just wasn't made to be good. Do you mind?"

"What I mind," he said, "is not knowing how you got that envelope."

"I like you to be rough with me." She kissed him again in a manner that all but turned his socks inside out. "Let's go in the other room and lie down."

"You haven't answered my question."

"Don't you want to go in the other room with me? We won't answer the door or the phone. Just us."

"My reflexes are all perfectly normal," Dan said. "But where did you get that envelope?"

"I'll be all yours. All of me." She kissed him again. "Give me the envelope."

"I still want to know how you got it."

She slapped his face and jumped to her feet. "Is that all I mean to you?"

"Why don't you tell me?"

"Does that mean more to you than I do?"

"It's pretty important."

She took another cigarette from the box on the table and lit it. "I got it from Glotcher. You know that."

"When?"

"What difference does it make?"

"Just that Glotcher was poisoned last night."

"Dan, this had nothing to do with that. You know perfectly well it didn't."

"Then why are you so cagey about how you got the negative?"

"I paid Glotcher five hundred dollars for it. He threatened to pass copies all around unless I did, so I paid him. He showed one to Kent."

"I know that."

"How did you know?"

"Never mind. When did you see Glotcher to get the picture and negative?"

"I didn't see him. He mailed it to me."

"You're lying."

Her eyes opened widely. "Oh, so now you're going to call me a liar!"

"All I want to know is how you got it."

"I suppose you think I poisoned him!"

"Not necessarily."

"I suppose you're afraid I'll poison you. If so, why are you drinking my brandy?"

Dan looked at the glass in his hand. "I haven't touched it."

She walked over and took the glass from him, drank a gulp, and gave it back. "Does that convince you?"

"Yes." He raised the glass to his lips. He needed it.

"If I tell you how I got the envelope," she pleaded, "will you return it to me?"

"That all depends."

"I met Glotcher yesterday afternoon. I paid him the money, and he gave me the picture and negative."

"Did you go to his studio?"

"No. I met him in a bar."

"What bar?"

"It was a bar—it—it was the Bali. The Bali bar on Montgomery Street."

"What time?"

"It was—it was about four o'clock."

"At four o'clock I saw Glotcher in an elevator downtown, in that building where Barney Price had his office."

"I guess it was earlier, then. It must have been about three o'clock."

Dan rose and began walking up and down. Marian's eyes followed him anxiously. "Another question," he said. "If you remember, when we were in Kipper's apartment, night before last, there was a telephone call. You answered it. You said it was Kipper and that he wouldn't be home that night. It couldn't have been Kipper. Who was it?"

She looked at her knuckles. "You must think I'm awful."

"Who was it?"

"I wanted to take you home. I knew it was all over between Kent and me. So I wanted to take you home. I didn't want to be alone. That's why I said it was Kent. So you wouldn't wait for him."

"Who was it?"

"It was Lance."

"How did he know you were there?"

"He didn't. He was calling Kent. He was surprised when I answered the phone. Then, later, when he was driving home, he saw the light in my house and dropped in."

"Is he in the habit of doing that?"

"Oh, Dan, don't be silly. I've known Lance since I was adolescent. He lives only a block away. Of course he drops in. He's been a dear. Especially since he's known I've been so upset lately." She smiled mischievously. "Sometimes it can be annoying, though."

"If you knew, as you say, that it was all over between you and Kent, why did you go to his studio that night?"

She snuffed her cigarette in an ash tray and shook her hair impatiently. "Why does anyone do anything? I don't know. I guess I thought that if we could have one more talk, it might change things. Maybe I thought I'd find him with another woman and make a scene. Anyhow, I found you there. And then—" She hesitated.

"Then what?"

"Then I didn't care so much about losing Kent anymore. If that makes you think I'm awful, then maybe I am. I don't care."

"I didn't say you were awful."

She spoke wistfully. "Dan, please give me back the picture."

"The picture's safe. You don't have to worry about it. If you're telling the truth, I'll give it back to you later."

"But, Dan, I am telling the truth. I've told you everything. Please give it to me."

"You'll get it in due time. And when I do give it back to you, I hope

you'll have sense enough to burn it, and not carry it around in your
purse."

She began to cry with the graceless abandon of an unhappy child.
It was startling to see her sophisticated face suddenly distorted in a
juvenile grimace. She ran to the davenport, threw herself on it face
down, and wailed with heaving shoulders. "Nobody cares about me,"
she sobbed. "Nobody has ever cared about me."

Dan shook his head. "I don't know what's to be done about you."

"I don't want to live anymore," she wailed.

Dan finished his drink and put the glass on the bar. "I wish God
would look after his own sparrows."

"You don't care what happens to me."

"What you need," Dan said, as he slipped into his overcoat, "is a good
walloping on your hind end."

"All right, beat me," she sobbed. "Go ahead and beat me, if that's how
you feel."

"The trouble is," Dan said, "you'd probably enjoy it."

He went out in the hall, and she came running after him. "Don't
leave me alone," she wailed. "I'll do anything you say, Dan. Anything!
Just don't leave me alone." She threw herself against the door and
spread her arms across it to block him. Her face was red and soaking
wet with tears.

"Don't be crazy." Dan tried to push her aside.

She wrapped her arms around him. "You want me, Dan. Take me.
Take me, Dan."

He managed to scrape her off and get the door open.

"I'll kill myself," she screamed.

He ran down the front steps. "You'll regret this," she called after him.
He walked quickly to the front gate, then paused and looked back. She
was standing there motionless, looking after him. Suddenly she ran
inside and slammed the door.

Out on the sidewalk, in the clear, bright day, he found it hard not to
run.

CHAPTER TWENTY-TWO

Dan walked out of the exclusive residential district and into an area
of cheap flats before he slowed his pace, and his mind began to adjust
itself to the commonplace realities of living.

If anyone had told him before he got out of the army that he would
live to scrape a beautiful woman out of his arms and run from her

house, he would have said they were crazy. Poor Kipper! She must have given him an awful buggy ride. And no wonder Gregory Fallon hardly knew whether he was going or coming.

The street sloped downward in a series of grades so steep that walking was difficult. Most of the houses in this neighborhood had round bay windows that poked out over the sidewalk.

It occurred to Dan that carrying the yellow envelope around in his pocket wasn't very sensible. He reached the bottom of the hill and a main artery of traffic. On the corner was a drugstore with its window full of whisky. Dan went in and asked for an envelope. The clerk, an old man with jowls like a St. Bernard, eyed him very strangely and said he couldn't sell one envelope. They came in packs of twenty, and you had to buy a pack.

"Then give me one out of a pack," Dan said, "and I'll pay you for the whole pack."

"I can't do that. It wouldn't be fair to you."

"All right, then," Dan said. "Give me a pack. I'll buy a pack."

Still eyeing Dan strangely, he dropped the envelopes in a paper bag, pushed them across the counter, and accepted a dime.

Puzzled by the way the man looked, Dan turned to see if there was anything behind him. "Anything wrong?" he asked.

Without taking his eyes from Dan, the man raised his hand to his lips. Dan looked in a near-by mirror. Around his mouth was a bright smear of lip rouge. He wiped it off without his handkerchief. "Thanks."

He took the yellow envelope from his pocket, put it in one of the new envelopes, sealed it, addressed it to himself at his hotel, stamped it with a stamp from a vending machine on the counter, and walked out of the drugstore, leaving the rest of the envelopes behind. The old man shook his head disgustedly.

As he slipped the letter in a corner mailbox, Dan remembered that it was a penitentiary offense to send such a picture through the mails, even if addressed to yourself. He mailed it just the same.

A block away, he was lucky enough to hail a cab. There was little doubt that Marian was lying about how she got the yellow envelope, he thought, but it was worth checking.

The Bali bar on Montgomery Street was supposed to look like a wind-beaten tropical shack. Bamboo trimmed its bright red doors. Inside, under soft orange lights, were many potted palms and large murals of brown women with alert bosoms that pointed accusingly at the customer wherever he looked. Several sipping couples talked quietly in the artificial gloom, or slouched silently in cushioned chairs around low tables meant to look like sawed-off barrels. The juke box was chortling, "Kiss me once, and kiss me twice, and kiss me once again. It's been a long, long time."

"What'll it be, mate?" said the bartender to Dan.

Dan ordered a beer and asked if he had been on duty at three o'clock the previous afternoon.

"Yes, mate. Why?"

"Do you know a girl named Marian Cleave, or a man by the name of Armand Glotcher?"

"No, mate. Never heard of them."

Dan described them and asked if he'd seen anybody resembling them.

"No, mate, I wouldn't know. They come, they go. You know how it is, mate."

Dan asked to speak to the other bartender.

"He wouldn't know, mate. That's a fact. You know how it is. Maybe she's your wife. I don't know. Maybe you're checking up on her. You know how it is, mate. Maybe your wife comes in tomorrow and asks us were you in here. We don't know, mate. We don't remember. You get it, mate?"

Dan got it.

"No hard feelings, mate. That's the way it's gotta be."

In the bamboo telephone booth, Dan called Lance Mallory's home. A Filipino accent informed him that Mr. Mallory was not in and would not be back that night. "He say going down Burlingame house down Peninsula. You leave message?"

"Never mind," Dan said. "Thanks a lot, mate."

Dan took the letter he had received that morning from his pocket and read it again: "The Crow, Laurel and L Streets, Redwood City. Ask for Agnes. Come alone. DOROTHY V."

From the Bali bar to the Exeter Building, where station KZY was located, was only a few blocks. Dan walked it. The girl in the reception room on the tenth floor said that Ike Miller was on the air right now in Studio C, right down the hall. "He'll be off the air in five minutes," she said.

Dan strolled along the hall and found a door marked "C." Through a glass panel, he saw Ike sitting before a microphone, moving his lips and gesturing with his hands as be read from a heap of papers. Not a sound came through the glass.

Presently Ike finished and came out.

"Don't you ever get tired of yammering that stuff into a microphone?" Dan asked.

"Well, for gosh sakes," Ike said. "A guy's got to earn a living, hasn't he?" He led Dan into the newsroom where six teletypes clattered frantically.

"Ike, I want you to do me a favor," Dan said. "Will you drive me down to Redwood City?"

"Tonight?"

"Yeah. When are you off?"

"I'm off now. That was my last broadcast. But I've got a date with Lorna."

"Why can't we bring Lorna along?" Ike suggested.

"That wouldn't be a good idea."

"Why not?"

"This is business. She'll only be in the way."

"What are you leading me into, anyhow?"

"Nothing for you to worry about. I just want to look up somebody down there."

"Then what's wrong with taking Lorna along for the ride?"

"Is it going to hurt you to break a date for one night?"

"That's not the point, Dan."

"What *is* the point?"

"I'm afraid she'll get drunk."

"When did you start worrying about other people's morals?"

"I don't want to see her make a mess of herself, that's all."

"Then bring her along, if it's going to break your heart."

"I didn't say it was going to break my heart."

"Then bring her along anyhow."

"She's a good kid. As a matter of fact, we were thinking of shacking up together."

"Why don't you marry her, while you're about it?"

"I've a darn good mind to do it, just to show you you're not so smart."

"That would sure put me in my place."

"A guy gets tired of livin' like an Indian."

"Put your hat on and let's get going."

Ike groped in a closet for his hat and overcoat. "Gettin' drunk every night. Livin' in a lousy dump. Comin' home to nothin'."

"I know. I know. Let's get going."

Ike put his hat on and struggled into his overcoat. "It gets so a guy's life is nothin' but a bunch of junk."

"Come on. You're breaking my heart."

They picked up Lorna Cargill at the Iron Cat. Dan waited in the car while Ike ran in and got her. She came out wrapped in her usual dreamy daze and a blue, mannish trench coat. On top of her long, tousled bob sat a blue beret.

She sat between them with her long legs wrapped around the gearshift.

"Who do you want to see in Redwood City?" Ike asked.

"Never mind," Dan said. "If it turns out to be interesting, I'll let you in on it."

"I get it. Mysterious stuff."

"Something like that."

"If you get us in a jam, you'd better be ready to dig up the bail. I've got to be at work in the morning."

By sundown they were well outside the city on a highway lined with roadhouses, bars, gas stations, and billboards. Great streaks of gold leaped in the sky ahead. As the light in the sky began to fade, Lorna suddenly began to sing in a soft, clear voice:

> "The Minstrel boy to the war is gone,
> In the ranks of death you'll find him;
> His father's sword he has girded on,
> And his wild harp hung behind him."

When she reached the last sad note of the ballad, Ike began to sing in a voice less clear:

> "Shoot me like an Irish soldier,
> Do not hang me like a dog."

Lorna took it up, and presently Dan joined them. One ballad followed another as the headlights of the car raced over the dark road ahead. For the first time in many months, Dan felt a warm, comforting glow inside him. Mingling your voice with others in song had a way of banishing loneliness. A person was not truly your friend until you'd sung a song together. Lorna seemed no longer just a skinny, walleyed clothespin with a mop of black hair falling over one eye, but a human being. He hoped Ike would marry her. Then, maybe, he could drop around once in a while. They'd sit in the kitchen, open a few bottles of beer, and sing together. Life would make some sense.

Their singing was interrupted when Ike turned in at a service station for gas.

"What place is this?" Dan asked, staring out at the houses.

"Burlingame," Ike said. "Redwood City is farther down the road."

"Isn't this where Lance Mallory has a house?"

"Yeah. His family's old house is down here. He doesn't spend much time in it, though."

"What do you say we drop in and see him on the way back?"

"Oh, he wouldn't be there. He doesn't come down very often."

"He's going to be there tonight. I happen to know."

"Well, fine. Now you're talking. We can be sure of a good drink if Lance is there."

"You've been there before?"

"Sure. I came down with him one week end."

When they reached Redwood City, Ike said, "When do we eat? I'm getting hungry."

"Drive past Laurel and L Streets," Dan said. "Then we'll get a bite."

At Laurel and L, Ike said, "All right, where do we park?"

Dan could see the neon sign of a bar, The Crow, down a side street. "Keep right on going," he said. "That looks like a business section up ahead. Maybe we can find a restaurant."

"More mysterious stuff!" said Ike.

Two blocks farther on, next to the sparkling entrance of a movie, a restaurant advertised fried chicken and charcoal-broiled steaks. "This ought to do fine," Ike said.

"You two go on and start your dinner," Dan said, getting out of the car. "I've got a little business to get off my mind."

Ike studied him suspiciously. "Sure you don't need any help?"

"Go ahead. Start eating. I won't be long."

"You got me curious."

"It's nothing, Ike. Go ahead and order your dinner. As a favor to me."

"Seems I'm always doing you favors."

"It's all bread on the water. You know someday you'll get it back double."

"Yeah. A lot of wet bread. What'll I do with it? Stuff a turkey?"

Dan saw them inside the restaurant before he turned back toward L Street.

CHAPTER TWENTY-THREE

The Crow was a tavern of the cheaper variety with a cement floor. The bar was a homemade affair, and the stools didn't match. Years of weary buttocks had flattened the stuffing out of some of the cushions. The walls were decorated with cardboard advertising signs given away by liquor firms.

About half the stools were taken up by people who looked as if they were going to sit there forever. Dan saw Dorothy Vane the minute he entered. She was seated down near the end of the bar talking to a fat man in a striped suit. She wore a checkered skirt and a fuzzy red sweater that fitted her like a sausage skin.

Dan straddled a stool and waited to catch her eye. When she saw him, she gulped her drink, said something to the fat man, and came over.

"Let's get outa here," she said, "and go someplace we can talk."

Dan followed her outside.

"You didn't bring nobody with you?"

"No. I'm alone."

"That's good, because I can tell you who done it." She walked down the street with Dan keeping step, and paused in front of a drugstore. "Will you buy a bottle?"

"Whisky?"

"Yeah."

Dan shrugged. "I guess so." H went in and bought a pint.

"Let's go to the joint where I'm stayin'," she said when he came out. "We can talk there."

"What was the idea of running away?" Dan asked as they walked.

"You don't think I want to be killed, do you?"

Presently she pushed open a gate in a picket fence and mounted the sagging steps of a cottage. A man with an unbuttoned vest lay on a couch in the front room. He stirred slightly and grunted.

"Don't get up, Monty," she said.

The floor was littered with mutilated children's toys, the furniture was scratched and battered, the close air smelled of babies' diapers. They passed through a narrow hall to a kitchen where an angry-eyed brunette woman was ironing clothes. Two solemn-faced children, a boy and a girl, looked up at them from the linoleum. The girl was reading an animal picture book. The boy was pushing a toy tank around the legs of the stove.

"We're gonna go to my room and talk," Dorothy said to the woman.

"Well, don't make any noise," the woman replied irritably. "The baby's asleep." As Dorothy opened the door of a room off the kitchen, the voice turned plaintive. "Dotty."

Dorothy turned. "Yeah?"

"Monty's drunk again."

"Yeah. I know."

The woman sighed deeply and picked up her iron again. "Don't make no noise, will you?"

"We won't Elvira."

Dorothy's room was large enough to hold an iron cot, a chair, and a white enamel dresser—nothing else.

"Elvira's an old girl friend of mine," she said. "I came down here last night. But I'll go crazy if I have to stay another day. Open up the whisky and let's have a drink."

Dan sat on the cot and pulled the pint out of the paper bag. Dorothy took it from him.

"Mind if I give Elvira a shot?"

Dan waved his approval. She went in the kitchen and returned in a few minutes with glasses and water for chasers. "It ought to be worth quite a bit to your paper to find out who done it," she said as she poured the liquor.

"You think you know?"

"Sure I know." She handed him a glass.

"Who?"

"How much is it worth to you?" She took a swig of her drink.

"Not a nickel." Dan reached over, took her glass from her, and gave her instead the glass she had poured for him.

"Say, what's the idea?" she demanded.

"Since you claim to know who the poisoner is, and I don't, I'm taking no chances."

"You don't think I did it!"

"You haven't told me yet."

"Is that so? And how do I know you didn't slip something in this?" She eyed the glass suspiciously.

"Well, you're supposed to know who the murderer is, and, of course, it's not me."

"I do know," she said.

"Spill it. Who do you think it is?"

"I'm not talking till I see the money."

"Don't be silly. You'd be smarter to tell me than to let the cops slap it out off you."

"I need dough bad."

"Who doesn't?"

"Can you slip me a couple of bucks anyhow? You could put it on your expense account."

"Tell me what you know. Then we'll talk about that."

She started to drink from the glass Dan had given her, then hesitated. "Say, you've given me the creeps."

"Go ahead and drink. There's nothing wrong with it."

She stuck her tongue in it cautiously, took a few experimental sips, then gulped and wiped her chin. "You can't trust nobody anymore."

"Who do you think the murderer is?"

She was thoughtful for a moment. "They've got a warrant out for me, haven't they?"

"The police are looking for you. They want to question you."

"Tell me, if they find the murderer, will they still be wanting me, or will they let it drop?"

"That all depends."

"Listen, if I tell you who did it, will you have to tell the cops who told you?"

"Not necessarily."

"Is that a promise?"

"No."

"I thought you said you'd help me."

"If you're not really guilty of anything, I'll try to see that you get a square break. That's all I can say."

"And that's a promise?"

"Listen, I can't guarantee you anything. I don't even know what you have to say. All I can tell you is that you'd be a lot more sensible to talk to me now and take your chances than to wait until the police catch up to you. Or worse than that, until the murderer catches up with you. Because, if you really have any information, the murderer is going to try to put you out of the way before you can spill it. That's one thing you can be sure of."

She looked frightened. "It was Gregory Fallon."

"What makes you think so?"

"He had a reason for killing Barney Price."

"What reason?"

"Barney arranged for—well, you know the business Barney was in."

"He was a private detective."

"Yeah, but he worked mostly on divorce cases. If somebody wanted grounds for a divorce, he arranged it."

A light clicked in Dan's mind. "Do you mean that Barney Price paid you and your husband to frame Fallon by having him caught in your bedroom?"

"Well, that's the way those things are done."

"Was that the way this was done?"

"Well, yes. I'd been doing odd jobs for Barney, and Howard, my husband, had just got out of the army. It was a chance for both of us to make a little money. We didn't see where it would do any harm."

"You mean that somebody hired Barney Price to frame Fallon, and he got you and your husband to do the dirty work?"

"You don't have to put it in such an insulting way. It's done every day. We have as much right to make our living as anybody else. If we hadn't done it, Barney would have got somebody else to do it. So what difference would it have made?"

"Who hired Barney to do this?"

"I don't know. I never asked. Maybe it was Fallon's wife. Maybe it was this guy Kipper who painted the pitchers."

"What makes you think it would be Kipper?"

"Fallon killed him, too, didn't he? He must have had a reason. You told me Fallon's wife used to be married to Kipper. Maybe Kipper wanted her back. Maybe he hired Barney to do the framing and split them up. Fallon found out. So he killed Kipper, and he killed Barney, and if the police don't arrest him, he may kill me. God, what dopes they are. Can't they see who done it?"

"If Fallon is the murderer, why do you think he killed Glotcher?"

"Glotcher? That was the guy who was poisoned last night, wasn't he?"

"Yes."

She shrugged. "I don't know."

"Did you ever meet Glotcher?"

"I never heard of him till I read his name in the paper this morning."

"All right, now tell me how you happened to be buying Kipper's paintings."

"That was for Barney. I did lots of little jobs like that for Barney. Barney was a square guy."

"Well, who was Barney buying the paintings for?"

"I don't know. I never asked. Maybe for Fallon's wife. Maybe for Kipper."

"Why do you say that?"

"I been trying to think it out. There must be some connection. I figure the same person who hired Barney to buy the pitchers, hired him to frame Fallon. It stands to reason."

"Why do you think Fallon's wife would have wanted the pictures?"

"Maybe she wanted to buy them on the sly because she liked Kipper and didn't want her husband to know. Maybe she hated Kipper and wanted to burn them. I don't know."

"Well, why do you think Kipper would have bought his own paintings?"

"I'm just guessing. Maybe he wanted to make it look like his stuff was selling good."

"Tell me, what did you do with the pictures after you bought them?"

"Barney would tell me where to go and buy them, and what name to give. He was awful good to work for that way. Everything was all thought out. He'd loan me his car, and I'd put the pitchers in the back seat. Then I'd meet him somewhere, and he'd drive me home. I don't know where he took them." Her brow wrinkled. "Oh yeah. I remember now. There was one night I met him in a parking lot near his office downtown. There was somebody there in a big station wagon. I couldn't see if it was a man or a woman. It was dark, and they stayed in the car. Barney took the pitchers and put them in the station wagon. Then he stood there and talked for a while with whoever it was."

"Did you notice anything particular about the station wagon? What kind it was, or anything?"

"No, just that it was a station wagon."

Dan got up and poured himself another drink from the bottle on the dresser.

"Now that you know who done it," she said, "can't you tell the cops, and have them pick up Fallon? They won't want me if they've got the murderer."

"What you've told me doesn't prove Fallon did it," Dan said. "All it proves is that Fallon was framed for a divorce. I think you ought to go to the police and tell them everything you've told me."

"Don't be crazy. They'd throw me in the can."

"You should have thought of that before you framed Fallon."

"What are you so sympathetic about him for? He's a murderer, ain't he?"

"That we don't know yet. If he is, it's partly your fault."

"I'm no murderer."

"That's right. I forgot. You have to earn your living."

"I certainly do."

"Use some sense. Let me take you back to the city. Talk it over with Inspector Gallagher. He might be reasonable."

"I don't trust cops."

"They'll pick you up anyhow. It's just a matter of time."

"I told you who done it. Ain't that enough?"

"No. You're needed as evidence."

"Jesus Christ! Are the police so goddamn dumb you've got to give them a blueprint?"

"They can't do anything without evidence."

"The hell they can't. You don't know those boys."

"I'll only have to tell them everything you told me, and where you're hiding out."

"You dirty goddamn stool pigeon!"

"Use your head. There's a murderer loose. If he isn't caught, he'll keep on killing. And you'll probably be the next victim. You'd be safer in jail than anyplace else."

"Oh yeah? That's what you say."

"Now come on. Put your things on and come back to the city with me. At the worst, you'll have to serve a little time."

She thought it over. "Okay. You win." She opened the top drawer of the dresser, then whirled around with a small nickel-plated revolver in her hand.

"Now listen—" Dan said.

She reached out an arm and opened a closet door. "Get in there."

"Listen here. Put that gun down."

"I said, get in there."

"You wouldn't be fool enough to get yourself in more trouble than you are."

"I said, get in that closet. Turn me in, will you?"

"You're making an awful mistake."

"Am I? I know your kind. At least I'll have a head start on you before you call a cop. Get in that closet before I start shooting."

"All right. I hope you know what you're doing." Dan took a step toward the closet. The room was so small, he had to pass within an inch of her. As he did, he lunged forward, flattening her against the wall so that she couldn't use the gun. He seized her wrist and began twisting.

"Monty!" she screamed. "Monty!"

"Let go of that gun," Dan grunted.

"Monty!" she screamed again. "Elvira! Monty!"

The gun clattered to the floor. Dan snatched it up and slipped it in his pocket. At the same time, Dorothy grabbed the pint from the dresser and brought it down on top of his head. The bottle didn't break, but glanced off, slipped from her fingers, and hit the floor. Dan was momentarily stunned by the blow. She started beating him with her fists, and he clinched with her.

Elvira came through the door with a hammer in her hand. Dan saw her out of the corner of his eye just in time to duck. The hammer missed his ear by a whisker's width. He pushed Dorothy out of the way and grappled with Elvira and the hammer. Dorothy ran out of the door and through the kitchen. Dan made Elvira drop the hammer. He picked her up, dumped her on the cot, and ran into the kitchen after Dorothy.

Monty came charging from the front room with his head lowered. Dan met him with a right to the jaw that sent him sprawling on the linoleum. The two children crawled under the stove and cried. Somewhere else in the house, Dan heard a baby bawling. The front door slammed loudly.

He ran through the hall to the front room, and out onto the porch. He saw Dorothy's red sweater disappear around a corner. He ran to the corner and looked down the street. The sidewalk was empty. He walked along looking in doorways and behind fences for a few minutes; then it occurred to him she'd only be a nuisance if he did find her. Let the cops pick her up.

He returned to the cottage. Monty was standing on the porch with his fists clenched, swaying on his feet. "Get out of my yard, you bastard," Monty said.

"Give me my hat."

"Get the hell out before I call the cops."

Elvira appeared in the doorway. "No, Monty. No cops. We don't want no trouble."

"All I want is my hat," Dan said.

"I'll get his hat." Elvira disappeared inside.

"I ought to beat the goddamn muck out of you," said Monty.

"You won't."

Elvira came back with the hat. The wailing of children still sounded inside. Monty took the hat from her, crumpled it in his hands, and threw it on the walk in front of Dan.

"Why, you lousy—" Dan took a step up the porch. Monty ran inside in staggering haste.

Elvira looked at Dan haggardly. "Please go away. Haven't we enough trouble?"

Dan picked up the hat, turned on his heel, and walked through the gate. Rage still singing in his ears, he tried to push the hat back in shape as he went down the street.

CHAPTER TWENTY-FOUR

Ike Miller and Lorna Cargill had finished eating, and were loafing over their coffee when Dan came in the restaurant.

"What happened to your hat?" was Ike's greeting.

"Your necktie's out," said Lorna.

Dan tossed the twisted hat on a hook. "I've been having a heart-to-heart talk with a wild animal."

"Where were you? We were just about to shove off."

"Never mind. Let me see the menu."

"You look beat up," Ike said. "Is anything wrong?"

"I just got socked with a bottle, that's all." Dan turned to the waitress who was hovering expectantly. "Bring me the special steak and a mixed green salad."

"Who socked you?"

"Stick your necktie in," Lorna said.

"It's nothing." Dan tucked the errant tie into his coat. "I just ask too many questions, that's all."

"I'm glad I'm not a leg man anymore," Ike said. "All I have to do on my job is sit and tear the news off the teletype as it comes in. You've got a tough head."

"Either that or a soft head," Dan replied. "The bottle didn't break."

Ike pushed a basket of rolls toward him. "Hurry up and get some food in you. We want to drop by Lance's place on the way back. Remember?"

Dinner restored Dan's composure. As they drove up the highway, he rearranged the facts in his mind to accord with the new information he had received from Dorothy Vane. The pieces were beginning to fit together in a definite pattern.

Lorna rode silently, watching the headlights dance on the road ahead.

"You'll get a kick out of Lance's place," Ike said. "It's old- fashioned. He keeps it that way for sentimental reasons, I guess.

When they came to Burlingame, Ike turned left onto a narrow, curving road. By the intervals between window lights, Dan guessed that the houses were some distance apart. Presently Ike drew to the side of the road and stopped. He squinted across a dark lawn toward a group of tall, lighted windows. "You're right," he said. "Lance must be there."

As they walked up the gravel, Dan estimated the dark shape from which the lighted windows gleamed to be a two-story wooden mansion. The smell of grass was in the cold air. Wide stairs led them onto a broad veranda. Lance Mallory answered the doorbell. He seemed startled. "Well, Ike. And Dan. And Lorna."

"We were just driving by," Ike said. "We were on our way home from Redwood City, and thought we'd drop in."

"Well, it's rather a surprise." Mallory's voice was a little uncertain. "Come in. As a matter of fact, we just arrived about ten minutes ago."

"Are we interrupting anything?" Ike said.

"Well, no, not exactly. You see, Marian's with me. She's been quite upset and I persuaded her to come down here for a few days. Rest her nerves."

He led them through a somber hall where a few white marble statues gleamed nakedly. A fanlike spread of savage spears bristled on the wall under the staircase. A thick, flowered carpet absorbed their footsteps noiselessly.

The room they entered had dark red wallpaper and crystal chandeliers. A lot of oil paintings of sheep and mountains and lakes and bearded old men hung in gold frames. The furniture was elaborately carved and ornamented in the manner of the last century. A fire was just getting started between brass andirons.

"It hasn't quite warmed up yet," Mallory said, rubbing his hands together. "Marian is in her room. Let me take your things."

"We can only stay a minute," Ike said, but he wrestled out of his overcoat.

"I hope you'll excuse the mess things are in. I haven't been able to get a housekeeper since the war started."

"I can't even get a house," Ike said. Dan noticed a film of dust on the table. The fire was sputtering weakly because the grate was clogged with ashes.

"Don't let the furnishings frighten you," Mallory said, with a little laugh. "They were my parents' idea of luxury. I haven't had the heart to change a thing. How about a drink?"

"Now you're talking," Ike said, settling into a cruel-looking chair with studded upholstery.

Mallory soon returned with a silver tray that tinkled with glasses and bottles. "It never occurred to the last generation to put a bar in the parlor. Seltzer or plain water? Name your pois— er, choice."

"Just beat Dan over the head with the bottle," Ike said. "He won't know the difference."

"You know, Dan and I had quite an experience last night. I'm afraid it was a little hard on my nerves." Mallory looked up from the tray on which he was fixing drinks. "Come in by the fire, Marian."

Dan turned from the fireplace where he had been warming his hands. Marian stood in the doorway watching him, a slight sneer on her lips. Lorna Cargill sighed, grimaced, and looked the other way. Ike made motions as if to rise.

"Don't get up." Marian walked to Mallory's side. "Can I help you, darling?"

Mallory appeared strangely ill at ease. "Well, yes. Hand Lorna a drink, will you. And keep one for yourself."

As Marian gave the glass to Lorna, she said, "That suit looks lovely since you cut those ugly pompoms off it."

"We all can't shop at Ransahoff's," Lorna snapped.

Mallory raised his glass. "Shall we drink to peace? No more wars?"

"And to us," Marian said.

"Oh—ah—yes." Mallory seemed confused.

"Haven't you told them, darling?"

"I didn't think we were ready to tell people yet." Mallory's embarrassment was plain.

"We're going to be married." Marian's voice was challenging, and she looked at Dan as she spoke.

An amazed silence followed the announcement.

Marian looked at Mallory. "We are, aren't we, darling?"

"That's right," Lance said, rather sheepishly. "Now you know."

"Well, I'll be damned." Ike started to drink from his glass, then, as an afterthought, lifted it. "Congratulations. By all means, congratulations."

"Congratulations," Dan repeated.

Lorna said nothing.

They drank.

As if to make their relationship more convincing, Marian took Mallory's hand, pulled him onto the divan, and leaned her head against his shoulder. Mallory patted her self-consciously.

"How long has this been going on?" Ike said.

"He asked me today. Or, rather, I asked him. Didn't I, darling?"

"Right," Mallory said.

"Well—" Ike paused as if not knowing what to say. "That's fine," he finished lamely.

Again an embarrassed silence settled over the room. The ringing of the doorbell rescued them. Mallory excused himself and left the room. When he was out of sight, Marian gave Dan one of her appealing, helpless looks. Dan looked away.

Out in the hall a voice boomed, "I don't give a damn what you say, Mallory. I know she's in there, and I'm going to see her."

"That's Greg Fallon," Ike announced to nobody in particular.

Marian looked frightened. Lorna smiled. Three men entered, literally pushing Mallory ahead of them. Gregory Fallon was in the lead. Arnold Winkleman, his eyes still tired and red at the corners, was close behind. Mark Wiener, the psychiatrist Dan had met at the Hobarts' house, trailed in the rear.

"See here," Mallory shouted, "this is my house. You can't break in here."

Fallon sighted Marian. "There she is."

"I'm warning you, Fallon." Mallory's face was flushed with anger.

"Marian, I must have a word with you." Fallon appeared sober, but highly excited.

"Why can't you leave me alone?" Marian pleaded.

Mark Wiener said to Mallory, "I'm terribly sorry we had to break in on you this way. But I assure you it's of the utmost importance. I wouldn't have come down here otherwise."

Fallon's eyes were intense. "Marian, please be reasonable. I must talk to you alone."

"No, Greg. I've told you before that there's simply nothing to talk about."

"It's for your own sake, Marian."

Mallory stepped in between them. "I'm warning you for the last time, Fallon. She's had all she can stand."

"For God's sake, Lance," Fallon pointed a thumb at Winkleman and Mark Wiener. "These men have information, and if you don't listen to reason, they're going to the police with it. I begged them to come down here and give Marian a chance to explain."

The doorbell rang again. Fallon sagged dejectedly into a chair and buried his face in his hands. "That's probably the police."

Winkleman and Wiener exchanged startled glances. Mallory hesitated for a moment, then walked slowly toward the door, as if not certain whether he'd open it or not.

More voices sounded in the hall. An instant later, Inspector Gallagher burst into the room, followed by Mack and the gray-hatted plain-clothes man. He gave the room a quick scrutiny. His eyes pinched at the corners when they lit on Dan. Without saying a word, he walked to the fireplace and warmed his seat. All eyes watched him apprehensively. When the silence had soaked in enough to satisfy his sense of drama, he said calmly to Marian, "Get your things, young lady. You're coming along with us."

Mallory's face was aghast. "See here, there must be some mistake."

"Sorry, Mallory." Gallagher turned and warmed his hands at the blaze. "That's how it is."

Marian's eyes were wide. She pointed at her breast. "Does he mean me?"

"But I don't understand." Mallory gestured futilely with his hands.

Mark Wiener advanced with an unhappy expression. "I'd like to point out, officer, that this young lady is ill."

Gallagher surveyed him critically. "What's she got?"

"Her ailment isn't physical."

"Are you her doctor?"

"I'm her psychiatrist."

"Oh, that." Gallagher whirled his hands to indicate a mix-up. "You mean she's a little—"

"A definite psychiatric case."

"Well, aren't we all?" Gallagher shrugged and returned his attention to the fire.

"I'm really sincere," insisted Wiener.

"You can appear in court," Gallagher said, indifferently. "That's not my end of it."

Mallory assumed an authoritative voice. "See here, you've got to have a warrant."

Without a word, Gallagher flashed a warrant. His manner was as bored as a five-star general showing his credentials to a doorman.

Dan had been watching Marian. She had turned sickly pale, and there was panic in her eyes. She had been sitting perfectly still. Suddenly her body inclined to the left. Dan caught her in time to keep her from falling to the floor. Mallory was at his elbow immediately, and Dan rolled her into his arms.

Ike came hurrying with a glass of water.

"Tsch, tsch, tsch!" Gallagher shook his head. "Better take her upstairs and throw her things together." He nodded to his assistants. "One of you boys go along."

Marian came palely to her senses. Mallory patted her hand. "Don't worry, my dear. You leave everything to me. I'll get an attorney. There's been a mistake, that's all."

"Get her things together," Gallagher repeated.

"My God! Can't you see she's ill?" Mallory's eyes flashed fiercely.

"I'm sorry, Mallory, but she's got to come along."

"Well, give us time to let her collect herself." Mallory helped her to her feet and guided her toward the hall. "Now don't you worry about a thing. I'll take care of it all." He looked back at Gallagher. "You're going to have reason to regret this. I happen to know a couple of members of the police commission."

When they were out of the room, Gallagher flipped Dan's coat lapel and led him to the far end of the room where the others couldn't hear. "Well, you pretty nearly beat me to it."

"I'm not trying to beat you to anything," Dan said.

"I bet you pretty nearly had it figured out, though."

"Not quite."

"It's all over but the court rigmarole. She'll probably plead insanity. That bug specialist over there is paving the way for her."

"Know why she bumped off Glotcher? He was blackmailing her. I prowled around his studio today. What I found would bug your eyes out. Some of these respectable dames can hand you surprises, Banion."

"Do you mean photographs?"

"Well, one photograph in particular."

"That doesn't mean she killed him."

"No? Wait till you get the rest of it. Do you know what the connection with Barney Price was? Barney specialized in divorces. He framed Fallon with that blonde Dorothy Vane so that Marian Cleave could divorce him. That's why the blonde skipped out after you called on her. Don't tell me you didn't have that figured out?"

"Not exactly. What about Kipper's paintings? Why was Barney buying them up?"

"I figure that was for Marian Cleave, too. She was having Barney buy them up for spite, so she could burn them. She had a couple of Kipper's pictures in her house, and they were burned."

"She accuses Fallon of burning them, doesn't she?"

"Yeah, but you know how women are."

"I thought she was up at Lake Tahoe at the time the paintings disappeared in her house."

"Is that a fact?" Gallagher looked worried.

"I'm pretty sure that's how it was. You'd better check on it."

"Hmmmm! That's a nuisance. Maybe she drove down to the city one day. I'll have to check that."

"You still haven't explained why she killed Kipper."

"Well, that's obvious. He'd thrown her over. That letter he left in his joint indicates that."

"Maybe you know what you're doing, but I'd go easy if I were you."

"For God's sake, Banion, I can't wait until I have everything down to the last detail before I make an arrest. The picture I found in Glotcher's joint is enough to hold her on. You mark my words. She'll confess when we begin to pile the evidence in front of her."

"You're forgetting about the spaghetti case, aren't you? I don't think she could lift a crate of that spaghetti, let alone nail a corpse up in it. And how would she find out all those particulars about where the cases were being taken?"

"Don't bank on that. These dames have more brawn than we credit them with. I've been fooled that way too many times. I remember a dame who hauled a stiff up five flights of stairs and dumped him on the roof. And she couldn't have weighed more than ninety pounds." Gallagher looked toward the fireplace. "By the way, what are all these characters doing here?"

"I came with Ike Miller and his girl. You'll have to ask the others."

Gallagher stomped back to the other end of the parlor. He confronted Mark Wiener first. "How do you happen to be here at this time, Doc?"

Wiener had been examining an old family album on the table, marveling at the psychiatric cases he had been born too late to grapple with. "I came down with these gentlemen." He nodded at Fallon and Winkleman.

"Why?"

"I believe I explained that I am the young lady's psychiatrist. I felt it was my duty to come."

"Why your duty?"

"In a case like this there is never any certainty. I felt it advisable to be along. There might be something I could perceive. The young lady is still my patient."

"I'm asking you exactly why you came down. I don't want all this rigmarole."

"Perhaps I ought to explain," Arnold Winkleman cut in.

"He came with me. I told him I was coming down, and—"

"Why were *you* coming?" Gallagher interrupted.

Winkleman turned to Fallon, who was still sitting with his head in his hands. "Greg, I'm going to have to be perfectly frank."

When Fallon looked up, his eyes were wet with tears. "I don't know what to say, Arnie. I wish I did, but I don't know what to say."

"I'd been reading the papers and giving the matter some thought," Winkleman said to Gallagher, "and it seemed to me there were a number of matters concerning Marian Cleave that needed explaining. I had no evidence. I wasn't accusing her. I want that understood. But I thought—"

"You thought she might have committed these homicides," Gallagher said.

"I didn't say that."

"What was the real reason you and Fallon called on Glotcher last night?"

"Well, you see, I'd been told about a certain photograph Glotcher had. I mentioned it to Fallon. Glotcher had evidently been showing it around. Fallon asked me to meet him at Glotcher's place. We thought we might reason with him."

"I know about the photograph," Gallagher said.

"Oh."

"Then why did you come down here?"

"Well, when Glotcher was poisoned, I talked it over with Greg. There was also the matter of Dorothy Vane and this man Barney Price. It seemed to me that Greg might have been framed in regard to that scandal with Dorothy. We knew that Mark Wiener was Marian's psychiatrist, and we thought he might be able to advise us."

"Why didn't you come to me?"

"Well, you're not a psychiatrist."

Gallagher looked as if he were going to explode. "God damn it! Everybody goes to anybody and everybody except the police."

"Well, we didn't like to say anything unless we were sure."

"You three had better come along with me." Gallagher scrutinized Ike.

"Don't look at me," Ike said. "I just dropped in because I thought I might get a free drink."

"I'm with Ike," Lorna said, when Gallagher's eyes fastened on her.

Marian's frantic voice came from the hall. "But, Lance, I didn't do anything. I didn't do a thing. What can they want with me?"

"They probably only want to question you," Mallory said, soothingly. "I'll get hold of Phil Wernham right away and have him straighten it out."

Gallagher buttoned his overcoat. "All right, let's go." He led the way to the hall.

Mallory was carrying Marian's overnight bag. "At least let me drive her up in my car," he insisted.

"Sorry, Mallory. It has to be this way. Come on, boys."

Mallory followed them out the door protesting. Fallon, Winkleman, and Wiener tagged along. Ike and Lorna were about to leave also, but when they saw Dan take out his pipe and walk back in the main room, they hesitated.

CHAPTER TWENTY-FIVE

When Mallory returned to the room, his eyes were distraught, and he kept punching one fist into the palm of the other hand nervously. "I must get hold of Phil Wernham right away. Let's see. I wonder if he'd be home now?"

"Is there anything I can do?" Ike said.

"No, I don't believe so. If I can reach Phil, he'll know what to do."

"Why don't you drive back to the city with us?"

"Thanks, Ike, but I have my car here."

"You don't look in shape to drive."

"I'm all right. Let's see now. Dan, maybe you'd drive back with me? Do you mind?"

"Not at all," Dan said. "You and Lorna go ahead, Ike."

"The first thing," Mallory said, "is to call Phil." He went out in the hall.

When he was gone, Ike said, "You'd better drive for him, Dan. He's got the jitters bad."

"I'll stick with him," Dan promised.

In a few minutes, Mallory returned. "I couldn't get Phil. They're going to locate him and have him call me back."

"They're probably just going to question Marian," Ike said. "They do that lots of times. Bring a person to the station as if they've got the evidence, and hope they'll confess when they get the light on them."

Mallory appeared alarmed. "You don't suppose they'll third-degree her, or anything like that?"

"Oh, no. Not that bad."

"Her nerves are just about at their limit. She's been through enough as it is."

"I don't think they'll pull any rough stuff."

"Come to think of it," Mallory said, "I know Trent Green, the District Attorney. I think I'd better call him right now."

"Well, Lance, if there isn't anything I can do," Ike said, "I think Lorna and I had better get along."

"Thanks, Ike. I think I can manage. You'll stay, won't you, Banion?"

"Sure. I'll stick around."

Mallory saw Ike and Lorna to the door, then remained in the hall where the phone was, trying to reach the District Attorney. Dan was alone in the parlor. The fireplace, clogged with ashes, was not burning very well. Dan took the poker and tried to scrape aside some of the ashes under the grate to start a draft. When he withdrew the poker, he noticed a small L-shaped piece of charred wood caught on the end of it. Evidently it had been buried in the layers of old ashes.

Dan raked the piece of wood onto the hearth. He tried to pick it up, but it burned his fingers. From the hall entrance, he heard Mallory say, "Trent's not home either. Damn it! They would be out at a time like this."

Dan pushed the piece of wood back in the fireplace, but to one side, where the flames could not reach it, and raked some ashes over it.

"Don't build up the fire," Mallory said. "We'll be going soon. Phil Wernham ought to be calling back in a few minutes."

"Is he your attorney?" Dan stood the poker in its rack, and settled himself in one of the chairs.

"Yes. And a good one. Have a drink while you're waiting?"

"No, thanks."

Mallory uncorked a bottle. "I can use one." He poured a stiff drink and gave it a shot of seltzer. "I guess it surprised you to hear that Marian and I are going to be married."

"A little."

He took the chair opposite Dan. "I've given it quite a bit of thought, and I think it will be the best thing for both of us. While there's some difference in our ages, I think she needs the understanding of an older man."

"You're not so old."

"I've known Marian since she was sixteen. The difference in our ages was more pronounced then than it is today."

Dan knocked his pipe ashes out in the grate. "You're tackling quite a problem in Marian. I guess you know that."

Mallory stared into his glass and smiled ironically. "Banion, when you've seen as much life as I have, it makes you very tolerant. You can laugh at a lot of things that a younger man would take too seriously."

"I don't know why you keep thinking you're so old. You're not really. By the way, you went to Stanford University, didn't you?"

"That's right. Why do you ask?"

"What year were you there?"

"Class of '22. Why?"

"I was just wondering. It's so nearby."

"Yes. I went there." Mallory looked at his watch. "I wish Phil would call. We ought to be getting up to the city."

"What kind of car are you driving? A station wagon?"

"Why, no. You know my car. You were in it last night."

"Oh, I thought you had another one."

"Why do you ask?"

"I thought someone said you had a station wagon."

Mallory eyed him strangely. "Who said that?"

"I don't remember. You do have a station wagon, don't you?"

"Yes, I have one. What about it?"

"Nothing. I've always wanted one myself. They're pretty handy, aren't they?"

"Yes, in a way." The phone rang. Mallory jumped to answer it. "That must be Phil now."

As soon as he was out of the room, Dan seized the poker and raked the little L-shaped piece of wood out on the hearth again. It appeared to be the charred corner of a picture frame. It was cool enough now so that he could pick it up. He dropped it in his pocket. Poking among the lower layers of ashes, he brought forth a charred stick with a piece of scorched canvas fastened to it by flat-headed tacks. He pulled it out on the hearth to cool. The tacks gave him an idea. He began scraping the bricks with the end of the poker, and soon had raked out a dozen or more flat-headed tacks. As he reached to pick them up, he heard

Mallory's voice close behind him.

"You may leave those right where they are, Banion." Mallory had a small automatic pistol in his hand. "Get up from there."

Dan straightened up. Mallory reached out, felt his pockets and under his arms. "All right. Sit down." Mallory's voice was cool. He walked around to the tray of bottles and began mixing another drink, meanwhile keeping the gun leveled in Dan's direction. "You wouldn't care for a drink, I suppose?"

"No, thanks," Dan said, with emphasis.

"You know, Banion, I was afraid we were coming to something like this when you began asking about my college life and, my station wagon." He eased a little seltzer into his glass.

"You met Barney Price at Stanford," Dan said.

"Right."

"He was a boxing instructor."

"Right."

"Later, you probably patronized the speakeasy he opened in San Mateo."

"Right. In fact, I loaned Barney the money to open the place." Mallory, a half-amused look on his face, walked around to the fireplace and took the chair opposite Dan. In one hand he held the drink, in the other the automatic, its small, round nose pointed menacingly at Dan.

"In a way," Dan said, "it's too bad you found me messing through those ashes. I was closing in on you without that. I'd have nailed you anyhow."

Mallory grinned sardonically. "Oh, no, you wouldn't. I had plans for you later on tonight. This doesn't change anything, really."

Dan looked at the fireplace. "When did you start burning Kipper's paintings?"

"Oh, about a year and a half ago."

"What was the idea?"

Mallory shrugged. "It amused me. I never liked Kipper or his paintings either. I never expected to kill him, of course. As a matter of fact, I rather took it for granted he'd be killed in the war."

"What did you expect to gain by burning his work?"

"He took something away from me. I don't forgive things like that easily, Banion."

"You mean when he married Marian?"

"Yes. Marian and I had been rather close before that."

"So, burning his paintings was a kind of revenge."

"Oh, not altogether. As I said, it amused me. I was bored with hearing people talk about his work. One night I gave a dinner. It was

my birthday. One of his pictures was hanging in the restaurant. I had
to sit for hours and listen to a stupid discussion about it. In the end,
I bought the picture and burned it. It gave me a kind of satisfaction.
Later on, the idea of burning all of them occurred to me. It was a kind
of game."

"And you hired Barney Price to buy them for you."

"Yes. Barney needed work. It gave him something to do. Sort of a
WPA project in reverse." Mallory grinned sarcastically.

"You think you're very smart, don't you?"

"The important thing in this world, Banion, is to get what you want.
Most people never get anything they want. They haven't the courage
to take it."

"Mallory, you're nothing but a cheap heel."

"I'd watch my language, Banion, if I were you." The sneer left
Mallory's face and his jaw tightened.

"I'll bet when you slipped him the poison it was in a drink that you
offered him as a friend. That's the way it was, wasn't it?"

"Shut up, Banion."

"You said, 'Here, Kent, have a drink. Step in the car and have a
drink.' And you handed him a bottle of poison."

Mallory rose to his feet. His face was flushed and his eyes were
narrow. The gun in his hand trembled. "That'll be about all from you."

Dan rose to face him. "That's how you did it, wasn't it, you sneaking
worm."

Mallory motioned with the gun. "Get moving."

"Which way, Mallory?"

In his excitement, Mallory pointed the gun toward the hall. Dan
seized the split second. He was on Mallory before his senses could
react. He gripped Mallory's wrist and the gun went off harmlessly.
Simultaneously, he brought his knee up in Mallory's groin with
brutal force. Mallory gasped. Still holding the wrist, Dan beat
Mallory's arm against the edge of the heavy mahogany table until he
felt the bone crack. The automatic fell to the floor. Dan brought his
right up and sent Mallory sprawling on the carpet like a bag of
bones. The whole action took less than thirty seconds.

Dan picked up the pistol and dropped it in his pocket. Mallory sat
up dazed, holding his fractured arm. Dan bent over him, seized him
by the knot of his necktie, dragged him to the divan and threw him
against the cushions. Mallory groaned at every bump, but Dan
handled him as indifferently as if he were a side of beef.

"My God," Mallory gasped. "My arm."

"Now we'll get the straight of things," Dan said. "The night Foisie and

Winkleman stayed in this house you doped their drinks, didn't you?"

"For God's sake, Banion, my arm!"

Dan reached down, pulled him within convenient reach, and slapped his face sharply five or six times. "Are you going to answer my questions?"

"Yes. Yes." Mallory gasped and tried to avert his face.

Dan threw him back on the cushions. "You doped their drinks to make certain they wouldn't wake up in the night. Then you pretended to pass out, and let them put you to bed. When they got drowsy and turned in, you sneaked out and drove to San Francisco, probably in your station wagon. It *was* your station wagon, wasn't it?"

"Yes."

"When Kipper came back from the war and Marian began chasing after him again, you couldn't take that, could you?"

"See here, Banion, this is all beside the point. I can make it worth your while."

"Besides, Kipper was looking for his paintings, and if he discovered you'd been burning them, it would have gone hard with you. Incidentally, where did you get hold of that screwy poison?"

"In Europe, years ago."

"And you kept it all this time!"

"It fascinated me. I don't know why. What does it matter?"

"Ask Kipper what it matters. Ask Barney Price."

"Listen to me, Banion. How would fifty thousand dollars seem?"

"When Kipper's body was found, Barney Price began to put two and two together, so Barney had to die."

"You can make a good thing for yourself out of this, Banion. Think it over."

"Barney was a handy little man to you. He framed Fallon for you, and he got that picture and negative from Glotcher for you. Isn't that right?"

"Fifty thousand dollars is a lot of money, Banion."

"Are you going to answer my questions, or shall I break your other arm?"

"Yes. Barney got the picture."

"Incidentally, Glotcher double-crossed you. He gave up the negative and one picture, but he kept a print for himself. Inspector Gallagher found it in his studio. That's why he arrested Marian."

"The dirty liar!"

"You were afraid Glotcher would associate Barney's murder with the photograph, especially since he delivered it only a short while before Barney was killed."

"He would have. There's no doubt about it."

"So you sneaked into Glotcher's studio and put poison in his whisky bottle."

"You're a man of the world, Banion. All this is no concern of yours. You could do a lot with fifty thousand dollars."

"What, for instance?"

"Travel. Enjoy life. Have plenty of women. You could quit work."

"Quit work. Is that your idea of bliss?"

"Women, Banion. You could have all the women you wanted."

"Except the ones I wanted in the way I wanted them. Look, Mallory, you're the one who's having women trouble. Not me."

"Let's say seventy-five thousand."

"That's better, of course, but look at the way prices are going up."

"A hundred thousand. Banion. But that's the top."

Dan stood up. "Oh, well, if you're going to haggle over the price, I'm not interested." He leaned over and grabbed Mallory's necktie again.

"A hundred and fifty thousand," Mallory gasped.

Dan pulled him off the divan and dragged him across the floor toward the hall.

"Banion, my arm! For God's sake, my arm! Two hundred thousand. Anything. Name your price."

"You've got more than that." Dan dragged him out in the hall, dumped him on the floor, and lifted the phone receiver.

"Name your price," Mallory screamed.

"How about a million dollars?" Dan said. He spoke in the telephone. "Get me the San Francisco Police Department."

"Banion, I can raise seven hundred thousand, but that's all."

"If I couldn't be a millionaire, I wouldn't want to be a lousy petty bourgeois," Dan said. "Connect me with Inspector Gallagher, Homicide Bureau."

"I might be able to raise seven hundred and fifty thousand. I'm not sure. I'd have to sell this house and the one in the city."

"Well, there you are. I wouldn't want to put you out in the street." He spoke again in the phone. "Tell him it's important Tell him it's Dan Banion of the *Journal*, and it's very important."

"For God's sake, Banion, don't be a fool. You're throwing away a fortune."

"I guess I just don't like you, Mallory .... Gallagher? Yes, this is Banion. Hold the line a minute, will you?"

Mallory had scrambled to his feet and made a dash for the assortment of spears and knives hanging on the wall under the staircase. He had hold of a large Malayan kris. Before he could turn and use it, Dan kicked him in the seat of the pants so hard that he crumpled to his knees groaning in agony. The kris fell from his hand. Dan grabbed him by the necktie and dragged him back to the phone.

"Oh, my God, you've broken my back!"

"I don't think so," Dan said. "But I guess I'll have to break one of your legs."

"No, Banion! No!"

Dan gripped one of his legs by the ankle and braced a knee against it, as if ready to crack it.

"Don't. Don't. My God, Banion, don't!"

Dan relaxed the pressure. "Do you think you can lie there long enough for me to finish this phone call?"

"Banion, I'll give you anything. Listen to reason. Think of your own interests."

Dan unbuckled Mallory's belt and pulled it out of his pants, made a loop through the buckle and fastened it around his neck like a dog collar. Then he tied the other end of it to the leg of a heavy table. "If you try to get out of that, I'll have to take you apart," he warned.

"Think, Banion. Seven hundred and fifty thousand dollars!"

Dan returned to the phone. "Gallagher?"

"What's the idea of keeping me hanging on this line?"

"Just a little interruption. How you coming with your third degree?"

"We just got here. I haven't time to waste, Banion. What is it?"

"Nothing much. I've got your murderer here. He offered me seven hundred and fifty thousand to let him go. Shall I take it? You and I could split it, you know."

"Cut the damn foolishness."

"I'm not kidding you. It's a fact. I'm still down in Burlingame. It's Lance Mallory."

"What about him?"

"He's the murderer."

"What are you trying to pull?"

"I've got it all cold turkey. If you don't want to believe me, I'll call the local sheriff. But I thought you'd like to make the arrest."

"Where are you?"

"Here in Mallory's house. I've got him tied to a table leg. I had to break his arm. Maybe I broke his back too, I don't know."

"You stay there, Banion. I'm coming down."

"Take your time."

"What about this girl Marian?"

"Turn her loose on humanity again. Or give her back to Wiener. That's his department."

CHAPTER TWENTY-SIX

Chuck Leary the bartender in The Wreck, looked up at the sepia print of the giant redwood over the bar, and winced. "You shoulda seen it," he said. "Pretty enough to pinch. All laid out there, pink and delicious. Just like askin' you to come and get it. Guys used to come in feelin' all frayed and petered out, their eyes stale as cigar butts. They'd take one look at her and perk up. It sort of made 'em feel like goin' on livin'. Gave 'em hope. Reminded 'em of what life is all about."

"You'll get another picture," Ike said.

Chuck sighed. "Not like that one. That's gone. Any lousy heel who would burn a pitcher like that ought to be hung." He put his cigar in his mouth and bit it to indicate he had said something.

"Drink up," Dan said. "I want to buy one for the bride and groom."

Chuck snapped into action. "Oh, no. Not tonight. It's on the house. Strictly on the house."

Lorna was sitting with her hand looped over Ike's arm and a brand-new gold band around her finger.

"It sort of reminds me of when the missus and I got hitched," Chuck said, dropping ice into glasses. "I rented one of those soup-and-fish outfits. The whole works. Split tails and a foldin' hat. Never had one on since. We got our pitcher taken, though. I could show it to you. Those days I thought I was gonna get up there among the foldin' money." He shook his head regretfully. "It didn't work out that way."

"It's just as well," Ike said. "You'd probably have been a pain in the neck. You're right the way you are."

"I never had any time to make money," Chuck reflected. "I was always too busy earnin' a living. Well, here's to the future."

"Let's drink it to Kipper," Dan said. "A good guy who wanted to make sense out of things."

"Right," Ike agreed.

"And to the doll that went up in smoke," Chuck added, lifting his glass to the redwood tree.

They drank.

"Tough break for that Marian Cleave dame," Chuck said, wiping his chin.

"She'll get along," Lorna said dryly.

"Maybe she'll go back with Fallon," Ike suggested. "I saw them together this afternoon. What do you think, Dan?"

Dan shrugged. "It's a great big world, and it's cold, cold, cold."

Lorna shook her head. "She won't go back to Fallon if she can snare anybody else with those bedroom eyes of hers."

An annoyed man a few stools down the bar was drumming his fingers and gesturing to Chuck.

"Excuse me," Chuck said. "Larry wants his stick." He fished the length of wood from under the bar and walked toward the impatient customer.

In the door came a gray little man talking to himself. He took a stool a few feet away from them. "Chuck them," he said. "Chuck them all. Chuck the big guy too. Would they listen to me? No. Coconuts! What's a coconut? Why, Christ, the world is full of coconuts. Keep your eye on the valve. That's what I told them. Keep your eye on the valve. Never mind the coconuts. Bang! Up she went. Would they listen to me? No. Would anybody listen to me? No. All right, chuck them. Chuck them all. That's what you get."

Lorna rubbed her head against Ike's shoulder. "Don't drink too much, will you, dear?"

Ike seemed surprised. "Why, I never drink too much."

"Just tonight, for me. I don't want you to be too drunk."

Momentarily ignored, Dan took some papers from his pocket and studied them. One was the address of Janey Navarro, which he had scribbled on the back of an old envelope. The other was a letter, addressed to himself in his own handwriting, which had been delivered to his hotel that afternoon. As he stared at them, the strains of Tchaikovsky's "Dance of the Sugar Plum Fairies" burst from the juke box.

Larry made curves in the air with his stick and leaned forward to coax the best from each instrument.

Dan slipped the letter back in his pocket, but still held the envelope with Janey's address on it. He tapped it against the knuckles of his hand for a moment, considering, then stepped down from his stool.

"Wait a minute," Ike said. "You're not going to leave us."

"Have another drink," Chuck urged. "It's still on the house."

"Thanks, another time," Dan said. "I have a little call to make."

"This is a hell of a time to walk out on me," Ike complained. "I've just been married."

"Yes," Dan said. "But I haven't."

THE END

MANY A MONSTER

by Robert Finnegan

CHAPTER ONE

As the waitress placed the cups on the table, her hand shook and slopped coffee into the saucers. Four men were crowded into the small restaurant booth. Three were big, hearty men who laughed gruffly and ordered enormous meals. The fourth was a dark-haired youth with brooding eyes and large, long-lingered hands. The waitress dared not look at him, yet could not keep her eyes away. It was fear of insanity that made her hand shake and filled every nerve in her body with anxiety.

The three big men were police officers. Reason told her that she had nothing to fear from the dark youth who was jammed into a corner and handcuffed to one of them. Yet, the very word insanity was frightening to her, and the presence of a lunatic in the restaurant gave her a sense of personal insecurity.

The waitress was not the only one emotionally affected by the men in the booth. The attention of the entire restaurant was concentrated on them. Patrons at other tables whispered solemnly, and their eyes crept again and again toward the booth. As the other waitresses moved from table to table, they whispered the information in voices full of awe.

The restaurant proprietor took a strange satisfaction in spreading the morbid sensation. He leaned over the nippled rubber change pad, and whispered to a customer, "Over there in the third booth where the waitress is. It's Rogan Lochmeister, the fiend."

The customer stood transfixed in horror, a forgotten five-dollar bill in his hand.

"The three men with him are officers," the proprietor explained. "They're taking him to the Wainley Prison for the Criminally Insane." He said this with a kind of eagerness, as if the weird novelty reflected some distinction on his establishment.

"My God," the customer gasped, "why bring him in here?"

"It's perfectly safe," the proprietor hastened to assure him. "It's quite a long drive. They had trouble with their car, and they stopped off here for dinner."

The patron stared at the booth in fascination. For many months he had been following the Rogan Lochmeister case in the papers. In fact, from the discovery of the first murdered and mutilated girl, long before Lochmeister had been apprehended, the case had intrigued him.

It was a smart-cracking radio commentator who had dubbed the unknown murderer "Gus the Grue." From then on it stuck. Washroom wits even made a craze of penciling "Gus the Grue was here" on the walls of public lavatories.

Public demand for the capture of Gus the Grue became a constant storm beating at the windows of the police department. Failure of the authorities to discover this warped mind among the teeming populace that flooded the sidewalks and crowded the buildings became a humiliation that seemed to tarnish the star of every policeman on duty.

Ultimately, the arrest of Rogan Lochmeister silenced, but hardly satisfied, public anxiety. They looked to the photograph for a face and stature distinct enough from their own to give them a sense of security. Rogan Lochmeister, unfortunately, had very much the face of an ordinary citizen. Certainly his eyes had a preoccupied and introspective look, but such eyes were common these days.

Now the patron of the small-town restaurant stood with a forgotten five-dollar bill in his hand and stared at the living flesh of the fiend who had occupied the headlines for so many months.

"It's hard to imagine," he said to the proprietor.

The proprietor shrugged. "Well, that's how it is. You never can tell, can you?" His business instinct snapped him back to reality. He reached out and plucked the five-dollar bill from the patron's hand, fingered the keys of the cash register, and broke the spell with a down-to-earth clang.

Meanwhile, in the booth that attracted so many uneasy eyes, Rogan Lochmeister forked his food with little appetite. His left hand, manacled to the big man beside him, experienced a restriction which seemed to reach up his arm and into his brain, frustrating every effort at thought. His mind was a sea of pain. The front of his skull felt fogged with weariness. The back of his head ached. It was his heart that he longed to still, for in his heart a strange defiance still throbbed. He could numb his brain with cynicism or despair, but he could not still the fight in his heart. His brain, still echoing the screams of jungle monkeys and the ripping whistle of enemy sniper bullets, could doubt itself. His brain, still blurred by the melting warmth of malaria, could question its own efficiency. But his heart pounded an unreasoning defiance.

It was strange. Although he could no longer understand himself, he still understood other people. When the muscular, red-haired man next to him tugged at the handcuffs by which the two of them were fastened together and said, "Come on, kid, we gotta move," he said it with a peculiar tenderness. Rogan knew that in his heart the man hated and feared him. But Rogan was on his way to be locked for life in a pit of broken brains. And the man could see that he, Rogan Lochmeister, ate his food no differently than the others, moved quietly and politely toward his hell, and was, for all anyone could see, a human being. And, although gentleness was not a normal characteristic of this man, he was awed by a tragedy that he could not understand, and was being considerate for his own comfort more than that of the victim who was manacled to him.

A small crowd was gathered on the sidewalk outside the restaurant door, for word had passed through the pool halls and barrooms up and down the street. They watched the four men leave the restaurant in fearful silence. Rogan Lochmeister didn't mind their presence. It didn't seem to matter. Public scrutiny is a matter of indifference to a man going to hell. Or would the Prison for the Criminally Insane be hell? Was it not more like going from one hell to another? From the hell of life, in which a man was tortured by vague things he did not comprehend, to the tangible hell of prison, where every blow and torment was an understandable pain.

The crowd followed them to the parking place where their long coffin-like sedan was waiting. Rogan half climbed, half was pulled into the back seat between the two big men where he had been sitting on all the long ride from San Francisco. The big man who was driving started the car with an angry roar and very quickly they were on the highway again, speeding toward what the court had decreed would be the final destination of his life.

The three big men talked rhythmically of things familiar to themselves, but never addressed Rogan. It was as if he were a ghost in the car. They talked of ball games, their wives, the relative qualities of various brands of beer, the mathematical chances of poker hands, the comparative charms of movie actresses, and the probabilities of race horses. But they never spoke to Rogan.

The headlights of the car danced over the road ahead illuminating fences, trees, signboards, and hedges. To the men who were taking him to hell these things were so commonplace as to be meaningless. But to Rogan they were last glimpses of a frantic world. When the headlights picked up a family stranded by the wayside repairing a tire on a dilapidated car, Rogan considered where they were going, how much money they had, what they would do when they got there, and what they wanted.

The steady roaring of the motor imposed a rhythm on the talking of the three men and upon Rogan's own thoughts. He could remember having told people in the past that a man's mind worked best when wheels were under him, yet it seemed tonight that his mind could not think clearly at all.

Some influence of the flashing road inspired the man at the wheel to discuss life from his viewpoint. The average bum, he declared, was born to be a bum. Just as the average successful man would have been successful regardless of circumstances. In the end, he said, it was fate that ordained the destinies of men. Whatever a man was, he was meant to be. It was all part of a higher plan. He said that he didn't believe in everything that religion taught, but he did believe in God. And that if any sonofabitch didn't believe in God he had no use for him. It stood to reason that there was a God or there wouldn't be a world. And if a man said he didn't believe in God it was like saying that there was no sense in anything.

The man to whom Rogan was handcuffed said that was about the way he'd figured it, and, although he hadn't been in church since he was baptized, he'd always paid his debts. And, by God, if you loaned him any money he would pay it back even if he had to steal it.

The headlights dancing on the road ahead and the rhythmic conversation in the warm interior of the sedan lulled the men to a sense of lazy security. It seemed that they would always be rushing over this smooth highway to the comforting drone of the engine and their own voices. Rogan, too, felt the numbing effect of talk and vibration. It was in a supreme moment of after-dinner languor that the crash came. No one had any sense of warning. To Rogan, two blinding headlights suddenly sprang out of the night. There was a deafening, metallic violence, then everything was gone.

When consciousness returned to him, Rogan felt as if he had been asleep for a hundred years. His brain seemed clean and rested. His whole body was refreshed. He lay quietly wherever he was for some time. Then, gradually, the context of events reshaped in his brain. He opened his eyes, and he could see the stars through one of the side doors of the sedan. He moved in that direction, but the handcuffs, still locked to the wrist of the big man, restrained him. His brain then grasped in full what had happened.

He groped through the man's pockets until he found a key ring. One of the smaller keys unlocked the handcuffs. However warped and thick his brain may have been, it could still grasp the possibilities of freedom. He groped farther through the man's pockets and found a wallet. In the proper compartment he felt what he knew were bills. It occurred to him to go through the pockets of the other men, but he dared not take the time. He pressed the handle of the car door, which was angled toward the sky, and climbed out. As he did so, the stars seemed to come so close he felt as if he were sticking his head among them.

CHAPTER TWO

"This is something you can really get excited about," Rolf Burgess said. "It's right down your alley."

Dan Banion was intent on watching a little white louse that was crawling along the edge of the city editor's desk. "I'm tired of living in an alley," he said. "I'm wondering if I'll ever graduate to a boulevard."

The city editor laughed generously but without amusement. "This really isn't anything to joke about. Suppose you had a sister living in this city with that fiend loose?"

The louse crawled under a row of books braced up on the city editor's desk, leaving Dan devoid of amusement. "I don't have a sister, and there's no reason to believe the fiend is in this city. Furthermore, you're so delighted that he escaped, you can hardly contain yourself."

Rolf Burgess was irritated but tried not to show it. In his heart he was afraid of Banion because he did not understand him. To Burgess newspaper publishing was a business. Business came first and the writhing chaos of human existence which comprised the news was only raw material from which to realize a return on the publisher's investment. To Dan Banion the news itself was a passion, and the newspaper was a kind of necessary nuisance from which one could draw a salary while probing the confusion of human lives. Burgess realized that without men like himself newspapers would soon cease to be a paying proposition. But he also realized that without men like Dan Banion they would have no news to print. "I wouldn't be so glib about it, Dan," he said. "There's every reason to believe Lochmeister will head straight for San Francisco. He's been loose for over twenty-four hours now, and the police haven't even a whisper of him. It's my bet, Dan, that if anyone alive can pick up his trail, you can."

"You mean it takes a bug to catch a bug." The louse had unexpectedly reappeared from under a dictionary and was legging frantically along the edge of the desk blotter looking for an opening. Nothing was pursuing it, yet it fled from an instinct of intangible peril. Dan became engrossed in its infinitesimal frenzy, and was listening to the city editor with only half an ear. Every microscopic fiber of the insect was motivated by a sense of insecurity as it frantically sought dark places in which to hide and soft objects on which to feed.

Burgess was annoyed by Dan's concentration on the desk top. "What the hell are you looking at?"

"A louse." Dan looked him straight in the eye.

"Where?"

"He just crawled under your desk blotter."

"Well, why didn't you squash him?"

"Why? What's he done?"

Burgess leaned forward and began beating the desk blotter with his fist. The very word "louse" grated on his nerves.

"I understand this guy was a Marine," Dan said.

Burgess stopped pounding the blotter. "Yes, a psycho. You know the story."

Dan stuffed his pipe with concentration. "The Marines had pretty tough screening. They didn't accept any psychos."

Burgess sensed that a touch of humanity in his reply would be diplomatic. He shook his head and looked unhappy. "You know, Dan, a lot of boys went into that fight straight as you or I, and came out pretty badly twisted."

Dan looked at him curiously. "As a matter of fact, Burgess, when you come right down to it, do you think you and I are so damned sensible?"

"I realize, Dan, you went through it too. But you're tough. Some of these kids, you know," Burgess shook his head, "they sort of went to pieces."

Dan scratched a match under the edge of Burgess' desk, and jerked angrily. "The guy probably came back so sex starved his head was a merry-go-round with pin-up girls riding every horse. He couldn't buy any and he didn't know how to get any free, so his brain went loony. You want me to find him. All right, what have you got? What's your information? What color were his eyes? Did he have any birthmarks? Did he smoke cigars? Does he play the pinball machines? There are only a couple of million people living in this Bay area, you know."

Burgess adjusted a pair of horn-rimmed glasses to his ears, and began scanning a folder of typewritten pages. "I suppose you know the general facts of the case?"

"Yeah, three cops were escorting him down to the prison for criminal nuts. A drunken joy-rider banged into them. The drunk has a broken spine and a fractured skull. One of the cops is dead, another is in an oxygen tent and it's anybody's guess. The third has a broken arm and three fractured ribs. Lochmeister got away and you want me to find him."

"Yes, it was an unfortunate piece of business." Burgess selected a paper. "Here's a little of the background. There were three girls, as you know, brutally murdered. The conditions in each case were so identical that it was obviously the work of the same man. It was not until the third murder that the killings were traced to Lochmeister. He was almost trapped at the scene of the crime but escaped by fatally shooting a police officer. They did, however, succeed in tracing Lochmeister to his apartment. His clothes were stained with blood, and he had the revolver with which the policeman had been killed."

Burgess selected another paper from the file folder and handed it across to Dan. "I've had a list typed of all the addresses of people he might be looking up. It's pretty complete. You'll notice I've even listed the witnesses who appeared against him at the trial, and as many of his personal friends and associates as we could get a line on."

Dan studied the list. "The police have all this stuff. They must be watching these places. What else have you got there?"

Burgess pushed the whole folder across the desk. "Here are a few photographs and a factual summary of the case. Take them along. They're not much to go on, I realize."

"It's like handing me a peanut shell and asking me to find the nut."

"Well, if you locate Lochmeister, fine, but that's not the only thing we're interested in. There's the human-interest angle too. A fiend at large. Witnesses who testified at his trial afraid for their lives. Former friends, uneasy that he may look them up. The emotional reaction of his sister, and there's even an ex-wife on the list, you'll notice."

"I'm not a sob sister, if that's what you mean."

"You know what we want, Dan. Do it your own way. Play around with it and see what turns up."

CHAPTER THREE

According to the information on Dan's list, Rogan Lochmeister's sister lived at an address on Clay Street, just off Fillmore, under the name of Florence Lock. She had evidently changed her name to avoid the stigma created by her brother's crimes.

As Dan parked his car in front of the house, he noticed a familiar black sedan at the curb across the street. He walked over and looked in. Mac McCracken, one of Inspector Gallagher's men, was lounging irritably in the back seat. "Excuse me," Dan said, "I just escaped from the insane asylum. Can you direct me to the nearest girls' seminary?"

"Beat it, Banion," Mac grunted, "I'm on duty."

Dan looked across the street at the big three-story wooden dwelling that was once a mansion but had now declined to a dilapidated rooming house. The curtains in the windows looked like cataracts in tired old eyes.

"Watching the place?"

Mac shrugged. "Gallagher thinks that bug might contact his sister."

"Well, don't go to sleep or you might wake up with your head wrapped in a paper bag and thrown in some garbage can."

"You're telling me! These loony cases give me the creeps. A guy that kills people for money or because he's sore I don't mind. But somebody who goes around killing people because he gets a kick out of it you can't figure."

As Dan climbed the worn steps of the old house, he noticed a room-for-rent sign in the window and got an idea. A gray-haired woman with large, beefy arms opened the door and looked at him questioningly through rimless glasses.

"Do you have a room to rent?" Dan asked.

Satisfied that he wasn't selling anything, she beamed warmly and said in a gentle voice, "Yes, won't you come in?"

When he stepped into the hall, she turned toward the rear of the house and bellowed, "Eddie, you keep an eye on Elizabeth. I'm going to show a gentleman the room."

A battered child's tricycle was parked in the hall. From the kitchen came smells of cooking. As the landlady toiled up the stairs ahead of him, her great hips swerved from side to side like loose melons in a sack.

She threw open a door on the second floor. "It gets the sun all day long, and we're right handy to the streetcar. Do you work in town?"

"Yes, I'm an insurance adjuster," Dan lied.

"Oh, isn't that nice. I have a nephew who works in insurance. Pete Reilly. Do you know him?"

"I don't recall him at the moment."

The room had an enameled iron bedstead, chipped in a number of places. The rug had long ago lost its grip on its pattern. It was vague in color and worn through in many places, but clean. A veneer-board dresser, an old rocking chair, and a two-burner gas plate on a stand made of orange boxes completed the furniture.

"I don't suppose you'd be doing much cooking," she said.

"Maybe a cup of coffee now and then."

"Well, I've just had a new tube put on the burners. Of course, you've got to be sure you turn them off tightly."

Dan poked his nose in the closet and then tried another door that was locked.

"That doesn't open," she said. "It used to connect with the next room. It's rented to a young lady who works at Wyler's department store. A Miss Lock. A very nice girl. We have a very nice class of people in the house."

Dan eyed the door with interest. "How much is the rent?"

"It's seven dollars a week. I know that seems high, but that's what we've been getting. You know how prices and everything are nowadays."

"It costs more to live than it's worth," Dan said. "Staying alive is an extravagance."

She fanned one hand at him. "Isn't it the truth. Land sakes, you're lucky you don't have any children."

"I'll take it." Dan reached his wallet out and extracted the right amount. As he did so, he saw a tall brunette girl, who had evidently just come home, pass the open door, and he heard the rattle of a key in the lock of the adjoining room.

The landlady wiped her hands on her apron and plucked the bills from him politely. "I'll give you a receipt for this, and you'll want a key. I always advise people to lock their doors when they go out. Of course, there's really no need for it, because we have a lovely class of people in the house. But I always say it pays to be on the safe side. I'll just take this downstairs and be right back."

The sound of someone moving about in the adjoining room came through the locked door. While waiting for the landlady to return, Dan looked out the window onto a patchwork of tiny fenced-in back yards that comprised the interior of the block. In some of the yards half-hearted attempts at gardening had been made, but the little individual squares of ground were really too small to be of use to anyone. All together they covered enough space to have made a beautiful community park if the people had only had sense enough to tear down their fences.

Dan went over and examined the keyhole in the locked door. It was plugged up with some kind of putty. The bottom edge of the door, however, had not been sealed, and there was about an eighth of an inch clearance through which he felt a draft. The landlady's footsteps, creaking on the staircase in the hall, caused him to straighten up.

She gave him his receipt, a key to the front door, a key to his room, a brief history of her family, an analysis of the postwar situation from the viewpoint of a rooming-house landlady, a résumé of the rules of her establishment, which definitely restricted tenants to one bath per week and made them responsible for cleaning out the tub. The telephone, it seemed, was answered by whoever got there first and, if it wasn't for them, it was their duty to shout the name of the person called in a loud voice.

When the landlady, whose name was Mrs. Murchison, left him alone, Dan pondered what would be the best means of getting acquainted with the girl in the next room. He could knock on her door and ask some silly question, but that would make him look like a masher. And Rogan Lochmeister's sister, at least at this moment, would probably not be in a mood for flirtation.

He could just wait around until an opportunity offered itself, but that might take days. He knew from experience that people in these rooming houses could sometimes live right next to each other for years and never achieve more than a speaking acquaintance.

As he stood thinking it over, the doorbell rang in the hall below. Soon the voice of Mrs. Murchison soared upward calling, "Florence." Dan heard the door of the next room open and a girl's voice call down over the banister, "Oh, Myrtle, come on up. Thank you, Mrs. Murchison."

Creaking stairs indicated someone coming up. Soon another voice said, "Hello, darling, have they been bothering you?"

"A little, yes," Miss Lock said. "I just got home a moment ago." Their voices quieted as they moved into the room next door. Dan tiptoed to the adjoining door and put his ear against the panel. He could hear fairly well. Miss Lock's voice had a weary quality. Myrtle spoke with an accent that Dan decided could only have been acquired at a girls' finishing school.

"Darling, there'll be no argument," Myrtle said. "I've talked to Papa and we've both decided you're coming home to stay with us. Now there's no use in your saying anything, 'cause we won't take no for an answer."

"Myrtle, I don't know what to do," Miss Lock's voice said, "but I'm going to stay here. It's the last address Roggie had. As long as there's a chance that he might come, I want to be here."

"But, my God, Flo, the police are watching the house. You have your own nerves to think of."

Miss Lock's voice became bitter. "I know how you feel about it. I know how you all feel about it. I tell you Roggie didn't do it. He couldn't have done it."

Myrtle's voice was soothing. "Now, dear, let's not talk about it. Come home to dinner with us anyhow. Papa's expecting you."

The rest of the conversation consisted of efforts on the part of Myrtle to conciliate Miss Lock in what seemed to be a difficult situation. Obviously Miss Lock had a sister's reluctance to believe her brother capable of evil. Myrtle did not try to argue otherwise, but it was plain she did not share this feeling. Miss Lock mentioned that several newspaper reporters had been bothering around the department store where she worked. Myrtle suggested that she take a few days off and that "Papa would not mind," which seemed to indicate that "Papa" had something to do with the department store.

When they were almost ready to leave, Dan stepped out in the hall and went downstairs to the telephone, which rested on a little stand below. He picked up the telephone book, and thumbed through it pretending to be looking for a number. Almost immediately the girls came down.

Miss Lock was a tall brunette with a long pointed nose and troubled, introspective eyes. Myrtle was a healthy-looking blonde with a determined expression. Dan guessed that she was used to having her own way. Her clothes were plain, but obviously expensive, and she wore them to advantage. They went out the door without giving him so much as a glance.

Dan looked out the front window and saw them get into a maroon convertible and drive off.

That was that. Getting acquainted with Miss Lock would have to await her return home, and no one could tell when that would be. Myrtle might even succeed in persuading her to stay at her house.

Dan studied the list of names that he had in his pocket. One of them was described as a "pal" who had served in the Marines with Lochmeister, a Mr. Clyde Ennis, listed at an address on Turk Street. A "pal" might know more about a man than his sister. Furthermore, if he was really a "pal," he was a likely person for Lochmeister to look up.

CHAPTER FOUR

The address on Turk Street was a masterpiece of bad taste—a cheap apartment house designed to look extravagant. The front door had iron grillwork over the plate glass, which served the double purpose of preventing drunks from lurching through it and giving what the designer hoped was the appearance of a Spanish palace.

As Dan was squinting at the name plate to see which buzzer to press, the door opened violently and a weeping blonde came hurtling through with a small handkerchief pressed to her nose. She took one look at Dan, then thumped down the stairs and away.

Dan found the name of Clyde Ennis and fingered the button. Soon the electric door latch began to click. A man was standing in the second-floor hall, waiting. "Are you Clyde Ennis?" Dan asked.

The man nodded without altering his expression. He was lithely built, of medium height, and dressed with fanatical care.

A tight-fitting double-breasted blue suit with pin stripes, a loud striped tie braced up with a collar pin. His hair was greased straight and perfectly combed. His features were neatly proportioned and his eyes were like black marbles.

"I wonder if I could have a word with you?" Dan said.

"Are you a cop or an ink hawk?" Still his face did not change expression.

Dan considered the question and decided the phrase fitted. "I'm an ink hawk."

"Sure, come on in." Ennis led the way into a small apartment in which the overstuffed furniture bulged like so many gluttons full of bicarbonate of soda. "You want to know about Lochmeister," Ennis said before Dan had a chance to ask a question.

"That's right."

"Strictly a nut." Ennis lit a cigarette, shook out the match, and dropped it in a glass tray.

"You were in the Marines together."

"That's right." Ennis blew smoke through tight lips.

"You were sort of pals, weren't you?"

"There was a war on," Ennis said, dryly.

"But you were pals, weren't you?"

"In a sense." His face was still controlled and expressionless.

"In what sense?"

"All heroes are pals. We were heroes."

"And what about now?"

"He's strictly a nut."

"And now you haven't any use for him. Is that the idea?"

"Figure it out your own way."

"I was in the 90th Division," Dan said. "If you saw any worse than we did, you saw plenty."

Ennis' face relaxed slightly. "Did you ever see a guy go nuts?"

"I did."

"Then what the hell are we talking about?"

Dan shrugged. "I just want to get your opinion."

Ennis sneered slightly. "You want to know if Rog will be looking me up. Well, he won't. He knows better. I've seen plenty of guys go off their noggins. Good guys, at that. But when it happens there's only one thing to do. Turn them in to sick bay. Let the bug doctors work on them. What can you or I do? It's a mucking mess. Will you have a drink?"

"Thanks," Dan said. "Do you know his sister?"

"I've met her. I don't know her very well. Just enough to recognize her on the street."

"She seems to think he's not guilty."

Ennis poured whisky into glasses. "Well, you know sisters. It's pretty hard for them to face facts. Do you want water or straight? I don't have any seltzer."

"A little water will be all right. You think she's just imagining things then?"

"There's no doubt about it. It's just one of those things. Something jarred loose in him, I guess. You never know what's inside you."

"From what you say, he was evidently a pretty good guy, before."

Ennis rolled his drink around his mouth and swallowed. "Whatever was before doesn't seem to matter. It has to be written off now. You look at any guy in the can or down on Skid Row. They're all good guys gone wrong. I don't know the answers, guy. You tell me about it."

"You don't think he'd be apt to look you up, then?"

Ennis pursed his lips in a positive way and shook his head. "Not a chance."

"I understand he had a wife. Did you ever meet her?"

"Oh, yes, I met her."

"Well, they weren't together, were they, when all this stuff began to happen?"

"Oh, no, they'd broken up."

"Do you think he'd be apt to look her up now that he's loose?"

Ennis' face had assumed its expressionless control again. "Uh, uh."

"You think not?"

"No, it's not likely."

"Why did they split up?"

"Well, the enemy isn't the only one who loses the war. Sometimes things go to hell behind your back, you know."

"It was that way, then."

"Well, it's nothing unusual."

"Was she interested in somebody else?"

"Everybody else, you might say."

Dan's eye was attracted to a headline on a late afternoon paper lying on the table: GIRL'S LEG FOUND IN PARK. He picked up the paper and glanced over the story. There was little more to it than that. The severed leg of a girl had been found in Golden Gate Park. Police were considering the possibility, the story said, that it might be the work of Rogan Lochmeister, the insane criminal who had escaped two days before. Dan held up the paper. "Did you read this?"

Clyde Ennis nodded.

"What do you think?"

"I don't have to think about it one way or another."

"But you must be interested."

"Listen, guy, I'm looking after myself. You asked me how I felt about Lochmeister and I told you. He's strictly a nut, and nuts are out of my line. He knows better than to look me up. But if he did I'd turn him over to the nut department where he belongs. Now if you've finished your drink, I'm going to have to ask you to beat it. I've got a date for dinner."

"Okay. You haven't any idea where he might head for now that he's on the loose?"

"I don't know and I don't care, and I'm sick of hearing about the thing."

"There's nothing for you to get on your ear about."

"Look, I let you come in here. I gave you a drink. I answered all your questions. What the hell more do you want?"

"Being a nuisance is how I make my living." Dan got up and walked to the door. "I'm inclined to agree with you, though."

"About what?"

"He won't be coming to you for help."

"That suits me fine," Ennis said.

CHAPTER FIVE

When he left Clyde Ennis' apartment, Dan drove to the Press Club for a drink. He found Nix Peters, a reporter from the *Express*, a rival paper, leaning on the bar well advanced with his evening drinking. "Say, Nix, what was that leg they found out in Golden Gate Park today?" Dan asked. "Did you get anything on it?"

"Oh, it was a leg," Nix said. "A dame's leg. It had a nylon stocking on it."

"Any connection with the Lochmeister case?"

"Oh, that. So you're on the nut hunt now." Nix beamed with interest. "That's what they have me running my tail off about. Had any luck?"

"Not yet, but what about the leg?"

"Oh, it was just an old leg that had been lying around for some time," Nix said. "Down at the morgue they figure it was hacked off a couple of days before Lochmeister escaped. It's some other nut, no doubt.

There's an epidemic of them, you know. I guess you've been making the rounds of Gus the Grue's old haunts same as I have."

They compared notes. Nix Peters had little of interest to report. He had tried to interview Florence Lochmeister in the music department of the store where she worked, but a floor-walker intervened. Finally two house detectives escorted him out of the place. Next he had called on several of the witnesses who had testified against Lochmeister at the trial. One of them had apparently gone into hiding and could not be located. The others were terrified that Lochmeister, now at large, might take revenge by dismembering them. After that, Nix had wearied of the pursuit and retired to the bar of the Press Club to soften the hard edges of life with alcohol. He was a large man, past middle age, with ill-fitting clothes and a placid face. News reporting, to him, had long since become a monotonous habit. He went about his work automatically and with the utmost economy of effort. "I'm supposed to interview his ex-wife too," he said. "I was thinking of looking her up after dinner. Her name is Enid Hoyte. She works as an entertainer in a joint on Turk Street. Why don't you come along and we'll kill one bird with two stones?"

They had dinner at an Italian restaurant and remained discussing the turmoil of life over two bottles of wine until nine o'clock. The case of Rogan Lochmeister seemed a faraway and unimportant thing by the time they piled into Dan's car and headed for the joint on Turk Street where Gus the Grue's ex-wife was employed as an entertainer.

The place was called Roscoe's Riviera. It was a square front of neon-illuminated glass bricks cut into the front of a dingy, soot-stained building. Inside was a gigantic bar built in a half circle around a drum-shaped platform on which a few musicians were playing while a blonde girl moaned into a microphone. It was one of those honky-tonks hastily and gaudily thrown together to catch the payrolls of the Army, Navy, and Marines during the war. Although once jammed with careless-spending servicemen, it was faring less profitably in times of peace. No more than a dozen bored-looking customers were ranged around the circular bar.

As they entered, Nix Peters jerked his head in the direction of the blonde singer on the platform. "That's Enid Hoyte," he said, "Gus the Grue's ex."

Dan's interest in the story revived with a surge when he recognized her as the same blonde girl he had seen exit weeping from the apartment house in which Clyde Ennis lived, earlier that afternoon. She was trying to sing "Doin' What Comes Naturally" with suggestive verve, but the customers weren't paying any attention and she was struggling against the dead weight of her own disinterest.

They took a table in the gloom around the edge of the room, and a girl in blue slacks came and asked them what they'd have.

After ordering drinks, Nix Peters slipped her a dollar and said, "We'd like to buy Miss Hoyte a drink when she's finished singing. Maybe you could invite her over for us."

The girl accepted the dollar without yes, no, or thank you, and swayed off to the bar to get their drinks. When she returned with the tray, Nix said, "You won't forget about the little songbird?"

The girl said, "Jesus, honey, give her a chance to finish the song."

"Okay, okay," Nix said.

"Maybe we could buy you a drink, too," Dan suggested. The wine at dinner had mellowed his brain and made him susceptible to tight silk slacks.

She grinned with a hard mouth. "You're cute. I like champagne cocktails."

Enid Hoyte sang several numbers. When she had finished, the girl in blue slacks went over and whispered in her ear. She looked toward Dan and Nix, and in a few minutes came to the table. Nix rose gallantly and Dan followed his example.

"You have a beautiful voice," Nix said.

"It was lousy and you know it. Bring me the usual, Judy," she said to the girl in blue slacks who was hovering nearby.

"We might as well tell you we're newspaper reporters," Nix said, settling in his chair.

"Anybody could see that," she replied.

"Naturally we understand how you feel," Nix continued.

"Oh, do you?"

"Well, if you're going to quibble about it," Nix said, "maybe we don't. Anyhow, no offense intended."

"I wish I was dead," Enid Hoyte said in the same tone of voice she might have said, "I wish I had a hamburger sandwich."

Nix tried to appear sympathetic. "I guess it's been tough." He looked hopefully to Dan, inviting him to take over; but Dan puffed contentedly at his pipe.

Enid Hoyte placed her red-tinted fingernails dramatically on her forehead. "When I realized that I was married to a monster—" she began.

Nix was struck suddenly by an idea. He straightened up. "That's a wonderful title, 'I Married a Monster.'"

"I will never feel the same way about things again," she sighed.

Nix was enchanted by the artistic possibilities. "'I Married a

Monster'! Say, that title is worth a million dollars. What d'ya think of
it, Dan?"

"It stinks."

"It would sell like hell," Nix insisted. "Just think of it. 'I Married a
Monster.' It's a natural."

Enid Hoyte studied her fingernails. "I could never bring myself to
write it. Besides, I can't write. Do you think there would be any money
in it?"

"Money?" Nix gasped. "Holy suffering catfish! It's just what people
go for. Isn't that right, Dan?"

"Nix, you can always steal money," Dan protested. "You don't have
to get it that way."

Enid bit a fingernail thoughtfully. "Maybe if somebody else would
put the words together for me, and if it would really help other
people to know—"

The girl in the blue slacks plunked a tray of drinks in the center of
the table. "Gosh, business is lousy. There's nothing but creeps in the
joint." She pulled up a chair and began sipping her champagne
cocktail.

Enid Hoyte's drink came in two sections. A shot glass of clear liquor
and a green glass that was obviously crème de menthe.

"What the hell are you drinking?" Nix asked.

"It's straight vodka with a crème de menthe chaser," the girl in blue
slacks volunteered. "Enid learned it from a Russian duke who used
to clean out the spittoons after the place closed."

"I can't write, myself," Enid said. "I just haven't got the knack. But
if you could just put the words together for me."

Nix's acquisitive instincts were roused. "Hell, I can write it. You just
give me the dope."

"I don't care about the money," Enid said, "but I feel I owe it to others
to tell what I've been through."

"Sure, we could split fifty-fifty."

"Isn't that kind of high?" she asked. "After all, I was the one who
married the monster. All you got to do is write it up."

"What's so tough about marrying a monster?" the girl in blue slacks
wanted to know. "I married a guy who saved postage stamps. Jesus,
it was awful. He kept picking around at those little things with a pair
of tweezers while I was waiting for him to come to bed."

"Well, we can figure out a percentage later," Nix said. "The main
thing is that it's a sure-fire proposition."

"Where did you meet Rogan Lochmeister?" Dan asked Enid.

"Oh, that was a long time ago. I was working in Wyler's department store. I was modeling in their dress department. He worked in the advertising department. We went out on a few dates together and, though he always seemed very cruel and sinister, somehow he must have hypnotized me. He kept insisting we get married. I didn't want to get married because of the strange feeling I got every time I looked in his eyes. But he kept insisting, and I was young and inexperienced, and so finally we got married. After that, he criticized everything I did, and I couldn't look at another man but what he got jealous. One day he took me by the throat and forced my head into a cold basin of water. I realize now that he was trying to drown me."

"Had you been drinking?" Dan asked.

"Certainly not," she snapped.

"He just all of a sudden grabbed you by the neck and ducked you in the water," Dan suggested.

Enid Hoyte looked annoyed. "Yes."

"The way I heard it," the girl in blue slacks said, "you came home at three o'clock in the morning stewed to the eyeballs and he tried to sober you up."

"You don't know a goddamn thing about it," Enid said.

"It doesn't matter," Nix interjected. "The fact remains you were married to a monster. That's good copy. It will sell like hell."

"When did you and Lochmeister split up?" Dan asked. "Well, after he went to war," she said, "I hoped it would straighten him up and give him some character. Instead, whenever he came home on leave he began to act more and more like a fiend."

"In what way?"

"Well, he accused me of going with other men while he was away."

The girl in the blue slacks gave a little ha-ha. Enid Hoyte turned on her with blazing eyes. "Just because you ran around with anything that wore a uniform is no reason to believe that every girl did the same."

"You mean Kilroy was here?" The girl in the blue slacks laughed.

"Now let's not get argumentative," Nix pleaded. "The war is over, and what you do when you're drunk, or in foreign countries, or during a war, doesn't count. The main thing is that you've been through a cruel experience, and the world deserves to hear about it."

"When did you actually break up with Lochmeister?" Dan repeated.

"That was after he got back from overseas," Enid said. "I realized then that I had married a monster. I don't suppose anyone would understand what I've been through."

Nix assumed an expression of profound sympathy. "By the way, now that Lochmeister is on the loose, how do you feel? Do you think he'd be apt to look you up?"

"I'm certain of it," Enid said. "I'm in terror almost every minute."

Dan decided that Enid Hoyte was a waste of time. He turned his attention to the girl in the blue slacks and let Nix discuss without interruption the possibilities of collaboration on the inspired work "I Married a Monster."

CHAPTER SIX

It was almost one in the morning when Dan returned to the dilapidated rooming house on Clay Street. They had stayed drinking at Roscoe's Riviera until the midnight closing hour. Nix Peters had dated Enid Hoyte to take her to an after-hours bootlegging joint for a lengthier discussion of their literary project. The girl in blue slacks had a previous date with the trap drummer in the orchestra. Nix wanted Dan to come along, but he pleaded weariness.

He went first to his hotel room and was on the point of turning in when he remembered that he had a seven-dollar investment in another residence. He hastily packed a suitcase and drove out to the address on Clay Street. A black sedan with lights out was parked in front of the rooming house. Dan ignored it and started to climb the steps when a gruff voice shot across the sidewalk: "All right, fella, stand right where you are."

Dan recognized the voice of Dink Buford, another of Inspector Gallagher's men, who had evidently relieved Mac McCracken for night duty. Dink got out of the sedan and came lumbering across the pavement with all the grace of an orangutan. "I'm a police officer," he said, "where you going?" He turned a flashlight in Dan's face. "Oh, for crissake!"

"I've got a bunch of human heads in this suitcase," Dan said, "and I'm looking for a place to dump them."

"What the hell you doing around here at this hour, Banion?"

"I live here."

"In this dump?"

"Sure, I rented a room." Dan held up his suitcase. "These are my clothes. I'm moving in."

Dink put both fists on his hips and began nodding his head. "Pretty goddamn smart. That's all I gotta say. Pretty goddamn smart."

"If anything happens on the inside I'll let you know," Dan aid.

"Wait till I tell Gallagher about this."

"Any objections?"

"Oh, hell, no. Go on in and get your ears cut off. It ain't my funeral."

"I don't see why I have to worry with you protecting the place," Dan said. "By the way, is anybody watching the back door?"

Dink shook his head. "We can't watch all doors. How many men you think we got on the force?"

"Well, let me ask you, if you were a fugitive on the loose, would you walk right up to the front door and ring the bell or would you sneak in the back?"

"Now, don't you give me any of those fancy ideas, Banion. I do what I'm told. That's enough. I don't think that nut's going to come around here, anyway."

"Why not?"

"Nuts are smart," Dink said. "They're not dumb like you and me. You take some of the smartest people in the world are nuts. It stands to reason. They think too much. You try it someday. You get to thinking about things and pretty soon you feel yourself going nuts. We got sense enough to stop thinking. They go right on thinking till they drive themselves goofy."

"I'll have to ponder that a little," Dan said. "Try and keep your eyes open, Dink. I wouldn't like to wake up tomorrow minus any of my important parts."

"Aw, you got nothing to worry about," Dink assured him. "That guy only slices up dames."

As Dan put the key in the lock and entered the dark hall, a variety of smells came to him that carried him back to his late teens and early twenties, when he had picked up a scant living at odd jobs and lived in a dozen or more places like this. In a sense, the creaking stairs and the odors of crowded living made it seem like coming home.

When he had felt his way upward to the second-floor landing, he saw that there were no cracks of light under any of the doors. If Florence Lochmeister was at home she must be asleep.

He groped to the door of his room and fumbled for the key. There was probably a light switch somewhere in the hall, but he didn't know where. When he put the key in the lock it rattled ineffectually, and he remembered that he had left the door open. He turned the knob and entered. Moonlight beaming in the window threw a sharp pattern of light across the floor and the foot of the bed.

Now where would the light switch be? He began feeling along the walls near the door, when he heard the bedsprings creak. An almost painful streak of fear shot down his spine. He looked in that direction and saw a form on the bed faintly revealed by the moonlight. He stood motionless for a minute, not knowing what move to make. The form on the bed was also motionless but seemed to be sitting up. He reached again to feel for the light, when there was a faint click and the room seemed to jump at him in full illumination.

He recognized Florence Lochmeister sitting up in his bed with a tiny automatic pistol gripped in her hand. With the other hand she had snapped on a light beside the bed. In the panic of the moment the hand with the pistol stood out beyond anything else in the room. It was businesslike and long-fingered. Each knuckle had separate prominence as the fingers wrapped awkwardly around the too-small gun. Her eyes were serious and hard.

"Don't move," she said.

Dan didn't move. He sensed that he was being mistaken for someone else. "I live here," he informed her.

"Where?"

"In this room. I live here. I rented it this afternoon."

Her face seemed to lose some of its tension, but the gun remained rigid in her hand.

Feeling that he was on the right track, Dan pointed to his suitcase on the floor. "There are my clothes. I'm moving in. I know it's late, but that's the fact."

She did not move or say a word.

Dan sensed that the only way to break the deadlock was to keep on talking. "You are Miss—the girl who has the room next door. I saw you in the hall this afternoon. I don't know what this is all about, but you are evidently making a mistake."

Her words jerked. "Why did you rent this room?"

"Well, for a place to live."

"What do you do?"

"I'm an insurance adjuster downtown."

"You're lying."

From the look in her eyes and the steadiness of the gun in her hand, Dan realized that any effort at deception was foolish. But he felt that he had broken the spell sufficiently to make a move. He walked a couple of steps to the rocking chair and sat down. As he did so, the gun in her hand followed him with an air of mechanical precision.

"Yes," Dan admitted, "I was lying. The truth is I'm a newspaper reporter on the *Journal*. You are Florence Lochmeister. I rented this room because I thought your brother might try to contact you. I was after a story. I rented the room this afternoon just before you came in. Right after that, some girl friend of yours named Myrtle came, and you went out. I went downtown and had some drinks with a friend of mine. Then I went to my hotel room, packed a grip, and came over here. I opened my door and there you are pointing a gun at me."

Dan wanted to take his pipe and tobacco pouch from his pocket, but the unusual steadiness of the gun suggested that he'd better wait until a better understanding had been established.

"Let me see your wallet," she said coldly.

Dan reached out his wallet and threw it on the bed beside her. She was fully clothed but had thrown the top blanket across her for warmth. Now she pushed the blanket aside and sat erect on the bed with her legs over the side. They were exceptionally long legs but not badly shaped. She was a tall, lanky girl, but with a little more meat on her would have been very attractive, Dan thought.

She groped at the wallet with her left hand, fingering out the contents on the bed. She examined his police pass, his guild membership card, his driver's license, and other identification.

"Are you satisfied?" Dan asked.

She looked terribly tired and said nothing. Dan took his pipe and pouch from his pocket and began loading tobacco into the bowl with a feeling of a crisis past. "Who did you think I was?"

"It doesn't matter."

"You thought this room was still unrented."

"Yes, I did."

"You were afraid that your—well, that someone might come looking for you. And if they did, you didn't want to be asleep in your own room. You thought it would be safer to come in here and sleep."

Her eyes fixed on him with hatred. "And who do you think I was expecting?"

Dan remained silent and waited.

"You think I was expecting my brother," she said with contempt.

Dan still kept quiet.

"You think I'd be afraid of my brother? I love my brother. I love him, and he didn't do these things. He didn't do them, I tell you. I've hoped with all my heart that he would come to me, but the police are outside in a car watching. I know it. And now you're right in this room. What can I do if he comes to me?"

Her voice ate deeply into Dan. This girl was a fighter and she believed in something. "Who were you expecting?" he asked.

"Why are you so sure I was expecting anyone?"

"There are only two reasons why you would be in my room. One would be that you were expecting someone you were afraid of. The other would be that somebody else was sleeping in your room."

She rose and opened the door to the hall. "Maybe you'd like to look for yourself."

"All right." Dan followed her while she opened the door to her room and snapped on the light. She had it fixed up pretty comfortably, with a studio couch instead of a bed, her own drapes, and some nice pieces of furniture. At first he thought that someone was lying on the couch. Looking closer, he saw that the covers were held up by pillows to give the appearance of a sleeping body.

"Are you satisfied?" she asked.

Dan eased himself into a chair and inclined his head toward the pillow-stuffed bed. "What's the idea of that?"

"Maybe I was expecting someone. But it wasn't my brother."

"Then who?"

Her eyes narrowed. "I don't know."

Dan studied the arrangement calmly. "It looks to me like you've set a trap."

"I was hoping the man who really committed those murders would come."

"So that you could trap him and clear your brother? Is that it?"

"Yes."

"What made you think he might come here?"

"To kill me."

"Why?"

"Because I've been doing some investigating on my own, and whoever is guilty knows that I'm going to discover him."

"Sit down," Dan said. "I have a completely open mind. If you have any good reason to believe your brother didn't do these things, I'd like to hear about it."

"You won't believe me any more than anyone else."

"Maybe not, but if you think your brother is innocent, then the only thing you can do is keep on trying to convince others. I'm somebody to convince."

She sat on the edge of the dummy-stuffed bed, took a cigarette from a pack on the side table, and beat it on the back of her hand. "I wish you hadn't rented that room."

"Wishing is a waste of time. What makes you think your brother didn't do it?"

"I know he didn't do it."

"According to my understanding, he confessed."

"No, he didn't. Roggie never confessed."

"Well, didn't they find the gun that had killed the police officer in his room? And wasn't there blood on his clothes?"

"That's true, but Roggie hadn't been wearing those clothes."

"Were they his clothes?"

"Yes, it was his suit, but I'm sure somebody else had been wearing it."

"Why?"

"Because it was an old suit and didn't fit him anymore. Besides, he never liked it. It was one he'd bought before the war. He'd lost a lot of weight when he was sick, and it didn't fit him anymore."

"How about the gun? Was that his?"

"Yes. But I'm sure someone else took it from his room and later put it back."

"What makes you think so?"

"It's the only possible explanation."

"Is there any evidence at all to indicate this?"

"Yes. Several times before, Roggie had complained that things were missing from his room. Later, he'd usually find them. Other times he told me that he'd found things rearranged and that he was sure someone had been in there. At the time I didn't pay much attention, because I thought it was only his nerves. He had been pretty sick, you know. Once when I was in his apartment with him and we were leaving to go to dinner, I suggested that he wear his overcoat. He told me that his coat had been stolen, or at least that he couldn't find it. I looked in his closet, and there it was on a hanger. He swore that it hadn't been there the last time he had looked for it."

"And that's the only reason why you think somebody else wore his clothes and used his gun?"

"It's enough, isn't it?"

"No, it isn't. Where had your brother been that night? How did he account for his time?"

"He couldn't remember."

"You mean to say that he couldn't remember where he'd been!"

"I know it sounds ridiculous, but Roggie is sick. He's terribly sick. His nerves were shattered by the war. He'd been trying desperately to pull himself together and live normally. He has spells during which he can't remember things very well."

"He's a psychiatric case, isn't he?"

"Yes, but he's not insane, and there's certainly nothing violent about him. Given a chance, he'd get over it. You don't believe me, do you?"

"I believe you mean what you say, but whether there's any truth in it, I don't know. You say you've been investigating. Have you found anything wrong?"

She bit her lip and nodded her head several times. "That's why I thought someone might come."

"You mean come here tonight?"

"Yes." She fumbled in the pocket of her suit. It was plain that she was laboring under intense excitement. She took out a ring of keys and held them up. "These. I took them." There seemed to be quite a number of keys of different sizes.

The telephone rang in the hall below. Her long fingers closed tightly over the keys. "That might be—" She opened the door and Dan could hear her footsteps creaking rapidly on the stairs.

Dan walked to the banister and looked down into the dark hall. She caught the phone in the middle of the third ring. He heard her voice in the darkness. "Yes. Yes, it's me. Yes, I want to see you in the morning. I've got something. No, I can't talk to you now. The first thing in the morning. No, I'm not going to work. You'd better not come here. I tried to get you earlier. Never mind, but I think it's important. Yes. Thanks for calling."

When he heard her hang up the receiver, Dan stepped back into her room. He resumed his place in the easy chair and proceeded to knock his pipe out in a near-by ash tray. As he did so, he noticed a red stub lying among the cigarette butts. He picked it up, examined it idly, and threw it back. It was the torn half of an admission ticket to some theater called the Regent. Probably a neighborhood movie. The bottom of his pipe bowl was a little mucky. He reached in his pocket for a pipe cleaner but discovered that he didn't have one. So he cleaned the bowl as best he could with a matchstick.

On the dressing table, a framed photograph of a young man in uniform attracted him. He went over and examined it. It was Rogan Lochmeister. The chin looked a little weak, and the eyes slightly dazed. On the whole, however, he was an agreeable-looking guy.

It struck Dan that Florence was taking an unusually long time returning from the phone. Most likely she had stopped by the bathroom on the way back. A copy of the evening paper was lying nearby. He read the police alibis on the search for Lochmeister, and reread the story about the leg that had been found in the park. Still Florence had not returned.

He stepped out in the hall but didn't hear anything. That is, nothing but a roomer snoring on the floor above. He tiptoed to the door of the bathroom, which the landlady had pointed out to him earlier. The door was open and it was dark inside.

He returned to the banister and looked down into the hall below. It was dark and silent. He listened for a few moments, then started down the stairs. He was almost to the bottom when the lights snapped on. Mrs. Murchison, the landlady, was standing with her hand on the switch near the front door. Her bulbous figure was wrapped in a cheap cotton bathrobe. Her gray hair was as scraggly as the end of a mop and her eyes were stupid from sleep. "Did you hear it?" she asked.

"Hear what?"

"I don't know. I thought I heard something in the hall. Or maybe it was in the kitchen."

A bumping sound, as if something had been knocked over, came dimly to their ears through the boards of the old house.

Mrs. Murchison started. "That was in the basement!"

Dan yanked open the front door. "Hey, Dink!" he yelled. "Wake up! Hurry!" Then he snapped at the landlady, "Which way?"

Her eyes bulged with alarm. "Through the kitchen."

Dan raced to a door in the rear of the hall and entered the dark kitchen. Mrs. Murchison followed quickly, slopping along in her slippers, and turned on the light. An open door showed a dark flight of stairs leading down.

"Someone opened that door," Mrs. Murchison gasped.

"Where's the light?"

"It's downstairs near the furnace on a cord."

There was no time for fumbling. Dan seized a broom, quickly struck a match, and ignited the straws. Holding it in front of him like a torch, he ran down the dark stairs. The rapidly burning straw threw a hellish, dancing light over the junk-littered basement. Dan got a quick glimpse of a man in dark glasses leaning over something behind the furnace. The man straightened up and pulled a gun. The basement roared with the noise of a shot, and Dan had a sensation as if someone had slapped him across the side of his face with a red-hot poker. He held the flaming broom like a lance and charged.

The man fled into a back room. Dan got through the door in time to see his leg disappear over the sill of a window. He ran to the window and stuck the broom out. It illuminated the yard enough for him to see the man scramble over the back fence.

By this time the broom was burning up toward the handle and losing some of its flare. Dan pulled it back into the room and returned to the main part of the basement still holding it in front of him. Its flickering light revealed the side of the furnace where the man had been stooping.

Dan's jaw clenched and the muscles in his face tightened. His brain reeled with anger and his heart turned sick. He felt responsible. This had happened while he had sat cleaning his pipe. This had happened while he might have prevented it.

As the flaming broom began to flicker out, the scene grew dimmer. Dan was distracted by the beam of a flashlight dancing over some old trunks at the foot of the basement stairs. He ran over. Officer Dink Buford was standing gingerly at the head of the stairs flashing his light downward. He turned the beam on Dan, "Don't move," he said. "Stay right where you are."

"For crissake, do something. He got out the back window and went over the fence."

"Oh, it's you," Buford said. "God, you've been knifed!" He came slowly down the stairs flashing his light slowly in circles. In one hand he held a big blunt revolver.

"He got out the back way," Dan shouted angrily. "For crissake, go after him! Or give me that gun and let me go after him!"

"Who? Where?"

The broom had burned out. Dan threw it on the cement floor and ran to the door of the rear room.

Buford followed cautiously. As he passed the furnace, his light flashed unexpectedly on the gruesome scene, and he backed away in such alarm he almost fell into a coal bin. Exasperated by his blundering slowness, Dan tried to grab the gun from him.

"Give it to me, you damn fool, and let me go after him."

"Le'go, Banion, or I'll slug you."

"Then for God's sake, come on." Dan led him through the back room to the window, climbed out, and ran to the back fence with Buford puffing after him. They climbed over and followed an alley between two apartment houses till they came out on the next street. There was no one in sight.

"He's gone now," Buford said. "There's no telling which direction he went. You're bleeding like hell, Dan. Did he cut you?"

Dan put his hand to his face and pulled it away. By the light of a street lamp he saw blood on his fingers. "Didn't you hear that shot? I think he just grazed me." He put a handkerchief to his face, and they returned to the basement the way they had come.

Mrs. Murchison had turned on a dim light bulb that dangled from a cord in the ceiling and was stamping angrily on the embers of the broom. She had evidently not yet looked behind the furnace. "You could start a fire that way," she complained. "You could burn the whole house down. And a new broom, too. A body should have better sense." She looked at Dan. "My God, Mr. Banion, you're hurt!"

CHAPTER SEVEN

Inspector Neil Gallagher sat at an old-fashioned round dining-room table stirring a cup of coffee which Mrs. Murchison had provided. Dan sat opposite him over another steaming cup. A strip of bandage was fastened to his left cheek by cross tabs of adhesive tape. Gallagher watched Dan's face closely. Although their work had brought them together many times, he had never seen Dan so disturbed.

Gallagher had spent the past hour examining the basement and questioning Mrs. Murchison's roomers. It was a fruitless procedure. Some of the light sleepers had heard the shot in the basement. Others had not. A few said they had been awakened first by the ringing of the telephone, had dozed off, and been reawakened by the shot.

Gallagher had found most of them crowding the lower hall when he arrived. They were wrapped in the cheap robes and kimonos which hard-up people buy at bargain sales and wear until they fall to pieces. Most of the buttons were off and sashes lost, so that they clutched their coverings around them in fearful modesty. A few, lacking bathrobes, had thrown their overcoats about them. Life had battered them into strange shapes and grooved most of their faces with permanent expressions of anxiety.

Mrs. Murchison assured Gallagher heartily that they were all "a very nice class of people." Having glimpsed the horror behind the furnace, she had forgiven Dan for the burned broom and accorded him the tenderness she felt owing to a hero. The bandage on his cheek was her handiwork. For Officer Dink Buford, however, she had nothing but contempt. She explained to Inspector Gallagher that after Dan had run down into the basement with the blazing broom, Buford had come cautiously into the house, walking as slowly as if he sore feet. "Then," she said, "he stood at the head of the basement stairs squirting that silly flashlight on a lot of old trunks."

When asked about Florence Lochmeister, she described her as "a very nice, refined girl who always paid her rent," then burst into tears.

Having made his examination of the premises, talked the matter over with the coroner, and disposed of the roomers, Gallagher was able for the first time to turn his attention to Dan. He was a big man with graying hair and sharp blue eyes. He had broad, bulging shoulders that made him seem to hunch forward as he sat in the chair spooning his coffee with a large clumsy hand. After studying Dan for several minutes, he said, "All right, Dan, my boy, start talking."

Dan snapped angrily, "What kind of damn craziness is it to put a man watching the front of the house and leave the back wide open?"

"You know, Dan, what I'm up against. I haven't enough men to cover the whole city. Crime's been increasing as fast as prices."

"If you can't watch everything, you can at least watch something."

"All right, take a crack at me in your paper if you want. I don't give a hoot. What if I'd surrounded the block? He'd have gone somewhere else and killed somebody else. You were right here in the house and it didn't do much good."

"I know," Dan said bitterly, "that's what makes me sore."

"You're taking it pretty hard."

"What did the coroner say?"

"It was Lochmeister all right. The same signs. The same screwy technique. Jesus! Imagine a guy doing that to his sister."

"He didn't look like Lochmeister to me."

"You just got a glimpse of him by the light of that broom, didn't you?"

"Yeah. But he didn't look like Lochmeister."

"Have you ever seen Lochmeister?"

"No, but I've seen pictures."

"Well, that's not dependable. Besides, it's a cinch he's done all he can to alter his appearance. It stands to reason, Dan. The coroner knows his stuff. The marks are the same. Who the hell else would do a thing like that?"

"Let me ask you something," Dan said. "That gun you found in his room when you first arrested him, did it have his fingerprints on it?"

The muscles pinched around Gallagher's eyes. "What are you getting at now?"

"I'm just asking."

"You and I know each other well enough, Dan, to be frank. If you've got anything on your mind, spill it."

"I'm only asking if his fingerprints were on the gun."

"No, they weren't. He'd wiped them off."

"Did he say he'd wiped them off?"

"No, but it stands to reason."

"How?"

"Well, hell, he'd just shot a cop. Wouldn't you wipe your prints off the gun in that case?"

"Not if I was going to stick the gun in my bureau drawer. There wouldn't be any sense to it."

Gallagher took a long gulp of his coffee and thumped the cup on the saucer. "Listen, Dan, he was screwy. He was a nut. And, besides, there's no doubt he intended to get rid of it later. Say, what's eating you, anyhow ? Come on out with it."

"I was talking to that girl just before she was murdered."

"You mean the one in the basement?"

"Yes, I was in her room."

"When was this?"

"Just before she was murdered. I was in her room talking to her when she went downstairs to answer that phone call. I was waiting there for her to come back upstairs when that guy grabbed her in the hall and dragged her down to the basement. He must have knifed her or gagged her or done something, because I didn't hear any struggle."

Gallagher pulled at his lower lip. "That makes it even clearer. You didn't hear any struggle because there wasn't any struggle. Young Lochmeister had come in through the basement window, and she found him in the hall below when she went down to answer the phone. She never did believe he was guilty, so naturally she wasn't afraid. Knowing that you were waiting upstairs in her room, she couldn't take him there. So she took him down to the basement without making any noise. But what were you doing in her room at that hour of the night?"

Dan told him the circumstances of his finding Florence Lochmeister in his room when he came home, her confidence in her brother's innocence, her belief that someone might come there to kill her, and the trap she had set for him.

Gallagher listened patiently, nodding his head occasionally. "Well, Dan," he said, "you know enough to figure that out. The girl was very fond of her brother. It's pretty hard to believe the worst of someone you love. I've been in this business a long time, but I've never yet been able to really convince anyone that a person they loved was guilty. Either they don't care, or else they won't believe it. Their opinions don't mean a thing."

"But, those keys," Dan said. "She had them in her hand when she left the room. Did you find them on her?"

"No. And we didn't find them in the basement, either. We went over the place pretty thoroughly, too, as a matter of routine."

"Then, don't you think that man could have murdered her to get those keys?"

"Dan, you're trying to convince yourself of something that's nonsense. That girl put a cockeyed idea in your head. You're a sucker for people in trouble."

"Show me the keys and maybe you'll convince me."

"I just told you we didn't find any keys."

"That's what I mean. A bunch of keys wouldn't evaporate. If you didn't find them on her, and they're not around any place, then it's a cinch that guy took them."

"Are you sure she took them with her when she left the room?"

"Positive. There isn't any doubt about it."

"All right, then they're around here somewhere. If it will make you feel any better, let's have a look."

They went out in the hall and examined every place where the keys could have dropped. Then they examined the kitchen floor and the stairway leading to the basement. Finally, they went over the basement thoroughly. The body had been removed, but a great, anguished stain marked where it had been.

Gallagher said, "This is senseless, Dan. There are a thousand explanations. Maybe young Lochmeister thought they were his own keys and put them in his pocket."

"Lochmeister wouldn't have had any keys, so he couldn't have thought they were his own."

"Well, maybe one of those keys was to a safe-deposit box or a locker somewhere that Lochmeister had some dough or clothes or stuff stashed away in."

When they had returned upstairs to the dining room, Dan said, "I think this thing deserves investigation."

"There isn't anything to investigate," Gallagher said, "until we find Lochmeister. Then, if he has the keys, that's that."

"And if he hasn't?"

"Dan, you're making a lot out of a lousy bunch of keys. I tell you, that coroner knows his business. This job was done by Lochmeister. The marks are unmistakable."

"I don't doubt that it was done by the same man who killed the other girls, but are you sure that man was Rogan Lochmeister?"

Gallagher fished a cigarette out of a crumpled pack, stuck it in his mouth, and struck a wooden kitchen match along the underside of the table. "What do you know about the case, Dan? You didn't cover the early part of it."

"That's true. They had me on another story but—"

"Well, he was caught cold. Caught in the act. Isn't that enough to satisfy you?"

"That's not the way I heard it. I heard he was arrested in his apartment."

"Listen, Dan, here's how it was. A guy by the name of Jansen—a longshoreman—came home to his apartment house at about ten o'clock at night. He accidentally went into the wrong apartment and found Lochmeister in the act of murdering this girl. Lochmeister ducked out a window and went down a fire escape. Jansen went after him. He's a big guy and could have torn Lochmeister apart if he'd ever got his hands on him. He chased Lochmeister about a block up the street. Officer Stranahan happened to come around a corner and tried to head Lochmeister off. Lochmeister drew his gun and shot him through the head. Jansen stopped to take care of Stranahan, but a couple of other people took up the chase, and pretty soon he had a regular mob after him, including another police officer. He ran into an alley, and they lost track of him. So they surrounded the block. It was a pretty fair bet he was trapped somewhere in that block, so we began searching every house and every apartment, every basement and every yard. It was a helluva job, I'll tell you. Along about one-thirty in the morning, we got to Lochmeister's apartment. He pretended he'd been asleep and came to the door groggy. When we searched the place, we found the gun and we found the clothes he'd been wearing stained with blood. The gun proved to be the one from which the bullet was fired that killed Officer Stranahan. The blood was analyzed and found to be the same type as that of the murdered girl."

"Did this fellow Jansen identify Lochmeister as the man he'd seen committing the murder?"

"Well, more or less. The killer was wearing dark glasses and got out of there pretty fast when Jansen came in. Jansen identified the suit all right."

"Was Jansen drunk at the time?"

"Well, he'd been having a few drinks."

"And that was why he got into the wrong apartment. Am I right?"

"Yes, that's right. But that's a small matter with all this other evidence. On top of everything else, Lochmeister couldn't account for his time that evening. He claimed he couldn't remember."

"His nerves were all shot to hell from the war. He'd been suffering lapses of memory. Didn't his doctors tell you that?"

"Listen, Dan, you're trying to stretch the benefit of the doubt beyond all reason."

"Didn't his doctors tell you that?"

"Yes, and they also told us that he was a mental case, which is more important. Dan, this guy's insane."

"I wouldn't be surprised if he was, after you guys got finished with him. He'd just been through a nervous breakdown. What did you do? Take him down to headquarters, throw a light on him, and give him the works?"

Gallagher's voice took a defensive tone. "Well, we gave him a pretty stiff working over, I'll admit that."

"And slapped him around plenty, I'll bet."

"Dan, this is neither here nor there. If you're going to argue that this guy's innocent, you'll just make a damn fool of yourself."

"I've been a damn fool plenty of times for less reason. Taking everything you say at face value, there is still at least a one per cent chance that somebody else might have been wearing Lochmeister's suit and might have borrowed his gun without him knowing it. Did you investigate that angle of it at all?"

"Certainly I did. There wasn't anything to it. There isn't any sense in it, either. Why would anyone do that?"

"You're not supposed to ask why. You're supposed to find out."

"Dan, this thing has thrown you off balance. You're ranting."

"I'm not saying Lochmeister is innocent. I'm saying there's a one per cent chance."

"Well, you've never taken any of my advice yet, so I don't expect you'll take it now. What makes you so interested?"

"I owe that girl something."

"Lochmeister's sister?"

"Yes. I should have had sense enough to have waited in the hall until she came upstairs. You don't know how that makes me feel."

"My God, Dan, it wasn't your fault."

Dan's jaw was stubborn and his eyes were hard. What he had seen behind the furnace still burned in his brain. "Let's just say I have a score to settle, and I want to be damn sure it's with the right guy."

CHAPTER EIGHT

Late though it was, it took Dan a long time to get to sleep. When he finally dozed off, he slept until noon. Before leaving the rooming house, he stopped at the telephone downstairs to call the office of the *Journal* and check on any new developments that might have turned up. Rolf Burgess was ecstatic about the story Dan had phoned in the night before. "Wonderful work, Dan," he said, "wonderful work. It's better than the original story of Gus the Grue. Keep right on it. It's just what we want."

Dan slapped down the receiver, cutting Burgess off in the middle of a sentence. He had his hand on the knob of the front door ready to leave when the voice of Mrs. Murchison stopped him. "Oh, Mr. Banion. Did you sleep well?"

"Well enough."

"You'll be late to work, but I suppose when you explain they'll understand. I would have waked you, but I didn't have the heart."

"It's all right," Dan said.

She fished in the pocket of her apron. "By the way, Mr. Banion, are these your keys?" She held up a tinkling ring.

"Where did you find them?"

"In the hall here, on the telephone stand. I found them last night while all the excitement was going on. Are they yours? I've been asking everyone."

"Yes," Dan said. "I must have left them there. Thanks a lot." He pocketed them eagerly.

At the corner lunch counter, where he had his breakfast, he took them out and examined them. It wasn't certain, but in all probability these were the keys he had seen in Florence Lochmeister's hand. There were six keys in all. Several looked like front-door keys. One was apparently the key to a padlock; another, made of white metal, had a number stamped on it, 297-J-6.

Why had Florence Lochmeister considered this ring of keys as evidence? The answer would be in the doors or locks which the keys would open. Apparently Florence Lochmeister knew what locks they were. But did anyone else know? She had said she had taken these keys from someone or someplace. But from whom?

There was also the question of the telephone call she had received in the middle of the night. She had made arrangements to meet someone early in the morning. But where? And who was it?

Dan put the keys back in his pocket. He considered turning them over to Inspector Gallagher, but decided against it. Gallagher was thoroughly convinced by the overwhelming evidence against Rogan Lochmeister. In that frame of mind, he could not be expected to make any diligent search for the doors that these keys would open. More than likely, he would turn them over to one of his not-too-bright assistants, who would walk around the block a couple of times, then return and toss them back on Gallagher's desk. Gallagher would throw them in a drawer, and there they would remain.

Dan took out the list of addresses Rolf Burgess had given him on the previous day. Among them was the apartment house where Rogan Lochmeister had lived and where he had been arrested. If he was innocent, then the guilty person must have had access to that apartment—must, in fact, have had a key to it.

He finished his coffee, got in his car, and drove to the address. It was a three-story apartment building on Taylor near Vallejo, old-fashioned, with protruding bay windows in front, but well kept up. He studied the name plates on the mailboxes and estimated that there were four apartments on each floor. Somebody by the name of Dison now occupied the apartment where Lochmeister had lived. He rang the bell several times, but there was no answering click at the door. That was good. Apparently Mr. Dison was out. In which case, Dan could try the key in his door with reasonable safety from embarrassment. He knew that places like this operated with individual keys for the various apartments and a lock on the front door arranged so that it could be opened by any of them.

Dan took out the ring of keys. The second one he tried fitted. The latch rolled smoothly, and the door opened. Number five was on the second floor. The key went into the lock all right, but wouldn't turn. Dan tried it several times, but it was obviously the wrong key.

This was a disappointment. But maybe this apartment house was different. Maybe here they had separate keys for the front door and the individual apartments. Another key on the ring looked very similar to the one that had opened the front door. He tried it in the lock of number five, and it turned smoothly. The door opened, but he pulled it shut again and removed the key. There was not likely to be anything inside to examine that would be worth the crime of burglary.

Another thought struck Dan. Since the grooving in both keys was identical, possibly this apartment house had the usual arrangement after all. Possibly both keys would fit the front door. In that case, the other key might fit still another apartment in the building. This was an interesting idea. Who would be more likely to borrow a man's clothes than someone who lived right in the same building?

Dan went downstairs and tried the key to number five in the front door. It fitted. The latch turned. That settled it. In all probability, the other key fitted one of the other apartments. But which one?

There were twelve apartments in the building. He could hardly hope to go around trying them all without getting caught. And what conceivable explanation could a man give for sticking a key in another man's door?

He unfolded the list of addresses again and studied it. A couple of the witnesses at Lochmeister's trial had lived at this same address, a Mr. Fergus Villiers and a Miss Alice Sweetser.

He examined the mailboxes again. Mr. Fergus Villiers' name did not appear, but Miss Sweetser's name was still there on number nine. He pressed the button several times and waited. The front-door latch did not click. Apparently Miss Sweetser was out, too.

He entered again and went up to number nine. The key fitted. He glanced into an ordinary and very feminine apartment, then closed the door. He debated going in and having a look around, but decided it wasn't worth the risk at this moment. A few minutes later he was glad of his decision.

He had walked only a few steps toward the stairs, when a neatly dressed man in a gray suit came up, brushed past him, fitted a key in the door of number nine, and entered. Dan hesitated a few moments, then went back to the door and knocked. The man opened it.

"I was looking for Miss Sweetser," Dan said.

"She's not here."

"Are you her husband?"

The man blushed. "No, I'm a friend of hers. She's out of town. She gave me her key and asked me to look in every once in a while to see that things were all right." He was a middle-aged man with a round, baby-like face and shy eyes.

"Can you tell me where Miss Sweetser is?"

The man looked down and rolled his head. "Well I—to tell you the truth—ah—may I ask what your business is?"

"I'm a newspaper reporter, from the *Journal.*"

The man smiled weakly. "Well, you see, that's just it. Under the circumstances, I'd rather not say where she's gone."

"By 'circumstances' do you mean the Lochmeister case?"

"Yes. I don't know that there's any real reason to worry, but with that fellow loose, you know—well, she was one of the witnesses at the trial, and there's no telling what spirit of revenge might motivate him."

"I can assure you that it would not be published."

"Just the same, it's better to be on the safe side."

"May I ask your name?"

"Well, I don't think that has any bearing on it."

"Just for the record," Dan said.

"I don't think that's necessary."

"Well, if I knew your name and that you were a friend of hers, there would be no point of mentioning it in the paper. But if you prefer to remain an unidentified man who was found in her apartment, that's news."

He looked annoyed, but not angry. "I'm sorry, I don't mean to be secretive, but I wouldn't want my name to appear in the paper. I'm Raymond Mills."

"And your address?"

"Is that necessary?"

"If anything should happen to Miss Sweetser, I'd naturally want to get in touch with you."

"My office is in the Medical Center Building. I'm a dentist."

"Is that so? As a matter of fact, I've had a tooth that's been bothering me for some time. I may drop in on you anyhow. Did Miss Sweetser leave before or after Lochmeister escaped?"

"She left a few days before. Of course, we didn't foresee this. As it happens, I'm very glad she's not around."

"Were you acquainted with Rogan Lochmeister?"

"I'm happy to say I was not."

"But Miss Sweetser was?"

"Only in the most casual, neighborly way."

"Do you recall the nature of her testimony at the trial?"

"It was extremely incidental. It concerned a violent quarrel he'd had with his wife shortly after he'd returned from the service."

"Oh, then his wife lived here too."

"Well, not after the quarrel. They had the apartment since before the war. When he went into the service, his wife stayed on. They split up soon after he returned. He kept the apartment, and she moved out."

"Do you know what they quarreled about?"

"Oh, I really can't say. I didn't follow it all that closely. The usual things, I assume."

"What did Miss Sweetser have to do with it?"

"Nothing at all. One evening she heard Mrs. Lochmeister screaming. She went down and found him struggling with her. He was evidently trying to kill her, because he had a knife. When Alice—that is, Miss Sweetser—intervened, he dropped the knife and went out of the apartment, banging the door."

"And that was her testimony?"

"Yes, but you can understand how it could motivate a spirit of revenge in him. That's why I'd rather not have Alice's whereabouts known."

"Of course. Well, thank you very much. I may be dropping in on you at your office."

"If that tooth has really been bothering you, you ought to have it looked at. It doesn't pay to let those things go."

Dan returned to the front door of the apartment house. The quarrel, if true, did not sound very encouraging. Still, on the other hand, what were keys to both Lochmeister's and Miss Sweetser's apartments doing on this ring? If Lochmeister's ex-wife, who now called herself Enid Hoyte, had lived in his apartment during the war, she would certainly have had a key. Dan decided that from now on he would try the keys in every door and every lock he encountered that had the slightest possibility of connection with the case.

The white-metal key stamped with the number 297-J-6 still puzzled him. It didn't quite look like the key to a safe-deposit box. He had seen such a key before, but he could not remember where.

Dan studied the mailboxes again. Underneath them was a buzzer marked "Janitor." He pressed it. Presently, through the glass of the front door, he saw a small, gnarled man with a brushlike mustache emerge from a door under the stairway and come forward. He opened the front door cautiously and peered out, saying, "Ya?"

"Are you the janitor of the building?"

"We ain't got no vacancy."

"I'm a newspaper reporter from the *Journal*."

"Ya. Nudder faller from de paper come yesterday."

Dan guessed that the "nudder faller" must have been Nix Peters from the *Express*. "Were you the janitor of the building when Rogan Lochmeister lived here?"

"Ya."

"You appeared as a witness at the trial, didn't you?"

"Ya."

"What's your opinion now that he's escaped? Do you think he might come around here?"

"Nope."

"You don't think he might want to take revenge on you for testifying?"

"Nope."

"Why not?"

"I say he's a fine faller."

Dan hadn't counted on this. "You mean you testified in his defense?"

"Ya."

"Do you mind if I come in and talk to you about it?"

"I give de answers here."

"Did you know his sister, Florence?"

"Ya."

"I was there last night when she was killed." Dan pointed to his cheek where the bandage still clung. "Whoever did it shot at me. That's how I got this."

"Aye, ya. Yer de faller burned de broom. I read in de paper."

"That's right."

"Brave faller."

Dan couldn't tell from his tone whether it was sarcasm or praise. "I talked to her just before it happened. She didn't believe her brother was guilty."

"Nope."

"You don't believe he's guilty, either?"

"Nope."

"Neither do I."

The little man laughed sourly, and his huge brushlike mustache danced up and down.

"You don't believe me?"

"Newspaper guys all boss' stooges—all damn liars."

"I'm telling you the truth," Dan insisted.

"You wait here." The little man shuffled back to the door under the staircase and disappeared. Soon he returned with a newspaper in his hand and again opened the front door. He shoved it out to Dan. It was a copy of the *Journal* headlined: *FIEND SLAYS SISTER*.

The story carried Dan's by-line and began:

> I saw Rogan Lochmeister murder his sister. By the light of a blazing broom I had seized for a torch, I saw the fiend leaning over the brutally mutilated corpse of one who loved him and who had believed until the last terrible moment that he was innocent of the long series of murders for which he had been convicted. As I lunged at the fiend with my blazing broom, he drew a revolver and fired. The bullet grazed my left cheek. With the hideous snarl of a trapped animal, he turned and fled into a rear room of the basement. He had committed what is undoubtedly the most horrible crime in the annals of our city.

Dan read no farther. "I didn't write this."

The little man sneered.

"I didn't write it, I tell you. This is the first time I've seen it. I phoned in the story early this morning, and I phoned it in straight. They wrote this and put my by-line on it. That's my name but I didn't write it. They often do that when you phone in a story, but I didn't expect them to twist it around like that. I didn't say anything like that over the phone."

The little man was still sneering.

"Let me use a telephone. I've got to have a telephone."

"I got no phone."

Dan reached in and pulled him out the door. "You're coming with me." The little man shook himself loose. "You're coming with me," Dan repeated. "You're going to hear what I say." Dan started down the stairs, but the little man remained where he was. "You called me a liar," Dan said. "At least you owe me the chance to prove I'm not."

The little man's mustache worked up and down as he seemed to chew over the idea. Then, without a word, he followed.

At the corner grocery there was a pay telephone on the wall. Dan inserted a nickel while the little man stood by. The fat grocer, alarmed by the angry look of Dan, stopped arranging tomatoes in the window and stood listening.

Presently Dan had Rolf Burgess on the line. "What the hell do you mean by running that goddamn story about me seeing Rogan Lochmeister!"

"Well, you did, didn't you?" Burgess said.

"I didn't say anything of the kind. I said I saw a man in dark glasses. I have no idea who he was. As a matter of fact, I wouldn't be able to identify him."

"Well, Dan, for the love of heaven, it's perfectly clear who it was."

"I said in the story I phoned in that there seemed to be a measure of doubt and I was going to look into it."

"Well, Dan, we can't run anything as ridiculous as that. You were emotionally upset when you phoned that story in. You were higher than a kite. But it was a wonderful story, and I think Hammond did a magnificent job of rewrite on it."

"Well, you tell Hammond he's a crap heel, and you can take your story and take your newspaper and your pen-and-pencil set and shove them all up your lousy ego! I'm quitting!"

"Now, Dan, be temperate. Reason this thing out. Don't do something you'll regret."

Dan gave elaborate expression to his opinion of Burgess himself and banged up the receiver. "I'll show that guy where he heads in," he told the little man. He put another nickel in the phone and soon had George Lederman, managing editor of the *Morning Courier*, on the line. "This is Dan Banion. I've been reporting for the *Journal*."

"Oh, yes, Banion," Lederman said. "We met one night at the Press Club, I believe."

"That's right. Did you see that story with my by-line on it in the *Journal* this morning?"

"Yeah. Great story, Banion. You scooped us pretty badly, though. Ha, ha! Can't exactly forgive you for that."

"Well, that's just the beginning. I'm going to have more on this case. Plenty more and bigger than that. I just quit the *Journal*, and if you want the follow-ups you can have them."

"Why did you quit the *Journal?*"

"They didn't run that story the way I phoned it in. As a matter of fact, there's a measure of doubt whether Rogan Lochmeister is Gus the Grue at all. He may be innocent of all these crimes."

"Well, that's a pretty unusual opinion, Banion. What's it based on?"

Dan suddenly realized that, after all, his arguments were weak. "Well, I talked to his sister just before she was murdered, and she was sure her bother wasn't guilty. She'd been doing some investigating and was convinced someone else had worn Lochmeister's clothes and borrowed his gun that night."

"What I mean is, Banion, have you any proof or any evidence?"

"Not yet, but I'm working on the case from that angle."

"Well, don't you think, Dan, that you're wasting a lot of good time?"

"Look, this is worth gambling on."

"The police say that there is no doubt whatever that it was Lochmeister."

"They've been mistaken before."

"Banion, the whole city is worked up about this thing. They want Lochmeister's head on a platter. If my paper started taking his side, people would cancel their subscriptions right and left."

"That's not true," Dan said. "People are always ready to give the benefit of the doubt."

Lederman laughed into the phone. "That's a hot one. Besides, there's no doubt to give anyone the benefit of."

Dan realized that he was floundering. "Then you won't handle it?"

"Can't handle it, Banion, Say, you've been drinking, haven't you?"

"Not at all."

"You go home and sleep it off, Dan. You'll laugh about this when you're sober. Give me a ring again tomorrow and we'll both have a laugh."

"You're turning down a good bet."

"If Burgess wouldn't handle it, it's a cinch it's no good for us. Burgess is a shrewd head."

"A lot of shrewd heads fell at Nuremberg."

"Don't lose your sense of humor, Banion. Get yourself a bromo and go to bed."

Dan hung the receiver up grimly. The fat grocer was standing motionless, with his mouth wide open. The little man said, "No go?"

"No go," Dan admitted.

The little man reached up a hand and patted his shoulder. "We go and have a drink on me. I'm Souzas Tsvirka." He led the way back to the apartment house and down into the basement. As they passed the furnace, Dan was reminded bitterly of a similar scene the night before.

Tsvirka's basement room was neatly furnished with odds and ends;

most of which appeared to have been constructed by himself. A colored photograph of a foreign-looking woman with a sad expression hung in an oval frame over his cot. When he saw Dan looking at it, he threw it a kiss. "My angel. Gone now. My wife, Stasia. She died many years ago." From a cupboard, he took a bottle of cheap whisky and a couple of thick jelly glasses. "I lose many jobs. It is nudding."

He had built bookshelves of orange boxes. Dan roved an eye over the titles and concluded that Souzas Tsvirka was an advanced social thinker.

"Like me, you cannot keep your mout shut," Tsvirka said. "In Lithuania, when I was little like dot,"—he indicated the proper height with his hand—"my fadder says to me 'keep your mout shut and you stay out of trouble.'" He poured generously into the glasses. "My fadder kept his mout shut all his life, and all his life he was in trouble. One day dey killed him. And as he lay dere dying, he cursed dem wit all his breath. But it was too late." He handed Dan a glass. "But I learned de lesson, and I keep my mout shut never. It means nudding to stand erect when your words are crawling. We shall drink to men who speak bravely." He held his glass high and smiled.

Dan returned the smile, and they downed their drinks. Tsvirka hastened to supply water chasers from a sink in the corner. "Now you are not a reporter and I like you better. But what will you do?"

"You're wrong there," Dan said. "I'm still a reporter, and I'm going to find out the rest of this story. If Lochmeister didn't do it, I'm going to find out who did."

"You're a good faller."

"What makes you so sure Lochmeister didn't do it?"

Tsvirka pointed to a shelf where a coconut shell with a face carved on it was smiling at them. "He was my friend. He brought me dat from de war. He's a good faller, I know."

"Is that the only reason you believe he's innocent?"

"He was my friend. I look him in de eye. 'Did you do dese tings,' I asked? He says no. I believe him."

Dan told Tsvirka the story of his conversation with Florence Lochmeister the night before, and of how he had tried the keys in the two apartments before ringing the janitor's bell. He showed Tsvirka the keys. "Do you recognize them?"

Tsvirka shook his head. They looked like any ordinary ring of keys. It was impossible to say whether he had seen them before. Of course, they might belong to Miss Sweetser, since one of them fitted her apartment. But why she would also have a key to Lochmeister's apartment he did not know. For that matter, he suggested, they might have belonged to Lochmeister himself. But in that case, he did not know why Lochmeister would have a key to Miss Sweetser's apartment. Also, they may have belonged to Lochmeister's ex-wife. Having lived there so long, she would naturally have a key. Furthermore, he explained, Lochmeister's wife had been very friendly with Miss Sweetser. There had been much visiting back and forth, and they seemed to have mutual friends. He recalled now that Mrs. Lochmeister did not have a phone and frequently went upstairs to use Miss Sweetser's. Since they were good friends, perhaps Miss Sweetser had given her a key so that Mrs. Lochmeister could use the phone when she was out. Miss Sweetser, he said, was a representative of a factory that made women's underwear. Her business took her out of town a lot, and she was frequently gone for weeks at a time.

As to who else might have possessed a key to Lochmeister's apartment, Tsvirka couldn't guess. There had been a constant stream of men going in and out of there while Lochmeister was away in the service. His wife had been a very loose woman, and that's why they split up. In such circumstances, any number of men might have had keys. On the other hand, that was unlikely, because there seemed to be so many of them that if they all had keys they would have been constantly bumping into each other. As Tsvirka pondered the problem, he hunched forward, wrinkled his brow, and tugged at his thick mustache.

Dan asked about Dr. Raymond Mills, the man he had seen upstairs in Miss Sweetser's apartment. Tsvirka was familiar with him but did not know much about him. He was Miss Sweetser's gentleman friend. He had been in and out hundreds of times during the past few years. He obviously had a key to her apartment, but Tsvirka could think of no reason why he would have had one to Lochmeister's.

Tsvirka threw new light on the quarrel between Lochmeister and his wife, which was the subject of Miss Sweetser's testimony at the trial. Lochmeister, he said, had told him all about it. He had found a package of marijuana cigarettes in her purse and had taken them away from her. She grabbed a kitchen knife and tried to stab him. He struggled with her and took the knife away. Just then Miss Sweetser came in and saw him with the knife in his hand. To all appearances, he was the attacker. Tsvirka had tried to explain this at the trial, but since he had not actually seen the incident himself, it was ruled out as hearsay.

"What about this fellow Fergus Villiers?" Dan asked. "He was one of the witnesses at the trial, and he's supposed to have lived in this building."

"Aye, him. He moved."

"What kind of a guy was he?"

"A music-listener. Always listening to music on the phonograph."

"Did he know Rogan Lochmeister?"

"He knew everybody." According to Tsvirka, Villiers was a very foolish man who was in and out of everybody's apartments. He didn't know where Villiers worked. He'd never asked. But he did have his forwarding address, and obligingly fished it out of an old cigar box. Villiers had moved shortly after Lochmeister's arrest.

Dan asked him if he knew Lochmeister's friend, Clyde Ennis, who had been in the Marines with him. Tsvirka did. Once when Ennis had been on furlough, he had come to see Tsvirka. Lochmeister had asked Ennis to look him up and say hello. Tsvirka and Rogan Lochmeister had been close friends ever since he had moved into the apartment long before the war. Lochmeister's parents were dead, and the old Lithuanian janitor, with his orange-crate bookshelves crammed with volumes that yearned and argued for the brotherhood of man, had become a friend and confidant who filled the place of a father.

Ennis had brought Tsvirka a bottle of whisky and told him many stories of what Lochmeister was experiencing in the service. He had also visited Lochmeister's wife upstairs. But Tsvirka had not been present at that meeting. Tsvirka did not get along well with Mrs. Lochmeister, and his friendship with Rogan seemed to have been somewhat of an annoyance to her.

With Florence Lochmeister, Tsvirka had not been very well acquainted. Rogan had told him much about her, and he knew that she was a fine girl who could play the piano. But they had only met personally on a few occasions. He believed, however, that Florence Lochmeister had known Miss Sweetser, because he had seen her visit Miss Sweetser's apartment a few days before Rogan Lochmeister escaped.

Dan asked him if there was any possibility of there having been a relationship between Rogan Lochmeister and Alice Sweetser.

Tsvirka doubted it. Miss Sweetser was his wife's friend and had been cool to him after having seen them in that violent quarrel. "More likely de gal downstairs," he said.

"What girl downstairs ?" Dan asked.

"De gal in number two. Dey were sweet togedder."

"Who was she?"

"Gal by name Viola. First-class swall gal." He shook his head and clucked his tongue.

"You mean she was his girl?"

"She love him very much. I think he love her. Nobody know much, but I know." He explained that sometime after his wife had moved out, Rogan had become acquainted with a "very swall gal" who lived downstairs in apartment two. The relationship had become very close. "By gad, I hoped dey'd get married," Tsvirka said.

Dan asked if she still lived there, but Tsvirka shook his head. "She's very sick. Nerves. Her uncle come and take her away. He put her in de hospital."

"Do you mean she had a nervous breakdown?"

"I guess dat's so. She lie in bed, don't eat, don't talk, don't get up, stare at de wall."

"Did all this happen after Lochmeister was arrested? I mean, was she all right before that?"

"Oh, she fine before dat. Her heart broken. She no more wants to live."

"I didn't see anything in the accounts of the trial about his having had a girl friend. Did she appear at the trial?"

"Nobody know much about they be in love. But I know. I say nudding, Rogan say nudding. Nobody ask her."

"Didn't you ask her anything? Maybe Lochmeister had been with her the night that murder was committed. It might have been important."

"I ask her. She say no. She know nudding. She stunned. She too sick to do anything. When I go see Rogan in jail, say nudding, he tells me. Don't let dem know about Viola. So I tell nobody. But I tell you 'cause you good faller. Nobody bodder her. Her uncle come take her de hospital."

Dan questioned Tsvirka further and learned that the name of the young lady who had lived in number two was Viola Adler. The uncle's name was Warren Braddock. Tsvirka fished around in some papers and found his address. "He some kind businessman. He look like boss."

Dan accepted another shot of Tsvirka's whisky, then folded his notebook and put it back in his pocket.

To Tsvirka, who had evidently never been more than a couple of dollars ahead most of his life, the loss of a job could mean only immediate destitution. He urged that if Dan were short of money he move into the basement with him and he'd get another cot. Dan thanked him but said that he'd get along.

"You one swall fighting fool," Tsvirka declared.

"That still leaves me a fool," Dan said.

CHAPTER NINE

Viola Adler represented a new element in the case that Inspector Gallagher had not inquired into. Dan decided to place her next on his list for a call. The only address he had was that of her uncle, Warren Braddock. If she had suffered a nervous breakdown, she might or might not be still in the hospital. In any event, Braddock's address was the first bet.

It turned out to be a house designed to look like an Old English cottage in the exclusive Forest Hills residential district out beyond Twin Peaks. The door was opened by a fat maid, who said nothing but lifted her chin and looked intent as a signal for him to start talking.

"Is Miss Viola Adler at home?"

"No, she's out. Who shall I tell her called?"

At that, a man dressed in white ducks, who had just parked a delivery car at the curb, came smiling up the steps with a large bundle in his hand. "Dy-Dee Wash," he sang out pleasantly.

"Oh, yes, thank you." The maid seemed rather embarrassed.

"Have you got the soiled ones?" he asked.

"Yes, er—just a minute." She disappeared inside and returned immediately with a bulging laundry bag.

"They sure do use 'em up, don't they?" the man said, cheerily. "How is the little fellow?"

"Oh, he's fine. He's just fine."

The man went humming off down the steps.

"Can you tell me when Miss Adler will be in?" Dan asked.

"No, I can't. I really couldn't. Who shall I say called?"

"Is Mr. Braddock in?"

"No, he's not in, either. Will you leave your name?"

"When do you think Mr. Braddock will be in?"

"I don't know. He went downtown this morning. He may not be home until dinner. What did you say your name was?"

"Just tell him Mr. Banion called. I'll try to find them in later."

"Was it about something in particular?"

"Yes, you can tell them it's about something particular. I'll be back later."

She stood watching him all the way to the gate and did not close the door until he was out on the sidewalk.

It was a corner lot, and a stone wall higher than Dan's head ran all around Braddock's property. Dan walked down the side street until

he came to the part of the wall that enclosed the area behind
Braddock's house. He grasped the top of the wall and pulled himself
up until his elbows were resting on it and he could see into a pleasant,
well-kept garden. A dark-haired girl was sitting in a lawn chair
reading. Nearby, on a spread-out blanket, a naked baby was sunning
and kicking. The girl seemed intent on her reading and did not see
him.

Dan watched her for a few minutes, then whistled softly. She raised
her eyes from the book and looked around. He whistled softly again,
and she saw him.

She did not seem to be alarmed. She stared at him for a moment,
then put her book down and came over to the wall. She was a scrawny
girl with dark, anxious eyes.

"Are you Viola Adler?"

"Yes."

"The maid said you were out."

"They always say that."

"My name is Banion. Do you mind if I come over and talk to you?"

"What is it about ?"

"It's about Rogan Lochmeister."

Her eyes darted toward the house. "You'd better keep out of sight."

Dan pulled himself over the wall and jumped down inside. There
were bushes growing near the wall which he hoped would shield him
from the rear windows of the house. "I'm a friend of Rogan's," he said.
"I'm trying to help him."

"Is he all right? Do you know where he is?"

"No, I don't. I'll have to talk fast. Have you any idea where he'd been
that night he was arrested?"

"I don't know. I've tried to think of where he could have been, but I
don't know."

"Then he wasn't with you?"

"No, I'd been with some friends. I don't know where he was."

"Did he often have lapses of memory like that?"

"Not very often, but he did have them. He'd been sick, terribly sick.
But he was getting better. Every day he was getting better. I know he
didn't do it. I know he didn't. I wanted to do something. I wanted to
say something. But they wouldn't let me, and I didn't know what to
do."

"You mean your uncle wouldn't let you?"

"Yes, you see there was—" She looked toward the baby sunning on
the lawn.

"Is it yours?" Dan asked.

"Ours," she said. "We were going to be married as soon as his divorce papers were final."

"Did you talk to his sister after it happened?"

"Yes, she told me not to say anything on account of the baby. She said that Rogan asked her to tell me that. I'm afraid I took it hard. I was sick for a long time." She looked toward the baby. "I almost lost him. We came here from the hospital a week ago."

Dan started to ask her if she knew Alice Sweetser, but a harsh voice barked from around the bush. "All right, you. Put your hands over your head." Dan recognized the big man as Foxy Schlutz, who worked for the Eagle Private Detective Agency. He had crept along the wall without their seeing him and was holding an ugly revolver.

"Well, Foxy, I see you've a job."

Foxy tried to look grim. "You, eh? Just get your hands up and come along with me."

Dan reached in his pocket and took out his pipe. "Go ahead and shoot me, Foxy."

"How would ya like a slap in the puss with this iron?"

"Go ahead and slug me. That's a swell idea. I'll see that you get your picture in the paper and everything. I'm here as this lady's guest. What's your business?"

"My job's to keep wise guys off Mr. Braddock's property."

"Is this young lady a prisoner here?"

"That's not the idea."

Dan turned to Miss Adler. "Have I been bothering you?"

"No," she said.

Dan calmly scooped tobacco from his pouch. "Put that gun away, Foxy. Don't be silly."

Schlutz looked dubiously at the gun and slid it into a shoulder holster under his coat. "You know I'm only trying to do my job, Dan. Why don't you be reasonable?"

"What's on your mind?"

"Braddock seen you from the window and bawled hell out of me. I'm supposed to be watching this joint. You ain't supposed to be in here."

Dan turned again to Miss Adler. "Do you want me to go?"

"No," she said.

"Do you want *him* to go?" Dan asked.

"Yes."

Dan grinned at Schlutz. "Beat it, Foxy, You're annoying the lady."

"Aw, come on, Dan, have a heart. Braddock wants to see ya."

Dan thought it over and decided he'd also like to have a look at Braddock. "I think I'd better go and have a talk with your uncle," he said to Viola.

"He'll be angry."

"That's all right," Dan said. "So am I."

Foxy led him across the lawn to the house.

"What are you watching the place for?" Dan asked when they were out of hearing of Miss Adler.

"Search me. I'm just watching it. I think she's got an ex-husband or something that might want to steal the baby. Whatever it is, they don't want to bring the cops in on it."

Foxy led Dan to a room that was fixed up as a sort of office or study. There were framed sporting prints on the walls and a collection of old pistols over the fireplace. A sturdily built man with thinning reddish-brown hair and rimless glasses stood behind a large desk. As they entered, he opened a drawer, took out an automatic pistol, and laid it on the desk top. "You can go now," he said curtly to Schlutz, who backed out obediently, closing the door after him.

The man seated himself with the attitude of an army officer about to interview a prisoner. "Before I call the police I want to know what you were doing in my garden."

"I'm newspaper reporter from the *Journal*." It was a lie, but since no one knew about his quitting, Dan decided to continue in the role.

"That still doesn't give you license to trespass on my property. What were you discussing with Miss Adler?"

"Is Miss Adler a prisoner in this house?"

"Certainly not. That's very impertinent."

"Then why shouldn't I discuss anything I please with her as long as she doesn't object?"

Warren Braddock appeared annoyed. "Perhaps you don't realize that my niece has been very ill. She's had a nervous breakdown and—well, I'm doing everything I can to protect her from disturbing intrusions. May I ask what impelled you to talk to my niece?"

"Certainly," Dan said. "I know about her relationship with Rogan Lochmeister and I know about the baby."

The man swallowed and gritted his teeth. His hands gripped hard on the edge of the desk. He was quiet for a moment, then said, "My God, you're not going to publish that, are you?"

"That all depends. May I ask you a favor? Either shoot me or put that gun away. One or the other."

Braddock picked up the automatic and weighed it in his hand as if debating. A faint sneer curled his lip. He dropped it back in the drawer. "You want money. Is that it?"

"No, not money. Just a little cooperation."

Braddock's eyes were cynical. "What does that mean?"

"Just this. I have reason to believe Rogan Lochmeister may not have committed any of these crimes, and I'm trying to find out the truth."

"What is your interest?"

"For one thing, I knew his sister. But even without that, I wouldn't want to see a man suffer for something he didn't do. Would you?"

"What leads you to believe he didn't do it?"

Again Dan found himself obliged to explain his doubt without much to back it up. Because he didn't like Braddock's looks, he decided not to mention the keys. In the end, he had little reason to offer aside from the fact that Rogan Lochmeister's sister had believed her brother innocent. When he had finished, Braddock said, "Don't you think that's a rather ridiculous assumption to make on the basis of no evidence at all?"

"Did you know Rogan Lochmeister personally?" Dan asked.

"I met him a number of times through my niece. I wouldn't say that I was very well impressed."

"Apparently you didn't approve of his friendship with your niece."

"Certainly not. She's my sister's child. Her mother has been dead for a good many years, and I have been her guardian. It hardly pleased me to have her take up with a mental freak."

"You understand, I suppose, that his nervous trouble was owing to the war. He wasn't a mental freak."

Braddock smiled ironically. "I'm afraid that you have a very unusual viewpoint."

"Whatever the case may be, you didn't like him."

"I did not. And I certainly am not inclined to any sympathy for him now."

"Your niece feels differently."

"The girl has suffered an emotional shock. I think you should take that into consideration."

"You evidently think it likely he may try to contact her. Is that the reason you have the place guarded?"

"Of course."

"And what would you do if he did come here?"

"I would certainly kill him."

"May I ask why your niece happened to be living in that apartment house downtown?"

"That was her own idea. She wanted to earn her own money, be independent, find out about life. I tried to reason with her, but she was of age and there was nothing I could do. She got a job with an advertising company."

"And she met Lochmeister in the apartment house?"

"Either there or in the course of business. Lochmeister was also in the advertising game. He had a job with Wyler's department store, I believe."

"Did you visit your niece often in her apartment?"

"I don't know that I care to answer all of these detailed questions."

"They come under the head of 'cooperation.'"

"Am I to understand that you intend using your knowledge of my niece's relationship with Lochmeister as a means of intruding into my affairs and invading the privacy of my home?"

"I suppose that's what it amounts to."

"In other words, blackmail."

"I told you all I want is cooperation."

"And if I refuse?"

"Get this straight. When I ask you a question, it's information I want and need and intend to get. If I don't get it one way, I'll get it another. And the other way may be a damn sight more annoying to you. Did you visit your niece very often in her apartment?"

Braddock was silent for a moment, then answered sullenly. "I visited her whenever I pleased."

"Were you acquainted with any of the other people in the building?"

"I met Lochmeister."

"Any others?"

"Certainly not."

"May I ask what your business is, Mr. Braddock?"

"I'm a real-estate operator."

"And you have an office downtown?"

"Of course."

"Your company doesn't happen to own that apartment house, does it?"

"It does not."

"You wouldn't happen to be acting as an agent for the owners?"

"I couldn't say. We are the agents for a hundred or more dwellings and apartments all over town. I don't keep track of them all."

Dan reached across the desk and pulled the telephone toward him. "I don't suppose you mind if I check on that. What is the number of your office?"

"See here, I object to this."

"Why make me go to the trouble of looking it up in the book? Or would you rather have me call my newspaper?"

"Well, as a matter of fact, we are agents for that apartment house. What difference does that make?"

"Well, why didn't you say so?"

"Because I—because I object to this cross-examination and I don't like your attitude. I'm not accustomed to being bulldozed. Here." He opened the top drawer of his desk, took out a checkbook, and began writing. In a moment he tore out a check and handed it to Dan. "Take that. It ought to be worth something to you. Drop this confounded foolishness of playing detective. I won't consider it blackmail, because you're entitled to something for keeping your mouth shut about a story that the newspapers would probably be glad to get."

The check was for three thousand dollars. "And what am I supposed to do for this?"

"Just go away and leave me alone. If I never see you again, the price is cheap. Take it and go to Europe. Buy yourself a car. Do anything."

Dan tore the check in pieces and threw it on the desk. "I'm just one of those guys who love cooperation," he said. "I'll be satisfied if it's understood that the next time I call on either Miss Adler or yourself I won't be told that you're not in."

"See here, if you keep poking your nose into this business you're just going to cause a lot of misery for everyone, including yourself. The thing is settled. There's nothing to be gained by reopening it. They'll locate Lochmeister in due time, and that will be the end of it. Don't you think my niece has been through enough, without subjecting her to this nonsense?"

"And suppose Lochmeister isn't guilty?"

"That's the most absurd notion I've ever heard."

Dan rose and picked up his hat. "Well, if we can't agree, at least we understand each other. Don't get up. I know my way to the door."

Braddock, however, accompanied him not only to the door but all the way out to the sidewalk. He seemed unwilling to let Dan out of his sight. His parting words were, "Will you assure me that you won't do anything without consulting me first? I am not asking you for my own sake but for Viola's."

The best Dan could tell him was that if there was anything he could do to help Miss Adler he would certainly do it.

CHAPTER TEN

Seated at the wheel of his car again, Dan studied the list and decided that Mr. Fergus Villiers deserved a call. Aside from Viola Adler, he was the only tenant who had moved out of the apartment house since Lochmeister's arrest. Dan drove to Villiers' new address,

which Tsvirka had given him. It was an old residence on Post Street
that had been remodeled into modern studio apartments.

Having pressed the button under Villiers' name and been admitted
by a clicking of the latch, Dan became lost in a tangle of hallways in
the old house. He climbed one flight of stairs and was looking for a
likely door when a voice from over his head said, "I'm up here, old
man."

Dan looked above and saw a man in a green and yellow dressing
gown leaning over the banister of the top floor. "These halls confuse
everyone. Come on up."

Dan climbed the stairs. "Are you Mr. Villiers?"

"Yes."

"My name is Banion. I'm a reporter from the *Journal*."

Villiers laughed lightly. "Oh! Another one. Well, come on in. You'll
have to excuse my condition." He was limping on a cane. "Sprained
my damn ankle. Some fool child left a baseball lying on the porch.
Almost broke my neck." He led the way into a pleasant room with
large windows and a couple of small skylights. Yellow and green were
evidently his favorite colors. There were yellow drapes, a green rug,
and green cushions thrown around liberally. "Sit down," he said.
"Can I fix you a drink?"

"I don't mind."

He was a bland-featured man of middle age with youthful eyes and
yellow hair. "I suppose you want to know if I'm barricading my door
in fear that young Lochmeister will be around to butcher me. That's
what the others wanted to know."

"Well, you don't seem worried."

"Haven't any talent for worry. Never was good at it. All I have is
brandy. A little soda?"

"Okay, a little. Did you know Lochmeister very well?"

"Yes. Rather. Odd chap. Knew his sister better. Tsch, tsch, tsch. Awful
thing. Had rather a crush on her for a while. Fascinating girl. Splendid
pianist." He handed Dan the drink.

"You testified at his trial, didn't you?"

"In a minor way. I don't really know why they called me in. My
relations with him at the store, I suppose."

"What store?"

"Wyler's. He worked there, you know."

"Do you work there?"

"Yes, of course. I thought you knew that. I'm in their interior
decorating department. Out today, of course, for this damn foot.
They'll dock me, too. Damn! How is a person to live with prices the

way they are? How much do they pay you?"

"Not enough. What was the nature of your testimony?"

"Oh, nothing special. I had the apartment next to his, you know. Damn stuffy place. This is much better. I happened to see him leave his apartment shortly after eight o'clock that night. And I must say he had a weird look on his face. Very odd."

"Did you see him come back?"

"Oh, Lord, no. I was asleep by that time." He leaned over a large, well-filled record cabinet. "Like to hear a little music? I have a wonderful new Brahms." Without waiting for an answer, he selected an album and began placing records in an automatic changer.

"What did you think of Lochmeister? Did you like him?"

"We got along. But I get along with everyone. Listen to these opening notes. Do you like Brahms?"

"When I'm in the mood. Did you know Alice Sweetser?"

Villiers wrinkled his brow and studied Dan. "You're an odd character. What does that have to do with it? Everybody knows Alice. She didn't care for Lochmeister."

"You say you knew Florence Lochmeister very well. Did she ever talk to you about her brother?"

"Oh, of course."

"She didn't think he was guilty, did she?"

"No. She didn't."

"What did you think about that?"

"Good Lord, how should I know?"

"It would be pretty awful if there were any mistake."

"Awful! My God, it would be terrible."

"You don't think there's any possibility, do you?"

"Of his being innocent?"

"Yes."

Villiers looked bewildered. "Well, how would I know? I suppose such things do happen."

"What's your feeling about it?"

"Mine? Oh, I'd feel terrible."

"I mean, from your own association with Lochmeister—from what you know about him. Is it your feeling that he's guilty?"

"I haven't the slightest idea. That's what I told Flo."

Dan asked him a number of questions about the other tenants of the apartment house, and about Lochmeister's associates at Wyler's department store, but invariably Villiers said he "hadn't noticed," or "didn't know," or "wouldn't be apt to know," and tried to turn the subject to music. Finally, Dan asked, "What happened between you and Flo?"

"You ask more damn questions. What's the idea? Those other reporters didn't ask me these things."

"I have the soul of a fishwife and a brain like a corkscrew. That makes me different."

"Well, I don't mind answering. Flo was a very serious-minded girl. I'm more or less of a fool. I guess you can see that."

"Did you have a quarrel?"

"My dear fellow. I never quarrel with anyone. I'm the most even-tempered person in the world."

"Did she get angry?"

"Of course not. She just thought I was a fool. She was here the night before last listening to records. She often came and listened to records. What are you getting at? Did you think we had an affair or something?"

"I usually ask as many questions as a person will let me."

"Well, by all means, amuse yourself. I must say I was getting bored sitting here all alone. Another drink?"

"No, I don't think so." Dan walked over and examined the albums in the record cabinet. Beethoven. Mozart. Shostakovich. Grieg. Rachmaninoff. "These men weren't fools," he said, meaningly.

Villiers twisted his mouth and nodded his head a couple of times thoughtfully. "Perhaps not."

"I may come back another time and listen to some records. Okay?"

"By all means."

"Maybe Lochmeister will drop in on you, too. You can't tell."

"My God, I hope not."

On the way out the front door, Dan took out the ring of keys and tried all the likely ones. None of them fitted.

CHAPTER ELEVEN

Back in his car, Dan studied his list again and decided that Wyler's department store rated the next call. The name kept popping up all along the line. Rogan Lochmeister had worked there. Florence Lochmeister had worked there. Rogan's ex-wife, Enid Hoyte, had worked there at one time. Fergus Villiers worked there. The list named Jason P. Wyler as Rogan Lochmeister's former employer.

Wyler's department store was a four-story building on Grant Avenue in the heart of the downtown shopping area. Dan wove his way through a maze of counters to the elevators and went up to the fourth floor where the business offices were located. There were windows where you paid your bills, windows where you made complaints, and windows where you opened charge accounts. Dan was directed from place to place until he found an auburn-haired girl in a starched blouse, who was apparently Jason P. Wyler's secretary. It disturbed her somewhat that he had neither an appointment nor a business card.

"Just tell him that Mr. Banion of the *Journal* would like to see him regarding a certain news story. I feel that he's entitled to see it before we publish it." Dan knew from experience that this approach was likely to open even the most difficult doors.

She returned in a moment and said that Mr. Wyler was busy with a gentleman but would see him in a few minutes.

Dan took a chair and passed the time marveling at the efficiency of the young lady. She held her head erect and flipped crisp white pages in and out of her typewriter with almost mechanical precision. Her fingers hit the keys with the rapidity of a machine gun. The carriage of the typewriter would glide to the right, and she'd slap it back, glide to the right, and she'd slap it back. Then presently she'd rip the page from the machine, jerk out the carbon, deposit the duplicate and original in separate piles, and insert a new page almost quicker than your eye could follow. And this, seemingly, without effort, a calm, bored expression on her face. After a while, a buzzer sounded on her desk, and she said, "You may go in now, Mr. Banion."

As Dan opened the door marked "J. P. Wyler," he heard a high-pitched voice declare, "Never mind telling me they'll sell eventually. How soon will they sell? If we had a stock of button shoes and kept them on display for twenty years, we might eventually sell them. But we'd be out of business before that. Fast-selling merchandise! That's what our business is based on. If it doesn't sell in a couple of months, get rid of it. Take a loss on it. Throw it out the window. Keep the merchandise moving."

A round-shouldered little man with an armload of imitation fur coats was standing in front of Mr. Wyler's desk. "But I thought in this case," he said, "we might take the gamble. You see—"

"What good is a gamble when you've already lost?" Mr. Wyler demanded in his high, cackling voice. "Get rid of them in the bargain basement. Sell them for junk. Give them to Greek Relief. Do anything, but get rid of them. You'll have to go now, Morris. I must talk to this gentleman."

The little man stomped out dejectedly with his imitation fur coats while Mr. Wyler turned his attention to Dan. "Mr. Banion, sit down.

You'll pardon my keeping you waiting."

Mr. Wyler was one of the baldest men Dan had ever seen. The hairless dome of his head gleamed like polished ivory. He offered his hand, meanwhile looking Dan up and down with shrewd business eyes that seemed to be calculating the cost of his shoes, the quality of his suit, and the brand of his shirt.

"I'm a reporter from the *Journal*," Dan said. "I wanted to talk to you about—"

"You needn't explain. I'm very glad you called. Will you excuse me just a moment?" He lifted the phone from his desk and asked for a Mr. Seeman. When he had Mr. Seeman on the phone he said, "Arthur, I'm sending a Mr. Banion down to see you later on. I want you to fix him up with a couple of suits. See that he gets the best. Show him those imported tweeds we just got in. Don't let him take anything but the best, and there's to be no charge. Anything he wants. Absolutely."

As he hung up the phone, Wyler smiled recklessly at Dan. "Just a little something I want you to let me do."

Dan was confused. "What's the idea?"

"I read in the paper about your experience. That was a noble thing to do, Mr. Banion. You made a fine effort."

"You mean last night?"

"Yes. I don't know whether you've been told or not, but Florence was rather dear to me."

"I didn't know that."

"Her mother was one of the finest women I've ever known. I must say this whole thing has hit me rather hard."

"You knew Rogan Lochmeister pretty well too, then."

Mr. Wyler picked up a paper knife and studied the tip of it He sighed. "I don't know how to explain it to you. I've known the boy since he was a child. He always had peculiar ways. He had a tendency to withdraw into himself. Was the thoughtful type. But I certainly never foresaw anything like this. It leaves you wondering what you can trust and what you can believe in."

"Lochmeister worked here, I understand."

"Oh, yes, in our advertising department. He did very excellently, too. I think, Mr. Banion, there's a great deal about these things that we do not understand. The war had upset his mind. You know that, I suppose."

"I know his record."

"Florence worked here, too. I would rather, of course, that she had let me help her in another way. I wanted to send her on a trip. Get her away from the city and the atmosphere of the whole thing. It was impossible. She was very proud. She wouldn't accept anything she didn't earn. I must say in all fairness that Rogan was the same way."

"Didn't Florence have dinner at your house last night?"

"Yes, Myrtle brought her home. We tried to persuade her to stay with us, but she wouldn't listen to reason."

"She still believed her brother was innocent."

"Yes, well, I think you can understand that. She was tremendously attached to him. Her mind simply refused to accept any evidence pointing to his guilt. Of course, I never tried to contradict her."

"Did she ever tell you her reasons for thinking her brother innocent?"

"Yes, but they were sheer imagination. Of course, I never argued with her about it. I let her cling to the idea that there was a possibility of error. I thought it would comfort her. I realize now that I was wrong. I realize that my attitude must have helped put her off her guard."

The buzzer on his desk sounded. "Yes, by all means, send her in." As he hung up the receiver he said, "That's my daughter. I'm sure she'll want to meet you."

In a moment the blonde girl Dan had seen in the rooming house came in.

"Myrtle, this is Mr. Banion," Wyler said. "He is the gentleman we read about in the papers."

Myrtle Wyler studied Dan with quizzical eyes as she removed her gloves. She was wearing a brown beret and tweed sport suit with a high muffler fastened by a silver pin. "Oh, yes." She nodded slightly.

"I was telling Mr. Banion that Florence had dinner with us only last night."

Myrtle continued studying Dan. "I've seen you somewhere before."

"It may have been in the rooming house yesterday afternoon," Dan explained. "I was at the telephone when you and Florence Lochmeister came downstairs."

"That may have been it," she said.

"By the way," Wyler recalled, "my secretary said something about a story you wanted me to look at before you published it."

Dan smiled. "Well, that was just a way of getting in to see you."

"Oh, I see." Wyler grinned. "Well, that wasn't exactly necessary. What did you want to see me about?"

"Oh, I'm just making the rounds of everyone Lochmeister knew, to see if I might get some idea of where he's apt to turn up. Have you any ideas?"

Wyler pursed his lips and studied the chandelier. "It's rather odd.

One would think that in his condition he wouldn't get far. But he seems to have dropped out of sight very successfully."

"It inclines me to think somebody must be helping him," Dan said.

Wyler's eyes jerked from the chandelier and looked curiously at Dan. "That's a strange thought. It never occurred to me."

Myrtle had eased one hip onto her father's desk and was perched there lighting a cigarette. Her sharp blue eyes moved from one to the other as they spoke.

"From your knowledge of his acquaintances," Dan said, "is there anyone who you think might help him?"

Wyler shook his head. "It seems incredible. Good heavens!"

Myrtle exhaled a long puff from her cigarette. Her eyes watched Dan's face closely. "Why would anyone do that?"

"Yes," Wyler said, "why would they do it? My God, under the circumstances it would be criminal. And what would be the point?"

"It would have to be someone who believed him innocent," Dan said.

Wyler seemed bewildered. "I can't imagine how anyone could think that."

"His sister did," Dan reminded him.

"Did you talk to Florence before she was killed?" Myrtle asked.

"Yes, I did."

"Well, his sister. That's understandable," Wyler said. "But after last night, how in the world could anyone have any doubt?"

Myrtle smiled and inclined her head toward Dan. "He does."

Wyler appeared startled. "Who does? Banion? What do you mean?"

Myrtle looked at Dan. "Florence told you her ideas, didn't she?"

"Yes, she said what she thought."

"You really didn't come here to look for Rogan," Myrtle said. "You came because you think someone else might have done it, and you're trying to get an idea who that might be."

"Partly, perhaps."

"I don't understand this at all," Wyler said.

Myrtle flicked her ashes in her father's tray. "You're very dense, darling."

Wyler looked at Dan curiously. "You don't really believe this thing, do you?"

"There's a possibility," Dan said.

The door opened and a serious-faced young man in an expensive tweed suit entered with a roll of papers in his hand. "Excuse me, J. P., can you take a glance at these layouts before I okay them? Hello, Myrtle." He looked at Dan. "Am I intruding?"

Wyler fanned one hand at him. "Just a minute, Alex." He fixed his eyes on Dan. "That's a very serious statement to make. If there's even the slightest possibility, it should be looked into thoroughly."

Dan was watching Myrtle. Her cheeks flushed noticeably, and a self-conscious look had come into her eyes as the man in the tweed suit entered.

"If you want, I can go," the man said.

"No, wait a minute," Wyler said. "You should hear this. On what do you base this conclusion?" he asked Dan. Realizing that his arguments were weak, and that if he mentioned the ring of keys Wyler would insist on having it turned over to Inspector Gallagher, where it would more than likely be pigeonholed, Dan simply said, "On the same reasoning that Florence Lochmeister based her belief."

Wyler leaned back in his swivel chair and sighed. "Good Lord, we've been all over that so many times."

The man in the tweed suit looked from Wyler to Myrtle. 'What's it all about?"

"Excuse me," Wyler said, "this is Mr. Banion of the *Journal*. Mr. Groton is our advertising manager."

"Oh, yes, I believe I read in the paper about you." Groton offered a hand and Dan rose slightly to grasp it.

Wyler took a soothing tone. "I can understand how you feel, Mr. Banion, after your experience last night. I assure you this s something I have given every consideration. And it is absolutely futile. I even hired private detectives to investigate every possible angle. There is simply nothing to it."

"Nothing to what?" Groton asked.

"Mr. Banion talked to Florence last night before it happened," Wyler said. "She told him that theory of hers about someone else wearing Rogan's suit and using his gun."

"Oh, that."

"I wish that it were so," Wyler said, "but I'm afraid we have to face facts. We have a lot to learn about the human mind."

"Darn pity," Groton said.

"Rogan worked in Mr. Groton's department," Wyler explained.

Groton was shaking his head. "Darn shame. Very good copy writer. Showed a lot of imagination. That's very often the case, they tell me. Sensitive mind. Something breaks. You'd better look at these layouts, J. P."

"Oh, yes." Wyler began to unroll the papers.

Groton patted Myrtle on the shoulder. "Good golfing, old girl. Knew you'd win. Where do you keep all those trophies?"

Myrtle looked accusing. "You promised to drive me home after.

Where did you go?"

Groton snapped his fingers. "That's right. By God, I did. Say, I'm sorry. I met Leonard and Francie. We had a few drinks and—"

"Oh, you needn't apologize."

Wyler shook his head over the layouts. "I don't understand, Alex, why you want all this white space around the corset figure. That costs money. Couldn't we use it for something?"

"White space is important. It draws the eye."

"It seems to me the girl's figure would draw any eye. Why don't we put the fishing tackle ad right next to the corsets. The girl would attract men's eyes, then they'd see the fishing gear."

Myrtle bit her lip and turned to Dan. "You'd better come along with me and let these two buzzards make money."

"So that you can spend it, eh?" Groton laughed in a forced way.

Dan followed Myrtle as she strode to the door.

Wyler called after them, "Don't forget about your suits, Banion. Just ask Mr. Seeman in the men's-clothing department. Pick anything you want."

As they waited for the elevator, Myrtle studied a framed advertisement on the wall and let Dan stand there as if he were a child she had consented to escort. Dan said nothing. He could see that the conversation with Groton had disturbed her. He thought it best to give her time to cool off.

Out on the sidewalk she said, "There's a bar around the corner," and led the way with a willful stride. When they were seated on the leather cushions of a booth in the dimly lighted bar, she said, "Tell me the rest of it."

"The rest of what?"

"You didn't get an idea that Rogan was innocent just from listening to that story of Florence's."

"I might have."

"Don't be ridiculous. You're not a fool. You wouldn't think what you do unless there was good reason."

"I might think that was good reason."

"No, you wouldn't. She told you something else."

"What makes you think so?"

"I knew Florence very well, you know. She had dinner at our house just before this happened. She told me she had some kind of evidence."

"What kind?"

"She wouldn't say. But she had a reason for wanting to return to that rooming house last night. I could tell."

"What's your attitude about Rogan Lochmeister?"

"I'm not ready to leap to any conclusions."

"Do you think there could be anything in Florence's belief?"

"Up to now I would have said no."

"And now?"

"You are not a person who would act without reason. You know something."

As the waiter put down the drinks, she said, "Bring us two more."

"There's no use getting me drunk," Dan said. "This stuff only makes me talk about myself."

She ignored his crack. "If you have any information, I feel entitled to know. Florence meant a great deal to me."

Dan pondered the problem. If he showed her the keys, she might recognize at a glance whose they were. On the other hand, if she didn't recognize them, she would certainly insist on turning them over to the police. That was something Dan intended to do in his own good time. "Believe me," he said, "if I had any convincing evidence, I'd take it straight to the police. I have nothing but a hunch. As it happens, I usually follow my hunches. If there's anything in Florence Lochmeister's story, I intend to find it out. If not, I have nothing to lose." Dan remembered that he had already lost his job, but decided to overlook that.

Myrtle sipped her drink thoughtfully. Dan sensed that she knew he was holding out on her and could see that she wasn't accustomed to being balked. Finally she said, "I want to help."

"Do you believe there is a possibility that he is innocent?"

"Yes."

"All on the basis of what Florence believed?"

"No. Because you believe it."

"What gives you such strange confidence in me?"

"That's not the point. Perhaps I have confidence in myself."

Dan could readily believe that. "You think I know something?"

"You wouldn't be acting the way you are if there wasn't something to it. I can see that."

"You must have known Rogan Lochmeister pretty well."

"Of course. I knew Rogan very well."

"Do you think he was capable of a thing like this?"

"If there were any way of telling which people are capable of things like this and which people aren't, life would be a lot simpler."

"That's an evasion. You must have some opinion about it."

Her face showed that she didn't like being accused of evasion. "Rogan was pretty much like all men. There didn't seem to be anything extraordinary about him. That is, until he came out of the war. Then he was nervous, of course."

"Did you like him?"

"He wasn't an easy person to know. Of course, I was fond of him, just as I was fond of Florence. Florence always seemed closer to me, though. I guess that's natural. We were together a lot as children."

"Did you know Rogan's friends?"

"A few of them. I didn't know them all."

"Would any of them have had keys to his apartment that you know of?"

"Some of them might. His wife must have had a key. Clyde Ennis might have. Clyde was with him in the Marines. Clyde stayed with him in the apartment for a while until he found a place of his own."

"Do you know Clyde?"

"I met him two or three times. He was a rather strange sort of friend for Rogan."

"What do you mean by that?"

"Well, Rogan had a good education. Clyde was rather a slick type. A pool hall sort of person. You'd understand what I meant if you saw him."

"What does Ennis do for a living? Do you know?"

"Yes, he owns a little theater on Third Street. Rogan had me drive him by there one night. It's called the Regent, I believe."

The color red flashed in Dan's mind and took the shape of a ticket stub. He remembered the stub he had found in Florence Lochmeister's ash tray the night before. He tried to hide his interest in the information by looking as casual as possible. "Who else might have had a key?"

"In those kinds of apartments," Myrtle said, "there is no telling who may have had a key."

"Did you know Alice Sweetser, the girl who had the apartment just above Rogan?"

"Alice? Oh, yes. She represents some garment firm. Father buys quite a lot from her. Why? Do you think she may have had a key to his apartment?"

"Do you know any reason why she would?"

"Certainly not. I was asking you."

Dan finished his drink. "You really want to help, do you?"

"I'm going to help," Myrtle said definitely.

Dan grinned. "All right, here's an assignment for you. Find out where Alice Sweetser is. She's out of town somewhere. There's a Dr. Raymond Mills who seems to be her boy friend. He evidently knows but won't say. Maybe your father knows. You don't happen to be acquainted with

Mills, do you?"

"Oh, yes. I know Ray."

Dan studied her well-formed face. If only she didn't have that spoiled, willful look! He shrugged. "Well, get busy on it. That's a definite assignment. I'll call you up tomorrow to check on it. You see, I'm taking you at your word." He stood up to indicate that their conference was over.

Her mouth tightened in determination. "I'll find her." She followed Dan out to the sidewalk. "Can I give you a lift?"

"No, thanks."

"Where are you going?"

"Never mind. You get busy on Miss Sweetser."

"I'm going with you."

"No, you're not. You do as I say." Dan took a kind of malicious pleasure in bossing her. He could see that it irritated, but figured it would be good for her. He walked a block, and she followed right along.

"I mean what I say. Beat it!"

"You're very rude."

"You'll probably be rude too before we're finished, if you really intend to follow through on this."

A taxi had just discharged a load at the curb, and the driver was about to take off. Dan hopped in, slamming the door behind him before Myrtle could follow. "Take me to the North Pole," he hollered at the driver.

"The North Pole. Right you are." The driver put the car in gear. Myrtle was left fuming at the curb.

"I figured you wanted to ditch her," the driver said a block away.

"You guessed it."

"Hell, these dames," the driver said, and stopped there as if the words constituted a full and adequate statement.

Dan let him drive around in circles for a while to be sure Myrtle hadn't found a way of following him. Then he said, "Take me to Third and Market."

CHAPTER TWELVE

At Third and Market Dan had a sandwich and a plate of beans at a lunch counter. Then he looked up the address in the phone book and started walking out Third Street toward the Regent Theater. His car was still parked near Wyler's department store, and he decided to leave it there for the time being.

Third Street—commonly called Skid Row or Skid Road—was the
street of down-and-outers, lined by pawnshops, junk stores, cheap
saloons, and gaunt-looking hotels. The conglomeration of worn tools
that crowded secondhand store windows, and an occasional shop
displaying overalls, work aprons, or sturdy shoes, indicated that it was
also the gathering place of itinerant workers. Old men walked slowly
on bunioned feet, puffing quietly at pipes. Here and there a ragged
drunk slept in a doorway with an empty bottle clutched to his breast.
Prostitutes, fat and dowdy, thin and tuberculous, wandered in and out
the barrooms on crooked heels. It was just getting dark, and yellow
lights were cutting weakly into the gray atmosphere.

Farther up the street, Dan could see the neon sign of the Regent
Theater projecting over the sidewalk. Before he reached it, he caught
sight of Clyde Ennis chalking a cue in a poolroom next door. As Dan
entered, Ennis leaned over the table and banked a ball into an end
pocket with casual skill, then backed away to study the position of the
remaining balls. He was about to lean to another shot when he
noticed Dan standing nearby. His eyes narrowed and he grinned in
a bored way.

"You again."

"Did you read about what happened?" Dan asked.

Ennis took careful aim at the cue ball. "I read it."

"You said yesterday you knew his sister."

"Just casually." Ennis shot and the ball just missed the pocket. "Too
bad."

Dan couldn't tell whether he referred to Florence Lochmeister or
missing the shot. "I was there when it happened, you know."

"Yeah, I read about some newspaper guy. Was that you?" Ennis
studied the balls for another shot with complete indifference.

"I was there, and I got a look at the guy. He didn't look like
Lochmeister."

"No?" Ennis aimed again.

"I talked with his sister just before it happened."

"You don't say?"

"You don't seem to be much interested."

Ennis shot again; this time the ball flopped neatly into a pocket. He
straightened up and looked Dan in the eye. "You've got it exactly right,
fellow. I'm not interested, and I don't intend to get interested. I
happened to know the guy in the service. Okay. I knew a lot of guys
in the service. The war's over. I'm not interested in getting myself
mixed up in any of their messes. They've got their headaches; I've got
mine."

"All right, if that's how you feel about it. How about a game of pool?"

"What do you think I am, a sucker? Why don't you beat it and leave me alone?" Ennis' tone was nasty.

Instead of going, Dan took out his pouch and stuffed his pipe in a leisurely way. "I can't quite figure you."

Ennis pointed to his chest. "I'm looking after number one. See? Maybe you can figure that out." He poked the cue angrily in the rack, turned on his heel, and went to the rear of the room where there was a bar.

Dan debated whether to follow him, and decided against it. He went outside and examined the Regent Theater. It was a small hole-in-the-wall place, blazing with posters. The double feature was Betty Grable and Hopalong Cassidy. Dan went up to the small window and bought a ticket from a fat blonde girl. Inside, a trim brunette tore his ticket in two, eyed his pipe, and told him smoking was on the left side only. He groped his way into the darkness and found an aisle seat.

On the screen, Betty Grable was stomping up and down in a lace negligee, pulling a tantrum and telling another girl that she never wanted to see somebody-or-other again. To the left of the screen was a big illuminated clock with a sign, "By courtesy of Dr. Leonard Katz, painless dentist." Below the clock was a sign, "Ladies and Gents Rest Rooms."

Dan watched the picture for a few minutes, then got up and made his way to the rest room. A squeaky door led him into a dingy hallway. A door just to the right was marked "Ladies." Another door was marked "Men." Midway between them was another door fastened by a large padlock. At the far end of the hall was a fire exit.

Dan took out the ring of keys and tried the likely ones in the padlock as rapidly as he could. None of them fitted. He walked to the door marked "Men," and had it partly open when he heard the hinges of the door leading from the theater squeak. Dan had a fleeting glimpse of the brunette girl who had taken his ticket at the door. She was carrying a paper bag.

There was nothing unusual about the men's room or even about the scribbling on the wall. Dan waited a few minutes to be sure the passage was clear, then returned to the hall. As he passed the center door, he noticed that the padlock was now unlocked and the hasp open. The girl must have gone in there.

Dan thought it over. What excuse could he make for opening the door? He could act stupid and claim that he was looking for the men's room and accidentally opened the wrong door. It was silly, but then people do silly things like that.

He turned the knob. There was a stairway leading to the basement. Somewhere below, a dim light was burning. He hesitated again. Well, he could use the same excuse for descending the stairs. He closed the door after him and went down cautiously. A single light globe was burning over an area of cement floor. Old signs, broken seats, and other pieces of junk were heaped against the wall. This would be almost directly under the movie screen in the theater above. Over to one side, a dark passage led up forward. At the far end of this passage Dan could see a crack of light where a door was partly opened. For going up there he couldn't think of any excuse. Nevertheless, he advanced quietly along the passage.

As he got nearer to the crack of light, he heard a girl's voice say, "I'm afraid the coffee got kind of cold."

A man said, "That's all right. It's fine."

The girl said, "It's the late edition of the paper. There doesn't seem to be anything new."

Behind him, Dan heard a door close and feet descending the stairs. There was no escape anywhere along the passage. Someone else was coming. Whichever way he turned, Dan would be caught. In a moment of panic he had to think quickly. It was a choice of being caught either trying to get out of the dark passage or in the lighted room ahead of him. Dan preferred the lighted room. He stepped forward and pushed open the door.

A man seated on a cot with a sandwich in his hand raised startled eyes. Dan recognized him immediately. The girl was sitting on an upturned box, but rose to her feet.

"Now take it easy," Dan said. "Just take it easy." He heard quick steps in the passage, and Clyde Ennis burst in.

Ennis stood looking at him quietly with hard eyes and a tight mouth. For a minute nobody said anything.

"Now take it easy," Dan repeated, "and give me a chance to explain."

Rogan Lochmeister, the man on the cot, continued to stare wild-eyed with the sandwich still poised in his hand. Ennis closed the door and leaned against it. "I told you never to stay down here with that door unlocked," he barked at the girl.

"It's all right," Dan said.

"I knew you were trouble the minute I looked at you," Ennis snapped. "I ought to bash your goddamn face in."

A number of boxes were scattered about the room. Dan pulled one over and sat down. "You're a good actor, Ennis."

"Is he a cop?" the girl asked.

"He's a goddamn ink hawk," Ennis said.

Lochmeister threw his sandwich down on a box he was using for a table. "I shouldn't have come here. I told you I shouldn't have." His dark eyes were sunken and his cheekbones prominent. Dan could see that he'd lost a lot of weight.

"Why don't you listen to me?" Dan said. "I'm not going to give you away. You're Rogan Lochmeister, aren't you? I talked to your sister last night. She was a fine girl."

Lochmeister ran his long fingers through his hair and began to cry.

"Leave him alone," Ennis snapped. "He's feeling lousy. Finish what you were saying."

"I'm not going to turn him in. I don't think he's guilty. What I'm trying to do is find out who did do it."

Ennis pulled up a box and sat down. "Keep on talking."

Dan told of his conversation with Florence Lochmeister the night before, and explained how he had lost his job.

Ennis looked at the girl. "What do you think?"

"He's telling the truth," she said.

Ennis jerked his head in her direction. "She can tell. She's got an instinct." He indicated Lochmeister. "That guy dragged me out of a tough hole on Saipan. If it wasn't for him, I wouldn't be around."

"How did he get here?" Dan asked.

"After that wreck, he stole a ride on a truck—hid himself under a canvas in back. The truck came all the way through to San Francisco. He phoned me and I hid him down here. He's been here ever since."

Lochmeister took his face out of his hands. "I don't want to get you in trouble. I've got to get out of here."

Ennis grinned at him. "Shut up, Rog. Eat your sandwich."

"Did Florence Lochmeister know he was here?" Dan asked.

"Sure. She'd been around a couple of times."

"Does anyone else know?"

"Just Pat here." Ennis inclined his head toward the girl. "She's my sister."

"How about the blonde in the box office?"

"She don't know anything."

"You wouldn't be the one who telephoned Florence at her rooming house last night?"

"Yeah. That was me."

"Then you knew she had been doing some investigating."

"Sure. We've both been trying to figure the thing out. She seemed to have found something. She said so over the phone."

Dan told him about the ring of keys. He took them from his pocket and handed them to Ennis, who examined them carefully. "Do you recognize them?" Dan asked.

"Not that I know of." Ennis handed them to Lochmeister. "Ever seen these before?"

Lochmeister looked them over and shook his head. "I don't know. I don't remember them."

Dan explained how he had tried them in various doors at the apartment house where Lochmeister had lived, and how one of them fitted Lochmeister's apartment, and another the apartment of Alice Sweetser on the floor above.

Lochmeister strained his mind over it but could not imagine why Alice Sweetser would have a key to his apartment. He agreed that it was quite likely his former wife, Enid, had a key to Miss Sweetser's apartment because of their friendship and the fact that she so often used the phone up there. "They might be Enid's keys," he said, "but I don't recognize them."

"Do you know of any particular person," Dan asked Ennis, "whom Florence suspected, and from whom she might have taken these keys?"

"Well, we were both keeping an eye on Ray Mills, that is, Dr. Raymond Mills, who runs around with Alice Sweetser. Florence had been having her teeth fixed by him just to see what she could find out. I followed him around several evenings to see where he went, but didn't learn anything. He's got a bunch of dirty post cards in his apartment and his address book is full of names. That don't necessarily mean anything, though."

"How do you know that?" Dan asked.

Ennis grinned. "I just happened to sort of go in there one night to case the joint. Never mind the particulars."

"Was there anything else you noticed in his apartment?"

"Nothing that seemed to suggest anything. I've got a couple of others on my list, too, that I've been following around a little. Alex Groton—he was Rog's boss—and a guy by the name of Fergus Villiers, who lived in that apartment house."

"You don't happen to have just sort of looked around their apartments, do you?"

Ennis grinned again. "No. But they're on my list."

"How about Warren Braddock?" Dan suggested.

Ennis looked startled. "How the hell did you know about him?"

Dan turned to Lochmeister. "I saw Viola this afternoon. She's all right. And she still thinks you're tops."

"You sure get around," Ennis said. "I thought we had that pretty well sealed up."

Lochmeister's eyes brightened. "Did you see the kid?"

"First-class," Dan said. "A real little champ."

"How the hell did you get by Braddock to see her?" Ennis asked.

"Well, I just happened to sort of climb over his garden wall."

"My God! You're another!" Ennis' sister said.

"Well, what about Braddock?" Dan asked.

Ennis scratched his head. "He's a heel. But I never thought of him as a candidate for this deal."

Dan turned to Lochmeister. "Would you mind telling me that business about your not being able to remember where you were the night you were arrested?"

Lochmeister squinted his eyes and rubbed his knuckles on his forehead. "It isn't just that I can't remember. I can in a way. I'd had a couple of drinks. I wasn't supposed to be drinking. I was crazy to touch anything, but it was the anniversary of the store, and everybody was having a few drinks after closing hour. I thought a few wouldn't hurt me, but they hit me pretty hard. That was early in the evening, of course. I began to feel kind of sick, so J. P. drove me home."

"Who do you mean by J.P.?"

"Jason P. Wyler. He's the owner. He was an old friend of my mother's. The celebration was in his office after work. All the department heads were there, and pretty nearly the whole staff from the advertising department. J. P. drove me home, and when I got in my apartment, I felt dizzy."

"Did J. P. go in with you?"

"No. He just dropped me off at the door. I had felt better when I was out in the air, but then I got dizzy again when I went in the apartment."

"About what time was this?"

"Oh, it must have been about seven o'clock when he dropped me off. I remembered that I had felt better when I was out in the air. I thought fresh air was what I needed. I remember going out, and I think I remember going to that little park on top of the hill about a half block away. I'm pretty sure that's where I went. I often used to go there to sit, so I must have gone there. I think I sat there on a bench, and then that's all that I can remember, except that I have a feeling that somebody helped me home and put me to bed. I don't know who, but I have that feeling. I seem to remember it. I remember somebody helping me off with my clothes, and I remember saying that I was sick. But that's all. When I woke up, the police were banging at my door. They came in to search the place and took me down to headquarters. They got me so confused that I couldn't answer any questions straight."

"Did they examine you to see if you had been doped?"

"No. It never occurred to me that I'd been doped. I don't think I was. You see, I wasn't supposed to drink anything."

"Who else was at that celebration in Wyler's office? Was Alex Groton there?"

"Yes, of course. Nearly the whole advertising department was there."

"Was Fergus Villiers there?"

"Yes, I remember him. He was there."

"How about Miss Sweetser?"

"Yes, come to think of it, she was there. She represents one of the manufacturers the store deals with, so I guess J. P. invited her. It was a big party; they hold it every year."

"And how about this Dr. Raymond Mills?"

"He was there with Miss Sweetser. I remember because they both snubbed me. That was because Alice Sweetser came in once when I was having a quarrel with Enid. She was a good friend of Enid's."

Ennis was thoughtful. "This dope angle interests me. I hadn't thought of that."

Lochmeister shook his head dubiously. "Oh, I don't think I was doped."

While they were talking, Clyde Ennis' sister, Pat, had taken the keys from Lochmeister's hand and was examining them. "I think I know what this is," she said, holding up the white-metal key that had a number stamped on it. "It looks like one of the keys to those checking lockers they have in bus stations and places. You know, where you drop a coin in a slot, put your bag inside, and the key is your check."

"Certainly, that's what it is." Dan took the keys from her and examined the numbered one carefully. "I knew I'd seen one before."

"Leave it to Pat to furnish the brains," Clyde said. "It's a cinch. All we have to do is phone the company and find out where that number locker is located."

"No, no," Dan warned. "If we do that, they'll think we found the key, or stole it, and be down to open the locker before we can locate it."

"Then what shall we do?"

"We'll just have to go around and find the locker for ourselves," Dan said.

CHAPTER THIRTEEN

Pat Ennis insisted on going with them. Dan's car was still parked near the department store, but Clyde had a battered old sedan at the curb. First they tried the Southern Pacific railroad station at Third and Townsend Streets, but none of the automatic-checking lockers there bore the number 297-J-6, which was stamped on the key.

Dan dropped a coin in one of the empty lockers and extracted the key to compare it with the one on the ring. They were identical except for the numbers stamped on them and the filing. The way these lockers worked was that the key would not come out until you dropped the coin, then you could unlock the small metal door, put your suitcases or packages inside, lock the door, and keep the key for your check.

From there they tried the Santa Fe bus station at Fourth and Market. Then the Greyhound station at Fifth and Mission. At neither place was there a locker numbered 297-J-6. Next they tried the San Francisco-Oakland Bay Bridge terminal, and then the ferry building at the foot of Market. In the ferry building they found it.

Dan inserted the key and opened the door. Instantly he became aware of something. Inside were two suitcases, one large and one small. On the end of the large one were the initials "A. L. S." Clyde Ennis reached for one of them, but Dan held his arm. "Wait a minute. Smell?"

Ennis hesitated and sniffed. Pat also wrinkled her nose. "It does smell funny," she said.

Dan closed the locker door and locked it again. "Recognize it?"

Ennis nodded.

"What is it?" Pat asked.

"There must be a stiff in there," Clyde said. "I'd know that smell anywhere."

"You're not fooling," Dan agreed.

"Hadn't you better look?" Pat suggested.

Clyde patted her on the shoulder. "We don't have to look, sweetheart. We've smelled too much of that in the past few years." He looked at Dan. "What'll we do?"

"We'll have to call the police," Dan said. "But you two shouldn't be around."

"Why not?" Pat asked.

"Because you've got Lochmeister in your basement, and you're not supposed to be this interested in the case. One thing leads to another, and if they find you here, you're apt to have cops stomping all over that theater of yours."

"He's right. We'd better beat it," Clyde said. "But we want to know the dope on this."

"I'll let you know as soon as I find out," Dan assured him.

"I don't care how late it is," Clyde said. "We'll either be at the theater or at my place. You know where I live."

When they had gone, Dan went in a barroom and had a straight shot. Then he phoned Inspector Gallagher from a booth in the corner. "I've got something, Neil," he said.

"You've got what?"

"Before tell you, I want it understood that we're going to cooperate."

"We always cooperate, don't we? You know me, Dan."

"I also know that we don't see this case the same way."

"Differences of opinion are what make horse races, Dan."

"Yes and horses' rumps."

"Don't get personal. What have you got?"

"Just a little corpse, probably unjointed."

"For crissake, where?"

"Wait a minute, Neil. I wouldn't go busting out of the place with a lot of sirens blowing and a herd of reporters on your heels. This had better be kept quiet for a while. Can you kind of sneak out and come quietly?"

"I've got to tell the coroner."

"Tell him quietly. Bring him along in your own car. He doesn't need the morgue wagon. Everything's conveniently packaged here."

"Where the hell are you?"

"Just come down to the ferry building. I'll see you by the flower stand."

"I don't see how anything could be secret there."

"It's quiet. Nobody knows. If you're wise, you'll take my advice."

"If I was wise, I wouldn't need advice. Stand by, Dan, I'm on my way."

Gallagher arrived with Mac McCracken and a coroner's deputy who looked like a college boy on his way to a football game in a huge overcoat and a sloppy hat.

"All right, Dan. What's the mystery?" Gallagher said.

Dan took them to the long row of checking lockers. He rattled the ring of keys significantly for Gallagher's benefit, selected the white-metal one, and opened the door of number 297-J-6.

Gallagher peeked at the suitcases, then sniffed. "Something for you, Harold," he said to the coroner's deputy.

The two other men leaned toward the opening and made phooey faces.

"Take 'em out easy," Gallagher cautioned. "Don't touch the handles. We want any fingerprints that are on them. Put them in the car."

As Mac eased the cases out, the coroner's deputy said, "They must have been here quite a while. These suitcases are practically airtight, but you could smell it anyway."

Dan rapped a knuckle on a sign above the locker.

Time limit for checking is 24 hours. If you wish to leave your luggage for a longer period, another coin must be deposited before the time elapses. This will renew your checking privilege for another 24 hours. If no coin is found in the lock, the locker will be opened and your property removed to the National Automatic Checking Company office, 314 Battery Street, San Francisco, California. You may secure your belongings by calling there and paying the storage fee due.

"According to that," Dan said, "if they've been here several days, somebody must've been coming by every day and putting a coin in the slot."

"Smart boy," Gallagher agreed.

"In that case, you'd better keep it quiet, and have a man stand by here to watch. If they don't think the body's been discovered, then sometime tonight or tomorrow they'll be along to put another coin in."

"I could figure that out myself. Where'd you get those keys?"

"Let's discuss that later," Dan said.

"Have you any idea who it might be?" Gallagher asked.

"The initials on one of those suitcases are A. L. S. The only person I can think of they might fit is Alice Sweetser."

Gallagher scratched his head. "Let's see, now. That name seems familiar."

"She was one of the witnesses at Lochmeister's trial. She lived in the apartment just above him."

"Oh, yes. Oh, yes. What makes you think they're her cases?"

"Well, she's kind of dropped out of sight. It isn't certain, but just to be on the safe side, why don't you have a certain Raymond Mills brought in right away for questioning. He's Alice Sweetser's boy friend. He told me this morning he knew where she was."

"We'd better find out if they're her suitcases first, don't you think?"

"You'll want him anyhow to make an identification of the body."

"You mean you think this Alice Sweetser might be in her own suitcases?"

"It's just sort of a hunch."

"What would I do without you to tell me how to do my job?" Gallagher asked sarcastically.

"Probably hang half the innocent people in the city."

"You may be right at that. I hate this job." Gallagher closed the metal door and locked it again. He shook the ring of keys in front of Dan's nose. "We'll be talking about these later."

Mac McCracken returned from the street. "We've got the grips in the car, Neil."

"Good. You stay here and watch this locker, Mac." Gallagher banged his knuckles against 297-J-6. "Somebody's been coming by every day putting coins in it to hold it. He'll probably be back again."

"Is it Lochmeister?" Mac asked.

"It might be Hitler for all I know. No matter who monkeys with that box, nab him."

CHAPTER FOURTEEN

Seated behind the scarred and footworn desk in his office, Inspector Gallagher threw the ring of keys in front of Dan and said, "All right, son. Start talking."

"How about Dr. Mills? Are you going to have him picked up?"

"I'm having him brought in. He'll be along in a minute. What I want to know is where you got these keys and how you happened to stumble onto that checking locker."

"What did you find in the suitcases?"

"It was a dame—that is, various parts of a dame. They're trying to fit them together now."

"Are all the parts there?"

"Most of them, I guess. It was a hell of a hash. There was only one leg, though."

"One leg? Say, what about that leg that was found in Golden Gate Park yesterday?"

"I thought of that. They're trying to match it up now. They'll have a report soon. What I want to know is about these keys."

"Any identification?"

"None. There are some laundry marks on the clothes. We're having them checked."

"What does it look like? Gus the Grue?"

"It's Lochmeister's technique, all right. No doubt about that."

"I said Gus the Grue, not Lochmeister."

"Let's not get started on that again, Dan. I want to know what you've been up to and where you got these keys."

"If the leg you found yesterday fits this corpse, then Lochmeister couldn't have done it. According to the coroner's own report, that leg had been hacked off about two days before Lochmeister escaped."

"Nobody said the leg fitted. They haven't even tried to match it up yet. So that's beside the point." The phone rang, Gallagher ripped it from its holder. "Gallagher speaking. Yeah. Yeah. Yeah. No. Well, I'll be damned! Are you sure? That's impossible! No, no. I'll be down later. Do the best you can."

As Gallagher hung up the phone, Dan said, "So it fits."

Gallagher's face was a study in confusion. "Yeah, it fits."

Dan puffed contentedly at his pipe. "I'll just sit here quietly for a few minutes and give you time to figure out what that means."

Gallagher picked up the ring of keys, jingled it fitfully, and threw it down again. "You'll do, hell! You'll start talking about where you got these keys. Even if I have to shove you under a light and work on you with a rubber hose."

Dan straightened up and took the pipe out of his mouth. "Listen, Neil. That's a hell of a way to talk to a friend. It isn't funny and it isn't smart. I've already lost my job over this thing, but I could put through a phone call right now, give them the story, and get the job back. I'm not doing it, because I'm playing square with you. I'm keeping quiet so that whoever has been putting coins in that checking locker won't be tipped off and you'll have a chance to nab him."

Gallagher massaged his nose with his fist and cleared his throat. "You're right, Dan. Forget it. You know I wouldn't do a thing like that. But, damn it, son, I've got to have information."

"You've just received information proving that Lochmeister's innocent."

"It doesn't prove anything, Dan. This might have been done by somebody entirely different."

"Last night, because the murder showed signs of the same technique, you were insisting it had to be Lochmeister. Tonight, when the same signs turn up showing Lochmeister's innocent, you decide they don't mean anything."

"I didn't say they don't mean anything, Dan. This puts me in an awful hole. You know that."

"Listen, Neil. Lochmeister's the one who's in a hole. All this does to you is hurt your pride and cause you a little trouble."

"Dan, please. Where the hell did you get those keys?"

"Mrs. Murchison, the landlady in the rooming house, found them on the telephone stand in the hall last night. She thought they belonged to one of the roomers. I got them from her this morning."

"Why the hell didn't you bring them to me?"

"I did bring them to you. That's where you got them. You wouldn't even know they existed if it wasn't for me. One of those keys fits the apartment Lochmeister used to live in. Another fits Alice Sweetser's apartment on the floor above. That's as far as I was able to check. I don't know what the other ones fit. But come to think about it, maybe you'd better have Enid Hoyte, Lochmeister's former wife, picked up too. She used to live in that apartment, you know. She would have had a key, and she was a very good friend of Alice Sweetser. She used to use the phone in Alice Sweetser's apartment, and she might have had a key to that, too."

Gallagher ripped the phone from its nest again. "Now that's the kind of information I want." He barked an order to have Enid Hoyte picked up and brought in. "Now what else do you know?"

"That's all. But it's enough to indicate to me that this whole case should be ripped wide open, and your department should get busy trying to find out who has really been committing these murders."

Gallagher clasped his big hands and tapped his combined knuckles against his chin. He looked worried. "That's not going to be easy."

"For the love of God, Neil. You can't lock a man in the insane asylum for life just to get out of a little work."

"You know me better than that, Dan. If this boy, Lochmeister, didn't do it, I'll never stop fighting until I clear him. I don't give a damn if it costs me my job or anything else. But I'm thinking of Raglan, the district attorney. It's not going to sit well with him, and you know how he and I are. He reads the obituaries every day hoping to Christ I've dropped dead. There's an election coming up, and if things are bungling like this, it wouldn't do his office any good. He'll throw every difficulty possible in my way."

Dan grinned. "Don't worry, Neil. If you lose your job I know an old Lithuanian who will let us sleep in a basement with him."

"What the hell are you talking about?" The phone rang and Gallagher answered it. "Sure, bring him right in." He hung up. "That's your Dr. Raymond Mills. They've got him outside. You sit right there, Dan. You'd better be in on this. Something tells me I'm going to need you a lot before this is through. What the hell were you saying about a Lithuanian?"

The question was left unanswered. The door opened and Dink

Buford came in guiding Dr. Raymond Mills. Dink pulled up a chair, opened a notebook, and tested the sharpness of a pencil on his thumb. Dr. Mills stood, hat in hand, with a what-the-hell-is-this-all-about expression on his face.

"Sit down, Doctor. Have a chair," Gallagher said warmly.

Mills seated himself gingerly. He looked at Dan with nervous recognition. "I don't exactly understand," he said, "why I have been brought here."

"Oh, it's just a routine matter," Gallagher purred. "You are a friend, I believe, of a Miss Alice Sweetser."

"Has anything happened to Miss Sweetser?" Mills asked in alarm.

"We're just trying to locate her, that's all. You don't happen to know her whereabouts at the present time, do you?"

Mills looked nervously at Dan and back to Gallagher. "No. Frankly, I don't."

Gallagher was about to say something, but Dan interrupted. "You told me this afternoon that you did."

Mills was embarrassed. "Yes, I did tell you that, but it wasn't true."

"Where was this?" Gallagher asked Dan.

"This afternoon I called at Miss Sweetser's apartment. She wasn't in, but Dr. Mills here answered the door. He said she was out of town but that he didn't like to say where, because, since Lochmeister had escaped, he didn't want her whereabouts known. That was because he was afraid Lochmeister might try to take revenge against her for testifying in his trial."

"I know I said that," Dr. Mills admitted, "but it wasn't true. I really didn't know where she was. I said that because—well, you told me you were a newspaper reporter, and I didn't think it was any of your business."

"What were you doing in Miss Sweetser's apartment?" Gallagher asked.

Dr. Mills blushed. "Well, that's really not fair to ask."

"If you haven't any satisfactory explanation," Gallagher said, "we'll have to classify it as burglary."

"I was merely looking for Miss Sweetser."

"What business did you have entering her apartment if she wasn't home?"

"Miss Sweetser and I have been very close friends."

"How did you get in?"

"I had a key."

"And how did you happen to have a key?"

Mills was now blushing crimson. "Miss Sweetser gave me one. You see, we are very close friends, and very often when she is out of town, I look in to see that everything is all right. She had asked me to do that, of course."

"You knew, then, that Miss Sweetser was out of town."

"Oh, yes."

"Then why would you be looking for her in her apartment?"

"Well, I thought she may have come home. I wanted to see."

"Didn't she tell you where she was going when she left?"

"No."

"Was it usual for her to leave town without telling you where she was going?"

"No."

"But on this occasion she did."

"Yes."

"Why?"

"Well, I really don't know. To tell you the truth, I am rather worried."

"Why are you worried?"

"Well, not knowing where she is, it naturally worries me."

"How did you know that she had left town?"

"Her suitcases are gone. She is a representative of a women's clothing manufacturer. She travels up and down the state and very often leaves town."

"Had she ever gone off before without saying something to you?"

"No."

"There didn't happen to be any quarrel or anything between you and Miss Sweetser?"

"Not exactly—well, no."

"What do you mean by 'not exactly'?"

"I mean no."

"There had been no quarrel?"

"No. Of course not. I really don't understand why you're asking these questions. Has anything happened to Miss Sweetser? I feel entitled to know."

Gallagher rose. "Well, we might as well have a look. You come too, Dan."

After taking an elevator down to the basement, they turned a corner and started along a hallway toward a white door plainly labeled "Morgue." As the sign became visible, Mills' legs buckled under him. Dan grabbed him from one side and Gallagher from the other and prevented him from falling. They laid him out on the linoleum. His face was pale as cigarette paper. "Get some smelling salts, Dink," Gallagher ordered.

When Dink got back with the small bottle, Gallagher wafted it under Dr. Mills' nostrils, and he came slowly to his senses.

"That's a funny way for a doctor to behave," Gallagher said.

"He's a dentist," Dan reminded him.

Mills' eyes were full of terror. "I don't want to see her."

"You don't want to see who?" Gallagher asked.

"Alice. I don't want to see her."

"How do you know it's Alice?"

"I know it is. I don't want to see her."

"Oh! So you know, do you?" Gallagher said meaningly.

Mills hesitated. "Isn't it?"

"You were just telling us it was," Gallagher said.

Mills clutched at his arms. "It *is* Alice, isn't it? Tell me."

"What made you say that?"

"Don't torture me. Tell me."

"You better have a look," Gallagher said.

They hoisted him to his feet and guided him down the hall, Gallagher holding him by one arm and Dink by the other. When they got to within pushing distance of the door, his knees buckled again, but he didn't faint. Gallagher and Dink held him up, and half dragged him through. Dan held the door open for them, his eyes intent on Dr. Mills' face.

The morgue attendants were working over the body on a porcelain table as they entered. One of them stepped aside revealing the face. Mills screamed and tried to tear his arms free from Gallagher and Dink. He was moaning hysterically.

Dan couldn't stand it any longer. "Take him out of here," he said. "For crissake, take him out!"

Gallagher's jaw was clenched. "He's got to have a good look."

They held him there for several minutes, then dragged him into an adjoining room. He was struggling and gibbering wildly. They threw him in a chair, and Gallagher slapped his face several times, hard. That brought him out of it. His moaning stopped and he began to blink his eyes.

"Why did you kill her?" Gallagher roared.

"No! No! My God, no!" Mills sobbed.

"We know you did," Gallagher barked. "You don't have to deny it."

"What do you mean?"

Gallagher slapped his face again. "Why did you do it?"

Dan grabbed Gallagher by the shoulder. "Neil, use some sense. That's stupid."

"If you can't take it, Dan, get the hell out of here." Gallagher motioned to Dink. "Come on, let's get him upstairs."

They half pushed, half dragged him down the corridor toward the elevator, Dan following with a disgusted look on his face. On the way up, he said to Gallagher, "Whenever I begin to think you're different, you always do something to remind me that you're just the same as the rest."

"I know my job," Gallagher grunted, sullenly. When they got out of the elevator, he said to Dan, "You go wait in my office. This job isn't in your line."

They dragged Mills off down the corridor toward another room. Dan returned to Gallagher's office biting his lip. As he opened the door, he saw Nix Peters and Enid Hoyte sitting in the anteroom with a plain-clothes man standing behind them.

"Hi, Dan," Nix greeted him. "What's this all about? Do you know?"

"What's what all about?"

"Enid and I were sitting in her apartment making some notes on 'I Married a Monster,' when this guy comes along and says Gallagher wants to talk to her."

Dan shrugged. "I guess he just wants to talk to her, that's all."

"In a pig's eye. Something's up. What is it?"

"How should I know?"

Nix haw-hawed sarcastically. "How should you know? To you the world's a wide-open keyhole. Come on, brother, give."

"Wait'll Gallagher comes. Maybe he just wants to ask her some routine questions."

"Listen, Dan, I can't read your mind, but I can read your face like a first-grade primer. You've got that look."

"My mother remarked about it the minute I was born."

"Yeah, well, I'm the guy Abraham Lincoln was talking about when he said there are some fools you can't fool all the time. From now on I'm hanging right onto your coat-tail. I'm going to be just like a tattoo on your chest, till I find out what's up."

Enid Hoyte looked up with big, empty eyes. "You would think I had suffered enough."

"You don't know these boys, honey," Nix said. "They can always grind another groan out of your carcass."

Gallagher came in wiping his hands on a handkerchief. He jerked his head at Dan. "Come on in, Dan, I want to see you." He ignored Nix and Enid Hoyte.

When they were alone in his private office, Dan said, "What did you do, beat his brains out?"

Gallagher shoved the handkerchief in his back pocket and shook his head. "He won't talk."

"He won't say what you want, you mean. Did he definitely identify the body?"

"Yeah. It's the Sweetser dame. He looks like our man, all right."

"He looks to me like a guy who's heartbroken and getting as dirty a slapping around as I've ever seen."

"Don't talk like a goddamn fool, Dan. He knew who was in that morgue. He knew what he was going to see before he even got to the door."

"Of course he did."

"Well, don't that indicate something to you?"

"No. You bring him to your office and question him about Alice Sweetser. He'd been afraid something might happen to her right along. Then, without a word of warning, you march him down to the morgue. He'd have to be pretty dense not to be able to figure it out. Naturally he knew what to expect."

Gallagher thought it over. "There's something in that, maybe, but I can't afford to take chances."

"Why the hell don't you let him get over the shock before you begin questioning him?"

"Now that's where you're all cockeyed, Dan. That's just what you don't want to do. That's what you guys don't understand who aren't experienced in this line. You want to drive right at him before he's had a chance to think it over. Give a man a chance to cool off and collect himself, and you'll never get the truth out of him."

"You're not getting a damn thing out of him now, are you?"

"He's a tough case."

"Listen, Neil, if you'll give the guy a couple of slugs of whisky and let him calm down, he may have all sorts of information. But you'll never get it that way. He probably knows all about Alice Sweetser and the people who lived in the apartment house. Quit trying to slug a confession out of him and question him sensibly."

"All right," Gallagher said. "Let's skip it. Let's just drop the subject. You've got your ideas, and I've got mine. Let's let it stand at that." But Dan could tell by his tone that he'd got his point over. Gallagher would seldom concede you an issue in argument, but he was usually quick to take your advice when your back was turned. "Let's have that Enid Hoyte in here now and see what she's got to say."

"Wait a minute," Dan said. "Nix Peters is with her. If you let her know what's up, it'll be all over the front page of the *Express* within an hour."

Gallagher nodded his head. "I'll play it easy. She won't get wise." He lifted the phone and ordered them to bring in Enid Hoyte.

Enid slipped in with a grieved look and perched on the edge of a chair like a bird.

Gallagher threw the ring of keys in front of her. "Do you recognize those?"

Enid picked them up, turned them over in her hand, and dropped them. "No."

"Never saw them before?"

"No. I don't think so. They look like any other ring of keys."

"Look at the keys closely. See if you recognize any of them."

She picked up the ring again, examined each individual key, then shrugged her shoulders. "I don't think so."

Gallagher took the keys and dropped them in the top drawer of his desk. "You had a key to Rogan Lochmeister's apartment—that is, before you were separated, didn't you?"

"Yes, of course. But that was before I realized he was a monster."

"What became of the key? Did you take it with you when you left?"

"I don't remember."

"Try to think."

Enid Hoyte sat quite still for a minute with a blank face. They hoped she was thinking. "No. I can't remember. I don't remember leaving it, but then I don't remember taking it with me."

"Could it be possible that you still have it?"

"It may be. I don't know."

"It would be on your key ring, wouldn't it?"

"I don't carry a key ring. I just keep the keys in my purse."

"Is it in your purse now?"

She opened the purse and poked through it with a red-painted fingernail. "No. I only have the key to my apartment." She held up the key.

"You also had a key to Miss Sweetser's apartment, didn't you?"

"Yes, I did. I used her telephone, you know. She gave me a key."

"What did you do with that key when you moved?"

Her face looked blank again. "I don't know."

"Did you give it back to Miss Sweetser?"

"I don't know. Maybe I did. I never thought about it."

"You could have taken it along with you, though."

"Maybe. It never occurred to me. Why? What difference does it make?"

Gallagher questioned her about keys until he was exhausted. Probing the contents of her mind was like straining water. When asked if any men had visited her in her apartment while Lochmeister was away, she was indignant. Gallagher asked her if she knew Dr. Raymond Mills. She did, and thought that he was a very nice man. Alice Sweetser, she said, was a very nice girl. Finally wearying of throwing out questions and drawing blanks, Gallagher asked her a little about Lochmeister in order to give her the impression that finding Lochmeister was his only concern. She explained to him that being married to a monster had ruined her life, and that he couldn't possibly understand the suffering she had been through.

Gallagher admitted that he had never been married to a monster, and guessed that in that respect he was lucky, and escorted her to the door.

When she had gone, Dan said, "Listen, Neil, I realize you've got to keep the news quiet on this for at least twenty-four hours, but when the story does break I feel entitled to an advantage. I'd like to see a couple of editors eat their words."

"I've eaten a lot of grammar in my own time," Gallagher said, "but this is a dirty mouthful. I wish now I hadn't bragged so much when we caught Lochmeister."

"It won't hurt you much. People think cops are dumb anyway."

Gallagher sighed. "The people have a way of being right. I guess that's what's good about democracy."

"You haven't answered my question. Do I get a break on this story?"

"Hell, Dan, you can practically write your own ticket."

CHAPTER FIFTEEN

Nix Peters was still waiting in the outer room.

"Where's Enid?" Dan asked. "Didn't you see her home?"

"I put her in a taxi," Nix said. "I'm sticking right with you from now on."

"Well, isn't that nice. Have you got a car?"

"Such as it is. You've seen it."

"Fine. You can drive me to where I parked mine."

As they climbed into Nix Peters' rusty prewar coupe, Nix said, "Don't try to kid me, Dan. Something's doing, and I know it. Come on, give."

"You'll have to sit tight, Nix. I'm not talking. But I'll give you one little tip. Go easy on featuring Lochmeister as a demon."

"What do you mean?"

"It may turn out he didn't commit these crimes after all."

"Oh, that's impossible, Dan. Don't be a kill-joy."

"What do you want them to do? Hang an innocent man?"

"That's not the point, Dan. It's a hell of a thing to say just when I'm about to clean up some dough with 'I Married a Monster.' It's coming along fine. We knocked out two chapters this afternoon. The paper's going to syndicate it and run it serially. I've already got an agent working on the movie rights."

"Everything that's yellow isn't gold, Nix."

"Don't joke about it, Dan. It's my big opportunity to amount to something."

When they reached the dark street near Wyler's department store, where Dan had parked, Nix got out and followed him to his car. "Don't think you're going to ditch me," he said. "Where you go, I go. I'm tired of being a dummy."

At that moment, Nix felt a blunt object poke hard in the back of his ribs. A gruff voice barked in his ear. "Just be quiet, fellow, and you'll live to collect your Social Security."

Dan felt another gun in his own back. "Go on, you two. Get in the car. Not a word out of you. Understand?" The men pushed them toward a dark sedan that was parked near Dan's car.

"Wait a minute," Nix said. "I haven't any dough. I'm a newspaper reporter. Why don't you stick up the publisher?"

"Shut up, wise guy, and get in the front seat."

Nix was forced into the front seat between two men. Dan was in the back with a third man holding a gun on him. The man at the wheel drove as if he had borrowed the car from his worst enemy and intended to return it without gears.

"What are you guys? Gangsters?" Nix said.

"There ain't no more gangsters, bud. That was prewar stuff. We're the White Knights of the Flaming Torch. We're going to save the country from the Jews and niggers."

"Oh, that outfit," Nix said. "Supermen. Well, my mother was Irish and my father was Swiss. Not that I've got anything against Jews and colored people, but why are you picking on me?"

"You guys are biting off a mouthful," Dan said from the back seat. "We happen to be newspaper reporters."

"You mean you work for the Jew press," the driver sneered.

Nix hawed. "That's a hot one. My boss sees eye to eye with you guys. He's a heel too."

The man next to him gave him a loud slap on the side of the face.

"Just remember, fellow," Dan said quietly, "anything you dish out you're going to get back double."

"Shut up, kike."

Nix was quiet for a few minutes after the slap in the ear. Then he began to hum softly the "Battle Hymn of the Republic." The man next to him lifted an arm to hit him again, but the driver pulled in to a curb. They'd evidently reached their destination.

It was an old red sandstone building on Pacific Street just off Van Ness Avenue. Dan noticed the number, 1822, as they climbed the steps. The door was opened by a man in a khaki shirt with a felt flaming-torch symbol sewed on his sleeve. When they were inside the gaunt, sparsely-furnished hall, the man in the shirt clicked his heels and placed his right hand on his left shoulder. The three other men did likewise. The man in the shirt then did a neat about-face and led them to the rear of the house.

In a big room that had apparently once been a library but was now lined with empty shelves, a man in a white mask that covered his entire face was sitting behind a flat-topped desk.

The three men clicked their heels and put their hands on their left shoulders. The man behind the desk stood at attention and returned their salute.

"What did you do with all the books?" Nix asked. "Burn them?" One of the men belted him across the ear, and he shut up.

A White Knight took a length of rubber hose from a shelf. Another brought an American flag from behind the leader's desk and held it in front of Dan. The masked leader spoke in a strange tone. "Get down on your knees, Jew, and kiss the flag." He was obviously holding something in his teeth to disguise his voice.

"You can go to hell," Dan said.

One of the White Knights smacked him across the ear with the rubber hose.

"Get down on your knees and kiss the flag," the leader repeated.

"All this is going down in the books," Dan said.

The man with the rubber hose smacked him hard again.

"That flag," Dan said, "is the symbol of men who fought erect in order that other men could live erect. Any man who crawls on his knees to kiss it is insulting everything it stands for."

The man smacked him again with the rubber hose. "Put him in the chair," the leader said.

Two of the men forced Dan into a chair and held him there while a third tied his arms to the sides with a rope.

The man in the mask came around from behind the desk and slapped Dan's face ten or twelve times with a loose hand. "Where is that Jew Lochmeister?"

Dan said nothing.

The man walked to the desk and took a pair of pliers from a drawer. "You know where he is and you're going to talk. You're not dealing with dumb cops now. You're going to tell us where that Jew rapist is hiding, and this time we're going to take care of him ourselves." He returned to Dan and took a pinch of his hair in the pliers. "Where's Lochmeister?"

Dan remained silent.

The man yanked, and the hair came out by the roots. He took another pinch. "Where is Lochmeister?"

Dan said nothing.

He yanked again. "Where is he?"

Dan gritted his jaw and remained silent.

The man locked the pliers around one of Dan's fingers and began to squeeze.

"Christ! That's enough!" Nix said. "I'll talk."

Dan shot him a glance and caught the idea. "Shut up, you fool."

"I don't give a damn what you say. I'm going to tell them," Nix raved. "They're not going to do that to me. You must be crazy."

"You'll get yours if you talk," Dan said.

The man in the mask slapped him hard across the face. "Shut up, Jew." He turned to Nix. "Go on. Talk, and talk fast."

"Wait a minute," Nix said. "There was a lot of dough in this for me. I had a thousand bucks coming for my end of the deal. I don't give a damn about Lochmeister, but if I tell you, the deal's all loused up. I won't get a nickel."

"If you don't talk, you'll get your fingers broken," the masked man said.

"If you talk, Nix, I'll get you," Dan said, grimly. "So help me God, I'll get you if it's the last thing I do."

The masked man belted him again. "Talk!" he yelled at Nix.

"There's one other thing," Nix said. "Hiding this guy out has been a little against the law. I've only had a small hand in it, but if I tell you I'll want protection."

"You'll get protection," the masked man said. "Talk!"

"Shut up, Nix!" Dan shouted. "Don't be a yellow bastard."

"To hell with you," Nix said. "I value my knuckles more than a few lousy dollars. The guy's hiding in a barn in back of a residence at 1432 Eighteenth Avenue."

"You dirty, damn rat!" Dan screamed.

The man belted him across the mouth again. "What is this place?" he asked Nix.

"A Jew named Ballantine lives there. His name used to be

Weinstein, but he changed it. Lochmeister had a lot of dough stashed away in a safe-deposit box. He's paying Ballantine off, and he was paying us off."

Dan bowed his head dejectedly and muttered to himself. The masked man barked an order to one of his White Knights. "Assemble all men available. We move tonight."

"You better bring enough men to surround the building," Nix said. "There are a lot of ways for them to get out." Feeling that he had established himself in good graces, he took out a cigarette and lit it. No one seemed to object.

The man in the mask strode to his desk, put on a shoulder holster, and fitted a large black automatic into it. From the hall came the sounds of rumbling feet and excited voices.

"You two are coming with us," the masked man snapped. He looked meaningly at Nix. "And if you're lying, you'll get what we intended for Lochmeister. Come on, men."

They untied Dan from his chair and pushed him toward the door. Nix walked over to the desk and seemed to be snuffing his cigarette in an ash tray.

The masked man barked at him from the doorway. "Come along, you. Take charge of him, boys. We don't know if we can trust him yet."

Outside, three cars were drawn up at the curb, two of them crammed with White Knights. Dan and Nix were pushed into the third car, along with the three men who had brought them and the man in the mask. The three motors roared simultaneously and the cavalcade plunged forward.

The cars leaned on their springs at every corner, and the tires screeched on the paving. After a while, Nix turned to the man at the wheel and asked, "Did you ever drive a car before?"

"Shut up," snapped the masked man.

Out on Eighteenth Avenue, in the Richmond district, the cars stopped at a curb around the corner from the fourteen-hundred block. "You go ahead and reconnoiter," the masked man said to one of his Knights. "See if there is a barn in back of 1432, and see if the name on the mailbox is Ballantine."

The man came back in a few minutes. "It's right, Commander. That's the joint. This guy was giving it straight."

"Is there a barn in back?" asked the masked man.

"There's a barn in back, and there's a light in a little window up high. The name on the box is Ballantine, all right."

The man in the mask chuckled. He leaned forward and patted Nix on the shoulder. "Good man." He barked an order and the Knights began piling out of their cars.

"You two stay here and watch these men," the commander said. "If they make a move, let 'em have it."

"Oh, now, you shouldn't talk that way about me," Nix complained.

The commander ignored him. "Go up quietly, two and three at a time. The first squad is to surround the barn. Cover every entrance and every window where he might jump out. The second squad will surround the house. Cover front and back and all the side windows. Don't make a noise until I blow my whistle. Then we all move in at once. All except those who are assigned to watch the windows. Now, have you got it?"

They all placed their right hands on their left shoulders.

"Good. When you hear the whistle, pile right in. Grab whoever you see. Now get going."

Two or three at a time, they rounded the corner and sauntered up the street. Soon there were none remaining except the two men guarding Dan and Nix. For what seemed like a long time, the street was quiet. Most of the people had gone to bed, and there were few lights in windows. Suddenly a sharp whistle cut the night air.

"They're going in," one of the Knights said, excitedly.

"You boys go on up and see the fun," Nix suggested. "I'll watch this bastard."

"You shut up," the Knight ordered.

"You watch them," the other said. "I'm going to go up to the corner and have a look."

He wandered to the corner, and they could see him peeking up the street. Suddenly, three shots rang out in the distance.

The Knight who was guarding them looked instinctively in that direction. Dan was out of the car and on top of him before he could rally his senses. He ripped the gun from the Knight's hand and laid him out on the sidewalk with a fist to the jaw.

The man at the corner whirled around and reached for his gun. Dan fired, and he sagged into the gutter.

The other Knight had struggled halfway to his feet. Dan fired again, and he flattened out.

Dan ran to the corner, leaned over the man in the gutter, and took his gun. Hefting a revolver in each hand, he peered around the edge of the building and up the street. Two Knights, who had heard the shots, were running toward him. He aimed carefully and fired twice. One fell on the sidewalk and the other on a lawn.

There was another Knight standing in front of number 1432. Dan fired again. The man staggered but did not go down. Dan fired once more, and saw him crumple.

Nix had come up and was watching over Dan's shoulder. "For crissake, do you expect to get them all?"

"If I can," Dan said coldly.

"You're not in uniform now, you know."

"My kind of uniform doesn't come off."

"Let's get out of here, Dan, before they come back."

"Not till I get that guy with the mask."

Two more White Knights came running out of 1432. It took Dan four shots, but he dropped one at the gate and one on the stairs. Several more shots sounded from inside the house.

"Who the hell is this Ballantine?" Dan asked.

"Oh. Him?" Nix said. "That's Captain Ballantine of the Riot Squad. He has two brothers who are cops too. They all live there. I figured it was a nice place to steer them."

Lights had come on in every house up and down the street, and heads were poking out of windows. A siren screamed, and a police car ripped around the corner, burning rubber. It pulled in to the curb near Dan and Nix. Two officers piled out. "All right. Put your hands up—high—over your heads."

Dan and Nix obliged. As one of the officers took the guns, Dan said, "A bunch of Fascists are raiding Captain Ballantine's house up the street. I got seven of them. The rest are up to you."

Several Knights were running fiercely down the street. When they saw the police car, they turned and ran in the other direction.

CHAPTER SIXTEEN

Captain Ballantine had close-cropped red hair and a face that was a tapestry of freckles. He shook his fist at Nix Peters, who was seated on one of the hard chairs in Inspector Gallagher's office. "If I had one half the sense of a cockroach," he said, "I would tear you limb from limb and throw each piece out a different window."

"Now, Sam," Gallagher soothed, "let's not lose our heads."

Nix shifted uneasily under the threat of Captain Ballantine's gigantic freckled fist. He had reason to be thankful that Ballantine did not have half the sense of a cockroach. "You've got to have a sense of humor about these things," he suggested.

"Humor!" Ballantine exploded. "It's funny as hell isn't it? Every goddamn window in my house is broken."

"Now, Sam," Gallagher soothed, "he had to give them some address.

He couldn't very well send them to the Hall of Justice." One of the younger Ballantine brothers, a lean, muscular motorcycle cop, spoke up. "Neil is right, Sam. Cool yourself off. As far as I'm concerned, I was glad enough to get a crack at those bastards."

All of the Ballantine brothers had been at home when the White Knights of the Flaming Torch came crashing in. Three of them, who were police officers, were asleep in the house. A fourth, who was a chemist, had been at work in his experimental laboratory upstairs in the old barn.

"What is the casualty list?" Dan asked.

"Three dead, ten wounded, and two captured," Gallagher said. "The rest of them got away. I don't know how many there were in all."

"How about the man in the mask?" Dan asked.

"He was one of the first to blow," Gallagher said. "We didn't get our hands on him. The ones we have in jail and in the hospital claim they don't know who he is. They say they know him only as 'The Voice.'"

"Who are these guys? Have you checked up on them?"

"Most of them are pool-hall bums," Gallagher said. "A lot of them have police records. Some of them are gun-nutty clerks. They must have some dough in back of them. That shyster attorney, Cecil Jerome, has already showed up with bail for the whole lot of them."

Captain Ballantine jerked his thumb at Dan. "This fellow ought to be booked for manslaughter."

The lean brother protested. "If you do that I'll swear in court that I shot every one of the bastards."

Dan turned on Captain Ballantine. "Go ahead and charge me. It would make a nice case. Do you want to encourage a lot of bigots to run lynch mobs? There's only one way to fight such guys, and that is with their own weapons. They know that one man with a gun can handle a hundred men armed only with arguments and ideals. That's their trump card."

"Take it easy, Dan," Gallagher said. "You're not going to be charged with anything. You were within your rights."

"Since when does a man have the right to stage a massacre?" Ballantine demanded.

"He didn't do all the shooting," Gallagher explained. "As a matter of fact, he may not have killed anybody. We don't know at the moment which of them were shot out on the street and which were shot in the house. You fellows were spraying your guns all over the place in that house, you know."

"I took a couple of shots out the window, too," the lean brother said.

The chemist brother spoke up for the first time. "I pushed one out the window of the barn. He fell onto a lot of old bottles in the yard. That might account for one of them."

Dan had no inclination to evade responsibility. "I dropped seven of them," he said. "Make no mistake about that."

"Yeah, and how many did this guy shoot?" Captain Ballantine asked, jerking his thumb at Nix Peters.

"Who, me? I wouldn't harm a soul," Nix said.

Gallagher glared at Captain Ballantine. "It doesn't make a damn bit of difference who shot them. There's one thing you've got to get straight in your head, Sam. And that is that police officers haven't any exclusive privilege when it comes to protecting the lives and rights of Americans. If any Ku-Kluxer or two-bit Fascist attacks an American in his home or on the street, he has every right to blow the bastard's head off, and he's a damn fool if he doesn't. Dan and Nix didn't attack your home. Those Fascist hooligans did. If you want to be mad at anybody, get mad at them."

"What did you find out at their place on Pacific Street?" Dan asked.

"That joint? It burned down," Gallagher said. "I can't quite figure it. There's something screwy about it."

"Burned down?"

"Yeah, a three-alarm fire. It happened just about the time they were raiding Ballantine's place."

"You don't suppose they planned it themselves?" Captain Ballantine suggested.

"I don't know," Gallagher said. "But it was a hell of a fire."

Dan looked at Nix Peters. Nix had a very innocent expression and had become interested in reblocking his hat. He would pinch it and push it a little and then hold it off to study the effect.

"Was there anything in the wreckage," Dan asked, "that would indicate who the man in the mask was?"

"The firemen hauled out a bunch of junk. I haven't had time to look it over." Gallagher yawned. "And I'm not going to look it over tonight. I don't care what you guys do, but I'm going to get some sleep."

As they filed out the door, Captain Ballantine said to Nix, "I'll just be waiting until you step out of line once. Just you park too close to a hydrant, or let me catch you jaywalking on Market Street, and I'll beat your brains out for resisting arrest."

Gallagher held Dan's arm. "I want to speak to you for a minute, Dan." He closed the door on the others and went over to his desk. "Have you got any special hunches about this business tonight?"

"Hmmm, well, no."

"I think you're a liar."

"Well, at least nothing worth mentioning at the moment."

Gallagher bit his thumb and thought the matter over. "Of course, it might be just as these nuts say. They were out to get Lochmeister because they thought it would be good publicity for their organization. They figured if they nabbed him before the police, they'd be public heroes."

"In that case," Dan said, "what made them think I knew where he was?"

"Search me." A suspicious thought struck Gallagher. "You *don't* know where he is, do you?"

"What ever gave you that idea?"

"I wouldn't put it past you."

"Don't be crazy."

"They must have had some reason for thinking you knew."

Dan shrugged. "What gets me is how they knew my car was parked where it was."

"Offhand, I'd say somebody must have been following you."

"That's what I'm thinking."

"You're positive you don't know where Lochmeister's hiding?" Gallagher closed his left eye and peered at him from the corner of his right.

"Don't be ridiculous, Neil."

"You'd be wise to cut me in more, Dan. You know you can't keep this up forever. One of these days, I'm going to find you in an alley full of slugs, and I'm not going to like it."

"Thanks, Neil. That is, thanks for not liking it."

Gallagher opened a drawer, took out a small, blunt revolver, and poked it across the desk. "Would you mind keeping that in your pocket for me, Dan? It's an old family heirloom, and I'm afraid the janitor or someone might steal it. You know how careless I am about such things."

"No, thanks," Dan said.

"Why not?"

"I just don't like the idea."

"You seem to know how to handle one. That was a fierce little exhibition of marksmanship you gave tonight."

"Sometimes a man is good at a lot of things he'd rather not do at all."

"Suit yourself," Gallagher said. "But if you think walking around unarmed among a bunch of murdering heels is romantic or noble or heroic, you're just a conceited ass who hasn't any better sense than to give an extra advantage to his enemy."

Dan grinned and picked up the gun. "It's against the law to carry one of these."

"Not if I give it to you."

Dan slipped it in his pocket. "I hope I won't need it."

"One more thing," Gallagher said. "I sort of feel it in my bones that you're going to catch up to that guy in the mask before I do. I don't give a damn what you do to him, but don't shoot him. Leave enough of him for me to get some information out of."

In the outer office Nix Peters was waiting. "Do you still think it's a good idea to hang around me?" Dan asked.

"What the hell. I got a story, didn't I? Let's go up to Chinatown and get some noodles."

"Not me. I'm going to bed."

On the way down in the elevator, Nix said, "I think I'll go home with you."

"I've brought a lot of things home in my time," Dan said, "but nothing that looked like you."

"You're going to have a hard time shaking me. I'm not so dumb."

"That's a controversial subject."

"Well, at least I have sense enough to figure out one thing. You know where Lochmeister is."

"Don't be a damn fool."

"That fink wasn't pulling your hair out for nothing. You've got information, and he knew it."

"Listen, Nix. If I knew anything, I'd have better sense than to tell you."

"Is that any way to talk to a guy who just saved your life?"

"Well, I guess I do owe you a little something."

"Don't mention it," Nix said. "My God! I left my car down on that street where yours is parked. I don't like the idea of going around there again."

"Don't worry. They won't be back."

They took a taxi downtown. On the way, Nix said, "I'm beginning to see the light."

"You couldn't see any light if your nose was on fire."

"That crack you made about Lochmeister being innocent—there's something to it, isn't there?"

"Well, if I were you, I wouldn't waste any more time on 'I Married a Monster.'"

Nix shook his head. "This will break Enid's heart."

"By the way," Dan said. "That was quite a coincidence about the Flaming Knights' headquarters burning down right after we left it tonight."

Nix chuckled. "You remember when I put my cigarette out in the ash tray on his desk when we were leaving?"

"Yeah."

"Well, I didn't put it in the ash tray at all. I threw it in the bastard's wastebasket."

CHAPTER SEVENTEEN

By promising that he'd get in touch with Nix the next day, Dan managed to get rid of him. When he told Nix that he was going back to sleep at the rooming house where Florence Lochmeister had been murdered the night before, that clinched the matter. Nix had no desire to sleep under a roof where a murder had been committed.

After Nix had gone, Dan drove to an all-night drugstore and phoned Clyde Ennis at his apartment. He summarized the events of the evening, and Ennis asked him to drop by and give him more particulars, but Dan said, "Everybody's beginning to suspect I know where Lochmeister's hiding. In fact, I have good reason to believe I'm being followed. The farther I stay away from you for a few days, the better." Nevertheless, Dan agreed to get in touch with him the next day.

When Dan entered the hall of the rooming house on Clay Street, Mrs. Murchison stuck her head out of the kitchen and said, "Oh, Mr. Banion, I have a message for you." She came out clutching her cheap cotton bathrobe around her. "Miss Wyler has been phoning all evening. My lands, she's phoned every half hour it seems. I thought it was important, so I waited up for you. She said you must call her immediately, no matter how late it is. Here's the number." She handed Dan a torn-off piece of grocery paper with the number scribbled on it. Dan dialed the number on the hall telephone, while Mrs. Murchison stood waiting curiously. The phone on the other end rang a long while before a man's sleepy voice answered. "Yes, yes, hello."

"Is Miss Myrtle Wyler in?"

"Myrtle? Heavens, I don't know. What an hour to call! Who is this?"

Dan recognized the high-pitched voice of Jason P. Wyler. "This is Banion of the *Journal*. I have a message here from your daughter asking me to call."

"Well, good Lord, man, why don't you call in the morning?"

"She asked me to call tonight. Is she in?"

"Good Lord, I don't know. If she is, she's asleep. She's in bed. Listen, Banion, this is ridiculous. I'm standing here in my bare feet."

"You mean to tell me you own a department store and don't even have a pair of slippers?"

"Certainly I have slippers. I couldn't find them. Nothing is ever where it ought to be when I want to put my hand on it. This is insane, Banion, please hang up and call Myrtle in the morning. I'm not going to wake her up for any of your drunken foolishness."

"I'm sorry I got you out of bed," Dan said, and hung up.

"Isn't she there?" asked Mrs. Murchison.

"I don't know. Maybe she's asleep. I'll call her in the morning."

Mrs. Murchison was disappointed. "That's odd. She said it was so terribly important."

Dan went upstairs and started to get ready for bed. He had his necktie off when the doorbell rang. Mrs. Murchison had already answered it by the time he leaned his head over the banister. It was Myrtle.

"I gave him your message," Mrs. Murchison said. "He just came in. He phoned, but I guess you were out. Be quiet, dear. Try not to wake people up."

Myrtle saw Dan leaning over the banister, and started up the stairs.

"I shouldn't let you go to his room this hour of the night," Mrs. Murchison said doubtfully.

"It's important," Myrtle said. "It isn't personal."

Mrs. Murchison stared after her with an obvious longing to have whatever was important shared with her.

Myrtle strode breathlessly into Dan's room and sat on the bed. "Alice Sweetser has disappeared," she said dramatically.

Dan yawned. "I know. That's why I asked you to find her."

"You didn't say she had disappeared."

Dan yawned again. "You'll have to pardon me. I've had a hell of a night. What makes you say she's disappeared?"

"I've asked everyone, and no one knows where she is. Her office says she's on a two weeks' vacation."

"Well, maybe that's it. Maybe she's just out of town somewhere on a vacation." Dan decided there was no point in letting Myrtle know that Alice Sweetser was lying in the morgue.

"That's what Enid thought. She told me Alice had gone to Acorn Lodge at Lake Tahoe. But I phoned up there and they said that she hadn't arrived. She made reservations, and they were expecting her, but she hadn't shown up."

"Do you mean you talked to Enid Hoyte, Lochmeister's former wife?"

"Yes, she was a very good friend of Alice's."

"Suppose you start from the beginning and tell me what you found out this evening."

"Well, I phoned Alice's office, and they told me she was on vacation, but they didn't know where she was. Then I called Dr. Raymond Mills. He said that he knew where she was, but wouldn't tell me. He was lying, though."

"How do you know he was lying?"

"Because I found out from Fergus Villiers. Alice had had a quarrel with him. That was one of the reasons she was going away. To avoid him. He was the last person in the world she would have told where she was going."

Dan rubbed his sleepy head and tried to concentrate on the problem. "You get around pretty thoroughly when you're given an assignment. What made you ask Villiers?"

"Oh, Fergus is an old friend of Alice's. I went to him after I called Ray Mills. Fergus told me about the quarrel Alice had had with Ray and said he drove around the next day and moved her over to Enid Hoyte's with a couple of suitcases."

"What was the idea of that?"

"Well, Ray had a key to her apartment, and she didn't want to see him anymore. He was making a nuisance of himself. So she called up Fergus and asked him to help her move over to Enid's place."

"Didn't she have a car of her own?"

"Yes, but it was in the garage. She'd had a little wreck about a week before."

"She must be a pretty good friend of Villiers to tell him all her personal troubles."

"Oh, everybody is that way with Fergus. He's sort of an old grandma. He thought that Alice was still staying with Enid, so when I left Fergus I drove over to Enid's place. She told me that Alice had only stayed in her apartment one day and then had left for Acorn Lodge, but when I checked with the Lodge, she had never arrived there at all,"

"What was the reason for her quarrel with Ray Mills?"

"It was just a typical quarrel, you might say. I guess she was getting tired of him."

"Maybe so, but there's usually some incident that touches off the explosion in those cases."

"No, I think she was just tired of him."

"You don't think there might have been another man?"

"Well—ah—no."

"I'll bet you a new hat there was another man."

"I don't think that's the answer," Myrtle said, grimly.

Something in the way she said it made Dan suspicious. "It wouldn't be that you know who the other man is, and don't want to tell me?"

"Of course not."

"It won't do you any good to hold out on me. I'll find out anyway."

Myrtle closed her eyes for a moment, then opened them and said, "Well, to be truthful, I do know the other man. But he doesn't know where she is, either."

"I wish you'd tell me who he is. Believe me, I'll keep it confidential. Unless, of course, something has really happened to Miss Sweetser. In that case the police will find out anyhow."

Myrtle's voice thickened, and her cheeks flushed. "Well, it's Alex Groton."

"You evidently saw Groton this evening, too."

"Yes, I did. I went to Alex as soon as I discovered that Alice had not arrived at the Lodge."

"And what did Alex say?"

"As far as he was concerned, the whole thing was over, and he told Alice that."

"Did he know she was going to the Lodge?"

"Yes, she wanted him to go with her, but of course he refused."

"Did he think she had gone there alone?"

"He didn't know where she was. He didn't know whether she had gone to the Lodge or not. He hadn't seen her since the night before she left Enid's apartment."

"Well, it doesn't necessarily mean anything," Dan said. "Maybe she just changed her mind and went to some other lodge."

Myrtle snuffed her cigarette angrily in the ash tray. "You're not playing fair with me."

"I don't understand."

"You have reason to believe someone other than Rogan killed Florence, and killed those other girls. You're not going ahead on guesswork, because you're not the kind of man who acts without reason. This afternoon you told me to locate Alice Sweetser. You wouldn't have asked me to do that if it wasn't important. I discover that she's disappeared, and now you pretend it's of no importance at all."

"Listen, can't we talk this over in the morning? I've had a hard night. I want to get some sleep."

"Where have you been?"

Dan said nothing about his experiences at Clyde Ennis' theater, or the checking locker at the ferry building, but he told her briefly about his clash with the White Knights of the Flaming Torch. "None of your friends happen to be Fascists, do they?" he asked.

"Papa knows all sorts of fools," she said. "I'll bet I could find out something from him."

"Good. Suppose we call that your next assignment. Find out who that man in the mask is, and I'll promote you to my first assistant."

Myrtle nodded. "I'll find out."

"You were pretty fond of Florence, weren't you?"

A hard look came into her eyes. "She was about the only friend I had."

"Why didn't you listen to her when she told you her brother was innocent?"

"Because I was a fool. If I'd had better sense, Florence might be alive today."

"You're pretty fond of Alex Groton, too, aren't you?"

Myrtle rose and picked up her purse. She ignored the question. "I'll talk to Papa first thing in the morning. He may know something about that White Knights organization."

Remembering the experience of the night before, Dan accompanied her all the way down the stairs and out to her car, and did not return to his room until he had seen her drive safely away.

CHAPTER EIGHTEEN

The next morning, while breakfasting at the corner lunchroom, Dan read both the city's morning newspapers. The *Journal* featured the raid on Captain Ballantine's house as "A frightful mistake." It said, "While we do not condone citizens taking the law in their own hands, it must be recognized that bungling by the police department in the matter of the Gus Grue murders has public patience strained to the breaking point."

The *Morning Courier*, however, named the Fascists for what they were, and described them as a worse menace than a dozen Gus Grues. It warned that the public's understandable desire to see Rogan Lochmeister brought to justice must not blind them to the greater evil of Fascist lynch gangs.

Dan wasted no time phoning George Lederman, managing editor of the *Courier*. Lederman's voice came vigorously over the phone. "That was a good job you did on those bastards, Banion. I still think you're crazy, but I want you on my paper. You can consider yourself hired right now."

"I still say Lochmeister didn't do it," Dan persisted, "and I tend to handle the story from that angle."

"Let's agree to disagree on that issue," Lederman said. "What I'm interested in is these Knights of the Flaming Drawers, or whatever they call themselves. I lost my boy fighting those rats in Italy, and I'm damned if I'm going to see any two-bit Hitlers get started in this country. Have you any ideas for a follow-up on that story?"

"Am I on the pay roll?"

"You're on the pay roll."

"I'll have something for you this afternoon. I'm going to find that guy in the mask and put him in the hospital."

"Fine. Meanwhile, we can use more particulars on last night's business. We want a by-line story from you giving all the particulars."

"Put a rewrite on the phone," Dan said, "and I'll give him the works."

When Dan finished dictating his story, Lederman cut in on the wire again. "What made that guy think you knew where Lochmeister was hiding?"

"Damned if I know."

"Listen, Dan, you know more about this than you're saying."

"Well, I'll give you a tip," Dan said, "but, whatever you do, keep quiet about it. Sometime tonight you're going to have headline that Lochmeister is innocent."

"You're pipe-dreaming, Dan."

"If you had any sense, you'd take my advice and start planting the idea that he might be innocent right now."

"We can't do that on the basis of no evidence."

"All right then, but I'm giving you a straight tip."

When Dan finished the call, he looked up an address in the telephone book, and drove to the Braddock and Garley Real Estate Company on Post Street. As he entered the office, he saw Myrtle Wyler seated in a chair, apparently waiting to see someone.

"Oh," she said, "you must have known all along."

"Known what?" Dan asked.

"Didn't you come here to see Mr. Braddock?"

"Yes. What are you doing here?"

"I came to see Mr. Braddock, too. They say he's busy in his office. I'm waiting until he's free."

"Well, what am I supposed to have known all along?"

"Papa says he's the leader of the Flaming Torch organization. He once asked Papa to make a contribution, but Papa refused."

"Good for Papa."

"I phoned you, but you had left the rooming house, so I decided to come here and see him myself."

"What did you think you were going to accomplish?"

"I didn't know, but I thought I'd ask him some questions."

A young woman approached Myrtle. "Mr. Braddock will see you now."

"I'm with Miss Wyler. I'll go along if you don't mind," Dan said.

The girl led the way through a jungle of desks, at which clerks were typing, sorting cards, and squinting over maps.

Braddock seemed startled at seeing Dan enter with Myrtle. The young lady who had guided them backed out quietly and closed the door.

"You are—er—together?" Braddock asked.

"I thought you might like another chance to pull out some of my hair," Dan said.

"I don't seem to understand."

"Well, don't reach for those push buttons," Dan warned, "because if you press one of them, the building will cave in on you. I guarantee that."

Braddock jerked a revolver from the top drawer of his desk and leveled it at Dan. "Keep your distance, Banion. I think, Miss Wyler, that you ought to leave."

"You can't shoot your way out of this, Braddock."

"Banion, you're insane to bring this girl here. Let her wait outside, and we can talk reasonably."

"You had me followed when I left your house yesterday, didn't you?"

"Certainly not. I don't know what you're talking about."

"Then what are you doing with that gun in your hand?"

"Your tone of voice was very threatening."

Ignoring the gun, Myrtle walked over to his desk and lifted the telephone. "Unless you put that gun away, I'm going to phone the police. Papa told me you were the leader of that Flaming Torch group."

"I never heard of such nonsense," Braddock insisted.

Myrtle dialed operator, and Braddock quickly put the gun back in the drawer. She hung up the phone.

Dan walked over and leaned his knuckles on the desk top within easy reach of Braddock. "Why don't you open your checkbook and try to buy me off?"

"Don't discuss such things in front of Miss Wyler."

Dan remained leaning on his knuckles and staring at Braddock for some time. He was trying to figure out a problem. Although Braddock no longer had the gun in his hand, it was within quick grabbing distance in the top drawer.

Dan took a book of paper matches from his pocket and dropped it on the desk in front of Braddock. "You made the mistake of dropping those last night. If you want to know how I traced them to you, read what it says on the cover."

Braddock was puzzled. He looked at the matches from a distance, then up at Dan again.

"Go ahead, read it. It won't bite you."

Braddock had to reach far across the desk to pick up the matches. As he did so, Dan seized his wrist, braced one foot against the edge of the desk, and pulled Braddock clear across it, landing him with a thump on the opposite side.

Myrtle edged around and took the gun from the top drawer. As Braddock scrambled to his feet, Dan threw a hard fist into his right eye, and he went down with a clatter.

Instead of trying to rise again, Braddock lunged on his hands and knees, gripped Dan by the legs, and brought him down to the floor. Employees in the outer office, hearing the racket, opened the door and began to crowd in. Myrtle pointed the gun at them and held them at bay.

Braddock had Dan by the throat and was trying to choke him. Dan brought his arms up inside Braddock's, forced outward with his elbows, and broke the grip. He grabbed Braddock by the ears and wrenched so hard that Braddock screamed and writhed about helplessly. Still keeping a merciless grip on the ears, Dan rose and pulled Braddock to his feet. When Braddock was erect, Dan released the ears and shot another fist, this time into Braddock's other eye.

Braddock staggered but did not go down. He began swinging wildly. A couple of blows caught Dan in the face and chest.

Dan backed away a few steps and warded off blows until he saw his chance. Then he brought his right up and crashed his knuckles accurately against Braddock's upper lip, where they would be most likely to loosen a few teeth.

Braddock reached out in a bear hug and pinioned Dan's arms to his sides, then began rocking in an attempt to force Dan to the floor. Dan clasped his hands in front of him and forced out with his elbows, breaking the grip. Then he raised his clasped fists over his head and brought them down with crunching force against Braddock's forehead. Braddock groaned and went down in a heap.

At this moment, Inspector Gallagher elbowed his way into the room, followed by Mac McCracken. They stopped short when Myrtle leveled the gun at them in a businesslike way.

"Put it down," Dan said. "They're police officers."

Gallagher stared curiously at Braddock's battered hulk on the floor. "Well, isn't this a pity. No doubt he assaulted you and you had to defend yourself."

"There's your Fuehrer," Dan said.

Gallagher clucked his tongue. "Too bad we didn't get here sooner, but then that's how it goes. It took us half the morning to persuade one of his Flaming Troopers to tell us his name. How did you get a line on him, Dan?"

"Miss Wyler here was kind enough to look him up in the *Social Register* for me."

Nix Peters came squeezing through the crowd of clerks and stenographers, who were staring openmouthed. "Who killed him?" he asked, looking at Braddock on the floor.

"He isn't dead," Dan said. "That's Warren Braddock, the real-estate man. He was the guy in the mask we had dealings with last night."

"How did you get here?" Gallagher asked Nix.

"Hell, I'm not dumb. When I saw you leave headquarters, I followed you."

Braddock was beginning to revive. He rolled on the floor and tried to sit up. The young lady, who was evidently his secretary, kneeled down and wiped the blood from his face with a handkerchief. "Come on, El Doochay," Gallagher said, "the putsch is over."

Braddock muttered something about Jews.

"I'm going to see if Judge Goldstein can fit you in on his calendar," Gallagher said.

"I have a right to call my attorney," Braddock insisted.

"I'll phone Mr. Jerome," his secretary said.

But the phone was already busy. Dan was firing his story in to the *Courier*. Nix was taking notes so that he could repeat the same to his own paper. "My editor isn't going to like this," he remarked. "Braddock and Garley are one of our biggest advertising accounts."

CHAPTER NINETEEN

Gallagher turned Warren Braddock over to McCracken to deliver to headquarters, and remained behind to speak to Dan privately. So far, no one had shown up to put a coin in the checking locker at the ferry building, and Gallagher said that if no one appeared by eight o'clock that night, Dan was free to break the story.

Dr. Raymond Mills had responded much more co-operatively to milder treatment. He admitted that he'd had a quarrel with Alice Sweetser. He said he had been telling people that he knew where Alice was because he didn't want them to know about the quarrel. He named the other man as Alex Groton, head of the advertising department of Wyler's department store. Gallagher said he was having Groton brought in for questioning. He invited Dan to come back to headquarters and sit in on the session. But Dan said he had other plans.

Nix Peters and Myrtle Wyler were waiting for Dan outside Braddock's private office, where he had been having his talk with Gallagher. They were listening to a little bald-headed fat man, who was shaking his finger at them and talking vehemently. "I'm making a statement," he said. "Take this down. Warren Braddock is an outstanding patriot. He is being made the victim of a Jewish plot. If we had more patriots like Warren Braddock, our city would not be overrun with foreign rapists. If the police department will not deal with these fiends, there are red-blooded Americans who will."

"Are you one of these Flaming Knights?" Dan asked.

"I am an American citizen and a taxpayer," the fat man blurted.

"This is Mr. Garley, Braddock's partner," Nix explained.

Dan looked Garley up and down, then turned his back on him. "Come on, let's get out of here," he said.

At Nix's suggestion, they stopped at the nearest barroom to celebrate Braddock's arrest. "Well, that's one down," Nix said. "What's the next move?"

"The first thing to do is get rid of you," Dan said.

"No, you don't," Nix insisted. "You're indebted to me. I saved your life last night, and I'm never going to let you forget it."

"You're not going to get rid of me, either," Myrtle added.

"Well, I don't know why you shouldn't come along," Dan said. "I figured to drop in on Enid Hoyte and have a little talk."

"What about?" Nix asked.

"I thought I'd ask how you and she are getting along with 'I Married a Monster.'"

Nix wrinkled his nose. "I'm getting kind of cold on that deal. Maybe you're right. The idea does stink a little."

Enid Hoyte lived on Fulton Street in an apartment house that was covered with shiny white bricks such as are generally used to line bathrooms. The idea, apparently, had been that it would be easy to wash off. However, no one had bothered to wash it for a long time, and the bricks were streaked and dirty. Most of them had turned a sickly yellow color. They rang Enid's bell several times, but there was no answer.

"We're out of luck," Dan said.

"Maybe she's asleep." Nix held his finger on the button for a prolonged period. "Naw, I guess she's out."

Dan had been studying the opposite side of the street. "Wait here a minute," he said. He crossed the street and approached a black sedan parked at the curb. Slouched in the back seat was Al Rainey, another of Gallagher's men. "Seen any lunatics lately?" Dan asked.

"Aw, for crissake, this is a waste of time," Rainey grunted. "Gallagher's had me parked here for two days. I'm wearing out the seat of my pants."

"What time did you come on duty?"

"I relieved Sorenson at eight o'clock this morning. He has the night shift."

"What time did Enid Hoyte leave her apartment?"

"She ain't left."

"You must have dozed off. I just rang her bell, and she's not in."

"The hell you say! I've been watching all the time. I didn't see her come out."

"Well, she isn't in."

"Are you sure? I'm supposed to keep a record here of when she goes in and when she comes out."

"Maybe she left before you came on duty."

"No. I checked with Sorenson. He said she was still in there."

"Well, maybe Sorenson fell asleep."

Al Rainey got out of the car. "Come on. Let's have a look."

They crossed the street to where Nix and Myrtle were waiting in the doorway. Rainey put his finger on the button beside Enid Hoyte's name and held it there a long time. "By God, you're right, she don't answer." Rainey pressed the manager's bell. Presently a matronly-looking woman opened the door. Rainey showed her his badge. "I'm a police officer. Do you have a key to Enid Hoyte's apartment? I'd like to take a look in there."

"Have you a search warrant?"

"I don't want to search the place. I just want to take a squint and see if everything's all right."

"Is anything wrong?"

"I didn't say anything was wrong. I just want to see if she's sick or something."

The manager took them up to the fourth floor in an elevator and along a hall to Enid's door. She fumbled with a ring of keys until she found the right one, and opened it.

"You guys wait out here," Rainey said. He went into the apartment and the manager followed him. Through the open door they could see him giving the place the once-over.

The manager lifted a half-empty whisky bottle from the bar surface of the table and pointed to a ring it had caused on the varnish. "Will you look how people treat a place when they rent it. You'd think a pig lived in here."

"This Hoyte dame ain't tidy," Rainey agreed. He examined the kitchen, opened a closet door, and poked his nose in the bathroom. "She's out, all right." He returned to the hall.

"Has anything happened?" The manager asked as she locked the door.

"Naw, I just thought she might be sick," Rainey said.

As they went down in the elevator, the manager remarked, "You never can tell what kind of people you're going to get for tenants these days."

Outside on the sidewalk, Rainey said, "Gallagher's going to be sore as hell about this. I can't figure how she slipped out without my seeing her."

"I don't see what's the sense in watching the place, anyhow," Dan said. "Anybody could slip in the back way and out again while you were watching the front."

"It's just a matter of responsibility," Rainey explained. "If anything happened, and we didn't even have anybody watching the place, it'd look like negligence."

"And what if something happened while you were watching? Wouldn't that be just as bad?"

Rainey rubbed his chin. "Well, I don't know. At least we get a time check on who comes and goes and what they look like. I'm pretty sure I could spot that guy Lochmeister if he came around."

Nix pointed to Rainey's chin where he had rubbed it. "You're bleeding."

"What are you talking about?" Rainey asked.

"Your chin," Nix said. "It's bleeding." There was a streak of red where Rainey had rubbed his chin. He started to feel it again, but stopped when his hand came in range of his eyes. There was a wet smear of red on his hand.

"Did you cut yourself?" Dan asked.

Rainey examined his hand again. "No, but I'm damned if that ain't blood." He took out a handkerchief and wiped it off. "Look at my face.

Am I cut anywhere?"

Dan took the handkerchief and rubbed at his face. "No, it must have come from your hand."

"Well, what the hell!"

"You must have got it in that apartment," Myrtle suggested.

"There wasn't anything wrong there, and besides, I didn't touch anything."

"You opened a couple of doors," Nix said. "Maybe you got it off one of the knobs."

They returned to the doorway of the apartment house and rang for the manager. She was very irritable about it, but finally consented to take them up to the fourth floor again. Rainey spent quite a long while examining things in the apartment and then came out. "I can't find any blood in there," he said.

"Blood!" said the manager. "What about blood?"

Rainey reached out and felt the shoulder of Nix' coat, then looked at his fingers. "You're the guy who's bleeding," he said.

Nix looked startled and began to feel himself. "Where?"

"There's blood on your coat," Rainey said.

Nix felt his shoulder and looked at his fingers. "Holy cow!"

"Are you hurt?" the manager asked.

"I don't think so." Nix slipped his coat off his shoulder. There was no blood on his shirt.

"What the hell's going on here?" Rainey asked.

"That isn't my blood," Nix said.

Rainey eyed him hostilely. "You got some explaining to do, fella."

The manager backed away from Nix in fright. "Get him out of here," she said.

Rainey had his gun out. "Hold your hands up—high." He slapped Nix around the chest and hips to see if he was armed.

"Listen, this is crazy," Nix said. "I didn't accuse you of anything when I saw blood on your face."

Rainey motioned them all toward the elevator. "Come on. Somebody's going to do a lot of explaining here." He put the gun back in his shoulder holster. "And don't anybody get the idea of starting anything, or I'll finish it."

Going down in the elevator, Dan was standing directly behind the manager. Suddenly he saw a spot of blood appear on her neck. He looked above and nudged Rainey. Rainey also looked at the ceiling of the elevator car. There was a small, square trap door designed so that mechanics could crawl through to work on the cables. At the edge of the trap was a moist streak of blood.

When the manager opened the elevator door on the lower floor, Rainey said, "Get me a chair or something to stand on."

"What for?" she asked. Rainey pointed to the trap. She took one look, and turned white. Nix looked above and turned equally white. Myrtle clenched her jaw, as if determined not to show any emotion.

"There's a better way," Dan said. He took a pencil from his pocket and pushed the copper lever at the top of the elevator doorway into a position of contact, the same as when the door was closed. "Now somebody get in and run the elevator down far enough so we can see what's on top."

"I won't get in there," the manager said stubbornly.

"You do it, Nix."

"Do it yourself," Nix said.

Rainey gave Nix a shove into the elevator. "Go ahead. Do as he says."

Dan turned to Myrtle, "You'd better get out of here." Myrtle moved her lips as if to speak, but no words came. She walked to the front of the apartment-house lobby, turned her back, and stared through the glass door at the street.

"All right," Rainey said to Nix, "get the thing moving."

"What in the hell am I supposed to do?" Nix asked.

"Press the basement button," Dan said, "and when the elevator is down far enough for us to see on top, press that red button marked 'Stop.'"

Nix pressed the button. The elevator jerked downward. The manager ran around a corner of the hall and hid her eyes. As the top of the elevator came in view, Rainey bared his teeth. Dan felt the same cold horror he had felt when viewing the remains of Florence Lochmeister in the basement of the rooming house.

"Jesus, God!" Rainey gasped.

Nix jerked the elevator to a stop when his shoulders were about even with the floor.

Dan leaned a hand down and helped him climb out. As he scrambled to his feet, he looked around at the top of the elevator and fainted dead away. Dan caught him in time to ease him to the floor.

CHAPTER TWENTY

Inspector Gallagher had set up camp in the manager's parlor. "This much is clear," he said to Dan, "whoever did it was waiting in the hall upstairs on the fourth floor when Enid Hoyte came home last night. That must have been right after I'd finished questioning her. He probably came up behind her and grabbed her when she started to open her door. There's a sort of attic over the elevator shaft. He dragged her up there, killed her, and threw her down the shaft, where she landed on top of the elevator."

"About what time does the coroner say it happened?" Dan asked.

"It was around eleven or twelve. That would be just about the time she'd have been returning here."

A big freckled-faced blond man opened the door and entered. "Here's Sorenson," Gallagher said. "He may be able to tell us something."

Sorenson grinned. "Some mess, hey, Chief?"

"You were on duty in the car across the street last night, weren't you?" Gallagher asked.

"That's right, Chief."

"Let's see your list of who came and went."

Sorenson took out a notebook and frowned over it. "I relieved Downey at about nine o'clock at night. Where shall I start reading?"

"Start at nine o'clock," Gallagher said.

"Well, let's see. At about nine-twenty, a fat lady in a fur coat came home with a skinny guy in a brown overcoat. I guess she lives here. I see her going in and out all the time. They stood in the entrance and argued a while. I guess he wanted to go upstairs with her, but she evidently wouldn't let him, because after a while he went away and she went inside. While they were arguing, at nine-twenty-three, an old guy with a cane went in. I guess he lives here too. He's always going in and out. Then, at nine-thirty-six, the manager came home. At nine-forty-two, some guy came out stewed to the eyeballs. He wore a checkered overcoat. I guess he went in while Downey was on duty. Then at nine-fifty-one ..."

Sorenson continued through the list until he came to ten-twenty-one. "There was a guy in a gray overcoat with a cane. He rang one of the apartments, got a buzz, and went in. He was a new one. I hadn't seen him before."

Gallagher made a note of the man in the gray overcoat. When Sorenson came to twelve-nine, he said, "Then this guy with the gray overcoat and the cane came out. There were only three people who had left the building after eleven o'clock at night. The other two Sorenson recognized as persons he had seen visiting there before. The man with the cane and the gray overcoat seemed the most likely possibility.

"If he's our man," Gallagher said, "ten to one he pushed any old apartment number at random just to get somebody to buzz the latch so he could get in." He turned to Al Rainey, who was leaning against the wall nearby. "Go check whatever tenants are in, and find out if any of them had their doorbell ring at ten-twenty-one last night, without anyone coming to their apartment after they buzzed the latch."

As Rainey went out, Gallagher said to Sorenson, "Can you give us any better description of this guy in the gray overcoat?"

"Well, yeah. He had this cane, you see. Maybe there was something wrong with his leg. He walked with a limp."

Sorenson had reported Enid Hoyte as coming home at eleven-forty-three. The man in the gray overcoat had left the building exactly twenty-six minutes later.

Gallagher asked Dan, "Have you run across anybody in your rounds who walks with a limp?"

"One," Dan said.

"One is enough. Who is he?"

"Fergus Villiers. He works in the interior-decorating department of Wyler's department store. He used to live in the apartment house where Lochmeister was arrested. He was one of the witnesses at the trial."

Al Rainey came back into the room. "Yeah, Neil, there's a lady in 216 says her bell rang at about ten-twenty-one last night. She opened her apartment door and waited, but nobody came up."

Gallagher was putting his hat on. "Come on, Dan, you might as well be in on this. Where does that guy Villiers live?"

Because the lobby of the apartment house was crowded with reporters and cameramen, Gallagher had the manager let them out the back way. Dan remembered that Nix and Myrtle were also out in the lobby. It seemed a shame to ditch them, but there was no help for it.

When they rang the bell of Fergus Villiers' studio, the door latch clicked in response. Dan led the way upstairs, with Gallagher and Sorenson following. On the top floor, Villiers was leaning over the banister watching for them. "Oh, you," he said, recognizing Dan. "I tell you, old man, I'm busy right now. Could you come back later?"

Gallagher edged past Dan and continued up the stairs. "Are you Mr. Villiers?"

"Yes."

Gallagher showed his badge. "We'd like to ask you a few questions."

"You've got me at an awkward time. Could you come back a little later?"

"We want to talk to you now."

"Well, I suppose if it's important ..." Villiers led them into his skylighted studio room. He was wearing the same green and yellow dressing gown Dan had seen him in the day before. As they entered, Jason P. Wyler rose from one of the chairs and looked at them in a confused way.

"I'm sorry, J. P., but these chaps seem to be in a swivet about something."

"Who are you?" Gallagher asked, eying Wyler.

"This is my employer, Jason P. Wyler," Villiers said. Wyler extended his hand with a smile. "You're Inspector Gallagher, aren't you? I've heard a great deal about you."

"Sit down," Villiers said. "I think you'll find enough chairs. No, one of you will have to sit on the couch. Would you care for a drink?"

Gallagher seated himself heavily in a yellow upholstered chair. "No, thanks. When did you last see Enid Hoyte?"

"Enid? Last night." Still limping on his cane, Villiers moved over to a sideboard and began mixing himself a highball.

"What time was that?" Gallagher asked.

"I don't know exactly. It must have been around eight o'clock. Maybe eight-thirty. Why?"

"How long did you stay there?"

"I only stayed a few minutes. I was really looking for Alice Sweetser. I thought she was staying there with Enid, but Enid told me she had gone to the country."

"What did you do after that?"

"Why, is something wrong?"

"Maybe," Gallagher said. "Where did you go after that?"

"Well, then I came back here. What's happened?"

"And what did you do last night? Say from about ten o'clock on?"

"Nothing. I was in bed asleep."

"What time did you go to bed?"

"Oh, at about nine o'clock. Say, what's this all about?"

"Isn't that kind of early to go to bed?"

"Yes, but I was terribly tired. I guess this ankle got me down. Turned it, you know."

"You seem to get around pretty good on it."

"I manage, but it's rather a nuisance."

"How many overcoats have you got?"

"One. I'm not exactly a millionaire."

"Can I see it?"

"Well, certainly, but what's the idea?"

"I'd just like to take a look at it."

"Well, anything to oblige." Villiers put his drink down and limped to a closet.

"Bring your hat, too," Gallagher added.

"Why, are we going somewhere?"

"Maybe."

Villiers limped back with a gray overcoat over one arm and a hat in the other hand.

"Do you mind putting them on?" Gallagher asked.

"Isn't this rather foolish?"

"I hope so," Gallagher said, "but you never can tell. Do you mind putting them on?"

Villiers grinned and shrugged his shoulders. "There's more mysterious things going on these days." He slipped the green and yellow dressing gown off, elbowed into the overcoat, and put the hat on his head sideways in a kind of Napoleonic effect.

"Put the hat on straight," Gallagher said.

Villiers adjusted the hat carefully, buttoned the overcoat, and rammed his hands into the pockets. "Last year's model, but not bad, eh?"

"Would you mind walking up and down a little?"

Villiers picked up his cane and limped up and down in a kind of lopsided march, whistling "Pop Goes the Weasel."

Gallagher looked at Sorenson. Sorenson nodded. "That's the guy."

Villiers was still parading up and down. "Let me know when you get tired of this."

"You can stop now," Gallagher said. "You're under arrest."

Villiers stopped marching, and his mouth dropped open. "You're kidding me."

"You're under arrest for the murder of Enid Hoyte."

"Good God!" Jason P. Wyler gasped.

"Enid? You don't mean to say—" Villiers rolled his eyes in confusion.

"She was murdered between eleven and twelve last night," Gallagher said. He jerked his thumb at Sorenson. "This man was watching in a car across the street. He saw you go into that apartment house at ten-twenty-one and leave at twelve-nine."

"That's the guy; positively," Sorenson said.

"Why, that's insane. I was right here asleep in bed."

"Did you sleep soundly?" Dan asked.

"I never slept sounder in my life."

Jason P. Wyler addressed Villiers in an employer's tone. "Did you do this thing, Fergus?"

"I don't know what he's talking about. Why the hell would I kill Enid?"

Wyler shook his head sadly. "I never expected anything like this."

"But I tell you I didn't do it," Villiers insisted.

Gallagher jerked his head at Sorenson. "Have a look around the place."

Sorenson got up and began poking into drawers and peering behind the furniture.

"Where were you the night before last when Florence Lochmeister was murdered?" Gallagher asked.

"Well, let's see. I was right here in bed. That was the night I'd turned my ankle. It was very painful. I went to bed about eight or nine o'clock."

"And slept soundly, I suppose?"

"Yes, as I remember, I did. Are you trying to imply that I killed Florence?"

Sorenson came over from the closet with a blue suit on a hanger. He held it for Gallagher's inspection. Gallagher thumbed the cloth and looked closely. "This is your suit, I take it?"

"Yes, of course," Villiers said.

"It seems to have blood on the front of it. We'll have to have it analyzed, of course, but I can tell you definitely enough from the look of it."

"That's ridiculous," Villiers said.

Sorenson draped the suit over a chair and returned to the closet.

"You're just about the same build as Lochmeister," Gallagher said. "Did you ever borrow any clothes from him?"

"You can't do this," Villiers said. "I know what you're leading up to. I never wore any of Lochmeister's clothes in my life."

Sorenson hauled a large handbag out of the closet and brought it over to Gallagher.

"That's empty, don't be silly," Villiers said.

Sorenson opened it wide, plunged his hand in, and took out a fistful of rumpled women's clothing. As he did so, a blood-stained handkerchief became detached from the rest and fell to the floor at Gallagher's feet.

"That's not—something's wrong," Villiers said. "That stuff isn't mine. I didn't put it there. Somebody else must have put it there. I never saw it before."

Sorenson reached in again and pulled out a large, heavy-bladed clasp knife of the type used by yachtsmen.

"I guess we might as well get going," Gallagher said.

"I tell you somebody put that stuff there," Villiers argued. "I never saw it before."

"Does this mean," Wyler asked, "that Rogan Lochmeister didn't commit these crimes?"

"It's beginning to look that way," Gallagher said.

"Thank God," Wyler sighed. "Thank God."

Villiers looked at his employer in amazement. "They're taking me off to hang me for something I don't know anything about, and you sit there saying thank God."

Wyler gave him a look of disgust and turned away.

"Well, if you're going to be so quick to judge people," Villiers said, "why don't you explain to them what you were doing in Enid Hoyte's apartment when I called there last evening?"

Wyler clenched his jaw hard and glared at him. "You dirty cad."

"Well, you were there, weren't you?" Villiers said.

"That has nothing to do with the case in hand."

"Is it true? Were you there?" Gallagher asked.

"Well, yes, I was. She was a former employee of the store, you know, and Rogan Lochmeister's ex-wife. I felt, under the circumstances, that I owed her a visit to inquire into her welfare."

"That's a hot one," Villiers said. "Then why did you come here this afternoon and ask me not to mention having seen you there?"

"You're placing a vicious construction on a very innocent statement of mine," Wyler said.

"You were asking me to keep quiet about it when these people arrived."

"Well, I don't see that it matters," Wyler snapped. "I simply wanted to avoid a lot of senseless gossip."

"For the sake of the record, Mr. Wyler," Gallagher said, "what time did you leave Enid Hoyte's apartment yesterday?"

"Oh, I believe it was around eight o'clock."

"Do you mind, just for the record, stating where you were for the rest of the evening?"

"In view of the evidence you have here, I don't see that there's much point to it," Wyler said.

"Well, this man has made a very serious insinuation," Gallagher explained. "It would be a very good idea to clear it up right now, so that it won't come up again."

"Very well. I had dinner at Ferdinand's and then I went home. I guess I got home about nine-thirty or ten."

"Your wife or your servants can no doubt confirm that?"

"No, I don't believe they can. You see, my wife's away visiting in Los Angeles. It was the butler's night off, and the cook was asleep. Of course I didn't disturb her. My daughter was out."

"Well, it doesn't matter," Gallagher assured him. "We have our man."

"I'm not blind," Villiers said. "I didn't have to see him in Enid's apartment yesterday to know what was going on. I lived in the same apartment house as she did while Rogan Lochmeister was away in the service. Mr. Wyler was a very frequent visitor."

"This is ridiculous," Wyler said. "I believe I did drop around several times merely to inquire if she had heard from Rogan."

"You pick funny hours to make fatherly calls," Villiers said.

Gallagher put his hands on his knees and pushed himself to his feet. "Well, there's no use going into your neighbor's fields to look for a horse that's already in your barn. Wrap up your toothbrush, Villiers. You're coming along with us. Mr. Wyler, if we want to confirm anything from you, we'll get in touch with you at your office." While Villiers was getting dressed, Gallagher jerked Dan by the lapel, and took him aside. "You've got a great story now, boy, go to town on it," he said.

"I'm not going to town on it, and if you're smart you won't either."

"What do you mean?"

"I'll turn in a very reserved story saying that the circumstances of Villiers' arrest are almost identical to Lochmeister's."

"You don't think this guy did it?"

"Could be yes, and could be no. Probably no."

"What's your reasoning?"

"This stuff could have been planted in here. Somebody could have doped him just as they apparently did Lochmeister. They could have borrowed his clothes, borrowed his cane, and even imitated his limp."

"Don't say that, Dan, you're driving me crazy."

"I'm just telling you what it looks like to me."

Gallagher wanted him to come down to headquarters and talk it over, but Dan said he had other business. He promised, however, to be in Gallagher's office at eight o'clock, at which time Gallagher had told him he could break the story of Alice Sweetser's murder, if no one had shown up to put a coin in the checking locker at the ferry building.

CHAPTER TWENTY-ONE

Dan didn't wait to see Gallagher drag Villiers off to headquarters. He went to the nearest drugstore and phoned in his story, qualifying every particular very carefully. Lederman did not argue with him about the manner in which the story should be written. In fact, the whole chain of the day's events threw Lederman's mind into such confusion he welcomed any instructions that Dan could give.

When he had finished calling in his story, Dan grabbed a taxi, picked up his car from where he had parked it near Enid Hoyte's apartment house, and drove to Wyler's department store. He took the elevator to the top floor, found the advertising department, and asked for Mr. Alex Groton. In a few minutes he was shown to a large, airy room with big windows, in which Groton was seated behind a desk that was littered with advertising layouts, proofs, and photographs. He waved an arm cheerily at a chair. "Sit down, Banion. I'm sorry I can't spare you much time. What's on your mind?"

"Well, to come right to the point, I'm interested in locating Alice Sweetser."

Groton sighed through his teeth. "So that's it. Has Myrtle been talking to you?"

"She didn't tell me anything that I wouldn't have found out anyhow."

"She ought to have sense enough to keep her mouth shut."

"She thinks a lot of you, and I don't think she'd do anything to hurt you."

"That's not the point. It's rather embarrassing."

"When did you last see Alice?"

"It must have been a day or so before she was supposed to leave for some lodge at Tahoe. But this is a waste of time, Banion. I've been all over this with the police. They had me up there a couple of hours ago."

"You didn't happen to drive her to the station when she left?"

"Certainly not. See here, has anything happened to Alice?"

"Not that I know of."

"Then I can't see that any of this is pertinent. It's none of your business, and it's none of Myrtle's business. I wish to God she'd keep her nose out of my affairs."

"Blame me if you want, but not her. Anything she told me was in the strictest confidence."

"Listen, just because I work for her old man doesn't mean I have to have her in my hair all the time. I don't go in for the athletic type. I like my women willowy."

"There's nothing for you to get sore about. If you only knew it, you've got a pretty good friend in Myrtle."

Groton calmed down a little. "She's a nice enough girl. She's just not attractive to me, that's all. What business is it of hers who I run around with?"

"Do you happen to be acquainted with Rogan Lochmeister's ex-wife?"

"Yes, I know her slightly. Enough to say how-do-you-do. That's all.

Listen, Banion, you've put this bug in Myrtle's brain about Lochmeister's being innocent. I knew Lochmeister. He worked right here in this department with me. We were pretty good friends. If anyone would like to think he was innocent, it would be me, and if I thought there was the slightest chance of that being so, you could count on me to the limit. But I am not going to tolerate you or Myrtle poking your noses into my affairs. Particularly Myrtle. Now if you don't mind, Banion, I have a hell of a lot to do." Groton picked up an ad proof and started to resume work.

"It might interest you to know," Dan said, "that Enid Hoyte was murdered last night."

"What?"

"She was murdered in her apartment house and thrown down the elevator shaft."

Groton dropped the proof. "When did this happen?"

"Last night."

"Why didn't you say so?"

"Furthermore, Fergus Villiers has been arrested on suspicion, and there's already enough evidence in the hands of the police to indicate that Lochmeister didn't commit any of these crimes."

Groton's eyes took on a dazed expression. "Villiers! I don't understand."

Dan described the finding of Enid Hoyte's body and the clues that led to Villiers.

Groton nodded his head smugly. "I always did have Fergus figured for a weirdy of some kind. That childish gibbering of his gets on my nerves."

However," Dan said, "I don't think Villiers did it."

"You don't?"

"No. The thing had all the earmarks of a frame-up, the same as was worked on Lochmeister." Dan explained his reasons for thinking so.

"I don't follow your reasoning at all," Groton said. "Something's screwy here. I'll concede you that. But pardon me for saying that I don't think much of your talents as a sleuth. You ought to stick to newspapering."

"Then you think Villiers is guilty?"

"I'm not saying anything one way or another until I've had a chance to investigate for myself. For an outsider, Banion, you draw a lot of conclusions on the basis of very little knowledge."

"I'm willing to learn. What's your idea about it?"

"I think I can get along without your help. I'm sorry to have to be so frank, but you're one of these guys who don't get a thing unless it's put very bluntly. In plain words, Banion, if you'd just take your nose out of this affair and mind your own business, you'd be doing everybody concerned a big favor."

"I'm not in a mood for handing out favors right now. Least of all to two-bit advertising managers whose jobs have gone to their heads."

"See here, Banion, I've stood about all I'm—"

"Don't yell at me. I'm not one of the underpaid clerks around here."

"Are you going to get the hell out of my office, or am I going to have to throw you out?"

"Just lay one of your manicured hands on me and I'll wrap that goddamn desk around your neck."

Groton's face was crimson. "I'm telling you, Banion—"

"Tell it to the Junior Chamber of Commerce."

"I'll just call up Burgess about this, and we'll see how smart you sound when you're out of a job."

"I already quit the *Journal*. Better call up Lederman on the *Courier*."

"Thanks. I will. We're quite an important advertising account of theirs."

"Good. I'm sure he'll jump through a hoop every time you rattle your piggy bank." Dan got up and, walked to the door, "While you're about it, send a photograph of yourself over to Lederman. He'll probably need it for the evening edition."

"What do you mean?"

"There are a few things buzzing that you don't know about. Your love life is going to be entertaining the public very shortly."

"Wait a minute, Banion, I don't get you."

Dan opened the door. "People in glass houses should keep their pants on."

"Come back here, Banion. I want to talk to you."

"You're throwing me out. Remember?" Dan banged out the door. A few employees in the outer office, who had witnessed a snatch of the dispute while the door was open, looked at him with frightened eyes as he walked through.

He walked around the corner of the hall to J. P. Wyler's office. The secretary in the starched blouse told him that Mr. Wyler would not be in for the rest of the day.

Dan looked up the address in the phone book, and drove to the Wyler residence on Jackson Street, a two-story mansion, looking something like a wedding cake and something like an old colonial plantation. A tall, bald, uniformed butler, with a face like a squid and the manners of an undertaker, asked for a card, and when Dan couldn't produce one, accepted the name verbally with an attitude as if he was going to charge time and a half for having to carry it in his brain. He soon returned, bowed Dan into a hall as big as a basketball court, and led the way to a room hung with oil paintings in gold frames and lined with sets of books that looked as if they had never been opened. Jason P. Wyler was sitting behind a curlicue French desk. The gleam of his smooth, bald head was rivaled only by a crystal chandelier that glittered above it. He rose and offered his hand across the desk. "Banion, terribly glad you came. Wanted to talk with you. Pull up a chair. I really owe you my profoundest apologies."

"You're convinced now that Lochmeister is innocent?" Dan said.

"Good heavens, when I think of what that boy has been through. The thing we must do now is find him."

"I think he'll turn up when it's clearly enough established that he's innocent," Dan said.

"I sincerely hope so. By the way, that was rather embarrassing for me this afternoon when Villiers put that absurd construction on my visit to Enid Hoyte."

"Oh, well, I don't think anyone will pay any attention to him."

"Just the same, Banion, I'd appreciate it if you'd keep it rather confidential."

"I will, but I doubt if Villiers will."

"I have never seen a cooler hypocrite. He testified at Rogan's trial, you know."

"There is something I wanted to ask you about," Dan said. "If you will remember, there was a cocktail party at your store on the afternoon before Rogan Lochmeister was arrested."

"Come to think of it, there was."

"It was a sort of anniversary celebration, I understand."

"Yes, we have it every year."

"In your office?"

"Yes."

"Fergus Villiers was present, wasn't he, at that affair?"

"Fergus? Oh yes, yes. He was there."

"If I'm not mistaken, Rogan Lochmeister got sick at that party, and you drove him home."

"Let's see, is that right? Hmmm. I believe I did. Yes, come to think of it, my daughter pointed out that he was acting rather strangely. Pale and all that. So I took the boy home. Why are you mentioning this?"

"I was wondering if you had noticed whether Fergus Villiers was near Lochmeister at any time during that party?"

"Near him? Well, that's hard to say. People milling around the office, you know. It's quite a jolly affair. What are you getting at, Banion?"

"Well, it seems clear now that somebody doped Rogan Lochmeister that afternoon. Probably at that cocktail party."

"Doped him? What makes you say that?"

"The murderer wanted to be certain Lochmeister would be out like a light when he went into his apartment to put on one of his suits and borrow his gun. As it happened, instead of going right to bed, as the murderer expected him to do, Lochmeister went out to get a little air. He went up to that little park that's near his apartment house, and passed out on a bench. In some manner, the murderer found him there and helped him back to his apartment. That's why Lochmeister was hazy about where he'd been. He remembered going out, but he only had the vaguest sensation of coming home. He told that quite honestly to the police, and naturally they didn't believe him. Or, if they did believe him, they imagined he was in some kind of Jekyll-and-Hyde daze during which he committed the murder."

Wyler kept nodding his head solemnly as Dan talked. "Hmmm, yes, that sounds very logical. It never occurred to me."

"A Dr. Raymond Mills was also present at that party in your office, I believe. He was a friend of Alice Sweetser, and came with her."

"Well, I don't remember that. There were a number of people there who were not employed in the store. It would be impossible for me to recall offhand who they were."

"Alex Groton, the head of your advertising department, was also there, wasn't he?"

"Yes, he was."

"Did Warren Braddock, the real-estate man, happen to be there?"

"Braddock? I'm not certain. He may have been. He was bothering me at the time to get me to support that stupid organization of his. I can't say that I care for the man. But he may have been there. Why are you asking about these other people?"

"It just occurred to me that one of them might have seen Villiers put something in Lochmeister's drink."

"That's possible, of course. But I don't see that any further evidence is necessary."

"The evidence the police have indicates that Villiers killed Enid Hoyte, and the similarity of that murder with the others would lead anyone to the conclusion that he committed them all. But there is no actual proof of that, and unless he confesses, or unless some evidence of how he framed Lochmeister can be presented, then Lochmeister will never be entirely in the clear."

"By heaven, that never occurred to me."

Myrtle Wyler came in, pulling off her gloves. She eyed Dan sharply. "So this is where you are. Do you think that was fair, going off and leaving me standing in the lobby?"

"What lobby?" Wyler asked.

"The lobby of Enid's apartment," she said.

"What on earth were you doing there?"

"She came with me," Dan explained. "She was with me when we discovered the body."

"Myrtle, I asked you not to play detective. This sort of thing is dangerous."

"Well, it's all over now," she said. "You can stop worrying."

Wyler nodded. "Yes, I know. Banion was just discussing it with me."

Myrtle tossed her gloves on the desk and removed her hat. "The last person in the world I would ever have suspected was Fergus. Dad, I feel terrible about Rogan. I only hope that he's all right, wherever he is."

"Mr. Banion seems to feel that a little more evidence is needed to clear Rogan completely." He turned to Dan. "Do you mind telling her what you told me?"

Dan repeated his theory about Lochmeister's having been doped at the store celebration.

"Did you happen to notice whether Fergus was near enough to Rogan during the party to put anything in his drink?" Wyler asked Myrtle.

"Well, it's rather hard to say. It was quite a while ago. Everyone was moving around talking to everyone else. It wouldn't have been hard for him to do, though."

"Do you happen to remember if Warren Braddock was there?" Dan asked.

"Yes, he was." Myrtle turned her X-ray look on Dan. "Why do you ask?"

"I was just curious."

Wyler said he felt sure that when the police had finished checking up on all angles of Fergus Villiers, they would have more than enough evidence to prove he had committed all of the crimes, and that Rogan's name would be cleared. However, he told Dan, he was ready to cooperate in any possible way to speed the matter, and he sincerely hoped that Rogan, when he saw the newspaper account of Villiers' arrest, would come out of hiding.

When Dan was ready to leave, Myrtle followed him to the front door.

"Just one minute," she said, "I'm going with you."

"Why?"

"You're the poorest liar I've ever seen in my life."

"What do you mean?"

"Something's wrong, and you know it. Why were you asking about Braddock?"

"Just curiosity."

"You're not convinced that Fergus is guilty, are you?"

"What makes you think that?"

"Papa is pretty dense about things like this, but you can't fool me. Where are you going?"

"I'm going to dinner. If you want to come along, you're perfectly welcome."

Myrtle adjusted her beret before a hall mirror. "Also, I think you know where Rogan is hiding. If you were sure Villiers was guilty, why would Rogan still be hiding?"

Over a sea-food dinner on Fishermen's Wharf, Dan admitted to Myrtle that Villiers' arrest had the earmarks of Lochmeister's frame-up all over again. "I understand your father drove him home from that party," he said.

"Yes. I noticed that Rogan was looking rather pale. I knew that he wasn't supposed to be drinking. I spoke to Papa about it. He went over and talked to Rogan and then drove him home."

"Did you go into Rogan's apartment with him when you dropped him off?"

"Oh, I didn't go along. I had my own car there. I saw Papa home later, and he said that Rogan had felt better when he got out in the air."

CHAPTER TWENTY-TWO

After dinner, Dan drove Myrtle home. He had a hard time persuading her to get out of the car. She was convinced he was bent on more investigation, and she felt entitled to go along. He finally managed to get rid of her by being gruff, which seemed to hurt her feelings considerably. From there he drove to Gallagher's office in the Hall of Justice, arriving at about a quarter to eight.

"Nobody's showed at the checking locker," Gallagher said, "so I guess you can spill that story in a few minutes. Incidentally, ever since the Enid Hoyte murder and Villiers' arrest hit the streets, your old boss Rolf Burgess on the *Journal* has been calling up everybody in town trying to get a hold of you. He's called me three times."

Dan borrowed Gallagher's phone and called the *Journal*. Burgess' voice came bounding over the wire. "Banion, where have you been? I've been trying to get hold of you all day."

"Is your memory failing you? I quit yesterday."

"Oh, hell, Banion, you're not going to take that seriously."

"I'm working for the *Courier* now."

"See here, Banion, do you think that's fair to me?"

"I told you Lochmeister was innocent. You wouldn't listen."

"You didn't give me a chance. You hung up."

"You had your say before I hanged up on you."

"Listen, Banion, you're being very unethical about this whole thing."

"And when that band of two-bit Hitlers grabbed me last night, you came out with an editorial taking their side."

"We did nothing of the kind, Banion."

"Well, you whitewashed them. Called them impatient citizens yearning for justice, or something like that."

"Listen, Dan, Braddock and Garley are one of our biggest advertising accounts. I'm sure the whole thing was a misunderstanding on Braddock's part. He'd be the first to apologize if he thought he was wrong. You want to learn to see both sides of things, Dan."

"I can see both sides pretty well," Dan said, "but I can only be on one."

"I'm mighty disappointed in you, Banion. You're making a big mistake."

"Am I? I thought I was correcting one of yours."

When Dan hung up on Burgess, Gallagher puffed erratically at a cigarette and said, "Dan, I'm not satisfied. I feel like I'm floating around on a pink cloud."

"It's the Lochmeister case all over again with the same trimmings," Dan said.

"I'm beginning to agree with you. I've got my man. I've got the weapon. I've got all the evidence anyone could ask for, and I have an eyewitness who can identify him. And, damn it, I'm not convinced."

"Did you find out whose clothes those were that you found in Villiers' suitcase?"

"They belonged to Alice Sweetser. They were some of the stuff in her suitcases that the murderer took out in order to jam her dismembered body in."

"Why do you say only *some* of the stuff?"

"It couldn't have been all of it. There wasn't enough."

"That makes it look like somebody just grabbed a handful in a hurry to plant in Villiers' suitcase. The rest of the stuff must be hidden away someplace, if it hasn't been burned."

"It isn't easy to burn clothes. They make an awful stink and attract attention."

"What did you find out from Alex Groton?" Dan asked.

"Oh, he was in a hell of a stew. He admitted he'd had an affair with Alice Sweetser, but said he'd broken it off and hadn't seen her since the day before she was supposed to have gone up to that lodge at Lake Tahoe. Of course I didn't tell him that she'd been murdered. I just let him think we were trying to locate her."

"There's something screwy about the way everybody concerned in this thing turns out to be on Wyler's pay roll," Dan said. "They either work for him now or did work for him in the past."

"Well, I don't know what you can make of that."

"I think we're viewing this thing too much as the work of a homicidal maniac," Dan suggested, "and not paying enough attention to motives. For instance, in all probability Enid Hoyte was killed to keep her mouth shut. She knew something that would have given the murderer away, so he killed her."

"That's guesswork, of course."

"Well, sometimes you've got to dope a thing out wrong before you can discover what's right. There's no harm in theorizing."

"Come to think of it," Gallagher said, "we haven't let it out that Alice Sweetser has been murdered yet. Enid Hoyte didn't know that Alice Sweetser was dead. She may have known something that would have linked the murderer to that killing. The murderer naturally wanted to shut her up before she found out."

"That's possible," Dan said. "For another thing, Alice Sweetser had been staying in Enid Hoyte's apartment. It was from there that she left, presumably to go to Lake Tahoe, and there's no doubt that she was killed directly after she left that apartment. Her own car was in the garage from an accident she'd had not long before, so it stands to reason that she either took a taxi to go to the railroad station or bus station, or else somebody called for her in a car to give her a lift. It's more likely that someone called for her, and Enid knew who that person was. That's why she was killed."

"Now, that's not bad," Gallagher said, "not bad at all."

"But it doesn't explain why Alice Sweetser was killed or why any of the others were killed. What about those first three girls Lochmeister was supposed to have murdered?"

"Well, let's see," Gallagher said, "one of them was a little hairdresser. Her name was Fanny Owens. Another was Irene Du Boce; she was an elevator operator. The third one—by God, come to think of it, she worked at Wyler's. Geraldine Huneker was her name. She was a salesgirl."

"This isn't just the work of a fiend, Neil. There's some reason behind these killings."

"Yeah, but what about the gory technique of this nut? Why does he have to slash them up that way? Why can't he shoot 'em or choke 'em, and let it go at that?"

"Were any of these girls raped before they were killed?" Dan asked.

"No, that's a funny thing, no evidence of rape."

"That's interesting."

"It's a butcher, Dan, one of these guys that loves to cut."

"I remember a guy in the army," Dan said. "He was as quiet and calm as a Bible salesman, but when he got to killing he went crazy. He couldn't stop himself. Even after a man was dead he kept hacking and hacking and hacking. It got so we could identify the enemy casualties he'd worked out on. Finally they had to put him in the nut house."

"That may be some kind of an answer. But we're wasting time." Gallagher looked at his watch. "I don't see any sense in waiting any longer, Dan. You might as well go ahead and bust that story."

Dan phoned Lederman at the *Courier*, and the story was soon singing over the wire. When he had finished, Gallagher said, "That's as much of a break as I can give you, Dan. I'll have to go out now and tell the other reporters. Otherwise I'll be accused of some kind of a deal with you. They won't have all the intimate particulars, though, so you're still a mile ahead of them."

"That's good enough for me, but before you go, tell me one thing. Where is Braddock?"

"He's out on bail, of course. That fink attorney Cecil Jerome was up here with an unlimited financial budget almost by the time we brought Braddock in."

"And Dr. Raymond Mills?"

"I've been holding him so he couldn't spill the information about Alice Sweetser's murder, but I guess I'll have to let him go now."

When Gallagher left for the pressroom to give the other papers the formal story on the Alice Sweetser killing, Dan returned to his car. He drove a zigzag course for a while, circling several blocks to make certain Gallagher wasn't having him followed. Then he headed for the Regent Theater on Third Street.

CHAPTER TWENTY-THREE

An old man whom Dan hadn't seen before was taking tickets at the door. "Ennis is up in his office," he said. "There's a lady with him, but I guess it's all right. Go on up." He directed Dan to a narrow, walled-in flight of stairs, barely wide enough to let your shoulders through. It led to the projection room, and also to a narrow cubbyhole in which Clyde Ennis had a desk. Myrtle Wyler had one hip resting on the desk top. Her mouth was set in the expression of unyielding determination that had now become familiar to Dan.

"Come in, Banion," Ennis said. "I don't know whether you've met Miss Wyler."

"What are you doing here?" Dan said to Myrtle. "I thought I took you home an hour ago."

"He knows something about this," Myrtle said, "and I'm not going to leave here until he tells the truth."

Ennis sighed wearily and studied the ceiling.

"What's it all about?" Dan asked.

"Enid Hoyte was in love with him, and he knows it," Myrtle snapped. "I happen to know that he was seeing Enid behind Rogan's back while Rogan was in the service."

"That's ridiculous," Clyde said. "This dame is a screwball. Sure I called on Enid when I came to San Francisco on furlough. Rog asked me to."

"And she fell in love with you," Myrtle added.

"She tried to climb all over me, if that's what you mean. But that dame tried to climb all over every man."

"As long as the question has come up," Dan said, "I'd like to ask you something. When I first went around to see you at your apartment, the day before yesterday, Enid Hoyte came banging out the front door, and she was crying."

"Oh, you saw her, did you? I wondered about that. Since you didn't ask, I didn't say anything. She came to see me just before you did. She was batty with the idea that Rog would try to kill her now that he'd escaped. She pulled a lot of fake hysterics and tried to get me to take her away somewhere. It was all a lot of bilge. I told her so and kicked her out."

"Where were you last night between eleven and twelve o'clock?" Myrtle blurted.

"That's none of your business," Clyde said.

"You killed Enid Hoyte, and you killed Alice Sweetser," Myrtle accused.

"Don't be crazy," Clyde said. "I'll tell Banion where I was last night, but I won't tell you, because it's none of your business."

Ennis' sister Pat stuck her head in the door. "Clyde, can I see you for a minute?"

"What is it?"

"Can you step outside just a second?" Her face was troubled.

"Excuse me." Clyde got up and went out, closing the door behind him. In a minute he put his head in the door. "Come here a minute, Banion. Excuse me, Miss Wyler. We'll be right back."

Dan stepped out into the tiny hall at the head of the stairs.

"Rog's gone," Clyde said.

"What do you mean?"

"He's just gone, that's all," Pat said. "I went down to bring him some coffee, and he's gone. The door was unlocked, and he's gone."

Ennis led the way down the narrow stairs, and they went back to the hall where the rest rooms were. Dan noticed that a new tumbler lock had been fitted to the basement door since the day before.

"I put that on this morning," Clyde explained. "After the way you wandered down yesterday, I thought we ought to have a lock that would work from the inside. But Christ, I never thought Rog would take it on the lam."

The back basement room where Lochmeister had been hiding was empty, and his hat and coat were gone. Clyde noticed a piece of paper spiked on the nail where Lochmeister had hung is coat. He took it down, read it, and handed it to Dan.

> Dear Clyde [it read],
> I don't know what's going to happen, but whatever does, I'll never forget what you and Pat have done. But I know the risks you are taking, and I have no right to endanger you any longer. I'm going to turn myself in. Being here has given me the only rest I've had in months. I was sick and confused. Now I feel better, and I realize that this is the only sensible thing to do. I hate to go without saying good-by, but I know that if I tell you what I'm going to do, you'll talk me out of it.
> No one has ever had a better friend than you've been.
> Semper Fidelis,
> Rog

"Well, this is all right," Dan said. "The way the case is breaking right now, that's the best possible thing he could do."

"They'll kick the hell out of him up there," Clyde said. "He's a nervous guy. He's all shot. He can't take any more."

"They won't hurt him."

"The hell they won't. You know how they treat guys who take it on the lam."

"They won't hurt him," Dan repeated. "There's a guy named Gallagher up there who's on the level. I'll go right up now and have a talk with him."

"Christ! I wonder if he'll get there okay?"

"Best thing to do is go right up there and see."

As they emerged from the door of the basement, Myrtle was waiting for them in the hall. "I want to see Rogan," she said.

"What are you talking about?" Dan asked.

"Don't try to fool me. Rogan is down there. That's where you've been hiding him."

"You're crazy."

"All right, if you don't let me see him right now, I'll call the police."

"Don't be senseless."

"I'm tired of being lied to." Myrtle whirled on her heel and started for the front of the theater.

Dan ran after her, grabbed her by the arm, and pulled her back. "For God's sake, be reasonable."

"Are you going to let me see him?"

Pat Ennis tugged at Dan's sleeve and motioned him aside frantically. "Don't let her phone the police," she whispered. "They're sure to find out Clyde has been hiding him. Clyde has a police record. It will go hard with him."

"There's no use whispering," Myrtle said. "Either you're going to take me down there to see Rogan, or I'm going to call the police."

"I'm going to put it to you squarely," Dan said. "Come on. You can look for yourself."

They took her down in the basement to the room where Lochmeister had been. "Here's where he was," Dan said. "He slept on that cot. Clyde was hiding him because Clyde is the best friend he has. But we just discovered that he's gone. He left this note." Dan handed it to her. When she had finished reading, he said, "Now if you call the police, you're going to get Clyde put in jail for doing one of the decentest things a man ever did."

"Of course I won't. You should have been honest with me in the first place. I'm only trying to help."

Dan sighed in relief and patted her shoulder. "Good girl."

He handed the note to Clyde. "You'd better destroy that. It would be pretty husky evidence against you if anyone got hold of it."

"We'd better go to the police station and see if he got there all right," Myrtle suggested.

"That's where we were headed," Dan said. "Come on."

Clyde insisted on going along against Pat's worried advice. "Don't worry," he said. "If I just go along as an interested friend, they won't think anything. You stay here and look after the joint. I want to see that Rog's okay."

They went in Dan's car. Myrtle had her own car parked nearby, but when Dan asked her what she was going to do about it, she refused to consider it. She said that if she tried to follow along in her own car, she was afraid she'd be ditched, the way she'd been ditched a dozen times already.

As they climbed the steps of the Hall of Justice, they met Gallagher coming out.

"Now, what the hell?" he said. "I thought for once I'd get home and get some sleep."

"Let's go back to your office just for a few minutes," Dan said. "I've got a hunch the night isn't over yet."

"If there's anything on your mind, tell me right here," Gallagher insisted.

"No, let's go up to your office," Dan said. "It's too drafty here."

Gallagher sighed, cursed under his breath, and led the way back to the battered cubicle which the city dignified by the name of an office. "Now what have you done, Dan? Where have you been?"

"I just had a notion that Rogan Lochmeister might try to turn himself in tonight, now that the story of Villiers' arrest is out."

"He won't have to try very hard."

"Well, if he does come around, I figured you ought to be here."

"I can't be here twenty-four hours a day, Dan. Now tell me what's eating you, and let's get this business settled quickly." Gallagher jerked his head at Clyde Ennis. "Who's this guy?"

"This is Clyde Ennis. He was a friend of Lochmeister's. They were in the Marines together."

Gallagher's eyes narrowed. "Oh, yes. Don't I know you, Ennis?"

"I don't think so," Clyde said.

"I don't often forget faces," Gallagher insisted.

Clyde said nothing, but his mouth tightened. Gallagher continued scrutinizing him. "Ennis, Ennis, yes, yes. I remember you now. It's been quite a while, Marty."

Ennis sat quietly and said nothing.

"Market Street Marty! Well, well." Gallagher rolled the words around in his mouth as if they savored sweet. "I'd damn near forgotten you, Marty."

"Marty isn't my name," Ennis said.

"Of course it isn't," Gallagher soothed. "I knew that for a long time."

"Is there any complaint?" Ennis snapped.

"Oh, no. No complaint at all. None at all. I should say not. Where have you been keeping yourself, Marty?"

Ennis uncrossed his legs and gripped his knees with his hands. "I've been crawling around in a lot of mud and filth in the South Pacific so that a lot of fat asses like you could enjoy the Four Freedoms. And I'm not asking for any credit, either. But I'm trying to live up to the rules, and I haven't broken a goddamn law since I've been back." Ennis stopped in the middle of his discourse, as if he'd remembered something. He recrossed his legs and thrust his hands into his coat pockets. "What the hell am I talking to you for? It's a waste of time."

"It seems to me I seen this in the movies," Gallagher said. "Yeah, that's right. Some blonde dame with an uplift brassiere got a hold of the bad man and, by God, before he was through, he was elected mayor."

Dan interrupted him. "Listen, Neil, as cops go, you're a hell of a good guy, but you're no comedian."

"Listen, Dan, the day when an ex-con can come in here and call me a fat ass—"

"Neil, it's bad enough to be fat at that end without getting fat at the other," Dan said. "If Ennis has broken any law, arrest him. Otherwise, for crissake give him a square break."

Gallagher extended his hand toward Ennis, as if indicating the utmost unreasonableness in a human being. "Has anybody hurt him? Has anybody laid a finger on him? Who the hell is he that he can't take a little ribbing? So he served a little time. So what? Wouldn't I starve to death if all the crooks turned honest? All right, so he's reformed. Every crook that was ever hauled in here said he was reformed. So I'm a cop. So what of it? I didn't ask to be a cop. If you want to know the truth, I studied mechanical drawing, but I couldn't get a job at it. So now I'm a cop. That was years ago, of course. Now I make my living by asking people questions and believing the opposite. I have been in this business for thirty years. When I ask a man a question, I expect him to lie. If he tells me the truth, he throws all my reasoning out of joint. So a man comes in and tells me he has reformed. What am I to think? I like you, Dan. You know that. Maybe

I think you're a square guy. But that doesn't mean that for you or anybody else I'll sit here and let an ex-con call me a fat ass."

Dan touched a match to his pipe. "What the hell do you think you are? Pleasingly plump?"

Gallagher smoothed his hands over the top of his desk as if he were trying to calm strife on the face of the earth. "Look," he said. "I was on my way home. I was going to go home and open up the icebox and have a little feed. Then I was going to crawl in bed with my wife, and God knows I haven't seen her in so long I'd have had to introduce myself. I wasn't looking for Marty. I wasn't looking for you. I wasn't looking for anybody. But I can't get out the door without there you are, the three of you. And what's the proposition? Lochmeister is going to turn himself in. He can turn himself inside out for all I care. Will you please go home and let me do the same? Lochmeister can turn himself in in the morning. I'm sick and tired of the whole business. If I sit here ten minutes longer, somebody will murder somebody else out in that crazy damn city, and I'll be up the rest of the night again trying to stick it on somebody. Will you please go home, all of you?"

CHAPTER TWENTY-FOUR

When they had returned to Dan's car, Clyde Ennis said, "Those cops have memories like elephants and hearts like mice."

"Forget it," Dan said. "What we've got to do is find Lochmeister."

"Maybe he went to our house," Myrtle suggested.

Ennis bit his lip. "He's had plenty of time to get here."

"It's my guess he's gone somewhere else," Dan said.

"You'd better drive me back to the theater," Ennis advised. "He may have gone back there, or maybe he's phoned."

Dan drove back to the theater and parked in front. Ennis went inside and returned in a few minutes. "He hasn't come back, and he hasn't phoned."

"You'd better stick around here," Dan said. "I have a couple of ideas where he might have gone."

"Do you suppose he may have gone to our house?" Myrtle suggested again. "He may have wanted to talk to Papa."

"That's an idea," Dan said. "Maybe we'll try it."

They left Ennis at the theater, and Dan headed in the direction of Taylor Street on Russian Hill. As they neared the place, Myrtle said, "This is the apartment house where Rogan used to live."

"Right."

"You don't think he would have gone back there?"

"You never can tell."

He parked in front and told Myrtle to wait in the car. When she began to protest, he said, "I haven't any time to monkey around with you, and if you don't want to co-operate, I'll take you home and dump you." His tone was so serious she settled back in the seat obediently.

Dan rang the janitor's bell, and presently Souzas Tsvirka came shuffling through the hall in a pair of old slippers. "Has Lochmeister been here?" Dan asked.

"Ya. Come in. Ya." Tsvirka held the door open and beckoned him inside. He led the way downstairs and through the basement to his living quarters.

Dan took a quick look around. "Where is he?"

Tsvirka shrugged. "Gone."

"You mean he came here and then went away?"

"Ya."

An old trunk was lying open in the center of the room. Tsvirka gave the lid a kick. "He take something and go. Dat's his box."

After several questions, Dan learned that this was a trunk of Lochmeister's belongings that Tsvirka was keeping for him. Evidently Lochmeister had come directly here after leaving the theater. He had asked to see his old trunk, rummaged through it, and found something that he was looking for. Tsvirka saw him put it in his pocket, but couldn't quite make out what it was. He guessed, however, that it was a photograph. Lochmeister, he said, had, among other things, examined a photograph album. Then he had taken a newspaper from his pocket and compared a picture in it with one in the album.

"Did he say where he was going?" Dan asked.

"No. I tell him to stay here. Souzas Tsvirka will take care of you. But he puts something in his pocket and runs."

Dan knelt beside the trunk and looked over its contents. The photograph album was on top. He thumbed through it until he came to a page from which a photograph had obviously been torn. There were five other pictures on the page, and they had all obviously been taken on the same day at some beach. Lochmeister and Alex Groton were shown in various gag poses with a couple of shapely girls in bathing suits. The party had evidently consisted of the two couples, but no more than three at a time appeared in any of the photographs. One, apparently, had to stay out to operate the camera. It was reasonable to assume that the picture Lochmeister had torn out was one of this set.

Dan thought back over the newspapers he had seen that day and remembered that the *Journal* had run a full-page spread of background pictures on the case. He asked Tsvirka if he happened to have a copy around, and the old man produced one. Dan turned to the page of photographs and made some comparisons with the pictures in the album. Then he tore a couple of pictures from the album and put them in his pocket. Tsvirka watched with interest, but made no objection. Dan also tore the photographic spread from Tsvirka's newspaper and pocketed that.

He began turning the pages of the album, examining other photographs, and, as he did so, came upon a thumb-worn letter that had been inserted. It had been addressed to Rogan Lochmeister at San Diego when he was in the service and was from his wife, Enid. Inside was a letter and six photographs that she had enclosed. The letter combined effusive endearments with a resentful tone regarding his "suspicious attitude" about every man who was polite to her. It offered much testimony regarding her faithfulness and spoke of the arrangements she was making for a visit to his base at San Diego. Dan slipped the photographs and the letter back in the envelope and transferred it to his pocket.

"My God, I don't think I should be letting you do this," Tsvirka said.

"It's all right," Dan assured him. "Lochmeister is going to be in the clear very soon now, and this stuff will help."

He continued studying photographs throughout the album, some of which he scrutinized very closely. A set that had evidently been taken on a ranch interested him, and he tore one out. He removed another of a yachting party. Near the front of the album, the photographs dated all the way back to school days. Some were of Lochmeister, some of his sister. Dan removed a large group picture that had evidently been taken at some school function.

"By God, I don't like this," Tsvirka said, shaking his head.

"Well, that's enough," Dan said, closing the album. "If Lochmeister comes back here, you tell him to go to the Hall of Justice and turn himself in as quickly as he can."

"I tell him nudding of de kind."

"You tell him to do as I say. He's already enough in the clear so he doesn't have to worry, and the way things are shaping up, jail is about the safest place he can be."

Dan doubted if Tsvirka would obey his instructions, but there was nothing he could do about it. He returned to the car, where Myrtle was waiting impatiently.

"Was he there?" she asked.

"No."

"Who did you see?"

"Kilroy's great-grandfather. You ask too many questions."

"You don't think much of women, do you?"

"If I did less thinking about women, I'd be a rich man now."

"You never tell me anything."

"I don't have to. You're the nearest thing to a mind reader I've ever seen."

"Where are we going now?"

Dan already had the car in motion. "We're going to drop in on Mr. Alex Groton, your old boy friend."

"Why?"

"Just a social call."

When they reached the entrance to Alex Groton's apartment house, Dan remembered something. He told Myrtle to wait there a minute and returned to where he had parked the car. He opened the compartment in the dashboard and took out the revolver Gallagher had given him. He experimented putting it in various pockets to see which would have the least bulge, and finally decided that his hip pants pocket was best because the tail of his coat draped over it.

When he returned to the entrance of the apartment house, he found Myrtle already pressing the buzzer opposite Groton's name. "He isn't in," she said. "I've been ringing several times."

"Are you sure?" Dan pressed the button once more just to make certain. When there was no answering click, he pressed the button marked "Manager."

"What's that for?"

"We'd better have a look inside."

"Is something wrong?"

"Not necessarily."

An elderly, irritable-looking man opened the door.

"Excuse me," Dan said. "We are friends of Mr. Groton. We understand that he's been ill, and he doesn't answer his bell. I wonder if you'd open his door and just take a look inside."

"He's ill, you say?"

"Yes."

"I saw Mr. Groton this morning, and he looked all right."

"He took ill suddenly at his office this afternoon."

The old man looked unhappy. "Well, I don't know. I don't like to open people's doors, unless, of course, it's an emergency."

"I'm afraid we'll have to insist," Dan said. "Mr. Groton has heart trouble. He may be lying in there helpless and unable to call anyone."

"Is that so? I didn't know it was that serious. Come in." The elderly man led the way to the elevator. On the way up, he said, "Oh, I tell you, heart failure is a terrible thing. I had a brother-in-law went like that." He snapped his fingers and shook his head.

On the third floor, he fumbled his keys, found the right one, and opened Groton's door. The apartment had been fixed up to look like a Cape Cod cottage, with a lot of imitation colonial furniture about and a ship model in a bottle over an imitation fireplace. Dan eyed a long rack of expensive pipes admiringly.

"Doesn't seem to be home," the old man said, peering into the bedroom and then the kitchen.

A newspaper-wrapped bundle was lying partly open on a table in the center of the room. Dan flipped back the wrappings and revealed a jumbled pile of women's clothing.

"I wouldn't touch anything, if I were you," the old man cautioned.

Dan lifted a few of the garments and examined them. Myrtle Wyler had become pale and was staring hard at the bundle. "What is it?" she asked.

Dan picked up a lady's purse that was nestled in the pile and opened it.

"See here, I can't allow you to touch anything in this apartment," the old man rasped.

Dan removed a card from the purse and handed it to Myrtle. Her eyes were pinched, as if she were going to cry. It was Alice Sweetser's driving license. Dan took it back from her, returned it to the purse, and snapped it shut. "There are initials on some of the clothes, too," he said.

"I'm going to have to ask you to kindly leave," the old man snapped angrily.

"Sorry, fellow, but this is kind of important," Dan said. He went over to a desk and lifted the telephone.

Myrtle ran to him and held his arm. "Please, Dan, don't."

Dan hesitated and looked at her closely. "Why not?"

Her voice was thick with emotion. "He didn't do it. He couldn't have done it. Not Alex."

"He'll have a chance to explain."

"Explain what?" the old man asked. "I don't understand this at all."

"Please, Dan, give me time to think. At least you can wait a few minutes."

Dan put the phone back on its rack. "All right, let's go."

As they went down in the elevator, the old man said, "I don't like to be rude, but it's not right to touch things in another person's apartment. If you want to use the phone, you can go to a drugstore."

Out in the car, Myrtle said, "Take me home."

"You were pretty crazy about that guy, weren't you?"

"I want to go home."

Dan took the photographs he had torn out of Lochmeister's album from his pocket, selected one of the beach scenes in which Alex Groton had his arm around a girl, and handed it to her. He snapped on the light so that she could see it. "I'm sorry to have to do this to you."

She stared quietly at the picture for a few minutes, and then repeated, "Take me home."

Dan unfolded the newspaper spread of photographs. Pictures of all the murdered girls were arranged in a row. He pointed to the first victim, Fanny Owens. The face was the same as the girl Alex Groton had his arm around in the snapshot.

"I still don't believe it," she sobbed. "I'm sure Alex can explain."

"You wouldn't want to protect him if you thought he was guilty."

"Please take me home." Her voice was imploring.

Dan put the pictures back in his pocket, and drove to the Wyler residence.

CHAPTER TWENTY-FIVE

The pasty-faced butler met them at the door. "Mr. Groton is in the library," he said. "He wanted to see Mr. Wyler, but your father is out. He said he'd wait."

Before he had finished speaking, Myrtle was running toward the library. Dan and the butler followed, walking fast. In the library, Myrtle was circling the room with her eyes. "Where is he?"

The butler's dignity was undisturbed. "I'm sure, Miss Wyler, I don't know. He was here a moment ago."

Myrtle dashed from the room, and Dan heard her feet bumping on the stairs somewhere out in the hall.

The butler said in a mildly interested tone, "That's very odd. Miss Wyler seems disturbed."

Dan left him standing there and walked rapidly in the direction Myrtle had taken. He mounted a broad stairway to the second floor. The hall above was empty. He opened a couple of doors, but the rooms were dark, quiet, and apparently empty. He was about to try the third floor when he heard a sound behind one of the doors near the landing. He opened the door, but the room was as quiet as the others. He felt along the wall until his fingers found a switch, and turned on the lights. It was probably J. P. Wyler's bedroom. There was a huge four-poster bed, and a litter of men's toilet articles on a large mahogany dresser. A door that led to an adjoining room was open. Dan walked over to it and looked into a large, glistening bathroom with a tub big enough for a polar bear. Dan flicked on the light and peeked into an elaborate stall that had a dozen or more sprays. On the opposite side of the bathroom was another door that led into still another room. Dan went over and tried it, but it was locked. As his hand relaxed from the knob, he heard the door behind him slam loudly and a key turn in the lock. He whirled around and made a dive for it, but it was wasted effort. The knob rattled uselessly in his hand.

He threw open a large frosted-glass window and stuck his head out. As nearly as he could determine in the darkness, there was a sheer drop to the ground two stories below. Without any further delay, he picked up a heavy metal bath stool, and began wielding it like a sledge hammer against the locked door. The noise was terrific, but he continued pounding with all his might. The wooden panel splintered, gave a little, and then split. Dan gave it a couple more wallops, and the split widened two or three inches—enough for him to look through. He was about to continue banging away at it, when a slight motion that he could see through the crack attracted him. He moved his eye closer to the opening, and saw the frightened face of the butler. "Open this door," he shouted.

The butler was frozen by fear and indecision. He remained staring with his mouth wide open.

"Don't stand there like a chump. Unlock this door."

"What are you doing in there?" the butler gasped.

"I'm locked in. Open up."

The butler moved forward cautiously, turned the key, and Dan kicked the door open. "Where's Miss Wyler?" he asked.

"Why, I don't know. I was in the kitchen. I heard you pounding and—"

Five shots sounded in quick succession from somewhere on the lower floor, followed by a shrill scream.

Dan raced down the stairs three at a time, with the butler jigging along behind him. As they reached the lower hall, Myrtle came slowly out of the library, biting her fingers and moaning. One side of her face was red with blood from a long gash in her cheek. In one hand she carried an automatic pistol.

Dan quickly took the gun from her hand, then went to the door of the library and looked in. Alex Groton was lying face down on an expensive rug, in a wide pool of blood. Dan returned to Myrtle. She was still hysterical, her eyes rolling wildly. He forced her fingers from her mouth, and slapped her face hard several times. She gasped for breath and recovered her senses, then pressed her face into her hands and wept.

"What happened?" Dan asked.

"He tried to kill me; Alex tried to kill me."

The butler, who had taken a look in the library, mopped his face with a handkerchief. "Good heavens, what shall we do?"

Myrtle took her hands from her face. They were stained with blood from the cut. She screamed again.

Dan gripped her firmly by the arms. "You're all right, it's just a cut. Better come upstairs."

The butler led the way to Myrtle's bedroom, a modernistic affair with angular furniture devoid of any ornament. Then he excused himself for a moment and returned with a small first-aid package. Dan had eased Myrtle onto the bed, where she was trembling with her hands over her eyes. The butler efficiently wiped the blood from her face, applied antiseptic to the cut, and fastened a neat bandage with adhesive tape. While he did so, Dan examined the automatic he had taken from Myrtle. He slipped the clip out. All the cartridges had been fired. He put the gun on a table, and went over to watch the first aid.

"I think that will be all right," the butler said. "The cut is not very deep. But she'd better have a doctor."

"You'd better call the police, too," Dan said.

"She should be kept as quiet as possible."

"I'll watch her," Dan said. "You go call the police."

The butler gathered up his bandages and antiseptics and went quietly out.

When the door closed behind him, Dan pulled a chair up beside the bed, took his pipe out, and began scooping tobacco into it from his pouch. Myrtle was still lying silently with her hands over her eyes, breathing deeply. "I was a fool to have let you out of my sight," Dan said.

"I didn't believe you. I should have believed you," she moaned.

"We haven't much time before the police arrive," Dan said.

"I wish I was dead. I wish I had let him kill me."

"This evening, when I found you in Clyde Ennis' office, you accused him of killing Enid Hoyte."

"Yes, I thought that he had. I suspected everyone, but not Alex."

"You also accused him of killing Alice Sweetser."

"I know I did. I thought he must have done it."

"What made you think Alice Sweetser was dead?" Dan asked.

Myrtle's regular breathing halted for an instant, then continued. She still had her hands over her eyes.

"I assumed she was. She's disappeared, hasn't she?"

"You said she was dead."

"That was just an assumption."

"As it happens, she is dead. She was murdered, just like the others, but the newspapers announcing it hadn't hit the streets yet, when you accused Ennis of killing her. I had just finished phoning in the story a few minutes before I went there."

"She'd disappeared. I assumed she'd been murdered. I didn't know."

Dan took the letter he had found between the pages of Lochmeister's photograph album from his pocket. He looked again at the six photographs that were enclosed in it. "You were apparently much more friendly with Enid Hoyte and Alice Sweetser than you led me to believe."

"Why do you say that?"

"These pictures seem to indicate it. I wish you'd look at them."

Myrtle removed her hands from her eyes and slowly leaned up on one elbow. She took the photographs from Dan. They showed Myrtle, Enid, and Alice in various congenial poses on a sun porch. In one of them Myrtle had her arms around both of them, and they were laughing together. "I remember when these were taken," she said. "It was a long time ago."

"Yes, during the war. Enid sent them to Rogan Lochmeister when he was based at San Diego. Here is the letter she sent with them." Dan unfolded it and read, "'I hope these snapshots will convince you that I am not running around with other men, as you seem to imagine. In fact, I am thoroughly chaperoned. Myrtle is staying with me now. Her father is in New York, and she says she gets lonely in their big house. She is going to look after the apartment for me when I come down to see you next week. She sends her love.'"

The butler knocked on the door and put his head in. "I phoned Dr. Stinson, and also the police. Can I get you anything, Miss Wyler?"

"No. Please leave us alone."

"If I may suggest a little brandy or perhaps some coffee."

Myrtle's voice was sharp. "No. Please go away."

The butler backed out, closing the door. "I don't understand why you're reading me this letter," she said.

"We haven't much time, so I'll be brief. If you stayed in that apartment while Enid was down in San Diego, she must have left you keys to both her apartment and Alice Sweetser's so that you could use the phone up there."

Myrtle sat up and took a cigarette from a porcelain box on the bedside table. "What difference would that make?"

"As a matter of fact, if you stayed there any length of time, you must have had your own set of keys to both apartments."

"I don't understand what you're getting at."

"Rogan's civilian clothes were still in the closet of that apartment. They must have fitted you pretty well."

Myrtle took a long, calm drag of her cigarette and exhaled slowly. "That's a strange thing to say."

Dan took out another photograph he had torn from Lochmeister's album. "You'll pardon my saying it, but you are not a very feminine type. Women who wear their hair in such a close-cut boyish bob generally aren't. Here is a picture, for instance, that was taken of you on some ranch. You are wearing men's clothes, and if I didn't know you I'd mistake you for a man. Here's another taken on a yacht, in which you look like the captain himself. But here's one that interests me particularly. According to the writing in the corner, it's a group photograph of the dramatics club of Oakdale Girls' School. You're all in costumes for a play called 'Tomorrow's Garden.' I recognized Florence Lochmeister as one of the girls, and I had to look closely to see that you were cast in one of the men's roles. You certainly look the part."

Myrtle's jaw was clenched in the capable, determined expression that was now familiar to Dan. "Go on," she said, "that isn't all you have to say."

"You're as strong as most men. That's why you excel in athletic sports."

"Is that all?"

"No. You asked me some time ago if I knew what evidence Florence Lochmeister had that her brother was innocent. Well, I did know. It was a ring of keys, and I've found those keys."

"Yes?"

"Florence returned to her rooming house with those keys immediately after having had dinner here. One of the keys fits Rogan Lochmeister's apartment. Another fits Alice Sweetser's apartment. Another opened a checking locker at the ferry building, where we found most of Alice Sweetser's body. The rest of them we haven't checked yet. But I think when the police get here, we'll find that one of them fits the front door to this house."

Myrtle calmly snuffed her cigarette in an ash tray. "Go on, is that all?"

"A guilty man doesn't leave the evidence of his crime wide open on a table in his apartment and go off visiting. Alex Groton found that bundle of clothing somewhere, and the manner of his finding it either told him, or led him to suspect very strongly, who was guilty. You realized that the minute you saw the bundle on his table. You knew he would go straight to your father before he told the police. That's why you were so anxious to get home. It was you who locked me in that bathroom so that I'd be out of the way while you killed Groton, and it was you who put that gash in your cheek to make it look as if you'd been attacked."

Myrtle rose thoughtfully from the bed and began walking slowly toward the door. Dan pulled the revolver from his pocket. "I think you'd better come back here and sit down."

Myrtle turned and looked at him coldly. "You haven't the nerve to kill me."

"I wouldn't be too sure of that. At least I might trim off a little of your ankle. I'm a pretty good shot."

She smiled sarcastically. "You won't do any harm with that. I took the bullets out of it while you were in seeing that stupid old janitor."

Dan pointed the gun toward the fireplace and pulled the trigger several times. It clicked harmlessly.

Myrtle walked to the door, locked it, and put the key in a pocket of her skirt. "Are you afraid of blood?" she asked.

Dan ignored the question, and asked one of his own. "Did you really care so much about Alex Groton?"

"Blood is warm," she said. "I was once afraid of it. But now I know that it is warm." She walked to a chest of drawers, opened one of them, and began poking around inside.

"Did you love Alex Groton?" Dan repeated.

"He was the only man who ever attracted me," she said. She took a long hunting knife from the drawer and felt its edge. "But he preferred Fanny Owens, or any other little chippy he could pick up. He didn't care for me that way, he said."

"How did you know about Fanny Owens?"

"I followed them one night when he took her out. I followed them all evening. When he took her home, I waited all night for him to come out. It was morning when he left. He looked horrible, like a pale worm drained of blood. I decided to kill her."

"And the other girls?"

"Irene Du Boce and that Huneker girl, they were two more of his harlots. Alice Sweetser was another. Florence and Enid I had to kill. They knew things, and they would have talked." She moved slowly toward Dan, holding the knife cradled in her two hands as if it were a baby.

Dan was still hefting the empty revolver in his hand, although he had let his arm hang down beside the chair where it would not be noticed. "And what about—"

Before Dan could finish, she had gripped the tip of the blade and was swinging it back for a throw. Dan's arm came up like a catapult and hurled the revolver with all his force. It caught her in the side of the head, and her knees folded under her.

Dan sprang forward prepared for a struggle, but she was out cold. He examined the bruised place over her eye where the revolver had struck. It was a nasty blow, but it didn't look serious. He slipped the gun back in his pocket, picked up the knife, and tested its sharp point with his thumb. It was a well-balanced weapon, and he could tell from the way she had gripped it that she knew how to throw. He was debating whether to tie her up, when the door chimes sounded in the hall below. That would be either the police or the Dr. Stinson the butler had phoned.

It seemed a long time before anyone came up. Dan could picture Gallagher examining the corpse in the library and questioning the butler. At last he heard footsteps in the hall. There was a knock on the door, and the knob rattled. Gallagher's voice came through. "Open up, Dan."

"I thought you went home," Dan called through the door.

"This is no time to kid, Dan. Open up."

Dan leaned over Myrtle and took the key from the pocket of her skirt. As he opened the door, Gallagher said, "What's the idea of locking yourself in?" He spotted Myrtle lying on the rug. "What's the matter with her? What's happened here?"

Mac McCracken and the butler were right behind him. The butler ran to Myrtle, examined her, then went out, apparently to get his first-aid equipment again.

"What's been going on here?" Gallagher demanded.

"I had to sock her," Dan explained.

"What for? Are you crazy?"

"She was hysterical."

"You ought to have your head examined."

"She shot Groton."

"God knows she had reason. What are you doing with that knife?"

The butler came back with his kit and a basin of water. He began daubing Myrtle's face.

"You'd better get handcuffs on her before that guy brings her to," Dan advised.

"She's not at fault," Gallagher said. "Groton was Gus the Grue. You ought to know that, Dan. You were up in his apartment tonight ten minutes before we got there."

"Who led you there? Lochmeister?"

"Yeah. He turned himself in."

"I told you he was going to."

"Never mind about that. What's the idea of socking Miss Wyler?"

Myrtle was beginning to stir. "I'm warning you to put cuffs on her before she comes to," Dan said. "She's the Grue, not Alex Groton."

"Dan, you're daffy."

"She tried to stick me with this knife." Dan handed it to Gallagher.

Myrtle sat up, rubbing her head with her hands. "What kind of a gag is this?" Gallagher asked.

The butler carefully helped Myrtle to her feet. She looked around at them with sullen eyes. Gallagher held the knife in front of her in the palm of his hand. "Did you try to stab Banion with this?"

She made a wild grab for it, and got it in her hand before Mac McCracken could throw an arm around her neck and clench it tight. It took all three of them to get handcuffs on her.

CHAPTER TWENTY-SIX

"In Lithuania," declared Souzas Tsvirka, "it is an insult not to get drunk on a friend's wedding day." He leaned far over the crowded restaurant table with a bottle of wine, pouring generously into every glass that was empty or even not quite full.

Viola Adler, who had been Mrs. Rogan Lochmeister for more than an hour now, put her hand over her glass. "A wife must stay sober," she said, "to look after her husband."

Nix Peters pointed his fork at Rogan Lochmeister as if the meat of human wisdom were impaled on its prongs. "Think it over," he said. "'Mistaken for a Monster.' That's a wonderful title. It would clean up plenty of dough. All you'd have to do would be give me the facts. I'd write it up, and we'd split fifty-fifty."

"Leave him alone," Dan told Nix. "You've got a brain like a dirty old five-dollar bill."

Nix smacked his lips and shook his head. "I hate to see an opportunity like this passed up."

"Opportunity isn't in the past," Clyde Ennis said. "It's in the future."

Souzas Tsvirka was delighted. "To the future," he cried, and raised his glass. When they had all drunk, he leaned forward again with the bottle and began filling their glasses to the rims.

"Please tell me this," Nix said to Rogan. "What made you remember that photograph of Groton and Fanny Owens you had in your trunk?"

"I thought her face looked familiar ever since it first began appearing in the papers," Rogan said. "But I couldn't place it. The one they printed that afternoon was a new one that I hadn't seen before. The way she had her hair done made me recognize her as a girl Alex had brought along to the beach one Sunday a long while ago. I wasn't positive, but then I remembered the photographs, and thought it was worth checking. That's why I went to see Tsvirka instead of going directly to the Hall of Justice. When the photograph checked with the picture of Fanny Owens in the newspaper, I jumped to the conclusion that Alex was guilty. I took it straight to the Hall of Justice."

Gallagher, who had been quietly chewing the bones of a fried chicken at the other end of the table, boomed out, "I'd gone home. I had my hand on the latch of the icebox and was ready to fix me a little feed when they phoned me. I had to go all the way downtown again. I was sore as hell. When Rogan showed me the picture, I grabbed a couple of men and shot over to Groton's apartment. We found all that junk on his table, and—"

Fergus Villiers interrupted him. "All this time, remember, I'm sitting in jail playing solitaire with the most unsanitary deck of playing cards I've ever seen in my life. What makes me mad is nobody bothered to come and let me out, even after they had discovered I wasn't a monster. They let me sit there until the next morning, and I don't recall that anyone has ever even apologized."

"We were busy," Gallagher said.

"Let's stop rehashing it," Rogan pleaded. "Let's not talk about the past on my wedding day."

Souzas Tsvirka was up with his glass again. "To the future," he cried, "to a well-fed future."

"We've already drunk to that," Clyde Ennis' sister Pat reminded him.

"Then to Banion," Tsvirka proposed, "and to all men who speak and act with boldness."

They drank the toast, and as they put their glasses down, Nix's face became pensive. "Dan, an idea just struck me," he said. "Did you ever remember to go around and collect those two suits of clothes old man Wyler offered you?"

THE END

Classic hardboiled fiction from the King of the Paperbacks...

Harry Whittington

A Night for Screaming / Any Woman He Wanted $19.95
"[*A Night for Screaming*] is pure Harry. The damned thing is almost on fire, it reads so fast." —Ed Gorman, *Gormania*

To Find Cora / Like Mink Like Murder / Body and Passion $21.95
"Harry Whittington was the king of plot and pace, and he could write anything well. He's 100 percent perfect entertainment."
—Joe R. Lansdale

Rapture Alley / Winter Girl / Strictly for the Boys $21.95
"Whittington was an innovator, often turning archetypical characters and plots on their head, and finding wild new ways to tell stories from unusual angles." —Cullen Gallagher, *Pulp Serenade*

Black Gat #1 **A Haven for the Damned** $9.99
"A wild, savage romp and pure Whittington: raw noir that has the feel of a Jim Thompson novel crossed with a Russ Meyer film."
—Brian Greene, *The Life Sentence.*

Trouble Rides Tall / Cross the Red Creek / Desert Stake-Out $21.95
"If these three Whittington novels are the only westerns crime fiction fans ever read, they will have experienced some of the best the genre has to offer." —Alan Cranis, *Bookgasm*

"Harry Whittington delivers every time." –Bill Crider

STARK HOUSE

Stark House Press, 1315 H Street, Eureka, CA 95501
griffinskye3@sbcglobal.net / www.StarkHousePress.com
Available from your local bookstore, or order direct via our website.